The Deep Well At Noon

It was not a smartly dressed young Pimlico business woman who lived in this room. It was Holly Beckman, Leo's daughter. She looked as drawn and tired as any working girl after a hard week in Cavanaugh's factory.

But I'm not a factory girl.

I'm different.

I did what I am capable of doing.

I will do it again – and more.

Still holding the mirror, she seated herself in the tub chair and leaned her elbows on the card-table.

'Just who are you?' she spoke aloud to her reflection . . .

She saw only a person, not the Lambeth girl that David saw, not a shabby little servant, not Maury's sister, Leo's daughter or Tal's granddaughter. Perhaps what she recognised was the woman her mother had never had the chance to become . . .

About the author

Jessica Stirling was born in Glasgow and still lives in
Scotland. She has enjoyed a highly successful career as a
writer, beginning with the bestselling trilogy *The Spoiled
Earth*, *The Hiring Fair* and *The Dark Pasture*. Her most recent
novel, *Prized Possessions*, is set in Glasgow in the 1930s.

The Deep Well at Noon

Jessica Stirling

CORONET BOOKS
Hodder and Stoughton

Copyright © 1979 by Jessica Stirling

The right of Jessica Stirling to be identified as the
Author of the Work has been asserted in accordance with the
Copyright, Designs and Patents Act 1988.

First published in Great Britain in 1979 by Hodder and Stoughton
A division of Hodder Headline PLC
First published in paperback by Pan Books in 1978
First published by Hodder and Stoughton in paperback in 1999
A Coronet Paperback

10 9 8 7 6 5 4 3 2 1

A CIP catalogue record for this title is available
from the British Library.

ISBN 0 340 70833 6

Printed and bound in Great Britain by
Mackays of Chatham plc, Chatham, Kent

Hodder and Stoughton
A division of Hodder Headline PLC
338 Euston Road
London NW1 3BH

For Janice

Contents

The shoemaker told him that retreat was inevitable. Jerry had finally blown the bridge at Etalon. On this side of the river only the fort at Marguiller remained in British hands. The Germans were expected to advance again after the all-night bombardment and bite off what remained of the salient north of Bullecourt. The captain was a veteran of eleven campaigns and had lost interest in the progress of the war. He had been thirty-seven hours in the redoubt on the ridge above the ravine and he knew he would have to return. He could not hold anything in his head except the memory of the redoubt and the two scratch platoons he had left there. The shoemaker spoke with a flat Fenland accent and did not understand the officer's indifference to his news.

With the shoemaker they had sent up four cooks, four storemen, a farrier and two boys from a Bantam battalion who had returned to the front from the field-hospital at Noyer only that morning. The boys were rested and cheerful and said they were not afraid of the guns. They gave him half a tin of bully beef which he ate with his fingers while they waited in the ravine for a lull in the shelling. One of the boys was called George, the other Freddie. He never did discover the shoemaker's name.

By half-past eight, the captain guessed that the bombardment was not going to let up. He said they had better make a run for the redoubt in case Jerry started chucking over gas shells. Thick mist hid the wire and spilled down into the ravine. Crouching, the captain led the replacements along a trail of broken duckboards and through what was left of the netting. As he passed he peered down at the faces of the dead French gunners, but he did not think any of them had been gassed that morning. He had marked the ladder with a pile of empty grenade boxes, and went up ahead of the men. The mist was very white and thick. It rolled off the ridge and crept across the mud, blotting out the redoubt. The barrage was deafening. The captain could hear nothing but the guns. Signalling with his revolver, he hopped over the top and ran, stooped, into the mist.

9

The Maxim opened up before he had covered fifty yards.

Although he had two Mills bombs in his pouch, it did not occur to the captain to use them. He still thought of the redoubt as his place, and could not bring himself to destroy it. Tacking left, he ran on until he could see the shape of the ridge in the mist. He had almost reached the edge of the wire. One of the boys and three of the men were staggered across the line of fire behind him.

The captain flopped on his belly. He could just make out the light chatter of the Maxim now. He had no fear of it. He was thoroughly familiar with the gun and understood its nature. He was furious with himself for stopping to eat the bully beef. He was even madder with Jerry for commandeering his machine-gun. Pushing forward, he ran again towards the ridge. The boy, Freddie, charged past him, yelling. When the boy screamed and went down the captain did not stop running.

There were five Germans in the redoubt. They had swung the Maxim and braced the muzzle against the backs of the Tommies he had dragged in last night to help shore up the walls. The Germans were just like the ones who had come yesterday and the day before. They were very young and eager and wore brand-new uniforms. Off to his left, in thinning mist, he spotted stormtroopers among the tree stumps on the shoulder of the ridge. There were more than yesterday, many more. If only he could get to his Maxim he would have plenty of targets to pop at today. He was a couple of hundred yards shy of the redoubt when the bullet punched into his thigh.

Its impact surprised him. He stumbled and fell into the wire. He lay motionless, teeth clenched, weeping. It was not the pain of the wound that made him weep. He wept because he realised that he wasn't going to reach the redoubt now. He had held the position damned well, really, but he shouldn't have left it, not even for an hour. He had been a fool to come down to collect replacements. There were forty-six dead men up there already. What did he want with more? He had been quite comfortable where he was, with his Maxim and ammo boxes and two platoons of odds-and-sods for company. It embarrassed him that the shoemaker found him in tears.

The flat Fenland voice said, "Easy, easy now, sir. I'll have you off there in a jiffy."

When the shoemaker pulled him down, the breast and sleeves of his uniform tore. He lost a glove. He saw the glove suspended on the wire, growing smaller and smaller as the shoemaker lugged him away by the ankles. He slid smoothly through the mud on his back. Mist closed over the tiny black dot of the glove. He lifted his head and *watched the shoemaker's buttocks bobbing ahead of his legs. They sailed past Freddie. They sailed past George. They sailed past a huddle of corpses only some of whom he recognised. They were just a few yards short of the ladder when the shoemaker let out a shout.*

The captain felt his legs drop and there was a great deal of pain. To take his mind off it, he twisted on his hip and fired his revolver blindly into the mist. When the gun was empty he tossed it away, rolled onto his stomach and began crawling towards the trench. The shoemaker had been shot several times in the back. He had fallen on his side. His helmet was over his face and his arms were folded across his chest in a peaceful sort of way. The captain crawled past him and slithered down the ladder to the floor of the ravine.

For a while he sat on the duckboard and watched his thigh bleed. He wondered how he could possibly make it back to the ridge without help.

Thinking of the journey, he took a penknife from his pocket and cut the webbing strap off his pouch. He wrapped the strap tightly round his leg and tied it in a knot. He got to his feet and started off down the ravine in the hope of finding replacements to take back with him.

The French gunners were hopeless. They gaped blankly and hadn't even the savvy to clear out of his way. By the time he got to the north-west corner of the British sector he was beginning to think that nobody would answer his demand for volunteers to man the forward post. He kept walking, quite slowly, asking everybody he met if they would help him back to his redoubt. Nobody replied. When the boards gave out he could not manage to walk in the mud and climbed a shallow gravel slope and started down the hill towards the fort at Marguiller to look for replacements there.

Stretcher-bearers found him an hour later not far above the fort. He was the only survivor of the dawn attacks on the salient north of Bullecourt. Clearing out, they ferried him down river on a crowded barge and he reached the hospital at Noyer soon after dark.

At Noyer the doctors assured him that his wound was not serious and would heal with hardly a mark. The captain smiled up at them from the table as they put the ether mask over his face. He had decided to say nothing about the shoemaker, the Maxim or his lost redoubt.

Already he was planning how he would return to take his rightful place among the dead.

PART ONE

1918

1

Armistice Day

FROM THE INTERIOR of the Admiral's Hat cheerful shouts of song and laughter wafted into the street. A piano, two accordions and a banjolele were going great guns. Annie Pirelli, a big-bosomed warbler with a voice that could crack coping stones, was belting out "I Don't Want to be a Soldier's Gal" in competition with a decrepit quartet who were rendering "Keep the Home Fires Burning" in lugubrious harmony. Children barged in and out of the pub's scrolled doors. Grandmas and grandpas, wrapped in shawls and greatcoats, huddled on wooden benches along the wall out of the wind. Trestle tables had been carted round from the Salvation Army hall in Bucks' Walk and the womenfolk of Ambraham's Terrace were bustling about with teapots and borrowed crockery, setting up a spread for the evening street party. Like every other London borough, Lambeth was determined to celebrate the end of the war in style.

Twenty yards from the public-house door, a group of six young people had rather aimlessly converged round a lamp post. Holly Beckman was among them.

At nineteen, Holly's dark eyes and oval face had a character that made her seem beautiful, even in an era where the preference was for dimples and retroussé noses. Her sober grey jacket and skirt set her apart and, since she had gone to work over the river in Pimlico, she had acquired a certain poise that contrasted with the busy-bee coyness of the three other girls.

In the three years she had worked in James Aspinall's Antique Shop she had seen little of her former schoolmates and had drifted away from them. She knew that they suspected her of patronising them but she could not explain that she had found a purpose, and that every moment away from the pursuit of that purpose was a moment lost – even on Armistice Day.

Holly's brother, Ritchie, emerged from the Admiral's Hat with a tray. Briskly he brought the drinks to the group by the lamp post and handed them round.

"What is it?" Holly asked.

"It ain't rat poison," Ritchie said.

Holly took the glass.

Ritchie stood in the centre of the circle and raised his glass.

"Here's t' victory, then." he said.

"Victory."

"T' all our brave soldiers."

"Here's to peace and prosperity."

"Specially for us," said Ritchie, with a grin.

The three girls had been Holly's chums at school. They worked now in the Park Road tram depot. There was little to choose between them. Dressed to kill in costumes of mauve, crimson and petunia, all with their hair up, they demonstrated how effectively four years of war had lowered the age of womanhood.

Holly noticed that Dora Leyton's lips left a cupid's bow of bright red Tangee on the rim of the glass.

"Thanks, Ritchie," said Dora. "It's lovely an' warmin'."

"You don't need much warmin', Dora," said Ritchie.

Dora blushed.

Holly knew that her brother's compliment had no sting. Though Ritchie could be charming, and was handsome enough in his way, he really had no time for the ordinary run of Lambeth girls like Dora, Violet and Cissy. At home, she had often heard him pour scorn on them for their silliness and lack of ambition.

"They want one thing – a man," Ritchie would say. "Husbands. Can't they see, year or two after the weddin' he'll be down the pub every night, an' the only contact between them'll be when he blacks her eye for not having his grub ready."

Over the years, Holly had grown used to her brother's sly cynicism. It was one of many elements of life in Ambraham's Terrace that she disliked.

"Drink up, Hol," said Ritchie. "Nothin' like hot port'n' lemon for puttin' a smile on your face."

Holly sipped the strong drink and glanced down the street.

The women were going gaga trying to make Fray Bentos look like Bradenham ham. Everybody had been saving their meagre rations for the Armistice celebrations and the street party that would begin sometime towards dusk. Holly felt no more affinity with the wives and mothers than she did with the trio of snappy tram girls in their casque hats and hobble skirts.

Was it the war that had changed things so radically for them all, or was it the inevitable process of growing up, growing away from your roots? Just a half dozen years ago, at Harmon Street School, Dora had been her best friend; now they had nothing, except the past, in common.

"Well, Ritchie," said Violet. "What's the programme?"

"Programme?" Ritchie had been thinking of other things. He had not realised that the three girls were looking to him for a lead.

"Thought we might hang round 'ere," said Dora, "until they dish up the food, then we could all buzz up West."

"Everywhere'll be packed tonight," said Ritchie.

"That's half the fun, ain't it?" said Cissy.

What would become of tram depot girls when the troops returned, Holly wondered. They would probably be forced back into low-paid jobs as servants or waitresses or into sweatshops like Cavanaugh's Patent Medicine factory, whose blank brick wall sealed off the backs of the Terrace. Inevitably high wages would dry up and they would no longer be able to afford bright clothes and make-up – and, she realised, they would resent it, would, perhaps, wish that the war had not ended so soon.

Holly was lucky. Her job in Aspinall's Antique Shop would not be at risk. Mr. Aspinall would not sack her in favour of a returning soldier. It wasn't that kind of situation. At least Pa would stop nagging her to give up shop work and sign on at the munitions plant in Hatfield, where staggering wages could be earned by girls of her age.

"Do you fancy a fling up West, Holly?" Stan Nuttall asked.

More than any of the others in the group, Stan carried the visible evidence of war's great changes. He had fought at the Somme and had lost an eye and three fingers to a whizz-bang. When he was discharged and returned to civilian life in Lambeth, his mates dubbed him the Baron of Bishop's Row because he wore a black leather glove and a black leather eyepatch. Stan took the banter in good spirit and declared that he considered one eye and three fingers a fair exchange for his neck.

"I'm not much of a one for crowds, Stan," said Holly. "I'd rather stay here, in the Terrace."

"Spoilsport," said Dora.

"I'm not stoppin' you, Dora," said Holly.

"Seven's a crowd, anyhow," said Cissy.

"Yer, but Stan'll stay with her ladyship, won't he?" said Violet.

"Ritchie can cope with three of us," said Dora.

"What about me then?" asked Jeff Horsfall.

"Oh, yer, there's Jeff," said Cissy, without a spark of enthusiasm. Jeff would be bound to tag along with Ritchie, and the prospect did not please any of the girls. Unlike Stan, neither Jeff nor Ritchie had seen military service. Conscription had passed them over on medical grounds. In Jeff's case a tubercular hip threw his body out of kilter and he would never have survived basic training, let alone a single day in Flanders mud. As a child Ritchie had suffered from severe asthma and even now was prone to occasional attacks. His ribcage and shoulders had been slightly malformed and, in damp winter weather, his voice changed to a chummy wheeze.

Ritchie, Stan and Jeff all worked in O'Connor's Tannery in Bermondsey, helping to meet the demand for boots and belts. Though only twenty-two years old, Ritchie's smartness had brought him speedy promotion to acting foreman of the tannery's despatch department.

"What about it, Holly?" said Stan. "Will we wait for the dancin'?"

"That's best," said Holly.

"Hells bells!" said Jeff. "All the old dears doin' the knees-up, ain't what I call celebratin'."

"Got any money, Jeff?" asked Violet, teasingly.

"Yer, some."

"Some ain't enough," said Violet. "Anybody walks me out gotta be able t' do it in style."

Style: Holly's interpretation was different from the other girls. She was drab by comparison, in a grey skirt and jacket and a white blouse. Best shop wear. Everything in her life, this last year or two, had turned in upon the shop, upon pleasing the gentle Mr. Aspinall, in furthering her worth to him. She cared deeply, almost passionately, about the shop and the antique trade but there was nobody to whom she could impart the reasons for her preoccupation with Aspinall's Antiques. Ritchie thought she was giving herself airs and graces. Her father, Leo, considered she was squandering her time for no return. Only her grandfather, Tal Kirsanoff, understood; he was shrewd enough to leave her be, to let her work out her own salvation and come to terms with the split that the job had caused in her.

"You can do it in style," said Dora to Ritchie.

Then Holly knew how this odd council would end; Dora, Violet and Cissy would trot over the river to pirate a Canadian or American soldier, or any uniform they could find who was willing to throw out money on a spree. Ritchie, Stan and Jeff would seek refuge in the Admiral's Hat along with most of the other men in the Terrace. They would be quite drunk before the street party started.

"Sure," said Ritchie. "But I . . . I feel you should hang around the street on a day like this. Celebrate at home."

"Oh, patriotism, is it?" said Cissy, who was sharper than the other two. "I thought you was lookin' for an excuse t' ditch us."

To Holly's surprise, the girls' disappointment turned into hostility directed at her.

Violet said, "I suppose if Holly'd said she wanted t' go up t' Trafalgar Square an' join in the high jinks you'd all've been runnin'."

"She ain't exactly dressed for an outin', is she?" said Cissy.

"Dressed for her precious bleedin' shop, by the look of it," said Dora.

"Stop it, you lot," said Stan.

"Workin' the trams for the good o' the country ain't for Holly Beckman," Cissy persisted. "Gotta be dif'rent, her."

Holly did not defend herself, or retaliate. She was aware of the anxiety that lay behind the remarks, the uncertainty that the final signing of a peace treaty with Germany had brought. Strange that the newspapers talked of 'relief and gladness' when there was so much else, so many other emotions bound into what most people were really feeling.

"What's special about an antique shop, anyhow?" said Dora.

"All 'nice' things; ladies' things," said Violet, sarcastically. "I saw the place once, out walkin'. It's a little hole in the bleedin' wall."

It was Ritchie who came to his sister's defence.

"Lay off our Hol," he said. "She's got more brains than you lot put t'gether."

"Hark at 'im!" said Cissy. "All tarred with the same brush, them Beckmans."

The years at the tram depot had coarsened them. With independence had come liberty; they did not know what to do with it. Schoolgirl animosities had roughened into viciousness.

"Bet she's never been kissed yet," said Cissy.

"Only by Stan," said Dora.

"An' that's cause he can't see proper," Cissy added.

It was not anger that prompted Holly; she acted out of a sense of outraged justice, coupled, in part, with guilt.

"Take that back, Cissy Seaver. Apologise to Stan," Holly snapped.

"She loves him! Oh, she loves him!"

"Gawd!" said Jeff Horsfall. "Armistice Day! It's like any other, nothin' t'do but bicker an' squabble."

"I ain't stayin' 'ere to be insulted by the likes of 'er," Cissy declared.

Holly caught her arm. "An' you aren't leavin' until you apologise to Stan."

"What's so special, he needs an apology?"

"He fought for his country," said Holly. "That's what's special."

"Go on, Ciss," Dora sighed. "Don't argue with her. She ain't worth it. Tell Stan you're sorry."

"Sorry," said Cissy sulkily then, tearing herself from Holly's grip, flounced off up the Terrace towards Joshua Street.

"Stuck-up cow," said Dora to Holly, then, to Ritchie. "Wouldn't go out with you, Ritchie Beckman, if you was the last man in Lambeth."

Linking arms with Violet, she wheeled and followed her companion out of the confines of the Terrace.

"Ritchie, I'm sorry," Holly said. "I spoiled it for you."

Ritchie shrugged. "Little tarts. I didn't want t'be stuck with them, like. Better things t'do."

"Like what?" said Stan.

"Stay 'ere in the Terrace," said Ritchie, grinning again. "Have a few pints, a feed, dance with the old dears, make them happy."

"Gawd! Armistice Day!" said Jeff Horsfall again. "Come on, Stan, let's fight our way int' the Hat."

Stan hesitated. "What about you, Holly? Want to go for a walk, see what's doin' in the High Street or along the embankment?"

"Later," said Holly. "I'll still be here, Stan. Go an' have a pint with Ritchie an' Jeff."

Stan looked at her. He knew only too well that he had lost her. When they had been no more than children there had been a tacit understanding that one day they would become sweethearts. But that had changed too, like so many other things. Holly felt sorry for Stan but had sense enough to realise that sympathy was no basis for a permanent relationship.

"Come on, Stan," Ritchie said. "You're buyin' the first round."

"Right-o," Stan said. "Keep me a dance, Holly."

"As many as you want."

"An' . . . thanks."

"For what?"

"Stickin' up for me."

"You . . . you deserve it," Holly said.

He searched her face for a moment, and she could see the wistful sadness in his eyes.

"Stan," Jeff shouted.

"I'm comin'."

Picking up the tray of empty glasses, he carried it into the pub, leaving Holly alone by the lamp post.

She glanced towards the benches, hoping that Grandpa Tal would be there. He would be sure to cheer her up. He understood what it was to be out of place. And she was out of place here. There was no denying it. She could not otherwise explain her mood and, dispirited, strolled aimlessly down the Terrace.

The brown brick cul-de-sac, known locally as Abraham's Box, was draped with cheap bunting that fluttered listlessly in the chill wind that funnelled up Vauxhall from the Thames. It should have been a golden day, November sky glazed blue as porcelain, the sun over St. Thomas's like a copper warming pan. Instead it was raw and overcast.

The blare of a brass band made her look round.

The Borough Engineers had been marshalled and were touring the high streets, playing all the triumphant marches in their repertoire. Children flooked out of the Terrace, the women looked up and waved and a few drinkers, pints in their hands, came to the step of the Admiral's Hat to cheer the cornet players and the trombones and the big drummer. The martial sounds reminded Holly of her eldest brother, Maury; she wondered if he was at the back of the inexplicable foreboding that lurked in her. But it could hardly be; Maury's battalion had been withdrawn from the lines weeks ago.

The band passed, the music faded.

She was a creature of habit, that was it. She did not like being stuck in Lambeth. Given a choice, she would have spent the holiday in the antique shop doorway, with Mr. Aspinall. The Pimlico shop was close enough to Victoria for revellers to be rolling past. But, like all shops, Aspinall's was closed. Besides, Mr. Aspinall had been laid up with a mild Spanish influenza and, if sufficiently recovered, would be spending the day with his family.

It began to rain again, a soft drizzle.

Holly drifted down towards the door of No. 5 – the Beckman house.

Rain and wind would not matter tonight when the street parties wound into full swing. Only the grieving, the ungenerous and a handful who had reaped profits from the war would grudge Londoners their celebrations. Yet Holly felt out of it. And for no good reason except that she had been shown another side of life – and had come to prefer it.

She stopped at the door of No. 5 and reached through the letterbox for the string to which the door key was attached.

A cheer went up.

Holly, key in hand, hesitated and glanced up the street.

The taximeter cab, rattling like a biscuit tin on wheels, was bearing down on her, threading a route between trestles and gangs of children.

"Holly? Holly Beckman?"

The woman leaned from the cab window like a tattered black parrot caught by the claws. Her hat was of black straw, her gloves of thready black lace and her overcoat had a scruffy collar of dyed bunny fur. She waved an umbrella at Holly in a state of frantic disarray.

The cab was brought to a halt by a platoon of Terrace wives all armed with teapots. They steadfastly refused to allow the vehicle to navigate among their tables.

Holly dropped the string.

The woman in the taxi was Mrs. Hodge, the Aspinalls' "daily", who had charge of the cleaning of the apartments above the shop. The notion of the Cockney woman entering a cab, let alone riding all the was over from Pimlico, was inconceivable.

It augured an event of such importance that Holly's faint sense of foreboding bloomed instantly into fear.

She ran to the woman's side. Holly's first thought was that the shop had gone on fire. She had a silly vision of the Kaiser's last Zeppelin, released just before the Armistice, dropping its bombs straight through the Aspinalls' windows. Mrs. Hodge was breathless. Puffing and wheezing, she laid her thready glove on Holly's shoulder while the cabbie, fag hanging from his nether lip, yelled at the urchins who pranced around the bonnet.

"What is it, Mrs. Hodge. What's wrong?"

"Poor man, poor feller."

"Who?"

"Mr. A – he's a-dyin'."

As two boys tried to stand on the Cowley's bumper, the cabbie roared, "Get ter 'ell, y'bleedin' little perishers."

"But . . . but I thought . . ." Holly stammered. "On Saturday Mrs. Aspinall told me he was on the mend."

"The influenza went for 'is 'eart." Mrs. Hodge dabbed her eyes with the back of her glove. "Been sent t'fetch yer, Holly. He's been a-askin' for yer, special."

Grandpa Tal was suddenly by her side, bulky and reassuring in the sheepskin coat that was the last relic of his Russian youth. Its big winged collar was bald now, the skin ticked. He put his arm about Holly's shoulders. "What is it, child?"

"Mr. Aspinall. He's . . . he's dyin'."

"The woman has come for you?"

"Yes."

"Do not dawdle." Grandpa pulled open the cab door. "Go at once."

"Yes." Holly climbed into the cab.

"Take these, you may have need of them." The old man pressed two half-crowns into her hand.

It was cramped in the back of the cab. Holly was fenced in by Mrs. Hodge's hat, the meter-clock – already showing a debt of three shillings and eightpence – and by the cabbie's irate visage.

"Where?" he demanded.

"Cardwell Place, Pimlico," Holly said.

"I just come from there, for Gawd's sake."

"Do yer drivin'," Mrs. Hodge told him waspishly, "an' never mind yer lip."

The cab edged its way back up the narrow terrace.

Children were optimistically begging pennies, as if it was a wedding party. Holly saw their gaunt little faces distorted by the screen, saw Grandpa, arms folded, balaclava pulled low on his brow. Already three nosy neighbours were clamouring for information about what Holly was up to now. Grandpa remained resolutely silent, holding up his hand in salute as the cab found course and, bouncing on the cobbles, crawled past the Admiral's Hat. Pints in their hands, squinting with curiosity, Ritchie and Pa, Jeff and Stan were all out on the step. Then the cab went round into Joshua Street, headed for Kennington Lane and the Vauxhall Bridge.

Holly had no idea how long the journey would take. The streets were glutted with pedestrians. Floats, horse-carts, buses and trams were like islands in the throng.

Mrs. Hodge sniffed and dabbed her eyes once more.

"I prays we're in time, lovey," she said.

Only then did it come home to Holly that James Aspinall, her friend, mentor and one of the few people in the world who cared about her welfare, was dying. Without him, in Cardwell Place and out of it, she would be lost, deprived of purpose – and a job.

* * *

"What's *she* doing here?" Andrea Apsinall's whispered question sounded particularly vicious.

Oval shadows under her eyes and a dragee-shaped mouth, even more hooked than usual, transformed her humourlessness into a savage kind of anger.

As always, she was immaculately and expensively groomed. "Half the profits from this shop," James Aspinall had once confided, "seem to go on my daughter's back." The Radley's outfit had been tailored to her statuesque figure. It was as if she had prepared for the role of grieving daughter. Holly could not believe that Andrea felt any genuine emotion.

"I don't want *her* here."

"Daddy asked me to send for her," Andrea's mother explained, apologetically. Thora Aspinall had more than enough to contend with without Andrea's bullying.

Formally attired in an Edwardian morning coat and pearl-grey trousers, an elderly doctor stooped over the bed. Light from the broad window, narrowed by faded velvet drapes and parchment blinds, imparted a quality of sombre chiaroscuro to the large low-ceilinged bedroom. Holly had been in the Aspinalls' domestic apartments only a half dozen times; never in the bedroom. It seemed oddly familiar, though. Involuntarily she separated the pieces from the whole. That bow-fronted chest-of-drawers had been picked up for a song at a bailiff's sale in Marmington, Surrey; this convex mirror with delicate girandoles at an auction in Silverdale's Salerooms. The bed had a long, fine needlework panel set into the headboard. Three Hepplewhite shieldback chairs and a worn early Georgian wing chair made up the furnishings. There were no stray ornaments or *objets d'art*; Mr. Aspinall had never been one for needlessly cluttering up rooms.

Thora was perched on one of the chairs. Andrea stood behind her, like a guardian. Holly was aware of Andrea's hostility. It made her acutely uncomfortable. She would have left at once, if it hadn't been for Mr. Aspinall.

Gingerly the doctor lowered the patient's arm to the quilt and, turning, shook his head.

Mrs. Aspinall buried her face in a cambric handkerchief.

"Is he . . . dead?". Andrea asked.

"It's only a matter of time, I'm afraid."

The doctor's snow-white hair fanned back from a domed forehead in two crests that bounced slightly as he moved to Thora's side. "There's no more that medical science can do. His heart is failing rapidly. I would prepare myself for the worst, if I were you."

"Can't you take him to a hospital?" Andrea demanded.

"He wouldn't survive the journey."

Thora rested her brow against the doctor's arm and wept soundlessly, while Andrea sailed from behind the chair to the bed. Scowling, she stared down at her father as if to command him to step back from the grave. In spite of the ominous presence of the daughter, Holly was drawn to the bedside. Andrea said nothing. Two tears, like crystal peardrops, clung to her cheeks.

"May . . . may I?" Holly asked.

Andrea did not reply.

From the chair, Thora said brokenly, "It's what he would have wished, dear."

Mr. Aspinall's normally rubicund cheeks were waxen. He no longer appeared cheerfully distracted. Stillness made him seem smaller. The embroidered pillow was smooth, sheet smooth, quilt smooth, the needlework panel, just above his head, rich in texture. He looked, Holly thought, like a porcelain figurine in an ornate box. On the chest-of-drawers glassware rattled as Holly knelt on the rug and gently touched the man's hand.

He gave no sign of recognition.

She wanted to kiss him – for the first and last time. But such a bold gesture would surely have provoked Andrea. There had never been anything physical in Holly's relationship with Mr. A. It was the rapport of two people, one quite old, the other quite young, who shared a mutual passion, expert and apprentice drawn together by love of craft in a bond that was difficult to explain to the Twentieth Century's give-and-get society.

Five years – almost. Six days a week. Ten to fifteen hours each day. She had spent more time with James Aspinall than she had with her own father – he more time with her than with Andrea or David.

It had been by chance that she'd obtained a position as shop servant in Aspinall's Antiques. Her father had had her marked for a job in Cavanaugh's, filling bottles with cough linctus or boxes with liver pills. In the months prior to the outbreak of war, however, Cavanaugh's hadn't been employing labour. There was no question of Holly being allowed to continue her education. It was unthinkable to a man like Leo Beckman. None of Grandpa Tal's barbed hints found a target in the surly little docker. Holly must work. Holly must bring home money. Holly must contribute to the housekeeping, like Maury and Ritchie. Time enough for lolling about when Holly snared a hubby, if the geezer was fool enough to let her. Holly must make the rounds, find something that paid well. Sweet shops, cafes, clothing warehouses – plenty to choose from, warn't there? Though she was slender and good-looking – if not exactly a Kirchner girl – Holly lacked the assured manner that would get her into one of the better-class gown shops. Nothing much else appealed to her. She was drifting, with a doomed feeling that, in a fourteen-year-old, seemed like a boulder pressing on her shoulders. Ten months later, Britain was at war and she could have had her pick of highly-paid jobs. She thanked God that she had not been ten months younger or she would never have passed the shop in Pimlico on that warm spring afternoon, found her vocation and, with it, the will to fight her father's boorish dictatorship.

Aspinall's Antiques; the window first attracted her and made her linger. In it was a human hand. Supported in the fingers of that hand was a glass goblet. A waterfall of maroon velvet trickled through a landscape of bric-à-brac. The hand hovered. The pinkie tickled the velvet survace to make it ripple then, with great delicacy and precision, the fingers set the goblet down. The hand snaked back under glass shelves laden with carriage clocks, vinaigrettes, cigar boxes, scent bottles, snuff mulls, tarnished candelabrum, jasper plaques, commemorative mugs and a dozy-looking faience duck with a cracked bill. The goblet was quite different from the other "treasures" that the window contained; Holly knew it instinctively. It was finer, richer in colour, and, strangely, not so pretty as some of the other glass items, yet she stared at it with awe because she sensed the incredible skill that had gone into its making.

"Got money to spend?" Come out to admire his handiwork, the owner of the arm was suddenly beside her.

"No, I . . . just . . . looking."

"What would you buy?"

"I don't have any money."

"Never mind. Imagine you're well-off. What would you buy?"

"That glass."

"Why?"

"It's worth a lot, ain't it?"

"Why?"

"I just think it is."

"So, you'd buy it cheap, sell it again, an' take your profit?"

"No, I'd keep it," Holly had answered, firmly.

"Why?"

She had glanced at him, smiling. He was portly and jovial. She had realised that he was playing a game with her, one that gave him teasing pleasure.

"Because it's beautiful."

"That's for true." They had studied the goblet together. "What makes it beautiful? You like the colour?"

"It looks as if somebody'd taken care makin' it."

"That's also for true. Go on, have a guess. Who made it?"

"How'd I know a thing like that?"

"I don't expect you to know. Guess."

"Is it Italian?"

"You're in the trade! You must be!"

"No, no I'm not. Honest!"

"That was no lucky guess."

"I read about it in a schoolbook – I think."

He had scrutinised her closely. She did not feel threatened by his scrutiny, not there on the doorstep of the shop. She had loitered willingly.

"It *is* Italian. Venetian. Famous glass-makers in Venice. Like to guess its age?"

"Oh, no. I've no idea," she'd said.

"Probably made about 1700."

"Is it whole?"

The man's eyebrows had risen in surprise. "I beg your pardon?"

"I mean, is it chipped or cracked."

"Does it look it?"

"I thought, excuse me, I thought perhaps that's why you'd put it in the window so careful, t' hide a crack in it."

The man had grinned. "Smart girl. But that's not my style. I'm an honest dealer. Trickery doesn't pay in the long run. Customer loyalty. You understand?"

Holly had nodded.

"Let's see your hands," the man had requested.

"What for?"

"Hold them out, that'll do."

He had inspected them critically, then glanced up, head cocked. "Straight out of the schoolroom, ain't you?"

"Yes."

"Got a job?"

"Not yet."

"Want one?"

"Doin' what?"

"Sweepin' floors, dustin' china, polishin' brass."

"A servant, y' mean?"

"Shop servant."

"It doesn't sound much cop."

"If you buckle in, you could learn the trade."

"Trade?"

"Antiques."

She had hesitated.

"I've been lookin' for the right girl," the man had said. "Come inside. Poke about. Take your time. Think about my offer. Jobs don't grow on trees, y'know."

Before she'd left Cardwell Place, an hour later, she'd accepted. It was only when she returned home she remembered that she hadn't asked what the wages were. It hadn't seemed to matter. James Aspinall had pegged her correctly. Across the threshold of the cluttered shop, and in its dismal back warehouse, she had found exactly what she was looking for.

Her father had cuffed her ears, making her head ring. But, for the first time, she'd refused to cry or kow-tow to his wishes. Adamantly she had stood her ground while Leo Beckman raged and shouted. In the end – being that kind of father – he did nothing positive to deter her from taking the job. He was calmed a little by Maury's assurance that it was a "good trade, with plenty of gelt in it after Hol gets to know the ropes". Grandpa Tal and Maury had backed her to the hilt. But it was her own self-assurance that had persuaded Leo to leave well alone.

From that day on, inch by inch, she had moved out of Leo's influence into a world in which men like her father had no proper place.

Eight until six, Monday to Saturday, she belonged to James Aspinall. She was more than a sweeper and duster. Soon she became his pupil, his confidante, his disciple. The business – the profession – of antique-dealing swiftly absorbed her. She soaked up knowledge like a sponge.

Now Mr. Aspinall was dying. She could not tell him how she felt, could not express her gratitude. He was not a sentimental man. "Hard-headed, Holly, m'girl. Feet on the ground. Honest, but sharp; that's the ticket for the likes of us." Only now, as Mr. A. lay dying, did she appreciate all that he had done for her. It had never been put into words, never would be. But she understood, as she had not understood before, and realisation brought tears to her eyes. It was too late to say anything, to make a gesture that Mr. Aspinall could grasp.

Andrea put a hand on her shoulder. "He can't hear you. Don't you see, he's unconscious."

Holly released the man's hand. It was almost weightless, like the tiny dried bundles of feathers, made up to look like humming-birds, that came with foliage under glass and which she, like Mr. A., abhorred for their pointless artficiality. "I'm . . . sorry, Miss Aspinall."

"Sorry?" Andrea did not understand. "What have you to be sorry about?"

Holly got to her feet. She looked down at her employer for a moment longer. She did not doubt the doctor's word. There was no hope of a recovery. She could see death already on him. Leaning away from Andrea she stooped and kissed him quickly on the brow, then, turning, hurried from the room. She would have gone on downstairs by the back staircase into the shop, if Andrea's voice had not halted her.

"Wait, Beckman. I want a word with you."

Holly stopped. Holding the iron rail at the top of the stairs she waited. She wanted to run, to fly from the claustrophobic atmosphere of the Aspinalls' apartments. There was nothing she could do now – except leave. She had never lost anybody close before. She'd been too young to remember her mother's death. In spite of the war's win nowing of many men, she'd known none of them well enough to mourn; though, when fighting was intense along the Marne and newspapers were listing staggering numbers of dead, she had been haunted by the recurring nightmare of Maury lying dead in the Flanders mud. Now she recognised the tightness in her chest, the hollowness in her heart as sorrow for the plump little trader.

As Andrea advanced from the bedroom, Holly fought back tears.

"You'd better find my brother," Andrea stated.

"But, I. . ."

"Oh, yes, Armistice Day. I suppose there's some chap waiting to pick you up and take you off to a public house for a good time?"

"No, but. . ."

"Then – please – do this for us. Find David. He should be here at the . . . the end."

"Where is he?"

"That's the problem," Andrea frowned. "Mrs. Hodge has already been to his club, his office, and the barracks. He isn't at any of these places."

"How will I find him, then?"

Glancing furtively behind her, Andrea produced a slip of paper from her sleeve. "You might try this address. It's in Mayfair. I'd go myself, but I daren't leave Mother."

"Will David be there?"

"He might. If not, sombody's sure to know his whereabouts."

Holly was puzzled. "This address. . .?"

Andrea hesitated. "It's his lady friend's flat, if you must know. He hasn't been home since yesterday morning. Personally I'd leave him, but . . . well, no doubt it's better if he's here."

"Yes," Holly said. "I'll find him, if I can."

"Thank you," Andrea said, grudgingly. "Tell him to hurry. And, Beckman, I beg you – be discreet."

*   *   *

In making her request of Holly, Andrea could not have been aware of the unpleasant ironies that she had stirred up. In asking the girl to be discreet, she had touched a loyal nerve that Holly had kept etherised during her years of service to the family. Holly had loved James Aspinall with the respect and affection of a surrogate daughter, but she had tumbled head-over-heels for David in a manner less subtle and more romantic.

It was, however, a private emotion. She hadn't even confided in Grandpa Tal. The impossibility of allowing herself to fall in love with James Aspinall's son made the dream less, not more, solvent. While other girls of her age mooned over Lewis Waller or Francis X. Bushman, the object of Holly's desire lay dangerously close, a breathing person who knew of and occasionally even recognised her existence. David was not a figment of a dark picture palace or distant stage; he occupied a world that interacted with Holly's own in a peculiar planetary arrangement of orbits, zeniths, nadirs and conjunctions.

But David – like Andrea – had "background". For a start, he was a public-school chap, an old Lydanian, and had attended St. Peter's College, Oxford, for a couple of years before retreating, bloody but by no means bowed, to study Advanced Bookkeeping and Accountancy in the City of London Institute, a slide from pinnacles of academe that secretly rather pleased his father. A career as a very junior manager in the mammoth insurance firm of Spencer, Lucas & Andrews had been interrupted by the war. A client and drinking companion in high post in the War Office had fiddled him a commission in the Royal Army Pay Corps which kept him safe out of the trenches for the duration. All this education, this "falling on his feet", had swung David on to a wobbling course that carried him far from the ambit of dark-haired Lambeth girls – and almost as far from his father, mother and the apartment over the shop where he only occasionally deigned to spend a night or two.

At twenty-six a whole year David's senior, Andrea was a cultivated, implacable snob. But David's good humour and a generous streak, inherited from his father perhaps, made him indulgent towards those less favoured by fortune – including the little mouse that his father had rescued from the tedium of poverty. For all her colourlessness, the Beckman gal seemed to be a winner, at least in Dad's book. Being female, Andrea naturally resented young Beckman. But David was jolly relieved that his father had finally found somebody *simpatico* to drone on at. Personally he considered endless conversations about tatty second-hand junk very yawn-making indeed.

When their paths did cross, David was not too stuck-up to reward Beckman for putting up with the monotonous old buffer. At various times over the years, he had given Holly a pasteboard Easter egg filled with Beech's chocolates, a bunch of daffodils that a persistent vendor had foisted on him, a casket of cheap perfume won on the Wheel of Fortune at a Chingford garden party, a Union Jack cushion, and odd Red Back romances that one or other of his sweethearts had "donated" for the comfort of soldiers and that he hadn't the neck to drop in the book bag. Also, once, a fine fat hen, plucked and dressed, that he'd bought for a couple of bob from a nervous private soldier who'd accosted him after a bibulous supper party at Rumpelmayers. All his gifts, except the hen, were hidden away in Holly's bedroom in the terrace house in Abraham's Box; Red Backs unread, perfumes still stoppered, chocs untasted, the daffs dried and withered now like a collection of seagulls' bones.

The girl's gratitude was obvious. She would look at him as if she thought he was the elephant's eyebrows – which, of course, he was; especially in his tailored service uniform from Pope & Bradley's, with his moustache grown full and mature. It would have been a piece of cake to apply a touch of the old languishers, sweep Beckman off her feet, educate her in *l'amour*. She was really quite pretty, and had a good figure under her drab workdress. Most of his fellow subalterns wouldn't have thought twice about seducing her, but David Aspinall, was basically too decent to tumble an employee that his father depended upon. Besides, he had as much of "this-that-and-the-other" as he could cope with. Plenty of chic young ladies were willing to go to the bother of seducing *him*, and that was much more flattering to the ego and much less exhausting in the long run than tumbling servants. Since taking up with – or being taken up by – Linsey Leigh-Jennings, Captain David Aspinall had no energy left to play the field. He found Linsey so demanding, so devouring and so damnably depraved that languidity was no longer just a fashionable pose but the exhaustion of a bather carried by unseen currents into very deep water indeed.

Vaguely Holly realised that David Aspinall was a participating member of the dissolute society crowd whose strength had been increased, not diminished, by the travails of war. She regarded David's private life as mysterious and somewhat glamorous, though Mr. Aspinall occasionally complained about the amount of borrowed money that his son was wasting in the pursuit of unmentionable pleasures. The painted face of London's smart set, bright and new, had never been revealed to Holly in close-up. Her confrontation with its lesser personages that evening was coloured by the afternoon's sorrow. The contrasts changed Holly, stripping off layers of illusion and inhibition as rapidly as acetone peels varnished wood down to the original grain.

She reached the address that Andrea had given her just as the lamps were being lit. She'd had to struggle through celebrating crowds at Hyde Park Corner and along Piccadilly. It was a relief to clear the public thoroughfares and slip into the backwaters of Mayfair that nestled between Curzon Street and Grosvenor Square. Ahead of her she glimpsed a comforting symbol of routine, a lamplighter in cape and billed hat padding from lamp to lamp, pole like a lance, the misty auras of the mantles blooming behind him. Shouting and singing from the Park was more distant; to Holly it still seemed threatening, like the din of riot, less jubilant than angry in the melancholy dusk.

In Larder Mews cobbles were flanked by recently converted cottages and new constructions. Warm red brick did not show in the darkness and it was the wrong season for the soft touches of window-gardens and creepers. Slotted between the still-used stables and carriage houses that backed on to the quadrangles of inhabited town-house mansions were the new establishments where the sons and daughters of the rich had sown seed and taken hold. The listing old windows of livery cottages had been replaced by bows of bulls' eye glass. Horseposts were painted in garish reds and yellows. The modish picturesqueness of Mayfair had, even then, begun to take on a quality as synthetic as cheap lacquer. The Mews was long. Sloping kerbstones were hidden by carriages and raffish motorcars. Before Miss Linsey Leigh-Jennings's doorway were ranked a Lanchester and a Silver Ghost. Two Prince Henry Vauxhall sporting machines awkwardly blocked the narrow pavement.

Against the house wall, beneath an open window through which floated clouds of smoke, squatted a Scottish major. He wore a kilt and a pair of patent leather dancing pumps and was naked to the waist. Fine rain glistened on his squat body and dewed the matted hair on his chest. Draped over his shoulders was his tunic jacket. Bare brawny arms rested on bare knees. His head hung as if he was asleep. In one fist, like an Indian club, he clutched an almost empty bottle of

Gleneagles whisky. He was seated so close to the step of the house that Holly could not avoid him. The door was painted crimson with a fleur-de-lys inset of stained glass and a brass knocker in the shape of a suspended dove. Though the door was ajar and there was considerable row inside, Holly rapped tentatively and waited to be admitted.

The hand gripped her suddenly on the calf of the leg, rucking up her skirt and stocking. With a gasp of shock, she tried to jerk away. The major held her fast. She stared down into his swarthy unshaven features with compassion and dread.

"They've occupied the house, lass. They're crawlin' all o'er it."

"I . . . I have a message to deliver."

"Give it here."

"It's for . . . for Captain Aspinall."

"You're no verry trustin', are you?"

"It's about his father. It's urgent."

"You speakee good English."

"Please, let me go."

"Nice wee bit o' leg there."

The fist shifted upwards to her knee.

"French, are you?" the major asked, in a low, intimate growl. "A native?"

"I'm a . . . a friend of David Aspinall."

"Aye, lucky bloody David! Who the hell's he when he's at home? Are you Belgian?" Though his gaze was fixed on her face and his mouth twisted in a crooked grin, he was not addressing her at all. He swung the bottle. "Will you be havin' a drop, lassie, to keep a soldier company, a soldier far from home."

She thought quickly. "Yes, I'll take a drop, sir."

"Aye, there's a nice lassie. Here."

"I can't get the cork out."

When the major took his hand from her leg to draw the cork of the whisky bottle she stepped swiftly away from him into the house of Linsey Leigh-Jennings.

Holly leaned against the door, closing it, and turning, shot the stout metal bolt. The major roared, and battered upon the door with the bottle, swearing obscenely, then, abruptly, fell silent. A moment later Holly heard him sobbing.

The hallway was tiny. Tense and trembling, Holly was afraid of the grotesque things she might find in the dolls-house chambers at the end of the corridor. Prominent beams were painted the same shade of crimson as the door. At the foot of a miniature staircase lay a handsome walnut longcase clock, splintered and stopped. Twisted hands jutted from the face like waxed moustaches.

Holly moved from the door, away from the sobbing. She trod gingerly over a rumpled tricolour, and peered into an anteroom, hoping that she might find the servants' quarters and somebody who would tell her what to do. Bundles of overcoats, capes and furs were mounded in the little room. On them, curled like a child, was a young woman, either unconscious or deep asleep. Dressed only in a corded corset and lace-edge petticoat, her silken legs twitched as she slept. Her pretty face was half-hidden beneath an organdie hat, her head resting uncomfortably on a brass scuttle that bristled with sticks and riding crops. Holly stepped past the sleeping girl, paused and called out as loudly as she dared.

"David. David Aspinall. Captain Aspinall."

In drawing attention to her presence, she increased her fear.

"I say. I *do* say!"

The man was not in uniform. He wore the trousers of a dinner suit and a stiff-fronted, short-collar skirt, bow-tie askew. The stub of a cigarette adhering to his lip scattered ash down his dickey when he spoke. He was very tall, with an equine nose, and Holly surmised that he was not much older than she was.

"Rah-thah ado-rah-ball!"

"Please, sir. I've been sent to fetch Captain Aspinall."

"Hev yah rally!"

She had heard the accent mocked; Ritchie did a top-notch imitation. But the true intonations were more ugly than any mimic could catch.

"Is Captain Aspinall here, sir?" Holly said. "I've been sent to fetch him on a matter of extreme urgency."

"Sent? Oh, dear God! A *servant?*"

"Yes, sir."

Strings of paper ribbon were attached to the young man's legs trailing endlessly back, like shackles, around the corner of the hallway.

"Captain Aspinall, is he here?" Holly persisted.

"Aspinall, Aspinall, whaw faw art tha, Aspinall?"

With a casual waggle of his slender fingers, and no other clue as to David's whereabouts, the young man drifted back along the corridor and vanished from sight. Gathering her courage, Holly followed him into a brightly-lit room filled with people.

The room was larger than she would have guessed from the Lilliputian scale of the entrances. It was decorated in shades of blue and orange. There were several chairs and settles of Indian wicker. In one corner a horseshoe-shaped bar was lit by two pagoda lanterns. The bar-top was strewn with bottles, glasses and bamboo ice-shakers. In the midst of the smoke, twenty or thirty people were arranged in a series of tableaux. For all the attention Holly received she might have been invisible, though, dressed in sober skirt and jacket, she stood out in that luminous company.

By the horn of an American gramophone a stately colonel, in full dress uniform, did his duty. He was about sixty, ramrod straight. Only his right fist moved, remorselessly cranking the handle of the Victrola, while a petite young thing in a silk afternoon suit crouched at his feet, snapping up at him, "Left, right, left, right – and left and turn." From the machine's fluted bell emerged a quixotic martial air to which couples in the vicinity danced in romantic – or erotic – defiance of the crisp military tempo. Penned in the window corner two adult women and a young boy were executing the steps of the "Hullo Tango" at furious pace. The women passed the boy between them, like lionesses sharing a kill, squeezing him against their breasts, sweeping him backwards to be kissed by the other. Moon-faced and smooth, the boy showed no emotion at all, but danced – and kissed – with hideous expertise.

Holly's impulse was to turn on her heel and flee. But the drunken Scottish major, like Charon, would be waiting outside. Besides she could not abandon her mission, could not surrender to her revulsion without a struggle. Hesitantly she edged between the dancers in search of David. It was the thought that David was completely at home in such bizarre company that shocked Holly most of all.

"My God! Fancy dress! How original!" The couple spun on the spot, following Holly's progress.

"Perfect! How utterly perfect! Ain't the hair perfect?"

"Who *is* she?"

"God knows!"

Perspiration freckled Holly's brow. She felt as if she was choking. The reek of smoke was both sweet and acrid, interlaced with cloying perfumes and the sharpness of spilled alcohol. From behind the bar came the explosion of a champagne cork. A hand rose, holding aloft a fizzing bottle that sprayed foam in all directions.

Somebody caught her elbow and spun her round.

She was confronted by a puffy little gentleman in a purple smoking jacket. He was her father's age, and, like her father, had handsome features made venous by drink.

"Brought the 'amper, 'ave yer?" he demanded.

"No, I. . ."

"From Fortnum's, ain't yer?"

For an instant Holly thought he was mocking her, then she realised that the accent was quite genuine.

"No, I. . ."

"Out front, round back, down the cellar steps." The man made to turn away, then, with a nod, swung round on her again and put out his fat hand, stuffing a one-pound banknote into the vee of her jacket. "Good gal, 'ave one on Charlie Hallet. For all them as was lost at sea. Right-oh?"

"Sir, please?" But Hallet had rolled off towards the bar.

Holly followed him, holding out the banknote. It was then, from a corner of the bar, that she saw David.

Four men and two women were hidden behind the bar. Two of the men wore bits and pieces of army uniform, the other pair dinner jackets. Not much older than Holly, the women were dressed in evening gowns. Though both were pretty and their gowns expensive, there was no elegance in the way they squatted on the floor, showing their legs up to the garters. None of them was particularly drunk. Concentration gave them an air of sobriety at odds with their rowdy surroundings. A bar-stool, laid on its side, made a table for the Crown & Anchor board, a creased and tattered square of painted canvas, relic of barracks and tents. On it lay silver coins and notes.

The woman holding the dice-cup was golden-haired, with violet eyes and a heart-shaped face on a slender neck. At that moment her features were strangely elongated, stretched out of shape by a need of such intensity that it appeared like pain. Neck tensed, eyes narrowed, lips compressed, it was as if she was thrusting to give birth, not merely to roll dice from a tortoise-shell beaker.

David's head was in profile to Holly, his lips slightly parted as if the vision of the blonde woman entranced him. She shook the cup and with a backhand toss shot dice along the floor.

Heads bent. A cheer went up. David's mouth closed. He nodded in fatalistic resignation, rubbed his mouth with is wrist, forced a grin.

"You'll have my socks before long, darling," he said.

"And your trowzies, no doubt," the other woman remarked archly.

"How *does* she do it?" asked one young man. "Every time, a winner."

Obviously he had also lost on the throw. Only Linsey Leigh-Jennings had won. She pressed the cup to her breasts to keep it warm, scraped notes and coins towards her and tucked them possessively between her knees.

"Truly, she is favoured of the gods," said the third young man.

"It's unfair," said the woman.

"Virtue," said Linsey, "is being rewarded, that's all. Now pay your money, dears, and set up the stakes for. . ."

Linsey's brows rose in astonishment as she noticed Holly.

"What on earth is that creature doing?"

They all looked up at Holly who was hoping to catch David's eye without drawing attention to herself. She was more embarrassed by the intimacy of the gamblers than by the dancers' antics.

"Good God," David said. "It's young Beckman."

"You actually *know* this person?"

David scrambled to his feet. "What's wrong?"

"Your father," Holly answered.

"Relapse?"

The others got to their feet, Linsey still holding the dice-cup to her breast. Her cheeks were flushed and her eyes empty in that moment of transference from the heightened reality of gambling to the squalid business of duty.

"It's . . . it's very serious," Holly said. "I've been sent to fetch you."

"How did you find me?"

"Miss Andrea gave me this address."

"Did she, indeed?" murmured Linsey.

In spite of the alcohol he had consumed David was instantly in control. He lifted his tunic from the tap of a sink below the level of the bar.

"Take the Prince." One of the young men tugged a wire keyring from his pocket and chucked it to David.

"Shall I come?" Linsey asked.

David kissed her on the cheek. "Best not."

"Call me," the young woman said.

"I will."

A clap on the back from his friends and, buttoning his uniform, David hurried from behind the bar. Guiding Holly by the elbow, ignoring the jibes that were thrown at him, he ushered the girl from the house.

It was raining. The drunken major had gone, leaving only an upright empty bottle where he had been, like a little glass gravestone. The leather upholstery in the Vauxhall motorcar was damp. Nobody had thought to cover it.

"Get in," David told Holly.

Holly did so. Hardly had she seated herself and gripped the ledge beneath the sloping shield, than David started the machine. Jerkily he reversed along the mews.

"How bad is it with Dad?" David asked.

"He's . . . he's dyin'."

"Heart?"

"Yes."

"What did that sawbones, Adair, say?"

"There's no hope, I'm afraid."

"Damn! Damn and blast! Poor old buzzard! What a time to go." He glanced at Holly. "Did you see him?"

"Yes, but he was unconscious."

"Oh, hell!"

David said no more. He concentrated on threading the Vauxhall out of Mayfair and, with much stopping, starting and violent use of the horn, navigated through shoals of pedestrians by Hyde Park Corner and Grosvenor Place, down into Pimlico. In the end they could have walked it faster. Eventually they drew up in front of the shop in Cardwell Place.

Andrea was waiting on the step by the door of the stairs to the apartment. Leaving Holly to climb over the side of the motorcar, David got out. She could see the brother and sister only indistinctly – Andrea had not lighted the electric globe above the door – but could tell by their gestures, and the manner in which Andrea silently drew her brother to her before allowing him to pass upstairs, that they had arrived too late.

Disorientated by the events of the evening, by the ride through teeming London in an open motorcar, and dismayed by the realisation that her life had been robbed of its centre, Holly loitered on the pavement, not quite knowing where to go or what to do.

Andrea, who had entered the doorway after her brother, returned. Holly could not see if there were tears in her eyes. Her voice, though, was as strong and commanding as ever. Her statement left no room for question.

"Go away, Beckman. We don't need you now."

With that Andrea Aspinall slammed the street door, shutting Holly out.

*   *   *

Old Tal Kirsanoff had no difficulty in predicting his granddaughter's movements. The roistering terrace with its lights, bunting and noisy bands would not merely make Holly uncomfortable – it would repel her. She would enter the house by the back lots and scullery door.

Tal's room was next to Holly's, at the very top of the stairs, jammed on to a landing no larger than a postcard. Each had a window as narrow as a vent, a view of warehouse walls, the "lanes", lavatory roofs and narrow gardens that bristled with the skeletal remains of last summer's cabbages. Like Holly, Tal enjoyed the comparative privacy of a room set above the main quarters. He found the window rewarding, especially in the small hours of the night when insomnia troubled him and brought too many remembrances of the past; then he would sit in his wooden rocking chair in the dark, close to the glass, and observe the nocturnal doings of the good folk of Abraham's Box.

If Tal had been more gregarious, greedy for attention, like Leo, his neighbours would have found in him a source of gossip as deep and wide as a lake. But Grandpa Tal told no tales on the drunkards who slept off their excesses in the wash-houses when their wives had barred the doors on them, or of lovers' trysts in the lanes. He revealed nothing of desperate assignations, the adulteries of the wives of soldiers – Faye Yeaman, Jan Mavorski, Netta Corcoran – who slipped out late, when their children were asleep, and returned just before dawn; nothing of his knowledge of the thieves, fences and bully-boys who met to plan jobs, or slithered past pushing handcarts covered by tarpaulins. He was a passive witness to the underground history of the neighbourhood, as once he had been a silent spectator at less trivial events in Russia, long before the October Revolution had torn his native land apart. In many ways he found the parochial misdeeds of Lambeth more interesting and more significant.

Nobody, not even Holly, knew of Tal's night watches, or that he had gleaned from them a detailed awareness of his family's secrets. He could name the girl that Maury had been seduced by at the age of nineteen; name the young widow that Leo frequently "consoled"; give date to the day of Ritchie's first real venture into thieving, and identify the boy's less skilled accomplices.

All such history was grist to the mills of Tal Kirsanoff's memory which – alas – was as rugged and enduring as his body.

Though he had the blunt features of a peasant, education had sharpened his mind. He had his father to thank for that. His father had not been ashamed of education, as Leo and most fathers in Lambeth were, through fear of being thought swank, of losing the respect of the community. In Russia, Tal's father had been praised for teaching his sons to read and write. It had not been his father's fault that the world had collapsed, that the Act of Emancipation sponsored by Nicholas had come too late. Instead of reforming the lives of the peasant classes, enforcement of the Act served to treble their obligations, raise taxes, stir up political clashes, increase the effects of crop failures with evictions and near famine. It was his father who had persuaded Tal and his brothers to leave Russia. His father stayed behind. He had obligations, debts to his own father and mother, aunts and uncles, even to nephews. By remaining, Tal's father had finally "emancipated" his sons.

How different from Leo Beckman, that godless, once-charming little immigrant who had seduced Tal's only daughter. But it was not Leo who had kept him a prisoner in the council house in Ambraham's Terrace all these years. He stayed to be near his grandchildren. They were his flesh and his blood, as Leo Beckman was not. Where else could he go now? Not to New York, in America. His brother Peter had been dead these ten years. Ilek – if still alive – would be over ninety; he had last been heard of in Berlin forty years ago. Perhaps Ilek's grandsons had fought for the Kaiser as willingly as Maury fought for the King of England.

Tal was stuck, had been stuck here since the money he had saved had run out. His wife, Huldah, had been sick when they first arrived in England. He had accepted charity, food and beds in the Poor Jews' Shelter in Leman Street until he got work; not, as he had hoped, with his nimble fingers, but with his muscles, his broad back, as a hauler in the coal-dock in Shadwell.

Tal blinked.

Huldah came around the corner from Harmon Street. Under the lamp, he saw her just as she had been before they left Russia, when she used to come to the corner by the Platonov Gate to wait for him finishing work. Before their marriage. Young and lithe and dark and beautiful, she would pause – like so – to glance left and right in case the careless carriages of the rich ran her down. It was not Huldah, of course, but Holly.

Holly was so like Huldah.

Tal pushed himself from the rocker and opened the door of his room. He listened. Noises from the terrace were abrasive. He could hear nothing in the house itself. No Leo, no Ritchie. He could smell the stew he had set to cook on the stove two floors below. He stepped back to the window and watched Holly slip through the door in the wall from the warehouse lane, hurry across the garden, through the second door into the terrace lane.

Huldah: Holly – perhaps the good God provided old men with such beautiful ellipses as compensation for having lived too long.

Buttoning his woollen vest, Tal went downstairs.

The living room was chock-a-block with bits of furniture, none of Holly's choosing. She had long since given up trying to keep the rooms tidy and had settled, with Tal's help, for a general Sunday cleaning. Nothing she could do ever got rid of the overpowering odours of tobacco, beer and boiled mutton. Three overstuffed armchairs and a sagging settee that Leo had ambitiously re-covered in cheap cut moquette defended the hob grate. Four wooden chairs were propped against a drop-leaf table against the inner wall. Out of necessity, the scullery door had been replaced by a greasy curtain. Scuttle, footstool, mushroom ashtray and a writing bureau, in which crockery, cutlery, sauce and pickle bottles were kept, chopped up the limited space even more. The overmantel was littered with pipe racks, cigar boxes, match holders, dented mugs, candlesticks, broken clocks, framed photographs, and a big ugly tin tea-caddy that Leo had won in a shuffle-board competition many years ago.

Cooking and eating were messy procedures in the Beckman household. Stewpot, frying pan, soup pot and kettle were usually balanced on or around the hob. The new gas stove in the scullery was hardly ever used, for reasons of laziness rather than economy. Tal could not recall when last the five of them had sat round a table to break bread together. It had been so different in the old days. However much she bowed to Leo's will, Holly's mother had always insisted that certain proprieties be maintained. She had been a wonderful cook, able to make much out of little and to see to it that he, Tal, had food appropriate to Jewish observances. Now Leo and Ritchie, Maury too, just grabbed a bite from plates balanced on their knees. He, being an old man, had not the will to concern himself with the strict observation of Jewish festivals. Over the years he had been infected by Leo's slovenliness.

He had not seriously opposed his daughter's marriage to Leo Beckman. Perhaps that had been the one fault he had made in bringing up his daughter. He had been too understanding. In spite of her intelligence and apparent coolness, there had been a hot fire of physical passion in her. Leo had been strong then and so ardent in his love-making that few girls could have resisted him. Besides, Leo's family had been decent Polish Jews, though Leo had relinquished the faith at all levels. He had even refused the Jewish wedding ritual, though Tal had fought him bitterly on that score. Young Huldah was too enraptured to take sides. Perhaps, Tal thought later, she had been over-confident of her ability to tame and civilise her wild husband, blind to his stubbornness and his growing laziness. It was sloth, not theology, that undermined them all.

Leo had gone from bad to worse. The children, Ritchie, Holly, even Maury, had been brought up as Gentiles, not even as Christians. Following a creed meant self-discipline; Leo would have none of that, not for himself or his offspring. To his shame, Tal had gradually capitulated too in time. The only consolation he could find was his belief that even Holly's mother, for all her shrewdness, would not have been able to withstand Leo's implacable ignorance. Holly had so many of her mother's qualities, including, Tal suspected, the irrational urges of a passionate nature; but in Holly they were held well in check, reined in by a preoccupation with "trade business" and by her ability to rule her body with her mind.

Pale and red-eyed, Holly entered the room from the scullery. She had taken off her jacket and laid it on the settee. Going to her grandfather she lifted her cheek to his kiss. His arms went around her and she sagged against his chest.

"He's dead. Mr. Aspinall's dead."

"There, there, child." Tal put his hand on her hair. "He was a good man and he will be mourned."

"What shall I do?"

"First, you should eat supper."

"I'm not hungry."

"But you haven't eaten since this morning."

Tal took down the tray from its hook by the grate, spread it with the white tablecloth he'd brought down earlier from his room and set it with fork and spoon, plate and cup.

Obediently Holly seated herself in an armchair, Leo's chair, by the fire. She was chilled. As Tal served stew from the pot, cut bread and infused tea, he encouraged her to tell him of the events of that day. With the warmth of the fire upon her, Holly relaxed a little and, with unaccustomed garrulousness, poured out all that had happened, from the sombreness of Mr. Aspinall's deathbed to the obscene gaiety of the Mayfair set.

The stew was thickened by cornflour: it contained little meat, but sliced carrots, dumplings and the inevitable onions made it rich and filling. Holly mopped up the gravy with bread. Not until her plate had been wiped clean and only tea-leaves remained in her cup did she recover control of herself. Tal removed the tray and left it on the draining board by the cold-water sink in the scullery. When he returned, Holly had taken off her shoes and had sat back, head against the cushion.

Quietly she said, "What a hypocrite I am, Grandfather. I was so unhappy at Mr. Aspinall's passing that I wept all the way home.

But a plate of stew and a seat by the fire. . ."

"Listen," the old man said. "You hear them? Singing, shouting, dancing. You would not think half a million men had died. What do *they* celebrate? Their own survival."

Without the jacket, the girl seemed younger.

"I promised Stan I'd dance with him," Holly said.

"Stan an' your brother went up West."

"Sober?"

"What do you think?"

She sat in silence for a minute or two while Tal reached down a cigar box and raked among the stubs until he found one to his liking. He lit it with a kitchen match and took his seat in Ritchie's chair, opposite the girl.

At length Holly said, "I'll be given notice."

"You are sure?" Tal said.

"The daughter – Andrea – hates me."

"*She* will run the shop, I suppose?"

"No, not her. David might."

"From what you say of him, he will not be content to be a shopkeeper."

"It makes money, you know."

"Because of good buying."

"And sellin'. Mr. A. had lots of 'special' clients."

"Do you want to leave?"

"No," Holly said. "But it's unavoidable. At best, they'll sell out. I wouldn't want to work there, not for somebody else."

"Then you must look for another position."

"I suppose so."

"Do you have friends – in the trade, I mean?"

"Yes, but there will be tens of thousands of young men comin' home soon, all lookin' for work, trained dealers among them."

"Maury will also be coming home," Tal reminded her. "If he is still of a mind to go into the brick trade maybe he will find something for you to do for him."

"Employ me?" said Holly. "Maury will barely be able to keep himself. Anyhow, Maury may have changed his mind."

"Maury has a head on his shoulders. And he's a worker. Heaven knows, there will be much scope for bricks and sellers of bricks."

Good times just around the corner? Tal had too much experience of the upheavals that came in the wake of war to be genuinely optimistic. But he tried to sound it, to draw Holly out of her depression. Maury *was* a worker. If there was any scope for opportunity in the post-war world, then Maury would forge ahead. It was true, though, that the labour market would be flooded, that girls like Holly would not find it easy to obtain jobs. He had witnessed instances of this in Russia, where the balance of society and its money-providing machinery were easily sent skew-whiff.

"It will take time, Holly," he said. "Time for you to find out what you really want to do."

"I know that already."

"Your own shop? Holly Beckman – Antiques?"

"I want it more than anything."

"Then stay with the trade."

Holly nodded.

There was evidence of an assurance in her that Tal had not detected before, not in such large measure. James Aspinall had done wonders for the girl. Tal now wished that he had managed to meet the man who had so changed Holly. But he had never found the courage to cross the bridge that separated Lambeth from Pimlico, shop-owner from dock labourer.

Holly's lids were heavy, her eyes somnolent.

Sounds from the street vibrated through the walls of the house, like spirits from the Volga that, with the onset of winter, beat ghostly fists upon cottage doors, seeking entry and a warm billet – but if they were admitted out of pity for their plight, they would oust the family, one by one. Some things you did not give in to.

Holly seemed oblivious to the din. But Tal knew enough of her character to realise that she was aware of the uninhibited sounds of the crowds in the upper Terrace. There was no reason why she should be gregarious. So many people considered it a virtue; instinct was to follow the crowd. Holly was different.

Tal wondered if she was at all conscious of the conflicts that lay within her. She was a Gentile by upbringing, Jewish by heritage; a Londoner with echoes of Moscow, Prague, Budapest and Vienna sounding in her. Her mother had been different too; he had made sure of that. He had reared his daughter without regard for the mores of the English backstreets, inculcating in her respect for independence of spirit gained through knowledge. It had been all the rage, at the turn of the century, to endow boys with practical knowledge, mechanistic knowledge suited to the sons of artisans. But girls, young women – ah, there he had flown in the face of fashion. He had raised Huldah as he would have raised a son, had almost forgotten that she was a woman and, by her very nature, vulnerable to passions that the intellect could not control. Independence of mind had caused young

Huldah to defy his wishes, to take what she wanted – Leo Beckman; lover first, husband second – and to the devil with the consequences.

How much of Huldah was in Holly? How much of himself? In the sciences, learned men explored the very structures of the cells, the atoms that composed the individual consciousness. It seemed that uniqueness was a myth; every man, every woman was the sum of all that had gone into their creation, not an end but a mere mark in evolutionary time. That philosophy rather depressed him. Holly was one year older than a century that had already bred a surfeit of disruption, suffering, bloodshed and change. Though she was totally unaware of it, the Kirsanoffs' cosmopolitan attitudes were wound into her character like threads into fine cloth. What was now, for Holly, preoccupation could so easily become passion, all-consuming as white flame.

For a moment, Tal felt sorry for her.

"I must help the child," he promised himself. "Holly and Maury, I must help them in any way I can, for they are Kirsanoffs under the skin. Ritchie is not; he is Leo Beckman's son. But Holly, beautiful Holly, she is more Kirsanoff than Beckman, more like my own wife and daughter than I dare to believe." Tal nodded to himself. "I remember how resentful it makes one, when one is young. They wish to find things out for themselves, just as I did, as her mother did. It will be doubly difficult for Holly, though, in these changed days."

The old Russian felt his muscles tighten. He longed for a peep into the future – if only to relieve him of the burden of the past.

Holly was watching him.

Just for an instant, sleep made her eyes seem secretive, like Ritchie's.

Suddenly he was anxious, and confused.

Sucking on the cigar stump, he growled aloud, "It will work out, child. In its own good time it will work out for you."

Holly smiled wistfully, and closed her eyes.

Grandpa Tal was bewildered by the enigmatic smile.

What did Holly really and truly desire? A shop with her name above the door? Wealth, security, a fine lover? Entry, perhaps, into the gaudy world she had glimpsed that Armistice night, to share the tinsel and transient glitter, the careless laughter of the diamond hearts of Mayfair?

Within minutes Holly had fallen asleep, and her dreams were safe from an old man's curiosity.

2

The Shadow of Mr. A.

FROM THE SHELTER of the shop window Holly watched the funeral procession depart. Procession was really too grand a word for it; a shiny black hearse with two uniformed men on the open seat, three other carriages containing the family and a few of James Aspinall's closest colleagues. Holly knew them all by sight. She was surprised that such august members of the profession as Kennedy King and Simon Black had forsaken their Bond Street shops to say farewell to Mr. A. of Pimlico. None of David's intimates, except the young lieutenant who had loaned him the Vauxhall, turned up. There was no sign of Linsey Leigh-Jennings, though Miles Walshott, Andrea's "intended", was present. After the internment service in Castle Hill Cemetery the mourners would return to the Cavendish Hotel to eat lunch and toast the memory of the departed in wine and spirits.

The shop had remained closed during the two days in which James Aspinall's body had been laid out upstairs. On Andrea's instructions, however, Holly had returned to the premises on Tuesday and, behind locked doors, had begun an inventory of the stock. On Tuesday, without interruption, she had listed the contents of all shelves and cupboards, and made note of the heavier furniture in the back store. On Wednesday, she had covered the four glass-topped showcases in the body of the shop and had moved into the store to complete the list of small objects in the huge fly-blown collector's case.

Carefully she had propped open the lid with four volumes of *The Poetical Works of Lord Byron*, tomes that served all kinds of useful purposes, from wedges to doorstops. Slipping her hand into the case she removed each item, inspected it, entered a brief description and the label price against the purchase price code of the lot, and laid the object on the scarred oak packing bench. She carried about with her a little teakwood tray with two inkwells and a penrack fixed to it. Her writing had become smaller and neater over the past couple of years and had a solicitor's meticulousness on the lined foolscap sheets that were used for cataloguing and stock records. So engrossed did Holly become in her task that she did not hear the Aspinalls' return at twenty minutes after three o'clock. She was startled by David's sudden appearance in the doorway behind her.

He looked drawn, almost ill, and moved without his usual languorous ease – trying to be silent and respectful, perhaps.

He did not venture beyond the doorway.

"Come upstairs," he said.

Holly put the pen on the tray and glanced at her dusty, stained hands and shabby skirt. She took off her overall and would have gone to the back where the sink was, if David's voice had not floated back from the shop.

"At once, please."

Wiping her fingers on the back of her skirt, Holly followed David up the iron staircase and along the corridor. He held the door for her and nodded for her to enter the sitting room.

Red-eyed, Thora was seated at an occasional table. Andrea stood behind her mother. David moved from the door to stand, awkwardly, opposite. At the head of the table sat a man Holly hadn't seen before, a saturnine gent with barrel chest and big hands. Documents were arranged on the table. The stranger peered at Holly from under bushy brows.

"Come in. Be seated." Brusquely he indicated a vacant chair at the table.

Andrea said, "I really must pro. . ."

"Not now, Andrea," David spoke sharply, silencing his sister.

"Please do sit down, Miss," the lawyer advised.

Holly took the chair he indicated. She fixed her gaze on the centre frond of one of the fleur-de-lys patterns on the wallpaper behind the solicitor's head.

"Miss Beckaman – you are Miss Beckaman?"

"Beckman, sir. Just Beckman," Holly answered.

"I'm Mumford, solicitor to James Aspinall. You have been invited to the reading of his will and testament, in accordance with the courtesy afforded all benefactors. Do you understand, Miss Beckman?"

"Yes, sir."

Mumford folded his arms and, without more ado, read from the document before him. He rapped out each word in a loud voice, to override interruption.

Holly listened in bemusement.

Mumford read, "I James Aspinall, of Cardwell Place, Pimlico, dealer in antique objects and works of art, revoke heretofore all other wills and testamentary dispositions made by me, and declare this to be my final will and testament."

Thora uttered a deep dry sob.

Mumford continued: "I appoint Sebastian John Mann Mumford of Gray's Inn Court, executor and trustee . . ." The voice droned a little now, dispensing legal mumbo-jumbo, arriving at length at important matters without pause or special inflexion. "I bequeath to my beloved wife and companion of these happy years, Thora Cropper Aspinall, free of legacy duty, my personal belongings, books not of a trade nature, clothing and all intimate effects, along with one quarter part of the business concerned with the purchasing and selling of antique objects, and of the proceeds that may be raised by sale of such objects, and the dispersal of stock purchased previous to the date of my death."

"Good God!" said Andrea.

Hastening on, Mumford read, "I bequeath to my only son, David James Aspinall, one quarter part of the said business on all terms equal to those designated in the foregoing disposition to my wife. To my daughter. . ."

"Oh, really, it's too much!" Andrea was running ahead.

"To my daughter, Thora Andrea Aspinall, one quarter part of the said business on all terms equal to those designated in the foregoing disposition to my son."

"Only three quarters," said Andrea. "I insist that you go no further."

"Please, Miss Aspinall," Mumford ordered, then said, "I bequeath to my employee and loyal shop servant, Holly Beckman, one quarter. . ."

Andrea jumped to her feet. David reached out to grip his sister's arm. ". . . one quarter share in the said business on all terms equal to those designated to my wife, daughter and son. Relentlessly Mumford went on, "In witness whereof I, the said James Aspinall, have to this will and last testament set my hand on this Twenty-first day of March, in the year of Our Lord one thousand nine hundred and eighteen."

Andrea and David were shouting at each other. Across the table Thora Aspinall lifted her head and looked directly at Holly in a curious manner.

Holly sat quite still.

"Will witnessed by Oliver T. Smithers, and. . ."

"Making that . . . that ragamuffin *my* equal," Andrea shouted.

"The will is available to anyone who may wish to inspect it."

Mumford got to his feet.

David had come around the table. He swayed then swung round to glance at Holly. "Four ways! The old devil!"

"*Monstrous!*" Andrea cried.

"Hush it up, Andrea," David said. "You're upsettin' Mother."

The lawyer now took a hand. "I may say that I felt it incumbent upon me to point out to your father that the terms he wished to express might cause considerable distress."

"Distress! That's putting it mildly," David remarked.

"Your father assured me that he'd given the matter, in all its ramifications, long and serious consideration," Mumford added.

"Somehow *she* got round him," Andrea said.

Holly found her voice. "I did not."

"You see! She spoke back to me. She addressed me as if she were my equal."

"What do you expect her to do, Andrea?" said David. "Sit tight while you cast silly aspersions? It isn't *her* fault, you know. Father's to blame."

"So you're siding with her, are you? I suppose you're looking for another cheap conquest, another slut with a bit of money to splash. . ."

"If you're implying that Linsey. .?"

"Stop it at once." Mumford slapped the table.

Andrea drew herself up. In a more even voice she said, "We'll fight it; the will I mean. No court in the country will uphold a disposition of that nature."

"'Fraid it will," David said. "Father may have been . . . eccentric, shall we say, but he wasn't careless. Besides, Mr. Mumford advised him on the draftin'. That means it's tied up nice and neat, the way Father wanted it. Am I right, sir?"

"There's no breach of the heritable property law," said Mumford.

"I can't understand why James did it." Thora spoke for the first time.

Mumford gathered his papers and stuffed them into his brief case. "I can answer you that one. James wanted the business to survive as a going concern, Mrs. Aspinall. In confidence, your husband informed me that he had trained Beckman – Miss Beckman – to take over in the event of his death. To keep the shop open, the business ticking. It's just as plain and uncomplicated as that. Perhaps, if I might be so bold as to suggest it, you'd do better to congratulate Miss Beckman rather than berate her."

"Don't talk rot," said Andrea. "Look at her – smirking."

"For God's sake, Andrea!" David exploded.

"Get her out of here." Andrea said.

"Allow me, Miss Beckman." Mumford gave Holly his arm.

It was an odd gesture, courtly but stiff, an indication that he did not approve of the Aspinall children's petty squabbling, or of Andrea's crass behaviour.

To David he said, "If you will be good enough to call at my office on Monday, if that's convenient, perhaps we may go through the other points of business in a calmer frame of mind."

"Yes, Mr. Mumford." David glanced at Holly. "What about you? What d'you say, young lady?"

"I . . . I'm sorry it had to happen."

"So you should be – sorry," said Andrea.

Mumford escorted the girl away before arguments could flare up again. He led her down the iron stair into the shop, holding her elbow as if to prevent her making a run for it.

It was strange coming down into the semi-darkness of the shop again. It seemed like an alien place now, not her fortress, her sanctuary.

"Thank you, sir," Holly said. "I'm . . . I'm all right."

Mumford glanced behind him up the spiral staircase, then in a confidential tone said, "So this is your domain, is it?"

"I suppose it is – or used to be."

"I've some advice for you, young woman, if you'll listen."

"Advice is somethin' I could use," Holly said.

"Don't apologise to them."

"What?"

"You owe those spoiled brats no apology," Mumford said. "Stand up to them."

"I . . . I can't."

"Then learn; learn quickly," Mumford told her. "Now, fetch your coat. Do you have a key?"

"Yes, but I've got work to do, inventories to finish. It's only half-past four."

"You're no longer a servant: you're co-owner of this establishment. Close up early, go home and rest."

Holly hesitated.

"Go on."

When Holly had put on her coat and switched out the lights Mumford accompanied her into the street. He waited while she locked the door and put up the stout wooden gate, padlocking it to two metal bars. When all was secure, he took her by the arm and escorted her to the corner of Cardwell Place and Sefton Street.

"You *do* want it, don't you, Miss Beckman? A share in the shop, I mean?"

"More than anythin', sir. But I'm not sure I'm ready for it."

"James Aspinall was no fool," said Mumford. "Oh, I'm not claiming that I supported his wish. On the contrary, I tried to dissuade him. He was adamant, however; quite adamant. His only concern was that you would not be able to stand up to a concerted attack from 'above' – if you take my meaning."

"*Is* the document legal?"

"Watertight."

"What d'I do now?"

"Do what you were trained to do – make profit," said Mumford. "If you make money for them, then they'll have no leg to stand on. Certainly, they'll try to get rid of you; Andrea in particular." He stopped on the corner, glanced up at the traffic that flowed along towards the Vauxhall Bridge Road, in search of a motor taxi. "How old are you?"

"Comin' up for twenty."

"Very young."

"Sometimes," said Holly, "sometimes I feel older."

"Hm, don't we all these days!" Mumford raised his arm, shaking his briefcase. "Taxi!"

"Thanks, sir," said Holly.

"Don't thank me," Mumford said, as the taximeter cab growled to a halt by the kerb. "For James Aspinall's sake, however, make a go of it."

Holly watched the lawyer climb into the taxi and slam the door. He leaned from under the canopy and smiled. "No fool was he, after all."

The taxi departed leaving Holly alone on the corner.

Behind her buildings loomed up into foggy ducts. Flags draped windowsills and, high up, wound limply round poles. She glanced into Cardwell Place. She was tempted to run back, to assure David and Andrea that it was all a dreadful mistake, that she wanted no share in their father's estate. But she knew that that would be a denial of Mr. A.'s intentions. She was filled with a heady mixture of fear and exhilaration.

She had a piece of what she had always wanted. She had taken a giant step nearer to the day when she would have a shop to call her own, her name in gilt letters above the door. Why was she so apprehensive?

She knew what her acquaintances would answer to that question:

Holly Beckman is too young, too inexperienced. The only possible rebuttal was to prove to everybody, including herself, that she could do it, could run Mr. Aspinall's business. She had few illusions as to what would be required of her. Kennedy King, Simon Black and Miss Emma Chubb, the up-town dealers, would be quite ruthless. They would scalp her without a qualm if she faltered. Profit was not so easy to coin. She could afford few errors of judgment – and her judgment was only half formed. In five years she would be equal in skill and knowledge to any of them. But she didn't have five years. When he had drafted his will, Mr. A. obviously hadn't supposed that he would die so soon.

Holly strolled slowly along Sefton Street towards the bridge. The air was cold and motionless, a dead, raw, nipping atmosphere that preceded the onset of November fogs. On the river the barge horns lowed already, though there was still faint light in the sky.

Walking cleared Hollys head. She sorted out the week's events as meticulously as she had arranged the items in the collector's case back in the shop.

If she paid herself the same wage as Mr. A. had paid her, the family could hardly quibble. After all, she would be better off, for, after the quarterly accounting, she would be entitled to withdraw a share of the profits.

She toyed with the idea of having money to spend, thought of dresses and shoes, hats and handbags that she had seen in shop windows and briefly coveted. She might be able to afford some of them now. The caress of silk underwear; she could almost feel it against her skin. The long-collar shirt-blouse in DuParry's window at four pounds fifteen shillings; it would suit her figure perfectly. She visualised herself as a fashion plate, stunningly elegant; what effect would it have on David? Would he fall suddenly in love with her?

Holly switched off the thought.

Profits must be ploughed back into purchase of stock. She had more practical ideas on that score.

For a minute or two, however, her mind flirted with several thoughts at once, a jumble of desires, in which the sensual appeal of DuParry lingerie, the beautiful symmetry of Chinese porcelain, David and money became confused.

How much had David skimmed from the profits over the years?

Mr. A. had hinted that the sums had been large enough to restrict adequate stock purchase. With another wave of apprehension Holly recalled the black-backed notebook in which Mr. A. did his personal calculations in the midst of auction sales or before totting up an offer to a private client. Frowns, sighs, muffled groans, occassional muttered curses accompanied his reckonings. David and Andrea had been indulged at the expense of stock, the health of the business. But now that Mr. Aspinall was gone, would they still expect the shop to mint money for their personal use?

That was another problem she would have to come to terms with.

How on earth could she tell David and Andrea that she could not allow them to dip into the cash box whenever they felt inclined. It would mean storms ahead, and she would run the risk of seriously antagonising David.

Crossing the bridge Holly confronted the sprawl of Lambeth along the riverbank, rows of council houses cowering behind the railway embankments, chimneys of South London's gas works belching out plumes of smoke and lurid gusts of hot cinders. She had never found the scene picturesque. How could she when she lived in the midst of it, tasting smoke, feeling grains of soot on her skin? It was all very well for the Kennedy Kings of this world to stand on the Chelsea side and admire the further shore as they would admire a vigorous and dramatic painting; Holly doubted if they would find it so attractive if they lived there.

She remembered one winter's afternoon walk with Maury; she couldn't have been more than eight or nine. He had taken her across the bridge and had stopped to lean on the rail and look back at the prospect of Lambeth lying exposed under the hard bright sun. She had been engrossed with things close at hand, as children are; seagulls on the mud, boats, people. Standing by Maury's side, his big adult hand on her shoulder, she had felt secure, then, abruptly, and with almost frightening vehemence, Maury had exploded. "Gawd, but it's ugly!" She had looked up at him, then away across the river to Lambeth. At that precise second, she had sensed the meaning of their station in life. It *was* ugly – yet it was their home. All the rest of that afternoon she had been fretful and peevish and had given Maury a roasting, so much so that he had come close to losing his temper with her. Neither the man nor the child had understood the reason for her uncharacteristic ill-humour.

Thoughts of Maury lead her on to Abraham's Box, to Leo and Ritchie. She had almost forgotten about her family. How would they react to her astonishing news?

Leo would resent her good fortune.

Ritchie would scheme to make use of it.

Only Grandpa Tal would rejoice with her.

Her apprehension congealed into dread.

She faltered, hesitating, hand on the bridge rail. She felt a totally irrational urge to turn about and run back to the north bank of the river, not to return to her father's house in the mean Lambeth cul-de-sac, not ever again.

But she had no choice.

"Not yet," she said aloud. "Not just yet."

Squaring her shoulders, she stepped out briskly to drop her little bombshell in No. 5 and take the consequences, whatever the consequences might be.

* * *

Leo Beckman had never placed much value on his daughter. The truth was that he hardly spared her a thought. She cleaned house, made beds, sewed shirt buttons, darned socks, eked out the family's coupons, kept pans simmering on the stove, and, mercifully, didn't nag him. In other words she did all the things a wife was expected to do – and that was enough for Leo.

If ever Leo dared to recall Huldah, which he did not often do, he thought of her as she had been before marriage, not after. He remembered the fieriness of her desire for his body. How vain he had become of his person during their rapid courtship. He had been flattered by her persistent attention, gulled into wedlock. It had not taken long for the trap to close.

Huldah attended his welfare as dutifully as any wife in Lambeth, but she was different from the neighbours' wives, very, very different. She wanted to change him. The more she tried, the more he resisted her until something ripped between them. In later years, after Maury and Ritchie had been born, Huldah's attentions to his well-being had been blackened by hatred. There was no other word for it: hatred, deep and not obvious to outsiders, had given a core to their marriage.

The more he ignored her, abused her, the more attentive she became. They would fight, he would roar at her, slap her, then stamp out to the pub. When he returned, the house would be shining, not just neat and clean, but shining. The table would be set before a blazing fire, the boys asleep in bed upstairs. Huldah would be dressed in her best frock, collar and cuffs as white as milk, her hair combed and pinned, her skin pink with scrubbing. She would serve him, wait on him mutely like a servant; a gourmet supper of black bean soup, Russian eggs on triangles of crisp toast, a dish of *tokany* or goulash, made from leftovers but so done that the fragrance made the mouth water, or an Aunt Nelly pudding, so golden and light that it seemed to float on the plate. And he would hate her all the more. None of it was done to please him, only to inform him that she was more worthy than he was, that no matter what he did to her she would never flag in her duty. He would be possessed by fury, pretend to be drunker than he really was, would hurl food about, lurch over the table. When he had spent himself, Huldah would quietly begin cleaning up.

Sometimes he would force himself upon her, right there in the living room. She would not resist. On that ultimate battleground he was, occasionally, the victor. Sensing that her responses were no longer stiff and dutiful but womanly, he would laugh and taunt her. It was out of just such a coupling that Holly had come into the world.

Dying on him had been Huldah's final revenge. She had saddled him with a daughter, a little female brat to raise on his own, with the boys hardly old enough to look out for themselves.

When he looked at Holly, sometimes Leo saw in her the pretty girl that his wife had been, and, with a slow, diffuse coiling of ancient shames, the wife that he had made of her. In defence, he chose to pretend that Holly hardly existed. It was easier than making amends.

Leo was not exactly in the best of spirits when Holly arrived home from Aspinall's. Three days of celebrating down at the Admiral's Hat had soured even Leo's iron constitution, and he was faced with the grim prospect of having to drag his bones out to the dockside tomorrow morning; victory didn't last forever. He looked at the girl blankly, and listened to her story without real attention.

Ritchie had always been a go-between. Anything that Leo was required to know about Holly he gleaned from his son. So out of practice he had become in even tuning in to her voice that he did not completely absorb her news about the inheritance. It was only when Ritchie let out a whoop of delighted amazement that Leo's common sense told him that he had better take his bearings quickly and start to assert his authority.

"What d'you think of that then, Pa?" said Ritchie, an arm entwined round his sister's waist. "Ain't it a real windfall?"

Leo bestowed a wink on his daughter. "Should make a bob'r two outta it, I suppose."

"A bob or two?" said Ritchie. "Pa, don't you see? Holly's gone an' got herself a real slice of pie. The old geezer she worked for left her in clover."

Leo wiped his mouth with his hand and drank a draught of tea. Hemmed in a corner, he twisted his head to observe his children then glanced at Kirsanoff to see what the old Russian thought of it all.

"It is wonderful opportunity for the girl," Tal told him.

"How much gelt will she make?" Leo addressed Ritchie.

"It's a drippin' roast, Pa," Ritchie explained. "Now she's a part owner nobody can pay her a slave's wages an' get off with it. What she don't make one way, she'll make the other."

"How's that?" said Leo, puzzled.

"Because she'll collect a quarter of the audited profits," said Ritchie, speaking as he might have spoken to a child. "What they cheat her out of in wages, she'll get back in hard cash end of every quarter. Ain't that right, Holly?"

"I suppose it is," said Holly. "I never stopped to work it out."

"Take yer brother's word for it," said Ritchie.

"So what's it all come to, in gelt?" Leo put in.

"Well, it'll never be a fortune," said Holly.

To Ritchie, Leo said, "They won't let 'er keep it."

Ritchie said, "She saw a wig, talked straight t' a bleedin' lawyer. Pa, don't you ever listen? The wig says it's iron-clad."

"Wigs," said Leo. "Don't trust wigs."

Kirsanoff said, "Holly, they'll fight it. No matter what the lawyer told you, they will fight it."

"See!" Leo, vindicated, said. "Listen t'yer Grandpa."

"Holly can fight back," said Ritchie.

"Make 'em pay, y'mean?" said Leo.

"No," Holly said. "No, I want to keep my share."

"Grab what yer can while yer can," said Leo. "Best motto."

"Not this time," said Ritchie. "Anyhow, sis *wants* t'stay on, workin' in the shop. Don't yer, Hol?"

"I *am* stayin' on."

Leo inched his way out of the corner. He was put out by Ritchie's championing of his sister and by the girl's defiance. He knew that look in her eye; he'd seen it once or twice before. He felt threatened by it. It had never occurred to him before that Holly might have hob-nobbed with this Pimlico crowd, not just worked for them.

"What'd he do t'yer?" It was out before he could censor it.

"I don't know what you mean, Pa?"

"Left yer plenty, di'n't he? Must be a reason for such gen'osity."

"Stop it, Leo," Kirsanoff advised.

"Nothin' for nothin'." Leo's temper rose. He was being patronised. That much he could recognise. "What did yer *do* for it, gal?"

He didn't give two pigs' feet *what* she'd done for it, especially since the geezer was dead and buried. But he didn't want no other man takin' over the privilege, skinnin' her out of what was due. He had to

look out for her, di'n't he? He was her Pa, responsible for her welfare.
Ritchie didn't understand. Ritchie hadn't seen the things he'd seen,
had his experiences. He knew how it was in places like bleedin'
Pimlico. She was fair game for any fancy dan that came along. They
would screw her out of whatever they could. Toss her aside. Fling her
back, broke, maybe with a kid inside her. Who'd look after her then?
Not bleedin' Ritchie. Not her bleedin' fancy pals in Pimlico.

Blood rose to Leo's face. He could feel it glowing hot as a coal.
Choleric outbursts cleansed his system, made him feel strong. Noisily
he breathed through his nostrils.

"Minute me back's turned, y'go wrong." He pumped the bellows,
getting up steam. "Just's well he kicked the bleedin' bucket, or he'd
'ave 'ad me t'answer to."

What right had *she* to collect his windfall?

There was no justice.

Elbows cocked, he hooked his fingers into his leather belt. He
should have paid more attention to her. Should have hammered
respect into her. Would have too if that old Russian hadn't been
around to protect her.

"This Aspinall lot. . ." he roared.

She got to her feet, lips white. She did not weep, did not protest.
She stared at him. He felt himself wither. There was no respect in her
eyes, no anger. What he saw there dried up his authority. What he saw
there was pity. He wanted her to give him sauce, at least defend her
fancy-man, her posh friends. But with a dignity that floored him
completely, she moved past him and went upstairs. It was not
surrender, not escape. She had cut him off, cut him dead. And he
didn't know what to do about it.

"Now you've torn it," Ritchie said.

"But she . . . you said she. . ."

Ritchie opened his mouth, then, glancing round at the old man,
changed his mind. He grabbed Leo's coat from the sofa, and a scarf
from the chairback and threw them at his father.

"I'll stand you a pint, Pa." He spoke with strained heartiness.
"Come on, let's get outta here."

Blustering, Leo permitted his son to jostle him towards the living-
room door. Before he could go into the hallway, however, Kirsanoff
called out his name. Coat half on, half off, Leo paused.

The old Russian was sitting smugly in the chair, legs crossed, big
head tilted, a smile plastered over his chops.

"What?" Leo demanded.

"You're a bigger fool than I took you for," Tal Kirsanoff told him.

"Come on, Pa, let's shove."

And Leo, having no ready answer to Kirsanoff's insult, meekly let his son lead him off to the public house.

* * *

The Shears and Mallet was an ancient hostelry that, in more romantic days, had been a post stage and haunt of highwaymen. The original tavern was preserved within a new brick structure that provided refreshment for the thousands of workers who had moved into the area to earn their daily bread at the factories. Leo Beckman did not feel comfortable in this public house. He was surprised that Ritchie was so at home in the establishment. The Shears and Mallet had itself a reputation – nothing historical, nothing to do with the phantom shades of Red Mask, Causeway Tom or Moll Reagan. It was the more substantial presence of their professional heirs that made Leo uneasy.

Leo had not known that Ritchie was that well in with the fraternity. The fact that the boy received nods of greeting from several of the men at the tables and long bar both pleased and disturbed Leo. He knew that the boy did a spot of snafflin' from time to time, but he had no idea that Ritchie had done enough to merit acceptance by big fish like Vince Shotten. Shotten was a mature crook who held feudal sway over underworld activities in Bermondsey, Walworth and parts of Lambeth town. But even Shotten's lordly boys deigned to give his son the nod.

"What'd y'bring me here for?" Leo asked as soon as they were closeted in a high-backed booth towards the rear.

"T'make you see sense."

A taproom boy limped up with two boilermakers on a tray.

"On the slate, Ritch?" the boy asked.

"Yer, chalk it up. I'll be flush, Thursday."

Smoking coal fire, a transom the colour of tobacco leaf, an arched cowling over a slot to the public bar, like a confessional window; in two of the nine booths men supped beer, murmuring in low voices, caps almost touching. No flags or victory rosettes were visible in the Shears and Mallet. Its customers did not welcome an end to war, to the specialised lines of demand and supply they had built up over the years, when a case of tinned pineapple or a sack of sugar fetched as much as sterling silver candlesticks or twenty-two carat cufflinks.

As soon as the boy had gone, Ritchie leaned on the table and gripped his father's wrist. "Listen, Pa." he said in a soft persuasive drawl. "Go easy on Hol, will you?"

"Did he 'ave 'er, though? That's what I got t'know."

"The old boy, Aspinall? Nah, he didn't lay a finger on her. Wasn't that sort. Neither's Hol. Don't y'know her better'n that? She's got it screwed on, I tell yer. It's a genuine windfall – for all of us."

"She's a tight little cow," said Leo, sourly. "She won't part with a brass ha'penny. She'll be up'n off like a greyhound when it starts t'roll in, mark me."

"Blood's thicker'n water," said Ritchie.

"What's on yer mind, son?"

"An outlet of me own."

"Uh?"

"I got it goin'," said Ritchie. "I got pals in proper places. What I ain't got is outlets. Don't y'see? I sell to Shotten. I sell cheap. A tenth retail value."

Leo sipped whisky, then beer. He was beginning to realise why Kirsanoff had called him a fool.

"Y'mean, Hol'll buy shady."

"She'll have to."

"Not 'er."

"She wants t'make a go of this shop. The Aspinalls'll try t'stop her. Only thing'll count with them is profit. She won't make a fortune sellin' brass monkeys an' plaster saints. She'll need quality stock."

"How'd the old geezer do it?"

"I asked 'round about him. Aspinall was sharp as a tack in tradin'. Hol's got flair, but she ha'n't got experience. Can't have. Stands to reason. The Bond Street mob won't give *her* a helping hand. Ain't enough jam t'go round. When she runs into red ink, she'll do anythin' to keep solvent, take gold, silver, sparklers, studs – anythin' small she can hive off smartish, under the counter."

"I think you've got 'er wrong."

"Our Holly's head's stuffed with big ideas," said Ritchie. "She won't give up."

"Don't mean she'll market hot stuff."

"She'll slip," Ritchie said. "One slip's all it'll take."

"You want me t'keep 'er sweet."

"Don't rile her, Pa."

"I still says the Aspinalls won't sit still."

"Then we'll just have t'move fast, won't we?" Ritchie said.

* * *

At that precise hour, the Aspinalls were holding a council of war in

Cardwell Place, Pimlico. Chairs were drawn around a drawing-room fire that, with nutty coal banked behind an iron "saviour", gave out more smoke than heat. The women wore deep mourning. Thora had draped a woollen gown over a tunic that reached to her knees, accentuating her dumpiness. Andrea had suggested that her mother splash out on a wardrobe of black garments. Thora had refused. She was frugal by inclination and had persuaded a dressmaker she had patronised for three decades to do a job on the sombre Edwardian cast-offs that had accumulated in wardrobes and chests over the years. In contrast, Andrea was elegant in a two-piece suit of corded black velvet, with ruched satin facings that gave it a military air.

Though in uniform, David's posture was anything but soldierly. He lounged in an easy chair, one leg negligently hooked over the arm.

"Andrea, we've been through it a dozen times," he said wearily. "In your view, Beckman is a scheming little minx who took advantage of father's gullibility."

Thora said, "Your father was neither a fool nor a philanderer. I won't hear a word against him. 'Specially not tonight."

"Nobody's slandering father," said Andrea. "But you can't deny that Beckman stands to walk off with a quarter of our business."

"How do you think I feel about it?" said David. "I've been helpin' our country win a war. I had no end of plans."

"Sitting behind a desk in a dusty office is hardly the same as fighting," Andrea sneered. "You've been here often enough, David. Why didn't you notice that Beckman was worming her way into daddy's good books?"

"I had other things to think about."

"Things," said Andrea, "like that Jennings woman."

David shrugged. "If you're so alert, Andrea, why didn't *you* put a spoke in Beckman's wheel. Too occupied with tea-parties and bandage-rolling, I suppose."

Thora said, "Holly helped your Dad."

"Didn't I help him?" said Andrea. "Opening crates, packing orders. During the holidays I did as much work as she did. You know that's true, mother. I often helped out – before that Jewish slut pushed her nose in."

"Ah-hah!" said David. "It's the fact Holly's a Jew that rubs your fur the wrong way, is it? Well, for your information, she isn't a Jew."

"How do you know?"

"Dad told me: I asked him point-blar.'<."

"And who told father?" asked Andrea.

David hesitated. "Beckman, I suppose."

"You see," said Andrea. "You don't think she'd *admit* it. She'd tell him what he wanted to hear. That's her style. Buttering up her betters so they don't know where they are."

"Good God, Andrea!" David swung his leg from the chair arm and sat up straight. "Right now it doesn't matter whether Beckman's a Jew or a damn' Confucian."

"It matters to me, David. I'm not prepared to introduce such a person as our business partner."

"Then don't introduce her. Don't say anything about her."

"What am I to tell Miles?"

Miles Walshott, Andrea's "intended", was as stuffy as a clubroom library.

"There's no need to tell Miles much about Beckman. I've a much more valid suggestion; show your beloved the books."

"What books?"

"Dad's account books."

"Have you seen them?"

"Of course I've seen them. First thing I looked at. We don't have a current finalising balance sheet yet, of course; the auditors will take their own sweet time disgorging that. But I've studied last year's figures, and records going back ten years."

"We're not insolvent?" asked Thora anxiously.

"That depends," said David. "I can assure you, however, that dad sailed pretty close to the wind."

"Nonsense," said Andrea. "We never wanted for anything."

"No more we did," said David. "But his Day Book – his Journal – makes depressing reading. I'd no idea that father had to do *so* much juggling. He didn't have much to begin with, you know."

"We started on next to nothing," said Thora. "We were very poor at the beginning."

"You don't mean poor, mother; you mean not well off," Andrea corrected.

"I mean poor," said Thora. "James always said that his children, you, wouldn't have to fret about money."

Andrea glanced at David, enquiringly. "What *does* this Journal say?"

"We demanded too much, Andrea. It was given willingly, without complaint, but that doesn't alter the fact that you and I received all the benefits of dad's hard labours. It would have been easier for him, much easier, if there'd been more capital around. He tapped it away almost as quickly as he made it – not to improve the premises or increase the value of his trading stock; to indulge us."

"I never asked for a thing," said Andrea, adding, "that I didn't need."

Staring into the smoke above the coals, David shook his head. "I didn't realise just how little dad was takin' out for himself."

After a moment's silence, Andrea asked, "How much is there?"

"In realisable assets," David answered, "there's held stock, the shop itself, this apartment, and a small pool of cash, most of it already earmarked for purchases."

"Debts outstanding?"

"Dad owes – I mean, of course, *we* owe – the Abbey Salerooms some forty-eight pounds. We are owed one hundred and four pounds from a Mr. Wilmott and, under the circumstances, can reasonably call it in. There are other minor outgoings."

"Insurance?" said Andrea. "You haven't mentioned insurance."

"That belongs to mother," said David. "It isn't much. There's an outstanding balance on the loan on the house and shop to pay. But that would be covered by a sale."

"You're not selling my house?" Thora cried. "How can you talk so and your father not cold in his grave. He worked his knuckles to the bone to keep making enough money to see you both right. But he loved the shop. He was proud of it."

"Which is where Beckman comes in," said David.

"Holly's a nice girl," said Thora.

"That's true, but it *was* injudicious of dad to treat her as one of the family," said David.

As usual, when he talked money, David's tone became clipped and impersonal, covering nervousness of financial matters. He had never *quite* grasped the significance of some of the terms used in his profession. The assured jargon of his colleagues, in and out of the Pensions Office, disconcerted him. They talked the language of money naturally. In a sense he had never cared about money as an entity. To David money was only a link in the barter system. It had no value apart from the pleasures it could buy. The mysteries of economics fascinated him, but he was no nearer genuine comprehension than he had been at the start of his training.

The Day Book – the equivalent of a Log or Journal – that his father had kept during his thirty years in business had shaken him by its revelations. *To David, extra: £30. To Andrea, clothing: £45. To David, mess bill, extra: £22.10s. To Andrea, carriage hire: £4.4s.* The sums were always higher than standard trade entries, telling a tale of extravagance, a quality that his father had unwittingly instilled in his children and one which they had failed to recognise. Now he understood why his father had never allowed him access to the accounts. They would have exposed weaknesses on both sides. Taken in conjunction with the others, the Proprietary Account had brought tears to his eyes. *To shirt cuffing: 10 pence. To one collar, celluloid: 1s and 2 pence. To cleaning of hat: 3s.* Double entry bookkeeping with a vengeance.

Beckman had been good for his father; David did not doubt it. In some inexplicable way, Beckman had also been good for business, that was a documented fact – unless the rise in profits had been entirely coincidental or due to extraneous causes not set down in the shop's annals. At no point in his life had David been more conscious of his lack of native wit. Unlike his sister, however, he was not impulsively inclined to dismiss Beckman out of hand.

"We must correct father's mistake," Andrea said.

"I'm not sure it is a mistake," said David mildly.

"So – you side with mother?"

"It's not a question of taking sides, dear," said Thora.

"It is, however, a question of making decisions," said Andrea. "Whether we sell or hold."

"Hold?" said David. "Hold what?"

"Hold on to the business, run it ourselves," said Andrea.

"Really?" David said. "That's ludicrous! I certainly couldn't devote much time to it. I'm a fighting . . . I mean, a soldier under orders. Can't sue for early release, not in my office. Not sure I'd want to."

"I see. You won't give up your sinecure?"

"Have it your way," David agreed. "My sinecure. It strikes me that my officer's pay may soon be an essential part of our total income."

"Why don't we employ a manager?" asked Andrea.

"Turnover doesn't justify it."

"Labour will be cheap, now the war's over."

"Honesty and experience are never cheap."

"Lease the shop as a going concern, then."

"What's buzzing in your lovely head, Andrea?"

"Buy the Beckman girl out."

"With what?"

"Money, of course."

"Where will the money come from?"

"Do you *want* to keep that wretched girl here?"

"All I'm saying is, it's silly to employ a manager when we already have Beckman."

"We are equal partners, you and I, David; equal partners with her. I propose that we offer her a lump sum for her share. You know what hard cash means to people of that calibre. She'll jump at it."

"I'm not sure," said David. "She loves the business."

"Mother?" Andrea appealed to Thora for support.

The woman glanced up, blinking, as if she'd only been vaguely listening to the conversation. "I want to stay here. Can I stay here, Andrea?"

"Of course, mother. But what about Beckman?"

"I'll be guided by your advice."

"Good!" Andrea said. "David, realise what money you can."

"Shall I turn out my pockets?"

"Don't be facetious. Between us we own seventy-five per cent of the business. We'll borrow against it. I'll consult Miles on the most suitable procedure. Besides, I have a little nest-egg put away – not much, but enough to help tempt Beckman."

"Are you dead set on this course, Andrea?"

"Yes, I want Beckman out. You, David, will make her the offer."

"Oh, now, I say! I'm not good at that kind of thing."

"As head of the family, it's your duty."

"Very well." David surrendered. "See how much we can muster, and I'll put it to her."

"Don't 'put it to her'," Andrea said. "Tell her."

"What if she won't agree?"

"Tackle her family. Spread banknotes on the kitchen table. That," said Andrea, with a firm nod, "will fix it for good and all."

In his heart, David knew that it probably would.

He would be sorry to see Holly Beckman depart, though he could find no valid reason for regret. After all, she was nothing to him, and, when all was said, done and settled, he would be better off with a third of his father's business than a mere quarter.

"Agreed?" said Andrea.

"Agreed," said David.

* * *

In the wake of victory celebrations which got so out of hand that the constabulary were finally called upon to disperse the riotous crowds, the weeks following the signing of the Armistice seemed a let down. Day-to-day living hadn't changed. Though there was much optimistic talk about an end to "meatless days" and a return of prosperity, bread and many other staples were still rationed. Influenza tightened its grip on Britain. Cold rain fell ceaselessly. There was a serious shortage of fuel. True, the very first of the fighting men were beginning to return home, uncertain smiles on their faces as they dumped their kitbags through doors and set about re-establishing relationships with families who, in four years, had learned to live quite well without them. In Cardwell Place it was business as usual – or so Holly tried to pretend, though "the dynamo was missing". The girl had not yet found confidence to evolve her own routines.

At nine a.m. on Saturday, November 23rd, Holly raised the green linen blind that covered the window and removed the board that protected the glass door. She turned a ticket to declare the shop "Open", lifted a scatter of letters from the lino behind the door and carried the morning's mail to the high wedge-shaped desk in the office under the stairs.

There were a couple of condolence notes addressed to Mrs. Aspinall; Holly put them carefully in the wire tray with its "Upstairs" label. She slit the other letters with a penknife, sorted out two trade notices of sales due next month – both sadly listed as *Possessions and Personal Effects of a Deceased Military Gentleman* – and the first letter of application.

It came from an obviously enterprising sergeant in an Oxfordshire Regiment, and had all the formal correctness of a circular. Holly wondered how many such letters the sergeant had sent out. How thorough he must have been to work down the *Dealers' Handbook and Directory* as far as Aspinall's which was only listed under "General". The sergeant catalogued his age – thirty-two – marital status – married, three children – previous experience – eleven years in Hallam's. An old-established furniture dealers in Islington, Hallam's had gone bust in 1917. Holly guessed that she would receive many such letters; she had no idea, of course, that it would eventually become a flood. She set it aside to draft a suitably regretful reply.

She had seen very little of the Aspinalls during the past ten days. Mrs. Hodge brought news from upstairs, collected letters, and expressed anxiety about her own future employment.

Oddly, Holly did not feel threatened. Every sign of unsettled circumstances made the gloomy shop more of a haven. On Fridays she drew her wages from the petty cash box and filled in an appropriate slip. Once, in response to a memo that she sent upstairs, two five pound notes were returned from David, via Mrs. Hodge, as tick-over money. Sooner or later, of course, one or other of the Aspinalls would have to descend from on high to make arrangements about banking accounts and the signing of bills. However, Holly had decided not to press matters. She busied herself with the completion of the inventory, duly posted it to Mr. Mumford, and got on with the sorting of various lots that Mr. A. had purchased in the week before his fatal illness.

There were more customers than usual, casual browsers in search of "nice" pieces for presents, trade clients from outlying stores come in to "see what was what" and pick over the stock in the hope of finding a bargain. Holly was firm with them. She would not barter or haggle. She sat on marked prices as adamantly as Mr. A. would have done.

"Look, gal, go fetch the boss."

"I'm the boss."

"Get off!"

"Sorry. But I'm in charge."

"You're workin' hard at losin' a good sale."

"It's only a good sale at marked price."

"Ten per cent, for trade?"

"Yes, ten per cent for trade – if you have a card."

"An' another ten per cent for cash."

"'Fraid not."

"Strewth!"

Sometimes she made a sale, sometimes not. She could spot bazaar merchants a mile off and knew that she must not yield an inch. She understood their double-talk, the "take-three-items-at-double-the-price-of-one" patter that was intended to confuse her and lure her into parting with good pieces at little more than cost.

In addition to buyers, trade and casual, she had a steady stream of sellers. Over the years she had learned to smother sympathy and reject worthless bric-à-brac so desperately offered, purchasing only items that had value, paying only market price. It was difficult and occasionally heartrending to be firm, but Aspinall's was not a "pop shop", a pawn-brokers. Buying and selling were the basis of the business, not loans and handouts, however pathetic the seller seemed. Widows, children, limbless soldiers, a parade of the victims of war and poverty became Holly's cross, the price she had to pay for "keeping out of it".

In the latter part of November, she bought nothing. The situation was too uncertain. She would concern herself with problems of re-stocking only when David and Andrea consented to sit round a table with her and devise a cost-effective scheme based on turnover and profit margins. Buy she must – she was more scared than she would admit about buying – but not yet. There was enough in store to keep the shop energetic for three months, though private dealing and special-client offers had dwindled to a trickle.

Finding nothing in the mail that required immediate attention that Saturday morning, Holly made herself a cup of tea on the gas ring that was Mr. Aspinall's one concession to luxury. She finished it quickly, rinsed the cup at the sink in the back store, then proceeded to drag from the niche where out-going and in-coming orders were stowed, a lumpy burlap-wrapped package some three-feet square. It was the very last purchase Mr. Aspinall had made before his illness, a job lot of English china. Holly had been saving it for a quiet morning. Unwrapping and transporting had been rendered difficult; she hadn't a man's strength, had no means of hoisting the package from floor to work table. With really heavy wares, furniture for instance, a couple of strapping lads from the Carriers' Quarters in Dignam Street were summoned, at an hourly rate, to do the unloading. Since the beginning of 1917 though, the lads had become much less strapping, much less youthful, and the team had increased from two to four. Thoughtfully, Holly surveyed the package. She had it in mind to construct a ramp from floor to table; another chore that would have to wait. In the interim, she would be obliged to open the package on the floor and transfer the items one by one to the table.

"May I help?"

Holly started and stood up.

Engrossed, she hadn't heard David come down stairs. He was not in uniform. He wore a cord-fronted cardigan, khaki trousers and a collarless shirt. He looked, Holly thought, no different from any Lambeth work-dog, except for his spruce moustache and sleekly combed hair. He hadn't shaved, and the day's stubble was apparent. A Gold Flake hung from his lip. Without awaiting her answer, he stooped and hoisted the package to the table.

"Is that what you want?"

"That's fine." Holly was aware that she sounded stand-offish, as if she was reprimanding him. "Thank you."

"Ah . . . how are you finding your way about?"

"There's nothing I haven't done before."

"Good. Good."

"Except. . ."

"Go on. I won't bite your head off."

"I need to know what your plans are."

"Plans? What sort of plans?"

"There's a sale in Buckinghamshire, next Tuesday. Mr. A. – your father – had priced several lots in the catalogue."

"Do you want to go? To buy?"

"Twenty lots are commissions for Dr. Royle."

"Dr. Royle?"

"Private collector; very rich; lives in Dorset. He often buys through us," Holly explained.

"How much do we make on each commission?"

"Five per cent of the lot price, plus twenty-five per cent of the difference between Royle's top figure an' what we get it for."

"That's a generous sort of thing," said David. "Bit of a lottery, though, for us."

"Not if y'know what you're doing."

"Do you know what you're doing?"

"I've done it before."

"What about the rest of the marked items?"

"For stock – if we get them cheap enough."

"How much will it cost?"

"Depends. The more we get cheap, the more it costs us, if you see what I mean. The way your father handled most auctions was to try to cover the cost of our stock purchases by the commission on Royle's items. Send Dr. Royle a bill immediately; receive his payment before the bill from the auctioneers arrived here. Could always trust Dr. Royle to come through quickly."

"That gives us stock, though, not cash."

"Stock is money."

"Yes, I'm aware," said David.

"Well, do I go, or not? If I do go t' Buckinghamshire, it'll mean fare, an' carriage – in advance. But either somebody'll have to come down here an' keep an eye on the shop, or else we close up while I'm gone."

"You know, I hadn't thought of that."

"About the money required for. . ."

"Not so fast, my tiger; you're making my head spin."

Holly said, "If I don't attend the sale, I'll have t' push the commission out; that's only fair to Dr. Royle."

"And we'll lose his custom?"

"He might give us a second chance."

"Where would you lay off the commission?"

"On short notice, probably to Kennedy King."

"Why?"

"He'll be goin' to the sale for certain. His firm is large enough to cover the capital outlay," said Holly. "But he'll pinch Royle from us. He's wanted in on Mr. A.'s client list for years."

"King – how well does he know you?"

"Your father's done lots of buyer trade with. . ."

"Know *you*, personally?"

"King knows who I'm with," Holly answered, puzzled.

"Would King take you on?"

"What d'you mean – take me on?"

"Employ you?"

"I don't need a job."

"If . . . if the family decides to sell."

"Oh!"

"You'd have some money, of course, a cash settlement – probably about four or five hundred pounds, lump sum; a fat little nest-egg for a girl your age, Holly." David did not lie well. "If you invested it, it could bring you several pounds each week – to swell your wage. You could live really rather well. I'd call on King personally, if you think it'd do any good, give you a glowing testimonial."

"That won't be necessary," said Holly. "I'm not sellin'."

"If we – the family – vote to sell. . ."

"I'll take what's due to me, an' think about it then."

David nodded, letting the subject drop. He did not leave, however. He leaned against the work table and studied the cobwebs that laced the rafters. Two electric bulbs hung from dusty cords, swaying slightly in the permanent draught. Holly waited, but when he said no more she pulled a cork-handled knife from a drawer in the table and hacked at the twine that bound up the package. The man watched as she deftly unwrapped the china, preserving the twine and burlap and even the wadded newspapers that made up the padding.

"What are they?" David asked.

China figures, eight inches high, glazed in pale blue and delicate lemon yellow; two shepherdesses held out their flounced aprons to form scalloped little trays.

"Sweet-dishes." Holly lifted each shepherdess in turn, blew the dust of travel from her dress and set her upright on her base. "Chelsea figures."

"Valuable?"

"Eighteen, the pair."

"Shillings?"

"Pounds."

"My sister was rather abrasive, t'other day. She didn't mean any harm, Holly. She was considerably upset at the time."

"Yes."

He leaned on his other elbow. "Thanks for coming to fetch me that night, to Mayfair, I mean."

"That's all right."

"What did you think of her? My fiancée."

"Very pretty," said Holly, stiffly.

"I won't have this to trade on much longer." He touched the regimental badge attached to the collar of his cardigan. "I'll be dependent on earning my living again. And, as you may have noticed, my young lady has expensive tastes."

Holly removed a Chelsea plate from the package. She held it between her palms, angled against the light, searching its rim and surfaces for blemishes. "D'*you* want rid of me, too?"

"No, not actually. But I do require a source of revenue, you understand."

"The shop *is* a source of revenue. Once things get back to normal, you'll see – it'll go. It'll make money for all of us."

"It isn't just that.'

"I know what it is."

"Holly, you're too young to understand."

"Too young t'cope, you mean?"

"It took Dad all his time."

"Only because you pair. . ." Holly stifled her outburst.

"Whether we're right, or whether we're wrong," David said, "it's still our decision, not yours."

"I didn't mean. . ."

"If I were you," David moved from the table towards the doorway, "I'd have a word with Kennedy King."

"I can't just give up, I. . ."

"About Royle's commission purchases."

"You won't let me go t'the sale; won't let me buy stock?"

"Not just at present," David declared.

"In a couple of months we'll dry up."

"In a couple of months," said David Aspinall, with more asperity than he had intended, "none of us may be here to worry about it."

She watched him pass out of the doorway, out of sight. This time she heard the iron staircase creak, the sound of a floorboard on the first landing. An upstairs door closed. The silence in the back storeroom was intense, fluid. Noises from the apartment dropped into it like pebbles into a still pool. Her heart was thumping. She did not know whether she was scared now or angry. Disappointed, perhaps disillusioned? Somehow she had expected more of him, had anticipated his support. It was weakness, not selfishness, that caused David to side with his sister. Holly was not sure that she could withstand them without an ally. She had been silly to hope that, when it came to a scrap, David would back her against Andrea. What did they have against her? Was it the fact that she was a girl or a usurper that made Andrea hate her and David side against her. Apparently even Mrs. Aspinall had made no sort of defence of her competence.

Carefully she laid down the Chelsea plate. Lifting one of the shepherdesses, she studied the merry expression that the artistry of the glazer made to suggest coy innocence. It did not appeal to her. It was too vacuous, too vain. She replaced the figure by its companion, took off her apron, washed her hands at the tap in the sink and tidied her hair before the fly-blown mirror that hung on the wall.

Five hundred pounds! Four years' wages at the going rate. Invested, interest from the Hearts of Oak Building Society, never mind anything grandiose, would bring in almost, if not quite, half her present weekly wage – and she would not have to work for it. When it came to cutting up the estate, she might wind up with less than that. She assumed that Andrea, David and their cronies would find a legal means of limiting her quarter claim.

She took her overcoat from the cupboard, put it on, added a hat and gloves that she had bought yesterday with a "loan" from Grandpa Tal, put out the lights, pulled down the blinds, turned the ticket to "Closed" and, locking the door and gate behind her, left to call on Mr. Kennedy King in his palatial premises in the Chalfont Arcade.

* * *

Clad in a smoking jacket of crushed mulberry velvet that indicated an informal approach to the chore of making himself richer, Kennedy King was both surprised and delighted to receive Miss Holly Beckman. Not only did Mr. King recognise the girl's name, he had even acquired certain crumbs of information regarding the "Little Man's assistant". "The Little Man" was a trade nickname for James Aspinall, who had been an acceptable little emissary from the profession's lower depths, an honest, eager artisan who, with damn' all else to occupy his mind, had devised many remunerative sidelines to keep his spendthrift children in peppermint. Much good it had done the fellow in the end.

Mr. King genuinely regretted Aspinall's demise.

Mr. King had rolled over quite a nice bit of chink in his twenty-year association with the little man. By inclination, if not by blood, Mr. King, however, was an aristocrat – therefore, he always wanted more than his agents were willing to give. Several times during the last decade, Mr. King had been tempted to wring the neck of the golden goose. But the relationship was too useful. Aspinall often put him in way of purchases and markets. Mr. King had shown gratitude by paying straight commissions on agreed percentages.

What Mr. King had always craved – and never got – was a peek at Aspinall's client-book. Aspinall had kept the black-backed notebook pressed in his vest pocket, close to his heart. Mr. King could only admire such caution. Much fuller and richer than Aspinall's, his own special-client file reposed in a safe in his Chelsea domicile, and was never aired in company.

The other thing that Mr. King coveted was the little man's assistant, Holly Beckman.

Girls were King's weakness. Having reached the age of forty-five, however, he was no longer content to gadfly from one pretty to another. He sought not just a bedmate but a companion. Many ladies would have swooned with eagerness if they had known what was on Kennedy King's mind. Many others would have offered up their debutante daughters just to dip fingers in the King account. Smart-set damsels and feather-brained matrons, however, were King's business, not his pleasure. Charming though he could be, he shunned their company after hours, except for necessary dinner parties and charity events. Being an astute and thrifty chap, what he really wanted was a girl with a figure who had nothing to lose and everything to gain from an unblessed association with an older man, a girl who would also contribute to the running of the business.

Simon Black had actually found such an angel, a shade long in the tooth for his taste but with a head on her shoulders. Black shared a big slice of his life with his mistress in defiance of his wife, children, mother, father-in-law and aged nanny. Miss Emma Chubb was more to Simon than all his relatives lumped together; they shared an all-consuming interest in antique dealing as well as other more private things.

Kennedy King was a bachelor, however, and consequently had to be careful. He did not want to find himself trapped into marriage with some little hand-on-hip heroine of the streets. As a result of board schools and compulsory education, the working classes had learned much about their rights, about writs and actions and the general paraphernalia of legal blackmail. The very last thing Kennedy wanted was trouble. He had sailed close to the wind on three occasions and on all of them it had cost him more than the dinah was worth to avoid the hint of scandal. After each near squeak he vowed to forswear girls for ever but, sooner or later, he was captivated by another neat little ankle or a pair of innocent brown eyes.

In sizing up Holly Beckman, Kennedy King had reached the conclusion that James Aspinall had found himself a treasure – and didn't quite know what to do with it. Miss Beckman was, as yet, without much polish and style but that could be developed. She was beautiful in an out-of-fashion way. Kennedy's father, a pupil of Rossetti, would have adored her oval face and solemn brows and the downcast mouth that, when she smiled, was so warm that it would have melted a less susceptible heart than King's. But it was not just her looks that Kennedy King admired. Good looks were not so uncommon. What qualities Holly Beckman possessed could only be surmised. Kennedy King was man of the world enough to recognise a passionate nature.

At the moment the girl might be totally preoccupied with business, with seizing the nettle of opportunity that circumstances had brought her – and who could blame her: ambition was a great virtue in his book – but in due course, when she had explored her potential for getting ahead in trade, she would divert her obvious determination to getting ahead in life.

And that, hopefully, was where he might step in.

In a period when it had been impossible to find loyal staff, Aspinall had stumbled on a winner. Kennedy had been pea-green with envy, the more so when it became obvious that Holly Beckman would have done anything for Aspinall, and all the staid fool asked of her was to tote up the books, dust the shelves and speak nicely to the customers.

But, now, here she was! And things had changed!

He would tread very warily, however, explore the possibility of persuading her to desert Pimlico for Bond Street. That would do for a start.

"Miss Beckman, what brings you to this part of town?"

She appeared slightly non-plussed, as if she had strayed into the gilded palace by accident.

She moved most charmingly, with natural poise. Kennedy could just imagine her in the Savoy or the Ritz in Paris, clinging to his arm while all heads turned. She would carry *haute monde* clothes well with that figure and probably had better taste than Simon's Emma, who did tend to be vulgar and showy. In his imagination, Kennedy King tried Holly in a brown tie-dyed summer dress of pleated voile with a turn-down collar and wide sleeves, a wide rose-petal sash about her slender waist.

The dealer sighed.

Confidence, that was all the girl really needed; confidence, money and a guiding hand.

She still seemed non-plussed.

Had she guessed what was on his mind? No, surely not! It must be the surroundings, nothing more.

Naturally the décor would overwhelm her, in contrast to Cardwell Place. It was all very well to see and handle fine items in sale rooms but to be confronted with a vast array of them all in one place – naturally she was entranced.

Indulgently, Kennedy watched the girl taking it all in. His private treasures clearly impressed her. He had inherited most of them from his mother's second husband, together with rather a lot of money in the form of gilt-edged shares. From the age of seven – when his father died as a result of over-indulgence in brandy spiced with chloral, and the family moved from Tithe Street to Kensington – King had been bathed in an atmosphere of impeccable good taste. Though he was not yet consciously the preserver of a tradition that would soon be seen as Romantic, he glided towards the high summer of his life under a panoply of Edwardianism. War had increased his sense of conservative isolation. War was something he equated with bad taste, Socialism, urban sprawl, self-denial and waste. Together with meatless days, coupons, rationing, drunken Colonials, and scarcity of fine teas and vintage wines, war was a crashing bore.

King had a sister-in-law with a son at the Front. Louise badgered him with talk of gore and unspeakable misery every time she was in town. That bored him too. He quite liked his nephew, though he was artistic, in the King family tradition; a poet, with something of a reputation. He had dined Christopher at the club once or twice during the subaltern's brief billeting at the former Duke of York's School, Chelsea. But the nephew had been so terribly full of military zeal that King had made a point of not repeating the exercise.

In sombre overcoat and black hat, the Beckman girl looked disturbingly like a young widow. If he ever became her "employer", he would change that image and smarten her up.

Running ahead of himself, he rose and drew out a chair.

He was a puffy figure, with smooth cheeks and thin sandy hair. He did not appear healthy in spite of his fleshiness. The paleness of his skin and fair brows gave him a naked expression. As a schoolboy, when he had been even puffier, he had squirmed under the nickname "Piggie". The acquisition of the shop – bought with his stepfather's money – had kicked the nickname into the cellar of his memory along with other slights and insults.

No, the girl was not rendered speechless after all. She was just taking her time, making a last rehearsal of her no-doubt prepared speech.

She held the Buckinghamshire sale catalogue in her hand, flat, not rolled like a Racing Pink.

She spoke with only the trace of an accent, not dropping her aitches too often. She said, "I take it, Mr. King, you've heard what's happenin' with Mr. Aspinall's business?"

"A few snatches of gossip."

"The situation is under review." Definitely rehearsed.

"Situation?"

"Mr. Aspinall left me a quarter share. I thought I should be manager, but the family ain't . . . haven't decided yet."

"How can I help?"

"The Buckingham sale, Tuesday first. Mr. Aspinall had a twenty-lot commission."

"What items?"

"The heavy silver; most all of it."

"Indeed!"

"Since the family haven't made a decision, I won't be attendin' the sale. Would you like t'take over the client?"

"I'll filch the client, if I can," warned King with a smile.

She nodded, hesitated, then offered the catalogue. "The top bid on each item is marked in red ink. Pay no heed to the other lots."

"Rather sad," said King, leafing through the catalogue. "The Little Man's last pricing.'

"Just the red ink items."

"He won't get the George Three matched salvers for that. I've a higher bid in my pocket."

"What about the modern rose bowl?"

"Yes, it should knock down under forty."

"Will you undertake the commission, Mr. King?"

"For Aspinall's, or the client – that's the rub, young lady."

"For the client."

"In that case, of course; I'd be delighted."

The girl extracred a printed card from the band of her glove and handed it to him. King scanned it. Dr. Augustus Royle, in darkest Dorset. The name meant nothing to him. But if the doctor was willing to trust Aspinall's on heavy stuff like silver, he must be a long-standing client.

Holly said, "I'll write to Dr. Royle an' explain."

"Do I bill him in advance? Is he a tardy payer?"

"He always pays by return."

"That's the advantage the little men have over us Bond Street chaps," said King, sighing. "Our lords and ladies are slow as the deuce when it comes to stumping up."

Holly got to her feet.

"Won't you stay a moment; drink a cup of tea?" said King.

"I've got to be gettin' back, sir."

"Must you? James usually stopped for a chat, you know."

"There's nobody in the shop."

"I see. Not pulling their weight, those offspring of his?"

Holly did not rise to the bait.

Kennedy King put his hand on her shoulder. He experienced a pang of physical desire, tender rather than possessive. It was all he could do to restrain himself from stroking Holly's neck with his fingertips. He guided her through the archway, round a sharp corner into the body of the shop.

Bronze steam radiators kept it moderately warm, in spite of the coal shortage that obliged him to feed the basement boiler vast quantities of scrap wood. Condensation veiled the windows. The bustle of the Arcade's Saturday traffic was decently remote. The floor was of wood-block, polished to a rich chocolate brown, bisected by a runner carpet in Indian pattern. On each side of the pathway, King's expensive wares were arranged in a series of open "rooms", four specific periods divided by watersilk screens. The bulbous structures of Tudor Gothic contrasted with lean, clean classical Adam, and "Chinese" Chippendale, more French than Oriental, and squared tapered Sheraton. Glasses and goblets, plate, snuff mulls, chambersticks, jugs, clocks and candelabra were precisely matched to the furniture. None of the items was price-tagged, not so much offered for sale as presented as part of an historical tapestry which the client, if well-cobbled enough, might weave for himself.

King studied the girl's face. All thought of her mission had flown from her head. She could not absorb enough of his trove, seemed to drink it in with a thirstiness that was close to greed. For all that, she had none of the slyness of the bazaarmen who, though discouraged, occasionally slouched in by the front door to offer him a "choice" item; they saw only the value of the goods, not their beauty. How on earth had a Lambeth gal, a docker's daughter, ever developed such an urgent aesthetic sense? It didn't seem right and proper, somehow; it was rare, and, being rare, intriguing. He supposed that quality had drawn Aspinall to her. He wished he had got there first, believing – probably correctly – that he would have spotted this talent in her too.

He stopped her just short of the door.

Mr. McDonald had doddered forward to open it but King brushed the ancient back to the mystic passes that McDonald called "dusting". King craved a little more of Holly's company.

He said, "I'm grateful to you, Miss Beckman, for thinking of King's in this matter."

"That's all right," the girl said.

"I trust you don't think I'm prying, but if there's anything I can do – for you, I mean – please don't hesitate to call on me."

"I don't know what's happenin' yet."

"Must be very unsettling for you."

"Yes, Mr. King. An' it's not good for business."

"Are the Aspinalls seriously contemplating selling out?"

"I think so."

"Would they consider an offer from me?"

Her dark eyes were amazed. "What would you want with a junk-shop like Aspinall's? You've got all this."

"Pimlico isn't a bad area. Besides, you have that large store at the rear; warehousing space is becoming increasingly more expensive to rent." King's voice softened. "I'd require a manager, of course."

"Mr. King . . . d'you mean . . . me?"

"Who better, Miss Beckman?"

Flustered, Holly said, "I . . . I don't know what to say, sir."

He risked putting his finger lightly against her lips, giving her his warmest, most avuncular smile. "Say nothing, Miss Beckman. Let the Aspinalls decide; I suppose they will – eventually. Keep my offer up your sleeve."

"Mr. King, I . . ."

He winked. "Consider me your trump card."

She thanked him again, not quite as profusely as he would have wished. But she was, without doubt, an astute child, would have begun to calculate the financial arrangements. If he bought Aspinall's, he would scare off the other interested parties, get it cheap, lock, stock, staff and barrel. If he got it cheap, her share of the proceeds of the sale would be reduced accordingly. On the other hand, she would be assured of a position, a responsible position, and a degree of security that the Aspinalls could never offer.

Standing at the doorway, neglectful of the fact that he was still clad in his smoking jacket, Mr. King watched the girl hurry down the Arcade beneath the vaulted glass ceiling. She glanced behind her, once, and waved tentatively to him. The youthful trust in that gesture quite made Kennedy King's day.

* * *

Cracking the Silver Thimble Fund's depot in Conniston Lane,

Kensington, turned out to be a simple piece of business for Ritchie Beckman and his reluctant accomplice, Leo. The purpose of the Fund's latest rake-around for gold and silver trinkets was to raise sufficient money to endow a ward in the Seamen's Hospital, Greenwich. Neither Ritchie nor his Pa had ever been to sea, and didn't have a high opinion of the jacks they'd encountered tanking it up in Bermondsey's pubs. In spite of his dockland background, Leo equated the perils and privations of a merchantman's life in war with a steamer trip on the Thames – a bit dampish and smoky and "umpty" round the bends; apart from that, a cushy number.

Ritchie considered the Fund's organisers mad to advertise in the newspapers. He could think of a billion better ways of "celebrating a victorious Peace" than lashing out valuable objects for free. He knew the kind of nobs who'd go in for that kind of charitable exercise. They'd react to the news that some "monster" had whipped the hoard by tugging out their chequebooks and fountain pens and posting off an even bigger donation, just to thumb their noses at the unpatriotic burglars. Charities, of course, were the biggest bloomin' racket of the lot.

Leo was not Ritchie's ideal as a helpmate on a big job. He would have preferred to take along one of his seasoned acquaintances but then the thing would leak to Shotten and Shotten would get huffy because he hadn't offered him the swag. Gingerly he had broached the subject of doing a bit of the dishonest with Stan Nuttall but Stan knew what shrapnel from a six-inch gun could do, could fill in from his imagination the horrors of torpedoes, burning oil slicks, freezing seas. He read Ritchie a lecture on the convoy system, explaining how the Admiralty had left Britain's cargo ships a prey to Bosche U-boats, Dreadnoughts and cruisers until late in the war. Ritchie prudently backed off.

There was no question of including Jeff Horsfall, who'd have come in like a shot. Jeff was too slow, too obvious for anything but simple snaffles.

It wasn't the first job that Ritch had pulled out of the area. He adored robbing the black-fur-muff brigade of Kensington and Knightsbridge whenever an opportunity presented itself. He took his time making the survey, toddling round South Ken on a Sunday afternoon, when cold winds and intermittent rain kept the fashionable indoors and the steps of the great museums free of students and seekers after truth and beauty.

Conniston Lane was conveniently sited behind Damaris Terrace. Private gardens and high brick walls gave first-rate protection. Four mansions in the Lane had been converted into offices under the thumb of the department of Home Affairs; outposts of Whitehall. The number given in the newspaper ads was that of a large four-storey mansion which had become a warren of offices. Ritchie walked boldly up the path and read the cards tacked to the doorpost. The temporary depot of the Silver Thimble Fund occupied the first floor back. Twenty minutes' research on Sunday convinced Ritchie that his target had been inspired and that a plan involving simple skills of housebreaking, plus a little protective camouflage, would see him through all right. He had shaken harder cribs with nothing but a rope, a chisel and a hammer.

He briefed his Pa thoroughly. "We do it Saturday evenin'. The rozzers'll be too busy nabbin' drunken soldiers to bother. We can take our time, slide away nice an' light, like."

"What's in there, though?"

"Gold, silver, small wares."

"Will it be worth our while?"

"Should be." Ritchie grinned.

To him thieving was no novelty. His Pa's nervousness made him more thorough in his preparations. He enjoyed the adventure as well as its rewards. Anyhow, it was time the old man was made to realise just how good he was; skilled as well as bright. He had worked out just how it was that the Lambeth blaggers got themselves hoisted, what mistakes they made. He avoided those mistakes like the plague. For instance, he carried no tools from job to job, kept nothing in-criminating in the house or his place of work. He didn't have his "meets" in public places, or associate directly with anybody who might be a nark.

For the Kensington job he acquired the tools from seedy market stalls up the East End, far from his home patch. He bought, piecemeal, a bent cold chisel, a screwdriver, a sharp steel knife, a gimlet, a glazier's blade and a glass-cutter, a length of new rope, a short coil of perished rubber cable, two peaked hats and two brown overalls, topping off with two large canvas haversacks. The lot came to two pounds and fourteen shillings; an investment. He had used similar implements before, though this was his first major burglary – by strict definition, a "housebreaking", since it would be over and done with before the witching hour of nine p.m. For years, he had augmented his wages by occasional acts of theft, usually from shops in Newington and Camberbell, stealing only cash. Once or twice he had acquired valuable goods that he had sold to Jack Renzo, Vince Shotten's fence. One time he had pulled a job that Renzo had put out for a likely lad – a daylight raid on a pop shop whose owner had been holding loot from a big robbery by the Salter mob, East Cheap heavyweights who'd no right to be operating on Shotten's patch. Though he had been nothing but a scout on that tickle he'd got paid a straight five nicker. While admiring their style, Ritchie was leery of Shotten. Big boys controlled the buyers; buyers paid dirt for the goodies. Only low-life twerps did regular trade with them, ran the risk of finding themselves shopped for crossing Vince. Cash takings were small beer, however, compared with what could be made from goods. Ritchie had always yearned for an outlet of his own, a safe, secure, clean-as-a-whistle selling agent who had no underworld connections – somebody like Holly, his own dear sister with her nice little shop.

Ritchie's job in the tannery was part of his cover, a necessary evil while he completed his apprenticeship in crime. He had no false modesty about his abilities as a criminal. In private, he regarded himself first and foremost as a professional thief. He wanted to be wealthy, to own fine things, to live in style with his lady. He also lusted for a taste of Shotten's muscular authority, to be a man who was feared. For such-like ends Ritchie risked the cat o' nine tails and long terms of penal servitude. So far, amazingly, he had not attracted the attention of the police. He had never appeared before the beak on any charges. He was imaginative, intelligent and cool as an iceberg.

Clad in peaked caps and brown overalls, each with a bag slung over his shoulder and Leo with the coil of rubberised cable conspicuously displayed, like a muffler around his neck, father and son walked into Conniston Lane at a quarter-past eight o'clock on that moist Saturday night, looking more or less like a couple of Post Office telephone engineers. In the shadows of the Lane, where it counted, they would pass for the real thing.

Leo waited by the gate while Ritchie marched up the path and hammered loudly on the mansion's front door. There was no caretaker in the building, and no answer. Ritchie signalled to Pa. Together they slipped round to the back of the building. There were two trade entrances. Both doors were secure. Ground floor windows were protected by wrought-iron grilles. A box drainpipe, however, dropped from the roof. It was firmly bolted to brackets embedded in the stonework. Behind the Beckmans, as they stared up at the rear façade, was a flagged apron and a long lawn that had been turned over and planted with spuds.

"Anybody there?" Leo asked in a hoarse whisper, like a medium at a spiritualist seance.

"Not a whisper."

"What winder?"

"That 'un."

"What d'yer want me t'do, son?"

"Give's a leg up, Pa, then go stand at the gable corner an' keep a weather on the gate. Anybody shows up, spin them the tale about how we're cable engineers. Keep them talkin'."

"Gotcher."

"Put on yer 'at."

"Right."

"Now – leg up."

Stooping, Leo braced hands on knees.

Wheezing softly with excitement, Ritchie mounted his father's shoulders. Tools clanked in the canvas sack. Weight pressed on Leo's back, then lifted. Ritchie shinned up the drainpipe as fast as a monkey up a coconut palm. Leo was impressed by his son's agility. Stepping back, he watched, open-mouthed, until Ritchie called down to him, "Get t'the bleedin' corner, Pa."

By now Ritchie had reached a window ledge twenty-five feet above the flagstones. He crouched on the ledge and cautiously secured himself by a loop of rope knotted around the pipe. Silent as a flea in a rug, he put two strips of plaster tape across the glass, cut round the pane with the glazier's knife, hinged the pane inwards, held it with one hand, unknotted the safety rope with the other hand, slid under the glass flap, and groped for the floor.

Down into the room. Lower the glass, draw in the sling and rope, lightly tape glass in place, bag the tools and take out the torch.

What a bleedin' cake-walk.

Temporary office, all right; two tables, wire trays, letters, a typewriter's machine, three filing cabinets, two large cupboards with padlocks like "Try Me" signs.

The cold chisel saw the padlocks off.

Inside, the goodies were stacked on shelves. The Fund organisers had even labelled the boxes to help him along – "Gold", "Silver", "Plated", "Precious Stones", "Semi-Precious", "Watches and Links", "Cases", "Odds." There wasn't much stuff in the boxes, though, except for "Odds" which was brimful of cheap junk. He took down the boxes and, sitting cross-legged on the floor, sorted through the contents, appropriating only items which he considered might have high value and which were not engraved or monogrammed. He put the bulk of the items back in the boxes and returned the boxes to the shelves. He had no intention of storing truck, or of being nailed for something worth only a couple of bob.

He checked out the table drawers and unlocked cabinets. In a cigar box he found sixteen pounds in banknotes, contributions sent through the mail. He took the notes, of course, but left the sheaf of uncashed cheques bedded beside them. It was tempting to "do over" the rest of the building. Ritchie resisted; he believed in a clean, quick hit. He made his exit by the window, lowering the swag down to the flagstones on the rope, then shinning down the drainpipe.

Leo's head popped round the gable corner.

"What's up, son?"

"Nothin', Pa. It's done."

"Yer? Then let's scarper."

"Easy, Pa. Just stroll away, easy like."

Ritchie put on his hat, slung the canvas bag over his shoulder, picked up the coil of cable then, nudging Leo ahead of him, made down the path and through the gate into the lane. His father, poor old bastard, was rigid with fear, walking stiff-legged like a tin soldier. Lightly, Ritchie clapped the old man on the shoulder.

"We knocked it off."

"Whatcher pull?" said Leo, squinting at him, greed overcoming terror.

"Twenty nice little pieces."

"No cash?"

"Nope," said Ritchie. "No cash."

They rounded the corner and headed along the road towards railings, trees, the bright crowns of gas lamps, towards people, motorcars, carriages, trams, across busy Old Brompton Road. Leo wanted to drop into a public house for a refreshment. Ritchie would have none of it. Right, along Fulham Road, left, into Park Walk and on down to an obsolete cab drivers' shelter that Ritchie had spotted in advance. There the two men divested themselves of the disguises and wrapped the overalls and hats into a brown paper bundle. The swag was small enough to stow in their pockets. Leo was disapppointed at its lack of bulk. Carrying the bundle, Ritchie led his father off again towards the Thames.

Somewhere along the Chelsea Embankment, Ritchie dropped the bundle over the wall into the muddy tide that seeped between the houseboats. He ditched the cable and – to Leo's astonishment – all of the burglar's tools as well. The bother of buying more was less than the risk of being caught with them.

Sweeping up the Thames, the wind was arctic. Leo carped and complained, demanding a drink. Sternly, Ritchie drove his father on

across the Suspension Bridge and round Battersea Park. They board-
ed an omnibus there and, with one change, rode home to Ambraham's Terrace.

"Come on int' The Hat, son?" Leo pleaded. "I'm dry's a bone, for
Gawd sake."

"No drinkin' for you tonight, Pa. I want you sober."

"One pint."

"Home."

Whining but obedient, Leo trundled down the Box by Ritchie's
side. They let themselves in by the front door, and stepped quietly
through the tiny hall towards the stairs.

The living room door opened.

Leo and Ritchie froze.

"See who's here," Grandpa Tal boomed.

Leo swallowed. "W . . . who?"

"See for yourselves." The old man pushed the door wider.

Maury was sprawled in the easy chair, uniform unbuttoned, boots
off. He looked round at his father and brother, not smiling, steady
eyes searching Ritchie's face.

"Blimey! It's our Maury," Ritchie wheezed. He rammed a smile on
to his lips, then, for a reason he could not explain, began to shake as a
sudden engulfing wave of guilt caught him off guard.

"Been out on the tiles, Ritch?" Maury asked.

The gold and silver trinkets in his trouser pockets weighed like
lead, burned like blobs of phosphorus. Leo, beetroot red, was
stammering and stuttering like a looney.

"We . . . been. . ." Ritchie fought giddiness, nervous shaking and, in
a moment, gained control of himself. His smile relaxed. "Yer; on the
tiles, my old son."

Brazenly pushing his father, he descended into the living room to
welcome his brother home.

*   *   *

With Leo Beckman, volume equated with warmth. Being hearty
meant being overweeningly loud. "I mean t'say, son, how couldn't yer
let us know you was comin'?"

"How? By sendin' postcards?" said Maury. "We've been on the
shift for twelve stinkin' days, movin' the battalion over from France."

"But are y'out, demobilised?" Ritchie asked.

"Gawd, no! Not yet," said Maury. "Caught the rumour the regiment was chalked up for a tour as an occupation force. Another that

we was all bein' sent t'Russia to tame the Bolsheviks 'fore they get out o'hand."

Frowning, Tal sat forward in his chair. "Russia! The Allies have no business in Russia."

"It's all right, Grandad," Maury assured him. "None of it's true. Looks like we're home for good. They got us billeted in tents in a field round back of the officers' hospital at Crofton Castle in Wiltshire. Students, coal miners an' farmers are getting' first release. Our adjutant told us, we been good boys an'll be in the next batch for the ticket. Might even be home by Christmas. Done, finished, *kaput*."

"Maury, that's wonderful," Holly said.

He smiled at his sister.

Even Holly could not sense how he felt, how strange it was to be there in the cluttered living room in Lambeth; not altogether comfortable.

Maury could not believe that the killing was over.

Ten weeks ago he'd been half-buried in a fox-hole with tanks thundering round him and rain falling. Since then, with a bout of influenza to blunt his awareness, it had all become like a dream. He still could not understand why, out of hundreds of thousands of soldiers, he and his mates had been set up for an early ticket. True, the battalion was nothing but a collection of rags, its strength chopped and chopped and chopped again by the Offensive campaigns of summer and autumn, by the drive to the Hindenburg Line. Even so . . . he told his mind to lay off it. He was home now. There was Grandad Tal in his ancient blanket-cloth dressing gown that did not reach his knees and exposed the puckered white flesh of his legs; like a venerable, pugnacious Russian monk; Holly, more mature, more reserved than he remembered her, more beautiful; Ritchie and Pa, too – there was some silly consolation in their trivialisation of his experiences, their lack of understanding. He knew how it would be. Leo would ask him on the q.t. about French women, Ritchie would angle to see what plans he had for the future.

Holly put two spoonfuls of precious sugar into a thick china mug and stirred it, handing it to him together with a plate of buttered bread and jam.

"Butter, not drippin'," she said.

"How'd you get that, then?"

"Out of Grandpa's store," said Holly.

Already divisions were beginning to re-establish themselves. It had been so for years; Leo and Ritchie on the one side, Holly, Tal and Maury on the other. Tiny wars, skirmishes, battles, played round the hearth, not the pride of nations but the vanity of individuals at stake. Ruefully, Maury viewed his family. Of them all, he had the most individuality. He didn't look like a Beckman, nor a Kirsanoff, not even like a Jew. He was large, square-faced, fresh complexioned with light-brown curling hair. Once he had had a photograph taken – in calm spring sunshine on the road from the Factory at Amiens – wearing a *Pickelhaube*, the spiked Bosche helmet so popular as a souvenir. To the camera he looked so much like a young Saxon that some wag had written *Siegfried Beckman* across the back of the picture – and he had torn it up. His hatred of Germans was almost pathological. Though nobody, ever, would be made privy to his secret, he had killed them with awful pleasure. Too many men had been torn apart by guilt and sorrow. Maury had stayed sane not just by obeying his officers and refusing to think about the stupidity of war, but by finding himself an enemy, *the* enemy, simplifying his instincts, around that ready-made point. Occasionally, he even believed the propaganda tripe and thought that being a fighting Tommy had, in fact, made a man of him.

"Betcher glad it's over?" Leo eyed up Kirsanoff's secret butter pile and wondered why the hell he hadn't scrounged for it, being a butter addict too.

"Sure," said Maury, biting into the bread.

"Couldn't 'ave been all bad, though?" Leo persisted.

"Had a great time," said Maury.

"We read about it in the papers," said Ritchie.

Maury swallowed, drank sweet tea. "Sure; the papers."

Called to the West Surrey Regiment at the beginning of 1915, Maury had disappointed his grandfather by not transferring to one of the three Jewish battalions that had been raised fifteen months later. By that time he couldn't have cared less. Though he humoured the old man, his interest in Jewish traditions had always been nil. In France it didn't matter what badge you displayed on your cap; he would be just as dead whether he wore the Menorah or not.

Now they were waiting – for what? God, what *were* they waiting for? Adventure stories? *Up the Nibblers, Tales of the Toffee-Apples, Crack Squadron in France?* Sentiment? *Some Poor Mother's Son?*

Leo was blabbering. "Starks – you remember Starks, him as worked the meat market – he come 'ome minus a leg. Said it was worth it t'keep the nation free. An' Ritchie's pal, Stan Nuttall, he don't seem t'mind what happened t'him. Ma Bennet's boy, the eldest, him as was at the Polytechnic 'fore the war, he wrote it up for the papers.

Read them stories, I did. Paid him ten quid. Good money, ain't it, just for scribblin' down rubbish?"

"Sure," said Maury.

"When did you last have a good night's sleep?" asked Tal Kirsanoff. "Holly has made up your bed. Don't let us keep you talkin' here."

"Sod off!" said Leo. "Let'm talk. S'what they tells yer t'do in the papers. Let 'em talk it out."

"Dad, Maury's worn out," said Holly.

Maurice emptied the mug, put it behind him on to the ledge of the dresser. He fished in his pocket, brought out a crushed packet of Black Cat cigarettes. He did not offer them around. He lit one from a match and shook the match out so that it left a signature of greasy smoke across his face. Raising his eyebrows ingenuously, he smiled.

"Yer, maybe I will jot down a few things for the papers, Da," he said, in a slow, deep drawling voice. "Big attack, right? Shellin' goes on for three days, four nights. Can't hear, can't smell nothin' but the guns. You sweat, an' the sweat freezes. You piss often, where you can."

"No, Maury," Holly warned softly.

"You get a thirst like you wouldn't believe. Tongue swells up. Can't swaller properly. Right? Waterboys, canteen carriers, they don't get through. Get shot, blown up, gassed, blasted. Stupid kids! You find a hole with water in it; brown water, thick, like gravy. You ignore the handbooks, the warnin's, the things in there, rottin'. You throw yourself down an' you drink. Once you get started, there ain't no stoppin'; you go on drinkin'. Right?"

Ritchie said, "Hey, Maury, we don't want to. . ."

"Four hours, five hours, you start t'swell. It's out t'here, your belly. One in the oven. Right? Your organs crushed t'gether. Right? Takes a day, usually, t'die. Put a bayonet in t'let the gas out." He stopped. "Not excitin' enough for you, Pa? I'll tell you about Pierre. Maybe that wasn't his name. We called him Pierre. Real hero, Pierre. Got t'know him well."

Leo cleared his throat loudly, and shouted, "Gotta bottle o' stout; you want that, Maury? Nightcap, like?"

Maurice ignored him. "Found Pierre in a shell-hole. Eighteen. Came from Lille. Blinded. Had enough eyes left t'cry, though. Not for himself. For his brother. None of us, includin' our Sarge, knew what t'do with Pierre, the Frenchie. We was far out, ordered t'stay dug in behind a church the tanks had gone through. Red Cross? Gawd knows where they were? Ridin' on the front o'the tanks, maybe. Anyhow, we took Pierre back t'the dug-out, an' bandaged his blind eyes. 'Louis,' he kept shoutin'. 'Louis.' Weepin' pink for Louis. Keeps it up for eighteen hours, while we're pinned down, the whole platoon pinned down. 'Louis. Louis. Louis.'" Maurice snorted. "Drive you bleedin' mad, that kind o' thing. We talked about pushin' him up the steps. But – well – Christ, we're *English*, ain't we? *We're* not the bleedin' Bosche."

"What . . . what happened to him?" Holly asked.

"We crawled up the sector an' got grog for the poor Frenchie bastard. Poured it into him, about a pint o' the stuff. He calmed down. Talked. Talked English, too. Pretty good. Educated. Been to London. Loved Kew Gardens. Father was a teacher in Lille. Louis was his brother. Nineteen. Pierre," Maurice shook his head, "talked about Louis. Poor old bleedin' Louis-the-Frog, ordered t'attack the German lines. Dozen in advance t'clip the wires. This in daylight, broad, beamin', bleedin' daylight. Get up there, Louis. You're only a Frog. Up they went, over the parapet into the middle of nowhere. Five o' them catch it, p.d.q. Bang-bang: five times. The rest freeze. Crazy bleedin' Frogs. Freeze solid. Can't go up, can't come back. Lie there for nine hours, 'till dark, then crawl back to their trench – an' get arrested."

"Gawd Almighty!" said Ritchie.

"Disobeyin' an order. Cowardice. Court-martial convened on the spot. Frog colonel in charge. Privates let off. Both corporals found guilty, toot-sweet. *Rapidement*. Report sent to the General. Brother Pierre brought up the line. Stunned. By-bye, *frère Louis*. Ta-rah. Dawn – they shoot the two corporals. Noon – runner from the General, wants further enquiries. Executions to be postponed. Pierre goes over the top. Lucky bogger t'get 'imself blinded."

"Lucky?" Ritchie said.

"The brass would've shot him on the spot. No eyes is a good excuse. Better than no guts. Right?"

"He survived then?" asked Tal Kirsanoff. "Your French boy?"

"British hospital at base. We delivered him there in the end," said Maurice. "You got any more o' that tea, Holly?"

The girl entered the scullery where she had left the teapot on the stove. Casually Maury rose and threaded his way between the furniture. Hand on the curtain, he paused.

"Think the papers'll buy my stories, Pa?" he enquired. "Reckon they're worth a tenner a piece?"

Leo did not answer.

Maury went on into the kitchen.

She was out in the back yard, standing on a patch of broken paving that bordered the cabbage allotment.

In the damp night the odour of gas was pungent, lights in the mazes of the Lambeth lanes gaseous too, like the slow fall of exploded Very flares suspended in cloud. The gable wall of the Patent Medicine factory had a dead fish-skin glow. Only at close range, in the yard's earthy shadows, was there any depth, any hint of colour.

Maury put his arm across her shoulders. He could feel the sobs, dry and muffled, that shook his sister.

"I had to, Holly. I had to tell them the truth."

"Did you have to tell me, too? I didn't want t' hear."

"Better t'hear it from me, luv." He tugged her against him. He felt huge, solid, strange. "You'll hear no more of it, not from my lips. That's all I'll ever say. But it ain't just me went through it, that's what you must remember. All of us who fought an' survived, every man you meet with, he'll have it locked inside him. It's better you know somethin', a part of it."

She turned against him, putting her hands to his face, to the stubble of his day-old beard. "Maury, I can't share that sort of thing with anyone."

"Then don't take up with a soldier."

"Maury, you're not the same."

"You can't expect it."

"I don't know what to expect these days."

"Cheer up, old luv," said Maury, flatly. "Things can't get no worse, ever again."

*   *   *

That night, evil dreams tormented Holly.

Caught in a sea of muddy images and blurred visions, she walked endlessly through a vast auction room under a great grey ceiling of hammered lead. The oblong room was jammed with dealers, backs turned as they pored over the lots. Across the table she glimpsed a face; Stan Nuttall stared at her, pale and serious, eyepatch raised like a tiny lid to expose an ivory cameo screwed into the hollow socket. More faces – Scottie Hansford had shared a school desk with her; his cap was too big for his impudent head. Scottie Hansford, killed at Mons. Mikie Pawle, Johnnie Botham, little Joseph Swart, all boys from Abraham's Box, all dead now.

The dealers' identical grey suits changed to khaki. She walked between soldiers towards the dais where the auctioneer's desk stood, complete with glass, carafe and record book. Mr. Aspinall was the auctioneer, Maury his clerk. Soundlessly they shouted out lot numbers, Mr. A. rapping his silent hammer, racing through the catalogue, hands moving with graceful haste, knocking down the lots fast as ninepins. Desperate to bid, frantic to buy, Holly called out. Inexorably the desk crept back from her, the ranks of soldiers lengthened. Among the uniforms she caught sight of women, not slumped and sad in widows' weeds, but gay as butterflies, svelte as leopards, the pretty, pained, hungry, haughty, desirable monsters of Mayfair. She saw David, the Scottish major – and Kennedy King tricked out like the Kaiser in cape, boots, sword and helmet. They were all laughing uproariously at her ineptitude. One by one, in quick succession, the lots were knocked down and vanished, until the room was bare.

Mr. Aspinall pointed his mahogany mallet. She turned to see what he had reserved for her. The final lot, identical to the others, stood on a plinth at the aisle's end. But a subaltern in bloodstained uniform had laid his torn hand on it. Holly shouted, and ran towards the plinth, aching to buy that one remaining lot – a plain pinewood coffin with an unhinged lid.

The soldier bowed and laughed, beckoning her on, then stepped up, lifted his prize and began to walk away, the coffin – marked "Sold" – hoisted on his back.

"Wait," Holly cried. "Wait."

No words came, except grunts. She fought in fear and frustration to utter a sound.

The cry wakened her from her shallow sleep.

Drenched in perspiration, her shift twined tightly round her stomach, she paddled down the blankets and let cold air flood over her.

Awake now, she heard the cry again, faint and plaintive.

Slipping from bed, she crossed to the window, lifted the net curtain and stared out into the still moist mist, half in hope, half in horror of finding the man who had uttered that desolate cry.

Even the back yard had no colour now. It stared emptily back at her, a soiled grey deserted place.

Whoever had made the sound, it seemed, had not expected a response.

Holly returned to bed. Hands on her breasts, head pressed into the pillow, she lay awake for an hour or more expecting the dream to return, the cry to sound again. She was ready to respond, to make her bid, half in horror, half in hope.

Eventually she drifted down into sleep.

And did not dream again.

Diamond Ear-rings

DECEMBER SEEMED TO begin well. Holly had no means of knowing that she was being steered towards events that would require all her strength of will to resolve.

Brother Ritchie had sorted out the collection of wares thieved from the Silver Thimble Fund and had appeased his father by paying him the sixteen pounds stolen from the offices. In the main the jewellery was not top quality, apart from one choice item that Ritchie intended to foist on to his sister.

In his shop in the Chalfont Arcade, Mr. Kennedy King had put his feet up and his thinking-cap on and, spurred by inexplicable impulses, mused over the possible acquisition of Aspinall's – and Holly Beckman.

Andrea found her plans to be rid of the Beckman girl brought to a temporary halt. And David, caught in the blizzard of work that Armistice had swept into Whitehall, had too much to cope with, including Miss Leigh-Jennings, to spare more than an occasional thought for the shop and its youthful manager.

But the first week of December belonged to Maury who, to make amends for his harsh lesson in reality, helped his sister settle down to the tasks on hand.

In contrast to all that Maury had suffered, her own problems seemed minor. Maury, however, would have none of that negative thinking. On Sunday, instead of sloping off in search of "a good time", he persuaded his sister to don her best bib and tucker and accompany him to dinner; a real dinner, none of your Lambeth eel-pie suppers. The invitation did not include Pa or Ritchie; Maury made no bones about the fact that he wanted Holly to himself. He took her to Hardesty's, an old-established chop-house off the Strand where the chefs had been tutored in the art of making much of little. It was not the kind of place that Maury should have known about, let alone had the gall to enter. But her brother's indifference to the queer looks that darted from the officers and their ladies at neighbouring tables gave

Holly confidence. After all, she had no reason to be ashamed of eating in a posh restaurant with a soldier. Her brother was as brave and gallant as any of the lieutenants or captains there. Besides, she was not just a lowly little shop servant now but a partner in a moderately successful business.

"Isn't it strange," Holly said, after they had been shown to a table, "you an' me dinin' together in a place like this."

"I've seen stranger things, Holly."

"But three years ago you'd never have guessed we'd be here, would you, Maury?"

"Three years ago I wouldn't have given tuppence for my chances of ever eatin' out in London again," said Maury. "Anyhow, three years ago you were just a kid."

"I suppose you get used to it," said Holly.

"Used to what, love?"

"This."

"It ain't hard," said Maury. "Gets easier every time."

"You done it before?"

"Sure I have," said Maury. "Up in town, not knowin' when you was comin' back, *if* you was comin' back. Couldn't be bothered with takin' on a skinful of beer and goin' lookin' for some little tart to blow your pay on; not me. There was a sergeant, Welsh; William Gwynn Pryce-Evans. Can't get more Welsh than that, can you? Anyhow, he was a toff, a blue-blood. Billy should have been an officer. But he was a wild man, brave as a lion but a natural rebel. He'd been flung out of half a dozen public schools, sent down from Oxford, disinherited by his father, disowned by his whole family, except his brother who was as wild as he was. When war broke out Billy enlisted. The authorities did everything to persuade him to join the officer corps, but the bold Billy would 'ave none of it. Into the ranks he went, an' nobody could stop him. He was given a lot of stick for his la-de-da accent – though he could curse better'n anybody – an' his nice manners. But Billy saw no reason to turn coarse just to save face."

"Was he your friend?"

"Yer," said Maury. "We were together for fourteen months, one way an' another. It was Billy taught me the difference between the classes."

"Money? Privilege?"

"Attitude," said Maury. "Look round you, Holly. See them? *We* make *them* uncomfortable. Not our fault. It's their attitude, not ours. Why should we inherit their prejudices. We're not dirty. We can pay for our dinner, an' our manners ain't that shocking. When Billy'd drag me along with 'im into fancy restaurants or bars, I used to cringe at first. Then I saw that Billy took stick there an' all – just because of his sergeant's uniform. It was all surfaces; know what I mean. Stripes not bars made all the difference. Billy had a pedigree that'd shame most of the so-called toffs in those places, but he didn't flaunt it, an' it didn't worry him. He had his gin in comfort, his roast beef well cooked, an' t' hell with what they thought." Maury paused. "He taught me a lot did old Sergeant Pryce-Evans."

"What happened to him?"

"Killed," said Maury. "Sniper's bullet. Last September. He nearly made it through."

"Do you miss him?"

"I miss a lot of them," said Maury. "The only consolation was, I got that bleedin' sniper personally, with a grenade."

"That didn't help Billy, though?"

"No," said Maury. "But it helped me."

Holly studied the menu in silence, not really taking in the words.

"Mother would've liked all this," Maury said, abruptly shifting the slant of the conversation.

"Do you remember her?" said Holly.

"Course. Not that well. But she was beautiful. Really she was. An' she had a mind of 'er own, I can tell you. I was a right cheeky little tyke, but I wouldn't dare cross Ma."

"I wish she hadn't died," said Holly.

"Well, if she hadn't, maybe dear ol' Pa would've murdered her by this time," said Maury. "Never did understand why she married 'im. She was too clever by 'alf for Leo. He knew it too. They used t' fight like cat an' dog."

"Lots of people do."

"I remember the shoutin'. He would thump 'er an' all," said Maury. "It was a last desperate resort. She could outsmart our Leo every time. You're like 'er."

"Come off it, Maury," said Holly. "You can't possibly remember 'er that well."

"No, you are. Grandpa says you're very like her. Ma would've loved to run a business. It would have suited 'er nature. She was far too clever t'be stuck in a box in Lambeth washin' a docker's socks an' wipin' kids' noses. Maybe Grandpa did 'er a bad turn bringin' 'er up the way he did, out of chip with the world she 'ad to live in. I dunno. But I tell you, Holly, she'd have been proud as Punch t'think 'er daughter – not one of 'er sons, mark you, but 'er daughter – was a business woman."

"Business woman," said Holly.

She liked the definition. It sounded classless, efficient and not too grand, even if it didn't quite relate to the shop in Cardwell Place and the grimier aspects of the trade.

"It's exactly what you are," Maury assured her. "It's what I'll be too, given a bit of time – a business man. There's no future in sweatin' blood for somebody else's profit. I'm strikin' out on my own."

"Doin' what, Maury?"

"Bricks an' mortar," Maury said. "Building's the comin' thing. I kept my ears open. I talked with officers, dozens of the poor bleeders. You've got t'talk about somethin' t'keep your mind off what might happen t'morrer." He shrugged. "I learned a lot talkin' to these so-called educated men. Some good lessons in how t'get on in this world. You don't need no silver spoon now, Holly. Next twenty, thirty years will be our time."

"Our time?"

"Anybody who's got guts enough t'seize the chance."

"You'd never know it, lookin' round Lambeth."

"They haven't wakened up yet, that's all. Anyhow, we was always different, you an' me – Ritchie too. Thought about it, but can't find a reason. Kirsanoff blood, maybe."

"Do you *feel* different?"

"Course I do. Always did."

"I thought it was me, just me. I felt bad about not bein' like . . . like them."

"You found somethin' t'hang on to."

"Mr. Aspinall?"

"Call it that, call it anythin'."

Across the aisle a young subaltern with a sprinkle of hair on his upper lip and an air of raging superciliousness was loudly complaining about the turkey pie. The waiter, old as Methuselah and grey as a whale, nodded patiently, rode out the officer's wrath, and removed the half-eaten plate of pie.

To his companion, a red-haired girl little older than Holly, the officer remarked, "Damned if I'm eatin' muck at these prices. Better off in the trenches, I say."

Methuselah returned with a silver dish of steamed turbot. The officer wrinkled his nose then, with suffering, accepted it.

The waiter came to Maury's side.

"Sir?"

"Well 'ave the turkey pie." said Maury.

"Sir," said the waiter inscrutably, and went away.

Maury continued, as if nothing had happened, though Holly was conscious of the subaltern's startled gaze, his knife poised over the steaming fish.

Maury said, "Learned a lot about strength, too, out there. It took a strong man t'say no." He was fleetingly grave, then shook his head. "Yer, maybe it is Grandpa Tal we've t'thank for our confidence."

"I don't feel too confident right now, Maury."

"Listen, they winkle this shop back from you, they got t'pay you your money. Start again. Start on your own. Adapt."

"I don't want t'adapt. I want t'do what Mr. Aspinall wanted me t'do – keep the shop open."

"Tell me about this son'n' heir."

"David?"

"Yer."

Holly told her brother a little about David Aspinall, guarding against phrases that might betray her secret.

When she'd finished, and as the turkey pie was served, Maury said, "If he's an accountant, he can't be exactly stupid. He must've twigged that runnin' down the stock ain't good policy, not if he hopes t'sell the place as a goin' concern."

"I don't think David knows what he wants. Andrea – she simply wants rid of me. It's David I feel. . ."

"Sorry for?" Maury grinned understandingly. "Young an' handsome, is he?"

"He's livin' with a lady in Mayfair."

"Mayfair ladies don't come cheap. He's the one you'll have t'convince. Make him see he's better off with you runnin' the shop an' bringin' in reg'lar boodle, than a lump capital sum." Maury took a forkful of pie and held it up, glanced to his left, put the pie into his mouth, chewed thoughtfully and said to the waiter, who was spooning out creamed potatoes, "Delicious! Better'n anythin' *I* ever tasted in France."

"Thank you, sir."

The subaltern made a trumpeting sound, and pointedly turned his back on Maury's table.

To Holly, Maury said, "So they've froze your workin' capital, won't let you buy?"

"Told me it's tied up," said Holly.

"It ain't," said Maury. "It's just that they ain't sure you know what t'do with it."

"I'm not sure I do."

"Only one way t'find out."

"How?"

"Put your own money into stock."

"I haven't got any money."

"I have."

"Maury, I can't take your hard-earned cash. You'll need every ha'penny when you're demobilised."

"That won't be for months yet. How long'd it take you t'turn a profit on any sum I invested with you? Say, thirty quid?"

"Thirty quid!"

"How would you make it grow?"

"Well, I'd wait 'til one or two really good items turned up, then I'd buy them and sell them again t'clients from the client-book."

"Quick turnover?"

"Exactly," said Holly. "I'd sink the profit into three or four more items. . ."

"Pyramid principle," said Maury. "What kind of items?"

"Nothin' big: not furniture, like," Holly explained. "If I buy heavy goods right now, I've got problems in meetin' carters' costs, and packin' and haulin'. I'm not strong enough, physically, t'do that kind of thing without help. Besides, it takes up a lot of valuable time. I'd be scoutin' for plate, china or porcelain. Singles or small choice lots. Thank God, Mr. A. didn't believe in specialisation. I've a smatterin' of knowledge in a lot of fields. I think I can buy an' sell across the board, without makin' too many mistakes."

"Right, I'll back you for thirty quid, Holly. I want it back, o'course; no interest."

"What if I lose it?"

"Better you than an 'orse," Maury said. "Keep tally, separate from the shop accounts. If the Aspinalls sell the business over your head, you've gotta nest egg. If they keep it goin', you can record the transactions reg'lar, like."

"It doesn't sound altogether honest, Maury."

"Nobody's lookin' out for you but yourself, Holly. Any case, there's nothin' illegal in usin' your expertise for private dealin'."

"Maury, are you sure you can afford it?"

"Sure, I'm sure. It's the army's blood-money."

"All right, Maury," Holly said. "You're on."

"I'll give you the money when we get home."

Holly nodded excitedly. "So I can start lookin' for just the right buy."

"Toot sweet," Maury said.

•   •   •

Andrea Aspinall was not used to set-backs. She had been accustomed to sail through life like a man o'war, armed with overweening confidence, sure of her motives. When all else failed she used her sexual attraction, an unacknowledged "secret" weapon, to get her own way. For three years her relationship with Miles Walshott had progressed on an even keel. It could hardly have been called a love affair. Both Miles and Andrea had a similar interpretation of the term. Physical contact between them was dutiful rather than passionate.

Walshott was a prepossessing thirty-six-year-old stockbroker. Apart from compulsive neatness, what made him so prepossessing was his position in life. Partner in the City firm of Michaels, Walshott, Dabney & Lodge, he enjoyed a reputation for soundness in business matters and agreeability in society. Selectively gregarious, he maintained a small circle of friends, many of them clients. He was considered slightly odd in only one respect – Miles Walshott never invited anyone to his home. He *had* a home, of course, a large detached villa in the outer orbit of Hampstead. But his social obligations were met by dinners at the club or, if ladies were in the company, at the Connaught Hotel. Not even Andrea, wearer of a solitaire diamond engagement ring hewn out of a Walshott family heirloom, had seen her betrothed in his domestic setting. Unlike his other friends and acquaintances, she had been given the true reason for Miles's foible. The facts were not mysterious and might even be said to be mundane; Miles did not live alone in the Hampstead villa. He shared it with an elderly maternal aunt who was alcoholic, incontinent, wickedly intolerant of strangers, scornful of her nephew, deficient in table manners, filthy in habit, and, apparently, immortal.

Females were the bane of Miles Walshott's life. If marriage had not been such a neat and respectable thing to do, he would quite happily have remained a bachelor. But Andrea had all the qualities that he expected in a wife. She filled the bill, you might say, and would do – in due course of time – as housekeeper, companion and mother to his children better than any other female he had ever met.

Miles's mother, Isabella, had been the youngest of five daughters, and the only one to find the route to the altar, but fate had paid the price of impetuosity. Fulfilling predictions of doom put about by her whiskered sisters, she had gone and got drowned in a boating accident in Norfolk, dragging with her to a watery grave her poor lightweight husband, Miles Augustus.

Miles Junior had been saved from the fate that befell his parents only because boats made him sick. He had been sitting, alone, on the bank when it happened. He had sat there obediently for twenty minutes waiting for his Mama to surface and tell him what to do. It was slow to dawn on the poor mite that he had been thoroughly and completely orphaned. Off he was whisked to Hampstead, back to Laurel Row, to conform with the role of orphan and confront the reminders of his eight years as a "normal" little boy bravely enough under the charge of the oldest of his aunts.

She was called Beatrice – all the names came from Shakespeare – and she had left her Shropshire cottage for London with an air of martyred suffering that had tinted young Miles's most impressionable years. In due course, Beatrice gave her soul back to God – ruining a half-term vac, as it happened – and was replaced in the wings of Miles's life by Portia.

Portia was a professional hypochondriac. She was so self-orientated that there were times when she couldn't even get her nephew's name right and called to him in a wisping, fey little voice, more suited to Ophelia than Portia, "Wiles, Wiles, bring me my green bottle," or "Niles, Niles, bring me my white pill box." Latterly, she took to calling him Stanley. She died on the very day he went up to Cambridge.

Aunt Hermione popped out of the Shropshire box to take up protectorship of Miles and, more importantly, of the Hampstead dwelling that had been her father's legacy to Isabella. Aunt Hermione was really rather a brick, an inveterate "diner-outer" and theatre-goer. She adored her nephew's company during vacations and, to some extent, partially redeemed his faith in the female sex. She didn't peg out too long, alas, and was smitten by "the fog" six months after Miles embarked on his career as a stockbroker.

Then came Cordelia.

Cordelia was already a viper, already addicted to brandy, already crazy enough to be almost certifiable – if Miles had had the heart. Instead of signing her over to proper medical care in some chintzy Bedlam, however, he managed to persuade her to become a recluse. He relinquished all but occasional tenancy of the villa, kept her in vittles and *vino*, and left the running of the establishment to servants.

Oddly, Andrea thought the entire arrangement ideal.

It suited Miss Aspinall to wait for death to overtake Cordelia and the Laurel Row villa to revert into Miles' possession, for the years to roll on in that pleasant state of limbo. It was a decent kind of engagement all round and, until her father's demise threw a spanner in the works, it suited both parties admirably.

The Shakespearean aunts, living and dead, had done Miles one huge favour; they had helped keep him out of the war. Early in 1915

Miles had been moved to offer his services to the army. He had been rejected on account of several minor physical defects that included a slight cast in the right or "sighting" eye, result of a boyhood accident with a cricket ball, and a "disease potential" classified, in those cautious recruiting days, as "fast heart". The latter condition was caused by imbibing an excess of the dark Brazilian coffee to which Miles was partial. With these strikes already against his name, and patriotic fervour diminished by statistics from the Front, Miles did not insist on being appointed to the officer corps but waited, with dread, for conscription to net him. The aunts came to his rescue. In the dank catacombs of the Manpower Office of the War Department, all four, including dear departed, were listed as current dependents. Miles' categorisation was dropped below cannon-fodder level.

As a face-saving excuse for not being a uniformed hero, Miles let it be known that he was engaged in work of National Importance. In fact, he sat on the boards of four companies that nursed fat government contracts for the import and distribution of ferrous metals and chemicals. He dined quite frequently with ministers. Though he occasionally made blimpish noises of regret at not being a fighting man, Miles Walshott came through the war unscathed, fit to tangle with his fianceé.

Andrea Aspinall, a tactician of considerable skill, had already read the lie of the land in respect of Income and Beckman, and had prudently prepared a second line of defence.

Fittingly, perhaps, the initial engagement took place not by candlelight in the Connaught's dining room or amid the steam of spinach and nut-roast in Martinello's intimate supper rooms in the Cornhill, but in Miles' panelled chamber in the offices of Michaels, Walshott, Dabney & Lodge, in Lower Lombard Street.

Miles was behind his desk, an empty half acre of polished walnut with a single folder set square before him, a slim thing in chestnut leather tied with scarlet ribbons – share portfolio of a fabulously wealthy Austrian emigré. Andrea occupied the client's chair, upright and dramatic in jet-black mourning ensemble. They drank coffee and discussed the weather while office formalities were cleared away. Miles issued orders to his clerk that he was not to be disturbed, then, in a diffident tone regretfully informed his beloved that Holly Beckman could not, alas, be erased from the page like an unfortunate error in arithmetic.

For once, Andrea did not bluster and rant. She resrected Miles' mastery of money matters far too much to interrupt. Though she listed a shade to one side as the explanation continued, she took in without protest as much as she was able of Miles' complicated reasoning.

"Don't think of the Beckman girl as a person, dear," Miles advised, in the middle of his apologia; "think of her as a possible bonus to the dividend."

"As far as I'm concerned, dear, Beckman *isn't* a person," said Andrea.

"She has the law on her side. The sums involved are piffling in respect of potential long-term return. By all accounts the girl will be content to manage the shop at a weekly wage sufficiently large to satisfy one of her station but that will, all told, not place a serious drain on the annual profit-loss. With your father, rest his soul, gone, there will be a little more money in the pot."

"Can't we buy her out, dear?"

"Andrea, I ask you to consider the circumstances – your brother, for instance."

"David? What's David got to do with it?"

"His . . . his habits. . ."

"Habits?"

"In my opinion it would not be to David's advantage to be presented with a lump sum of money. Such a sum could, of course, be re-invested at a decent rate of return but, dear, the antique trade in England will not be bearish for long. Given the incentive of insecurity, the Beckman girl will do well for you."

"Do you mean, Miles, that David will squander any capital sum that we might gain from the sale of the business?"

"Bluntly, Andrea, yes."

Andrea took it with a stiff upper lip. She did not hold her brother in high esteem. At the back of her mind was the thought that she might somehow become responsible for him. It was bad enough to be responsible for Mother. That was her duty; she could not shirk it. But David was another story. He had always been spoiled.

Nasty stories circulated about him, more especially about the Leigh-Jennings woman. If credence was to be given to rumour, then – yes – Miles had made a valid point. If David and Mother were settled with regular emoluments, then she could disclaim responsibility for their material welfare: an appealing prospect.

Andrea suddenly recalled the moment of her first awakening to the class divide, how it shocked her delicate system. Miss Leblanc, who taught drawing and painting at the Mallowan School for Girls, had taken her charges to the park to sketch "the limbs of trees", in lieu of the limbs of anything more vulgar. There, on a hot May afternoon,

Andrea and her trim little companions had been exposed to the sight of "others" bathing in the fish pond. She remembered the uninhibited glee with which the grubby children threw off their clothing, and, clad only in filthy undervests and knickers, plunged into the murky waters of the pond. Ribs, bony shoulders, buttocks like the small hard bread rolls served with luncheon at home. Crushed faces blossoming with laughter in the watery playground. Miss Leblanc had not – as one would have expected – hurried her charges away from such disturbing scenes. Deliberately, Andrea later suspected, the mistress had kept them there, intent on their nice white drawing pads, bowed by curiosity, embarrassment and – yes – by envy.

Miles said, "You seem pensive, dear. Do you understand what I have told you?"

"You mean, it might be worthwhile delaying action until we see just how useful the Beckman girl can be?"

Miles said, "I'm sure she can be satisfactorily exploited."

Andrea hesitated; the word "exploited" had a strong appeal. It suggested a restoration of inequalities, balm to the envy and guilt she'd experienced at her father's gesture of affection for the Lambeth girl.

Miles asked, "What do you say?"

Andrea chose her reply with care, strengthening her second line of defence. "It hardly matters to me, dear, does it?"

"I thought you were anxious to. . ." Miles frowned; an inkling of Andrea's next statement was transmitted by a sudden softening of expression.

"After all, Miles dear, I will soon be your wife, will I not?"

"Yes, yes, of course," Miles answered. "As soon as Aunt Cordelia . . . is no longer with us."

"That might not be for years."

"Aunt Cordelia is, as you know, an insoluble problem."

"I feel, Miles, that we have made too much of Aunt Cordelia."

"The house would not be our own."

"Do you not wish to marry me, Miles?"

"With all my heart, yes, naturally, of course, yes, I wish to marry you. I gave you a ring, didn't I?"

"It's time I met your aunt!"

"You will not enjoy the experience."

"It must be done, Miles dear," said Andrea, resolutely.

"She's . . . she's particularly unsettled just now. Later, in a month or two, perhaps."

"Soon, Miles." Andrea blinked from under the brim of her hat – blinked at him, Oh God, coquettishly.

Miles heart sank like an onion in inferior gin.

For the first time in months he was tormented by the vision of Andrea undressed. He was acutely aware that she was endowed with breasts, hips and. . . He experienced a constriction in the throat. Not desire – dismay. Anxiety caused him to blush. Andrea's misinterpretation of the blush, caused her, in turn, to blush. Miles, in turn, misinterpreted that blush as maidenly eagerness for the bridal bed. In neither case did the prospect please.

Miles imagined Cordelia cackling like a crow, toasting the nuptials from a bottle. Miles imagined Cordelia propped up in bed with a sour bib around her neck, Cordelia waiting for him by lamplight, grinning like a gutted mullet, Portia, Beatrice and Hermione ranked alongside; he pictured his father, Miles Augustus, going down for the third time while dearest Mama embraced him to death.

Outwardly he was as diffident as ever. He assured Andrea that he would soon arrange the meeting, would certainly love her until his dying day – no mention of "husband", no mention of "wife" – and, in the meantime, would turn his mind to what might be done to bring her affairs to a rapid and satisfactory conclusion.

He escorted her from the chamber.

"Thursday, dear?" Andrea asked.

"At the Connaught."

"Just the two of us, I hope?"

"Yes, dear," Miles said. "Just the two of us."

From the window of his chamber he looked down at the pavement, watching his fiancée step into the cab that she had extravagantly kept waiting at the kerb. Even from that angle, she appeared Amazonian. Miles shivered, turned, lifted the telephone on the desk and asked to be connected with Sebastian Mumford, Solicitor, of Gray's Inn.

What Andrea wanted, she must have.

Money no longer mattered.

He must prevent the Beckman girl spoiling his life, even if it meant buying out the blasted little junk-shop himself. Whatever happened, Andrea must be appeased.

*   *   *

On Monday and Tuesday much trade was done with travelling dealers. A gentleman from Weybridge was setting up a shop to incorporate his son, due home soon from the war. Generous in his relief at having his boy back intact, he picked a miscellany of items from Holly's front-shop stock.

It was around four-thirty on Tuesday afternoon when the woman came in from the street. Holly had noticed her hanging about on the pavement, apparently inspecting the goods in the window. Tall, straight and quite dignified in rusty widow's weeds, a half veil partly hid her features. Holly noticed, however, that her shoes were badly down at heel, her lipstick was garish and her powder cheap. She spoke in a clipped affected accent, that soon dropped into the squeaky dialect of South London street women.

"Do you buy all kinds of jewellery, miss?"

A gas lamp, four candles and a couple of wan electric bulbs made islands of light among the shop's furniture. Outside there was fog, not moist but harsh, catching the throat. The woman seemed mysterious, almost sinister. For no discernible reason Holly was instantly on her guard.

"We do." Holly answered.

"Is the b . . . manager available?"

Holly's wariness increased. There was something vaguely familiar about the woman. Holly informed her that she was the manager. The woman made no comment, but removed a cambric handkerchief from her sleeve and dabbed her nose with it.

"I got this to sell." Opening a gloved hand, she showed Holly a small box finished in scuffed green leather, like lizard skin.

Holly took the box and opened it.

Earrings; a pair of diamond earrings in a fine, though old-fashioned setting. She judged them to be early Victorian. Holly was inexperienced in evaluating precious gems. Mr. A. had taught her how to use a powerful magnifying glass to search a stone's surfaces for flaws. At least, Holly reassured herself, I can tell if they're fake. But what do I do if they *are* genuine? What sort of offer do I make? Dare I gamble with Maury's thirty pounds? It was hidden in a tea-caddy behind a warming-pan on a high shelf.

"Mind if I examine them?" she said.

The woman did more handkerchief work on her nose. "I suppose you gotter."

Holly carried the box to the desk, switched on the lamp and extracted Mr. A.'s magnifying glass.

The woman watched her closely. Holly could hardly blame her. Perhaps she was upset by the events that required her to sell the earrings. In her imagination, Holly charitably devised a history for the woman. She was concerned, of course, about being sold a pup, but also about cheating a widow by offering her less than the pieces were worth.

Lifting the rings from the box with stamp-tweezers, Holly laid them on a green baize pad. It was in her mind to ask the woman to hang on, then to run round to Simon Black and see what he thought of them. But something stopped her – independence? A kind of vanity? Or that inexplicable suspicion that all was not as it seemed? Holly wondered why the woman had chosen to sell to Aspinall's. London was packed with jewellery shops. Had it been pure and simple impulse? Carefully she lifted an earring in the tweezers and peered at it through the enlarging glass. She tried to recall the geometry of the half-dozen real diamonds that Mr. A. had shown her.

Yes, the rings were genuine. Good size. Each stone must weigh close to four carats. The settings were heavy red gold. The stones were backed with foil, glued into place. Under the lens the workmanship appeared crude. Probably Mid rather than Early Victorian; an heirloom handed down from mother to son, son to wife, widow to dealer. Holly concentrated on her inspection. Square cut, good colour; she could see no flaw in them.

The myriad mistakes that a valuator could make buzzed in her head. Particularly with gemstones. What did she know about diamonds? Very little, really. Oh God, don't let me be wrong. No, Holly, she told herself, they are real. I'm certain of it. But the size? Size is crucial to the offer. Wish I had an ivory gauge. Since I haven't I'll have to do it by eye. The woman's no expert. If she was, she wouldn't be selling them to me. She'd be up Bond Street or the Gardens. Oh God, I've got to back my own judgment – with our Maury's money, too. I only have that thirty. Isn't enough, is it? Two four carat diamonds in a gold setting *must* be worth lots more than thirty. What does she expect for them? What does she need?

To delay decision, Holly continued to study the rings.

Eventually, she sucked in breath and, carrying the baize pad, crossed the shop to the woman.

"What's wrong, miss? Don't tell me they ain't real?"

"Yes, they're genuine, ma'am," said Holly, solemnly.

"What are they worth?"

"I advise you to take them to an expert. I can give you the name an'. . ."

"Don't yer want 'em?"

"How did you acquire them?"

"Got 'em from me dear 'usband George." The widow hesitated, tongue out, tip touching her lip. "Dear 'usband George. He was killed in action."

Holly did not respond.

The woman laid a gloved hand on her forearm. "Got nobody 'ere. Me sister's in America. I need the money for the travel, like. See?"

"A Bond Street jeweller would give you a better price than I can."

The woman shook her head emphatically. "Steal me blind, they would, the toffs. What *are* the stones worth?"

"I would offer thirty pounds."

"Thirty quid! Blimey!"

She lifted the veil in astonished delight, crooking it up and tucking it round the brim of her hat. She looked haggard – and even more familiar.

"It's all they're worth to me," Holly said.

"I'll take it."

The alacrity with which the widow accepted the paltry offer was the last straw. Abruptly, almost rudely, Holly snapped shut the little box with the earrings inside it and handed it back. The widow stared down at it, uncomprehendingly.

"No, you won't take it," Holly said. "I don't want your jewels, ma'am."

"But yer told me. . ."

"Take them to Fielding's, Black's, or King's. Do you want me to write down the addresses?"

"You bleedin' said. . ."

"Your heirlooms are worth twice or three times what I offered," said Holly. "But I haven't got the money on hand to pay for them."

"You could get it, couldn't yer?"

"No," said Holly. "I'm sorry, I'm not in the market for antique jewellery, not at any price."

"Bleedin' suspicious cow!"

Clutching the box in her fist, the widow glared at Holly for a moment then, seeing that the girl had no intention of relenting, turned on her worn heel and hurried out of the shop.

For a fleeting instant, Holly was inclined to run after her, apologise, pay out Maury's thirty, risk it. But she restrained herself. She had obeyed her instincts and, later that evening, she would make some judicious enquiries on her own account about the diamond earrings.

* * *

In the tannery dispatch department, Ritchie passed ten hours of every weekday, five on Saturdays. He worked like a Trojan for approximately three hours each shift but, being a natural leader of men – half charmer, half bully – he had things so organised that everything was done by minions and he applied himself mainly to checking their mistakes. In this feudal system Ritchie protected his decrepit workers from the managers, took the snash on to his own shoulders and assumed responsibility for all the mishaps that occurred. In effect, the department ran like clockwork. Even the most embittered, or perspicacious, of managers thought twice before they crossed the Beckman boy. What got their hackles up was Ritchie's lack of respect for authority. If anybody in a hat happened to catch him in the clerk's hole with his feet up and the Pink 'un open, Beckman never jumped guiltily to his feet. Calmly he would fold the paper, put it to one side and, with a smile, ask the hat what he wanted. No guilt, therefore, no respect. Whatever the problem, Beckman was on top of it, had a solution up his sleeve, an answer ready. His very manner seemed to say, *I do not hurry, because I do not need to hurry.* Lord help the management if that attitude ever infected the workers. One like Ritchie Beckman was enough. Among themselves the managers of O'Connors' Tannery muttered about how relieved they would be when the men came home from the Front and Beckman could be relegated to the packing department floor, where he could be kept in line more easily. They'd clip his wings then, all right. No more clocking out at twenty minutes to six of an evening, bold as a cock-robin, with a smiling "G'night, Mr. Perrie. Have a good dinner, Mr. Lloyd. Another day over, Mr. Osgood."

On Tuesday evening, Ritchie punched his work card at five thirty-five. He left Jeff Horsfall in charge. Everything was in apple-pie order, anyhow, and there would be no emergencies at that time of the night.

At ten minutes to six, Ritchie entered the bar parlour of a public house in the Lambeth Road where he found Paula Henson, only partly divested of her widow's weeds, seated at a corner table near the fire nursing a port and lemon. Lambeth Road was not on Paula's regular beat, though she came up this way sometimes when pickings were lean and the battalions moved out of Newington barracks. At one stage in her career, when "rheumaticks" had gripped the small of her back, she had had a brief flirtation with Leo Beckman. Leo hadn't realised what she did for a living until he'd been "courting" her for a fortnight. She'd got to meet the kid that way, up in the Admiral's Hat on the edge of her territory. She hadn't seen Leo in six months, though. She'd been surprised when the kid picked her up in the Bull's Head. She understood the deal at once. She was tickled pink with the quid he gave her. She did a good job on herself as far as disguise went and even remembered the story he'd written out for her.

"What'd you get?" Ritchie asked, putting another port beside her and sliding into the bench.

"Sweet Fanny Adams!"

"What?"

"She wouldn't cough. Offered thirty quid, changed 'er mind an' went stone cold."

"Did she suss you?"

"Dunno," said Paula. "Sorry, son. I done me best."

"Yer, not your fault, Paula." He took her hand and squeezed it reassuringly, transferring the earring box from her palm to his jacket pocket. "She's smart, that 'un. Too bleedin' smart."

Oddly, Ritchie did not seem angered; he was rueful in defeat.

"What'll y'do now, Ritch?"

He drank off his beer, dropped a one pound note on the table and got to his feet.

"Find another muggins," he said.

* * *

In Victora, that tedious stucco annex of opulent Belgravia, Samuel Fielding, long years a widower, lived and worked in the basement apartment of a terrace house. Like its neighbours, the house was a model of architectural neatness. It had no history to speak of – as yet.

Dukes, baronets, Members of both Houses, and their ladies, were thick among Sam's clientele. Fragrant whiffs of best Havana sweetened the air of the showroom, though the august gentlemen and regal ladies never had anything but Sam's undivided attention and, mysteriously, never seemed to encounter each other there. Inevitably they would find Sam crouched over the sloping shelf that served as his workbench. Thin legs in shiny morning trousers were knotted round the spars of a tall stool, lens plugged into his right eye, rimless spectacles propped on his pink, hairless dome as if to report on what was happening on the pavement above.

Because of the need for daylight to execute his most intricate repairs, Sam's workshop was at the front, the showroom at the back. His domestic quarters – a single room like a bargee's cabin – was off to one side of the corridor. Sam at sixty-nine was hardly different from Sam at thirty-six. Once his delicate bones had set and his hair had fled, Sam, in appearance, was Sam for life – stock collar, wire sleevebands, warm woollen waistcoat, button boots, polka-dot cravat and all.

The showroom was a series of glass moth-cases set on legs hardly less spindly than Sam's own. Displayed on faded velvet within each case were ten or a dozen pieces of antique jewellery of finest quality. On a panelled wall, a case of pocket watches, all oiled and ticking, was surmounted by a cabinet of leaded glass in which were exhibited – strictly not for sale – rare portable timepieces; spherical oddities in gilt tambour cases of sixteenth century Germany up to nineteenth century French confections glittering with jewels.

Fielding's was a burglar's paradise, worth more than the rake-off from a hundred pop shops or ten West End emporiums. But no light-fingered luke dared tug old Sam Fielding's bell. The stuff was hotter than the coals of hell. It would be impossible to shift. Besides, Sam was protected by a crew of local constables and 'tecs from the Yard, having served the Crown as an "expert witness" in many a big trial.

At the bottom of five steep steps, the basement door was never locked during business hours. Holly entered, found a second door in the carpeted corridor and went through, under a chiming bell, into the workshop.

Sam turned on the stool and peered at her through the lens.

"It's Holly Beckman, Mr. Fielding."

"So it is, so it is now."

Untangling his legs from the spars, Sam sprung the lens from his eye and came towards her, chirping in welcome. Though he had not felt up to attending James Aspinall's funeral, he had sent along a spray of pure white lilies and a letter, in handwriting like musical notation, offering Thora his sincere condolences. Pleased to see Holly, he led her into the showroom where he presented her, in spite of her protests, with a glass of madeira wine and an Osborne biscuit. Gently he questioned her about the state of affairs at Aspinall's, with particular reference to the "poor widder", Thora, whom he had always rather admired.

Holly gave him what news she could. She did not mention the feud that existed between the family and herself. Only when the civilities had been put out of the way would Sam get down to business. At length he asked her what had brought her round to Snetterton Street on such a dismal night. Holly explained about her customer and the diamond earrings.

Sam listened, pinkie raised and set against his nostril as if he were taking snuff.

"Now, you didn't exactly buy these trinkets?" Sam asked, when Holly had finished.

"No, I turned them down."

"Wise child, wise child."

"Why do y'say that, Mr. Fielding?"

"Fishy all through, very fishy. A real story from Billingsgate, if ever I'eard one." Sam went to a little middle-grade bureau-bookcase at the rear of the room. "But," he asked, teasingly, "what'd y'come round to old Sam for?"

"I know you receive the Police Lists before anyone else," said Holly. "I thought the earrings might be recorded."

"They are, like fun they are." He returned from the bureau with a bulky file which he placed carefully on the nearest moth-case. "Hot from the presses, brought round this mornin' as it 'appens; the weekend's 'aul, stuff the naughty boys gotter 'way with."

"And the earrings are listed?"

Sam ran his finger down closely typed columns, nose almost touching the paper. On the second page, he found it. "Good description 'ere. One pair Lahue earrings, diamonds, exact four carats, in red-gold settings."

"Stolen?"

"Stolen."

"Are y'sure it's the same pair, Mr. Fielding?"

"Made right here in London. Three brothers named Lahue had a cutters' shop in Greenwich. Did lots of the red-gold work. Started up in business the year o'Waterloo. Closed down in 'Ninety-four. I was distantly acquainted with the youngest, Harold. Dead now. Between 'em, the three brothers 'ad eleven children. Scattered wide an' far. Four on 'em still in the diamond business, though; merchants." He consulted the list again. "Estimated market value; four hundred pounds. Flawless stones in foil."

"Crude-lookin' under the glass?" Holly asked.

"Ol' fashioned, I'd say."

"That's them."

"Thank your stars you didn't take 'em, young lady."

"Might I ask, where an' when they were stolen."

"From offices in Kensington, Silver Thimble folk; Sat'day night."

"Saturday night?" The woman's face rose in Holly's mind's eye again.

"Only item o'any real value: the rest was petty compared with them pieces," Sam told her.

"What'd have happened if I'd bought them?"

"Might 'ave got off with it, Holly, but not likely. You'd 'ave sold to trade, an' trade would've found out eventually. Police would come an' quiz you, smack your 'and and, make you give the money back an' take the loss."

"Suspected me of re-settin'?"

"Doubt it, doubt it," said Sam. "I'd 'ave given a character for you. You're young, inexperienced. Any roads, you'd sense enough not t'buy. What made you twig they was 'ot?"

"I . . . I don't know. What do I do if the woman comes back?"

"She won't, not if she's smart. Whoever picked over the Silver Thimble office 'as got a few brains in his head, didn't burden himself with junk. Didn't recognise this woman, by any chance? Be nice t'nail the devils." Sam said. "Did you have a glimmerin', Holly?"

Holly lied badly. She felt as if the old man could see into her mind as easily as he could penetrate the heart of a bright stone.

"No, no, Sam. Why should I have recognised her?"

"Should report this t'the police, y'know."

"I'd . . . I'd rather not."

"Put yer stock up with the coppers."

"Do I have to, Sam?"

"No, don't 'ave to. What puzzles me is why y'won't."

"I just don't have *time* t'get involved."

"Got y'workin' 'ard 'ave they?"

"Do I *have* to report?"

Sam paused, then shook his head. "Not if you don't want to. It wouldn't be much 'elp, anyhow, not since you didn't recognise the woman."

"I didn't! Really, Sam, I didn't."

The old man nodded, scanning the girl's face in search of an explanation to the little mystery that had landed on his doorstep.

"I 'ave a friend in the Yard," said Sam. "I can let it be known the stuff's bein' offered, without givin' you away, Holly."

"Yes, Sam; please do that."

"That all the information you got for me?"

"Yes. That's all."

It was her first real lie, her first act of deceit; Holly despised herself for it. She thanked Sam for his help and left before his inquisitiveness forced her to lie again.

Putting Snetterton Street behind her, she soon reached main thoroughfares. At Victoria buses and trams lumbered through thickening fog. The shunting, volcanic whumping of trains was muffled. On the pavements Holly's heels sounded like mallets on parquet. Jostled by travellers, she crossed out of the station's crowds and went on down the Vauxhall Bridge Road. Eventually, she would catch an omnibus. Meantime, she needed an opportunity to think about the untruth and its implications, about the moment when she had suddenly placed the mock widow, and realised that her father might be involved in the miserable crime.

Paula – Paula – Paula something! One of her father's fancy women from out of Lambeth.

Behind her father would be Ritchie. The attempted off-loading of the stolen earrings would be his idea. Holly did not believe in coincidence. She needed no proof. Ritchie had tried to trap her into buying hot property. One slip and she would have been at his mercy.

Anger stirred in her.

She must not let Ritchie know that she had tumbled to his game. But from now on she must be on constant guard against her brother.

* * *

The buyer's name was Jack Renzo, brother of Sydney Renzo, that well-known sporting gentleman whose peacock plumage graced race-track enclosures from Epsom to Doncaster. If Syd's business was mostly open and above board, Jack's was done exclusively below the waterline.

It galled Ritchie to have to slip cap-in-hand to Shotten's principal fence, but the manner in which his sister had twigged that the stones were stolen made him uneasy. It was possible that the items had already been listed and circulated to London dealers. He had not expected the police to be so efficient, or the Silver Thimble Fund haul to merit so much attention. Wasn't Lady Astor's tiara, after all, was it? Weighing up the pros and cons, Ritchie decided that he preferred not to take the risk of holding on to the goodies.

That threw him to Shotten, who had infallible means of disposing of hot potatoes – smuggling them off to the Continent, most like.

He left word with the barman in the Shears that he wanted a word with Jack Renzo. In due course he received a verbal message through a lanky street urchin that Jack would meet him outside the synagogue at the Elephant & Castle 'round eight next night. In due course, Ritchie turned up there. He had knotted the earring box into a handkerchief and tucked it into his left hand. If – for any reason – Jack the Lad was "at it" – had it in mind to shop him – then he would drop the stuff into the gutter at the first hint of a nark.

Renzo was stationed across the St. George's Road, leaning against a railing scanning a racing form under a hanging lamp. On spotting Ritchie, who had already spotted him, Renzo turned and ambled north-west along the St. George's. Ritchie crossed between the traffic. He tailed Renzo for thirty or forty yards. The man stopped and let the youngster catch up with him. Ritchie had a Gold Flake in his mouth. He asked Renzo for a light. Renzo cupped a match in his palms, while Ritchie held the cigarette with his right hand, the left casually down by his side, ready to drop the knotted handkerchief should the Old Bill blow up out of nowhere.

Jack Renzo was forty-one and filthy rich, though careful to disguise both facts. When he wasn't engaged in conducting business, he dressed in a "countrified" style that made him look like a stable owner, and shaved ten years off his age. Tonight, however, he had on a navy gabardine and a five bob hat, though his hand-lasted boots would have given him away if you were observant. He had a round, fair sort of face, with frank brown eyes and a mouth that might have been geometrically drawn with a set-square. He was affable but never effusive. He treated all crooks as if they were dumb-bells, which most of them were. He did not make that mistake with Beckman, however. Shotten had had a quiet little word in his ear about the Beckman boy.

For ten or a dozen yards they made limping conversation about the weather, then turned down into Gibraltar Row where it was quieter, and embarked on the topic that had brought them together in the Newington wilderness.

Ritchie wheezed slightly – the air was dry and heavy and tasted of sacking – as he put his sales pitch and answered Renzo's questions about where the stuff had come from and who'd been along on the kick. Shotten insisted on details, unlike long-noses and creepers out of the East End who just didn't want to know anything, the theory being that what you didn't know you couldn't blab.

"What have you got?" Renzo enquired.

"Twenty pieces."

"Bring a sample, did you?"

They were down Eliot's Row now. It seemed about as safe a location as he was likely to find. Ritchie opened his fist and passed Renzo the knotted handkerchief.

"What's this? Stealin' wipes, are you?" Renzo chuckled at his own wit. He unpicked the knot, tossed the handkerchief to Ritchie and opened the box with his fingernail.

"Guaranteed genuine," said Ritchie.

"Yer, the Silver Thimble brings out the best in people." Renzo made no inspection of the merchandise. He clipped the box shut again and put it into his overcoat pocket. "What else?"

"That's the best of it," Ritchie said. "But what y'got there is prime."

"I read the Police List," Renzo stated.

Ritchie gave a snort of admiration.

"What that means, Ritch," said Renzo, "is burnt fingers, don't it?"

"You can shift it, Jack."

"Not so easy."

"What's your best offer, like?"

"Thirty."

"For the earrings, you mean?"

"Thirty, the lot."

"Gawd!" said Ritchie. "You're a worse thief than I am!"

"Best I can do."

"Earrings are worth more'n that alone. The rest's not junk."

"If it was, wouldn't give thirty," said Renzo.

They were walking down Eliot's Row towards Brook Street, away from the din of the mad traffic junction of the Castle.

"What happens if I say no t'your offer?" asked Ritchie.

"You get the stones back; we go our separate ways."

"An' then what?"

Renzo paused before answering. "I tell Vince you didn't care t'do business with him."

Two emotions warred in Ritchie; he was furious with Renzo for screwing him on the haul and, simultaneously, full of envy for Shotten's power. Ritchie knew that he had stepped into the ever-open trap. It was a buyer's market and he did not dare withdraw – not if he hoped to make Lambeth his stamping ground.

"I'll take it, Jack," he said.

"Thirty buys a lot o'grog, Ritchie."

"Yer." Ritchie sounded cheerful. Mentally he was calculating the kind of profits that Shotten would make on his hard labour, his high risk – five, six, seven hundred per cent, maybe even more. Someday, he promised himself, he would stand above Shotten and would reap that kind of profit for himself and his lady.

Renzo gave Beckman specific instructions. They parted at the corner of Eliot's Row and Brook Street.

The following night, in the upstairs billiards room of the Shears and Mallet, Ritchie handed a brown paper parcel to Henry, the barman. In exchange he received an envelope containing thirty grubby one-pound Bank of England notes. Ritchie was not elated. Indeed, he felt cheated. Because there was no other available outlet he turned his anger on Holly, his bleedin' smart-nosed sister, who could have made him twice as well-off at a stroke.

He stayed out late that night, drinking himself into a state of mute depression at the thought of how the world was set against enterprise and bravado, and how difficult it would be for him to climb up to the top. It would be a lot more arduous than shinning up a drainpipe to hoist a pair of diamond earrings that, in the end, had brought him no more than beans.

4

A Fabric of Compromises

LIKE EVERYBODY ELSE, Paddy Elkins seemed to have grown older than the years warranted. In a mere couple of years, strappin' Paddy had visibly shrunk. It was clear that it would soon be time for the Irish hod-carrier to be put out to pasture. In his day Paddy had been as wild a boyo as ever crossed the Irish Sea. But blarney and braggart had waned in the strain of war when he had run the yard virtually single-handed. Unaided he had fed the ponies, shovelled sand, ripped timber and loaded bricks.

Maury had timed his visit well. Paddy had stopped for breakfast in the sloping hut by the railway wall. He was standing bow-legged by the iron stove with a frypan and a jar of brown dripping in his hands. On a piece of yesterday's *Sketch* lay four sausages, pierced and sprinkled with celery salt and black pepper. Paddy's entire meat ration was blown on bangers; and all Paddy's bangers were blown on breakfast. For the rest of the day he was sustained by a doorstep of bread and treacle washed down with Guinness.

His first view of Paddy, who, deafer than ever, had not heard his apprentice's entry, gave Maury no comfort. It raised in his mind the philosophic question "What's it all for, really?" – and he had been dodging the answer to that for months among corpses and barbed wire. Once Paddy too had been young and ambitious, yelling how he would use the yard in Firebrick Street as a base to conquer London.

Maury had served Paddy Elkins for many years; first as a "boy", then as an apprentice, at four shillings and sixpence per week. From Paddy he had learned how to line up, lay out and dig a foundation, all about soil, sand, gravel, clay, shale and bloody blasted bedrock; later, about wood, plaster, mortar, paint and limewash, and the mathematical exactness of frames, struts, lathes and beams. In all things practical, Paddy was an admirable teacher. Maury supplemented the Irishman's rough-and-ready courses with books borrowed from the Borough Library. Once he had considered taking night classes in building trade subjects, but he could not find the time.

Spring, summer and autumn he worked a fifteen-hour day. In the winter months, after dark, he practised by gaslight with the tools in the big bleak shed. In those days Paddy had had ten or fifteen men working for him. Each gang was shipped out to a site in its own long cart drawn by two ponies. Paddy picked his employees with care. He supervised them, and did all estimating and costing personally. Costing, though, was the rock on which Paddy Elkins' ambition foundered. Not even Maury, who had a good head for figures, was allowed to help out. The Irishman was secretive about money.

Things had started to run down even before the war drained away all the young navvies, tradesmen and casual labourers. Since then, so Maury had heard, Paddy had worked himself to the bone to keep the yard open.

"Do one for me, Paddy," Maury said. "No pepper."

The Irishman turned.

"Father in Heaven! It's Maury."

"I smelled them bangers all the way out in Union Street," said Maury. "Got bread t'dip?"

"Maury, Maury!" Rolling on bowed legs, very slow now, Paddy hobbled over. His hair had turned white. His flesh was pared off the bones of his face so that it looked pixie-like under the woollen cap with its dirty green bobble. "Maury, Maury!"

"Yer, well, leastways y'remember my name."

The old man put his arm about the young man's shoulders and hugged him. He laid an ear against the buttons of the tunic as if to ascertain that a heart beat there, and lungs pumped air, and that Maury Beckman was no phantom.

"It's me apprentice, sure an' it is," Paddy said, with a little groan. "God spared me me apprentice."

Apart from Tal and Holly, the old Irishman was the only other person in the world that Maury cared about. He was moved by Paddy's emotional greeting. He put his hand on the old man's skull and held him a moment, swallowed the lump that had come into his throat, then gently pushed Paddy back.

"Are ye comin' in for t'work, then, Maury?"

"Hoi, hoi, y'greedy old slave-driver; I'm not free o'the bloomin' army yet."

"When?" Paddy could not disguise his eagerness. "I could do wit a strong arm. God, could I not!"

"Yer, I heard things was sticky," said Maury.

"Sticky? Things's terrible. Not that the work ain't about. God, aye, the work is there, sure'n it is. But. . ."

"Nobody t'do it, right?"

Paddy crimped his false teeth together. Slipping the upper plate out a little, he swallowed too. "What're we talkin' like this for, now, wit you just fresh home. Step over an' eat a sausage wit me, drink a dish o' tea."

"Sure'n I will," said Maury, grinning to hide his dismay at the changes in his employer and the poor state of the yard. "But tell me, how's your good lady? How's Nora?"

"Ailin'."

Nora Elkins had been ailing since the day Paddy married her.

"An' Georgie, an' Luke."

"You ain't heard, then?"

Chill clutched Maury's heart.

"No, I ain't heard."

"Georgie's dead. Last year, we had the letter. Killed in the battle o' Ypres. Ye didn't see him over there, Maury?"

Maury shook his head. "What about Luke?"

"Lost a leg. Safe, though. Gone back t'farm in Mayo."

"Luke was always a country boy at heart," said Maury.

The men looked down into the little lake of fat that had formed in the frypan, as if it was a pool in which they might see shadows of the past and shapes of the future. Silently, Paddy slid two sausages into the pan and skated them around with is fork. He heaved a great sigh, then glanced up at Maury.

"But what about yourself, then? Sure'n it's grand t'be seein' you again."

Maury had come here with the specific purpose of making Paddy Elkins an offer for the business. It was run right down now; he could pick it up for nothing. Paddy would take what he could get and be grateful to Maury for ever more. During long black bitter nights in the trenches, Maury had whiled away his watch imagining how he would come striding in, dump down two hundred pounds and tell Elkins to take it or leave it. But, now that he was here, saw old Paddy and the broken-down state of the place, his arrogance vanished. He could not, at any price, throw the Irishman on the rubbish dump.

"I'm lookin' for work, Paddy. Will y'take me on again?"

"Aye, an' ye know I will. Not a day too soon, Maury. Ye might've been sent from Heaven."

"Or the other place," Maury said.

He looked round.

Strewn timber in the damp corner going to waste, bags of plaster, bought before the war, hardened by weather; racks of rusty tools; overhead, lathings stored along the beams were twisted like corkscrews. He wondered what the ponies were like. Had Paddy, in his desperate struggle against the clock, let the beasts go to skin and bone too? A sudden sense of urgency possessed the soldier. To Paddy's surprise, he thumbed the buttons of his tunic jacket and almost ripped it off. Beneath he wore a khaki pullover over a regulation shirt. He threw the jacket on to the table, and clapped his hands together.

"What in God's name is it ye're doin', Maury."

"Startin' work."

"Eat your sausages; I can spare them. Sure, there'll be time for work later."

"No there bloomin' won't," said Maury. "I only got ten days' leave. Before I go back, Paddy, I want this place straight an' you out there in the streets with an order book in yer hand."

"But Maury. . .?"

"Since I'm out o'practice," Maury grunted, as he heaved up the old rock-hard plaster bag and staggered with it towards the door, "y'can 'ave me at the old rate."

"Maury. . ."

"But when I get out o'the Army for good," he pushed the shed door with his knee, "I'll want more."

"Sure, Maury, sure'n ye can have it," Paddy pursued his apprentice into the yard, wagging a sausage on a fork like an odd-shaped charm. "Anythin', any blessed thing ye'll be wantin'."

Like your business, old Paddy, thought Maury as he heaved the useless plaster bag onto the dump; that's what I'm really after. Not anything – everything.

* * *

Sebastian John Mann Mumford had three daughters. He did not understand them. When they were children he had taken great delight in their company, and had provided them with everything that money could buy. Rapport with James Aspinall was inevitable. Spoiled children had been the bond. Mumford's daughters had swept out of the nest with hardly a backward glance. They were scattered now through the Home Counties, each in a mansion, each with a battery of servants, a motorcar, a wardrobe of expensive gowns – oh, yes, and a husband and children of their own. Though S.J.M. Mumford would have been a marvellous grandfather, he was given little opportunity to put his funnybone into joint with the five little boys and four little girls that shared his blood. Margaret and he were allocated two visits a year from each daughter, plus the bonus of a Boxing Day get-together that was invariably spoiled by his daughters' petulant squabbling. Mumford could not abide his sons-in-law, lumpy business men who seemed to spend half their lives riding first-class carriages to and from the City and the other half kow-towing to their wives' social aspirations.

Mumford's initial impression was that Miles Walshott came from the same drawer as his daughters' husbands. Fifteen or twenty minutes of cautious sparring, however, indicated that there was a brain ticking inside Walshott's head, and that his grey matter had been activated by self-protective instincts; Andrea Aspinall was not the ideal consort for a man who liked a quiet life.

That dull afternoon in his chambers, Mumford pushed Andrea out like a queen across the conversational board.

"Don't you find it rather odd, Mr. Walshott, that Miss Aspinall reacts so vigorously against the whole idea of trade?"

"Odd?" Walshot was careful to get his definitions right.

"Peculiar that so much attention is being focused on a little piece of a shop in a not awfully proper part of Pimlico?"

Solemnly, Walshott said, "I'm a great respecter of trade, Mr. Mumford."

"But a shop, an antique shop..."

"What do you mean, sir?"

"I mean, Mr. Walshott, that I find it remarkable that a man of your ability should be bothering with this piddling little matter."

"Miss Aspinall is my fiancée; her affairs..."

"Yes, yes," Mumford interrupted. "But here we are in the wake of a frightful holocaust, bothering not just about a pile of bricks and mortar and a few bits of antique junk but about *attitudes*. Attitudes interest me."

Walshott looked at the solicitor as if he thought he'd gone gaga. He repeated his opening declaration. "I merely want somebody to buy the blessed place, to take it off Andrea's hands, to be rid of it once and for all."

"And the girl, Beckman?"

"Surely she can't be allowed to stand in the family's way?"

"What about Mrs. Aspinall?"

"Mrs. Aspinall? I don't see what she has to do with it."

"She has a say. In this new democratic age, she must have a say."

"Thora will be looked after," said Walshott.

"Will Holly Beckman be looked after too?"

"Mr. Mumford, I fail to understand why you keep harking back to the Beckman girl. She should not feature in this reckoning. Apart from the . . . the circumstance that caused James to leave her a share in the shop, she would have sunk back into Lambeth. Surely, she can be bought out."

"Of course," said Mumford. "If that's the wish of all the other partners."

"Partners," said Walshott, who was not usually so repetitive. "A rather grand word for a four-part division of a shop, don't you think?"

"I would be inclined to 'look out' for Miss Beckman," said Mumford, deferentially.

"A confusion of interests, sir?" said Walshott. "I assume that Beckman is not your client."

"Do you wish to make purchase of the shop and its contents?"

"How much would it cost me?"

"In the region of two thousand pounds – at the moment."

"Two thousand! It seems high, for what one would be receiving."

"Stock inventories suggest that James Aspinall bought shrewdly."

"Well, Mr. Mumford, if I arranged an agent to make purchase, I assume that you could present the offer to the Aspinall family without mentioning my name."

"You'd pay two thousand pounds for Aspinall's shop?"

"Yes. Yes, I would."

"And do what with it?"

"Re-sell it. I don't want it."

"And if the selling price was higher?"

"Do I detect a threat there, sir?"

"You're not the only interested party, Mr. Walshott."

"Really!" Walshott raised an eyebrow. "In that case, I would be inclined to withdraw my offer, not stand in the way of the other interested party."

"And thus deprive your fiancée, to say nothing of her mother and brother – and Miss Beckman, of course, mustn't forget Miss Beckman – making a larger profit on the sale."

"You want somebody to run up the price."

"I'm not the selling agent; I only vet any offers that come forth and pass them on to the family."

"This," said Walshott, "is becoming rather confusing, Mr. Mumford."

"I agree," said Mumford.

"The other interested party," said Walshott, "will he take it as it is, as a going concern?"

"Indeed he will. I'm not betraying a confidence when I say that the intending purchaser is already well established in the trade."

Walshott bridged his fingers over his nose and spent a minute in thought. "Another dealer wants the place?"

"Lock, stock, barrel – and staff."

"So it's worth something?"

"Without doubt."

Mumford observed Walshott's conflict. It was telegraphed by a corkscrewing of the brows and a matching twist of the lips. Mumford was enjoying himself. He did not give a hoot about Andrea's perplexed victim – the stockbroker was well able to take care of himself – but thought of Holly Beckman. The Lambeth girl, quiet and rather shabby though she was at present, embodied qualities that Mumford reckoned would come to the fore in the next few years. Deliberately he had put Walshott on the horns of a dilemma by introducing the promise of profit. Profit. Profit. Profit. A siren song. Walshott could not bring himself to withdraw from a venture that might make money, could not let go the red thread that would lead him deeper into the marshland of marriage and entanglement with the Aspinalls. Served him right, Mumford supposed.

"Have you communicated to the family the import of this other offer?" Walshott asked.

"Not yet: it isn't formalised. I haven't had it in writing."

"Can you get it in writing?"

"In time."

Walshott would not let go. "This other client, this interested party, what can he want with Aspinall's?"

"The site, the stock and, most of all, the expertise."

"Expertise?"

"Apparently knows a good thing when he sees it," said Mumford.

"You can't mean Beckman."

"I do mean Beckman."

"Wait," said Walshott. "Am I correct in thinking that it would be unwise for Andrea – for the Aspinalls – to buy Beckman out? Are you saying that the girl is part of the overall worth of the business?"

"That's exactly what I am saying."

"Why?"

"I'm informed," said Mumford, "that the girl has flair. That quality alone makes her of value to anyone concerned with antique dealing."

"Come now, Mr. Mumford. Holly Beckman is simply a young girl with no background or breeding and precious little experience."

"Background and breeding are irrelevant," said Mumford. "As to experience, she has received a sound basic training from James Aspinall, and he, I assure you, was an excellent antique dealer, hampered only by the scale of his enterprises and a throttling shortage of working capital."

"That doesn't answer my question about Beckman."

"Miss Beckman came into the business when the home labour market was at a premium. Do you suppose, Mr. Walshott, that all the professional valuators and dealers who went to war will return? Statistics are against it. The trade will be cluttered with 'amateurs', will become a refuge for men, and possibly a few women, who are seeking a quiet life. To them antiques will be a pastime that turns a little profit. Holly Beckman is a professional. She is no mere dabbler."

"You seem very well acquainted with her virtues," said Walshott.

"I've kept an eye on her," said Mumford. "What's more, I'm aware of the fact that several large and prosperous businesses in the city are anxious to employ her – if she should be driven out of Cardwell Place. Now, sir, if the Bond Street gang rate her as having high potential value to them, then it would seem to me that, young as she is, she might do very well for the Aspinall family. She has training, some experience, flair and ambition."

"There's no premium on ambition," said Walshott.

"Although you are not here in an official capacity, may I offer my advice in the hope that you may use your influence on my clients, the Aspinall children?"

"Please do."

"Do not underestimate the worth of Miss Beckman. Any trade that involves buying and selling is dependent upon judgment, and judgment can often be an instinctive quality. Oh, yes, experience is needed too, and it would have been better if Holly Beckman had been able to spend another four or five years as James Aspinall's assistant, to benefit from a longer period from his advice. But that was not to be. Don't, however, allow yourself to be swayed by ill-founded prejudices. Class – what did you call it; background and breeding – has nothing whatsoever to do with it. All craft and art-related trades and professions are supported by persons of no background whatsoever, and not a drop of breeding. Holly Beckman is not playing at shopkeeping; it is her livelihood, and her future. She will learn everything she needs to know to make a success of it, including – what shall we say – decorum. She will acquire polish as she acquires confidence."

"I take your point, Mr. Mumford," said Walshott. "What do you suggest I do, apropos Andrea?"

"Play for time."

"What do you mean?"

"Give Holly Beckman two or three years. Unless I'm sadly mistaken, in that time she will have increased the turnover of the shop and will have built up the reputation of the business."

"James Aspinall couldn't manage it," said Walshott, "not beyond a certain point. What makes you suppose that a young girl will succeed where Aspinall failed?"

"The young girl," said Mumford, "isn't burdened with James Aspinall's family."

"I'm not sure I like the tenor of that remark."

"She does not have domestic responsibilities," said Mumford. "She can afford to be single-minded, to devote all her waking hours to the shop and the business."

"If she wants to."

"Oh, she wants to," said Mumford. "She can't help herself. Her preoccupation may make her seem a little dull as a person, lacking in feminine sparkle, but you must accept that as part of the price that Holly is willing to pay for success. I believe that she will persist, will not be diverted from her aim."

"Which is?"

"To be the best antique dealer in London."

"And you truly believe that this is no mere pipe-dream?"

"I do," said Mumford. "In three years, if you still wish it, you may sell the business at a much higher price than you'd get for it now. In the interim, your fiancée and her family will reap the benefits."

"Dear me," said Walshott. "You make it sound very clear cut."

"The problem," said Mumford, clearing his throat, "is Miss Andrea's impatience, is it not?"

"It is."

"Take a firm stand, Mr. Walshott – and wait."

"Wait – how long?"

"Give it six months at the very least."

"And the other interested party?" said Walshott. "Will he wait too?"

"Lots of things may happen in the interim," said Mumford.

"That," said Walshott, "is what I'm rather afraid of."

"Play for time, sir," said Mumford. "I'm sure it's common practice in your profession."

Walshott nodded unhappily.

The stockbroker had triumphed over the suitor, practicality over instinct for survival. He wondered if Mr. Lawrence, his own solicitor, had had much experience with breach of promise actions, and how much it would cost him not just to play for time, apropos Andrea, but to sever himself from her finally and for ever.

Mumford got to his feet, offering his hand.

Rather limply, Miles Walshott shook it and made his thanks.

After Walshott left, S.J.M. Mumford sat back in his chair and drank the tea that his clerk brought him and felt the warm glow of the mischief-maker steal over him. Gallantry came in many forms; even if young Beckman never knew of it, he would continue to stand guard over her. She was, after all, tomorrow's woman, and must be given her chance.

Later that same afternoon, Mr. Mumford happened to call on a bed-ridden spinster, client of many years, who happened to live in Mandragore Mansions not a stone's throw from Chalfont Arcade. In passing, Mr. Mumford dropped in for a friendly word with Mr. King, mainly to inform him that, in his opinion, it would not be the best time to frame an offer for Aspinall's. Mr. King did not ask Mr. Mumford to explain the reasons behind the free advice. He accepted it as the word of a gentleman. Though disappointed, Mr. King indicated that he would exercise patience in respect of acquiring the premises in Pimlico.

As he rode home, at twenty minutes after seven, to eat a dinner with his wife, Mr. Mumford glanced out of the window of the taxicab at the throng of pedestrians on the pavements of Piccadilly, at the girls in particular. He had no desire for them, only a vague paternal concern for their well-being, a feeling that had somehow positively attached itself to Holly Beckman.

However, he would do no more for the girl at this juncture. After all, he had a busy practice to attend to and he hadn't earned a penny from his actions on the girl's behalf. He had, he hoped, gained her a modicum of time. Now it was up to her to take the bit between her teeth, to show the Walshotts and the Aspinalls of this world a thing or two about industry, application and ambition.

•   •   •

Holly had thought a lot about David Aspinall in the days since she had taken over the shop. Rationalising her feelings towards him worked, for a while at least. She felt herself almost cured of the silly romantic attachment that seemed to belong to a period that had ended with the reading of Mr. Aspinall's will. It was at this time that she discarded the trophies of her girlhood, the gifts that David had given her and that she, in mooning over them, had imbued with meaning far beyond the man's intentions. It did no harm at all to be rid of the perfumes, chocolates, novelettes and even the rock-hard patriotic cushion. It made more room for the new wardrobe of clothes that she had bought to smarten herself up and give her not only pleasure but added confidence. Besides, there was another reason. In the last few months her feelings for David had altered. She was intelligent enough to recognise that she wanted him, not just as a dream lover, but physically. Quickening of the sexual impulse dismayed her slightly; it was a compelling thing and distracted her from concentration on business matters. But it was undeniable, and its demands were not to be spurned.

She wished more than ever that her mother was alive. There were things she could only discuss with a woman, advice that only an intelligent woman could give her. It was not the introverted desires that bothered Holly so much as coming to terms with their proper place in her life.

Dora Leyton, Violet, her other schoolmates, they too were tossed about by physical longings, but had a tried-and-true pattern to follow. They could, and would, use their sensual needs to lure a young man, not just into their arms, their beds, but to the altar or the registry office. Dora and Violet happily confused the issues of maturity, sought satisfaction without proper thought. Far back in her mind, it had occurred to Holly that that was how her own mother, Huldah Kirsanoff, had been trapped into marriage with her father. She could not explain, otherwise, the disparity between them or a pairing that, from the outset, must have been obviously ill-matched.

It was not a topic she could broach with Grandpa Tal. He was too tied into the situation. He must have suffered bitterly at the time. Grandpa Tal had given his daughter an education. He had released her from the bondage of ignorance without freeing her from an environment where ignorance was often a necessary evil and, perhaps, even a virtue. He had given her the tools for liberty without providing the means to use those tools. Money was the one thing that her mother had lacked to realise her potential. She, Huldah's daughter, had been more fortunate. Opportunity had come her way by sheer good luck.

But she was a little afraid of it, shy of the degree of calculation that must accompany its use. She struggled against her inhibitions, subconsciously torn between the inculcated modesty of the poor girl and the needs and desires of a woman who might soon have the means to effect them.

Liberated from the limitations of penny-pinching, Holly had to confront her taste, to test it, together with her ability to choose what it was that she wanted in love as well as in business.

Silverdale and Baur's sale of household furnishings and antique pieces was one of the auction-room's occasional clearing out manoeuvres, when all sorts of assorted items were put under the hammer. There would be none of the nostalgic sadness that sometimes pervaded a private house sale when the collection was all of a piece and a man's life seemed to add up to nothing but a few hundred pounds and the props of his existence appeared random and tawdry. Holly looked forward to the sale with considerable interest and excitement.

She closed the shop at ten a.m. She had come in early that morning to check her prices once more. In a paper parcel she had brought her best slope-shouldered blouse and a new black skirt and jacket. She hoped that the weather would be kind; she had gone for smartness not warmth in choosing the outfit. She changed in the back store, spending some considerable time over it, tweaking and smoothing at the skirt and adjusting the sit of the jacket. She had a new hat too, plain and business-like. She pinned her hair very carefully so that the hat would sit right. When all was done, she applied the faintest touch of rouge to her cheeks and a little cool lipstick and stood back to admire the effect.

It pleased her inordinately.

She would not be mistaken for a Right Honorable but neither would she be taken for some little wide-eyed mouse sent out by her Ma to scrounge cheap lots of pans or secondhand clothing for a shilling or two. The new clothes made her feel more assured, caused her to tip her head up, straighten her shoulders. She felt that she would be able now to look anyone in the eye and not be intimidated.

Putting on her gloves, she returned to the shop and took down the warming-pan from the high shelf. From the tea-caddy hidden behind it she extracted Maury's thirty pounds, wrapped it with a rubber band and tucked it into her big purse, together with the catalogue and a dozen of Aspinall's trade cards. It was her intention to spend some of the profits made during the past week. She had marked down five lots to Cash; if she got them at or below her estimated price, she would pay for them with Maury's money and sell them to selected clients in her spare time. In spite of Maury's assurances to the contrary, Holly still felt that it was slightly dishonest. She was just angry enough with the Aspinalls to go through with it, however.

Before leaving, Holly called loudly up the iron staircase and informed Mrs. Hodge that she was going out to a sale.

Rather to her surprise it was Thora who answered. She came on to the landing and, with a pinched and harassed look on her face, peered down at her.

"Who is that?" Thora Aspinall asked.

"It's me, Mrs. Aspinall. Holly Beckman."

"Holly? It doesn't look like you."

Holly hid her smile of pleasure.

"It's my new outfit, Mrs. Aspinall. Do you like it?"

"It makes you look all grown up."

"That's the idea, Mrs. Aspinall. I'm not a little girl any more."

"No, no, I suppose you're not."

"How are you, Mrs. A.?" Holly asked.

"As well as can be expected," Mrs. Aspinall said. "Are you goin' out?"

"Yes, to Silverdale and Baur's."

"Interestin' stuff?" The catch-phrase was an echo of casual dialogue between husband and wife.

"Interestin' enough," Holly answered, just as James Aspinall would have done.

Holly waited; Thora did not volunteer to stand in as a shopkeeper while Holly was gone. Such a thing would have been unthinkable. James had actively discouraged his wife from taking any part in the running of the business. Trade was a man's work, a husband's duty, just as keeping a clean house and raising healthy children were the proper concerns of a wife.

"Good luck to you, dear," Thora said.

"Thanks, Mrs. A. I'll be back about half-past one."

Thora nodded, and withdrew.

At least, thought Holly, as she locked up the shop door, Mrs. A. came out of her depression long enough to talk to me; a sign that she bears me no animosity.

The salerooms were set deep into a series of office-capped warehouses under the railway wall in Cheedle Street, east of the Hampstead Road. Holly travelled there by omnibus. She arrived with an hour on hand before the scheduled starting time of eleven-thiry. There were one hundred and forty-four lots, sixty of heavy furniture, the remainder single items, plus a dozen "tail enders" listed only as "China, ten pieces", "Ornaments and Vases, twenty-one pieces", and the like. The damp low-roofed vaults of the auction rooms were crowded. The two tables that held the odd lots were hidden behind a jostling row of disreputable junk-stall owners hunting bargains. Holly noticed ten dealers from the trade's middle ranks among the crowd; no doubt others would arrive before selling began. Viewing had been permitted yesterday afternoon, but Holly could not spare the time to pick over all the lots. She concentrated on inspecting those items in which she had a special interest, revising her tentative pricings after each examination, shielding her catalogue from prying eyes.

Among the better-class items were a Bristol china card tray, a Regency watch-holder and a pair of Nankin bowls. Everyone would be after those. Holly's pricing was optimistic. She had reached the last marked lot in her catalogue and was wondering if she had time to push her way through the greasy raincoats of the junk merchants to have a look at the oddments, when a hand on her elbow caused her to turn from her task.

"David," she blurted out in amazement. "What on earth are you doing here?"

"Keeping an eye on you, of course."

Holly's heart thumped and she felt her cheeks flame. On top of her excitement at having money to spend and the thrill of wearing her new clothes David's presence was almost too much for her. He looked so relaxed, so debonair. He was not in uniform. Dressed in a tweed hacking jacket and corduroys, it looked as if he had ridden up here from Pimlico and might have his stallion tethered outside in the street.

"Don't look so dismayed," said David.

"How did you know where I'd be?"

"Mother told me."

With her pleasure Holly experienced a pang of guilt. Maury's thirty pounds were in her purse and the last lot, a small ornamented scroll in rococo style, had been marked for Cash purchase.

David grinned at her. Her plan to split the lots between Aspinall and Beckman suddenly seemed like an act of disloyalty.

"I've got a spell of much-deserved leave," David said. "I'd retired to bye-byes for the morning when I heard you bawling up from the shop. I decided that it might be fun to toddle along and watch the wand being waved."

"It won't be much fun," said Holly. "It's usually just boring."

"Spending money is seldom boring." David lifted the rococo

ornament. "Do you suppose you can sell this in Cardwell Place?"

"I doubt it," Holly answered.

"You've marked it in your catalogue, though?"

"I . . .I thought I might buy it for myself."

David's mild, amused expression did not alter. "Doing a bit of personal collecting on the side, are you?"

"I've a little cash of my own to spend."

"And what better investment than a cupid's head scroll?"

The import of Holly's confession had not been lost on him, but he was practised in the art of appearing cool, particularly in situations where he felt unsure of himself. It was a skill that Holly had not quite mastered. She could not emulate his light bantering tone. The truth was that she was carried away with him. For a few unguarded minutes she was caught in a web of guilt and desire. His appearance here in her world seemed to give him a new dimension, to bring him closer to her. Among the shabby dealers, David seemed positively raffish. What was even more disturbing was that he had followed her here; he had come after her. Holly tried to convince herself that it was the auction that interested him, that he was, as he'd claimed, just "keeping an eye on her", but she did not swallow the excuse whole. He had come here to be with her, had taken a step towards her.

Her confusion threatened to destroy her concentration completely – and what sort of a show would that make? She got a grip on her emotions and, tilting her head up, looked into his face with a boldness that she did not feel. To protect herself against his attraction she would focus on business very hard indeed, keep him at a distance.

"Have you been here before?" she asked.

"Once, with Father, years ago. He brought me as a 'treat' during the school holidays. It was his idea of a treat, not mine. I was more interested in the chestnuts he promised to buy me than in the sale itself. To tell you the truth, Holly, I find all this frightfully tedious. I always did."

"Is that why you want to pull out of the business?"

"*I'm* not particularly anxious to sell. I can see sense in holding on to the shop, especially as you. . ."

"What?"

"Well, you'll probably make a nice piece of gingerbread for all of us, won't you, Holly? You're far too determined to fail at what you do."

"If you think that, David, why don't you persuade your sister to give me a chance to prove myself?"

"Andrea would be furious if she knew you were buying for

yourself, you know," said David. "She'll never adjust to the idea that you are an equal – for all practical purposes."

"I'm not your equal, David," Holly said.

David shrugged but did not disagree or pursue the argument.

He said, "Spoke with Mumford yesterday. Met him accidentally in Rigg's Coffee Room. He sends you his best regards."

"That's kind of him."

"I'm beginning to understand what he sees in you," said David, tossing away the compliment. "Couldn't before: can now."

"Perhaps," said Holly, "it's the new hat."

"What?" He was a little startled by her teasing tone. "Yes, perhaps it is."

The arrival of the auctioneer and his bald-headed clerk brought the moment of intimacy to a close. Holly was glad of the distraction, to be pulled down to earth again.

Neither of the men was sleek or smart, though both wore suits and starched collars. The fusty, damp dust of a hundred thousand lots seemed to adhere to them and Mr. Hampden, the auctioneer, spoke like a man with ticking in his throat. He was brisker in manner than his brethren in Sotheby's or Christie's. He stood no nonsense from the stall-dealers who, if permitted, would try to confuse him and knock him back on his calls, especially with the drab little lots at the end.

The bald-headed clerk crimped spectacles on to his nose, arranged his inkwell, ledger and pile of invoices, shot his celluloid cuffs and lowered his head like a parson about to pray. The auctioneer's box was sixty or seventy years old, an antique in its own right, high and narrow as a gibbet. The clerk's desk was dove-tailed on to the side on a lower level so that the men were linked by carpentry, welded into a team. When Hampden used his gavel too vigorously the clerk's inkwell would leap up and squirt out juice. And Baldy would crank his head round to scowl at his superior over the tops of his spectacles. And Hampden would say, "Done it again, 'aven't I, Wilf?" And Wilf would tut, and dab with his big wad of blotting paper.

In front of the box twenty chairs were occupied by twenty dealers. The hierarchy was well established. The men seated themselves in the same order at every saleroom auction they attended. It made it easy for the hammer to pick up their names. As a group they looked hunched, bird-like, humourless and without much individuality. Even Mr. Preeble, very fat and prone to use an amber holder as long as a billiard cue for his Balkan cigarettes, was drained of eccentricity by the drabness of the surroundings and unceremonial cant of the proceedings.

"Goodmorninggentlemen, lotnumberoneinyourcatalogue."

Exactly on time, the eleven thirty-four train rumbled distantly behind Hampden's back. Automatically he paused for it, though the sound was faint and subterranean.

"Sold t'the passenger for Maida Vale," Mr. Hampden said, as he did almost every blessed morning. Theatrically, Mr. Preeble boomed three amused notes – *Hoh, Hah, Hoh* – then everybody got down to serious business, ignoring all interruptions.

"Lot Number One: Bureau in burr walnut veneer, bears the Bell label, authenticated. Start it at twenty-five."

Bidding on the first dozen lots was sluggish, but the prices eventually fetched were higher than Holly would have imagined. She stood to the left of the box, close to Mr. Preeble, and Mr. Dale of Finsbury. She could tell by their reactions that the prices surprised them too. David stood a little behind her, sheltering her from the push of stall-dealers, who were not above spying on her prices and running her up out of sheer devilment.

Soon Holly was completely caught up in the auction. She felt no nervousness at all as the block of items that she'd marked came close, only curiosity as to the accuracy of her estimates. In spite of the high prices taken for the furniture, she was not tempted to revise her bids. Once a dealer started on that practice, and many did, one either had to be very wealthy or very lucky not to get one's fingers burned. Holly's bids were calculated on the shop price of the lot, what she could readily hope to sell it for. She kept a running tally of margins of profit in her head as Hampden pushed up the pace.

"Lot number seventy-three: one pair Swansea plates, very pretty examples. Perfect to the eye," Hampden said. "Start at four. Four the pair."

"Five."

"Five pounds?"

An out-of-town dealer indicated that he meant five pounds.

"Guineas," said Mr. James, a private collector of independent means.

"Six."

"Guineas."

"Seven."

"Guineas."

"Seven, ten."

"Eight."

"Eight, ten."

"Fifteen."

A lull: Mr. Hampden said, "At eight pounds and fifteen shillings, on my left."

"Nine," said the out-of-town dealer, adding, "guineas."

"Nine guineas in front," said Mr. Hampden. "Once at nine guineas, twice at. . ."

"Nine pounds, ten shillings."

"Nine, eleven," said the dealer, desperately.

"Ten pounds," said Mr. James, calmly.

The dealer made a gesture like a cricket umpire signalling a no ball, and Mr. James acquired another piece for his collection.

Unusually, there was a little murmur of conversation throughout the room. Mr. Hampden clacked his hammer.

"Wonder what I'd get for the wife: she's from Swansea too," he remarked; a standard joke to indicate his surprise at the ridiculously high price fetched for the plates. "Lot seventy-four."

Lot seventy-four, a pair of Delft flat dishes, started at three shillings and soared to an eventual knock-down of eighteen pounds. The dealers, Holly included, gasped.

Confidence was not restored when a salt-glaze punch pot, supposedly eighteenth century, went off to an over-dressed, middle-aged woman for a mere fourteen shillings; the pot had been of "doubtful origin".

After that, the steep rise in prices paid for authentic items was sustained.

Holly heard Mr. Preeble remark to Mr. Dale, "An upward trend, d'you think, old man?" And Mr. Dale reply, "You want it, Preeble, looks like you gotta be prepared to pay for it."

The Bristol china card tray sailed away, to a dealer from Reigate, for eleven pounds. Holly did not even have an opportunity to enter the bidding. She scribbled furiously in her catalogue.

The Regency watch-holder came under the hammer and, to Holly's mortification, bidding opened at a figure higher than her estimate and went up by leaps and bounds to four times the sum she would have paid. Again she pencilled figures in the catalogue while David, craning his neck, watched over her shoulder.

"Not doing too well, are you?" he whispered.

"I won't get anythin'," Holly whispered back. "But that's not important now."

"I don't understand."

"Later, David. I'll explain later."

The young woman appeared to have lost all interest in the bidding itself. She concerned herself with recording the final figure and the name of the purchaser.

"Gone to Mr. Summersby: account."

"Sold to Mr. Adams: account."

"Mr. Adams: twenty pounds: account."

The Nankin bowls, the Sunderland jugs and, the cream of the sale, a teaset of Rockingham china all went in a flurry of bidding.

"The gentleman's name?"

"Fortescue – with a 'c'. I have a card. Account."

"New account: Fortescue, with a 'c'."

Philosophically Mr. Preeble sat back and lit the cigarette in his elongated holder, while Mr. Dale, like Holly, diligently marked each price in his catalogue.

Hampden did not have to hurry the provincial buyers along now. The pace of bidding had accelerated in a kind of frantic eagerness to obtain the lots and, much to the chagrin of stall-keepers and small-beer traders, even the grubby, "with all faults" tail-end lots went for exorbitant sums.

Holly did not wait to hear Mr. Hampden's benediction: "Thank you, ladies and gents. Next sale – books – in these rooms, Thursday, eleven a.m." By that time, she had grabbed David's arm and positively sprinted out of the narrow front door of Silverdale and Baur's.

Dragging the young man beside her, she flew along to the Hampstead Road and, with the authority of somebody to the manor born, hailed a taxi and bundled David inside.

"Where's the fire?" he asked, breathlessly.

"Listen," said Holly, "will you, or won't you release me money from the business account?"

"If you tell me what's got you all excited, I might."

She riffled the well-thumbed leaves of the catalogue. "Did you hear the prices? Not two or three ill-informed private spendthrifts. The buyers were *trade*, dealers an' shop-owners from out of London."

"Well?"

"Where on earth can they be selling the stuff at those prices, an' makin' profit?" said Holly. "Obviously, David, they've a ready market, customers willing to take anythin' decent, no matter what the price. The big money went on collectors' items – china, pottery and plate. It isn't scarce, that kind of stuff."

David sat forward as the taxi ploughed into lunch-time congestion at the junction of Euston and Tottenham Court Roads. "Where to?" asked the driver, for the second or third time.

Holly came out of her excited and distracted state. "Pimlico, Cardwell Place."

David slipped the catalogue from her fingers and turned the pages slowly, trying to decipher the girl's crabbed figures.

Holly said, "Do I get t' buy for Aspinalls', or don't I?"

"Buy what, my tiger?"

"Anythin' an' everythin' I can lay hands on within the next couple of days. How much leave d'you have, David?"

"Six days."

"Will you help?" she pleaded. "Will you man the shop while I'm gone."

"Now, now, one question at a time."

Holly took a deep breath then explained. "There's been talk of a boom, rumours in the trade: but it's happened very quickly. I'm not mistaken, David. Silverdale and Baur's sales are not particularly important. But they circulate their lists an' catalogues widely. All down the South coast, even up into the Midlands. Provincial dealers don't have the competition we have here in London; they know quicker than we do what's happenin'."

"And what's happening is a boom?"

"Yes, but it hasn't dawned on most dealers yet."

"You propose to steal a march on the competition?"

"I've thirty pounds of my own money; came from m'brother, Maurice. I'll put that in the kitty."

"Go on."

"They were buyin' today at two times, three times what I'd *sell* these items at. Caught me by surprise. Caught even experienced oldsters, like Preeble, by surprise. But it won't take long for it t' get around the trade – then what a scramble there'll be for stock. You'll have t'pay through the nose in every tupenny ha'penny auction room from here t' Lands End. House sales will be like battle grounds."

"I like that," said David. "Very evocative: battle grounds."

"David, don't you understand?"

"Of course I do."

"Today, now, this afternoon, with as much cash as I can muster, I want t'get off round the shops. There are hundreds of little shops like Aspinall's in London, not countin' market stalls. They all show pretty poor stuff, on the whole, but they do have some items, a few, of quality – usually small wares, collectors' pieces."

David nodded. "Still offered at yesterday's prices?"

"That's it, that's the thing," said Holly.

"Once you've spent all our money – then what? Supposing it's a bubble, that there's no lasting boom?"

"I don't intend t'wait. I intend t' list an' sell. That's the reason I took note of the dealers' names. I can look them up in district directories an' post off lists."

"Can you cope?"

"Have to. It's far too good a chance t'miss. If we're goin' t'be obliged t'pay a fortune for stock in future, then we'll need capital, quick capital. This is one way t'get it. Volume turnover, it's called."

"Yes," said David, laconically, "I do understand the principle."

She was very excited now. Her reserve had gone completely. She caught his hand, squeezing it. "Please, David, please, don't let the business just go t'seed. For your father's sake, help me do this. I'm sure it'll work. He put his whole life int' the shop."

"That," said David, "is my shooting finger you're intent on breaking, Holly."

"*Please.*"

He glanced at the catalogue then at the girl's shining eyes and glowing cheeks. He had never seen her so animated. It heightened her beauty to an almost irresistible degree, the more so, oddly, as she was unconscious of it and had lost the fleeting edge of calculation that had marred their first minutes of meeting that morning. She looked like a Russian princess stepping from a sledge after a brisk ride through the snow. It was Holly's beauty that softened David, not the logic of her argument or the soundness of her ideas.

The clothes made all the difference, lifting her out of the shabby background of her father's world, making her seem like a *parvenu,* certainly, but not brash. She was leading him, and he was willing to be led, though the dance might turn out to be a merry one.

"Oh, very well," he said. "It's like backing the house to win at roulette, I suppose."

"But we are the house."

David smiled and shook his head. "I'll require two signatures on the withdrawal form for the bank. I'll have Mother do it. You may also count on my services, for what they're worth, over the next three or four days, though the Lord knows what my sweetheart will say."

"Thank you, David."

"Thank me properly, Holly."

"What?"

"Partner to partner, a kiss on the cheek would be satisfactory."

Holly hesitated then touched her lips to the edge of his moustache. Infected by her recklessness, David Aspinall wrapped his arms about her and hugged her for a moment before, reluctantly, Holly drew herself away.

* * *

"Have one'n me, Ritchie boy," Seaman said.

"Pint o' mild."

The men watched as the barman drew beer from the kegs with a strong steady pull on the ivory pump. He tilted the glass so that the head rose evenly. Sliding the glass across the bar to Ritchie, he said, "Yourself, Aleric?"

Aleric Seaman, who answered to no nickname, and was proud of his unusual Gothic handle, shook his head. A huge, fresh-complexioned man, ten years older than Ritchie, he exuded robustness without, in any way, being hearty. He was not often seen in the Admiral's Hat. The Box marked the limit of his province, though he maintained a nodding acquaintance with every publican between Kennington Green and the Bricklayers' Arms. What running boy had informed Seaman that Ritchie was making a stop-off for refreshment on the route home from work was a mystery, one of a thousand little mysteries that surrounded Vincent Shotten's empire. Like Renzo, Seaman was one of Shotten's "labourers", no buyer but a bully. Ritchie had no desire to suck up to the man. He listened without appearing to give the visitor attention.

"Spent your haul, yet, Ritchie?" Seaman asked.

"Put it in me piggie-bank," said Ritchie.

"Mr. Shotten was pleased."

"Right."

"So pleased, he's gonna put another few quid your way."

"Not interested."

"Yer, Ritchie, you're interested."

Ritchie lowered his mouth to the ale, eyes fixed on the marble counter. The barman had gone off and there was nobody at all within earshot. If he lifted his gaze he could see himself in the coppery depths of the mirror, the image broken into fragments by an advertisement for Alsopp's Old & Mild. There were times when he almost wished that he was old and mild, like Kirsanoff, not young, not boiling with anger.

Seaman leaned close to the young man, cocking his big head so that he could stare into Ritchie's face, stare very hard.

"Domestic job, good for a solo sneaker, just a coupla doors, like." Seaman paused. "Mr. Shotten's anxious it's done proper. Want me t'go on?"

"Right," said Ritchie.

"Nineteen, Shadwell Road, behind Waterloo Station. Know it?"

"Yer."

"Top floor, under the roof. Only door on the landin'. Can't miss it."

"When?"

"Sat'day's best, after dark, but not too late."

"What's there?"

"Goodies; bulky stuff."

"How bulky?"

"Carry it in a suitcase. Bring the best."

"Sat'day gets me a clear run, does it?"

"Should."

"Right."

"When you've got, hold."

"I don't like holdin'."

"Three, four days. Jack'll get in touch."

"Right."

"Better do it, Ritchie boy."

"Is that a promise?"

"Keep y'flush," said Seaman. "Anyhow, the mark's nothin' t'shed tears over. Name's Steiner: a dirty Jew profiteer. Don't mind that, do yer, Ritchie boy?"

"Nah," said Ritchie. "Don't mind that one bit."

* * *

By Saturday afternoon, Aspinall's stock had swollen by almost half. Though Holly's forays into the shops and markets of central and suburban London had yielded only small wares, the sheer volume of her purchases seemed to represent value for money, at least to David's weary eye. The three hundred pounds that he had withdrawn from the shop's trading account – in defiance of the fact that Andrea, if not the law, regarded it as a "frozen asset" – had been spent, together with Holly's thirty pounds.

There was a controlled kind of madness in her, a feverishness that David associated with gambling sickness. Indeed he regarded the entire venture as some kind of grand game, an elaborate wager in which he had put up the stake without being aware of the rules. His uneasiness was far outweighed by his stimulation. Impulsively, he had cancelled his arrangements, shelving a furious Linsey in favour of the shop, lying to her, of course, by claiming army business. Andrea was more of a problem than Linsey. He could not cover up the fact that the shop had turned into a hive of industry, or that he, voluntarily at that, had elected to assist the Lambeth girl, thus "taking sides" against his sister.

He had lost a valuable hour of Saturday morning in a shouting match with Andrea, a high-pitched argument that had ended not in truce but in an armed lull. Vainly he had tried to explain to his sister that his motives were selfish, that he wanted enough in the kitty to be able to withdraw a pound or two when he needed it without feeling guilty.

"Wait until your next dress bill comes in."

"I will pay it myself."

"With what, may I ask."

"You may not ask."

An elderly man in search of a Christmas present for his housekeeper popped his nose in the shop door in the midst of this stormy scene, took instant stock of the situation, and promptly popped his nose out again. Andrea had stationed herself on the iron staircase, David on the floor of the shop.

David: "You're being incredibly petty about this."

Andrea: "Petty? Petty? I merely wish to protect you, that's all."

"Protect me from what?"

"That little schemer."

"That little schemer has been on the streets. . ."

"Ah-hah: found her level at last, I see."

". . . on the streets, working her fingers to the bone. . ."

"Just to impress you."

"To increase our turnover, to take advantage of a rising market. . ."

"Rubbish!"

"Rubbish yourself!"

"First father, now you. I can hardly hold up my head as it it."

"Because it's . . . it's so damned *fat*."

"Oooooooooooh!"

When he got back to the shelter of the nook under the stairs, he could hear Andrea slamming doors in the flat above, shouting at Thora, who was used to it and, he suspected, secretly rather enjoyed seeing her daughter in a state of consternation.

David chuckled. He lit a cigarette, sipped from the tin mug of Camp Coffee, and, leaning on the desk like a schoolmaster, totted up Friday afternoon's purchases. Nineteen items broomed in from shops within walking distance: total cost, £57.18s. With Holly he had worked until midnight unwrapping the packages that she had trotted home – home, to the shop. Setting the items neatly on the trestle in the back store, he had listed each one carefully, to her dictation, against cost price, leaving the final column – selling price – blank. Holly's inspections were thorough. Here she did not hurry, grime-stained fingers gentle and patient. She had been relieved that none of her purchases was flawed, satisfied that her judgment had not been impaired by the urgency of her buying spree.

James Aspinall had issued a catalogue twice in the year. The practice was not uncommon, particularly among London dealers. But Mr. A. had made it a major bi-annual undertaking. For months he bought and stored choice items and spent many evenings writing elaborate little "histories" to tout the pieces. The strips were arranged alphabetically under appropriate headings and the whole thing glued onto brownpaper sheets. The sheets were then sent out to a typewriter agency who made a rough draft that Mr. Aspinall checked and corrected before sending the proof round to Myers & Crawley, a local jobbing printers, to run off three hundred copies. Envelopes were addressed by hand, sent in banded bundles to the Post Office all at once, to be fair to the clients. The distribution list was largely – in fact entirely – composed of private customers. Only after two weeks did Aspinall send out copies to friends in the trade, offering them, in effect, the dregs.

Holly had no intention of producing a monument to industry and patience. Dispensing with sophistication she intended to issue her catalogue within five days of its conception. Distribution would be in the form of twenty pages, typewritten, sent off to fifty provincial dealers. Orders would be treated on a first come, first served basis. The cost of the job, from the Speedwell Typewriter & Secretarial Agency, was twopence per page.

David had done the arithmetic. He found that the "list" could be brought in at under ten pounds, including spare copies for shop use. He added letter charges and, enjoying the calculations, extended them to include parcel postage costs and carriage (in brackets) on each of the items. During one of her brief returns to Cardwell Place, he presented Holly with an accurate per item surcharge to absorb whole costs. In spite of his weariness, David felt quite functional as the weekend was swallowed up in such work.

"Our catalogue entries must be accurate," Holly had told him. "Date, if known, period, maker and condition. Can't deceive the trade. No need to waste paper with fancy notes. They'll know what we're offerin', an' what they can sell it at. Besides, we'll give them protection, agree to take the pieces back an' refund postage, if the descriptions are found to be misleadin'."

"Isn't there a risk that dealers will buy "on spec"?"

"Some might; most won't. We'll put a five-day limit on returns. That should stop any fun'n' games at our expense."

"How often do you intend to do this, I mean, issue lists of stock for sale?"

"Not often," said Holly. "Next time, I might do it proper; a printed booklet like your father always did. Make a special out of it."

"But if this method works. . .?"

"We won't need it," said Holly. "Haven't the hands to cope with a mailing-order business. What we might get from it is contact with specialist dealers. Mr. A. never really approved of selling among the trade. Oh, he did it – more'n half our business was with other dealers – but in his heart he never really liked it. He preferred t' think of pieces "going to a good home" not just bein' traded here, there an' everywhere."

"Don't you regard antiques as objects of beauty, then, as father did?"

"'Course I do. Half the time, I don't want t'sell them at all. But it's impossible t'hang on t'everythin'. It's not dealin', then, David, it's just playin' at it, being a sort of rich collector."

"Do you like the pieces that you've bought today? Are they to your taste?" he'd asked.

"Some of them. I mean, I wouldn't want t'own them. I admire workmanship, though, even in ugly objects like that Worcester porcelain basket an' stand. But it's too fussy for me."

He was beginning to realise why his father had valued the Lambeth servant so highly. Comprehension increased as they worked together throughout Saturday evening.

David wished that he might be here instead of back among dockets and uniforms in Whitehall when the orders came in. On that December weekend, he was almost tempted to throw up his civilian career in insurance and gamble his future on the selling and buying of antiques. The urge did not last. Besides, it was too much like hard work, and he could not retain facts as Holly Beckman did. It seemed that every single thing she had ever been told, had ever read, was filed away in that pretty head. It was, he supposed, a gift; one he did not possess. He had trouble holding facts in his head. Often, negligently, he forgot the name of the account he was working on, had to flip over the folder and check it – and then, within minutes, had forgotten it again. His desk, his life, was a quagmire of memos and reminders. Horses, jockeys and odds adhered without pressure, most of the rest didn't.

Lighting his fortieth cigarette of the day, he lifted his head from the desk. His eyes watered with strain and his neck ached, but the first five pages of the famous list had been completed. He would not be the one to shout surrender.

Holly stood by the table. One would never have guessed that, since Thursday noon, she had been travelling the back streets of London and, by his reckoning, had snatched only ten hours' sleep; perhaps less, since he suspected that she'd sat up all of both nights poring over magazines and handbooks. She looked dishevelled, yet gave no evidence of tiredness, except that she rested one hip against the table and would, occasionally, close her eyes and sigh in temporary indecision as some relative fact briefly eluded her.

The Beckman Collection, as he called it, was a sight to behold. One hundred and eighty separate lots; twenty-one had been culled from existing stock, the rest purchased in the course of the past sixty hours. He could hardly believe it. He hoped to God it wasn't all junk, that he hadn't put too much faith in Holly's "expertise".

Ranged along the tables, the Beckman Collection *looked* valuable. Holly had bought nothing in need of repair. Though he did not generally appreciate their jargon the Canadians had a phrase that seemed appropriate. "Smart as a beaver, and twice as quick".

Holly dictated, and David wrote: "Lambeth Delft – early to mid-seventeenth century: unusually fine condition, quaint-slip-warepot. . ."

He glanced up. "Slipper, did you say?"

"S-L-I-P ware," she held the pot in one hand. "See the auburn colour; that's typical. They put the decorative patterns over it from a pipe or tube, like icing a cake. Called 'slip'."

"Slip." David wrote it down.

"Mason's Ironstone China."

Again he raised his head. "How do you know it's Mason's?"

She turned up the eight-sided jug, deep blue and vermilion. It had a queer little lizard for a handle, coloured a very reptilian green. "Says so on the bottom: impressed."

"Ah!"

"Not china at all; it's earthenware. I've heard there's a dozen of these jugs in a whole set, ascending sizes. I was lucky t'pick up four." She lifted a ruler and measured the octagonal carefully. "Five inches, five and a half, seven an' eight."

"Shall I put that down?"

"Please."

Later still, she told him, "Cup and saucer, Derby Japan pattern in scarlet an' blue, Mark number four."

He asked, "Date?"

She scowled at the cup, peered into its depths, then shook her head. "I'd better look it up."

On the shelf was a volume bound in binder's buckram with a laboratory label stuck on it, stating, "Crown Derby Ware." She checked over the contents, which were covered in pencil markings in Mr. Aspinall's hand. David massaged his fingers and cleaned the pen-nib on the edge of the blotter. She nodded and, bringing both book and cup to him, offered him the china.

"What colour is that, would you say?"

David rubbed his eyes with his wrist, then peered at the mark on the base of the cup. "Rust?"

"Puce?"

"Yes, puce; that's it. Decidedly."

"Date," said Holly; "1790 to 1795."

He was too tired now to ask her to explain.

At half-past eleven, she called a halt. David rose stiffly from the desk, stretching his arms, hunching his shoulders and rolling his neck. Holly stretched too, hands on her hips, arching her spine so that her breasts pressed against her blouse, distracting him. He lit yet another cigarette, savouring the faint flicker of desire then, without energy to sustain it, let it wane into a feeling of rapport. If she had been a man, he would have touched her, put his arm about her shoulder in a comradely sort of way, but he did not dare.

She gathered her overcoat and scarf from the nook.

"Will you put out the lights an' lock up, David?"

He did not resent being given orders by her. "How will you get home?"

"Too late for the underground. I'll catch the last tram."

"I'll walk you to the stop."

At that moment, they were unguarded and vulnerable. He was in the first phase of curious attraction, she sliding up out of the trough, each suddenly wary of the other.

"No," Holly said, a little too loudly. "I'll be quite safe. It isn't that late."

"Let me. . ."

"I'd just as soon go by myself."

He nodded. "Be in tomorrow, I take it, even although it's Sunday?"

"About midday. I won't need you. I mean, I can manage now."

"Can you, Holly? Can you really manage all on your own?"

"Yes."

"I can lend you my trusty pen-hand, at least until dinner time."

She capitulated with his gesture and accepted the rekindling of hope. But it was different now; they were both aware of it. The balance of understanding had changed as a result.

"I'd like that, David," she said.

She looped the scarf about her throat. Going to the door, she unlocked it.

Outlined against the frosty mist that filled Cardwell Place she looked most unlike a Lambeth girl; more, he thought fancifully, more Russian, with that handsome, doomed erectness that made the heroines of Russian drama so appealing before the bloody, bewildering Revolution had put them out of fashion. If the wool had been fur, the scarf a capacious hood, the overcoat a cloak – God, I must be exhausted, David told himself, refusing to acknowledge the romantic in his soul.

Giving Holly a brusque "Good night", he stepped back into the warehouse to extinguish the lights.

* * *

The Jew, for Jew he undoubtedly was, caught Ritchie red-handed. It was Ritchie's own fault. He had observed the old man leave the house, had trailed him down as far as the entrance to the Shadwell Road Synagogue and had watched him limp on up the lane towards the side door – at least, that's what Ritchie had supposed. The reason for the Jew's return only twenty minutes after his departure was no longer important.

Ritchie had taken off the two locks in the outer door of the apartment with a jemmy and screwdriver and had done the bash on the big modern lock of the inner door. It had been crude work. He was not proud of it. If it had been his own toss-over he would have set it up much more carefully. But with profits mostly going into Shotten's pocket, Ritchie could not find a motive for the application of skill. In a word, he was careless.

The smell had almost choked him, a stink of lockshen, cabbage soup, gefilte and burnt blintzes emanating from the kitchen. All velour, heavy crushed velvet and uncomfortable furniture the flat dripped *mezuzahs*, rolls of sacred script.

Shaddai – Almighty – peered at Ritchie from a glass eye on the lintel, a defence against evil spirits. Ritchie had heard of the practice from his Grandfather. He could imagine the old Jew devoutly rubbing a wetted finger against the eye, again and again, with the grinding addiction to ritual that Ritchie detested in men of his grandfather's religion. On an oval table stood a half empty bowl of borsch; fat had been used instead of cream. Beside it was an open prayer book: *Yiddishkeit*.

With impulsive anger Ritchie grabbed the soft flock cloth and whipped it from the table, pitching book and bowl to the carpet. He felt better, more himself, more in control, in spite of the oppressive atmosphere. Like a fisherman spreading a net, he flung the tablecloth out on the floor. He attacked the tallboys and wardrobes that surrounded the walls of the huge bleak bedroom and the living room. In these receptacles Steiner – the fool – kept his treasure.

Ritchie saw Steiner exactly as Seaman had described him, without depth, without human compassion, as an archetype; a miserly Jew, haggling for silver and gold, taking bread from the mouths of the poor. Where Steiner had bought all the plates and mazers, fork sets, canteens of pistol-handled knives, chocolate pots, tumbler cups, tobacco boxes and quaichs, and why – when he was in the way of dealing in silver – he kept so many magnificent items in his drawers at home, Ritchie neither knew nor cared. Shotten's tip had been top-hole. There couldn't be another haul this good on this side of the Thames.

Yanking out drawers, tumbling the contents on to the floor, Ritchie carried the goods to the tablecloth on the living room carpet and mounded them up. It was his only concession to his habit of un-flustered precision. He had brought along two large carpetbags; one for himself, one for Shotten. Of course, the best of the bleedin' stuff must go to Shotten. For all Ritchie knew Shotten had an itemised inventory. But the bastard wasn't going to get it all.

When he had scoured both rooms – leaving tallboys and wardrobes gaping – he knelt by the pile and began to select the small, almost negligible items, that he intended to keep for himself. He picked out a plain mug with the harp punch of the Dublin Assay Office on the base, a mustard pot, a vinaigrette.

Concentrating on his work, he did not hear Steiner step through the outer door from the landing. Why the damned Jew didn't slink away to seek help was more than Ritchie could imagine; perhaps some of the silver had been stolen in the first place. In coming through the door to protect his hoard, Steiner put himself beyond mercy.

The first Ritchie knew of the man's presence was a faint creaking, followed in a split second by the clack of his walking stick. Steiner rushed forward, raising the stick. *Shaddai*: His eyes were piercing, beard bristling, seedy black hat tipped back, greasy black coat flapping like bats-wings.

Ritchie hid his face.

Bending, touching brow to knees, Ritchie took the full force of the blow across his shoulders. He reached round, snatched at the stick and possessed it. He drove it backwards into the Jew's stomach, then, using his shoulder as a fulcrum, jerked the man out of balance and flung him on to the pile of loot.

He mustn't see me.

He mustn't see me.

Lunging Ritchie caught the brim of Steiner's black hat and tugged it violently over the man's eyes. He kneaded the cloth into the Jew's flesh. Strangely, he was not afraid. Purified by that initial responsive act of violence, he felt as cool as a lily. He drove his right fist into the crumbled mass of the hat. Braced, he drove again, three times, until he was satisfied that the Jew was cold; then he got up and pulled the man from the pile and lugged him off to the side. He returned, crammed the silver into the carpetbags, and left the apartment just as Steiner began to moan and roll his head.

He thought of going back and hitting the Jew again, but it would have been superfluous. Instead, defiantly, he paused on the threshhold, put down the heavy bags, spat on his finger and rubbed it against the little glass eye on the lintel.

Shaddai.

Be hanged, Ritchie thought.

* * *

It was after ten before Ritchie reached the back lane of Ambraham's Terrace and let himself into the oblong garden by the door in the wall. The rear windows of the house were in darkness. He went at once to the broken-down shed that contained only a few rusty gardening tools and a spare tin of paraffin. He had already prepared the hiding place. Working in the dark, he lifted up the floorboards and squeezed the bags down on to the sacking he had put across the damp earth. He replaced the boards very carefully. He slipped out of the shed and into the house by the scullery, confident that nobody had seen him.

Nobody had – except Grandpa Tal Kirsanoff who had been staring out at the night sky from his window in the attic. But Grandpa Tal said nothing to anyone, of course.

Christmas with Cordelia

FIFTY COPIES OF Holly's list were posted by midday mail at the Moncrieff Road post office. The list did not appear in the least attractive. Typewriters did not give the finished look of print; tin staples were no substitute for stitches. But the brown manilla envelopes that Grandpa Tal had helped her address were sufficiently plump to be interesting. No dealer that Holly had ever encountered would be put off by appearances.

After slipping the envelopes into the slot, Holly heaved a sigh of relief and, by way of celebration, walked round to Miss Sinclair's and stood herself a slap-up three-course luncheon in the company of the senior clerks and maiden ladies who frequented the staid little restaurant. She was back in the shop, open for business, by one-thirty. As a good omen, she sold a "cricket" table and four rather shabby Windsor chairs before the clock struck two.

To the inhabitants of the upper floor of Aspinall's Antique Shop – Thora, Andrea and Mrs. Hodge – there was nothing special about the sight of the girl scurrying down the road with a basket of envelopes. It did not concern them that the "Closed" notice hung on the locked door for over an hour. Before Holly returned, Andrea had put on her severe pea-green uniform and round hat and had trotted off to dispense tea and buns at a war widows and orphans "treat" in Hoxton Borough Hall. It was part of her "duty" as a volunteer member of Lady Jane Graham's Catering Reserve, one of the seven charitible and patriotic organisations to which Andrea belonged.

Thora remained in the kitchen in Cardwell Place. Recently she had abandoned the use of the drawing room during daylight hours. She spent most of her time seated in the broad, countrified kitchen, knitting socks, scarves and over-vests for soldiers and sailors. Mrs. Hodge was company for her, though she seldom responded to the woman's remarks about the Armistice and "the 'orrible state o'the country". Mrs. Hodge prepared lunch and, before she went home at half-past five, left dinner ready for the oven.

Thora's days revolved around mealtimes, all that remained of the pattern of her life since James' death. She thought constantly of her husband, slid contentedly into recollections of their courtship and early married years. From a past that had not been at all exciting or colourful she fashioned a gay reality. What she made of it now was something wonderful – and very consoling. From below she would hear sounds, especially from the storeroom beneath the kitchen. She could imagine James still there; he would always be there, close to her. Only in the late evenings, with Andrea often out, the shop closed and Mrs. Hodge returned to her husband in Bayswater, would loneliness bite into her imaginings; then, still knitting steadily, Thora would shed tears for all the gaiety that had evaded her and the joys she had never really known.

If her daughter returned early and found her with wet cheeks and a red nose, Thora did not attempt to disguise them. Andrea would boom out, "Now, mother, don't be silly. Pull yourself together. You still have me."

It did not occur to Thora to descend the staircase and converse with Holly. Though she liked the girl well enough, the shop had always been James' territory. She was afraid to discover that it too was as hum-drum and shabby as the house upstairs. So Thora stayed in the kitchen. She ate her breakfast at eight-thirty, drank morning tea at ten forty-five, had lunch at one o'clock, more tea at four and, usually alone, disposed of dinner at half-past seven. She knitted. She read illustrated papers that David brought in, mostly the Court news, put on seven pounds in weight, and missed a golden opportunity to brighten the autumn of her life by making friends with Holly Beckman.

In turn, Holly considered going boldly upstairs and inviting Thora to come down 'and lend a hand'. But she was unsure where Thora's loyalties lay, could not be certain that Mr. A.'s wife did not resent her. So no contact was made. And when catalogue orders started flooding in, Holly had to cope alone, while Thora – alone – remained immured with her reveries and boredom.

Response to the "Catalogue of Choice Antiques" as Holly, rather grandly, had entitled the twenty-page list, was beyond her wildest expectations.

The first hint that the scheme would succeed came at eleven-thirty on Wednesday morning when a Mr. Tallis turned up, hot-foot from Brighton, with a hastily marked copy of the list. Holly made him welcome. She brought out the articles that he wished to inspect – some forty in all – and left him to it. While Mr. Tallis was diligently doing his stuff, three telephone calls bagged six, eleven and fourteen items respectively. Holly realised that much of her work would be in sending out "Sorry. Sold" postcards.

Tallis and almost all the callers pounced on Item 87 – a pair of millefiori glass scent bottles, bases and stoppers decorated with floral patterns woven with the initials S.L. Holly had been unable to date them or give any historical description, but had thought them pretty enough to sell at twelve pounds the pair. They had cost her only three at a covered stall in Bermondsey's Saturday market. She had the temerity to ask Mr. Tallis who S.L. might be and what was special about the bottles. But Mr. Tallis only looked inscrutable, as he filled out his cheque for the thirty-six items he had purchased, and replied, "Search me, youngster, search me."

During the course of the next ten days, Holly received a total of twenty-two visitors, fifteen telephone calls and nine letters, including, altogether, thirty-one requests for Item No. 87. Obviously she had missed something important about the scent bottles. It irritated her that – out of ignorance – she had let them go far below their worth.

Loss on the bottles was more than compensated for by the unqualified success of her catalogue. Not only did Aspinall's Antiques clear all but a handful of the listed items, the visiting dealers also bought other articles from the general stock.

Many of the men had been acquainted with James, and were pleased to see that Holly had "taken over". The rush of business, however, left Holly no time to feel smug. Packing and despatching, writing postcards and letters, making careful record of sales, all the chores tumbled on her shoulders. For over a week she put in a fifteen-hour day in Cardwell Place, hardly taking time to grab a bite to eat, falling into bed at night almost too tired to sleep.

During this hectic period she saw nothing of David. She missed him – not just his help but his companionship. Presumably he was billeted again in his girl friend's house in Larder Mews, making up for his neglect of her. Holly could not prevent a thin, peevish streak of jealousy entering her thoughts when she realised that David was in another woman's bed. In her was a tangle of emotions; fear of her own sensuality and desire to be with David Aspinall in every respect. Rightly or wrongly, she believed that David's love would be snared only by yielding, by giving herself to him with the fierce abandon that Mayfair women were reputed to turn on. Subtle suggestive passages in the more risqué romances that Holly had read came to have new meaning. She could not, however, relate them to the final surrender, nor could she imagine the act of love-making blending tenderness with physical needs so compelling that, even in thought, they could cause her mind to stray from the tasks on hand into a marshland of curious yearnings. Again and again Holly had to force herself to concentrate on shop business. Fortunately there was plenty of activity to keep her occupied; almost too much of it.

Only her energy kept her going in the weeks prior to Christmas. She was relieved when callers and orders eased off and she had an opportunity to draw a deep breath and take stock, figuratively as well as literally.

On the Saturday before Christmas she lugged home the account books and ledgers. She spent Sunday in her room, sorting bills and receipts, entering figures in appropriate columns, adding, subtracting, checking her arithmetic until she was sure no error had crept in.

She was amazed and delighted to discover that she had spiralled the three hundred into nine hundred and sixty-one pounds. From that sum she subtracted Maury's thirty, added another thirty and entered the total into the December return. It had been tempting to give Maury back a share equal to the two hundred per cent that she'd made for Aspinall's, but Holly resisted. Doubling Maury's money was good business – and enough.

The grand turnover for the first three weeks of December amounted to over a thousand pounds; an astronomical sum, more than James Aspinall had ever taken in a half year.

Stock was exceedingly low, of course. The shelves were almost bare. She must earmark a large proportion of the profits for replenishing and must somehow persuade David to allow her access to the bank account so that she might be able to judge the overall cash-flow picture. Only when operating costs were subtracted would she know exactly how much she could plough back into stock purchase.

General all round price rises would affect her now. Her hope, like that of all dealers, was that she would be offered private purchases or would unearth items that could be bought cheaply and sold for a high price. Her tour of London shops suggested that she might still be able to fill the shelves with choice items at a reasonably modest cost. The problem was that every time she attended a sale or went out on a buying trip the shop had to be closed and business lost.

Soon, very soon, she must convince David – and through David, Andrea – that the employment of a shop servant was essential.

The thought gave Holly pause.

Had her success run away with her?

One thousand pounds? Shop servants?

She rose from the card table before the gas fire, crossed the bedroom to the window and stared out at Lambeth's depressing greyness.

How far she'd travelled in a very short period of time.

Lifting a flyblown, broken-handled mirror she studied her face in the glass, searching for visible evidence of change. It was not a smartly-dressed young Pimlico business woman who lived in this room. It was Holly Beckman, Leo's daughter. She looked as drawn and tired as any working girl after a hard week in Cavanaugh's factory.

But I'm not a factory girl.

I'm different.

I did what I am capable of doing.

I will do it again – and more.

Still holding the mirror, she seated herself in the tub chair and leaned her elbows on the card-table.

"Just who are you?" she spoke aloud to her reflection. "How on earth did you manage to make a thousand pounds? And what are you doing here, in a back bedroom in Abraham's Box, when you belong elsewhere?"

The lips in the mirror repeated every word of her questions – but uttered no answers.

"Who *are* you?"

Examining her features, she saw only a person, not the Lambeth girl that David saw, not a shabby little servant, not Maury's sister, Leo's daughter or Tal's granddaughter. Perhaps what she recognised was the woman her mother had never had the chance to become. But the satisfaction of her achievements was smothered by the motion of her imagination. Imagination, determination, ambition; names for the unspecified longings that filled her and drove her on. Once more she wished that her mother was here, not just to offer advice and the benefit of experience, but so that she might see in the mature woman what she herself might become, how she might develop.

The sensual, self-originated demands of her body troubled Holly. In slack undefended minutes before sleep, she would twist and turn under the sting of needs that her intellect could identify but that were novel in their power over her emotions.

"How far have you come, really?" she asked her image.

Not far enough to be afraid of success yet.

As the Thames separated Lambeth from Pimlico, she was separated from David Aspinall, but now she saw that bridges could be flung up, rivers crossed.

"Where is he?" she whispered. "Right now?"

Rational answers did not please her, made her angrily impatient with herself. She flung the mirror on to the bed and tore a single lined sheet of paper from the back of the legal pad.

On it she printed bald facts and figures.

Expenditure.

Turnover.

Profit.

Though the exercise soothed her slightly, it could not for long be held to such a neat accountancy. For the time being, however, until she had a chance to explore her capabilities and measure them against her desires, paper terms would have to do.

Money, after all, was money.

Love was quite another matter; not an item she would buy blind, even if she could afford it.

But David. . .?

"That's enough, miss," Holly said aloud and, pursing her lips, reached quickly for her pen again.

* * *

They made love soon after he arrived from Whitehall at eleven o'clock in the morning; then again after lunch at Jules', back in the cottage bed in Larder Mews. The coral sheets were still rumpled, the air still impregnated with the smoke of her cocktail cigarettes. As he had expected, her brooding restlessness gave way to *tristesse*, symptom of boredom and uncertainty.

On his back, shoulders supported by a silken bolster, David watched Linsey's performance through half-closed eyes. Sated with her body, he found himself critical. He was able to admit that her slenderness had become pared almost to the point of scrawniness and that her white translucent skin was taut as parchment over her bones. The high colour that burned on her cheeks did not suit an English rose. It was as if she had worked a witchcraft to keep up with fashion, changing not just her clothes but her whole physical appearance; Gainsborough going out in favour of some impasto Parisian, a Fauve daub in patches of puce and green, like – what's the damned fellow's name – Van Dongen. Clouded blue eyes promised more passion, lean, whittled limbs were more agile, but Linsey had sacrificed the last shred of wholesome integrity that had made her so attractive.

No psychologist, David studied his lover subjectively. Sadly he wondered where her charm had gone, the beauty that had first attracted him. She no longer cared enough to be graceful, not even to be modest. She had discarded all outward mystery. Look how she squatted in front of the nursery grate, clacking the tongs, listlessly transferring knobs of coal on to the flames from the painted wooden hod. Against the white wall, tinted by fresh flames, hair tangled, features hollow and sunken, only a Fauve could do her justice. But if her beauty had deserted her, he had helped speed the process. For that, David Aspinall experienced sufficient guilt to keep him loyal.

"Now the war's over, he's bound to come back," Linsey said.

"Perhaps not: not if he's doing well out there."

"He'll come back. I know him. He'll want the house. And he'll want me."

"Will he get you?"

"He can have the house."

"And you?"

Still squatting, she whirled, naked feet making quick little duck-steps to keep her in balance.

"No, he shan't have me. He had the best of me. But that's quite enough, darling."

"Is the rent up to date?"

"Fish it is."

"How much do you owe?"

She shrugged her shoulders and assumed her most bored and vacant expression, promptly turning her back to the bed again, to hide her face. Piece by piece, scattering coal dust on to her flanks, she fed the fire wastefully.

David said, "How much are you in arrears – a month? Two months? A year?"

"Something like that."

"If you don't pay up, he'll have a claim on you, Linsey."

"Theodore won't mind."

"He let you have it cheap, didn't he?"

"How did I know the war was going to finish so abruptly?"

"By reading the newspapers, darling."

"Are we going out?" She turned again.

"If you wish."

"Christabel's?"

"I haven't been paid yet."

"Borrow. Charlie will come through."

"I don't really feel like Christabel's. I thought dinner, just us, and an early night might. . ."

"One grows old on early nights, darling." She was two years his senior. She threw the tongs into the hod and stretched, arching her lean back. Her breasts were large, with delicately shaded aureoles around the nipples. She leaned against the nursery mantelshelf and crossed her legs, warming her thighs.

"Let's go to Christabel's. Perhaps the Christmas fairy will bring me sackfuls of luck. Don't you think I deserve it?"

"Have you heard from him?" David, unmoving, said. "Is that why you're so down in the mouth? Has Theo actually told you when he's boarding ship?"

"Fish he has."

"Linsey?"

"God knows, Theodore was hardly a pauper when he departed, but he's *fabulously* rich now, darling. He won't expect me to be punctual with the rent on this place. It was really a parting gift, you know."

Theodore Willoughby had been Linsey's first lover. He had taken her, almost literally, from her mother's side during a cruise in the Adriatic when Linsey was a precocious seventeen. He had calmly ignored her father's raging threats of court action, and had lived with her as his mistress until the war intervened; then Willoughby, whose mother was American, decided that Europe was a little too hot for him and departed for a sojourn in New Hampshire. There he bought over Hollister Mills and, within a six month, the Feather Falls Manufacturing Company to keep him amused during his exile.

"I've been a sort of a caretaker, you might say."

"When," said David, "is Theo coming home?"

"In the spring. Cross my dickie-bow, darling; in the spring. But you know dear old Theo, he might decide to buy Alaska, or trot off to corner the coconut market in Tahiti."

David did not know "dear old Theo" all that well; well enough, however, to suspect that when Theo returned to England in the spring, he would not be as indulgent towards Linsey as she seemed to expect.

"How much *do* you owe him in arrears?"

"Oh, a hundred or so."

"Or two hundred?"

"Closer to three, actually. I haven't paid a bean into that silly account since he left, actually. Actually. . ."

"Then it's closer to four," said David.

Linsey shifted suddenly from the fireplace, striding towards the narrow whitewood wardrobe in which David had hung his uniform. It was her habit, her delight – though it delighted him no longer – to use his tunic jacket as a robe. She opened the wardrobe, took down the hanger and slid the jacket from it, put it on, letting it hang unbuttoned over her body. It came to the middle of her thighs. She giggled and closed her shoulders coyly, covering her breasts with an arm and her belly with a hand. "Wouldn't I have been a whizzer in the trenches."

"Did you put anything in writing?"

"How do I know?"

David got out of bed and stood before the door to the bathroom, barring her exit. "*Did* you sign any document, stipulating the agreed rental for this house, Linsey?"

"I suppose I did. Yes, I did scribble on some bit of damned paper that he waved at me."

David nodded. "What am I going to do with you?"

"Take me to Chrissie's, dine me, wine me and kiss the dice. I can win four hundred pounds in ten shakes, you know," she said. "Can do?"

"Can do," David capitulated. He could not stand up to such wild irresponsibility. It was one thing to be spendthrift and a tiny bit dissolute; it was quite another to be so without guilt or anxiety. He envied her that – and worried about it. It would be fine if Theo reclaimed her. But there was little hope of that. Theo was too long in the tooth to assume the burden of a fancy piece like Miss Leigh-Jennings.

She could not go to her parents for help. They wouldn't even let her near them, did not answer her letters, hung up the telephone on her. In desperation, she had once accosted her father on his way from his office in Regent Terrace but he had struck her with his stick and pushed her away as if she'd been a diseased street hag. Since then she had not spoken of her family at all, except to offer an occasional whimsical toast to a long-deceased aunt who had left her a small parcel of gilt-edged shares that brought her in a monthly income of sorts. No matter how broke she'd been Linsey had never done more than mutter about selling out this source of income for capital.

There were parallels here, David sensed, with his own situation.

She leaned up and kissed him on the mouth, insinuating her tongue briefly between his lips, trailing her nails across his naked chest. "Gotta, gotta, gotta go."

He let her past him into the bathroom. It was white and childish, like the rest of Theodore Willoughby's Mayfair establishment. He pulled the door closed behind her and returned, soggily, to sit on the side of the bed. He found and lit one of her perfumed cigarettes.

Do unto Linsey as she does unto others? If only he dared. He could follow her spoor into the jungles of Mayfair, into the private gaming clubs that had sprung up in the West End, into the salons of eclectic hostesses; he could even enjoy himself – but he could not embrace her morality. He could not shake off the feeling that he was in her debt and must be faithful to her, come what may, must tend her and attend her, as if she was a nice, normal fiancée and their relationship blessed. Living a lie made him unhappy; he fought the malaise by living it to the hilt.

Tonight – unless she got tight or won a large sum – she would be quiescent, passive and appeased. She would lie in the cottage bed with her arms locked about him, snoring slightly, cheek against his chest. And he would suppose that he loved her. And would worry about her future.

So – he stirred himself with a shake – Willoughby intended to return to England, to sell out or merge his New Hampshire companies, give up making duck cotton suits for doughboys. Perhaps Willoughby *would* take her on – and leave him free. Free of the army, free of Linsey, free to go straight, as it were, to be the kind of son he never was to his father. In the shop? Could the shop support him? Not in any sort of style. Not yet. There was no saying what the Russian princess might make of it however. No saying what they might make of it together. It occurred to him that he had deliberately avoided Cardwell Place because of young Beckman. Oddly he was more afraid of Holly than he was of Linsey.

Quickly he got to his feet and, to stop the flow of thoughts, padded downstairs to the lounge in search of a stiff drink. The more he thought of it, the more appealing Christabel's became after all. There, at least, he would not have to think of anything – except winning.

That's what he needed right now: four hours of nothing but fun.

"David? David?"

He put down the glass and ran upstairs. She had come out on to the landing, still with the tunic hanging slackly round her slender body. She held out her arms to him.

"Hold me. Please, hold me."

He held her close and kissed her, there on the landing, until it was all right again; then they dressed and, hand-in-hand, set off on foot for Christabel's and a riotous evening at the tables.

* * *

There was that day a stillness in which the odours of Bermondsey and the river hung suspended. Tanneries' salts and leguminous dyes mingled with the yeasty stench of brewers' wash and the faint fishy whiff of Billingsgate, all bound by smoke from the lugs of a small casting furnace in the foreground. From the window of the drying loft, Stan Nuttall looked out over sheds and seepage canals to Wapping Basin and the London Dock, a broad view snipped off just short of Tower Bridge.

Stan was eating a Sally Lunn smeared with watery rhubarb jam, drinking tea from a tin mug. Ritchie lay on a wooden bench like an emperor. Finishing his dinner with a bag of shelled hazelnuts, he popped the nuts into his mouth and chewed noisily. Far left, huddled away from tents of dampish hide, five or six old men were awkwardly seated on bundles of sacking round a tiny oil stove. A cauliflower of tobacco smoke hung over their heads. A jug of milk stout was going its last round among them.

Stan glanced at them, then at Ritchie, then, elbows on the window-sill and his face to the river once more, said, "Ain't seen much o' Holly, lately. Fact, ain't seen 'er at all."

"I thought you said. . ."

"She sleeps in the Box, eats supper there, but she ain't *here*, Stan; know what I mean?"

Stan nodded.

Ritchie said, "You gotta admit she's a looker. You should see 'er when she's rigged out for goin' to a sale. Gawd Almighty! She'd put yer eye on a plate."

"Maybe it's a soldier, an officer."

"Stan, Stan, there's nobody, I tell you. All Holly's interested in is makin' a success of that bleedin' antique shop. She works at it night an' day. When she ain't there, she's thinkin' about bein' there."

"I don't understand that."

Ritchie glanced at his friend and said quietly, almost under his breath, "I do."

Stan said, "An' when she's made 'er pile, what'll she do with it?"

"Be a dif'rent person," said Ritchie.

Stan grunted disapprovingly

Ritchie said, "She don't want t'spend 'er whole bleedin' life in Lambeth, no more'n I do."

Stan bridled. "Nothin' wrong with Lambeth."

"Never said there was. For some people."

"Meanin' me?"

"Ah, don't be so prickly, Stan. I don't want t' wind up like my old man, like bloody Leo. The boozer, bed, work. Bugger that lot for a lark."

"Yer, I know what you want, Ritchie. It's Holly I'm interested in."

"Well, if I was you, Stan, I'd try t'put 'er out of my 'ead. She'll ship out of 'ere as soon as she can scratch up the cash for a place of 'er own."

"Ain't right, young girl livin' on 'er own."

"Ain't right for who? You, Dora, Vi? Didn't it ever strike you, Stan, maybe its just right for our Holly."

"She'll go live with some bloke, an' no weddin' ring neither," Stan predicted with unusual viciousness.

"She ain't like that, I tell yer."

"She's still livin' at 'ome, ain't she?"

"Yer, for the time bein'."

"Don't even see 'er at the Palace, like I used to."

"Hasn't got time for the pictures now," said Ritchie. "Hasn't got time for anythin'."

"Is she really runnin' that shop on 'er own?"

"Yer."

"What's she after?"

Ritchie picked his teeth with a fingernail, his mind on other things. "Uh?"

"What does she 'ope to get out of it?" Stan addressed the open window.

"Money," Ritchie answered.

Stan pushed the last of the Sally Lunn into his mouth with a gloved finger and swilled the tea in the mug. He turned and seated himself on the end of the bench, close by Ritchie's feet. "Listen, has she got a boy friend over there in Pimlico?"

"Not 'er."

"Tell me the truth, Ritchie?" said Stan. "I just think it's bleedin' funny that nobody ever sees your sister any more. I mean, she could be livin' in China for all anybody in Lambeth knows. Dora ain't even seen 'er an' you know how thick they used to be."

"They was never that close," said Ritchie. "Nobody ever got close to Holly. Sure, she 'ad her mates like Dora an' Vi in school but it'd 've been funny if she hadn't. But close? Not our Hol."

"I thought she was close t' me once."

"Before the war; years ago. She was a kid then."

"Is it . . . is it what 'appened; my 'and; the patch?"

Ritchie said, "Doubt it. Our Holly's never been interested in men, not really. Never interested in anythin' much. I thought she was stupid, like most of the dinahs round 'ere."

"She ain't stupid. She's got more brains than the rest of us put t'gether," said Stan.

"Then she went t'work in that shop. Antiques, I ask yer! It was like she suddenly woke up. Like it suddenly all started 'tickin', you know. It ain't that she hates us – you, me, Dora, all 'er old pals – she just don't really live 'ere any more."

"Ritch?" Stan moved closer. "I heard you was int' the gravy."

"Where'd you hear that?"

"Jeff told me."

"That bleedin' little toad's gettin' too loose mouthed. What'd he say?"

"That you was int' the gravy."

"I ain't buyin' no gold-knobbed canes yet, Stan."

"Take me in."

"Can't."

"I ain't stupid, like Jeff. I can keep shut."

"Yer, I know that, Stan." Wide awake now, Ritchie patted his friend's arm. "But it ain't for me t'say who's on the corner with me. See?"

"You workin' for Shotten?"

Pause: "I done a job for 'im."

"Cut me in, Ritch."

Pause: "You ain't bent enough, Stan."

"I can learn."

"You ain't slippery enough. Keep out, Stan. Just keep pluggin' on 'ere."

"How long you think we're goin' t'last 'ere?"

"Our jobs is safe."

"Who's goin' ter buy fifty thousand bleedin' belts and a hundred thousand pairs o' boots every year."

"The bosses'll find new markets."

Leaning closer, Stan said, "I can see how it's goin', even with one bleedin' eye. Year, two years there'll be no sentiment left. Blokes like me, cripples, we'll be slouchin' on corners scroungin' for crusts. I thought when I come out o' the war alive, I was made for life. I thought it would be dandy, like, just t' be alive an' workin'. Now – for what? I can't get what I want, what I was promised. I want my share, Ritchie." He put out the gnarled glove, and closed it into a fist. "I want my bleedin' share, Ritchie. I earned it, didn't I?"

Pause: "It's our Holly y'really want, Stan."

"I could learn t' want somebody else."

"You won't ever get her, y'know."

"You goin' t'throw some nightwork my way?"

"How long can y'stay off the bottle?"

"Long enough t'do what's required."

"That ain't satisfactory." Ritchie pushed himself up and put his fingertips against Stan Nuttall's throat. "Keep out the boozers for a month. Keep the gag on, Stan. You can spill dangerous information without knowin' it when you've gotta skinful."

Suddenly, Stan wanted a drink. He licked his lips.

"Do it," said Ritchie, "an' I'll cut you in on whatever I get next from Shotten."

"Promise?"

"Promise."

"No booze for a month?" said Stan, thoughtfully.

"No hard booze while you're workin' with me: permanent."

"Right: then what?"

"Whenever I need a bagman," said Ritchie, "you're it."

"Shake on it?"

"Sure." Ritchie squeezed his colleague's right hand to seal the bargain.

It suited him very well to have Nuttall as an accomplice. After all, it would save him going through the risky process of storing the gains – and, if it ever came to it, would furnish a ready-made scapegoat to take the brunt of any blame.

* * *

The Times was adamant that there would be no snow for Christmas. Not even Mother Nature dared defy *The Times,* though the night was clear and cold enough to show that frost was on Her mind. It was a crystalline, rather magical night, shiny and ringingly still. The charming variety of Hampstead was shown to best advantage under a rimmed moon. Builders had mingled elevations and aspects cunningly and the presence of the winter Heath, Highgate Woods and Parliament Hill, together with picturesque eighteenth-century byways, spires and little churches, imparted a rustic element to the route that appealed greatly to Andrea.

Beyond Chalk Farm she was a stranger: it was all novel. She might have been a continental explorer, rather than the passenger in a taxicab taking her to dinner with her intended's maiden aunt.

Girlishly excited, she would have prattled on with unguarded enthusiasm if Miles hadn't dominated the conversation, allowing her hardly an edgewise word. Insistently, drily, he unrolled screeds of facts about the passing scene, talking of Keats and Constable, Besant and du Maurier, of Well Walk Spa, of the seventeenth century and other safe historical things. As a balancing feature, however, he decried the inflated pleasures of living out of the City and the stultifying effects of surburban attitudes on a cosmopolitan woman, like herself. Think of foggy nights, icy mornings, the distance from theatres, restaurants, quality shops; he droned on in this vein for long enough, as if to convince Andrea that Hampstead was nothing but a dusty museum perched on the edge of Mongolian wasteland.

Everything Miles said, however, was contradicted by the evidence of Andrea's senses: elegant mansions, gardens, parks, the feeling of "quality" in the scents and echoing sounds of that delightful rambling suburb.

Laurel Row was charming too. The houses were larger than she had imagined, not quite palaces but detached domiciles decently protected each from the other by squared privets and full, thick evergreens.

When the taxicab stopped and Miles handed her down to the narrow pavement, however, she had to confess that No. 12, the Walshott residence, came as something of a disappointment. At odds with all other evidence of Miles' well-groomed temperament, No. 12 had the neglected aspect of a mausoleum whose occupants have fallen out of favour with the times. Ragged crests of rhododendron broke against railings that surmounted a cracked, bulging wall. Through the aperture – it was hardly more – that showed the line of the drive, the house itself loomed in total darkness against the clear night sky.

"Is . . . are . . . we expected?" Andrea said, as Miles pushed open the main gate.

"Yes."

"But . . . the lights?"

"My aunt prefers darkness."

"Oh!"

"Andrea, there's still time to return to London."

"Certainly not, Miles."

"Very well: take my hand."

Apprehensively now, Andrea allowed herself to be led to the steps below the arched front doorway and listened to the hollow racket that the bell made in the depths of the house.

"Don't you have a key?" she whispered.

"Of course; but I think it best to warn my aunt that we have arrived."

"Miles, I . . ."

"If it's any consolation, my dear," said Miles, "I'm nervous too."

The door swung inwards. The pale features of a female servant were suspended in dusty darkness. She appeared to be a withered crone and carried no light. It was only when Andrea entered that she saw that the servant was in fact a very young girl, hardly more than a child, though she wore an expression of resignation far beyond her tender years.

"Evenin', zur, mum."

"Ah, Bridget: you may take our coats."

"Zur."

"Where is my aunt?"

"She be dressin', zur."

"And the lights?"

"Gone out, zur."

"Kindly tell my aunt that we have arrived, and ask her to be good enough to replace the main fuse – or do it yourself, Bridget, assuming that you have the spare fuse to hand."

Bridget did not understand fuses and electrical matters. She would have preferred to conduct the whole business of the house by candlelight or oil lamp, for she had been brought up on a Somerset farm where such new-fangled things as bulbs and switches did not exist. "Miss O'nnz haz the fuze, zur."

"Then," said Miles, with just a trace of impatience, "ask Mrs. Owens to do it – as soon as she has attended Miss Cordelia."

"Zur."

"We'll be in the library."

"Wine'z waitin', zur."

"Thank you, Bridget."

With the overcoats slung over her shoulder and her hands full of Andrea's bits and pieces, Bridget scuttled off across the darkened hallway with an assurance that, to Andrea, suggested supernatural ability.

"Does. . ." Andrea cleared her throat. "Does this happen often, Miles?"

He took her hand and led her into the blackness, like a blind man in familiar terrain. "Should be a fire in the library."

Before they reached the library, however, the lights went on and Andrea had her first sight of the house that she hoped, one day soon, to call home.

It was not Gothic, not sternly Victorian, not very much of anything really, with a bias, if at all, to the Tudor. She noticed that the rugs were all skew-whiff and that the panelling of the hall, of which she had just a glimpse, needed dusting. She would get rid of the girl, Bridget. She could not endure living with an accent like that.

The library was – a library: books in glass cases, a reading table, three parchment-shaded lamps, a nest of decanters from which Miles served her sherry, three large chairs – the leather oddly stained and scarred – and a very attractive mantel under whose eaves burned a bright coal fire.

Awkwardly, Miles dragged out festive conversation while they awaited Cordelia's entrance. Though it was unladylike in the extreme, Andrea perspired profusely under her powder. She was aware that her eyes had become, already, rather glassy, her smile marred by a tiny twitching tic at the left corner of her mouth. Miles too had that same look of glassy concentration, as if he was anticipating the first deafening boom of a bombardment.

Aunt Cordelia, however, did not appear.

Her ambassador, Mrs. Owens, brought profuse apologies. Mrs. Owens looked like a man. Big, raw-boned, whiskered and Welsh, she wore a tweed suit cut for the high hills and chill breezes of her native land. Her hair was twisted into a front knot that stuck out of her forehead like a horn. She could have been anywhere between forty and sixty. Her leathery complexion had obviously been tanned early in youth, her hair had become frosted. She was jovial in a weird clipped manner, a barker in a soft dialect, at odds with herself.

"Not up to it, sir."

"Is she . . . unwell?"

"Not proper unwell, sir, just partial unwell."

The degrees of "unwellness" were lost on Andrea; Miles understood the code perfectly.

Aunt Cordelia had been at the bottle, in spite of his instructions to keep her locked in her room all afternoon. It wasn't Mrs. Owens fault, of course. Aunt Cordelia could have found alcoholic beverages in the Mosque at Medinah. She seemed able to distil them out of the very air. He had tried every ruse, imposed every rule this side of cruelty to dry out the old trout but she was more inventive, and more motivated, than he was. Somehow, always, she defeated him. Even Mrs. Owens, who could have handled a platoon of Gunners with ease, was frequently at a loss when it came to matching her iron will against Cordelia's.

"Perhaps," said Miles, "she may be able to join us for coffee?"

"If she can, she will," said Mrs. Owens, with a sniff that indicated that Andrea and Cordelia would not meet that night.

"Very well," said Miles, "tell Bridget that we will dine in five minutes, if suitable to cook."

Miles used the five minutes to apologise to Andrea, though Miss Aspinall was nothing if not relieved to be spared the final revelation, in the light of what had gone on so far.

It was patently obvious why Miles was so reclusive when it came to "doing the domestic". He had turned his potentially lovely home into a sanctuary for his insane aunt. Infected by charity, indoctrinated by scores of Christian sermons and speeches, Andrea felt unusual warmth towards her fiancée at that moment and, involuntarily, kissed his brow as he approached to relieve her of her sherry glass. Miles started, stepped back, extended his arm and, without reciprocation, steered her in to dinner in the dining room next door.

Soup, fish, beef all passed: wine flowed fairly copiously. Bridget, the lone disher-upper, did not slop down anybody's neck or trip on the carpet or scoop up the mashed potato with her fingers. All in all it was going swimmingly, Miles thought. He began to relax just a little.

He would present the pudding – a treat for Cordelia since it was so close to Christmas – and get that out of the way, whisk Andrea into the drawing room, feed her coffee, marzipan oranges and crême-de-ménthe and have her back in the taxicab in ninety minutes, even less if he looked slippy. Once in the taxicab, he would be safe. Andrea would be out of harm's way, and their relationship would, he supposed, putter on for another year or two, provided he straightened out the affairs of the shop and got some sort of regular income for her.

Miles was absolutely certain that the events of the evening would have deterred his fiancée sufficiently to put all thought of an early marriage out of her head. Miles had misjudged Andrea's determination, however. For once, she was willing to compromise, to disregard the minor eccentricities of the household. Indeed, she had already begun to plan how she would confine the Welsh warder and the mad aunt to the upper floor, and what she would do by way of decor below. The cook, she thought, was probably good enough to stay. She sipped the Château neuf du Pape and smiled wistfully at Miles who was seated ten feet from her at the other end of the dining table, behind silver and glass. In her mind she had begun a mighty shopping spree, darting between furniture and fabrics and purchases for her trousseau. In the new Louvre de Paris in rebuilt Oxford Circus there was an exquisite gown, not too daring for a wife to wear. Andrea's smile was more or less natural now, the tic having gone as soon as she heard that Cordelia would not be gracing the table with her presence.

Miles said, "A penny for your thoughts, dear?"

Andrea said, "I was thinking how fine a house you have, my dearest."

Miles said, "It sadly lacks modern refinements."

Andrea said, "And a woman's touch, *n'est ce pas?*"

Miles raised himself from a slight, satisfied slouch.

"What – dear?"

"There's so much one could do."

"Andrea, I . . . what?"

The final question was in response to a knock on the dining room door.

"*What?*"

Bridget's face appeared round the door. "Will I be bringin' it in, zur?"

"What? Hm? Oh, yes, bring it in."

Andrea recognised a treat when she saw one. She sat up nicely with her hands in her lap, looking expectantly towards the door.

Bridget pushed the door with her knee and eased in a gigantic oval salver on which sat the largest plum pudding Andrea had ever seen.

What delighted Andrea most of all was that the pudding seemed, in its perfection, to embody all the illusions of Christmas that one cherished as a child, a three-dimensional portrait of every coloured plate in every Christmas album that she had ever greedily pored over. No plum pudding had ever appeared so grand.

It was dark brown, completely round and sat on a plinth of clotted cream custard, with a sprig of holly, red-berried holly at that, stuck in its cap. More impressively, it blazed with the steady blue flame of best brandy administered to the exact spoonsful. Daddy had only tried that once – and had lost his eyebrows for his pains. But the Walshott pudding was submissive, a feast for the eye, mouthwateringly displayed.

Andrea laughed delightedly and clapped her hands as Bridget began her cautious walk from door to table.

At that precise moment the lights went out.

Andrea assumed that it was intentional. She was not disturbed. Nor was she disturbed by scuffling sounds outside in the hall. It seemed only fitting that cook and the other servants would peep in at this wonderful little ceremony, take pleasure in the pleasure of their master and mistress. Assuredly, she would retain the cook.

Miles said, "Oh, dear God!" and got to his feet.

The pudding on the salver in Bridget's hands approached Andrea from the left side, gentle cornflower-blue flames making a corona round it, casting delicate patterns on the servant's chin, on the woman's cheeks.

Andrea sighed.

"How utterly marvellous, my..." she began.

The door barged open. Mrs. Owens' thunderous voice declared. "The bitch's loose. Watch out! Watch out!"

The beautiful plum pudding exploded.

Andrea screamed.

Gobs of hot pudding splattered her face and breasts. Custard rained down upon her hair.

Screaming like a mare, Andrea stumbled from the table. The remaining half of the pudding exploded too, blasting away from the silver salver. Bridget, who had taken her share of flak, joined her voice with Andrea's, then toppled backwards like a felled sapling and thudded in a dead faint to the carpet.

Ignoring the maid, Miles caught at his fiancée. But Andrea was hysterical and punched Miles on the chest and kicked him painfully on the shins as if she thought that he too might be booby-trapped and explode in her face. Frantically she flung herself away from him as, chirping in pain at the blows, Miles released her.

Aunt Cordelia sprang out of thin air.

Ancient taffeta and lace swirled about her. Her streaky amber hair flung about her skull like a Medusa's snakes and her baubles and trinkets rattled. She had plunged in through the open window; the heavy drapes puffed behind her like the wings of some huge moon-born creature. She flew straight at Andrea, grabbing a corner of the tablecloth in passing, whipping the cloth off. Dishes and cruets clattered around the insensible Bridget, but Cordelia's attention was fixed on Andrea. She twined the tablecloth round and round her victim, chanting gleefully, "*I've got you now, you upstart, you scarlet woman, you street gel, you succubus. Steal my Miles, would you? You shan't have my Miles, you harlot.*"

Seasoned by crisis, Mrs. Owens clipped the maniac with her fist, a neat uppercut that would have roused a cheer in any fairground boxing booth. She caught the sagging bag of bones and hauled Aunt Cordelia, insensible, away.

It took five minutes to restore any semblence of order in the dining room, to bring Bridget out of her swoon with a vial of sal volatile, dose her with a stiff whisky and accept her immediate notice, to ply Andrea with enough brandy to get her to stop screaming and reduce her shuddering to a steady humiliated trembling.

Miles edged her into the library, away from the scene of the crime, muttering soothingly, patting her with a napkin and, when Mrs. Owens returned to lend a helping hand, mopping her off with a moist sponge and towel. Another brandy got poor Andrea more or less on her feet and Miles wasted no time in removing her from the house.

A taxicab was summoned from the rank at Golders Green Station. Huddled in her fur-collared coat, clutching her accoutrement, Andrea was escorted out to the vehicle. Miles went with her, holding her head against his lapel. They said nothing, nothing at all, during the ride back to Pimlico. Only when the cab had growled into Cardwell Place did Andrea extricate herself from his stiff embrace and, drawing back, say quietly, "She called me an upstart."

"No, my dearest, no."

"I heard her. Am I an upstart?"

"You are a beautiful woman, with the patience of Job."

Andrea's lips quivered. There was a tear in her eye. "Darling Miles, I feel . . . I feel that our . . . our marriage . . . must . . . wait."

Miles delayed his reply, judging it to a tee. "Perhaps it's for the best."

"We will remain bethrothed, but marriage. . ."

"I understand my dearest."

"Are you terribly disappointed?"

"I understand completely."

"Do you?"

"Completely."

"You are a very fine man, my darling. I don't blame you for . . . for what happened tonight."

"And you are generous and patient, to a fault."

"We will wait, Miles."

"Yes," said Walshott. "If that's what you wish, we will wait."

• • •

Cordelia was not asleep. Her ugly old Gorgon's head was tucked down under a corner of the quilt and the pillow was built up against one ear. The table-lamp was lit. Her medicine – a magnesia solution – stood by a glass and spoon on a tray by the bed. Mrs. Owens loitered by the bedroom door. Miles seated himself on the slippery quilt, one hand behind his back. He craned his neck and peered over the pillow. One red eye, slitted, squinted back at him. Caught in Aunt Cordelia's hair was a single burned raisin.

"You may leave us, Mrs. Owens."

"She's had her dose, sir. She'll sleep soon."

"Shan't," hissed Aunt Cordelia.

Mrs. Owens left, closing the door behind her and, belatedly, locking it.

"She's a tart and an upstart, Miles. Wants your money and my house." The head did not move. She would wriggle away out of sight if he chided her.

He had no intention of chiding her.

He said, "How did you get out."

Cordelia simpered. "My secret."

He said, "Well, at least tell me how you booby-trapped the pudding."

"Two fireworks. Box in the attic. You'd forgotten."

"Yes, I'd forgotten." He made a mental note to check the contents of the boxes up there first thing in the morning.

"Cookie let me light the pud. Didn't want to see *her*. Put the squibs in then."

"And climbed in through the dining room window. Aunt, Aunt, you'll do yourself a serious injury one of these days."

She chuckled. "My, my, but it *was* a show!"

"You're a wicked old woman."

"Got rid of her, though, didn't I?"

"A very wicked old woman."

"Are you cross with me, Miles?"

"Of course." He brought his hand from behind his back, and laid the gift on the pillow.

"There's punishment for you," he said.

"Heh-heh," said Aunt Cordelia and, as her nephew stole away to find fresh coffee and a good cigar, brought the bottle of best Scotch whisky closer to her cheek and cuddled it to keep it warm.

*   *   *

Dinner had been a drab affair. David, who wished he was elsewhere on that Christmas night, had drunk a drop too much and slept in the armchair until his sister kicked his ankle and told him she'd no intention of listening to him snoring for the rest of the evening. Thora also napped, also snored, but there was an excuse for her; her "age" – to her children she was already senile – permitted it. Cardwell Place and the house above the shop were equally silent and solemn and contained no more than token trinkets to mark the festive season.

Andrea seemed more broody than usual. She had told her family nothing of her dinner with Miles and Cordelia; she saw no humour at all in exploding puddings, but suspected that David might.

The Aspinalls sat dourly together in the drawing room, pretending that filial affection rather than duty held them there. The "children" avoided mentioning their father who, when all was said and done, had at least had the gift of enjoying himself, with a bit of effort, when the occasion demanded it. Even the gifts that they had exchanged were tawdry, practical articles of winter clothing that hadn't cost much in money, time or imagination. David smoked too much, shifted in his chair, listened to the clock tick and his mother's purling snores. Andrea flicked listlessly through the *Savoy Christmas Album*, skipping the illustration of *Christmas Dinner at Devizes* which, in glorious colour, had as its focal point a you-know-what.

"Would you like to play some cribbage?"

"No," Andrea replied. "I don't feel like it."

"Draughts?"

"On Christmas day?"

"Dominoes?"

"David, please."

Eventually he got up and wandered into the kitchen and made himself a sandwich of cold breast of goose – which he didn't really want. He put it on a plate together with a large whisky and soda and went down the iron staircase into the shop.

The clock ticked there, too, telling him that it was only eight and that at least another couple of hours of tedium had to be endured before he could decently bid good night and hit the mattress. By the light of a single bulb, he mooched about the shop wondering what Linsey was doing and why he had not had the courage to bring her here for Christmas. He knew the answer to that question perfectly well. Chalk and cheese: Andrea and Linsey. The very idea of putting them at the same table, or in the same room, was preposterous.

Equally preposterous, but more appealing in a way, was the idea of sharing the goose with Holly Beckman. Perhaps he should have been outrageously bold and dragged her along to join the family. She would have provided divertissement, something to ward off the pall of gloom that enshrouded the house. But that would have been using Holly – who would hardly have been likely to enjoy herself – and he could not bring himself to use her, not in that flippant manner.

A stage whisper from the staircase startled him.

"What on earth are you doing, David?"

"Eating a sandwich."

Andrea came down into the light. "You drink too much, you know."

"I know. It stuns the senses rather effectively."

"It's cold down here."

"I'm wearing a whisky-soda muffler."

"I'm worried about you, David."

"I'm touched."

"What's going to become of you?"

"What's going to become of *you*, sister dear? Will you wed your nice little stockbroker in the next twelve-month? Will I have to turn up in my dickey-bow at the Connaught and give you away? Willingly, willingly, quoth he in gladness."

"You are . . . irresponsible."

"Don't you mean 'dissolute'?"

"I'm serious."

He discarded the heel of the sandwich, which was too greasy for his taste anyhow. He washed stringy meat from his teeth with the last of the whisky-soda and plunked the glass down on the nearest table. It *was* cold in the shop, cold enough for a Christmas haunting, for his father to materialise behind the grandfather clock or in the storeroom. David shivered. He was sober, completely sober.

"I'm serious, too, Andrea. Are you going to marry the fellow or not?"

He had put her at a disadvantage. "We've decided to hold off a while longer, David. Until Miles is better established."

"Good God, what do you want from him – Windsor Castle as a country retreat?" said David. "If wedding bells aren't in the offing, Andrea, perhaps we should declare a truce long enough to discuss *your* future as well as mine."

"What is your point, David?"

"Don't keep hectoring the Beckman girl." He held up his hand like a crossing policeman, to silence her protest. "She's valuable to us. We have, Andrea, very little talent or skill between us. We depended on father."

"Are you suggesting that we depend on Beckman?"

"I'll keep a close eye on her."

"Yes, oh, yes, I see."

He spoke sharply. "Andrea, put your personal bias to one side. The girl has flair in a high degree. For your information, we've made a large profit this year, in the past month, in fact. Do not, please, be negative about this matter."

"Twisted you round her fingers too, has she?"

"What advice did Miles give you? I'm sure you discussed it with him. Come, sister, tell me the truth."

"He advised me to wait – only until the business is on a solid footing and worth selling."

"For once, Miles and I see eye to eye," said David.

Andrea leaned against the post at the foot of the staircase and glanced around the shop. "I suppose this *is* all we have."

"It isn't so bad," said David. "But Beckman is the dynamo that makes it go."

"She comes cheaply enough," said Andrea.

"Mother will have the house to stay in – and you will have an income of sorts – and I'll have a bit of pocket money as an extra, if and when I require it."

"A thin ambition," said Andrea. "What about your girl friend: won't she want better?"

David said, "Let Holly hold the line, Andrea."

"Very well – but only for a limited period. Twelve months. In twelve months, come what may, David, I want to be shot of our association with Beckman, rid of this junk shop, and have my share of the proceeds sunk into something more secure."

"I'll tell her on Tuesday."

"Tell her what?"

"That she has the freedom to buy and sell, to run the shop, and that we will not interfere."

"For a year only."

"Do you want me to tell her that, too?"

"No," said Andrea, after a pause. "Let her think that she is safe. Let her – what is it – 'hold the line' for us until we're ready. Is that what you want, David?"

"It's a beginning," David said and, putting out the shop light, went past his sister and upstairs to pour himself another drink.

* * *

The hectic pace of the past month had disrupted Holly's perception of the passage of time. She could not believe that the waning weeks of 1918 had been so crammed with novel experiences. Not only had she inherited part of Mr. Aspinall's business, but she had acquired with it a certain inbuilt poise that enabled her to do things that would have been unthinkable for a mere mousy shop servant. The legacy had forced her to accelerate the pace of her flight from Lambeth and Leo, and had brought with it a measure of impatience with the idle, shiftless habits of the household and the squalid district. She supposed that she might, with some truth, be classed as a budding snob, but it was not the honest hard-working folk of her native borough that she had turned against, only the shallowness of character that it bred in those too weak or too lazy to come to grips with all life had to offer. Few, precious few of her contemporaries could be bothered to exert themselves; that was the flaw, the invisible crack in them. Much of their complaint against the inequality in society was a defence against inertia.

Very quickly Holly ceased to feel guilty as she progressed into social areas where, by the mores of Abraham's Box, she had no right to be. What law, after all, had set "her place" so immutably that it could not be changed? Even David Aspinall did not now seem beyond her reach; the glimpses she had had of his millieu, of Mayfair, Park Lane and St. James's, hinted that there too there was waste, more of it, perhaps, than in Lambeth, though of a different hue.

On the last day of the year, Holly spent the morning diligently polishing and dusting in the shop.

At noon she slipped into the back store and changed into a neat brown wool suit with a matching tobacco-leaf blouse. She put on hat and gloves and took herself to Miss Sinclair's for lunch. It was by no means the first time she had treated herself to lunch at the popular Pimlico restaurant and there, in company with business men and senior secretaries, she felt quite at home. Miss Holly Beckman, the proprietrix of a respectable establishment, smart but not showy, assured but not brazen, was surely entitled to enjoy a three-course meal in the middle of the day.

She wished only that David could be with her.

He had made a flying visit to Cardwell Place on Tuesday morning to deliver her a Christmas present, a large tin of Mackintosh's Chocolate Toffees. More importantly, he had brought along the bank forms that she was required to sign to allow her to draw freely from the trading account.

Though David had told her that she now had a free hand, Holly remained sceptical; in practice her hand might not be quite so free as David promised in that airy way of his. His light, off-hand manner was part of his charm and he looked more handsome than ever in his uniform, his cheeks flushed with celebrations and the need to meet "appointments" that had been hanging fire over Christmas. He was clearly in a hurry.

"David, I'll have to buy stock," Holly had said.

"Buy it."

"I'll need help – a servant – to keep the shop open when I'm out."

"Employ one."

"That's all very well, David, but what does Andrea have to say about it?"

"She's in agreement," said David. "We've had a corker of a year, after all – financially, I mean."

"Next year might not be such a corker."

"On the other hand," said David, on his way towards the door, "next year might be even better. I'm counting on you, tiger."

"David?"

He was gone.

As Holly walked back to Cardwell Place after lunch, the light was already fading down into a slow cold twilight streaked with spits of sleet. She did not change back into her overall when she reached the shop but settled at the tall desk in the nook under the stairs where it was warm and cosy. For the very first time, Holly was contented. She felt as if the shop really did belong to her and, for a few hours, ceased to be apprehensive about its future.

Though she sold a chipped decanter for a shilling and a not-very-good foxhead stirrup cup for five, the shop was quiet during the last hour of the afternoon.

In order on the high desk were catalogues of forthcoming sales, a handwritten list of "untapped" East End junk shops, Mr. Aspinall's client-book and a letter from Kennedy King.

In the letter Mr. King formally invited her to "scout" for him and promised to pay a generous commission on fair items of glass, porcelain and silver that she might not be in a position to buy for her own stock. He also thanked her for recommending Dr. Royle and implied that the gentleman had changed his allegiances from Aspinall's to King's. Holly was no longer intimidated by the scale of King's business. She had come to the conclusion that he was genuinely doing his best to see her through a sticky patch – perhaps out of a sense of debt to James Aspinall, perhaps because he liked her. Holly was not put out by the possibility that King admired her as a woman rather than as a fellow dealer. She was faintly flattered by the thought. In a postscript, Kennedy King left her an opening for further meetings: "If you are ever in need of advice, please do not hesitate to call upon me, with or without an appointment."

Next to King's letter, leaning on the toffee tin, was Grandpa Tal's present to her. The plump book on hallmarks had cost the old man two guineas. In return, Holly had given Tal a fine cedarwood cigar box engraved with the Imperial Russian crest. She had not yet had an opportunity to deliver her gift to Maury who had been on duty over the Christmas season. It was a nice cigar case in soft calfskin and into it, in fat rolls, she had inserted his sixty pounds. Maury was the first of the people she loved to benefit directly from her stroke of fortune and she looked forward to the day when her brother would be free of the army.

Seven eventful weeks had turned her life around and stood it on its head. But she had risen to the challenge and it would be false modesty to deny that she had succeeded in clearing the first hurdles amazingly well. Only at home did she feel oppressed. Ritchie had become even more sly and she feared his cunning more than a sister had a right to fear her brother. She had totally lost patience with her father and found the household chores tedious and – yes, she had to admit – demeaning. How frustrating it must have been for Huldah Kirsanoff, her mother, to be trapped with Leo in Abraham's Box. In an odd sort of way, Holly felt that she was making amends for the impoverished life her mother had lead.

She was a shop owner, and proud of it.

It was that factor that Dora, Cissy and Vi, even poor Stan, would not take into account when they met in the parlour of the Admiral's Hat or in the foyer of the Picture Palace and exchanged gossip about her. It was not vain of her to imagine that her name would crop up, for her friends would be spiteful in their discussion of the changes in her. Perhaps Stan would defend her still, but Stan was so much a part of Lambeth that he would not dare be her champion for long, not unless he too wished to be classed as a "stuck-up bleedin' snob", and shunned. What none of them could understand was that she was proud of her achievement and that it took more than a stroke of good luck, like picking a Derby winner, to separate her from them. She was a twenty-year-old slum kid who had seized her chance.

All the triumphs now would be her triumphs. The set-backs would be her responsibility. She would not have the easy excuses that they had, could not blame the government, the war, the borough council, the bosses for any reversals that occurred.

Yes, she told herself, David might be right: 1919 might be even more of a corker than 1918 had been.

She would work towards that end.

Destiny would not shove her around now like a pawn on a great big chessboard.

Precisely at six o'clock, she opened a crisp sweet-smelling new ledger and, with a ruler to guide her hand, printed *January, 1919* at the top of the first page.

Holly Beckman, one of society's dispossessed, had finally come into her own.

* * *

The captain put his key in the lock, turned it and entered the room. The curtains were not closed. Light from Shepherd Market slanted across the table. The captain closed the door behind him and leaned against it.

The air was cold. The room seemed hostile and not as he

remembered it, though all the parts were perfectly in place. During his absence his mother had acted as caretaker. Travelling up to town every two weeks, she had swept, dusted and polished, lighted fires in the grate, put hot bottles in the bed. If he had notified her of his return, she would have lit the fire, stocked the pantry and warmed the bed in dutiful anticipation. He should have told her, should have written. But he was too weary for generosity, too old to play the loving son, to do what was expected of him even if it was right.

Cigarette clinging to his lips, the captain remained motionless on the threshhold. The rim of his hat was low over his forehead. He had to lift his chin, inch by inch, to take in the table, the sofa, the boxes and furniture and shelves of books beyond the living room partition.

Two years ago, almost to the night, he had walked around the long table, patiently arranging the regiment that saluted his return.

Four Prussian dragoons headed the parade, followed by hussars from Dresden, grenadiers from Nuremberg, clansmen from Stuttgart and mounted Gauls from Leipzig. At the rear of the column came knights from Magdeburg, wild horsemen from Mignot and ten rare Hungarian rebels cast and painted two centuries ago in the workshops of old Vienna. They rode eagerly towards him under extravagant banners, waving swords and lances, trumpets, carbines and quaint musketoons.

Going forward, the captain faced the models squarely.

Flicking his eyes left, he was confronted by dioramas built into shelves over the Biedermeier escritoire. Painted glass perspectives swam with phantom landscapes, through which the Crecy archers stooped, and Pennefather's skeleton line repulsed the Russians at Inkerman.

The captain had prepared himself for this moment.

He turned abruptly on his heel.

Waterloo and Agincourt were dark above the Grecian sideboard. But faint glimmers from the window showed the Light Dragoons bucking and plunging under the guns in the valley of death, dying endlessly, vigorously, brave casts of painted tin.

Also on that wall was draped the gaudy jacket of a sergeant of Border Horse while on the sideboard, waiting for a head, was an officer's bell-top shako, its horsehair quiff spread out like a pennant in the wind.

The captain went into the bedroom.

His single bed, narrow as a beam, jutted from the wall.

Bookcases bulged around it. Two wardrobes and a dressing-table were buried in cliffs of books. Kinglake, Taine, Buckle, Prescott, Carlyle – a hoard of broken runs and scuffed sets in scholars' leather wedged by single tomes and slender inconsequential volumes gifted by Oxford friends.

On a pedestal table by the bed his mother had arranged his cigarette box, match holder, a pewter pot of hard-black pencils and a new pad of unlined stationery. There too she had placed his three collections, proudly done in pale blue doeskin.

The captain dropped the butt of his cigarette to the carpet and put his heel on it. He fished a tin from his pocket, picked out a fresh tube and lit it with a match from the box in the holder.

Outside the street folk of the Market murmured. A handcart trundled over cobbles out of Maxbridge Street and clanged against the galvanised dustbin that stood monumentally outside the butcher's shop.

London.

London: the captain had tried to ease himself into it by spending a night in Faulkner's Hotel, Villiers Street, next door to Charing Cross station.

It had been the acknowledged dream of every English Tommy to stroll the 'Dilly once again, to ride the open deck of an omnibus along the Strand. He had the 'Dilly and the Strand at his feet. He wanted to want them with raw and ruthless greed, an avarice for completion and fulfilment. But he could not.

Though his rooms were less than a mile from Charing Cross, he could not hurry. He must take his time, test each step, probing, probing like a sapper in a minefield.

All that day he had walked, following a circular route along the Victoria Embankment from Westminster Bridge to Blackfriars, along Fleet Street, the Strand and Whitehall. He did not wander aimlessly. He legged it as if he had a destination, a purpose, an appointment to keep. He was snug enough in greatcoat and gloves, comfortable in marching boots. Smartly, but mutely, he returned the salutes of men in uniform, not breaking stride, forging on – Whitehall, the Embankment, Fleet Street, the Strand – round and round from dawn until dinner time. With equal detachment he passed famous landmarks and inimitible vignettes of the world's greatest city. He was waiting for the clock inside his head to stop so that he could set it, wind it and begin again.

Standing by the bed, the captain finished another cigarette and ground it too out on the carpet. He returned to the living room. He put a match to the twists of newspaper in the grate. It was a high old-fashioned iron fireplace. Methodically his mother had built in paper and splinters, sticks and knurls of coal. She had filled the big brass scuttle with lumps of best domestic.

Hearth servant.

Fire ceremony.

Impinged upon by wit, the captain smiled to himself.

Mother, it seems I've been spawned by an old pagan.

Yes, dear, she would answer, *without argument, without understanding.*

Yes, dear.

The dry makings flared quickly.

Kneeling, the captain fed on coal from the scuttle. When the fire was roaring hot, he tipped the remaining coal into a corner of the fender and carried the empty brass scuttle to the long table.

One by one he dropped the model soldiers into it and carried them to the fire. One by one he took them out again and dropped them into the heart of the fire.

Solid lead and pressed tin instantly melted. Dripping lumps slid through white-hot ash and plopped to the grid below. A poker shook them free, made room for more. Knights, dragoons and grenadiers crumpled into grapeshot, releasing a faint whiff of molten metal and burned paint; Hungarian rebels two centuries old, Prussians, hussars, clansmen, one by one.

When they were gone, the captain lifted down his dioramas. With the poker he dismembered the plywood frames, smashed the glass perspectives and systematically melted down the many moulded figurines. He burned the wood to sustain the blaze, tore up the jacket of the yeoman volunteer and burned it too; finally, the shako. Its hair quiff filled the room with an acrid smoke that brought tears to the captain's eyes.

It was the captain's last act of destruction.

When it was done, the captain got to his feet.

He fetched water in a pail from the lavatory and dowsed the reeking grate. He left the pail on the rug with the scuttle full of broken glass. Remembrance of the mess would compel him to return tomorrow. He must be clean, he must be neat, no matter what. Now all the soldiers were gone, it might not be so hard to come back.

Tonight he would sleep in the secure anonymity of Faulkner's Hotel. He locked the door, went downstairs into Shepherd Market and found a public house. He stood himself a large whisky, then struck out for a turn around town before bed.

Whitehall, the Embankment.

Fleet Street. The Strand.

He was looking for something, he supposed; something or some one to help him back to earth.

He prayed to God that he would find it, before the Shoemaker found him.

PART TWO

1919

1

Sundry Lots

THE EARLY MONTHS of the year of 1919 brought strikes and riots in many parts of the world. The Bolsheviks were warring in Russia and labour unrest was rife in Paris, America and Britain. The railways ground to a standstill and many commodities became scarce. In addition, winter stung the land with a series of blizzards and bitter frosts.

Andrea was furious to learn that Indian tea-pickers had gone on strike, depriving her of her favourite Earl Grey. She complained loudly to Miles, who managed to find his fiancée a chest of the stuff on the black market but could not guarantee to clear up any world events that impinged on the lady's comfort.

Old Tal Kirsanoff was paid off.

"Paid off," said Leo. "What the 'ell d'you mean, paid off?"

"Younger men must have the work," said Tal.

"Bet the bosses mistook you for a Bolshie," said Ritchie.

"How long 'ave they given you?" asked Lee.

"I have until Friday."

"Ain't it bloomin' marvellous!" said Leo. "Strewth! It'll be my turn next."

"They can pay me off any time," Ritchie shrugged. "Who cares?"

"I care," Leo shouted. "I got rent t'pay, grub t'buy. I ain't made o' bleedin' money. I can't afford t' keep anybody in this 'ouse who don't pay 'is way. Hear me, old man. Best find yourself another job, double quick."

"Pa, he's past it. He'll never get work now."

"I am willing to work," said Tal, "but Ritchie is right. Nobody will employ me at my age."

"I will."

The three men stared at Holly.

"You will?" said Ritchie. "How?"

"I need a shopkeeper," said Holly.

"I won't accept charity, child," Tal said.

"It isn't charity. I need a shopkeeper to look after the place when I'm out at sales. There's no heavy work involved."

"Sounds like your cup of tea, Grandpa," said Ritchie.

Leo answered for his father-in-law. "You're on, gal. He'll take it. What'll you pay 'im?"

"Well, the shop can't afford to pay much."

"Typical! Ain't that typical?" said Leo. "She'd exploit 'er own flesh'n'blood without a qualm. That's what havin' power does. That's the corruptin' power of money for yer."

"Grandfather," said Holly, "will you come an' work for me in Aspinall's shop?"

Tal paused then smiled. "When do you wish me to start?"

"Monday morning, at nine o'clock, if it suits."

"It suits perfectly," said Tal Kirsanoff, and Holly kissed him on the brow to seal the agreement.

The spring of the year was wet. Social unrest was greatly increased by soldiers returning from the war, men who felt, rightly, that they had been cheated by promises of "A Better World, and a Land fit for Heroes". Surging undercurrents of cynicism and desperation were not calmed by the formal signing of the peace treaty with Germany or victory marches, civic pageants and pompous speeches, most of which took place in July.

In that month, Mr. Theodore Willoughby returned from America.

Linsey Leigh-Jennings wasted no time on calling upon her friend and landlord in his temporary headquarters, an opulent suite in the Palace Royal Hotel.

Theodore was tanned, slimmer than she remembered him but still with that thin-lipped reptilian coldness that she had once found irresistibly challenging. It took no more than minutes for Linsey to realise that Theodore had changed in his attitude towards her. He was no longer even faintly amused by her or inclined to indulge her. What was more he seemed to know an unconscionable amount about her doings over the past couple of years. She wondered just which of her acquaintances belonged to Willoughby's nest of spies.

It hardly mattered. He was on to her immediately, casting up her casual flirtation with David.

"David?" said Linsey, innocently. "You can't mean the Aspinall boy? I haven't seen him for ages, not since I heard you were coming back to England."

"You didn't know I was coming back to England, let alone when."

"Yes, I confess there was a bit of a thing going with the Aspinall boy, for a little while. You can't hold it against me, Theo. It's not like you to be prim. I'll bet you had your share of girls while you were in America, darling. I hope you didn't bring one back with you, not a special one."

"Out," said Theodore Willoughby.

"I do honestly believe you're jealous of young Aspinall."

"Out."

"Don't bark at me, Theo. I didn't come here to squabble."

"I know why you came."

"I came to give you a proper welcome home. Aren't I your best girl?" When the man did not respond, Linsey went on. "Is it my thing with David Aspinall that's upset you, Theo, darling? You have my absolute word that he means nothing to me. He kept me amused, paid a few bills . . ."

"Will he pay your rent?"

"Rent?"

"In case you'd forgotten, you're my tenant. You owe me rent, sweet, rather a lot of it."

"Oh, I thought we might come to an arrangement about that."

"All I want from you, Linsey, is my money."

"Money, money, money! Money can't mean that much to you, darling. I mean, you don't need it."

"No, I don't need it. It just happens to be mine, and what belongs to me I like to have in my possession."

"I used to belong to you."

"Not any more."

"Am'n't I worth a miserable two hundred pounds?"

"Four hundred and forty pounds: No, you're not."

"Why don't you try a sample, darling. I promise I've improved with keeping."

"With practise, you mean."

Willoughby gripped her by the arm, hurting her. He drew her towards the door of the suite, saying, "You've one month, four weeks, in which to clear out of my house in Larder Mews. Naturally, I'll require you to be present when my agent calls to take inventory, a document which, you may dimly recall, you signed at the same time as the lease."

"The house is fine, perfectly fine."

"I do hope so, Linsey," Willoughby said. "As to the matter of the four hundred and forty pounds, because I'm a generous and patient sort of fellow, I'll allow you three months to find it . . ."

"Theo, you're not throwing me out?"

". . . but if you don't come up with the dibbins, sweet, in

exactly three months I'll haul you in front of the beak."

"Theo, you wouldn't, not after what you did to me."

"You were a willing victim, Linsey."

"You bastard!"

"Make no mistake, I want my rent in full, not later than the first day of October."

"Oh God, you are a bastard!"

"Why don't you come to 'an arrangement' with young Aspinall. He's surely fool enough to fall madly in love with you, if you work hard at it."

"I don't *want* David Aspinall. I'm in love with *you*, Theo. It's *you* I want, *only* you."

"Well, sweet, it isn't you I want. Frankly, I wouldn't be interested in you if you served yourself naked on a clam shell."

"The four hundred – Theo, I don't see how I can possibly raise four hundred pounds . . ."

"You'd better have a damned good shot at it, Linsey."

"But how can I?"

"You know how, sweet," said Willoughby.

"But, Theo . . ?"

He yanked open the door and pushed her out into the corridor. She staggered and before she could recover her balance he had slammed the door on her.

"Bastard!" Linsey groaned, into her closed fist. "Bastard, bastard, bastard!"

Ritchie Beckman had been called by that name, and others even more obscene during the course of the spring and summer. But the men who cursed him blue blind didn't even know his name. They were the owners and managers of the four shops and three warehouses that the team of Beckman and Nuttall robbed during a nine week period of intense clandestine activity.

Stan was a good accomplice. He kept his fear well in check – at first. But as job succeeded job the anxiety in him grew and changed its character until, insidiously, he came to fear Ritchie Beckman more than he did discovery and arrest. Ritchie's violence manifested itself more and more openly; he would not hesitate to beat a caretaker or watchman over the head simply to expedite the work on hand. Stan was afraid that, sooner or later, Ritchie would murder somebody, and they would both be topped. For all that, Stan did not turn down the jobs. He took his share of the proceeds with a degree of satisfaction, deluding himself that this was no more than he was due, that wringing his rights from the capitalists was a fine form of revenge.

Holly and Maury Beckman were also concerned with capital, but their approach to its acquisition was honest and industrious and, in consequence, frustrating.

Maury in particular was finding out just how much things had changed in post-war society. During his leaves, just prior to demobilisation, the re-establishment of Elkins' as a going concern strained his patience to the limit. Merely acquiring materials had become a process so fraught with difficulties that Maury suspected a plot to put an end to private enterprise.

He learned to use the telephone and typewriting machine because it had become impossible to call in person on the men with whom he did business; there simply weren't enough hours in the day.

"Sand," said Maury. "I'm talkin' about sand, Harry. I'm not just after a bucketful. I need four full loads. None of yer rubbish shovelled up from South End neither. No beach stuff. No salty grit. I want best quality, coarse grain, an' I'd like it delivered to Elkins' yard next week."

"Cost yer a packet, Maury."

"Cost yer, Maury, cost yer, Maury – Gawd! That's all I hear these days. Harry, I know it'll cost me. Cost me even more next month, like as not."

"It's the haulage as runs up the price."

"I don't care what it is, Harry. Can y'get the bleedin' stuff delivered?"

"Need t'ask for cash down, Maury."

"Why? You've always given us credit before."

"Suppliers want cash from me, Maury. I can't afford t'lay out, like."

"Sand, I'm askin' for, not bloomin' gold dust."

"Like I said, it's the haulage what's expensive."

"Where's your pit, Harry?"

"Got several dif'rent sources," said Harry, cagily.

"Supposin' I collect."

"Comes from a long way off, Maury, the best stuff."

"Sand, not Italian bleedin' marble."

"Well, I gotta good deep pit on contract up by Malvern."

"Quote me for the load, dug out and piled."

"Pound the load, on the ground."

"Gawd Almighty! How much, then, t'the yard?"

"Tenner, thereabouts."

"Right. I'll collect."

"Maury, it's . . . I mean, it ain't done."

"Say three days. Can feed an' water two nags and m'self for a quid.

Save a fiver. Five for three days graft ain't a bad rate, Harry. Listen, you'd better not be sellin' me rubbish."

"Nah. It's a good pit. On Redroof Farm, three miles south from Malvern. Soon as you pay me, Maury, I'll have the loads dug ready for loadin'."

"Pay in advance?"

"That's the story everywhere these days."

"All right, all right. I'll 'ave the money sent round this afternoon."

"When'll you be up there, like?"

"Soon as I'm shot o' the army once an' for all. My final papers 'ave been promised for Monday after Victory Day."

"Yer, that's nice for you Maury. You'll be glad."

"Sure, I'm glad. Listen, you got a shoveller on this farm?"

"Can find you one. Cost extra, though."

"Gawd."

"Ten bob."

"Ten bob for a shoveller. Used t' get the spade for a shillin'."

"Before the war, that was, Maury. Things've changed."

"Don't I bleedin' know it!"

"You want the shoveller?"

"Yer."

"Pay in advance, Maury, sorry."

"Christ, what happened t' trust?"

"The Kaiser killed it," Harry said.

Maury did not often read newspapers, nor did he acquire a copy of the special issue of the government news sheet entitled *The Future*. Holly, however, was concerned enough over rumours of total national bankruptcy, with the government spending at the rate of four million pounds per day, to borrow the sheet and read it from cover to cover.

The government's glowing report and optimistic proposals had the desired effect on the young shop owner and calmed her anxieties about the whole country going broke. More experienced financiers, of course, treated the pamphlet as a joke, pointing out that the Prime Minister might shout as much as he liked about the need to end the "old world" but who would draw up the blueprint for the brave new world that would replace it.

Holly did not concern herself with politics. Soothed by the Prime Minister's dogmatic reassurances, she got on with running Aspinall's as best she could.

As with Maury, telephone and typewriting machine had become tools of the trade, important time-savers and, towards the end of July, she received a telephone call that was to have a profound effect upon her future.

"Miss Beckman?" said the voice on the telephone. "Ah, good! Kennedy King speaking."

"Yes, Mr. King, an' what can I do for you?"

"Have you received the catalogue for the Beaufort Grange sale yet?"

"Yes, I have."

"Going up?"

"It's a bit rich for my blood, Mr. King."

"Thought you might feel that way," said Kennedy King. "But I had a chat with the estimator yesterday. It seems that the job lots aren't to be sneezed at. The heavy stuff will go high, of course, but the job lots should come up just after lunch, when bargains can be had."

"Have you heard what's there, Mr. King?"

"Well it's listed as bric-à-brac, but I'm informed that it's of fair quality and might be worth viewing. You never know, Holly, do you?"

"Hm, I wonder," said Holly, into the telephone. "It'll mean stayin' overnight in Greesham; might not be enough in it to justify the railway ticket and a hotel bill at the end of it."

"Pope's the auctioneer: he hopes to do it in a day."

"Startin' time?"

"Ten o'clock."

"I suppose I could . . ."

"There's a spare seat in my motorcar," King said.

"That's kind, but I wouldn't dream . . ."

"Why ever not?"

"It . . . it wouldn't seem . . . right."

"Simon Black will be there, too, Holly, and Miss Chubb. I thought that we might . . . ah, discuss a little arrangement about bidding."

"An arrangement?" said Holly.

"Pool our resources, if you follow me."

Holly understood the principle; the "ring" system that enabled a consortium of dealers to undercut the market value of sale items and to squeeze out private buyers and other dealers on more valuable lots. She did not quite approve of it.

"I don't have the kind of resources you and Mr. Black have."

"I'll be blunt, Holly; I know what's in the bobtail lots. I don't want to be stuck with minor pieces but I could use six or eight single items; Simon could use the same. No point in us bidding against each other. We'll keep out, if advisable, if you'll let us have the articles we want at lot cost. The rest of the stuff is yours – in effect for nothing."

"I'm not sure I . . ."

"I know what you think, Holly. But it's not really a ring. Just four old friends looking out for their interests. Besides, it'll be a jolly jaunt for us, if the weather picks up. Greesham's very pretty this time of year."

"I don't know, Mr. King."

"No problems with the shop, are there?"

"My Grandfather can look after it."

"There you are then."

"Yes," said Holly. "Yes, I'll come – it it's not putting you out."

"Plenty of room in my motorcar," King said. "Can you be at my shop at a quarter to eight?"

"Yes."

"First class. It's a jolly accommodating motorcar, I assure you. It'll take the five of us in absolute comfort."

"Five?"

"My nephew's coming too."

"Is he in the trade?"

"Books: he's interested in books," said Kennedy King. "On the quiet side, but personable enough. Name's Deems: Captain Christopher Deems."

"I look forward to meeting him," said Holly, politely.

2

Property of a Gentleman

REDEEMED FROM A barn on a ramshackle estate in Somerset, the motorcar was a long-bodied 1908 Lanchester twenty horse-power open-drive landaulette. It had been "in a bit of a state" when King had purchased it. Peacock's, the Fulham coachbuilders, had done a wonderful job of refurbishing. She ran now as sweet as a nut, brasswork gleaming in July sunshine, tyres humming on the

macadamised roads that followed the Thames upriver towards
Greesham. King had taken a few lessons from one of the staff at
Peacock's. Full of technicalities he prattled away to Simon Black
about patent wick carburettors, pre-selective gearboxes and disc
transmission brakes, and demonstrated how to groove the lever
steering to hold the vehicle in something like a straight line. King wore
a tweed motoring cap the size of a tureen, goggles strapped above the
peak. He had supplied Simon Black with a similar outfit but the ladies
and the captain, in the open glass "cabin" at the rear, were well
protected from the breeze and had donned no special clothing.

It was undeniably exciting to skip along the highway at that hour of
a bright summer's morning. The party was in high spirits, particularly
Miss Emma Chubb, Mr. Black's "friend", an effervescent soul at the
best of times. Emma Chubb and Holly faced forward, but Captain
Deems had his back to the tall glass box so that, as in a railway
compartment, the ladies and the soldier were obliged to look into
each others' faces during the eighty-minute trip. Conversation was
difficult. Only Emma had no problem in making herself heard. She
bawled into Holly's ear quite happily, and addressed remarks on the
passing scene to the captain with eloquent gestures. The captain
nodded and smiled faintly in response, but said nothing. Occasionally, however, Holly noticed that he was scrutinising her, in preference
to tree-lined lanes or pretty views of distant riverside villages.

When they stopped at Sinnock to refresh themselves with a quick
cup of tea, Holly had no opportunity to engage the captain in
conversation. She was incorporated into a huddle at the table in the
tea-shop's parlour, with Messrs. Black and King and Miss Chubb.

Miss Emma Chubb, it transpired, was more than just a pretty face.
A dealer in her own right, Emma had premises in Spring Street, just
around the corner from Mr. Black's Antiques Emporium. Trade cards
were made out in her name and, once every year or so, she put out a
catalogue of one hundred "choice" items of furniture. The hundred
items were stored in Mr. Black's warehouse. Miss Chubb paid rental
for the use of the space. It was all, of course, a paper transaction, to
give Miss Emma Chubb "credentials", and security. More importantly, it enabled Miss Chubb to bid for – and, sometimes, against – Mr.
Black, cosily increasing the size of "the ring" by one member. Mr.
King was aware of the arrangement. He and Mr. Black were good
pals. In embroiling Miss Chubb in this manner, Simon Black insured
himself against the remote possibility of going bankrupt. The
relationship between the Bond Street dealer and the Bow Street
spinster was not confined to saleroom and emporium, however. It

had begun in the tester bed of a country hotel and, indeed, continued in beds of one sort or another in and around London. There was no doubt that Miss Emma Chubb greatly benefited from her partnership with Simon Black, or that Mr. Black received benefit in return. It was also apparent that the middle-aged Mr. Black and the not-so-young Miss Chubb admired each other and had acquired consummate skill in the art of sustaining an affair as a thing of the heart.

In appearance Black was not unlike Kennedy King. Laughter-lines webbed his eyes. He had a wide cheerful mouth. If anything, he dressed with more panache than King. That day he touted a chequered suit with a vivid yellow waistcoat and a pair of snow-white spats.

While the antique dealers convened over the cups, Captain Deems carried his tea to the low wall that surrounded the yard and, with one foot on the wall, stared at the trees and cottages across the river. Fleetingly Holly thought that he would have made a perfect illustration for *Vigilance,* that if she had been a Tommy in the trenches she would have trusted this man's judgment implicitly and would have obeyed him to the letter.

Kennedy King put his arm about her shoulders. He smelled of motorcar oil and leather from his new driving gloves. He handed her a copy of the catalogue of the sale. Opening it, Holly found that every lot had a bracketed figure beside it.

"But I thought . . . ?" she began.

Mr. King patted her cheek lightly.

"I'm sure you don't mind helping us out, Holly. Your Mr. A. was always co-operative. Many's the time we submerged our interests for the common good. Remember, Simon?"

"Many's the time," said Simon Black.

"Do you want me to bid for *all* the lots."

"It's better than sitting there dozing, Holly. Besides, it's good experience."

"It'll get your name known," put in Emma. "Who's this, stealin' a march on us, like."

"But what if I *get* the lots?"

"We'll buy them back from you," said Simon Black.

"It's simple, Holly," said Emma. "Everybody an' his wife will be at this sale. They'll be workin' in cliques, same as us. Four of us bid for everythin'. Some articles we get cheap, some expensive . . ."

"But we run each other up," said Holly.

"Only ten per cent of the time," said Emma.

She had a thin nose and arched brows, dark hair beginning to grey above the forehead. When she spoke of business matters she became electrically animated.

King and Black were content to let Emma do the talking.

"You're interested in the job lots, Holly," Emma said. "But you ain't seen them."

"I . . . I thought I'd price on the spot."

"Simon an' me went up Friday, did some viewin'," said Emma. "How much do you have to spend, Holly?"

"One hundred an' twenty pounds."

"That's fair, very fair," said Black. "Spend your hundred and twenty pounds. Buy anything you like. It doesn't matter what. We get what we can at the prices we've marked. We take it all back by carrier to my warehouse . . ."

"And we each scoop out what we want most," said King.

"See?" Emma asked.

"You bid very highly at first . . ." said Holly.

"She's got the idea," said Emma.

". . . an' frighten off the casuals. As soon as they see you, Mr. King, an' you, Miss Chubb, in at it, they pull out."

"And we cut off the bidding there and then," said Black.

"And the lot falls to us."

"No point," said Emma Chubb, repeating the dealers' creed, "in cuttin' our own throats."

"Nor in letting stuff go out of London," said Black.

"Provincial dealers have no idea of values," said King.

"Here, Kennedy, it's after nine now," said Black. "Best push on."

While King paid the bill, Emma took Holly's arm and escorted her outside saying, in womanly confidence, "It's a fine way of earnin' your livin', Holly. Look at us, out here in the sunshine, drivin' in a handsome motorcar with three gentlemen. Ain't it fun, Holly?"

Holly was not bewildered by the technique, nor apprehensive about her part. What disturbed her was the ease with which she had been drawn into the dealers' circle.

"He's a fine man, y'know," said Emma. "Simon. If it wasn't for him, I'd be stuck behind a table somewheres – or workin' my legs off; know what I mean?"

Holly was glad to reach the car.

Already seated, the captain was looking out at a vee of the river visible between two massy chestnut trees. Courteously, he rose and held the door open for the ladies, then seated himself again and returned to contemplation of the Thames.

With the sugary gaiety she would have despised in another, Holly leaned across the rear seat of the Lanchester and addressed him. "What company were you with, Captain Deems?"

It took him a moment to click his attention on to her. "Several."

"Oh, I see. My brother was in the war."

She knew she was being a foolish prattler, but she wanted to evade Emma's intimacies. Taciturn though he was, the captain happened to be the only avenue of escape.

"Did he come through it?" the captain asked.

"Yes, he's been out about a week."

"How long have you been out, Captain Deems?" Emma asked.

"Not long."

"An' what are you bidding for today?" Holly persisted.

"Some of the books."

"Ah, yes," she chirruped. "You're in the book trade aren't you?"

The captain did not deny it; no more did he confirm it. Conversation hung limply between them. Even Emma did not feel inclined to haul it along. She frowned at the captain and said, in a statement that ended the bout; "You don't look at all like your uncle."

Thank God for that, thought Holly.

To her relief the motor spluttered to life and, with a feathery belch of smoke, started off on the last leg of the journey to Beaufort Grange.

* * *

Tal was waiting for Holly when she returned to Lambeth long after ten o'clock, from Beaufort Grange. He had kept a cold meat salad for her but she declined it, informing him that she had eaten dinner in an inn on the way home.

"Did you get much stuff, Holly?" Tal asked.

"I don't know yet." The girl explained that she had had knocked down to Aspinall's Antiques some fifty lots. "I was part of Kennedy King's 'ring', Grandpa. But, you know, all the dealers were at it. Kennedy was right; we had to do it for our own good."

"But you were cheating somebody, were you not?"

"The owners of Beaufort Grange, I suppose. It's hard to think of them as people. It wasn't as if there was a widow standing about the place. The auctioneers ran everythin' very smoothly. Anyhow, as I understand it, the sold items were the property of a gentleman, a very old gentleman. It's his nephews who'll benefit. They won't go short, I reckon."

"When will you receive your share of the purchases?"

"At the weekend, probably Saturday. Mr. Black an' his . . . and

Miss Chubb stayed over in Greesham to arrange a carrier."

"You came back alone with Mr. King?" Tal managed to sound disapproving.

"No, his nephew was there too; a captain recently discharged from the army. He . . . he didn't say much. He bought half a dozen lots of books, that was all."

"Is he in the book trade?"

"Well, Emma Chubb told me that he was a poet, but it seems he intends to open a bookshop in Shepherd Market. He's buying stock at present."

"What is his name?" said Tal. "If he is a poet, I may have heard of him?"

"Deems, Christopher Deems."

"One of the Oxford crowd," said Tal, nodding. "I have read some of his stuff in the magazines."

"Is he a good poet, Grandpa?"

"I'm no critic; yes, he seems to me to be worthwhile."

"I wonder how he lives," said Holly, to herself.

"Is he wounded or shell-shocked?"

"He gave no sign of it."

"Perhaps poets from Oxford are tougher than those from Cambridge," said Tal. "It went hard with 'sensitive' young men. I have read of some who are still in hospital for diseases of the nervous system."

"Captain Deems seemed all right," said Holly. "He was such a quiet bloke, though. Didn't hardly say a word, not even to his uncle."

"Did you enjoy yourself today, Holly, being with these fine Bond Street fellows?"

"Hm, I suppose I did," said Holly.

"What do they want with you?"

The young woman looked up at her grandfather. Though he had not spoken sharply, she sensed a certain asperity in his tone. "Kennedy King wants me to be his assistant."

Bear-like shoulders hunched, brows furrowed.

"Where? In the Arcade?"

"I think his idea is that I'd stay in Pimlico, run the shop – for him. He'd like to buy Aspinall's, I'm sure."

"Has he said as much?"

"More'r less."

"Don't you want Mr. King to be your employer?" asked Tal.

Holly shook her head. "I want it to be my shop. Besides . . ."

"What is it, my dear?"

"I have the feelin' that Mr. King wants me to be more than an assistant?"

Tal laughed. It was easier to deal with a situation when it was out in the open. He had not been sure that Holly was wise enough in the ways of the world to understand King's motives. Men like King and Black did not offer "helping hands" to girls like Holly out of kindness. But the patronage of a Bond Street dealer would be rewarding. How could he make his granddaughter see the dangers? It seemed that he had misjudged her. She was not so naive, after all.

"I don't think it's funny," said Holly.

"Oh, are you 'considering his offer'?"

"Don't be silly."

"This Emma Chubb, does she appear to be suffering?"

"I'm not like Emma Chubb," said Holly. "Without Simon Black she would never 'ave 'ad – have had – anythin' at all. Thanks to Mr. A. I've got a piece of a shop to call my own."

"But if that was taken away from you – what then?"

"Grandfather," said Holly, "are you suggestin' that I should become Kennedy King's mistress?"

"Of course not, my dear." Tal stifled another chuckle.

"What *is* so funny?"

"Your confusion, Holly. You are flattered by King's interest, are you not?"

"Well . . ."

"And at the same time indignant that he should consider you in that light."

"It's true," said Holly. "When I sit here in Lambeth an' think about it, it's true. It is a bit ridiculous, really."

"What would he offer you?"

"Grandfather, I'm beginnin' t' find this conversation offensive."

"It is not intended."

"He would offer me a good livin'."

"Security, too?"

"I think so: Black's arrangement with Emma Chubb guarantees her that."

"Would you make a contract with King?"

"Grandfather, for Heaven's sake, stop it."

"There are many reasons for considering his proposal, are there not? It would get you out of this dump for one thing. It would involve you in the profession that you love . . ."

Holly cut in. "I can't stand the man. He's old. He's fat, an' he's . . . yeeeeeh."

"And you are in love with somebody else?"

"I'm not in love with anyone."

"But you would like to be. No?"

"If you mean David . . ."

She was blushing furiously. She was also becoming angry. Briskly Tal steered the conversation away from such sacred topics as love.

He said, "What did you have for dinner?"

"Fish," Holly stated. "Trout."

"And for pudding?"

"Strawberries an' cream."

"And real coffee?"

"An' real coffee, yer."

"I think I *will* eat your salad, if you have no room for it."

"Please do," Holly said. "An' while you're stuffin' yourself, tell me how it went today in the shop?"

"I sold the smoking chair with the spittoon attached."

"That hideous thing," said Holly. "We're well rid of it."

"The customer was delighted. He paid five pounds cheerfully. Collected it too. He also took the footstool and the decanters. I think it was the beginning of a bachelor room for a demobilised soldier."

"Well, it's all profit; an' I'm glad that stuff makes somebody happy."

"Your friend Miss Andrea also came to have a look at me."

"What did she say?"

"Oufff, she did not *speak* to me; there's no blue moon tonight. She leaned over the iron stairs and stared at me. I wished her a good morning, but she just stared, like I was a kangaroo in the zoo at Whipsnade."

"Or a Russian bear."

"Maybe that," agreed Tal, chuckling. "I disconcert her even more than you do, Holly."

"It's because you're so . . ."

"Jewish?"

"I was goin' t' say Russian."

"You were going to say Jewish. And it is true. It must offend her greatly to see me sitting in her father's place at the desk."

"Do you mind, grandpa?"

"I enjoy it," said Tal. "Now, I think I'll scoff that salad."

"Sit still," said Holly. "I'll fetch it. In Lambeth, you're not an employee, just my venerable old *Jewish* grandfather — and I must show you respect."

"In that case, *bubeleh,* you may also make me tea," Tal said and, with a contented sigh, sat back in his chair.

He was relieved to have talked with the girl, to learn that her ambition had limit. He would not have to worry about Holly. She was sensible and moral, in a peculiarly old-fashioned mixture. When it came to picking a husband, she would make the right choice.

In the meantime, she would let no man make her his property.

"Oil or vinegar?" Holly called from the scullery.

"Vinegar," said Tal.

* * *

"Feh! What a mess!" Tilly Erbach exclaimed.

"You are meanin' me?" asked her husband.

"I am meanin' the throne, stupid man." Tilly flicked a fringe of orange hair from her forehead with the back of her hand, winked at Holly, and added, "You, Mendel Erbach, are past repair."

Tilly was large limbed, not fat but plump. Her figure was enveloped now in a voluminous canvas apron whorled with varnish, freckled with sawdust and spangled with dried black paint. Bare forearms, even her cheeks, were stained with similar substances and pearls of paraffin wax clung to her improbable hair. Though rather comical in appearance, Tilly was a craftswoman of the highest order. In manual skill she was the equal of her big slow-moving husband, Mendel. Between them the pair could muster expertise in a multitude of arts. The board outside their workshop in Sayer Street, off the Waterloo Road, declared the Erbachs to be "Renovators of Fine and Antique Furniture"; that was less than half the story.

The article now receiving Mendel's particular attention was a commode that had been "ravaged" – Tilly's word – by the application of several layers of thick black paint. Part of the top and both doors had been stripped. The quality of the original rich walnut showed through now.

"I can't understand why folks do it, Tilly," said Holly, brushing the wood with her fingertips. "Coverin' up grainin' with hideous paint."

Assiduously Tilly enlarged the little patch of walnut on the topside surface with a fragment of glass. "Fashion an' style, it is. Ebony was all the rage in the 1830s in France. Those French! Louis-Phillipe started it. The crowd followed on. Black furniture! Feh!"

"Not everybody could afford ebony."

"That is true," said Mendel, still kneeling, his back to the women, his nose almost brushing the columnar section of wood between the doors. "But there is this to be said for the thing, they used such a good quality paint, like enamel, that the walnut was sealed and stayed unmarked. Hardly a blemish will you find on this piece, Holly, I guarantee."

"Unless my husband's hand slips," Tilly added.

Holly had not watched the Erbachs at work before. She was intrigued to see that the instrument used by both husband and wife was nothing but a crescent of plain glass sawn from a bottle. Tilly informed her that a cabinetmaker's scraper would soon become too clogged to be effective, its broad edge incapable of grooving out carved sections. Fine blades bent too much to give necessary purchase and more brittle tools had no "feeling". A piece of glass was ideal – in the hands of a skilled craftsman.

"Did you expect us to have your commode all stripped an' polished for you?" asked Mendel.

"Lord, no," said Holly. "But I have a buyer for it, if it's good enough in quality. What d'you think?"

"Sure, it's good," said Tilly. "Uh, husband?"

"Sure, sure."

"Take us another week," said Tilly. "Sorry, Holly, but we got other things to do, you know how it is."

"A week's not long," said Holly.

With forefinger and thumb, Mendel found a corner of the sombre paint, softened by white spirit application. He lifted a worm of paint away, clipped it cleanly from the underlying surface with the glass, and held it up. He looked round at Holly. "How is your grandpapa?"

"He's well."

"Good for him to work in the shop." Tilly nodded approval.

"Fine craftsman," said Mendel.

"Did he really once work for Ivan Sechenov in St. Petersburg?" Holly asked. "He used t' tell me when I was a little child that he made a miniature coach for the Tzar himself."

"I would not be surprised," said Tilly.

"I can't understand why he gave it up," said Holly. "I mean, why didn't he find that kind of work when he came to England?"

"You cannot understand how it was in London forty years ago; for Russians, for Jews, people like us," said Tilly. "It is as well you do not know, Holly. You took what you could find to feed you an' your family an' you thanked the Good God for it. You lost your ambition quick."

"But in goldsmithin' . . . ?" said Holly.

"Too many Jews, already," said Tilly. "Big man like your grandpapa, he don't *look* like a good craftsman." She wiggled her stained fingers. "Nobody willin' to believe it."

"Heh, you ever seen a Sechenov miniature?" Mendel asked.

"Only pictures. Grandfather has pictures."

"He never show you the carriage?"

"What carriage."

"He got a little gold carriage," said Mendel. "A Sechenov."

"Never," Holly exclaimed.

"Used to have," said Tilly. "I saw it once when my papa was alive an' Tal used to come 'round our house Fridays. He brought it once to show us. Little thing, so big."

"Not real Sechenov," said Mendel.

"How do you know, Mr. Stupid?" said Tilly.

"He made it to a design; only an apprentice work."

"Ach, but such workmanship," said Tilly.

"He never showed it to me," said Holly.

"Maybe he sold it," said Mendel. "You cannot eat filigree gold."

"Yer, I expect he sold it," said Tilly.

Mendel wiped his fingers on a rag and stooped again to his task. Tilly was restless; Holly could tell that she, too, wanted to be back at the patient chore of releasing the commode from its prison of thick black paint.

Holly said, "Well, I think that should come up fine. I'll tell my customer he can expect it in ten days. Mendel, will you bring it round to the shop when it's finished?"

"Sure, sure."

Tilly escorted Holly to the door in the huge wooden gate that opened on to the yard, a narrow coffin-shaped space surrounded by high brick walls, crammed with tiny tarpaulin tents and makeshift sheds in which, in summer, Mendel arranged his special woods to air and mature. Above the yard was a piece of blue sky out of which, foreshortened and leaning strangely, a tall chimney craned. There was no hint of greenery, except for clumps of moss growing in cracks of the wall and one ambitious spray of laburnum that peeked over from a garden to the left. Tilly wiped away an errant orange hair and glanced up at the sky as if speculating on what rich grains lay beneath its pale blue enamelling, what would be revealed if she could only get at it with her glass scraper.

"How is Ruth?" Holly asked.

"Ruth?" said Tilly. "Ruth is very well."

"How old is she now?"

"Sixteen."

"She'll be leavin' school soon."

"We keep her there for another year. We pay for it, Holly.

But . . . well, it is right she should have an education."

Ruth was the Erbachs' only child, a dark-haired, dark-eyed beauty that Holly had met only a half a dozen times. The Erbachs doted on her, and protected her over much – according to Tal – out of fear that something unpleasant would happen to her. "A cut finger," Tal had said, "would be a great tragedy, even. They treat that poor child as if she was made of glass. It is not right."

Certainly Ruth showed signs of a sheltered upbringing. She was reticent in company to the point of rudeness, and the strict all-girls day school that she had attended since the age of six had not helped to bring her out of herself.

"Isn't she on holiday just now?" Holly asked.

"Yer, we have her here with us."

"Oh, where?" said Holly.

"Upstairs. She likes to read. She is a great book-reader. I tell her it strain her eyes to read so much but Mendel he says her mind is better for it and her young eyes will come to no harm. That's what she likes to do, Holly. She likes to stay home an' read these books."

The Erbachs' house was built on top of the workshop; an odd place, like a hutment with a wooden staircase leading up from the tiny cul-de-sac of the Sayer Street stables, in the depths of which, amid more timber and other materials, the Erbachs' pony, Aaron, lived in semi-darkness, his fat well-fed little body packed comfortably into a stall. The house seemed to have grown by a process of accretion. Half-brick extensions were topped off by brightly painted wood set with circular windows. Holly had often thought that it should have been perched on a cliff overlooking the sea; a quaint, dainty eccentric retreat. But on the banks of the busy Waterloo Road it seemed out of place. Tilly had little time to spare for domestic routine, and Ruth was far too precious to be relegated to cook and dish-washer.

"Perhaps Mendel will bring her round with him when he delivers the commode," said Holly.

Tilly blinked. "What for, on earth?"

"An . . . well, an outin' . . . to see the shop, talk to Grandpa Tal, maybe. We might even allow her to serve a customer, if we have one."

"Our Ruth is nobody's shop servant," Tilly snapped. "Anyhow, she doesn't get to ride on the cart. It's not the right place for a girl of her class."

At a loss, Holly covered her gaffe as decently as possible, and made her goodbye. Tilly did not accompany her across the yard; Holly departed with the feeling of coldness, almost of hostility. She would not mention Ruth again. She liked the Erbachs, but was disturbed by that massive blemish, the Achilles heel in their friendliness – their cherished daughter, Ruth, locked away from contact with the rough world.

As she turned the corner out of the lane and cut across Sayer Street, Holly looked over her shoulder at the gable of the Erbachs' weird house, projecting outward from a blank brick wall. A single circular window stared at the wall opposite. In that window, like the face in a faded cameo, was Ruth.

Holly waved.

But little Ruth Erbach did not wave back, even though she recognised Ritchie's sister.

* * *

The war years had seen a serious slump in the buying and selling of antiques and art objects. The occupation seemed frivolous and unpatriotic while Europe tore itself apart. Money had been needed for more important things than the preservation of relics of former periods in history. In most of the towns and cities up and down the length of Great Britain shutters went up, in some cases permanently, as the fat pickings of the pre-war years dwindled and were finally gone, leaving in trade only dealers who were affluent, stubborn or particularly astute. James Aspinall, of course, had fallen into the latter category. He had often predicted that a boom would follow in the wake of war and had shaped his business accordingly, aiming "to remain on his feet" and reap benefits when the time came. With hostilities now ended and Victory celebrated with due pomp and ceremony, the increase of interest in "frivolous" subjects became overwhelming. Holly had not been the only young dealer to benefit from a degree of foresight, from an inspirational "flash" of what the future held. From the civilised pockets of Europe that had remained almost untouched by war and from the United States of America, enquiries and requests for fine English paintings, furniture, silver and gold wares, pottery, porcelain, tapestries and all the myriad objects of interest and beauty that people enjoyed, came in a flood. Combined with a dramatic rise in home sales, members of the trade were stirred to blithesome belief that they could sell anything. This heady thought led the avaricious and incompetent to swift disaster, but for conscientious dealers the new era lived up to its promise.

Towards the end of 1918, the British Antique Dealers Association had been formed. Its purpose was to safeguard both buyers and sellers of genuine antiques against the unscrupulous tricksters and charlatans that muddied the waters of trade by the introduction of cheap reproductions and outright forgeries. Though not yet a member of the Association, Holly was well aware of the developments that were taking place in her profession, and heartily approved of them. She was constantly on guard against "being took" by fakers and their products.

The shop was ticking over nicely, however. Grandpa Tal did not seem to mind the long hours spent there in Holly's absence, and got on well with Wilf Ackers, the gangling half-daft fifteen year old whom Holly employed to take care of the heavy labours of the shop. Wilf and his kind were a drug on the labour market. One of a family of fourteen, the boy could neither read nor write. He was a cheerful cove, though, and willing. He would do exactly what was asked of him and acquired the few necessary skills of his job by mimicry. Tal was patient with the lad, taught him how to tie knots, wrap china and how best to lift and lug heavy packages so that he would not injure himself. Wilf was not awkward, in spite of his lack of intelligence. In spare moments, he would apply himself to the stock with a duster, handling the fragile objects of glass and china as gently as Holly did. Unfortunately, he did not have it in him to learn the trade; he perceived the items as entirely functional.

"What d'you think of this then, Wilf?" Tal would ask him, offering a chased silver sauceboat for the boy's inspection.

Wilf would frown, hold the object carefully in the palms of his hands like a true expert, then brightly declare, "Big enough for me whole famb'ly, ain't it?"

Shown a fine Bristol plate depicting a pigtailed Chinese figure in a garden, he studied it long and hard, nodding sagely. "Me sister's gotter hair done like that."

Tal would sigh and go back to the knots.

Wilf cost little enough. Tal was paid the going rate, less than he had made on the docks, but quite sufficient for his needs. Though money was not discussed between them, Tal understood Holly's position; she did not dare pay him well. As far as the Aspinalls were concerned, it was bad enough that she had brought in a relative to be her shop servant without she should skim profits by paying him a decent wage. It was like one of the old music-hall jokes, the pointless ones: "I know that you know that I know that you daren't pay me any more; and you know that I know that you know that I don't mind."

Nonetheless Tal was delighted to be close to Holly at that period in her life, to watch over her without interfering. If she asked his advice, he gave it; otherwise, he held his tongue. His knowledge of the antique trade was limited, though he had once known much about metals and precious stones.

It was no fairytale; as a very young man he had served three years of an apprenticeship in the St. Petersburg workshops of Sechenov's goldsmiths. He had even seen Sechenov in the flesh once or twice. He could not recall now what the artist looked like, only that he spoke in a clipped and imperious manner and strolled through the workshop like a prince of the blood. Like the other apprentices, Tal had kept his head down over his bench and had pretended to be deeply absorbed in buffing down the pure silver wire that would, eventually, be transformed into the icing on one of the smith's exquisite confections. Because there was pride, though, and already a heritage among the workers, he had been given his apprentice work to keep – being docked a portion of his wage for a year to cover the cost of the materials. It was a crude trinket compared with the filigree jewels that were produced but it bore, for posterity, a tiny base plaque that stated, in Russian – *From the workshop of Ivan Sechenov, St. P's burg, 1858*. Tal had clung to it through every hardship, resisting every temptation to sell it. Now it was hidden at home, in the very place where he had secreted it before Holly's birth. Even in private he did not dare bring it out, for fear that Leo, or Ritchie, would thieve it. One day, when he found an opportunity, he might show it to Holly. He was afraid of her opinion of it, though, ashamed to admit that he had made this inferior object, even if it was fashioned from valuable materials under the tutelage of such a famous man. When he died, Tal promised himself that Holly would inherit the jewel. It was about all he had to leave her. He could be sure that it would be treasured by his granddaughter, and would stay with the family, at least as a curio. Maury would benefit from his demise by the sum of twenty pounds; it was already set aside. God knows, in a year or three Maury would hardly need the cash; he would probably be lighting his cigars with banknotes by then, if he didn't kill himself with overwork in the interim.

Tal's ability to cope with the run of customers in the shop meant that Holly was free to attend sales. Hence her trip to Drayman's End in Hertfordshire. It was a run-of-the-mill house sale, but such events were productive of modest lots that helped build the shop's resources.

From the Beaufort Grange sale – after the "carve up" – Aspinall's Antiques had done rather well. Simon and Kennedy had been generous. Holly had been given her choice of all the odds for a few pounds' payment, plus a very fine oak sideboard with carved boxwood panels that she thought she might sell to a Mr. Clarence of Edinburgh. That gentleman, a dealer, had asked her by letter to scout for late Victorian furniture; the sideboard in question was an authenticated piece that had been exhibited in the famous London Exhibition of 1873. Black and King had "let it go" to Holly for forty pounds, ten pounds less than the auction price. To make up, they had charged her, with her agreement, a little above knock-down price for a Pembroke table and a *bergère* cane-backed armchair. Mr. Clarence had taken the sideboard and paid a hundred and ten for it. She had sold the chair and table within a week of their arrival in the shop. Pretty pieces like that were always in demand. Simon and Kennedy had expressed themselves delighted with her participation. They had indicated that they would "incorporate" her into the travelling party next time there was a sale of note within range of London. Emma Chubb had winked, and added, "Or before, Holly, love, or before."

The sale at Drayman's End was not grand enough to attract the Bond Street brigade. Besides, no list had been issued. Holly had discovered it only by diligent scanning of local newspapers. She could imagine the scene — household articles being grabbed by greedy sale vultures, the good stuff going in a haze of resentment from the locals to the few genuine dealers who had turned up. It was hardly likely to be another "jolly jaunt", only a dreary trip that might yield up useful items of stock – if she was lucky.

Lately she had begun to re-establish contact with several private clients culled from Mr. A.'s book. She had waited until after Christmas before going through the book, memorising requirements and, whenever she could, picking up something particularly choice. In the guise of an offer, price kept low, she introduced herself to the customer and begged the favour of continued interest in purchases from Aspinall's. Nobody let her down; nobody except a Rippon parson who, she was formally told, was dead and buried and had no further use for copper and brass objects, thank you. Generally the clientele remained faithful. One or two even took the trouble to offer expressions of regret at Mr. Aspinall's death, and to assure her of their continued custom.

Holly had Tal compile an indexed file of customers' special requirements; this, with the original book, was kept securely in the safe that she'd bought, very cheaply, at a sale in Hounslow in March.

First off the train Holly walked briskly to the barrier, a slim, straight figure in grey coat and skirt. Though Drayman's End was not far from the station, Holly took a cab, one of the old horse-drawn variety that were still to be found this distance outside the city.

Anticipating that she would buy something, she made an arrangement with the cabby to return for her and to wait outside the house.

Drayman's End was a tight, perpendicular place set in an acre of untended garden. Once inside Holly wended her way through the crowd in the main hall and entered the dining room. She was relieved that few of the principal London dealers had decided to make the trip. Between dining room and drawing room were over a hundred ticketed lots, more set out in the library and in the hall. She did not like this peripatetic type of sale where buyers trailed the auctioneer from room to room; it was a casual way of doing it, typical of provincial firms who did not carry a large staff of porters.

Holly was thorough in her inspection of the lots that interested her, confident in making judgment of prices. She even had time to inspect the furniture. One dealer's features were familiar, Mr. Amiss from Puttick & Simpson's. He would be after the *famille verte* vase for sure, possibly the bracket clock, an eighteenth-century reproduction of one given by Henry VIII to Anne Boleyn on their wedding day. They were fine pieces, quite out of place here; heirlooms, Holly suspected. She would not be able to afford to compete against Mr. Amiss. Someday, someday soon perhaps, she would be able to bid for such fine works.

Holly completed her circuit of the rooms. Tables, chests and cases served as display counters for smaller pieces; Bristol and Worcester flowerholders and figurines, some not-too-good Wedgwood and Waterford glass, Victorian brass kettle, candlesticks, jelly pan, china, and a wicker basket classified as a single job lot. Holly marked a generous figure against it. She poked about among the contents and found that they included a large Sheffield Plate cruet, an ormolu clock, a knife box, tea-caddy, two framed pictures in muddy watercolours and a dozen or so books that had somehow escaped the library. Though the cruet was too large for modern tables, it was a piece that she could "move" quickly and would fit into the next catalogue. On separate tables, in the hall, were three full tea services, an early Coalport, and two good imitation Dresden attractively painted with flower sprays. She marked prices against the Dresden tea services, and also against a box of Victorian toys that lay partly hidden beneath the hall table.

Signs of activity indicated that the sale was about to begin. Holly made her way into the dining room where Lot No. 1 reposed. The locals were out in force. Some, perhaps, were acquaintances of the deceased; more likely, just nosey folk who had belatedly seized the opportunity to pry into Drayman's End. There were an uncommon number of women present, women in smart frocks and jackets, wearing shoes with dainty raised heels. Holly felt something of an antique herself. Moving to a position along the wall where she could catch the auctioneer's eye without too much fuss, she stumbled over long legs. She surveyed the woman in surprise. When had this metamorphosis taken place? She realised with a thrill that it was happening right now: 1919 was a post-war, emancipated woman's world, for sure. Changes in fashion and taste, in acceptability, invariably showed first among the moneyed classes. She glanced along the row of dining chairs. They were all occupied by women, their men standing attendance behind. Legs elegantly, daringly, crossed, one woman was a vision in fern-green marino. A loose necktie of saffron silk about her neck matched the under-lining of her fine straw hat. Holly had thought herself no end of a toff in her new clothes, but she had bought wisely, not daringly.

"Sold, to Mr. Bentley."

Holly pulled herself together.

"Lot the second, ladeez un' genulmen." Holed over by the window bay a porter held the lot aloft: a porcelain vase. "Persian manoofactur, copied in flawlez detail frum an orig'nal deezign of the . . . ah, the Kang Hsi die-nasty."

"A tenner."

"I have ten pound."

"Twelve pound."

"I have twelve."

Private buyer, aggressive and anxious; he jerked his catalogue as if it were a shotgun and, with every bid, drew a bead on the precious vase. Mr. Amiss was after the thing for Puttick & Simpson's, but the private buyer obviously meant to have it, whatever price he had to pay. Out of sheer devilment, Mr. Amiss ran the chap up, and up, and up. Holly would never have dared do such a thing in case she got stuck with the lot at an exorbitant price. Mr. Amiss, however, knew the ropes. He pulled out just as the private buyer was beginning to glow with fury and desperation, and left the "genulman" to fork out two hundred and thirty pounds for his Persian pot, a fantastic sum.

In due course the dining room was cleared and the auctioneer, his clerk and three porters carved a route through the buyers into the drawing room. Jostling and elbowing, the herd followed. The proceedings were conducted at fair speed. The auctioneer announced that there would be no break for luncheon, if that suited everybody, which it did. An hour later, with the drawing room cleared, the company assembled in the hall and the dozen lots there fell under the hammer. Holly acquired the wicker basket for nineteen shillings, the Victorian toys for ten. Mr. Amiss bid high on the Coalport tea service and got the first of the Dresden. With a wink, he pulled out of the bidding for the second and relinquished it to Holly at a reasonable sum. She had already picked up porcelain and china on the limit of her bidding, and congratulated herself that she had done very well.

It was in her mind not to bother with the final part of the sale, the library. In addition to a hundred and five lots of books, however, nine Globe bookcases were being knocked down too; bookcases were always good sellers. If she did happen to get one or more, she would have to find a carrier. She had intended to have a porter pack her purchases into a single large tea-chest, load it on to the horse cab, and "porter" it back to Left Luggage in Waterloo. It was cheaper than using a carrier for the whole trip. She would tip the porters down the line in advance to ensure that they weren't careless. But if she *did* manage to acquire a bookcase . . .

Close on the auctioneer's heels, she went into the library. Captain Deems was already in position, leaning against an empty case. Books had been spread out in various lots on two tables and along the box-seat of the window, from which stance the auctioneer elected to do the selling. Not many "casual" local buyers waited. It was after two o'clock and luncheon had more appeal than fusty old books.

Deems looked at home there. No, thought Holly, revising her first impression, not so much at home as at ease. He might have been left over as part of the household effects. He wore a tweed hacking jacket and light duck trousers. He looked lean, almost haggard, without softness. He had a classic profile, finely marked brows and lips. A heavy wave of blond hair hung over his forehead. His expression was diffident, private, exactly, she thought, as it had been during the jaunt to Beaufort Grange. There was no scar or mark on him, though he was man enough to have borne one with a touch of arrogance. He carried no catalogue but had, instead, a stiff-backed account book, tall as a ruler, which he consulted from time to time. Holly knew better than to disturb him. He was obviously intent upon bidding and, as far as Holly could make out, had a clear field.

As the auctioneer took his place, the captain turned away from Holly. It was not a deliberate act of rejection; he had not noticed her. He faced the window bay, left elbow resting on the little shelf of a bookcase, notebook held open with his thumb. His bidding technique was unostentatious. In a packed London saleroom he would have to be more assertive, Holly thought, recalling her one and only atten-

dance at an "All Book" sale and the furious cut-and-thrust of the
dealers. The captain's bids were not seriously challenged however.
Of the sixty-four lots on which he recorded bids, fifty were knocked
down to him in fairly short order. He bought, too, four of the
handsome Globe cases, letting the others go to a dour little Scotsman
who was on a buying trip from Glasgow. Holly did not even try for
one. Even before the tail-end lots came up, the room had emptied to a
mere dozen folk. Though she was hungry and thirsty and a little
fatigued with the strain of concentration, Holly did not leave.

"Mr. Deems, Shepherd Market; un'z agin," said the auctioneer,
knocking down the last lot with the ebony stick he used for a hammer.
"Muzt like readin', Mr. Deems."

"Very fond of it, sir," murmured the captain, as he went forward to
present his card and collect his invoices.

"You did well today, Captain Deems," Holly said.

Without surprise, he looked round at her. "Miss Beckman, isn't it?"

"That's right."

"Is my uncle here?"

"No, why should he be?"

Deems shrugged. He took the invoice from the clerk, consulted it,
signed a cheque, and returned both to the clerk.

"I'm not . . . I don't work for your uncle."

"I've been under a misapprehension," Deems said.

"Doesn't my uncle own Aspinall's?"

"I own Aspinall's," said Holly. "At least, a quarter share of it."

"I see; a young lady of substance."

"Have you opened your bookshop?"

"Yes, a couple of weeks ago," said Deems. "It isn't very grand, you
know."

"But it is your own."

"All my own."

"Well, I'd best sort out my lots and have them taken to the cab."

"Why don't you send them along with mine," said Deems. "I've a
carrier calling in an hour. You didn't purchase anything very heavy,
did you?"

"No, but . . ."

"You can pick your stuff up from my shop. Shepherd Market's
quite close to Pimlico."

"It's kind of you to offer. I'll admit it would be easier than man-
handling the stuff from here."

"Very well, give me the lot numbers and I'll arrange it."

Holly hesitated. She appreciated Christopher Deems' kindness and, if she had known him better, would have accepted with alacrity. But she did not wish him to think that she was in need of charity or even of help. The man disconcerted her by his civility.

"Right-o," Holly said, rather nervously, "but only if you'll allow me to take you to lunch."

"That seems like a fair exchange," Deems said.

They ate lunch in a restaurant close to the railway station. The food was fresh and wholesome and Holly, though faintly aware that it was unladylike to display a healthy appetite, could not resist tucking into soup, kidney pie and golden pudding.

The captain contented himself with a mushroom omelette. When the meal was over the couple made their way across the road to the station and waited on the platform for the London train. It was a cool, cloudy afternoon, fields and trees heavy, green and moist.

Out of doors, Christopher Deems looked paler and even more haggard. Holly studied him from the corner of her eye. She had never encountered a man so totally self-contained. In conversation, such as it was, he gave little of himself away. Again Holly found herself unnaturally bright and garrulous, driving on the talk as she might have driven a reluctant pony. It was not that the captain was edgy with her – but there was a rigidity in him that seemed almost unbreachable. Jaw clenched, hands clenched, lips compressed; she wondered if this was some manifestation of shell-shock. She had always supposed that nervous ailment to be a loud and obvious affliction, with twitchings and terrible tremblings, shoutings and outbursts of temper. None of these signs were evident in the captain, only an unyielding tautness. It was, she decided, like a kind of shyness, magnified. For all that he was not shy and, when she led him to it, answered her questions politely.

She saved up her curiosity for the train ride.

"My grandfather says you're a poet, Captain Deems."

"Now," Christopher Deems answered, "I'm a bookseller."

"I think you're puttin' me off with that answer."

"I did write poetry – once upon a time."

"I didn't know that writin' poetry was somethin' you could stop doin' that easily."

They were alone in the compartment, the train travelling at no great pace through the leafy tunnels of the English countryside, stopping frequently at rural halts. It would join a main line soon and would be in London in an hour. A faint flittering sunshine patched the shrubs and penetrated the carriage window.

Deems said, "You make it sound as if poetry is akin to alcoholism, Miss Beckman." He paused. "Do you mind if I smoke?"

"Not in the least." Holly hesitated; had he tried to cut off the questions, tie a knot in the conversation? Perhaps he was merely being modest, or was wary of ill-informed interrogation. She had never met a poet before; never met any kind of creative person – except craftsmen. She decided to persist. "When did you start writin', Captain Deems?"

"When I was too young to know any better," Deems said. "I think that you should call me Christopher. I'm really not fond of the rank thing. Not that proud of it."

"Will you call me Holly, then?"

"With pleasure," Deems said. "It's a pretty name, you know."

"My mother's choice. My grandfather, he'd have had me saddled with Rachael or Evie."

Deems phrased the question so that it provoked no offence. "Your grandfather is Jewish?"

"He's a Russian Jew," said Holly. "But my father: well, let's say the rest of the family are not. In fact, we're a Godless lot, not anythin' at all."

"Holly," Deems said. "It suits you."

"If . . . if I was Jewish, would it matter?"

"Why should it matter?" Deems said.

"I dunno. It does to some people."

"I've no prejudices of that sort."

Holly said, "How long were you at the Front, Christopher?"

"A long, long time," he replied, curtly, fists clenching.

Holly retreated: no talk about poetry, no talk about the war. The war: what else, thought Holly morosely. The truth was beginning to emerge, in little dribs and drabs, in articles and stories about the varieties of hell that fighting men had endured. Each man on his own Golgotha; the wounded psyche, slower to heal than the body. She had read that, been intrigued by the statement, had half-grasped it.

Christopher Deems bore no obvious grudges, unless reluctance to talk about his experiences with a chattering semi-stranger counted as "queer" behaviour.

Desultorily, Holly brought the conversation round to softer areas, the antique trade, the book business. Soon, she found that she was talking animatedly about herself. Instinct informed her that the flow of words soothed the man. When she talked of herself, he listened, not raptly, but intelligently. Only once or twice during the rest of the journey did he withdraw from her, become shuttered and curt as if to mark out the limits of the territory that enclosed them. She learned that he had never got on well with his uncle Kennedy King, and did not particularly admire the man. King's sister-in-law was Christopher's mother. She lived "out of London", quietly. Christopher had gone to Oxford, but had left to join up before taking his finals. Beyond that, Christopher was niggardly with personal information. Physically, he was attractive. More important, Holly felt sure that his opinions would be fascinating and unconventional. But he would not part with them. So Holly talked, revealing herself to the silent, attentive captain as she had revealed herself to few others.

Only when the train was grinding down to navigate the maze of points and lines that fed into Victoria, did he give away something of himself. As the platform skimmed into view, Christopher said, "I had forgotten what enthusiasm was, Holly. I think – yes, I think I once felt about poetry as you feel about antiques." He smiled bleakly, wistfully, as he reached past her to lower the window and open the door. "I hope it's never taken from you."

"Was it taken from you, Christopher?"

"I let it go."

"Perhaps it'll come back, now the war's . . ."

"No," he snapped, then, added in lower key, "I don't want it back. I don't ever want it back. Now – when will you collect your lots?"

"As soon as you let me know they've arrived."

"I'll telephone the shop."

"That's fine, Christopher," Holly said.

Curtly, he left her on the far side of the ticket barrier, saying that he had business nearby.

Holly watched him stride off into the crowd.

Christopher Deems was not like any other man she had ever met. She was not used to thinking of herself in relation to men. Apart from David she had forged no dreams for herself and lacked the burning vanity so common in girls of her age and class, that instant seizing upon and sizing up of "eligible" males, a testing of their own attractiveness. Her physical and emotional longings, her yearnings were kept in strict check; she saw in them a kind of weakness that made her less independent. It was not that she lacked warmth; she was afraid of the area where friendship waxed into need. She told herself that she did not *need* David. But that was a lie, or, at best, a half-truth.

As she headed out of the station into the late August dusk it was the captain who stayed in her thoughts, supplanting all the small busy details of shopkeeping that Holly had learned to use as a buffer against emotions that she did not understand or could not properly control.

Christopher Deems was different, so different. She was puzzled by him and, she had to confess, intrigued. There were depths to him that seemed impenetrable and dark; the sadness in him made her feel, for a moment, heart-breaking pity. He was, she felt, a man in retreat from life and she, by instinct, experienced the dreadful loneliness that marked him.

She had read an article once about famous Chinese philosophers, one of whom declared that impressions, when first received, are blanks; only when a person's breath touches them do they take on positive characteristics.

Captain Deems' breath, Holly suspected, would bring only sorrow.

For all that, and for no explicable reason, she hoped that they would meet again soon.

3

Dinner at the Connaught

SPRING AND SUMMER had come and gone. Now autumn tinted the streets of London. West of Chelsea the sky dulled to copper as dusk crept from the Pool. The sun extinguished itself softly, like an ember slipping into the Thames. Relief from the travails of war had turned, in some, to a frantic search for pleasure. Among rich and poor alike there was a feverish determination to look out for number one, not to be caught napping, not to be weak.

Holly was not totally immune to the contamination of the times. Her situation called for a degree of selfishness, a stilling of conscience and, prompted by her ambition, Holly subtly altered her attitudes, telling herself that rigorous honesty was gauche and that she could not hope to compete in trade if she did not do as the Romans did. She had always been aware that Leo and Ritchie received more admiration in Lambeth than Tal or Maury by building their miniscule reputations through qualities that she considered less than admirable. She did not want to be like them. On the contrary. Even so, her bright and shining scruples became a little tarnished during the course of the summer; she readily accepted Kennedy King's invitations to drive out in the Lanchester to country-house sales where the pickings might prove rewarding.

Holly fell in with the dealers' arrangements and profited by the association with King, Black and Miss Emma Chubb. She could see sense in manipulating the bidding as much as possible. Everybody was at it, even a group of the hangers-on, five disreputable stall-owners from the East End, who scooped up anything that could be had cheaply and actually threatened their down-wind competitors with reprisals for daring to cross them.

Holly had developed sufficient self-confidence to rebuke Emma for her suggestions that she should "play up a bit" to Kennedy. Holly did not dislike King but matchmaking seemed sleazy and sly and her direct responses to it were undoubtedly relayed by Emma to King who, happily, made no more covert advances. Though Holly would not have dreamed of embarking on a liaison with Kennedy King, she had developed enough awareness of the world King inhabited to realise that no insult was intended to her. On the contrary, King genuinely liked her and should not be condemned simply for that. Holly no longer denied to herself, out of false modesty, that she was attractive, particularly when she wore smart new clothes and took time to put on cosmetics and do her hair. She was better looking, by a long chalk, than Emma – and very much younger too. About this time, it occurred to her that she might set about impressing David by making herself as attractive as possible.

Shop turnover had stabilised. Profits were good.

Summer saw an influx of wealthy visitors to London and the return of emigrants who had evaded the war by slipping off to neutral territories across the seas. Re-establishing themselves in England, the latter class of person required household furnishings in quantity. When she could, Holly bought mirrors and screens, little tables and desks and other small articles of quality that would appeal to such people.

Soldiers of humbler means were also trailing back to Blighty to take up the labour of home-making. Holly caught only a corner of the caviare trade but a substantial part of local secondhand trade came her way. She sold many articles that could hardly be classed as antiques at all – clocks that kept time, copper pans and kettles, beds, stools, functional tables and chairs, tea services with a few cracked cups or plates missing. Sadly, this sort of dealing was a two-way traffic. For every husband who bought a little feathering for his nest, there was another compelled to sell domestic possessions to feed himself and his family.

Too many men were chasing too few jobs.

The railway strike had its effect. Food became difficult to get. All shops suffered, including Aspinall's. It was a relief when the strike was settled on October 5th, and some sort of order was restored.

With Tilly and Mendel Erbach behind her, Holly was not slow to purchase "hybrid" pieces, small items of furniture whose original woods or shapes had been altered by thoughtless owners. The Erbachs were marvellous restorers, worth every penny of the prices they charged. Beautiful little items – carefully labelled "restored by experts" – added tone to the Cardwell Place shop, and lured one or two aristocrats in to browse and buy. Lady Asterley, the Duchess of Moncrieff, and the Honourable George Groves, well-known collectors, all "dropped in" and made purchases. They were slow payers, however, and Holly's delight at having such high-toned clients was tempered by caution. One suave young gentleman, in duds that marked him as a major in the Greys, bought twenty-four poundsworth of goods – thank God that was *all* he bought – and paid by a banker's cheque that turned out to be made of rubber. The major was no major at all, so a weary detective constable informed Holly; the name on the cheque, together with all his credentials, were false. A trail of such cheques stretched right across London. Aspinall's name went down on the illustrious list, but Holly heard no more of the forger from the police, and wrote off the twenty-four pounds as a bad debt.

Ritchie, too, was "at it". Just what her brother was at, Holly could not be sure. He made no more approaches to her, though she was careful not to buy articles that might have been thieved. She dropped a hint to Grandpa Tal who, nodding, indicated that he understood the situation. At home Holly spent little time in the company of Leo or Ritchie. Working night and day at Elkins', Maury did little more than sleep at No. 5. The living room had become so dirty and untidy that even Leo was moved to complain.

"Look at this place. It's like a bleedin' pigsty. You ain't lookin' after it proper, gal."

The house had come to disgust Holly increasingly and she lost her temper completely.

"You're the chief pig, Pa," she shouted. "You can either live in it or pay a woman to clean for you."

"Pay a woman! Pay a woman! I ain't made o' money. Anyhow, why should I pay a bleedin' cleaner when you're 'ere?"

"'Cause I'm not your servant.'"

"High an' mighty little cow!"

He aimed a swipe at her but Holly had been expecting it and skipped out of his way. He was too lazy to pursue her and contented himself with roaring insults at her from his wallow on the sofa.

On other occasions, Leo was sweetness itself.

"I'm a bit 'ard up this week, luv," he would say. "Lend us five bob 'till payday."

To keep him quiet, Holly would give him a shilling. Instead of thanking her, Leo would whine that he was not being given the respect due him. "If it wasn't for Ritchie, I'd let you all stew, so I would."

Maury would laugh, sling his bag over his shoulder and, still laughing, would swiftly depart.

"Sweat'n'slave all me life t' keep a decent 'ome for you, an' what thanks do I get? Cast off like an old boot. Won't even keep the place clean. Won't even lend 'er old man five bob. What I've given you, what I've done for you don't count."

At which point Holly too would slip away, leaving her father muttering to himself.

The strange thing was that she felt no guilt. She was beginning to see Leo for what he was. Though she had been brought up in Abraham's Box, she was conscious that she had never been happy there; her father had contributed little or nothing to her welfare. It was not Lambeth that she had come to despise but Leo and those aspects of the workingclass that he typified.

Once the house's clock and calendar, Tal no longer bothered to keep account of who was on what shift or when so-and-so would be in for his grub. He too abandoned Leo. The house became more like a cramped lodging than a home, with Tal, Maury and Holly doing little more than sleeping there.

In all of this change, Tal Kirsanoff took pleasure.

Off her own bat, Holly had increased his wage. The shop could well afford it. She had received her dividend from the share of profits to December, and had salted them away in a personal bank account. She kept the bank book in the shop, in the warming-pan on the shelf in the back store; the pan now had a printed label on it saying "Not for Sale". What she earned, she spent. She felt confident that she would not starve, would not be out of a job, even if the Aspinalls decided to sell out.

At the age of twenty-one, Miss Holly Beckman was a woman of substance; recognition of that fact made her proud and self-assured.

There was no denying it; she was a shrewd, smart business woman.

Grandfather wore a dark blue corded jacket and a starched shirt with a crisp celluloid collar. She wore off-the-peg suits from Bedlington Modes, and a warm coat on cold mornings. Her shop servant, young Master Ackers, addressed her as "Mizz Beckman", or "M'm", and snapped to do her bidding. When she opened the door of the shop each morning she felt relief, confidence and energy, as if the whiff of the polish and leather, the wood and fabrics were the headiest ozone.

She dwelled, very comfortably, in her own bubble.

And she worked hard, doing what she enjoyed doing.

She was not aware that she needed more, that she was beginning to suffer from invidious loneliness.

But Mr. Aspinall's legacy included a solution to that problem too.

* * *

It was Sunday in the Beckman residence. Outside children skipped in the dry cool street, moving along the pavement as the motion of the earth caused shadows like wedges to shift down from the roofs, slicing off the sunlight inch by inch. The children followed the shrinking patches of sunlight, like sturdy weeds, gradually crowding into the end of the cul-de-sac with their games and old broken toys. In back lanes young men skulked in the shadows, where they had been most of the day, playing listless rounds with halfpennies or cards or chirping and cawing at girls, the bold and shameless ones, who dared run the gamut of that masculine preserve.

Fine weather did not tempt Holly out of doors. She had books and catalogues to amuse her during the late morning and early afternoon. It was only as evening approached that she became bored with reading and, in the privacy of her room, emptied her cupboards and wardrobe and spread out her new clothes. They were a vast improvement on what she had been obliged to wear when she was a poor shop servant and all the patched, over-washed garments had been flung out months ago. Even so, the new skirts and jackets, the modest suits struck her as being just too sensible and too dull.

She dragged out her shoe boxes and her two handbags and inspected them too. So strenuously had she avoided vulgarity in her choices that she had acquired the style of a middle-aged frump. Plain, sensible clothes were one thing, but she was young and, she now believed, pretty. She needed a measure of brightness in her dress, a counter to the sombre surroundings of Pimlico and the drabness of Lambeth.

Taking off her dress, she studied herself critically in the mirror. She was slender, her waist neatly pinched, her legs long, her breasts full and firm. She tugged out the pins and let her dark hair tumble about her shoulders. If David could see her now, like this, would he forget his grudging prejudices about her background and her accent? Would he find her irresistible – more sexually attractive, at any rate, than the Leigh-Jennings woman?

Thinking of David and of the things that a man and a woman did together, a heavy, heady mood of sensuality threatened to engulf Holly.

She sucked in a deep breath and let it out, then struck an outrageously artistic pose, tresses draping her breasts, her white arms raised.

I'm like something off a table lamp, she thought, plaster, not even proper alabaster. The threatening arousal of sexual desire was dispelled. Giggling, Holly dressed herself again.

The following afternoon, however, she left Grandpa Tal in charge of the shop and, giving no explanation, told him that she would not be back until closing time.

The beauty salon was a cavernous establishment in Upper Regent Street. Emma Chubb had spoken of it many times and had urged Holly to "try it for yourself; it'll make you feel marvellous." Holly's apprehension was not dispelled by the black glass windows or the interior's heavy gilt trim and scarlet carpeting. She felt as if she was about to commit a moral crime and had to force herself to go through with it.

The attention she received, the courtesy, soon put her at her ease. Holly's tweed coat and hat were removed and hung on a quilted hanger. She was taken into a private cubicle and wrapped in a smock of lilac crêpe-de-chine. A willowy lady armed with lotions and towels and bristling with combs and scissors proceeded to sit her in a chair like a throne in front of a shallow marble basin with two oval taps and a silver spray.

"Does Madam 'ave anything partic'lar in mind?"

"A short style for my hair," said Holly, who had studied pictures in the fashion magazines, "and . . . the . . . a full facial."

"Leave it to me," the woman said. "I'll make you even nicer than you are now."

Holly's hair was lathered, snipped and sculptured into the latest short style. The sight of her hair abandoned on the floor gave her a faint pang of remorse and apprehension, but she had no time to brood. Her features were now taken, literally, in hand. Her skin was creamed, smoothed, steamed, creamed again, and painted. Holly found to her surprise that she thoroughly enjoyed being coddled. She closed her eyes in contentment as fingers, silky brushes and doeskin swabs caressed her skin.

Eventually the smock was removed and she was presented with her reflection in the gilded mirror.

Voilà.

Holly had no inclination to giggle. At that instant her inbred self-deprecation and common sense received a mortal blow. Emma Chubb had not exaggerated: she *was* a different person. She *felt* different; more feminine, more confident. Her cheek bones were higher, her chin more pointed. Her eyes, under curving brows, were larger and more lustrous.

"What do you think?" the woman whispered in her ear.

"I can't believe it!"

"Oh, it's you, Madam," the woman said. "All I did was bring out the best. Your boy friend'll fall in love with you all over again."

Holly tipped the beautician generously and swung out into Regent Street. It was ten minutes after five. She found a telephone box, called the shop and told Grandpa Tal that she would not be returning to Cardwell Place. She asked him if he would lock up. That done, she headed for Madame Venard's in Oxford Street and there selected a wardrobe of skirts, blouses, dresses and two new coats. She bought shoes, gloves, three hats and handbags to complete the ensembles and paid the formidable bill without a qualm. The doorman whistled up a taxicab. Two assistants loaded up the vehicle's back seat with her purchases. It was after eight o'clock before Holly got back to Lambeth. To her vast relief, nobody was at home, not even Grandpa Tal who had probably stopped off to eat at the dockers' canteen.

She carried the boxes upstairs and opened them one by one, carefully putting the clothes away. She hid the boxes under her bed, and deposited the wrappings in the dustbins in the lane.

That done she cooked herself eggs, took a tray to her bedroom and sat there, a little stunned by her own temerity but very much looking forward to tomorrow.

It was the following morning before Holly revealed herself in all her glory. She managed to get up and out of No. 5 before Grandpa Tal stirred. She was waiting for him when he arrived in the shop.

"It is not my granddaughter!" Tal declared. "It is a witch."

The navy blue jacket and skirt fitted her to a tee, matching a soft peach blouse.

"Don't you like it?" she asked.

"Yes, yes, I like it. The hair makes you look like a boy, but the blouse – ah, the blouse says that you are very much a woman."

"That's a compliment, I hope?"

"Of course it is, but tell me, Holly, why are you so dressed up?"

"For absolutely no reason."

Grandpa Tal did not quite understand.

David Aspinall thought he did.

David had not yet been discharged from the army. He laboured daily in the War Office Pension Department in a gloomy building off Whitehall. Though the work was grindingly tedious, at least it brought him a regular salary. He needed it these days; money seemed to sift through his fingers like sand.

David's startled delight at the new Holly Beckman was all that the girl had secretly hoped for. His surprise was palpable. He could not take his eyes from her and his voice was no longer hearty and just a little patronising. It was as if she had undergone a total transformation, one which destroyed all memory in him of the drab little mouse that his father had employed.

"I can't believe it!" he murmured. "I turn my back for ten minutes and you blossom into a woman."

Holly had anticipated the moment, but now found herself tongue-tied. No quick, flirtatious remark came to her. His initial amazement had tempered down to a steady admiration, a keen but careful thing, as if he suspected that she had more such surprises in store for him and did not want to be caught off guard.

Holly said, "It's good to see you, David. Is there something special that brings you in?"

"What?"

She pointed to the parcel under his arm. "That, for instance?"

"What? Oh, yes! It's a little something I picked up for stock."

He tugged the string and let the wrapping paper fall to the floor. He held the object out on one hand. "What do you think of it?"

It was a good example of early Victorian nursery furniture, a bank made in the likeness of a Punch and Judy show. To operate it – as David demonstrated – a penny was placed on the ledge between the little lead figures, and Mr. Punch's truncheon tipped into action, triggered by an arrangement of weights and springs below stage. The penny disappeared into a slot in Dog Toby's stomach, a procedure that justified the highly indignant look painted on the animal's face.

There were three figures, Punch, Judy and Dog Toby, on the open stage: the painting was fresh and bright, and the soft lead moulding of the awnings and flags, as well as that of the figures, was remarkably free from scoring.

"How much do you think I got it for?" David asked.

"Tell me."

"Five bob."

"That *is* a bargain."

"What's it worth?"

"I think I can sell it to Mr. Byrne for three or four pounds."

"Fine: I'll take a pound for it."

"A pound? But you only paid five shillings."

"Scout's commission, Holly," said David. "Besides, you'll make two hundred per cent for the shop, won't you?"

"But it's your shop, too."

"Come on, Holly, don't be so stingy. It's worth a pound note to you, isn't it?"

"Well, I suppose it is."

"Take it out of petty cash: nobody'll be any the wiser."

"You haven't got a half-crown tiara behind your back, by any chance?" Holly said.

"Just ol' Punch and Judy."

Shaking her head, Holly extracted one pound from the Petty Cash box under the desk lid. She scribbled a note – "Casual purchase: £1.0.0. – H.B." – and gave David the money. He folded it with the fingers of one hand, like a conjurer, and tucked it into his breast pocket. "Little Emily *shall* have bread tonight."

"You can't be that hard up, David?"

"Skint: skint as a flint, my tiger."

"But the half-yearly dividend . . . ?"

"A mere bagatelle." Behind his breeziness was anxiety.

He reminded Holly of one of the Lambeth kids taking the Westgard Road hill in a battered perambulator "motorcar"; the thrill lay in the possibility of a spill, speed and danger mingled with fear. She had never ridden the hill in a barrow, though some of the bolder girls did, while the boys, like Ritchie, cheered and whistled and looked up the girls' flying skirts. One boy, she remembered, had broken his head badly on a lamppost but had become so addicted to the wild ride that he was back again two days later with a huge grubby turban of bandages around his skull. If David had lived in Lambeth instead of the more sedate Pimlico street, he would have been one of the Westgard riders, of that she was sure.

She had lost her awe of him; regarded him as an equal, really.

She was not too bashful to ask, "What on earth did you do with your money, David?"

"Blew it, my sweet, blew it just as fast as I could."

Holly said, "What about your future, David? What'll happen when you get married – with no nest-egg?"

"First, I've no intention of marrying, in spite of my so-called engagement. Second, if I do marry, I'll make sure it's to some young thing willing and able to keep me in the style to which I'm accustomed. Third, it's a chalk and cheese thing between you and me, Holly. Ant and grasshopper, if you know what I mean."

"I've read Aesop's Fables," said Holly. "Includin' the one about the Fox and the Grapes."

"Veeeeeery clever," said David. "You're almost as clever as you are beautiful."

She blushed but did not avert her gaze.

Holding up the Punch and Judy bank, she said, "If you come across anythin' else this good at a cheap price, I'll pay you scout's commission. How's that?"

"Can't ask for better," David glanced at his wristwatch and made towards the shop door, where he paused. "Ever eaten dinner in an hotel, Holly?"

"Yes, as a matter of fact."

"The Connaught?"

"Well, no; nothin' that grand."

"Friday: eight-thirty."

"Is that an invitation?"

"It's the least I can do," said David. "Let the grasshopper foot the bill, for once."

"Cost you more than that pound."

"Do you accept?"

"With pleasure."

"Pick you up here?"

"Eight o'clock."

After David had gone whisking out into Cardwell Place, Grandpa Tal emerged from his retreat in the back store. Holly feigned a coolness that she did not feel. All the old longings, strengthened by her new-found confidence, had returned in a rush. At that moment, she didn't care if David had to borrow from the account to pay for the dinner: she'd have stumped up herself. Dinner with David at the Connaught; what a thought!

She touched her hand to her coiffeured hair.

Grandpa Tal said, "So it worked, Holly?"

"I don't know what you mean."

Grinning, old Kirsanoff looked down at his own clothing, at his bulging stomach and the waistcoat with the egg stain on it. "Hm," he murmured, his grin broadening. "I wonder what would happen to me if I did myself over."

"Why don't you ask Mendel Erbach for an estimate?" said Holly.

Grandpa Tal laughed. "For dinner at the Connaught, it might even be worth it."

*   *   *

They stood by the pile at the end of the wharf looking down at seeping black mud that quaked at the return of the tide from the sea. Inch by inch the river was rising and the skeletal wreck of an abandoned wherry, still tied to its rotted painter, lurched suddenly, making the men jerk their heads in its direction. Across the Limehouse Reach, the Isle of Dogs basked in the waning rays of the sun, looking almost beautiful, like an Italian painting, full of sharp detail in a mellow setting. But the men did not take their eyes from the river at the base of the wharf, except, now and again, to glance down the lane that fed back between greasy walls towards the great ponds of the Commercial docks.

"Come on, Jack," said Ritchie. "I ain't got all night. What is it y'want?"

"Don't be so bloody impatient, Ritchie."

"Yer, yer, I know; there's supposed t'be a way o' doin' things, right? What the 'ell do you expect down 'ere? Think there's a nark in waterwings hidin' under the pier?"

"You're gettin' careless, sonny."

"I want a pint, an' my supper, Jack," said Ritchie. "It's all right for you, swannin' 'round all day long. I been floggin' my guts out in the bleedin' tannery."

"You don't have to, not now," said Jack Renzo.

"Who says?"

"Mr. Shotten says."

"An' what does Mr. Shotten know about my affairs?"

"You've made a bob or two, Ritchie, this past six months. Where is it?"

Ritchie laughed, then spat over the edge of the wharf into the mud, a little white fleck of saliva that sat on the silt like a daisy petal until the water absorbed it.

"Come on, Ritchie," said Renzo, "You ain't showin' it, not a penny."

Savagely, Ritchie turned on the fence. "'Course I ain't showin' it. What the bleedin' 'ell is this, Renzo? Shotten *want* me t' get shopped? I ain't shown it for the same reason I ain't quittin' work. I'm a poor, hard-workin' little lad from Lambeth, that's all."

"An' that mate o'yours, Nuttall, what's he doin' with his loot?"

"Ask him."

"Ritchie, listen, Vince has gotta know things like that."

"Stan's the same as me. Careful t' a fault. We don't go for this secretive stuff, like you, Jack; walkin' out on the bleedin' river for a simple bit o'chat. But we know how t' keep outta clink. No show. No flash."

"Then what's it for?"

"Say, the future."

"What about Nuttall?"

"He's my hire, not Shotten's. He does what I tell 'im, an' he takes the slice I give 'im. He's happy with it like that."

"You give away nothin', Ritchie."

"I give *service*," said Ritchie. "*That's* what Vince pays me for." He dropped another petal of spit into the Thames, watching it dissolve in the thick river water. "Now, what's on your mind, Jack, or d'you want us t' paddle out into the middle o' the bleedin' river first?"

"It's what you might call 'a standing order', Ritchie," Renzo told him. He came closer to the young man, who was leaning on the great dank wedge of woodwork that marked the butt of the wharf, his hands buried in his jacket pockets, his shoulders lifted. Anger had made him wheeze. He fought not to show the sign to Renzo; not even that much of his feelings. "Know what a 'standing order' is, Ritchie?"

"Come on, for Gawd's sake!"

"We don't want Nuttall in on this one, Ritch."

"Right."

"An' we've got nothin' particular in mind."

"You want me t' square the marks?"

"In your own time, Ritch."

"For what?"

"Clocks."

"Clocks?"

"Friend of Mr. Shotten's, from over the Atlantic, has it in mind to build a collection. He's not short of rhino, I can tell you, but he doesn't want truck. Only the best."

"Antiques, like?"

"Antiques. Take your time. Suss out the best places. Ask your sister for a list of marks."

Ritchie squinted at Renzo. "Leave 'er out of it, Jack. She's trouble."

Accommodatingly, Renzo shrugged. "However – it's clocks we can use right now. Not just your average tickers."

"Yer, I know what Shotten's after."

"Interested?"

"How many other hawks has Shotten put up?"

"Couple: but not on your beat."

"The Amcrican . . ."

"I didn't say he was American, did I?"

"The American," Ritchie persisted, "will he pay top for top?"

"Sure."

"An' Vince; will he see I get my proper share?"

"Sure."

"I know about clocks, see," said Ritchie. "I know what clocks is worth, even on the black market. I'm not takin' snuff for hand-picked antiques."

"I'll tell Mr. Shotten."

"Make sure he understands, Jack."

"He's gotta lotta respect for you, Ritchie."

"Let 'im show it, then, with his bleedin' wad."

"Bring me clocks, Ritch, an' you can buy your tannery."

"Hah!" said Ritchie, then, smiling with a modicum of his usual charm, asked, "How would the American fancy Big Ben?"

Relieved, Jack Renzo clapped his young friend on the back.

"Think you can get it?"

"Might be a bit too big for the bag, Jack."

Relaxed now, the fence put his arm about Ritchie's shoulders and led him back up the seamless lane. Shotten had been right; if anyone could target the antique market, it was Ritchie Beckman.

Clocks they would no doubt have.

By the score.

* * *

"One taxicab," David said. "One kiss."

He brushed her lips with his, the feathery touch of the moustache on her cheek. The cab growled into motion and David sat back, leaving Holly breathless, her heart beating loudly.

"David you . . . you mustn't."

"Why not?"

"It's . . ."

"You see, you can find no reason, Holly. I do wish you'd stop trying to rationalise everything."

"But you have a fiancée."

"No, no fiancée. If you mean Linsey, that's over; has been for weeks."

He looked authoritative in his dinner jacket, not raffish but solid. In her new silk dress, Holly felt herself to be more his equal than ever before.

"Holly, you're beautiful," he murmured. "Truly."

She said nothing.

"A Russian princess."

Still she said nothing.

"May I kiss you again?"

This time it was no fleeting kiss but a passionate coming together, as she crushed her lips against his. She forgot her reticence, the presence of the cab driver; everything. She had always been in love with David Aspinall, almost from the first moment of their meeting. But she had not understood the nature of her longing for him, or that, in the many months of their relationship, she had grown up, grown towards him.

When he drew away she sought his hand, and held it.

Strangely, David's face was pale. He – not she – suffered a pang of remorse for his impulsiveness. For Holly everything had been swept away.

"I'm sorry," he said.

"I'm not."

The journey was a short one. They reached Grosvenor Square and the imposing frontage of the Connaught Hotel far sooner than Holly would have wished. She did not want to share David's company tonight, not even with strangers. Besides, she was just a little nervous about her table manners, about her "style" in such opulent surroundings. Fleetingly, she thought of her dinner with Maury before Christmas and remembered her brother's enormous confidence. She tried to relax as David helped her from the taxicab, took her arm and escorted her up the steps into the reception area.

In the glittering, palace-like place, Holly found herself floating, her awkwardness gone. There were other women, other men, but none, she thought, as young and as handsome as David and she. The women had faces made of dough, the men were fat and ruddy-cheeked, like farmers or greengrocers. Her concepts of social divisions took a final knock, and tumbled like paper dominoes. Diamonds and fur stoles meant nothing; what counted was poise – and David had that, and she, by association, had it too. She straightened her shoulders and glided along by his side over thick cushioned carpeting under crystal chandeliers. She allowed David to take off her coat and pass it to a cloakroom attendant, to escort her on towards the door of the dining room.

There, a gentleman in a resplendent dinner jacket hovered by a gilded pillar, the *maître d'*; his purpose was to greet guests and conduct them to their tables.

"Sar, Madame; goot evenin'."

"The Walshott party," said David.

"Sar: Mr. Walshott an' hiz lady are in ze cocktail lounge."

The *maître* ushered David and Holly around the curved outer aisle of the dining room.

"David, you didn't tell me . . . I thought we were dinin' alone."

"I didn't want to scare you off."

"Is it . . . is it your sister?"

"'Fraid it is."

"David, what are you tryin' t'do?" Holly trailed the man in the dinner suit towards the arch of the cocktail lounge. "Did she invite me, or are you . . . ?"

"Miles, Andrea." They had arrived: it was too late. "How good to see you. Andrea, I think you know Holly."

"Good," said Andrea, "God!"

Though probably a little shaken too, Miles Walshott had more aplomb than his fiancée. He greeted Holly with something close to warmth.

"What would you like to drink, Miss Beckman?" he asked.

"I . . ."

"I do believe," said David, "that Holly would enjoy a Pink Pearl."

"Of course," said Walshott. "A Pink Pearl it is."

"I'll have my usual Green Dragon, Miles."

"Andrea, my dear: another of the same?"

Andrea was still staring at Holly. Miles extracted the glass from her fingers, and took it to the bar where the barman – who bore a distinct resemblance to Leo Beckman, only cleaner – greeted Mr. Walshott like a brother and set about the ritual of slinging up the exotic mixtures.

Holly looked around her. The cocktail bar was not busy.

She assumed it was too early for the "crowd". She was relieved of the worry of being stared at by others, as well as by Andrea. She quite understood – or thought she did – why David had brought her unannounced to dinner with his sister and her man friend. He was using her as a counter in a petty game against Andrea. Angry and resentful, her gaucheness returned. Biting her lip, she determined to say nothing, to go through with what promised to be a frightful and embarrassing evening. But it would be the last time. He would not use her again, would not turn her head with kisses and flattery.

She didn't know what to say.

But she had sufficient panache not to "drop any clangers", as Maury would have put it. Her silence, she hoped, was dignified.

Miles Walshott gave her the cocktail. It looked inviting, a creation of ice and pinkish liquid, exactly like a dissolved pearl.

"Mostly gin, Miss Beckman," Walshott explained, sipping his own dry Martini. "The colour is added in the form of one teaspoonful of *Crême de Noyau* Pink. Do you like it?"

"Yes, thank you. It's very pleasant."

While Miles Walshott engaged Holly in conversation, Andrea had pulled David to one side. She lowered her voice to a hiss, but did not attempt to make herself inaudible to Holly.

"What are you playing at, bringing *her* here?"

"Andrea, Holly's my guest; please don't be insulting."

"Bad enough . . . that Jennings creature . . . least she was . . . some polish, style . . . but that girl, here, and . . . Beckman. What will Miles . . . ?"

Smiling at Holly, Miles wheeled and, with effortless ease, scooped Andrea into the circle of four. She looked furious, but, warned by a glance from her fiancé, did not vent her spite against Holly openly.

Holly watched her, knowing that an attack would come, that it would be snide and sly.

"Have you been here before, Holly?" Andrea asked, in a loud voice.

"No, Andrea."

"Miles has a table more or less on permanent reserve, don't you, my dear?"

"The standard's beginning to pick up again, Miss Beckman," Miles said. "I think you will enjoy the quality of cooking."

Holly took another sip of the cocktail, then looking directly at Miles Walshott said, "As we will be dinin' together, perhaps you should call me Holly. It's a bit less formal, don't you think?"

"Indeed, I do think," Miles said. "Holly, and Miles, it had better be."

A minute or two later, the *maître* informed Mr. Walshott that the chef was ready to receive his order.

"Doesn't that sound awfully grand," said Miles to Holly, taking her arm. "It's a carefully rehearsed phrase, of course. The chef doesn't know me from Adam, and he is not at my personal disposal. Still, it's nice to think that he is, isn't it?"

Holly laughed and, leaving David to lead his sister to the table, went into the Connaught's luxurious dining room on the stock-broker's arm.

With Miles Walshott's gracious guidance, she would carry off the ordeal as flawlessly as possible.

To celebrate the end of her brief romance with David.

* * *

"I'll take a tram."

"Oh, don't be utterly ridiculous, Holly. Get in."

"So you can . . ." She suppressed her anger. "I'm perfectly capable of findin' myself a tram. Don't let me keep you."

"Holly, will you get into the taxi, please."

The cabby was grinning, leaning an elbow from the window. Miles and Andrea had departed only a moment before in another cab.

"I prefer not t'travel with you."

"Are you tiddles? Are you drunk?"

"No, I am not."

"*What is it?*"

She could hardly explain to him, standing there on the pavement bathed in the glow of the Connaught Hotel with fancy folk glancing at them, sniggering perhaps at her common voice. She had been shouting, very nearly.

"In'r out, miss?" the cabby asked. "Got more t'do than wait on the result o' this bout."

Holly was a little light-headed though she had been very careful not to drink too much wine at dinner and had refused liquors afterwards, contenting herself with coffee. She was, emphatically, not drunk, but the alcohol had loosened her tongue more than she would have wished. The very least she could do was to inform David in no uncertain terms what she thought of him, and that the kiss earlier that evening had been rendered meaningless by his betrayal. How dare he use her to spite on his sister! How dare he try to humiliate her!

She climbed into the cab and dumped herself down in the darken-ed corner.

"That's better, luv," said the cabby. "Kiss'n'make up."

David snapped, "Lambeth. Ambraham's Terrace," and jerked closed the glass divider, shutting out the driver. He turned at once to Holly. "Now what's *wrong* with you?"

"Why did you take me there?"

"Because I wanted to."

"To humiliate me."

"Don't be ridiculous! I wanted to go out with you."

"Why not alone? Why with Andrea?"

"Ah!" said David, sighing. "I see. I see what the problem is."

"The problem is that I'm nothin' but a shop servant, or so you think, an' therefore you can do what . . . what the *hell* you like with me."

"Holly, listen. I mean, that didn't cross my mind."

"You must've known she'd treat me like . . . like dirt."

"You showed her up. Yes, you did; you showed my sister up. You charmed Walshott. Andrea was pea-green. I mean it, absolutely pea-green."

Holly shook her head. "You're tryin' t'get round me."

He put his arm around her, to comfort her. She shook him off.

"I won't be used," Holly said.

"Do stop it. You're behaving exactly as Andrea expected you to behave. Only you didn't, not before dinner, during dinner, or after damned dinner," David said. "Won't you even listen to me?"

She slackened. She had been over-reacting. She should have been cold, distant, silent, should have parted from him with dignity. The strain of the evening had been too great.

In a soft, rapid voice, David explained, "If I had told you that you were going to be my partner at dinner with Andrea and Walshott, you'd have run like a little bunny-rabbit. Now isn't that true? Isn't it? Of course it is. So, I didn't tell you."

"You tricked me, David."

"I tricked you, yes; but for a very good reason."

"To annoy your sister."

"Do you think I'm *that* petty?"

"I . . . I don't know what to think."

"Andrea *is* my sister; no help for that," said David. "What's more important is that she's our partner. She will never like you, Holly, but she must be made to accept you."

"Why is that important, David?"

"One day Andrea may be more than your business partner."

"I don't understand."

"You're every bit as good as she is. Better. Andrea resents you for it more than anything."

"David, what are you saying?"

"I'm saying, in my round about way, that I think I'm falling in love with you."

She had seen little of him recently, though he had found excuses to drop into the shop whenever he was free. She had sensed a growing rapport between them, a quickening of interest in her. But the declaration was unexpected.

"David, are you sure you . . . ?"

Brusquely, he interrupted her, "Holly, I've come to the conclusion you're what I need. No, it's more than that; you're what I want. I'm a bit of an ass, really. Some times I've acted like a prime chump. But that phase is over, I promise. I want to prove I can match you, Holly."

"I like you as you are, David," said Holly. "Besides, we're not competing with each other. It's not a contest."

David said, "I'm not a boy any longer. In a couple of months I'll be shot of my commission. I'll be an ordinary civilian and will have to earn my living."

"The shop can support us."

"Oh, the shop's enough for you, Holly, but I'm not sure it's enough for me. Besides, I don't want to be dependent on you. I must find a job."

"What about the insurance company you worked for before the war?"

"I was only a glorified clerk, if you must know. The post only paid beans."

"Money isn't all that important, David."

Holly sensed in him a hesitation to confess the true reason for his reluctance to commit himself to her completely. Though he had announced that he was in love with her and hinted that he intended to marry her, his practical insistence on mundane matters indicated that he was still dogged by her class. He could not completely overlook her Lambeth background. It was natural that he should still hesitate. Once more need and desire had been reduced to talk of money. For all her excitement and the welling of love within her, Holly was chastened by the fact that David too lived by the equation, money equals happiness.

As if reading her thoughts, David explained. "I'm in debt, you see. I've certain obligations I must discharge before I . . . before we . . ."

"Is it the girl in Mayfair?"

"Linsey. Yes, it is."

"You told me you'd broken with her."

"I have," said David. "But it isn't quite that simple. I was so infatuated with her that I couldn't see how destructive she'd become. But I can't abandon her. She's in desperate bother, you see, and I'm partly responsible."

"Is she . . . expecting, is that it?"

"Good God, no!"

"What, then?"

"Debts," said David, "to the tune of five hundred pounds."

"Five *hundred*?" Holly was shocked. "Oh, David, five hundred is a lot more than I can extract from the shop account. Two hundred, perhaps three, but . . ."

"You see, you see! Already you're being drawn into my mess. I mustn't allow that to happen. It's my problem, Holly. I must meet my own obligations, my debts of honour, before I can be rid of Linsey and all she stands for. Be rid of her finally and completely."

"I do understand," said Holly, flatly.

Anxiously, he turned to her, seeking her hands with his. "When that's done, darling, when that's all over – and I must do it myself, to prove that I *can* do it – when I'm settled, then perhaps I might come to you again."

"Is that what you want, David?"

"It's all I really want," he said.

"Please, please, say it."

"I want you to be my wife, Holly."

"I will be."

"Will you allow me time, time to make changes, clear the debris?"

"Let me help."

"No, Holly. It's my mess. I've got to get out of it by my own efforts. I've something to work for now, to spur me on; make me less of an ass." Sardonically he smiled. "I must work, and I must save money; then I'll have something worthwhile to offer you."

"The shop's makin' money," said Holly. "You'll have your share of that."

"The shop's doing beautifully. But it won't be enough, or happen quickly enough. I must find a way of speeding things along."

Holly could understand his motive, sympathise with his pride. The strain of indulgent impulsiveness that had marred her idealisation of David Aspinall had gone. He was, that night, full of a determination and strength. She wanted to hold him, tell him that she would help him, wait for him, forever. She wanted to shout out that she loved him. She restrained herself. He must do it without her aid. Just as she must work even harder, build up the business even more rapidly. Their reward? It hardly seemed possible. In six months or a year, she might become David's wife.

David Aspinall's wife.

Between them they would own half the antique shop.

Leaning against him, she kissed his mouth.

"I'll wait," she promised. "But hurry, David; please hurry."

The cabby rapped on the divider, then opened it.

"This the place?"

Abraham's Box – the spill of men from the pub, the smell of cooking fat, the pervasive odours of Cavanaugh's factory, narrow windows hard against a broken pavement, the sound of a crying child: she was home.

"Yes," Holly said. "End of the row, please."

She did not invite him inside, though David seemed utterly oblivious to the squalor of the cramped cul-de-sac. He leaned from the cab window and brought her head forward, kissed her lingeringly on the mouth.

Away up the street an observant lounger spotted the event, and hollered, "Ol-ol-ol; 'nuffer that now; 'nuffer them carryin's on."

Holly drew away.

"I love you, tiger. Remember that. I love you with all my heart," David whispered.

"Where to now, guv?" asked the cabby.

David drew his head and shoulders back into the cab, and Holly crossed the pavement and let herself into No. 5 with her latchkey. She went straight upstairs, up the narrow creaky staircase, floating on a cloud of happiness, too full of joy to confide in anyone, not even in Grandpa Tal, that soon she might be married to the man she'd always loved.

Later, undressed, Holly lay under the covers and thought deeply of what marriage would mean, of how David would come to her and hold her, kiss her and touch her intimately and of how she would give herself up to him, unleashing the torrent of passion that she had kept dammed up for so long.

Whatever pleasure the Mayfair girl had given him, Holly promised herself that she would give him more.

Shivering with the heat of her need for him, Holly drew the bolster to her breasts and, hugging it tightly to her, eventually fell asleep.

4

Easy Money

"Is THAT IT?" said David. "Is that all?"

"Travel light, travel fast," said Linsey.

In the hallway of the Willoughby house in Larder Mews a single suitcase and a small battered trunk stood waiting.

"You didn't need me to help you move," said David, crossly.

"It was an excuse to see you just once more, darling."

"You dragged me from Whitehall just to lift those into a taxi? The driver would have done it for sixpence."

"I told you, it was an excuse. Besides, I don't happen to have sixpence."

"I see."

Feigning gaiety, the girl wheeled suddenly. She was dressed in an expensive outfit, which was ridiculously inappropriate for somebody who claimed not to have even sixpence to her name.

"Have a drink with me, David."

"At eleven o'clock in the morning?" David said; he glanced pointedly at his watch. "Listen, I have to get back very soon."

"One drink – a last little sup from Theodore's hoard, hm? For Auld Lang Syne?"

"I shouldn't be here at all."

"Please, darling; a loving cup, the last, the swansong, one for the road. All that gubbins, hm?"

She took his arm in both hands and dragged him out of the hall into the morning room where she had set up one bottle of gin, one bottle of bitters, a tub of ice, a saucer of sliced lemons and two tall glasses. The hospitable preparations were not in keeping with her "just help yourself" character.

"One drink, that's all. I'm not going to poison you, David, though I'd have every justification." She uncapped the Gordon's and poured liberally. "Absolutely every justification. It isn't every day a girl gets herself jilted."

"Don't be ridiculous," said David, gruffly, lighting one cigarette from the stub of another. He walked to the window and looked out into the rain-wet Mews; the Indian summer was drifting away, dying as softly as it had been born. The rain was misty, like gossamer and it was unseasonably warm, almost muggy. He felt sticky inside his uniform. The collar chaffed the ring of stubble that his razorblade had missed that morning.

"You've been avoiding me, David. I don't blame you, really. After all you've had your fun; no reason why you should pay for it, if you can get off with it. Do the same myself."

She came up behind him and handed him the drink, sitting herself on the box seat that squared the room's low bow window. She sat primly with her knees together, the drink held in both hands like a cocoa mug. Lemon peel and ice bobbed in a large measure of pure gin. She drank in melancholy gulps, looking up at him out of soulful eyes.

"What happened about the inventory?" David asked. "Did Willoughby send his man round?"

"Somebody came; couldn't have been his agent, not a ruffian like that. Yes, somebody came."

"And?"

"Wasn't so bad; fine, really."

"The clock, what about the clock?"

"Oh, yes, the clock. One or two silly little things. Theo really is making a fuss, isn't he? America hasn't improved his temper. I'm not pleased with Theodore."

"How much is he charging you for breakage?"

"The clock – a minor repair . . ."

"An antique piece," said David. "It'll cost a small fortune to put in order. It took a mauling, remember."

"Fussing about glassware, too. And china – his precious china plates."

"Come on, Linsey, tell me the exact extent of the damage. I can't bail you out unless I know what I'm in for."

She blinked, batted her lids. "Bail me out, David? I'm not going to Holloway jail. Oh, no; Theo isn't that sadistic. He'll come around soon, you'll see. Theo just wants me to make an 'arrangement' with him. But I told him, well, I told him that you and I . . ."

"Did you pay anything on the rent?"

"The total bill, according to Theodore's little bully, is five hundred. I mean, that's what Theo's asking for – at this present time. He'll climb down. He knows when to cut his losses, does Theo." She sipped gin, looked into the glass. "None of this would have happened, darling, if I'd been willing to . . . you know, go back to him."

"Why don't you?"

"David, you're even crueller than Theo. Don't you see how it is? Are you blind to my feelings for you? How can I go back to be Theodore Willoughby's plaything, after the love we've shared? Oh, yes, it may have just been fun for you, but you taught me that I have a heart, that I can feel. I didn't ask to fall in love with you. I know that you are not in love with me. But I'll . . . I *will* settle my affair with Theo in some other way. I'll pay him his money, but I can no longer give him my body."

David was not taken in by her string of cliches. He knew that Willoughby had spurned her.

"I thought he wanted his money by the first of the month?"

"Oh, I paid him something on account: quite a lot, actually."

"Where did you get it?"

"Sold dear auntie's shares."

"They were worth more than five hundred."

"I needed a little oil to light the lamps of China, David."

"You blew – what – three or four hundred?"

"Didn't say that."

"Linsey, you're mad."

"Don't call me that, David."

He could no longer bear to be close to her. He walked away, back to the table to refresh his drink, though he had hardly touched the first helping.

"Where will you go? Do you have someplace to go?" he asked.

"Friends, lots of friends who'll adopt a waif like me. Give me a chance to look around, find a lodging suitable to my status and true station. Haven't got a spare room going a-begging in Pimlico, have you?"

"Tonight? Where will you go?"

"Doesn't matter."

"Yes it does."

"Don't pretend you care."

"I do care; I don't want you to . . . to come to harm."

"Harm?" She laughed, got up and sailed down the side of the drawing room, waving the glass so that it spilled on the carpet. "Harm!" She laughed again. "Don't you think I've already come to harm? Trusting you, believing in you, *loving* you – that's where the harm came in."

"I'm trying to scrape up the money to pay off Willoughby. I'll bring it when I have it."

She came close to him, effecting a mood-change. "David, take me upstairs."

"For God's sake, Linsey!"

"Make love to me."

"I can't. I don't . . . don't feel at all like it."

"I need you, David; I need you inside me."

He glanced around the room, as if expecting to find an audience sniggering at his embarrassment. He drank a huge mouthful of gin, screwing up his face, then hastily placed the glass on the mantelshelf. He needed to stay stone-cold sober.

"There's a hotel, the Winslow, it's in Kensington. I've booked a room for a week; paid for it too."

"We'll go there then," Linsey said. "Now, right away."

"I'll drop you off."

"Leave me?" she said. "Oh, that *is* kind; deposit me, alone, in some fleabag dump in South Ken. What am I supposed to do there? Knit?"

"Give yourself a chance to think, Linsey. Perhaps your father would . . ."

"That pig; that rat-picker. I'd die first."

David nodded at the expected response.

He moved to her, took the drink from her hand and placed it on the table, then pushed her with his hip towards the door of the morning room. "You've got to get out of here Linsey. Lord knows, Willoughby won't wait for ever; you're days late in leaving. I'll take you to the Winslow. I'll pay the bill."

"Kiss me goodbye, sergeant-major."

He got her into the hallway, to the front door, nipped back and lifted the box and the suitcase and, crowding her with them, barred any possibility of a return into the house.

She kissed her fingertips. "Bye-bye, my sanctuary. You were nice while you lasted."

Tears streaming down her cheeks she went out ahead of him.

"Give me the key, Linsey?" he said. He went through the awkward process of locking the front door. He pocketed the key. He would see to it that it was returned to Willoughby that afternoon. At least he had succeeded in uprooting her. If he could only settle her in a quiet hotel for a day or two, find out just how much money she'd actually raised on the share sale and how much she'd paid Willoughby, how much was still due. God knows, he was strapped at present. He owed a sizeable mess bill not to mention thirty quid to his bookmaker.

Lugging the box and case, he escorted her along Larder Mews. She was still weeping. He thought that the tears were genuine. He felt sorry for her – and guilty.

Perhaps she did love him.

Without stopping, indeed quickening her pace, she said, "You're trying to get rid of me, David, aren't you?"

"No, not . . . no, but . . ."

"Is there another girl?"

He thought of Holly, steeling himself with the recollection of his promise to her. He had not known then that shaking free of his responsibilities would be quite so difficult. His problems, it seemed, were no nearer resolution. Why, oh God, *why* had he ever got involved with Linsey in the first place?

It was as if she'd read his thoughts.

"It was fun, though, David, wasn't it? Wasn't it wild, darling, while it lasted?"

Sweating, hoisting the box beneath his aching arm, he had to admit that it had been fun.

It was just after noon when the taxi dropped her at the front of the staid hotel in Kensington which looked, as Linsey accurately put it "as if it was infested with Methodists". David signalled an elderly porter to attend to the lady's luggage.

"Linsey, I must, simply must, get back to Whitehall. I don't want to collect a fizzer from the Colonel."

"Go, darling. Fly away."

"Listen, I . . ."

She put her fingers on his arm on the ledge of the cab window. "Don't leave me alone, David."

"I've *got* to get back to the office."

"Come and see me tonight. Please, please, David. I don't want to be alone, not tonight. Just tonight, for dinner. Just tonight, that's all I ask of you. I'll be fine after tonight."

"I . . . yes, all right."

"Seven-thirty?"

"Yes."

As the taxi whizzed away towards the Cromwell Road, David glanced back out of the rectangular window. She was standing where he had left her, at the edge of the pavement, her hand raised in farewell.

"God damn her."

She looked so waif-like, so lonely, that he knew he would keep his promise.

●   ●   ●

"Come on, Charlie, be a sport. You can afford it."

"'Course I can afford it." Charlie Hallet took the cigar from his mouth and studied the band on it, as if to say that a man who could afford to puff his way through twenty Coronas a day could bloody well afford a cheap tart like her. "But fifty quid don't grow on trees, love."

"I'll pay you back, Charlie. Cross my heart."

"I might've bleedin' known you was on the tap, Linsey. I should've had my gal tell yer I was out."

"Secretly, you wanted to stand me lunch. Secretly. Ain't I right, Charlie?"

She had caught Hallet at a fortuitous moment. He had only just hung up the receiver on Winifred, his lady wife, who had torn a piece off his ear because he hadn't been up to the place at Newminster at the weekend, though he'd sent up his chauffeur with a three-pound box of chocolates to make his apologies and personally tell her some whoppers about "business, business". The estate in Newminster hadn't been Charlie's idea of going posh. But Winifred had insisted that he buy it. So the fat cow could rot up there if she liked. Gave him more freedom. He was a city gentleman, entitled to live up in town, and do what the hell he liked.

As it happened, it *had* been "business, business". He was selling off the products of three manufactories to a swell, named Bourgas, who had come over to England specially to meet Mr. Hallet. What Mr. Bourgas wanted with shipments of long-rifle bullets, grenades, land-mines and mortar shells – very specific requirements – was more than simple little Charlie Hallet could imagine. Mr. Bourgas wasn't a Jerry; anyhow the Jerries had been licked. Charlie Hallet had bought the contents of the three manufactories at a knock-down sale held in Leamington Spa, of all places. He had got them very cheap. He already had necessary documents for the purchase and trans-shipment of weapons of war, a blank batch with the seal and rubber stamp of the War Office on them, that he'd prudently "saved" after his contract with His Majesty had terminated. It occurred to Charlie that perhaps Mr. Bourgas was a Bolshevist. But the huge diamond stickpin in his cravat and his solid gold cufflinks had dispelled that notion, though Mr. Bourgas had vaguely hinted that he did *know* some Russians who might be interested in munitions. Charlie had kept sober and celibate throughout the entire weekend in Leamington Spa. He'd been a real good boy, and collected a nice fat profit from his entrepreneurial presence. So, Willoughby's little pigeon got him at just the right moment, when he had buzzed off all

the letters, and was just beginning to think that he owed himself a
treat. Not that the Leigh-Jennings gal was much of a treat, in spite of
her having a double-barrelled name. But she was still young enough
to be appetising. She had been Theo Willoughby's tit-bit for a while,
and he had always respected Willoughby, almost worshipped him,
you might say. It might be enlightening to see what Willoughby had
taught her.

Fifty quid though?

He could have thirty girls and a jazz band for that.

But – no, he wasn't sorry that she'd invited herself to lunch.

He'd taken her up to Fredo's in the Rolls. Fredo's was a private
supper club that also did a short trade in luncheons, and had ten
elegant "lounging suites" on the upper floor. He had told the chauffeur not to wait; maybe that suggested that he was expecting the gal's
proposal. He did not suppose that she wanted his fatherly advice.

Still, he was Charlie Hallet and he had made a fortune by his own
unaided efforts. He could have taken fifty pounds from his wallet
there and then and put a match to them and not have shed a tear. Fifty
quid was nothing. Afterwards, he would be able to tell himself that he
had had his moneysworth out of Theo Willoughby's piece.

He signalled to the waiter and, leaning, murmured to the man while
Linsey watched. No money changed hands; the bill would be
presented later. Now that he had made up his mind, Charlie was as
direct as always. He saw no reason to spar with her. He swilled down
the rest of his brandy and got to his feet. Cheeks glowed with
anticipation, eyes were bright.

"Let's you'n' me trot upstairs an' discuss it, dear."

"Here? Upstairs here?"

"Why the 'ell not 'ere: it's as good a place as any?"

Linsey bit her lip.

"Charlie?"

"Foller me; it's this way."

"Fifty pounds, Charlie?"

The room was not large. Panelled walls, a heavy red drape over the
window, a faint aromatic perfume, a long quilted couch, two chairs
and a gentleman's "valet" in walnut; Linsey shivered, though the
room was, if anything, overheated.

Briskly Charlie switched on a lamp. He took off his jacket and his
tie and collar and put them on the valet. He hung his pocket watch
conspicuously from the knob, then turned.

"Right-o, dear," he said. "Let's see what you've got that's worth
fifty hard-earned quid."

"Charlie!" She glided to him and insinuated herself against him, her lips against his bulbous earlobe, hands tickling the fringe of bristling hair at the back of his neck. "Going to be nice to me, Charlie?"

He pushed her away.

"Never mind all that lovey-dovey stuff, gal," he said. "Just peel off, quick."

Linsey Leigh-Jennings nodded and obediently reached her fingers to the buttons of her dress.

* * *

As instructed, Ritchie left Stan Nuttall out of it. He sussed out the targets alone, and pulled two jobs in one night – alone. He had enough sense not to involve Holly, or the old man, not to raise the subject of tickers in any way, shape or form. What he did do was consult the journals and the tubby, well-thumbed directory that Holly kept on the mantelshelf above the gas fire in her bedroom. He picked his time, hooked the books, locked himself in his room, took the notes he needed, and put the books back just as he'd found them. Nobody in the house was any the wiser.

Ten targets, all in central London; eight shops, two emporiums. Saturday evening and Sunday, he did the first scout. He stroked off the emporiums as too risky, and put out three of the shops, too. Five shops left, all possibles. Through windows, large and small, Ritchie studied interiors crammed with clocks. From the five, he selected two that price-tagged their items. He also spent hours that week poring over books on Horology "borrowed", without tickets, from the Lambeth Free Library.

It was the following Saturday evening before Ritchie got around to casing Sam Fielding's establishment in Snetterton Street. He could see Fielding stooped over a bench in the window below street level. What he could not see was the stock. Whistling, Ritchie skipped down the steps and tried the handle of the basement door. It opened. He went into a corridor, very bright, brisk and noisy, calling out "Hulloa, Hulloa; anybody 'ome." He tried another door. It opened too. Ritchie went inside.

Immediately he realised that this was the Royal Mint of antique clocks. The man came shuffling over from a desk in an adjoining room, a feeble old cove with a jeweller's lens dangling from a cord around his neck. In his hand he had what looked like a surgeon's knife. Eyes darting around the room, taking in cases, shelves and general layout, Ritchie shouted, "Lookin' for Mr. Philips. You Mr. Philips?"

"Nobody 'ere of that name." The clock repairer prudently stopped short of his visitor.

"Number twenty-four," said Ritchie. "Mr. . . . Leonard Philips; gotta message for him."

"Twenty-four's further up; long way up, sonny."

"Oh, right you are, Mister." Ritchie was still at the door, holding it. "Thanks, an' sorry for givin' you the jumps." He grinned. "Hey, yer wouldn't 'appen t' have the right time?"

"Get on with yer," said the old man, relaxing.

Still whistling, Ritchie left again, hopping up the basement steps, while the clock repairer squinted at him from the window below.

That night, in the privacy of his bedroom, after Leo had fallen into a tipsy sleep, Ritchie made notes in a jotter. He put a large black lead asterisk against Mr. Samuel Fielding's name.

He would crack a couple of others first, just to test out the state of the clock market. But the top prize, he realised, was to be found in Snetterton Street, in sooty old Victoria.

* * *

Linsey was not at the Winslow Hotel in Kensington when David arrived there that evening at five minutes to seven. She'd left no note at the desk, no message with the porter. For a florin David bought the information that the "lady" had departed almost as soon as she'd arrived and hadn't returned since. David checked that the suitcase and the trunk were still in Linsey's room, then went down to the hotel's tiny disapproving bar and persuaded them to serve him a whisky and soda. He drank it slowly. Again he was tempted to abandon Linsey. But debts still had to be paid; all sorts of debts. He went home to Cardwell Place, shaved and changed out of uniform, ate a belated dinner with his mother, scraped what cash he could find from the drawer in his room and, at something after ten, left again for the so-called "Latin Quarter".

It was after midnight before David finally traced Linsey to the Green Parrot Club in Lemarck Street. He knew the owner, Rollo Roberts, fairly well.

"She's here," said Rollo Roberts. "I wish to God she wasn't."

"Tiddles?"

"Worse."

Linsey was in the chamber beyond the bar, an intimate dining room with a miniscule dance floor and a half-moon dais on which a five-man band crouched over their instruments, rendering a "blue-mood" arrangement that had crossed the Pond so recently that the lyrics hadn't caught up with it yet. The low moaning of a saxophone was appropriate to a scene in which scarlet-shaded table lanterns cast light up into the faces of the couples and a huge motor-powered fan, blades flecked with tiny mirrors, lazily rotated overhead, scattering reflections like stars falling languidly through a smoke-clouded sky. It was pretty, and decadently romantic – so long as the lights stayed dim.

Etheral in a gown of palest green chiffon, with a trail of red silk roses on the skirt, Linsey swayed soulfully on the edge of the floor, her slender body crushed against that of a very young man in evening dress. The young man, nineteen or twenty at most, was podgy, his thick hips miming an undulating, copulatory rhythm. His eyes were slitted, his lips slack, as, in a daze, he made love to the girl there on the dance floor.

"Who is that, Rollo?" David asked.

"Duke of Barclay's youngest: a damnable young pup."

"I'd better get her out of here."

"Yes," said Rollo Roberts. "If the police decided to drop in now there'd be no end of bother."

"Why?"

"Don't you see?"

"See what?"

"They've both been at the moonbeam."

"Moonbeam?"

"White dream; cocaine."

"Oh, God!"

"Peel them apart as discreetly as you can; I don't want a scene, you know."

David slid between the tables; the couples hardly glanced at him. The saxophone became louder, dry as bran, a husky sobbing sound. David put his hand on the young dancer's shoulder and forced a smile.

"Pardon me; may I cut in?"

Slitted eyes flicked towards him. "Hm? Ah! Noah, you may not. I'm almost there, you see. Almost there."

David's fist travelled twenty inches; a perfect straight right. The ducal nose split sprinkling blood on to nearby table cloths.

"Doh! Doh! He strubbed me."

The saxophone stopped. An indolent piano continued unaccompanied. Somebody screamed, shrill as a whistle, as the young man listed, thrust out his arm for support, found the table's edge and, falling, brought dishes and glasses down into the laps of the diners. They shot up and screamed too. A woman threw a champagne glass away from her as if it had turned suddenly into a serpent.

David caught Linsey.

"Daaaaaaaaavy; how maaaaaaaa'v'lous."

The vacuity, the fixed and staring eyes, the abandoned suppleness of her body – the moonbeam dream. Where the devil had she got the vile stuff? More relevant, where had she found the money? The purchase of cocaine was not difficult, supply was governed only by its high cost. Perhaps the duke's son had given it to her. The punch had caused blood to rush through David's veins. He felt a surge of righteous strength, of protectiveness.

"Daaaaavy, take me home."

She could not walk.

Green Parrot patrons were cawing and shrilling and, finding an excuse to relieve the tedium of the wee small hours, were having a fine time throwing glasses at the band.

David lifted the girl in his arms and, using his shoulder, charged through the bar, through the hallway and out into the street.

He put her down, her toes raised like a ballerina's, her body floating and weightless. He supported her, yelling for a taxi, yelling up at the rank at the corner of Lemarck Street until a vehicle detached itself and rolled backwards.

"Lady ain't goin' ter be sick, like, guv, is she?"

"No, no. I promise you. She's . . . she's fainted. It's just the heat in that place."

They were driven back to Kensington, to the Winslow Hotel.

Linsey lay across his knees, curled, thumb in her mouth, crooning some broken nursery tune that he couldn't identify. He stroked her soft golden hair.

When they refused to allow him to enter the Winslow Hotel, he had the porter bring down her bags and summoned another cab. It was a necessary madness; he could not desert her now.

He took her back to Mayfair, to Larder Mews, to the familiar house, to Willoughby's property. He broke a pane of glass in the morning room window, ripped his sleeve groping for the catch, lifted the window and stepped inside. He went through the dark and empty house, opened the front door, caught her as she fell inwards, and carried her upstairs to the bedroom.

He undressed her upstairs and put her to bed.

He went downstairs and helped himself to the Gordon's, sat, hunched, in an armchair and brooded about what he must do. *He must leave her.* With every return, every further involvement, a permanent parting became more difficult and more distant. *He must leave her where she was. Let her stew.* Booze was bad enough. Cocaine was deadly.

He got to his feet.

She's not my responsibility.

I want no more to do with her.

Let her sort out her own mess.

He stalked into the front hall.

And went upstairs.

In mid-morning, when Linsey Leigh-Jennings drifted out of drugged sleep, groaned and turned, she found David naked by her side, snoring out fine vaporous clouds of pure Gordon's gin.

Linsey chuckled, groaned again, stretched her body against his and, with her arms fast around him, slid back contentedly into sleep.

* * *

In the upstairs room in the Shears and Mallet, Jack Renzo switched on the lights above the billiards table, then went to the door and locked it with the key that the barman had given him. Aleric Seaman leaned nonchalantly on an iron steam radiator under the tattered linen blinds that kept daylight from the loft. Seaman's presence did not disturb Ritchie. It warned him, however, that he was about to be sharked again.

Two days ago he had passed on five fine clocks that he had lifted from two shops. He had broken in easily enough and, reverting to his favourite *modus operandi,* had disturbed the stock hardly at all, removing only three clocks from one shop and two from the other. He had poked about in search of loose cash but found none. He had ignored silver and china; he had no ready market. He had wrapped the clocks in old newspapers, bedded them in his hold-all, and slipped away into the night. He had held the goods for a day, then passed them on to Seaman. Now came the pay-off.

"Cut the chatter, Jack," said Ritchie curtly. "Tell me what the stuff fetched, straight off."

"You earned yourself fifty quid," said Renzo, taking a billfold from his hip pocket and tossing it to Ritchie.

Ritchie made no attempt to field it, allowing it to fall to the green baize under the lights. Seaman made a faint snorting noise; derision.

Ritchie said, "Jack, don't screw me. Those tickers are worth far more'n fifty."

"Not to Vincent they ain't."

"Look." Ritchie dug a hand into the pocket of his pilot coat and brought out five labels, like fish-bait, still attached to their threads. "Sellin' prices. Total, seven hundred an' eight pounds. One of those clocks was a Dutch museum piece, the one with the velvet dial. Two hundred guineas it was priced."

"He lifted marked goodies, Jack," said Seaman. "Ain't he the clever lad."

"The black ebony one was Turkish. Sellin' at one hundred an' twenty quid."

"Not that clever," said Jack Renzo. "Take the money, Ritchie. Don't give us no hard time, son."

"Hard *time*: that's funny, Jack," Seaman said. "Time: get it?"

"Fifty is fair. It's such easy money," said Renzo.

"Retail price – eight hundred, near enough," said Ritchie, twirling the price tags and tossing them on to the table. "Shotten sells for – be generous – half, t' this American toff. That's four hundred. Pays me fifty."

"Vince's got an organisation to run, Ritch."

"But he depends on me an' my like t' fetch the product."

"Watch it, Ritchie," said Renzo. "Vince wouldn't like t' hear that you're buckin' him."

Seaman had shifted away from the radiator at the table's end. The men flanked Ritchie now, one on each side of the table.

Ritchie gave no appearance of being intimidated. He had his hands back in the deep pockets of the pilot's coat. He wheezed slightly, and seemed vulnerable.

"Take the money, Ritchie, an' we'll forget all about this spot o' bother," Renzo suggested.

"Tell Shotten he can stuff his money," Ritchie said, conversationally.

Shaking his head, Renzo said, "I think you gotta teach our young friend some manners, Aleric."

It was too sudden for Renzo to follow. He flinched away from the first motion, the gigantic swing of the box-like light shade, as Ritchie leaped on to the billiards table. The knife in Ritchie's right hand was a foot long; none of your clean steel either. It had been whetted down by a butcher's stone so that the blade was concave and razor sharp.

Elbow to his side, feet spread, body balanced, Ritchie said, "Gawd, Renzo, you're a bigger bleedin' idiot than I am. Who's idea was this – not Shotten's. Who's creamin' off the extra? You? Tip Ally a fiver, do yer?"

"Now, now, Ritch! Don't do anythin' you'll regret," said Renzo.

"Stand still, you," Ritchie told Seaman. "I ain't wavin' this cutter for the fun of it. I'll use it t' write a message for yer boss, for Vince, printed right across your gob, Jack."

"You would an' all."

"Right," said Ritchie.

"You're in trouble, sonny." Seaman did not move.

"Not me," said Ritchie.

"Come down off the table; we'll talk about it. Civilised, like."

Stooping, Ritchie edged around the light-shade, keeping balance by holding on to the chain that supported it.

"Listen t' me, Jack," Ritchie said. "You – an' maybe Shotten too, for all I know – think you're dealin' with a common scruff. Well, you ain't. Tell me, Jack, what other mug brought you in what y'asked for – quality goods? I know what you got from the rest of the lads – junk. Right? I bring you five collector's pieces, an' you cheat me blind. You're *stupid*. Hear me? *Stupid*. Think I ain't got more? Think I ain't got better? I can lay 'ands on stuff that'd make yer Yank's eyes water. *But I know what I'm bleedin' doin' an' what I'm worth*."

"Sure, Ritchie. Nobody ever doubted you was good" said Seaman, placatingly, trying to catch the young man off guard.

"Put fifty more on the table, Jack, an' we'll think about the rest," said Ritchie. "An' if yer contemplatin' havin' that chimpanzee..." he gestured with the butcher's knife at Seaman, "... chop me up some dark night, forget it. I'm no brainless bantam, not yer usual run o'thief. I take risks; I plan jobs; I stay outta the clink. I'm an earner, Jack. Don't do yer boss an ill turn by switchin' me off."

"It's true, Ritchie. It's all true," said Renzo. "Maybe I was hasty."

"Get chimpie outta 'ere."

Renzo hesitated, then jerked his thumb at the door.

"Boss?" said Seaman, uncertainly.

"Best leave us." Renzo tossed Seaman the key. "Make sure we're not disturbed. Mr. Beckman an' me, we've got some serious talkin' to do."

When Seaman left, Ritchie climbed down from the table. He did not, however, put away the knife.

"Do I get the hundred, Jack?"

"If it ever got 'round that snafflers was namin' their own prices..."

"It won't get around," Ritchie promised.

"You get the hundred."

"An' you get more clocks."

"How many more? How good?"

"Ten, maybe fifteen – every one a prize."

"They'd better be."

"I'll know what they're worth," said Ritchie. "Remember that, Jack. Pass it on t' Shotten. I'll know what they're worth on the market. An' I want a quarter share."

"Cunning little bastard, ain't you?"

"Too cunnin' for you, Jack."

"What's it for, son? What's all the money for?"

Ritchie put the knife-point on the wooden bevelling of the table and made a tiny scratch.

"I gotta girl," he said.

"So?"

"It's all for her."

"She must be a stunner."

"She is," said Ritchie. "She is."

"And *all* the loot's for her?"

"Every last brass farthin'," Ritchie said. "So, shell out the hundred, an' let me get back t' work."

Meekly, Renzo counted out notes from his wallet and pushed them across the table. "Fifty in the fold, fifty here."

Ritchie took them and put them into his coat pocket.

"That's better," he said, going towards the door. "Now all you've gotta do is warn Seaman t' lay off me – permanently."

"Will do," said Renzo. "Hey – what's your dolly daydream's name?"

"Ruth Erbach," said Ritchie, before commonsense could smother his pride.

*   *   *

David did not dare let Linsey out of his sight. It was not that he was afraid she would do something deliberately self-destructive; girls like Linsey did not commit suicide by intention. He was drawn close to her by a sense of shame. Only in her company did he feel superior, in control of the direction of his life – even if that direction happened to be downward. It would cost too much effort to hoist himself up rung by rung, up to Holly Beckman, to the settled existence that he professed to desire. The role of scoundrel came easily. Complex motives could not be rationalised and altered. To add to his problems he was discharged from the army.

It happened almost cursorily.

The paperwork took four days.

He did not dare go home to Cardwell Place. He had sent his mother a letter informing her that he was "very, very busy" at the office and would be staying at the barracks. He had never properly explained that there were no barracks, that he had been the recipient of a boarding bonus since the day he had taken his commission. He had the use of a cot in a six-bunk dormitory in the old Siddons Street school, and could eat there if he wished. But the mess in Thrush Hall was effectively his home; he drank there, ate there, and slept with Linsey Leigh-Jennings in a sordid little no-questions-asked hotel in Old Compton Street. All of his terminal pay, plus twenty quid he'd scrounged from Peter Ulscroft, a brother officer, went on clearing the mess bill.

Shortly before midday on a bleak November afternoon, David Aspinall stepped into the street, one year and eleven days after the first signing of the Armistice. He had not actively sought discharge, had not badgered his superiors to release him. On the other hand he had not accepted the mandatory offer of a long-term commission in the Pay Corps. The insurance firm of Spencer, Lucas & Andrews would take him back, of course, but the very thought of drab offices, trivial people and grinding routine prevented him making an approach to his former employers. Only sheer desperation would drive him back there – and if things were that desperate the wage that Spencer, Lucas & Andrews would pay him would make no difference.

As it was, there were debts. Debts everywhere; his own minor ones as well as Linsey's whoppers. But there was also cash. Linsey had done fairly well from the sale of her shares. She had enough on hand to splash about. If she'd had her way, they would have established themselves in the Park Lane or the Goring and whooped it up for a month or so until they were flat broke – then she would have heaved the whole load of worry about their next meal on to his shoulders, and complained that he did not "look after her".

In January or early February, when the shop accounts for the six-month had been audited, he would receive a lump sum representing twenty-five per cent of the net profit for the period ending December 31st, 1919. However, he could not live in hope that Holly's effort would bring down five or even a couple of hundred. Holly had been ploughing profits back into stock purchase; the value of the business would have increased five fold, turnover would be record-breaking, but the take-away sum to be dispersed among the partners would not solve his problems. Having elevated his demands, he was compelled to think in pounds not pence, in hundreds not tens, when he did the mental arithmetic that told him what his madness was costing him.

Behind it was Linsey. Pity, passion, fury and fun – she was a kaleidoscope in which every emotional colour and shape could be experienced in a state of constant change. She made him feel alive. There was no real "love" – by which he meant romantic softness – like the feeling he had for Holly. He censored thoughts of Holly from his mind.

David had supposed that he had reached the bottom of a deep well, that the night of the dinner at the Connaught had marked the beginning of a climb back to the sweet fresh air of normalcy. But he had been wrong, quite wrong. The well was deeper than he had anticipated. He was still plunging downward, down towards unknown depths. He had no volition of his own. He could not even cry out for help. So he went along with Linsey in a haze of alcohol and sexuality, denying her – and himself – nothing.

Except "moonbeam". Cocaine sellers were well established in London. Mr. Chang built up his market by "cultivating" the hightoned whores of London's clubland. Jan Emeritus, a society hostess, supported a stable of racehorses and two Irish agricultural estates on the proceeds of her "medicinal" ministrations among the young, flushed debutantes of Chelsea and Belgravia. There was the mysterious Fish – Laurence Whiting – so thin and so tall that when Elisha Gray painted his portrait he had to do it in sections, like a stained glass window. It was Fish who swam in Linsey's particular pond; Fish who glided close from time to time. Linsey was friendly with Fish. David feared the man. In a temper one night, David had shaken a few loose truths out of his mistress. Yes, she had taken moonbeam before. Yes, she knew what it could do to her. But what did that *matter*, who *cared* about her anyhow? It was *so* pleasant. Why didn't he try it? What was he afraid of?

David cuffed her across the face for daring to suggest it, then pulled her to him and comforted her, dried her tears, told her that he did not want her to sniff the deadly fine white powder, nor even to talk to Fish or any of his brethren.

"But you don't know how good it is."

"I don't want to know."

Next morning she was sick and would not get up at all.

Next afternoon they got drunk together and made love while "respectable" Londoners trailed home from shops and offices.

Next evening, with the bruise on Linsey's cheek in full bloom, they went along to Christabel's to celebrate their "re-union".

And won a fortune at roulette.

* * *

Ritchie's run of easy money ended in the darkness of Sam Fielding's shop in Snetterton Street. Ritchie could not blame Shotten for what happened – though he did swing guilt that way eventually – and could not for the life of him credit that he had been responsible for the death of the old geezer. He made no bloody profit out of the break-in and it cost him nine months of freedom, to boot; quite enough punishment, to Ritchie's way of thinking, to lay Sam Fielding's ghost.

Darkness, silence, stealth. It seemed like a dream; because he was not afraid. In fact, later, when he had ample time to contemplate, he felt quite proud of himself for the coolness with which he had squared up to the piece of lousy luck.

Sure, he knew Sam Fielding slept on the premises. But Ritchie could move about with no more sound than a moth.

Three o'clock, he picked the outside lock.

He inched the door inwards, reached up on tip-toe, caught the stem of the bell, groped along the stem, and pinched the lead clapper inside the brass cup between finger and thumb. He rode the door inwards an inch at a time, muffling the tell-tale bell. He wore rubber pumps, an overall, a woollen sweater and a pair of cotton gloves. Once inside it was easy to hold the bell-tongue and close the door past it. He did not neglect to brace the tumbler lock with the wooden golfing tee that he carried for the purpose. He was relieved to be out of sight of the street.

The inner doors weren't even locked.

Three o'clock in the dark of a November morning; even the trains were asleep. It was bitterly cold. The old miser used no heating at all. He was probably a patriotic saver of fuel.

Ritchie had brought jute sugar bags into which he had sewn flannel linings. Paper, rags and string stuffed the bags at present, folded neatly into the bib of his overalls. The flat carbide torch, War Office issue, was lit only when he had to reconnoitre the position of shelves and cases. The quantity and quality of the haul gave him quite a jolt. He felt shaken by the knowledge that he was not sufficiently expert to do more than make a hopeful selection. It would have required a handcart to remove all of the clocks.

Methodically, unhurriedly, he started with the largest showcase.

Screening the beam of the carbide lamp with his palm, he studied the goodies carefully, made his selection, and placed each object on the floor. He took four clocks and closed the case lid gently. The brass lock made a faint squeaking noise.

He followed the same procedure with the second large case, stole five objects, including a couple of tiny mantel clocks set into porcelain figures, and one heavy carriage clock. Kneeling on the floor, Ritchie bagged the nine. He had room for three maybe four more in that sack. He was irked by the fact that he would have to leave so many tickers that Shotten's American would undoubtedly have paid through the snoot to acquire.

Next he turned his attention to a long shelved cabinet with a yellowing card tacked to it – *Not for Sale*. Though Ritchie did not know much about Sam Fielding's reputation, instinct told him that these were the old man's personal treasures and presumably the most valuable pieces in the place. He found a wooden chair, brought it over, climbed on it and, by the light of the shielded lamp, scrutinised each of the clocks individually.

It was then thirteen minutes after three a.m.

Nineteen of the things: some hefty.

Ritchie pursed his lips.

That one was silver mounted. He would have it.

That one was Viennese: he recognised the trimmings from one of the books he'd read. He'd have it too.

A Cartel in ormolu and tortoiseshell.

A Germanic-looking item, so ancient that he could hardly believe it was a clock at all.

Beside the Jerry number was a real beauty; a perfect square of a clock with a silver handle, chased silver face, and a glass case hung below. In the case was a miniature bird with yellow and blush-pink feathers and a gilded bill, even some leaves of grass done in a material that Ritchie did not recognise. He tilted the carbide closer. He saw diamond eyes. He reached up his hand.

It was a quarter after three o'clock.

Dutifully, cranking on its pedestal, the mechanical bird sang four liquid notes.

Only four notes.

Startled, Ritchie dropped the lamp..

Ritchie's hand froze on the clock case, his body rigid.

He heard a thump, running. The door slammed open to reveal old Fielding in striped knee-length nightshirt and limp nightcap. He heard a shout of *"Thief"*.

Stepping down, Ritchie slid a knife from the straight pocket of the overalls.

"Shut yer bleedin' mouth," he hissed.

There was nothing between them except three or four yards of floor and a skinny rug. Extending the knife Ritchie took a pace away from the cabinet.

"You're stealin' my . . ."

The old man grunted in mid-sentence.

Nothing that Ritchie could see by the faint light of the fallen lamp indicated that death came hard to Samuel Fielding. There was no change in his expression. He simply lost interest in Ritchie, in the shop, in everything. Still holding the door handle with his left hand, he clapped his right palm to the breast of his shirt, like a man taking a solemn oath, then fell forward, heavily, jarring all the clocks on all the shelves, making their filigree parts jingle.

Sam Fielding lay still.

Ritchie stood like an ebony statue for two full minutes, listening to his heart beating, lungs wheezing, then he laid the knife on one of the cases, picked up the lamp and went forward.

The old man's cheek crushed the rug. A dribble of saliva trailed from the corner of his mouth. Ritchie tried to avoid the staring gaze as he lifted Fielding's outstretched wrist and felt for the pulse. He found nothing. He tried again. Found nothing. Sliding his hand under the body on the left side, he discovered no heartbeat.

Sam Fielding had died of shock, it seemed.

Ritchie sat back on his heels.

Suddenly he was aware of the ticking of all the clocks and watches. The sound had been constant since his arrival. But it was only now, when silence turned against him, that he became conscious of the myriad tiny noises.

He could hardly think straight.

He got up and crossed the hall to the old man's bedroom. Spectacles on a table, teeth in a glass, a jeweller's eye-piece and a cheap novel with a smoking revolver depicted on the cover; the bed was hardly disturbed. He could still make out the indentation on the pillow where Fielding's head had lain. Blankets were stripped back in a single throw, where Fielding had flung them as he'd leapt out of sleep. No wonder his heart seized up.

Any other crook would have hopped it. Dumb-bells would even have snaffled the loot. Not Ritchie Beckman. Ritchie recognised trouble when it confronted him. A man was dead. Natural causes or not, the coppers would make it a murder charge, at best wilful manslaughter. What the hell did the charge matter? They would nail him to the mast. It could mean his neck, fifteen or twenty years hard labour in one of His Majesty's hellholes.

Fifteen years in clink. Fifteen years away from Ruth. Fifteen years out of circulation. Gawd! There'd be nothing left to come out to. It would be better, kinder to hang him.

Momentarily panic enveloped Ritchie.

He began to mutter to himself, to give himself instructions in a chummy whisper, cajoling himself. "Brace up, Ritchie-boy. Tighten your grip. Law ain't got yer yet. Nobody knows you're here, except the old man. And he's dead. Nobody even knows what you were planning. Give the coppers a real mystery. Even if they trace you, they'll never prove a thing. Right? Right you are, Ritchie-boy."

Now he acted swiftly, the plan complete in his brain.

Lugging Sam Fielding across the hall, he lifted the corpse and rolled it into bed. He positioned the limbs, folded up the blankets. He studied his handiwork by lamplight. Quite natural. Back across the hall, he straightened the rug then set to work replacing the clocks. He put them back more or less as he had found them, thanking his stars that he hadn't packed away more of the things.

The damned bird sang three-thirty; eight notes this time. Again it scared the wits out of Ritchie. Crouched low in darkness by the bottom showcase, fists clenched, he waited until the mechanical trill played itself out. Sweating heavily, breathing laboured, he talked to himself some more as he finished off the business of putting the stolen objects back in place. After that, he went over the room carefully by the light of the lamp.

It *looked* apple-pie. Deceiving? Might be small clues, tell-tales, crumbs of evidence that he'd overlooked. Still, couldn't afford to hang around any longer. Must get outside, push on with the hardest part of his plan – forging the perfect alibi. He reckoned he had about an hour.

Tearing himself away from the showroom, he closed the door after him. He let himself out by the front door, ignoring the bell chime. He locked the street door from the outside. Carrying the empty sacks under his arm, he crouched on the basement steps and surveyed the pavements.

All quiet.

Slinking up the steps he walked along Snetterton Street into Ranscombe Street. Two tipsy toffs strolled up from Buckingham Palace Road; did not appear to notice him. An encounter with coppers would be dangerous; he certainly looked suspicious in overalls and rubber pumps. He tossed the first sack into a green-grocer's doorway, the second into the gutter outside a grain merchants. In another shop doorway, he peeled off the overalls, balled them up and threw them over a wall beside a hoarding. The knife he slipped down a drain in Sophy Street.

At five minutes to four o'clock Ritchie reached Peacock Place, a short street not far from Cardwell Place. Here was The Clock Shop, a dismal dump, cramped, dusty and unattractive. He had cut it from his original list. It was perfect for his purpose now, however. It was protected by a Bramm & Williams' Mechanical Alarm, although there was nothing in the coffin-shaped shop really worth stealing.

A Bramm & Williams. What a joke!

Resignedly, Ritchie climbed over the wooden gate at the shop doorway. He had chosen The Clock Shop because he had already cased it and knew that it would be a simple matter to force an entry and that he would find nobody on the premises. The very last thing he wanted was to encounter another irate owner. Some people might think that he was creating a pretty feeble alibi; that would have been true if Sam Fielding had been lying back there with his head bloody or a knife sticking out of his belly. But Fielding had died natural, without a mark on him. Now who in their right mind would walk straight off and do another clock shop? Caution and subtlety; that was it. With a hangman's noose throwing its shadow, there could be no such thing as too much caution. Better a year in jail, if that, than a one way ticket to the gallows. It was very long odds that the coppers would even realise that Fielding had been scared to death, but if they did they would hardly look around for a petty thief daft enough to get caught red-handed.

Ritchie kicked the door open and, to the deafening din of the alarm bell, sauntered into the depths of the shop. He hauled open the till, which was empty, then stuffed handfuls of cheap trinkets and watches into his pockets and, with a sigh, leaned wearily on the counter to await arrest.

* * *

Nude body elongated, arms stretched, Linsey bathed luxuriously in five pound notes; two hundred and ten honourable Promises by the Bank of England, a crisp batch, unsullied by vulgar hands. The silken sheets of the Apollo hotel's bridal bed rippled as the girl rolled on scattered banknotes.

David shed his thigh-length robe. Naked too, he bridged Linsey's slender belly and brought his mouth to her breast.

"See, you *do* love me. You do. You do. You can't deny it," she crooned. "You love me as I am right now, in my natural habitat, smothered in money."

"You never looked more beautiful." Bubbly had a peculiar effect on him. It made him happy, plain ordinary happy, not depressed, deflated, defunct, devoid, demented or deintoxicated, not even drunk, really, just soooooo happy – and very Linsey-inclined. "Never more desirable, my loveliest one."

He licked her nipples. They tasted sharp. Perfumed soap. He pushed her left breast into a cone and nuzzled his mouth against the erect nipple, stimulating it with the point of his tongue.

She crooned, fingers flaring, banknotes crackling beneath her flanks.

It had never occurred to either of them before that large sums could be won at the gaming table. Cards, dice, gee-gees – all pastimes aimed to give one a thrill. But not money-making activities. Until that night in the upper room of Christabel's private salon at the long table that housed the new roulette wheel – imported direct from Deauville at great expense; a thing of beauty in its own right – neither Linsey nor David had considered gambling as a possible source of revenue, a solution to all life's tiresome problems. But it was a little clicking-clacking ball that had done it, had brought them the sum of one thousand pounds. More than David could earn in a year.

Winning was also magical, bestowing the bounty of good fortune. The gods had smiled on the innocent lovers. Showered down gifts. Blessed them.

It had begun with a simple one pound bet on the red.

Red. *Rouge*.

Double.

And left, and doubled; and doubled yet again.

For the fourth time the red came up.

Nothing could be simpler. Even the most inbred idiot of an earl, the most vacant-eyed debutante could understand it.

It had been David's pound note. Linsey was at another table, losing. Now he had sixteen pounds. The croupier, who spoke hardly any English and whose French was disgustingly rough-edged, held up proceedings while Linsey scrambled to her lover's side.

Red, Linsey had said, at his elbow, leaning over him to place one hundred pounds beside his sweet sixteen. Red. *Oui, Madame. Monsieur?*

Red. So be it.

Le rouge, s'il vous plait.

On that turn of the wheel they had wagered together, expecting to lose everything. Against the odds. Defiantly. Five reds, no black. Impossible.

Numero quartre. Le rouge.

Two hundred and thirty-two pounds.

"*Le rouge?* Linsey, for God's sake!"

"*Le rouge*, I say. Damn you, David. *Le rouge.*"

Four hundred and sixty-four pounds.

"Now stop."

He had turned his head and met her eye. There was a glazed look of disbelief in it, as if she had survived an accident. She was shocked by her run of luck, frightened. The pile of chips before them was mountainous. The low-roofed room buzzed with excitement. A gentleman on David's left rose and with a graceful bow yielded his chair to Linsey. She seated herself with an unladylike bump, still staring at David, he at her, neither of them daring to speak.

"One more, one more," she had begged at length.

"Pick a number."

"Red. Red will come up."

"It's with you, Linsey. *Pick a number this time.*"

"All of it. All of it on seventeen."

"Half."

"All of it, I tell you."

He refused, baulked and, with the croupier's white gloved fingers on the knob of the wheel, chopped his pile of chips in half and slid it out with his palm on to seventeen. She scrabbled by his side, but he held her back. He was oblivious to the mutterings of spectators and players. He knew he must not be *completely* mad, that the solution to all their problems lay on the suede cloth before them. The streak must be exploited, not flung away like a cheap toy.

"*Numero dix-sept. Numero dix-sept.*"

"Oh, God! Oh, darling!"

"We . . . we *won*."

"How . . . how much, David?"

"Over six thousand pounds."

"Put it all on; *all* of it."

"Stop it, Linsey. Don't be a fool."

"I won, I won. Put it . . ."

He split the chips and plaques, let her select the number. It did not come up. Again, he wagered a portion of their winnings on her choice. Again they lost.

"Linsey, let's . . ."

"Keep going, keep going. It will come. I *know* it will."

They lost.

Five hundred and twenty-five pounds remained. He found that he could evaluate the colours of the chips and card-sized plaques almost at a glance; a newly-discovered accomplishment.

"Win or lose, darling; it's our last spin.'

"Red."

"Are you sure?"

"Red. I tell you it's red."

There was, David had thought with a comforting pang of despair, a fine irony in it. Start on red. Finish on red.

Red came up.

He had scooped chips and plaques into his handkerchief before she could prevent him and positively leapt from the table. She had trailed him to the cash desk, mewing and yowling like a kitten. He had remained adamant. If they had only stopped when they were six thousand up. Still, one thousand and fifty pounds in virginal fivers was, by their standards, a fortune.

It gave them a stake.

They had swept out of the scruffy hotel in Soho in the wee small hours and checked into the Apollo, demanding the bridal suite. They were drunk with champagne and success.

Wintry dawn was far off yet. There was golden light from golden lamps, mother-of-pearl sheets, and *parfum* of kippers and scrambled eggs from silver dishes on a silver tray. And his lover's nude body, revived, made young again by her money bath. The thought burned in his mind, as lucid as any thought that he had ever had – he could do it again, do it again and again and again.

The thrill had been orgasmic, more prolonged than sexual release, more satisfying. For the hour of the run at the wheel in Christabel's, David had been oblivious to his sister, his mother, his weaknesses and failures; to the promise he'd made to Holly Beckman, his debt to Linsey Leigh-Jennings. He had lived on the very edge of experience, out where it was raw, male and challenging.

He would, must do it again.

He could make a living at the tables. He had control. Linsey had luck.

Between them.

Yes.

Now.

She wriggled. As he looked down to steer himself into her eager body, he saw the curled leaves of the banknotes beneath her, framing her belly.

"Now, David, now."

With a throaty cry of triumph, David pushed himself home.

5

The Princess in the Tower

AT SIX O'CLOCK on a cold winter's morning, the Beckmans' living room resembled a Crimean field hospital. Leo had thrown a greasy overcoat over his nightshirt. His eyes were baggy with lack of sleep and the effects of last night's beer. Maury was dressed in striped pyjama trousers and an army cardigan, Tal in flannels, sheepskin jacket and rubber galoshes. Only Holly, who treated the arrival of the police with resignation, had taken the trouble to dress.

A young plain-clothes detective accompanied by an experienced constable had brandished a warrant. Expertly they had searched the interior of the house from top to bottom, prying into every nook and cranny, while Leo growled and mumbled, "What the 'ell y'lookin' for 'ere? Ain't yer done enough damage, liftin' my boy for somethin' he ain't done?" The chant had grated on everybody's nerves. Finally the plain-clothes detective, losing his objectivity, had wheeled on the docker and snapped, "Somethin' he ain't done? Listen, mate, we nabbed the little beggar red-handed."

Outside the darkness was like a sodden blanket.

When the constable had moved out into the scullery, Tal had followed him, saying, "If you tell me, officer, what it is you're looking for, perhaps I may be able to assist you."

"'That'll be the day," the constable had said. "You're prob'ly as bad as the kid."

"What exactly did he do?" Tal had asked.

"Broke into an antique shop, stole some things."

"Where was the shop?"

"Peacock Place."

"How did you catch him?"

"Alarm went off; the silly beggar hadn't sense t'run for it."

Tal had frowned: he knew enough of his grandson to realise that Ritchie would not have triggered an alarm in the first place, let alone have hung around after it went off. He had recalled, with panic, the stolen goods that he had seen Ritchie hide in the garden shed.

The constable had yanked open the scullery door and was peering out into the garden.

"What's out there?"

"Garden shed," Tal had said. "It should be searched, too, should it not?"

The constable had hesitated.

"You must be thorough, officer."

"Don't tell me my business, oldster," the constable had said, shutting the outside door.

Tal had shrugged.

The policemen found nothing to incriminate Ritchie further. Holly could not understand why, if they had taken him red-handed, the police had considered it necessary to make a rapid house search at all.

"Been a rash o' shop break-ins lately," Maury explained. "I suppose they was just checkin' us out."

Tal said nothing about the garden shed.

Bemused, Leo lowered himself into the chair by the cold hearth. "Got caught. Can't see how he'd get caught. Not our Ritchie."

"Where is he being held?" asked Tal.

"Sutherland Street Police Station," Maury replied.

"In Pimlico?" said Holly.

"The shop he busted was in Pimlico," said Maury. "He'll appear some time this mornin' before the magistrate."

"Won't he be held over for trial, remanded in custody?" said Holly.

"Depends how he pleads," said Maury.

Tal saw that Maury was also puzzled by the facts of Ritchie's arrest.

"He's not bleedin' guilty." Leo thumped the arm of his chair. "My boy's innocent."

Maury lit a cigarette, shivering a little in the chill room.

"He was in it alone?" Tal asked.

"So it would seem," said Maury.

"Somebody had better go t'the court, hadn't they?" said Leo.

Maury and Tal exchanged glances; neither of them cared enough about Ritchie to volunteer.

"What about you?" said Holly to her father. "You'll be there, won't you?"

Leo's head jerked. "Me? In a bleedin' magistrate's court? He won't expect me there. I mean, what the 'ell good would it do Ritchie if I showed up? In a magistrate's court! Gawd strewth!"

"Spoken like a loyal father, Leo," said Tal.

"Afraid they'll recognise you, Pa?" Maury asked.

"Shut yer trap."

"Come t'think of it, where were *you* last night?" Maury said.

"In me bleedin' bed. In me bleedin' bed."

"Got witnesses?" asked Maury.

Leo sunk lower in the armchair, temper beginning to smoulder, but he would not stand up to his eldest son, nor to the old man. He squinted at Holly. "It's all 'er bleedin' fault."

"Gerroff!" said Maury. "Holly had nothin' t'do with it."

"Ritchie wouldn't 'ave needed no spare rhino, if she'd bought . . ." Leo bit off the accusation.

"If Holly had bought what?" asked Tal softly.

"None of you like 'im."

"That's true," Maury agreed.

"Starved o' nat'ral affection," Leo groused. "Poor kid."

"Gawd Almighty!" said Maury. "Here, I ain't standin' here freezin' half t'death an' listenin' t' this rubbish. He's your beloved bloody son, Pa; you go t'court, speak up for him, tell the beak how innocent he is, how 'starved of affection'. Right?"

"Can't. Gotta be at work." Mood shifting again, Leo looked up at Tal. "You go, old man. You look more respect'ble than the rest o' us."

"Thanks very much," said Maury. "Holly, do us a favour, love, throw some bread in the pan. Brew some tea as well. Now I'm up, may as well shove along t' the yard."

Leo shot to his feet. "Yer all abandonin' him. Yer own flesh an' blood."

Maury laughed. "Includin' you."

"Holly, Hol, lov; you'll go see what's happenin' t' your brother, won't yer?" Leo begged.

"I . . . No, Pa. I can't. I got the shop . . ."

"You an' your bleedin' shop," Leo shouted.

"I'll go," Tal said. "If Holly can spare me for the morning, I will go to the court."

Appeased, Leo grunted, "Right, right." He sat down in the armchair. "Right, right." He scowled round at Holly. "Come on, gal, where's that tea?"

Holly went into the scullery. As she filled the kettle and greased the frying pan and took a stale loaf from the bread tin, she heard her father's voice carping from the living room.

"Poor kid. Poor little kid. Outta a job for sure."

"He should've thought o' that before he burgled the shop," Maury said.

"What'll become of 'im now?"

"Clink," said Maury.

* * *

Metropolitan Police Courts were offensive places. Drunkards, brawlers, wife-beaters, prostitutes, tricksters, shop-lifters, lunatics, liars, embezzlers and thieves, some old, some young, some pathetically victimised, some steeped in the juice of wickedness, all somehow managed to make the tragedy of living seem like trivial hugger-mugger, so that even solemn coppers and considerate magistrates often appeared like clowns employed in the service of that king and queen of jesters – Law and Order. The system was not heartless, not of itself forbidding. On the contrary. The average householder had no concept of what police courts did, how they were governed, or realised that they existed to serve strayed citizens, not just to punish them.

In addition to charges and summonses, there was an opening period, immediately after court convened at ten-thirty a.m., when applications were heard. These proceedings were held *in camera*. Magistrates listened patiently and courteously to folk who came to make their wants known, and dispensed legal and often friendly advice.

Day by day, year by year, the almanack of domestic troubles and problems of the heart was written and rewritten in the books of the court. The clerks' writing grew more crabbed and the magistrates' voices more patient, souring some, sweetening others. The opinion that the fate of a man on remand before the magistrate depended on a magistrate's digestion was not quite so cynical as it seemed. Justice was often tempered by understanding, or distempered by sheer world-werinesss. It was a lottery, in other words, a situation that

Ritchie Beckman understood well. He had taken his chance only after weighing the odds on the scale of his knowledge of the law.

The prisoners' room had been reformed out of existence. Cells were allotted one to each man. Walls were faced with clean white tiles; ventilation adequate. Lavatory bucket had a bag of lime beside it and a mat beneath. There was an iron bedstead with a ticking mattress and two wool blankets that ponged just a little of sick.

Because Ritchie was sober, and declared intention to enter an immediate plea of guilty to the burglary charge, the officer of the court had put him on the list for breakfast. The meal consisted of a mug of tea, a bowl of porridge and a slice of bread. Ritchie had disposed of that lot at seven o'clock. By the time the old man showed up at eight-thirty he was hungry again.

Ritchie was conducted out of the police cell to a large room on the first floor of the court building where a crowd of garrulous prisoners endeavoured to explain their innocence to mothers, fathers, wives and solicitors. Four constables kept watch over the chicken-run but the babble of conversation was so loud that there was no danger at all of being overheard. Ritchie was escorted across the room and seated at the end of a long narrow table, directly opposite his grandfather. Tal looked more of a toff than most of the lawyers present, and must have impressed the officers who'd checked him through. He wore a suit with a waistcoat and stiff shirt, and had laced lily-white spats over his black boots. He carried a black overcoat over his arm.

"What'd y'bring me?" was Ritchie's first question.

Tal extracted a paper bag from the overcoat pocket.

"Ham roll and seed cake. Did they not feed you?"

"Sir?" Ritchie held the bag aloft. A copper came over, peered in at the food, nodded and returned to his chair. Ritchie guzzled the ham roll. "Where's Pa?"

"Refused to come."

"Just as well," said Ritchie.

"Why did you do it?"

"For the bleedin' money, 'course."

"I don't mean commit the robbery," said Tal. "I mean, why did you get caught?"

"Not slippery enough, I suppose."

"Look at me."

"Yer, very posh."

"Look at me, Ritchie."

"Yer – what?"

"Why did you allow yourself to get caught?"

"No flies on you, Gran'pa." Ritchie grinned. "Well, I'm glad it was you what came. Pa wouldn't 'ave done."

"You haven't answered me."

"Ain't got no answer."

"Do you want me to employ a solicitor?"

"What for? I'm pleadin' guilty, soon as they take me upstairs."

"Under the circumstances that is wise."

Ritchie wiped his mouth with his cuff and lifted the seed-cake. He nibbled it like a squirrel.

"Plead guilty 'fore His Worship," said Ritchie. "Throw m'self on the court's mercy. A deposition from me, one from the copper. Won't be taken too seriously, not since I confess I done it. Better than tryin' to slide off the hook an' havin' them pokin' an' pryin' int' our affairs."

"Two policemen searched the house this morning."

"Did they now? Wouldn't find anythin'."

"No," said Tal. "I assume, Ritchie, that you removed the stolen goods from the garden shed?"

"How'd you know 'bout that?"

"I know much more about you than you suppose," said Tal. "Enough to realise that you *wanted* to get caught last night."

"You're dreamin', old man," said Ritchie. "Anyhow, the coppers wouldn't find nothin' in the house."

"What have you done with your money?"

"That's my business." Ritchie dusted crumbs from his cardigan. "Listen, it'll be the middle o' the afternoon 'fore His Worship gets round t'me. I want you t'do somethin' for me, Gran'pa."

"What is it?"

"Deliver a couple of messages by word o' mouth, on the q.t."

"Messages – to whom?"

"First one to the barman o' the Shears and Mallet public house. Tell 'im to tell Jack Renzo I want no trouble. No trouble, an' I'll take my medicine with a closed mouth. Got it?"

"Were you thieving for Vince . . . ?"

"Got it?" Ritchie interrupted.

"Yes."

"The second message." Ritchie folded his hands on the table and stared at them, his cheeks fired with anger or embarrassment; Tal could not determine which. "The second message is for Ruth Erbach."

"*What?*"

"Yer, your friend Tilly's daughter."

"You . . . you and little Ruth Erbach?"

"That's about the size of it."

"God in Heaven!"

"Steer clear o' Tilly." Ritchie's thumbs tapped nervously together. "Mendel too. Gawd, if they knew that Ruth was in love with me, she'd be made t' suffer 'ell."

"In love with you? Ruth Erbach? What have you done to her?"

"I ain't done nothin' to Ruth. What do yer take me for? I'd never do anythin' to 'arm 'er. We met when she came t' the Box one time with Mendel. Remember? It's been a struggle t' meet since then. But we get t' see each other whenever we can, whenever Ruth can sneak out, or bleedin' Tilly ain't with her. Is it wrong?"

"But you, Ritchie, what can a girl like Ruth see in you?"

"I'm not so bad lookin'. But what she likes about me is I'm different from the pansy types 'er mother'd have her meet. She's lead a sheltered life, so I suppose I'm an adventure. Now, the message . . ."

"No, Ritchie, I will not be a go-between."

"Please, Gran'pa, please."

"How long have you known her?"

"Must be nearly three years."

"She was only a child then; she's little more than a child now."

"Listen, I love her."

"And she loves you?"

"It's the truth." Confession was a relief to Ritchie; he was both proud and anxious in the admission. In talking of Ruth his features had lost their innate cunning. "I could show you letters."

"You risk sending letters?"

"Not through the post. I leave them at a drop near the school gate, in a hole in a wall. Ruth leaves 'er answers there too. I tell you, you got doubts about whether she loves me, you should read her letters."

"No thank you, Ritchie," Tal said.

"I know what you think. You think I just *want* her. But that ain't true. I . . . I love 'er, Gran'pa. I could 'ave girls by the bushel, but I don't really want none of them. I want Ruth, an' I'll wait for her, like she'll wait for me. Will you deliver my message?"

Tal stroked his moustache thoughtfully. He had been totally unprepared for this turn of events. It was ironic that his grandson was able to cope unaided with all the vicissitudes of arrest and charge, to be calm and unruffled at the prospect of a court appearance and a probable jail sentence, and yet be unable to handle the simple matter of a courtship. On the other hand, given the circumstances, recalling Tilly's tigerish defence of her daughter, perhaps Ritchie had coped with his wooing rather well.

How did the child really feel about Ritchie. Was it, for her, just a romantic diversion? Clearly, it was much more than that for Ritchie. Tal could sense the sincerity in his grandson's statements, and the honourable manner in which he had so far treated the girl; Tal did not, on this point, doubt the young man. Ritchie was handsome, and a favourite with girls, who seemed to like the mixture of charm and hardness in him, to find it not just attractive but almost compulsive. Three years? Yes, it was about that time that Ritchie's passionate "affairs" began to tail off. Tal had supposed it was a sign of maturity; it had not occurred to him that Ritchie had found a true love and would be sufficiently infatuated with her to behave like a perfect gentleman towards her, and to keep himself chaste for her sake.

Tal said, "I will give her your message."

"An' say nothin' to Tilly?"

"I wouldn't dare."

"Tell Ruth I . . . I haven't changed my mind. Tell 'er I love 'er. Ask 'er to write t' me in jail."

"How long do you imagine you will get?"

Ritchie did not even hear the question. He was absorbed in an inner vision of little Ruth Erbach, the beautiful Jewess, dark and unspeaking, of the bitter-sweet pain of separation from her; perhaps, too, of a future reunion.

"Ritchie?" Tal said. "How long will the magistrate give you by way of sentence?"

Ritchie blinked. He drew in a long shuddering breath, brought himself back to the present. "I'll ask for consideration under the First Offences Act."

"Showing such a precocious knowledge of the law," said Tal, "may not go down well with the magistrate."

"I'll try t' get 'im t' suggest it," said Ritchie. "But if the dumb-bell act don't work, then I'll bring it up when he gives me a chance t'speak 'fore sentencing. The copper that brought me in, he'll have t'vouch that I didn't get away with nothin', an' didn't resist arrest."

"And the house search?"

"Since they found nothin', I'll play innocent."

"You may find that hard."

Ritchie leaned on his elbows. "Gran'pa, cut off now an' do what y' can with the messages I gave yer."

"Do you wish me to come back – to be in court?"

Ritchie nodded. "Sure, come an' see the show." He shook the old man's hand with unusual formality, then got to his feet. "An' tell me what Ruth said. Will yer?"

"I will," Grandpa Tal promised, and watched his grandson being led away to await his first appearance in an English dock.

* * *

Delivering Ritchie's personal messages was not such an easy matter as Tal imagined it would be. Despatching himself to the Shears and Mallet, Tal found the building, at that hour of the morning, still securely locked and no sign of anyone on the premises. He hung around for twenty minutes, stamping his feet to keep them warm, then he walked all the way to Paddy Elkins' yard in Firebrick Street to share his news with Maury. He would say nothing about Ritchie's infatuation with Ruth Erbach; the Erbachs had been friends for too long. He had no wish to bring down Tilly's wrath upon his head or, at this stage, to antagonise Mendel. Apart from anything else, the Erbachs were useful contacts for Holly. The longer he could defray the day of revelation the better. Perhaps with Ritchie off the scene, Ruth would find another young man, somebody more suited to "her station", a suitor gentlemanly enough to please Mama and Papa. Tal doubted it – unless, of course, young Ruth had worn blinkers in respect of her secret beau and didn't know that he was a thief. Would Ritchie's arrest disillusion the child, or would it make him appear more glamorous in her eyes? Pondering these questions, Tal entered Elkins' yard.

He headed across it, stepping around blocks of bricks and wigwams of timber. Though Maury was not much of a talker – not, at least, at home – Tal had gathered from casual remarks that all was rolling along well in the building business. There were certainly healthy signs of activity that December morning; a motor-driven saw howling in the shed, young employees hurrying to load a flat-cart with shaped battens. Two donkeys stood between the cart's shafts, chewing on hay, quite unperturbed by the wail of the saw. Staggering under the weight of a sack of nails, a boy rushed from the office shed and deposited his load on the cart too.

Paddy Elkins' inimitable brogue urged him on. "Y'll be gettin' that stuff around t' Mr. Warren at the shop in Bywaters Street as fast as the devil. Then ye'll be comin' right back here wit the cart – an' no takin' the long road round – an' no dawdlin'. We've a casement frame for t'go t' Easter Street then."

"Right, Mr. Elkins."

"An' don' ye be maltreatin' me mules, McGuire."

"Noah, Mr. Elkins."

Within the office, Maury was standing by a tilted board on to which were pinned sheafs of plans and elevations, yellowish onionskins covered in pencil numerations and comments. Rulers, tee-squares and triangulators and two Bournville tins bristling with pens and pencils hung from the spar of the sloping board. Daylight barely penetrated the grimy window. As Tal entered, Maury was speaking in a loud voice to a man of his own age, a large, handsome fellow with a crutch tucked nonchalantly under his left armpit and empty trouser leg neatly pinned above the knee.

"These bloody local buildin' inspectors don't 'alf make life difficult," Maury was saying. He leafed through a clip of letters, found the one he wanted and consulted it, checking a detail against the drawing pinned to the board. "What can y' do about this, Georgie? The council clerk's bleatin' about interference with the sewer. We're nowhere near his bloody sewer, are we?"

"Clerk's got it wrong, Maury," Georgie answered, calmly. "He's read feet for inches. I think he thinks we're strippin' out the baffle wall, not just the wall around the boiler."

"Is he bleedin' blind?"

"Just careless," said Georgie.

"Well, what y' think? Go ahead, or try explain' t'him?"

"Go ahead."

With forefinger and thumb Maury detached the drawing from the board, folded it neatly and passed it to Georgie.

"Take it round t' Sangsters, then. Tell 'im t' get bashed in on the wall."

"I'll do that, Maury."

"Find out when he'll be ready for the bricklayers, an'what his estimated requirement'll be."

"Yes, Maury."

Maury grinned and dunted his fist on his employee's shoulder. "Go on, then, lad, 'op to it."

Georgie took no offence. As he filed the drawing into his breast pocket and pushed himself round on the crutch, Maury noticed Tal waiting by the door and came over to him.

"It's a hive of industry, Maury," said Tal.

"One step ahead o' the bailiff all the time," Maury said. "We've got the work, an' I've splurged out on the men t' do it, but squeezin' payments outta the clients is tricky. Paddy'n'me can't afford even a week's delay in collectin' our fees."

"What kind of work, Maury?"

"Guttin' an' refittin' shops, mostly. We've got four big jobs on –

includin' replacin' frontages at street level. Means argument with all sorts o' officials – an' bringin' in a glazier. Not equipped t' do the glasswork ourselves; not yet."

"How many men do you employ?"

"Apart from glass an' sanitation, I don't sub-contract," Maury said. "I carry men in all trades, even plumbin'. Four teams, workin' round the clock."

"All ex-servicemen, like your friend?"

"Yer," said Maury. "Twenty men."

"What a wage bill!"

"Wages, materials, transportation – week after bleedin' week," said Maury. "Still, we got the work, Grandpa, an' we do it fast an' properly. I have t'turn down offers, though. Not big enough t'handle them. Turnin' down business sticks in my throat."

"Better than having to drum it up?"

"That's true," Maury said. "Now, what about me dear little brother?"

Tal explained Ritchie's position, and outlined the substance of his interview with his grandson. He told Maury of Ritchie's request that he deliver a "message" to the barman in the Shears and Mallet.

"Bloody 'ell," said Maury. "He's been workin' for Shotten."

"I do not understand."

"The Shears is Shotten's castle. Ritchie's worried in case Shotten's pug-uglies try t' force him t' keep his trap shut." Maury grimaced. "Nasty, grandfather. Nasty."

"Do you mean they would threaten us, his family?"

"Holly'd be the obvious target; they might wreck the shop, that kind o' thing."

"My God!"

"What was the message?"

Tal told him.

Maury nodded. "I'll deliver it. When'll Ritchie show before the magistrate?"

"He thought it would be after noon."

"But he is pleadin' guilty?"

"That is what he told me."

"I hope the little begger does plead guilty," said Maury. "If he insists on remittance t' a higher court, then Shotten'll get very nervous."

Remembering Ruth Erbach, Tal realised now why Ritchie had not resisted arrest, why he had apparently decided to take his punishment without complaint. He was afraid that the underworld lordling would harm his sweetheart. The importance of delivering the message quickly became clear now.

"Will you go to the Shears and Mallet soon, Maury?"

"In case Ritchie knows more about Shotten than is good for 'im, I'd better shoot round there just as soon's they open."

"I feel that you are more able to . . ."

"Bloody little swine!" said Maury. "T' think that my brother'd work for a bloke like Shotten. I hope the beak sends 'im up for ten years. Keep 'im out our hair."

"Maury, don't lose your temper with this Shotten."

"No, no, old man. I'm not that stupid."

"There will be no danger for you?"

"Not if Shotten believes Ritchie."

"But will he?"

"I'll see that he does."

* * *

"Aleric: gent 'ere 'as a message for a Mr. Shotten. You 'eard of Mr. Shotten?"

"Mr. Shotten ain't 'ere. Who's askin'?"

"Maury Beckman's askin'."

"Is that a fact."

"Maury Beckman's tellin'."

"Snotty bastard, ain't yer?"

"Snottier than my brother. Ritchie. Bigger, too. An' not so bleedin' shy, either."

"Oh, yer!"

"Ritchie got 'imself done last night. Nabbed in the act."

"Should be more careful, like, shouldn't he?"

"I gotta message – which is; he'll take his medicine without a word o' complaint."

"So *he* says."

"Well, mate, if y' won't take my brother's word for it, maybe you'll take mine."

"I eat geezers like you."

"No, mate, no y' don't. Not like me. I'd stick in yer craw, believe me I would."

"Threatenin' me, are yer?"

"Just makin' a promise, *mate*. Our Ritchie keeps his trap shut – an' he will – does his stretch, an' comes out clean. That's the whole story. We don't need no 'messages' from your kind. Whisper that in yer boss's ear, mate."

"What if my boss won't listen?"

"In the war, were yer?" Maury asked.

"Nah!"

"Didn't collect no souvenirs, then. Well, mate, I did my bit. Collected a few trinkets. Brought them 'ome an' all. Like these."

"Jesus!"

"Know what these are? Not whizz-bangs. Nope, whizz-bangs is 'armless compared with these beauties. Thus 'un's a Jerry stick grenade. Maybe you've 'eard about them. A Potato Masher. Unscrew this cap, pull the string, an' there's five seconds between you an' kingdom come."

"Live?"

"Wouldn't bring 'ome a dummy, would I? An' this other, that's Mr. Mills's little boy. Grenade, Hand, Number Five. Operates by spring-loaded striker. You just pull out this safety pin an' . . ."

"I got the message, Beckman."

"Makes an 'ell of a mess."

"I say I got the message."

"Blow a room like this apart, in a split second."

"Beckman, put them things away, eh?"

"All my employees 'ave used 'em, Aleric, old son. Every last man jack o' them."

"Yer, yer, Beckman . . ."

"Mister Beckman."

"Mister Beckman."

"Message received an' understood?"

"Yer."

"Say it."

"Message received an' understood."

"That's a good lad."

"Mister Beckman."

"What?"

"Ah, er – give young Ritchie our best regards."

"Yer, I'll do that," said Maury. "I'm sure he'll be deeply touched."

• • •

In the playground, through tall iron railings, Tal observed the girls at their dinner break. The younger ones were hectically involved in skipping and ball games, but those who had reached beyond puberty behaved with bored secrecy, gathered in twos and threes in sheltered corners of the school yard, whispering and giggling. Ruth Erbach was alone. Engrossed in a book, she was seated on her school satchel on a stone prow below a memorial to the school's founder. She did not look in the least like the child Tal remembered from his last encounter with her, just under a year ago. She was a woman now, a beautiful young woman, dark, solemn and self-orientated.

He called out her name, attracted her attention and motioned her to come to the railings. The teacher on duty in the playground raised her head like an antelope who has become aware of a predator. Politely, Tal raised his hat and smiled at her. The teacher waylaid Ruth who explained who the man was and was then permitted to come to the railing to talk with him.

"How are you, Ruth?"

"I am well, Mr. Kirsanoff."

"I have a message from my grandson, from Ritchie."

The young woman's eyes told him that Ritchie had not deluded himself, that Ruth Erbach was passionately in love with his grandson. Her response was not that of a silly romantic girl; no blushes or breathless flutterings. There was a kind of ferocity in her that almost scared the old man. Ritchie had not misconstrued Ruth's feelings for him. If anything they were more intense than Ritchie's were for her.

Tal said, "Ritchie has been arrested . . . for . . . for theft."

The girl's frown deepened into a scowl. She gave no other visible sign of astonishment or of distress.

Tal continued. "It is probable that he will be given a term of imprisonment."

"How long a term, Mr. Kirsanoff?"

"I cannot be sure. It depends upon the will of the magistrate. Ritchie has decided to plead guilty, so the magistrate may go easy on him."

"Where is he now?"

"In the police court."

"Have you told my father or mother?"

"No."

"You won't tell them, will you?"

"So, it's true; they know nothing of your . . . your association with my grandson?"

"Nothing. They'd go hoopla if they did."

"Then it is not my place to intervene," said Tal. "Has he treated you like a gentleman should treat a lady?"

Ruth smiled fleetingly at the quaintness of the question, then with due solemnity, said, "If you mean have we been to bed together, the answer is no. I would . . . go to bed . . . I would let him take me, but

Ritchie won't do it. He says we must wait 'til we're married. Yes, he wants me to be his wife."

"It is not just a game for you, Ruth, is it?"

"It's only a game because Mamma would not allow us to see each other. She wouldn't understand Ritchie. He's always gentle with me, Mr. Kirsanoff. I know he is not gentle with other people. But I'm not gentle myself, not inside."

"I see."

"What's Ritchie's message?"

"He says that he loves you and asks that you write to him in prison."

Dry-eyed, firm-lipped, the girl said, "What's the name of the prison?"

"I will let you know," said Tal. "But now that he has been proved to be a thief will you not give him up? Forget him?"

"No, sir. Never."

Sadly Tal nodded. "He may be in prison for some time."

"I am in prison, too, Mr. Kirsanoff." She glanced down at the horrid brown school uniform then put her hands upon the railings. "Do you see?"

"I'll bring you the name of the prison," Tal promised.

"Miss Erbach: Miss Erbach." The teacher called to her.

"I must go now. I thank you for coming."

"I . . . I don't approve, Ruth."

"Of course not," the young woman said and, turning, walked away from him across the playground and into the school building.

A wave of sadness enveloped Tal as he walked back to the bus stop in the Waterloo Road. He had grown too old to understand this manifestation of youth, the total lack of illusion that marked the twentieth century's children. Even their romances were hard as little hob-nails and, to the elderly Russian, inexplicable. For all that, he would keep his promise to the pair. He would be their go-between, and tell Tilly nothing.

•　•　•

Before Tal found his way back to the Metropolitan Police Court, Ritchie had been summoned before the attending magistrate. He had entered a plea of guilty and had made a statement that he had been carried away by an impulse, that he had realised that he had done wrong; the alarm bell had brought him to his senses. He had not resisted, had not tried to run away. The police constable's evidence reluctantly corroborated the prisoner's story. For all that, the magistrate, a downy bird, was not deceived. He had Ritchie marked from the moment he opened his mouth. He had a report from the police and the fact of the warrant for house search which was uncommon enough in the circumstances to suggest that the police had had their eye on young Beckman for some time. All of this the magistrate dropped into the balance. He did not believe a word of Beckman's "impulse" story.

"Were you in a state of alcoholic intoxication?"

"Nossir; I'm not a drinkin' man."

"What did you hope to gain by breaking into The Clock Shop?"

"Don't rightly know, your worship."

"Money?"

"I suppose so, sir."

"By selling the stolen objects, you hoped to make money; is that substantially correct?"

"Yer, I suppose it was money."

"Had you a ready market for the objects you hoped to steal?"

"Nossir."

"Are you sure you had no buyer waiting to take the objects from you and pay you cash?"

"Don't know no buyers, sir."

After another six or eight pointed questions, it became clear to Ritchie that the old bastard wasn't swallowing the innocent act. He asked for his case to be considered under the First Offences Act. In so doing, he realised, he had simply confirmed the magistrate's suspicions that he was a whole lot smarter than he pretended to be.

The magistrate wasted no more time on him.

"Do you wish to change your plea to one of not guilty?"

"Nossir."

"If you do, I may then remand your case for hearing to a higher court of law, and you may be advised by a solicitor. Do you wish it?"

"Nossir."

"In that case, I accept your plea of guilty on the charge of burglary and, with consideration to the amendments contained in the First Offences Act of 1911, sentence you, without the option of a fine, to serve twelve months as an ordinary prisoner in His Majesty's jails. The twelve-month period may be shortened by remission for good behaviour on the recommendation of the wardens of the prisons." The magistrate made a note in his personal ledger. "Have you anything you wish to say, Beckman?"

"My . . ." Ritchie thought better of it. A year inside was more than he had bargained for. He would serve nine or ten months, bleedin' interminable months in which he would make no money, would progress not one step further towards his objectives. Nine or ten eternal months in which he would not see his Ruth, not even for a few stolen hours in the week.

"Well, Beckman?"

"Nossir; nothin' further to say – 'cept, thank you, yer Worship.'"

Thanks *were* due, Ritchie supposed. It had not been the best of ruses. There had always been the outside possibility that the coppers would pry further into his doings that night, would calculate that he could have been in Fielding's. But, of course, no violence had been committed on the old man and the shop certainly didn't look as if it had been tampered with. He had made the best choice under the circumstances. He had made almost sure no police spotlights would turn in his direction. Fielding's body hadn't even been discovered yet. By the time it was, and a coroner's report was filed, he would be tucked well out of harm's way. It was possible but improbable that some bright bluebottle might detect evidence of a break-in and pursue the possibility that the stupid old buffer had been scared to death. Though the plan might not appear convincing to an outsider, Ritchie was confident that he had shortened the odds so much that they had become virtually negligible.

He smiled. "Yes, thank you, sir."

"Take him down, constable," the magistrate said.

*   *   *

Tal sank back into the gigantic armchair with broken springs in the back store of Aspinall's Antique Shop. He accepted the cup of tea that Holly handed him, laid it on the edge of the packing bench while he loosened his tight collar and unlaced his spats.

"Brixton: twelve months."

"Did you see him after sentencin'?" asked Holly.

"I had a couple of minutes with him before the black van arrived to transport him to jail."

"How's he takin' it?"

"Better than I would have expected."

"Ritchie's a fool," said Holly, heatedly. "He didn't need the money, surely. O'Connor's won't ever have him back now. He'll find it very hard to get a job when he comes out of prison."

"He may not need a job," said Tal.

"Grandfather, what do you mean? D'you think Ritchie will go on thievin'?"

"I do not have an answer, Holly. For all our sakes, I hope he will have learned his lesson."

It was late that afternoon, approaching closing time, when Holly received a telephone call from Kennedy King. He informed her that Sam Fielding had been found dead in bed.

"It would seem he died of a heart attack," King said.

"Poor Sam. Was nobody with him at the end?"

"Nobody. The police are satisfied that he died as he lived, alone."

"The shop," said Holly. "What will become of his shop?"

Respectfully, King hesitated, trying not to sound too eager. "I expect there will be an auction – eventually. What a sale that will be, Holly. Sam had many rare pieces, you know."

"But nobody will gain."

"Oh, there's a nephew somewhere. It's lawyers' business to track the lucky dog down. What a surprise it'll be for him, receiving a windfall like that."

"Poor Sam," said Holly again.

The police made no impediment. The official report listed Samuel Fielding as the victim of a coronary seizure. He was buried in the St. Silas's churchyard nine days later. Holly attended the funeral service and, later, when the menfolk had gone off to the burial, took lunch with Emma Chubb.

Nobody, it seemed, made even the remotest connection between Sam Fielding's death and Ritchie Beckman's arrest.

Only Tal Kirsanoff wondered at the coincidence, but, like so many other things, he kept his doubts on that score to himself.

*   *   *

Andrea – and the hapless Miles – had much to contend with during the last month of 1919. Since the disastrous dinner party with Aunt Cordelia almost a year before, their relationship had become so brittle that its survival was threatened. For all that, the couple found themselves drawn out of a mutually-shared Victorian stance and nudged along towards an acceptance of "moral insecurity" – the phrase was one of Miles' coining – by the adventure of self-exploration.

Revealing fashions in ladies' wear tempted Andrea, who was by nature vain, into a franker utilisation of her charms. *Tête-à-tête* dinner parties and quiet twosomes at the opera no longer really satisfied her. She had begun to enjoy the admiration of men – a safe plurality of admirers, of course, out of which the more libidinous emerged only at their peril. Many an interested nose was bitten off by the exquisite Miss Aspinall that summer and autumn, many an ambitious swain sent packing by outraged invective. For all her indignant protests and rapier-like thrusts at "cads with only one thing on their minds", Andrea revelled in the knowledge that she was capable of arousing desire in the male sex. Even Lord Partridge, a dessicated gentleman with a Tudor pedigree and High Church connections, had suffered a rush of blood one summer night and, during a croquet match in the long shadows of Marston Park, had patted her ardently on the *lower* lower back. On reporting this incident to Miles during the drive back to London, Andrea was not at all pleased by her intended's explanation that "old Partridge" must have been too tipsy to distinguish her from the maid whom he'd been patting all afternoon.

Not being given to self-analysis, it did not occur to Andrea that what she wanted from Miles was a *physical* response to her beauty. His apparent gallantry had become tiresome and very slightly insulting. Companionship and respect were all very well but just occasionally Andrea wished that her fiancé would shed his control and give some signal that he too found her alluring. She respected his respect of her and sought to sweep away boredom with the relationship by encouraging him to be generally gregarious. But, as the year waned, croquet, boating parties, opera evenings, charity tea-dances, and many dinner parties no longer substituted for the kind of fulfilment that Andrea, unknowingly, craved.

To sublimate her frustration, Andrea forced her fiancé to be a conspirator in acts of petty spite, her champion in the pygmy contests that occupied her waking hours. Though she had genuine cause for concern over David's apparent disappearance, the rest of her life ran smoothly enough. Most of the slights and insults that Miles was obliged to redress were inventions of the woman's inflamed ego. Though she dined and wined with certain members of the aristocracy, thanks to Miles' connections, she had no reputation of her own to uphold in society. Few hostesses really knew who she was; even fewer cared. Therefore Andrea's struggle to uphold "her position" was in itself an illusion. To everyone that mattered she was Miles Walshott's intended bride. Why Andrea's venom should concentrate on Holly Beckman was something that nobody – not even Andrea – could rationally explain.

During December the couple visited the theatre several times. Andrea had dragged Miles to the Opera-in-English season at Covent Garden: Miles had grumpily dismissed Rimsky-Korsakov's *Coq d'Or* as "Bolshevik twaddle", and retaliated by obtaining tickets for

Summertime, a silly frippery in which Miss Fay Compton conquered the heart of Mr. C. Aubrey Smith in the space of twenty-four hours. Andrea's Christmas treat for Miles was a seat in the Grand Circle for Arnold Bennett's *Sacred and Profane Love*. Hoist by her own petard, she found the play as offensive as her beloved found it dull. It served to set the proper tone, however, for the discussion that followed, over shellfish and Dover sole in Reynard's, not far from the Haymarket.

Out of the blue, half-way through supper, Andrea came out with it.

"Well, my dear, the year is almost up."

"1919, yes."

"Beckman's year of grace, I mean."

"Oh, that."

"I will have discharged my debt to father," said Andrea, "and kept my promise to David."

Miles filled her glass with white wine. "I say, do you mean to throw her out? She's been doing rather well by you, hasn't she?"

"Rather well by herself."

"We needn't worry our heads with it for a time yet," said Miles, trying to steer off the subject.

"You still side with this girl, I see."

"It's not a question of siding with her. She's good, she's capable. . ."

"And pretty?"

"Andrea, really! The point is that she's turning a decent profit from the shop. Your dear mother benefits, you benefit, David . . ."

"David – Lord knows where he is. None of us have clapped eyes on him for weeks."

"Tried his office?"

"I'm not concerned enough to go chasing after him."

"Is your dear mother concerned?"

"Of course."

"I'll try to lay him by the heels, if you wish," Miles offered.

"Not bothered."

"Is he . . . ah, still in cahoots with that Leigh-Jennings gel?"

"I do not know, and I do not care. To my way of thinking, dearest, my brother has abrogated . . ." Andrea surprised herself with the word, she repeated it, "abrogated his responsibility. I mean, if he doesn't care enough to come visiting, then he can hardly call the tune in family affairs."

"I think you're being unfair on David. He's probably busy."

"You have too generous a nature, Miles," said Andrea. "You see good in everybody. It's a fault of your character."

"David isn't a villain; a little unruly, perhaps, but . . ."

"I wasn't referring to my brother: I know perfectly well what *he* is."

"To whom were you referring?" Miles asked, with sinking heart.

"Beckman."

"She's . . . she's . . . all right."

"Her brother is a convicted criminal."

"*What?*"

The little bombshell had its desired effect. It left Miles without much of a leg to stand on.

"How do you know?" he muttered.

"Mrs. Hodge let it slip – to me, not to mother, thank God. I don't know what mother would say to harbouring the sister of a convict in our house."

"When did this occur?" asked Miles. "When did you hear the story?"

"Last week," said Andrea. "Naturally, I made further enquiries. I obtained a clipping from the *Record*, you know that vulgar rag where the morbid curiosity of the populace is appeased by the publication of police court . . ."

"Yes, quite," interrupted Miles. "What exactly did it say?"

Andrea's eyes narrowed. "Richard Beckman pleaded guilty to a charge of burglary before the North London magistrate and was sentenced to one year in prison. His crime, Miles, his crime was breaking into an *antique shop*."

"Ah," said Miles. "Oh!"

"Now what do you say to that, my dear? Do I have to be more explicit? Isn' the implication, the *repercussion* obvious?"

"Now, Andrea, we can't be sure that Holly Beckman was personally involved."

"The sister of a thief? The sister of a thief who *specialises* in stealing *antiques*? Come now, Miles. There's a point at which generosity degenerates into silliness."

"Do you really think that Holly was re-selling articles stolen by her brother?"

"What else *am* I to think?"

Miles pushed his fish to one side and called for coffee. Without even asking Andrea's permission, though she was still nibbling through a Dover sole, he lit a cigarette and puffed on it for inspiration. Finding none, he was obliged to concede. "Certainly looks . . . black."

"Next thing you know," said Andrea, "some clod-hopping policeman will be dragging mother and I from our beds in the dead of night and carting us off to a cell."

"I doubt if . . ."

"Mother and I are Beckman's partners, remember."

"Sleeping par . . ."

"Living on the premises."

"Yes. Yes, yes."

Miles was confused. He would check the facts for himself, of course. He would also find David and discover what relationship there might be between his discreet disappearance from the domestic environment and this business with Beckman's brother. The more he thought of it, the more Miles had to admit that Andrea, for once, had right on her side. There was no proof that Holly had been selling stolen goods in Cardwell Place. But he could not understand why the police had failed to check the stock. The Beckman boy had pleaded guilty, of course, to keep the spotlight from his sister. Noble? Smart? Tomorrow, first thing, he would begin to probe into the affair. If it was true, if evidence pointed to Andrea's shop having been used to fence off stolen articles, then he would advise her to be rid of it immediately – or rid of Beckman. It came to the same thing.

Pity – he liked Holly Beckman and had judged her to be honest. First he would track down the errant David. If there was dirty work to be done then David Aspinall was probably better suited to do it than he was.

The coffee pot was put down on the table and Miles poured himself a cup, strong and black. He drank it. It cleared his head.

Andrea was regarding him with an expression of smugness tinged with challenge.

"Do you see, Miles – it *is* serious."

"Yes, it is, my dear."

"How will you set about it?"

"First I will try to find and talk with David."

"David? He'll defend the little bitch. He's half in love with her, don't you know?"

"First I will talk with David," Miles went on, "and if it all turns out to be true, then I will instruct your brother to buy Miss Beckman out."

"David . . . buy . . ."

"In the circumstances," said Miles, sadly, "young Miss Beckman can be had for an old song."

Andrea beamed. "Forced out. For next to nothing. How marvellous!"

"And David will clinch the deal."

* * *

Miles traced David with ease. Aspinall had made no serious attempt to cover his tracks to the Apollo Hotel. It was there, esconsed in the bridal suite, that stockbroker and ex-officer confronted each other in an aura of astonishment.

It was eleven thirty in the morning of a grey day. In the sky, dark skeins of cloud threatened snow, and the hotel was busy with Christmas visitors to the capital.

Through the connecting door of the two-roomed suite, Miles glimpsed an ivory and gilded bed, silken sheets, a girl peeping over the coverlet at him, blonde hair tousled. David had donned a robe, an Oriental creation that swirled about his lean body as he played at being a good host in that temporary palace.

On the dressing table, like icons, were jewels, gold links, a gold wristwatch, and two crisp wads of banknotes with rubber bands around them. Huge vertical mirrors reflected the two men in endless variety, giving the effect of a crowded gathering.

David ordered breakfast by telephone, and an extra pot of coffee for his guest. He then invited Miles to be seated. Out of place in this room and uncomfortably conscious of the girl in the silken bed, still visible if he turned his head, the stockbroker could not relax.

David made the first move. "Andrea sent you, I suppose?"

Miles said, "Your family were worried."

"How's mother?"

"She seems well enough."

"And here you are, Miles," said David, perching himself on an arm of the chaise longue and folding his fists under his armpits.

"You're out of the army." It was a statement, not a question.

"I am – a free man."

Miles nodded. "Your position with the insurance firm, what of that?"

"Later," said David. "Perhaps I shall apply for reinstatement after Christmas."

"Is this by way of being a period of celebration?"

"Well, we won't be living in the bridal suite for ever."

"That's not what I meant, David." Miles flicked a glance behind him. The girl was sitting up in bed, listening to every word. She gave him a quick, flirtatious smile. He looked away quickly. "I say, you're not, not . . . ?"

"Married?" said David. "No, of course not."

"You pretend to be."

"Only for the benefit of the hotel staff."

"I see. David, I must ask you if you intend to return home soon."

"Yes, of course I do. I'll toddle round to see Mother in a day or two. I expect I'll be there for Christmas din-din. You know."

"Effectively, however, you won't be residing in Cardwell Place in future?"

"Is that my sister's question, Miles?"

"Naturally, Andrea is deeply concerned."

"I've been . . . busy."

"Seeking employment?" said Miles, with irony. "As you seem reluctant to return to the insurance company, I assume that you must be seeking employment."

"I have employment."

Miles raised an eyebrow. "Really?"

"Investment, you might say."

"Your brokers?"

"I handle my own . . . ah, portfolio."

Miles did not pursue the line. He was interrupted by the arrival of the waiter with the breakfast trolley. It gave him a little time to think. He suspected that David's "investments" were on dice and cards and the staying power of horses. He did not ask for a direct answer, however. Signs of affluence – gold trinkets, money – might have been related to the girl's income; though he had heard that she was actually in debt to the speculator Theodore Willoughby.

Coffee revived his flagging concentration. David had taken the trolley into the bedroom. Cringing a little, Miles heard the sounds of the girl's laughter, like crystal pendants stirred by a breeze, tinkling and fragile. He heard too the girl's injunction. "Go on, David; tell him the truth."

Miles lit a cigarette.

His hand was as steady as a rock. He felt reassured. After all, what right had the Aspinall boy to expect courtesy, even reticence, when he had made no attempt to disguise the evidence of his decline? Miles sat back in the rococo chair, cup and saucer balanced on his knee. When David returned from the bedroom, Miles rose, placed the cup and saucer on the table, deliberately walked to the bedroom door and closed it.

"How long do you intend to go on living with this girl?"

"Come on, old chap," said David. "You've no call to tick me off, as if I was a truant from school."

"Perhaps you'd prefer to talk with your sister."

"No," said David with a tight smile. "Come to think of it, I'd prefer to talk with you."

"Very well: straight answers to straight questions?"

"Right-o."

"Where's the money coming from?"

"Currently," said David, "from Benson's the bookmakers, via Lord Granley's The Panther. Have you heard of The Panther?"

"How much did you win?"

"Eight to one: one hundred pounds. Eight hundred."

"Eight hundred pounds? You *won* eight hundred pounds on a horse race?"

"That's not all."

"How long," Miles drew himself together. "How long will it last?"

"Plenty more where it came from."

"The girl . . . your . . . Miss Leigh-Jennings, does she have independent means?"

"I support her."

"Will you marry her?"

David hesitated. "Possibly."

"David, David; I'm saddened to see you in such straits."

David laughed harshly. "What damned straits, Miles? I'm richer now than I've ever been in my life. I live a life of positive luxury."

"For two weeks, that's all. For two brief weeks."

"No reason why it shouldn't continue."

"Gamblers – if that's what you intend to be – never prosper."

"An old wives' tale: I can name you half a dozen gentlemen who not only scrape along but got rich – as rich as you, Miles – on the proceeds of their wagers. Acumen and caution; bit of flair, that's all that's needed."

"It's a . . . a bubble."

"Then I'll float along in it, thank you, until it bursts."

"And when that day comes?"

David shrugged. "I'll find something else to do."

"Very well," said Miles. "I have one or two things to say, David."

"It's too early in the day for sermons."

"Concerning Andrea, your mother, and the home you've abandoned."

"Don't be so pompous."

Miles ignored the insult. "Andrea is still of a mind to sell the shop."

"Determined, do you mean?"

"Certain . . . certain incidents have taken place." Miles explained about Holly Beckman's brother, and Andrea's fear that the family would somehow be tainted by contact with a criminal.

"Rot!" said David. "Holly isn't like that. The brother may be a scoundrel, but Holly? Never. She's as honest as the day's long. Too honest."

"Setting aside Miss Beckman's character," said Miles. "Andrea has a very valid point. If you wish to obtain Beckman's quarter share, then this is an ideal moment to press a bid."

"Take advantage of her, you mean."

"Her share – the obvious success of the business notwithstanding – can be had for a few hundred pounds."

"Let Andrea buy it, then. You can lend her the money."

"I . . . I can't become too deeply involved in the transaction."

"Oh-ho! You want me to do it?"

"You know Holly Beckman better than I do."

"Holly will never accept."

"She has little choice."

"With her brother in jail." David nodded. "Stealing antiques? God, yes! The implications could be serious."

"Will you make the offer – you, personally?"

"To Holly? No," said David.

"Then I must."

"Make the offer to her father."

"What?"

"He's bound to be feeling the pinch. From what I know of the Beckman household, the father will leap at an opportunity to pocket a few pounds."

"But the father has no legal . . ."

"If," said David, "you really insist on being rid of Holly Beckman – and Andrea won't rest until she has ousted the girl from Aspinall's – then I suggest that an offer is made directly to her father. But I tell you this, Miles, I don't approve. The shop's doing nicely. If Beckman goes, then I will sell my share, and if Andrea wants it too, she'll pay through the snout for it, let me tell you."

Miles was silent for a moment, then said, "For the sake of peace, David, it would be as well to be rid of the shop. The capital can be re-invested."

"I'll take my slice cash-in-hand, please."

"Re-invested to bring a reasonable annual return. Your mother can be found more suitable accommodation, perhaps in the country, and Andrea . . ."

"Will marry you?"

Miles had anticipated the question. He nodded. "Probably."

"How much will the business fetch?"

"In all, with the lease attached, some three thousand pounds."

"More, Miles: much more. The shop stock alone is worth over fifteen hundred."

"I see you've been keeping record?"

"It's not some little pop shop we're talking about, Miles. In one year Holly has increased the value of the business threefold. The value of the unexpired lease has increased, too, thanks to wild inflation in property prices. All of this my dear sister wishes to throw to the winds simply because she can't abide Holly Beckman."

"It isn't as simple as that."

"It's not far off the mark, old chum."

"Beckman's brother . . ."

"Beckman's brother has nothing to do with it. Don't you see? What Andrea wants now is *change*. She wants a man between her legs, to put it crudely."

"You foul-mouthed . . . You daren't . . . How dare . . . !"

David seated himself on the chaise longue, knees apart. With the Oriental robe folded about him he looked like a mad emperor newly come into his kingdom, spilling over with reforming zeal.

"I can't arrange *that* for my dear sister," David said. "But I can, otherwise, give her what she wishes. You may be sorry that you came here today, Miles."

Miles Walshott was on his feet. "You are . . . you are . . ."

"You have no idea of what I am, Miles," said David. "You have no idea what I learned during my occupancy of that dismal office in Whitehall, what effect the daily rote of figures had on me. Surprise, then shock – a thousand men dead, two thousand, three, five, ten, ten times ten. Oh, no, I didn't see them drown in mud, smashed by shells, gassed, dismembered, torn up by barbed wire. None of that. Only tallies, figures; pensions to poor wives, the army's dispassionate settlements. Blood money. After a while, no shock, no surprises; only apathy. I can no longer *bear* apathy. I have no belief in security. I want something *now*. Not a rock, an anchor, a gilt-edged investment. I want . . ." He shrugged. "I know what you think of me, what Andrea thinks of me. You're right, both of you." He raised his right hand, forefinger jutting like a bayonet. "I don't give a damn, not one *good God damn* about Andrea, or you. But the shop is as much mine as it is my sister's, and my mother is as much my responsibility."

Lamely, Miles said, "I'm glad you admit it."

"So, Mr. Walshott, I would be obliged if you would leave it to me. I will do what Andrea wishes done. I will buy out Beckman. I'll sell the shop and the property, and divide the money evenly between my mother, my sister and myself."

"Come now, David, you've no experience of these . . ."

"Experience? All that counts these days is know-how. Have you heard that phrase yet, Miles? American, I believe. *Know How*."

"I'm more than willing to handle the . . ."

"I'll do it."

"What shall I tell Andrea?"

"Tell her that she'll be rid of Holly and the shop, and will have as large a gain as possible – all within the month."

"You can't possibly . . ."

"Thank you for calling on me, Miles," said David, stiffly. "Now that you've been good enough to bring the matter to my attention, I'll deal with Miss Beckman, and the selling of Aspinall's Antiques."

"Andrea will . . ."

"Remind my sister that I'm still head of the household."

"This isn't what I expected."

"I know it isn't," said David. "But we live in an age of surprises, don't we, old chum?"

• • •

David lay in the deep white bath. Daylight sheened the tiled walls and made the overhead electric light seem pallid. Reflected in the tiles he could see segments of his naked body, pale and insubstantial, quivering in the swirl of pine-green water. He slumped down out of sight of himself, the waterline rippling against his moustache, lifting the hair on the nape of his neck. The hot bath did not ease the tremendous tension in him, the odd, dogged excitement that had stolen over him immediately after Walshott had departed and the import of his boast had come home to roost.

Outside, Linsey was scratching on the door with a bone comb. "Why did you say that? Why did you tell him those lies?" she demanded.

"Darling, I meant it."

"It has nothing to do with us."

"Yes, yes it has."

"You're doing it for *her*, aren't you. It's just for *her* sake."

"Linsey, do shut up, there's a good chap."

Scratch, scratch, scratch: whine, whine, whine.

"*Shut up, damn it!*"

"I don't want you to do it. I don't want you to have anything to do with them. You're mine, darling. I want you to be mine."

He sank his head under water, nose projecting. Her voice was far, far off, faint, almost soothing. But his nervous exhilaration would not be stilled. His mind was spinning like a gyroscope on the edge of a china plate, wobbling this way and that.

He breathed through his nose, steadily, rhythmically.

No harm in backing a sure thing?

No harm in having one's cake and eating it?

First he had to close off all that the past held, as effectively as sealing a vault. He had to take that to the table tonight and put *that* down on a number and watch the little ivory ball spin and hear the *rickle-rickle-rickle* as it bobbed and tossed along the slots and stopped, knowing that it *mattered*, not to him but to her, to Holly.

Surging out of the bath, coughing, he grabbed the big pink bath towel from the rail and wrapped it round him toga-fashion, unlocked the bathroom door and whipped it open.

Linsey fell back.

"What's all that infernal racket about?" David said, as he strode past her towards the wardrobe, pulled out his new black suit, threw it on the unmade bed. "I've paid your debts, haven't I? Every last penny you owed. Paid your debts, darling. Now I intend to pay my own."

"Where . . . David, darling, where are you going?"

"Out," he said.

"Where?" She shrieked in panic.

Naked he took her in his arms, and held her shivering body close against his. "I'm not deserting you. I've business in the City, that's all. Family business. You can understand that, can't you? I'll be back in time for tea."

"Promise, David, promise."

"Yes, yes, I promise." He pushed her a little away from him and frowned. "Now, you must make me a promise, too."

"What?"

"When I come back, I want to find you fed, watered, groomed to the nines – and sober as a judge. Promise."

"But . . ."

"Tonight we'll dine in Claridge's, then go round to Christabel's. I want you with me, Linsey."

"Of course, yes, but . . ."

He kissed her lingeringly on the mouth, then turned to find himself a shirt and a suitably dignified tie.

"To bring me luck, my love," he said.

* * *

The crowd that gathered in Christabel's that Wednesday night had no notion that high drama was being enacted before their jaded eyes. David Aspinall and the Leigh-Jennings girl were habitués of the supper club's upstairs room. Even those whose bread was buttered by "observations" and the satisfying of strange appetites – sly-eyed men and women who stood alone in the shadows – would have been hard put to it to identify the purpose that brought the couple to the roulette table an hour earlier than usual. If they had watched intently they might have detected a setness in young Aspinall's jaw, or thought it strange that the girl was not half seas under. But the gaming room was quiet and only the croupier, Daniel, suspected that Aspinall had come along not just to gamble but to win.

In dinner jacket and bow-tie, newly-acquired trinkets glinting in the circular overhead light, David seated himself at one of the eight vacant chairs and arranged chips and plaques into four neat blocks before him. Linsey stood behind him in an evening gown of ivory silk that clung to her like a serpent's skin.

Daniel eyed her body as he spun the wheel, chanting his sing-song litany. Aspinall had been a big winner these past three weeks. Twelve nights he had gone home in pocket. Three times he had raked in several hundred pounds. Twice he had lost over all. Born into the croupier's trade, seasoned in Monte Carlo before the war, Daniel recognised in the young man that loss of *élan*, that stiffening which suggested he had transferred from a belief in luck to the conceited notion that he had done it himself. Tonight, perhaps, he would fall into the pitfall of *trying* to make it happen, would sacrifice intuition for system. Fatal! Systems seldom paid dividends. In a week or so, Aspinall would produce a little note book covered in scribblings, figures waltzing with figures all across the pages, as if gambling was a business that could be toted and analysed like a balance sheet. Some men tried; a tiny minority succeeded. But even the most successful of them ultimately relied on feeling, not mathematics.

Daniel spun the wheel again.

David met the croupier's eye. He smiled uncertainly.

Be positive, *mon ami*: Daniel smiled silently back.

"*Faites vos jeux*," he said.

The ball bobbled, chattered and fell. Daniel worked the rake expertly, hardly giving it thought.

Seven or eight hundred pounds in bone tokens were arranged before David, plaques and chips equally anonymous, values denominated only by colour.

"Place your bets," said Daniel, in English. "Mr. Aspinall?"

Twenty pounds: four chips. It would be a long, agonising night for the English captain as he see-sawed in and out of profit and his brain calculated odds against need. If Daniel had been advising him he would have limited his wagers to four, each of two hundred pounds, on the even bet of red and black. Runs of four were unusual. If a loss was sustained three times, the final bet would restore half the original sum wagered. Split the winnings into four, and stick with the colour. They had won well on red less than a month ago. If he won with the first bet, he would pull out the winnings and place four smaller bets. But, alas, there *was* no infallible system. The little ivory ball had a mind of its own. It was a replacement for people who had no will, no volition. Those who came to the wheel to change their lives got what they deserved.

David lost.

Linsey covered her hand with a wager of her own.

Red again.

David did not bet.

Red came up. She took twenty pounds off the board, split it and returned two counters each worth five pounds to the black.

Black came up.

Linsey let the four counters rest on the black.

David covered black too, with one hundred pounds; a single bright yellow plaque.

Black showed.

Linsey played black a third time. David followed her wordless lead.

Red showed.

Linsey placed twenty pounds on black.

"*Faites vos jeux,*" droned Daniel. "*Faites vos jeux.*"

Fingers clicked the plaques, spilling the cheaper chips out in a line. Dexterously Daniel nudged the chips back towards their owner with the tip of the rake.

"*Les jeux sont faits. Les jeux . . .*"

Four one-hundred pound yellow counters placed on black.

Black showed.

"Ride it, David," the girl said, huskily. "Ride it with me."

"It isn't . . ."

"Please, please. With me."

Young Aspinall could not stand the pace. He would never effectively gamble to a system, Daniel realised with relief. He would take his stick, win, and more often lose, but he would retain his innate faith in random fortune. As the Canadians said, he would back his hunch to the knell of doom.

"*Rien ne va plus.*"

Black gave them sixteen yellow plaques, and a scattering of chips.

David nodded and gestured. Daniel pushed the counters towards him.

"Again, again. Don't wait, David."

The sides of her dress were patched with perspiration. Does she want to lose? Daniel frowned. He delivered the opening phrase of the ritual. Drifting over from the Crown and Anchor table, seven or eight regulars watched the activity at the roulette wheel.

Oui: the lady is willing her lover to lose everything. She drives him to it by force of will. Here, she is stronger than he.

"Look, I'm putting everything on . . . on red," Linsey said.

Glancing round, panic flickered across David's features. His eyes were wide, lips parted.

"The bets are placed," said Daniel, slowly, holding the little uneven ball in his fingertips, wrist cocked. He spun the wheel with the tip of the handle of the rake, backhandedly whipping it into motion on its oiled bearings. "*Rien ne . . .*"

"Black," said David. "All of it, Daniel. Everything on black."

He pushed with both hands. Dispassionately, the croupier cocked the rake, brought the pile of counters neatly into the arena and, with his other hand, lobbed the ball against the wheel's rotation.

Linsey's nails sank into the back of David's hand.

Violently David dragged his hand away, ripping the surface of the skin. The girl's face was a mask of spite and fear, twisted viciously out of shape as if some demon had taken possession of her.

David Aspinall closed his eyes.

"Black," said Daniel. "*Numero dix-neuf.* Black."

David slumped.

Behind him Linsey pinched her earlobes with her nails and dragged on them as if to punish herself with pain for having guessed wrong.

"Oh . . . you . . . you are in form tonight . . . darling," she gasped. "Do it again. Keep going. Again."

David got to his feet. He filled his lungs, pushed out his chest and squared his shoulders.

"You are leaving, *monsieur*?" asked Daniel.

"I am."

"*Bon soir.*"

David tipped the croupier fifty pounds and carried the rest of his winnings over to the cashier's window, while Linsey trailed pitifully behind him.

"How much?" David asked the horse-faced man behind the metal grill.

"Three thousand, three hundred, fifty."

"That's fine," said David and, with shaking fingers, lit himself a cigarette.

* * *

"What did you do, David?" said Mr. Mumford. "Rob a bank?"

David lolled in a chair in the lawyer's office, smirking down at the wad of banknotes that Mumford slid from the fat brown envelope.

"I came by it honestly, sir, you may be assured."

"To be frank, young man, I didn't believe you yesterday."

"You made that plain, Mr. Mumford."

"Do you wish me to go ahead with purchase?"

"Of course," said David. "You will make an offer, through Miles Walshott, to my sister and my mother; fifteen hundred pounds each for their quarter shares in Aspinall's Antiques, as it stands, together with the unexpired portion of the lease on the property."

"Have you informed them of your intention?"

"No," said David. "And, sir, I do not wish you to do so."

"Fifty per cent of the business may not – probably isn't – worth three thousand."

"I'm being generous, you understand. Besides, I wish to make an offer that Andrea will find difficult to resist, one that will stop her asking too many questions."

"What of Miss Beckman?"

"She will retain her financial interest, and her position as general manager of the shop."

"Will she be told of the changed ownership?"

"Not at present," said David.

"It affects her quite considerably, David."

"How? I don't intend to make changes."

"But as owner of three-quarters of the business, you will have right of sale. I mean that you can sell without her consent. It's not what your father intended."

"My father," said David, "was a shrewd old buffer. I appreciate that now, Mr. Mumford. I doubt if he would object to my owning the shop – provided that Holly remains in charge. Unlike my sister, I am fully aware that Holly *is* the business."

During the past year Mumford had been occupied with other matters and had spared the Aspinalls and Holly Beckman hardly a thought. He asked, "Is she making a go of it?"

"Better than anyone could have predicted," said David. "I think Holly will make me a lot of money."

"Have you explained this to your sister?"

"Andrea is too much of a bigot to listen."

Mumford nodded. "What are you doing with yourself these days?"

"Resting."

"Profitably, it seems." Mumford glanced down at the envelope on his desk. "Are you . . . employed?"

"I'm in business; investments."

"Really? Is the shop another investment?"

"My . . . ah, fall-back position, shall we say?"

"The domestic quarters above the shop," said Mumford, "are worth almost as much as the shop itself. I don't know if you are aware of the dreadful increase in property values?"

"I'll meet the mortgage obligations out of shop profits," said David, airily. "My mother – and Andrea, I suppose – may continue to stay there."

"Will you charge them rental?"

"I'm not a profiteer, Mr. Mumford. No, of course not."

"They will ask questions, and expect answers."

"Yes, I see what you mean," said David.

"It will be next to impossible to keep your . . . generosity secret for long."

"Can you attend to the business of purchase without revealing my name?"

"Yes, that I can do – particularly as your sister is keen to be rid of the business, and you are paying cash."

"Walshott may baulk."

"I'll handle Mr. Walshott. I imagine he'll employ a fellow solicitor. Estimations, valuations will be required."

"I want it done quickly, very quickly."

"It's not something that can be hurried."

"Do your very best, Mr. Mumford."

"My clients always receive my best, David."

"When will you make the initial offer?"

"I'll write today."

"Good," said David.

•   •   •

"Well, my dear," said Miles Walshott. "It seems to me to be fortuitous in the extreme. I had nothing whatsoever to do with it, though the letter did come to me. As you'll see, it is in effect a firm offer, in very explicit terms, for purchase of your holdings in Aspinall's Antiques, plus the unexpired portion of the total lease, for a cash price payment of fifteen hundred pounds to you, Andrea, and to you, Mrs. Aspinall. Three thousand pounds in all. Mumford has had an interested party in his cupboard for almost a year now; I expect that it is he – or she. Apparently the client is interested only in the business and is willing to rent the domestic quarters as they stand at the very reasonable sum of three pounds and ten shillings each week. I stress, ladies, that this is a *very* reasonable sum indeed. The client is also prepared to give you an iron-clad sub-lease for ten years, thus ensuring you of a modicum of security. There's no mention of rental review periods, but I will raise that point with Mumford, if you are agreeable in principle to the whole transaction."

"I don't have to move, do I?"

"No, Mrs. Aspinall. You may remain here, just as you are," said Miles, patiently. "If you do elect to accept the offer, then I will invest the capital sums in certain securities that will bring you each a well-protected, though necessarily modest, monthly income."

"Has David been offered the same sum?" Andrea asked.

"I really couldn't say, dear," Miles answered.

"And Beckman? What about her?"

"The only means of discovering that, is to ask her," said Miles. "But it seems to me that Mumford's nameless client wishes to retain Beckman as manager and may, therefore, offer her retention of her twenty-five per cent interest as an inducement to remain."

"Who do you think Mumford's client really is, Miles?"

"My guess would be Kennedy King."

"Yes."

"As you have already expressed a desire to be quit of the business, in the light of Beckman's brother's imprisonment and the possible reflections on your good name," said Miles, roundly, "I would recommend that you accept this offer under the stated terms."

"I'd like to know more about it."

"That may jeopardise the . . ."

"I'd like to know how much David's getting."

"It is possible, Andrea, that David instigated this offer."

"I beg your pardon."

"I reported on my conversation with your brother."

"How could he . . . ?"

"Quite easily."

"Is he so desperate for cash?"

"I really couldn't say," Miles answered. "My advice is to leave

David to his own devices. Obviously, if an offer has been made to him for his share, then it has been made separately."

"Will he come home for Christmas, did he say?"

"Yes, Mrs. Aspinall, he assured me that he would call round for Christmas Day dinner, as usual."

"I'll believe it when I see him here," said Andrea.

Miles said, "You've read the solicitor's letter, and you have heard my opinions on the matter, my dear. Do you wish me to proceed with the sale?"

"Beckman will still be downstairs?"

"Really, Andrea," said Miles, with a trace of irritation, "I can't for the life of me see that it matters, she never comes up here; indeed, you have little or no contact with . . ."

"But I know she's there."

"Andrea, that's quite irrational. Do you wish to sell out, or do you not?"

"Yes, I do."

"Mrs. Aspinall?"

"You're sure I won't have to leave my house?"

"Quite sure."

"Then I'm willing to do what Andrea thinks best."

"That's settled, then," said Miles, with a sigh. "I will discuss the finer points with Mumford – I see no reason to employ another solicitor – and instruct him to draw up the relative documents forthwith, for your perusal and signature."

"Miles, are you sure we're doing the right thing?"

"Andrea, you have made your decision."

"Yes, of course I have. I just wish I knew what that brother of mine is getting out of it all."

"That," said Miles, "is for you to find out."

"If I can," said Andrea.

"The important thing is that you are rid of the responsibility of the business."

"And Holly Beckman," said Andrea.

* * *

Holly was aware that changes were in the wind. It hurt her that David had disappeared. She missed him terribly and could not understand why he had failed to communicate since that November night when he had declared himself to be in love with her. Had he lied? Had it been a cruel deceit and, if so, what purpose could there be in hurting her? He had asked her to wait for him and to be patient. She must resist silly imaginings. From Mrs. Hodge she learned that Thora and Andrea too were worried because David hadn't spent a single night at home since his discharge from the officers' roll and this aspect of the situation increased her anxiety even more.

After a restless night and a scanty breakfast, Holly slipped out of No. 5 very early with the intention of walking to the shop. As usual she was up and about before Tal; it was seldom that they travelled together from Lambeth to Pimlico. It was a fine morning, cold but with no trace of wind. Smoke from house and factory chimneys rose straight as pencil lines against the rising sun. Early workers seemed oblivious to the pretty weather, shuffling towards tram stops or queuing for bus rides. Men and women, muffled and drab; Holly recognised some of them – neighbours, the sons and daughters of neighbours, boys she'd been at school with. A few noticed her and nodded glumly. Lambeth in the morning, in any weather, did not encourage good feelings. Sometimes, at night, when pubs were lighted and music drifted down the rows of terraced houses, the packed life of the borough could be sensed and there was a cosy, comfortable sense of community. In the Picture Palace, in the Co-operative Halls, at Borough Hall dances, Lambeth would emerge as an entity and its honest working-class citizens would shed their inhibitions and forget what it cost them to survive, ignore hard fact that the future would hold no material changes for the better no matter how much they dreamed, how earnestly they believed in a bright new tomorrow.

Holly had always been a round peg in the square hole of the district; perhaps because the Beckman family had been without a head. Women, mothers, were the true community leaders; families revolved around them. They shaped streets and terraces into little villages, encouraged tribal legends in the form of gossip, and set codes of cleanliness, industry, decency and the practice of the helping hand. All of this the Beckmans had lost out on. A widow had her role in the narrow pattern of street life. She could fulfil herself in the face of terrible hardships and be admired for it. But a widower was ab-solved. He had too many acceptable excuses and was expected to be no more than a man. Leo Beckman, of course, had made full use of every excuse. He was at home only in the Admiral's Hat, no-where else; there he was given due admiration for having raised a family unaided, and was volubly envied for having no wife to tie him down.

If Huldah Beckman had lived, how different everything would

have been, Holly thought, as she cleared the oppressive gable of the Trinidad warehouse and saw the bridge before her.

The brightness of the day showed on the river. The wintry beauty of London-across-the-Thames perked Holly up considerably.

She had much to be thankful for.

The shop was doing well. Grandpa Tal protected her from Leo's worse moods and Maury was there, strong and solid and sensible, if she ever needed advice.

Ritchie? Holly could find no pity for her brother and was relieved that he was safe out of harm's way for a while. The mutterings from the Aspinalls no doubt had something to do with Ritchie's imprisonment. Holly had a clear conscience, however. She thanked God that she'd been smart enough to avoid the pitfalls that her dishonest brother had laid for her. If the Aspinalls tried to imply that she'd been party to her brother's thefts, she would show them the books, impeccable in the accuracy of their accounting, with nothing hidden away.

Even so, mud was bound to cling.

From the bridge, she glanced behind her at Lambeth. If only she did not have to return there ever again. She was coming dangerously close to hating it, seeing only its squalid aspects and not the many good qualities it possessed. There were many similar boroughs around London, each with its own character, but Lambeth was her place. It distressed her just a little that she longed to desert it, but she could find nothing in childhood or youth to cherish, nothing that she could not have found elsewhere. Now, however, she had all but given up the wistful search for roots in the borough. She had decided that her past lay in her family, in the Kirsanoff blood that flowed in her veins, not in the square half mile of crowded houses that had been her home, her cage. She would have to live without the affectionate nostalgia that so many people had in them for the place where they had been born and raised.

Holly wanted out.

If only she could take Tal with her, she would set about breaking ties with Abraham's Box immediately.

If only David would come back, she was sure she could make him understand that she didn't care about his prospects and was more than willing to be his wife.

But she remained confused by the mixture of selfishness and love, caution and impulsiveness that milled in her heart and mind. In an odd sort of way she realised that she no longer feared the future, with or without David Aspinall. Though she longed for him, and wanted him sexually, she did not regard her whole life as bound up with his. It puzzled her that she could still hang back from a total commitment. Perhaps she was preparing herself for disappointment.

She had proved her abilities. If it ever came down to a break with the Aspinalls, Kennedy King would give her a post as manager. She was confident of being able to avoid an Emma Chubb-Simon Black type of relationship with Kennedy, who, as a seducer, had more bark than bite.

Single-mindedness was not an unmixed blessing, Holly had come to realise. She wanted everything on a silver salver. In this golden age of opportunity, there was a danger that freedom would become licence. The thought made her uncomfortable.

"I must be completely practical," she told herself. "I must do my work and let events over which I've no control take care of themselves."

She reached the shop just before eight. Curtains were still drawn over the Aspinalls' front windows. Laying aside the heavy gate for Wilf to put away when he arrived at half-past the hour, she let herself in. Picking up the early mail, she carried it through the darkened shop to the store. She switched on the lamp at the packing bench, put the kettle on the gas ring and lit the two paraffin stoves. The walk through the dawn air had refreshed her. With a growing feeling of security she applied her mind to the business of the day.

For months now Holly had implemented her belief that ordinary men and women were interested in antiques. To encourage "non-collectors" she occasionally dressed the window with bargain lots, nice inexpensive items of bric-à-brac picked to appeal to the eye. She had had several large cards printed to augment the displays – "Antiques for All" – and arranged two long tables close to the doorway packed with small items. She made sure that all the objects were perfect, clean and polished. On some she hung a label giving information, a piece of history. All of this professional attention, far from putting lay persons off, attracted their interest, particularly as the prices were low. Other colourful show cards read: "Magpies Welcome", "Nothing Over Five Shillings," "Quality Christmas Gifts". She maintained the displays for one week at a time. The bulk of the goods in the bargain window were Georgian, with a sugar basin, a Nelson's head mug or a late 19th century paste-pearl brooch thrown in for variety. Mostly, though, it was Zodiac napkin rings, feather flower posies, picture frames, perfume bottles, brooches in coral and agate, and imitation Wedgwood pottery.

Such a window was presently on display. There were several holes in it where late-night selling had left gaps on the shelves. From a basket of oddments, Holly selected a dozen objects and carried them to the back of the window. She had just stretched to place a pair of Victorian fish trowels in a prominent position, when, to her astonishment, she saw David at the window.

Through the lace-like ribbons of frost on the glass, she hardly recognised him at first. He was dressed like a toff in a black alpaca overcoat, silk scarf and topper. He placed his gloved hand flat on the window and beckoned to her to open the door which she had locked after her.

Excitedly, she opened it at once.

"David, what on earth are you doin' here at this hour of the morning?"

"Waiting for you." He clapped his hands and stamped his feet. "It's freezing out there." He glanced down at the bargain tables, not meeting her inquiring gaze. "It's the best time for me. I didn't want to be spotted from upstairs. Thank God you're an early riser, Holly."

"David, what is it? Why all the cloak-and-dagger stuff?"

He laughed. "Is that how it looks? Not intended. I just wanted to have you to myself for a while. When's grandad due in?"

"Not for an hour; but Wilf . . ."

"I must talk with you, Holly. Come and have breakfast with me?"

"Breakfast? David, where . . . ?"

"I'm living not far from here. I've a room of my own; a little pied-à-terre, round in Wolfenden Street. By a stretch of the imagination, you could call it Belgravia. There's a rather decent hotel nearby, the Consort. It does a late breakfast, for chaps like me."

"Chaps like you?" said Holly.

"Night birds."

"Is *that* what you are?"

"You sound miffed? Well, I can't blame you," said David, looking at her now. "It's been hectic, really hectic. I just haven't had a chance to call round, Holly. Besides, I don't want to run across my sister. Look, come and have breakfast, and I will tell all. Doesn't that persuade you?"

"I can't leave the shop."

"Your grandad, can't he . . .?"

"He won't be here until nine."

"That'll do." David glanced over his shoulder at the doorway. "Listen, I must haste away, Holly. I'll expect you at the Consort, Wolfenden Street, in about an hour. I'll wait for you in the foyer. Will you come? Please, it's important."

"David, I'm . . . Yes, yes, I'll come."

He smiled warmly and touched her cheek. His fingers were icy. "Thank you."

Pivoting, he hurried out of the shop. Holly ran to the window but by that time he had vanished into the dim light like a spectre. Never before had she regarded her lover as a man of mystery. It amused her, but it also intrigued her.

Promptly at eight-thirty, Wilf arrived. Holly gave the lad explicit instructions and left him to fill the gaps in the window. Grandfather Tal could tidy it up later. She could not contain her impatience to be with David, to hear his news, to learn why he wanted no contact with his family and why he had gone to the expense of renting a room when there was a largish apartment at his disposal upstairs. She tried to convince herself that he was teasing her with an elaborate performance, a kind of play. But beneath his easy manner had been a nervousness that indicated that he was in deadly earnest.

From the cupboard in the back store, Holly took out a new dark green coat with a single large button fastening and fox fur collar. She washed the dust from her fingers, put on the coat and a trim hat to match, changed her shoes and, with final instructions to Wilf, left the shop and set off for Wolfenden Street.

The Consort Hotel had a dreary frontage with square windows topped by chiselled eaves. The entrance was up four worn steps through a swing door that would have been more appropriate in a swimming bath or public art gallery. Inside there were potted plants, brass spittoons, leather armchairs and wall sofas, like a gentleman's club; also an air of sleepiness, as if the day had not yet begun for the occupants of the hotel's bedrooms. The only cheer wafted from the dining room; the aroma of grilled kippers and piping hot coffee was fresh and appetising enough to coax the most languid guest from his hangover and bring him rolling down the stairs to brace himself for another day.

Though she was early, David was already stationed on one of the sofas. He had taken off the topper and overcoat and was seated in a tense position, watching the door. He wore a splendid hand-cut suit in dark worsted. His hands and wrists glinted with gold – a wristlet watch, rings, links. He rose, came towards her and greeted her cordially but with peculiar stiltedness, as if his mood had changed again and he was less sure of his purpose in inviting her here.

"Have I told you before," he said, "that you are as beautiful as a princess?"

The phrase sounded false in the echoing foyer, a whispered insincerity rather than a compliment.

"I don't feel like a princess, not at this hour of the mornin'," said Holly.

"Breakfast will put you right."

In the dining room, lined by two "bars" of old-fashioned hot-dishes, were fifty tables. In isolation, ten or a dozen solitary gentlemen, and three elderly married couples, were doing justice to food selected from the buffets. Coffee, tea, toast and other essentials were conveyed to the tables by young waiters.

"The graveyard shift," said David. "God, it is solemn, isn't it?"

"Why did you invite me here, then?"

"The food's good, and we'll have a modicum of privacy for an hour or more. The Consort serves breakfast until eleven-thirty. There's usually a last minute rush about twenty past. Until then nobody will bother us. At least, it's warm; not like some of the hotels in London, these days, where you can freeze to death in the cocktail bar, or where you have to wear mittens just to work your knife and fork."

David led her round the buffet, urging her to heap her plate with kidneys and creamed potatoes, poached haddock, bacon, pork sausages, or even palm-sized pieces of fried beefsteak. There was no sign of shortage in this establishment.

They found a table adjacent to the window, and were duly attended by one of the youthful waiters, who, in the buttonhole of his coffee-coloured jacket, wore a bombardier's badge.

"Virtually all ex-servicemen," said David. "The pay's miserable, the hours are long – but it's work, I suppose."

"Are they allowed to wear regimental badges?"

"Strictly speaking, no. But it's a useful ruse for extracting tips from ex-officers."

Holly cut her hot buttered toast into segments.

David said, "You really do look marvellous, tiger."

"Thank you, kind sir."

"I brought you here," David said, "because I want to tell you a secret. Nobody else, except Mumford, knows the truth. I'm depending on you not to breathe a word in the wrong quarter."

"Secret?" Holly pretended to be deeply interested in the contents of the pork sausage on her plate.

"For the time being, it's between you and me."

"Don't keep me in suspense, then."

David sat back in the chair, hands on the edge of the table. A big signet ring reflected light from the window; a dress-ring with a ruby stone glittered in the overhead light. She could hear the loud *tick-tick-tick* of his heavy wristlet watch on its gilded bracelet.

"In a very short space of time," David said, "I've made a bundle of money."

"That's good. I'm glad for you."

"I'm not being modest, I admit, but I tell you, Holly, I'm on my way to being rich."

"You certainly look rich."

He glanced down at the jewellery. "Oh, these. A little bit of advertising, you know; not to be taken seriously."

"How did you strike the Klondike?" asked Holly.

"I'm coming to that," said David. "Holly, I think that you inspired me."

"I did?"

"The reason I've been avoiding Cardwell Place is that I didn't want Andrea catching me by the scruff of the neck and trying to tell me what to do. You see, I've been investing in stocks and shares – and you know what she'd think of that. I mean, she'd have her dear Miles dogging my heels days and nights foisting all sorts of sound advice upon me. I don't want help. I want to prove I can do it all on my own."

"And you've succeeded?"

"Absolutely!"

There was danger here, and Holly sensed it. It overlaid her pleasure at being in David's company, the omnivorous yearnings she had for him that became almost overpowering of reason when she was close to him – almost but not quite. Kirsanoff passions and Kirsanoff intellect warred in her as they had warred in her mother and, for all Holly knew, in every woman back down the family tree. She fought to maintain an intelligent balance, to apply it to the situation in which she now found herself. David had no reason to play games with her, yet she had the disquieting doubts that came with contests, with the confused wrestling of men and women who wanted to give all for love but could not discard the realities of life bound to a material plane.

Holly steeled herself, then asked bluntly. "Is Linsey Leigh-Jennngs your housekeeper in this pied-à-terre you talked about; are you still sleepin' with her?"

David appeared to be scandalised. "Good God, no! Do you take me for that much of a cad? I haven't seen Linsey in weeks; at least, only when I had to, strictly for business purposes."

"She helps with your business?" Holly said. "I thought you were independent."

"Holly, you've no reason to be jealous of Linsey now."

"I'm not jealous of her," said Holly.

"It would be natural if you were."

"Well, I'm not," said Holly, then shifted closer to the truth. "Perhaps I was, but not now."

"It's all over between Linsey and me. Really it is. There was never much to start with, and what there was has gone," David said. "You're my one and only girl now, Holly."

Holly sprinkled salt on her poached eggs and forced herself to eat a mouthful or two.

How desperately she wanted to believe him, but the vehemence of his assurances and his denials created an echo of mystery, of a sinister covering up of the whole truth.

Intuition warned Holly to respond with caution, not to allow herself to be swept away by her physical need of him. David's arrogance, she realised with a start, had been transformed into a desperate craving for her approval. For an instant, it diminished him in her eyes. She rejected the assumption, the judgment, because it too was unfair and unsettled the balance of her emotions.

She loved him more than ever before and was willing to concede that perhaps he had become his own man at last.

"What do you mean?" asked Holly.

"In six months or less, we can be married."

"Is that a proposal, David?"

"I'm not much of a one for romantic approaches."

"I'd noticed."

"Holly, can't I make you understand that I want you?"

"You've made that plain enough, David."

"Tell me about your brother."

She was taken aback. "Ritchie?"

"Yes, Ritchie; the one who got caught in the act."

"He's . . . he's in Brixton prison. Can't say I'm sorry. He's a bad lot."

"I assume he didn't sell you anything, at any time."

"He tried, but I wouldn't buy."

"Sensible," said David. "I suppose you know that Andrea got wind of it."

"Oh?"

"Ruffled her feathers, yet again."

"Oh?"

"Insisted on selling her share in the shop; mother's too. Didn't want to be associated with thieving Jews.'

"Sold their shares? Who bought them?"

"I did."

"You bought . . . you own . . . ?"

"Right," said David, smugly. "I'm your one and only partner now, Holly."

"Seventy-five per cent? You're the owner."

"Don't fret. I've no intention of changing a thing. You carry on as you're doing – with a twenty-five per cent guaranteed stake. By the way, Andrea and mother don't know that I bought them out. It's our secret, for a while."

"Why did you do it?"

"I could lie and tell you that I did it to keep Aspinall's in the family," said David. "But that wouldn't be true. No, Holly, I did it to prove that I care for you, that I meant every word I said that night."

"How did you find the money?"

"Finding the money was the easy part," said David. "I made a killing on some share dealing. Before the profits could slip through my fingers, I put them into Aspinall's. Andrea was creating *such* a damned song and dance about wanting rid of you and the shop: I took her at her word. Bought them out. Gave them a very decent price, too. I had to, didn't I? I couldn't have you going to work for Kennedy King."

"David, what do you want from me?"

"Whatever you're willing to give."

"Meaning?"

"Aren't you pleased, Holly? I thought you might show just a little gratitude."

"Why should I be grateful?"

"Once upon a time – and it seems a long time ago – you told me all you wanted was to own Aspinall's Antiques. When you marry me, Holly, that will be my wedding gift to you."

"We'll run the shop together?"

"I'll certainly lend a hand," said David. "But, no, it'll be your shop to manage how you will."

"What will you do?"

"What I'm doing now."

"Tell me, since you seem t'have sorted everythin' out very nicely, where will we live?"

"Not above the shop; I've given that to mother. It would be cruel to make her decamp. I thought we might start housekeeping in my flat in Wolfenden Street. In a year or so we can look for something better."

"All planned. When is the wedding?"

"June, I thought. Holly, you'll make a lovely June bride."

"Why wait until June, David? Why not next month?"

"Affairs won't be completely settled until June."

"Your affairs, you mean?"

"Our affairs, Holly.'

"David, is the shop a bribe."

"Really, that's unworthy of you. No, the shop's not a bribe. I need a centre in my life, a home, a wife and a family."

"I'd give you all of those things, David, without the shop."

"The shop will provide for us, Holly, in time of need."

"That's a strange way of putting it."

"Once I'm established, we can expand. Look for bigger premises closer to the West End."

"I'll be happy enough to stay in Cardwell Place, with you."

"What's wrong, Holly?"

"It doesn't seem real, none of it."

David glanced at his watch. "If I showed you our flat, would that make it seem more real?"

Holly's throat was dry. She knew what the invitation implied. David was no bashful boy. He had made love to many women, she supposed; certainly to one who would have no inhibitions. Holly swallowed. She felt her cheeks heat up, reddened by acknowledgment of the fact that she was eager to be alone with him. "Our flat"; it even sounded like an invitation to the private, intimate world of lovers.

"The shop," Holly said, lamely.

"Hang the shop," David said. "Look, let me pay the bill, then we'll stroll round to Wolfenden Street."

"And?"

David smiled and shrugged. "Talk about curtains and carpets."

Holly studied his face; his hunger for her was apparent, and the fact that he was unsure of her, and anxious. It was in his searching eyes, the pursed line of his lips, and the little freckles of perspiration on his brow. He wanted her. His desire released in Holly a slow uncoiling passion, darker and more subtle than the man's but no less demanding.

"All right," she said.

He covered her hands with his, pressing her fingers to the table.

"Are you sure?"

"Yes."

Heart hammering, Holly let David lead her out of the hotel and round to the apartment he had leased in nearby Wolfenden Street.

There, a half hour later, she allowed him to lay her on the narrow bed and become her lover in reality as well as imagination.

* * *

Cheap pea-green curtains screened out the morning light. On the narrow iron mantelshelf a tin alarm clock ticked. Below it the gas fire purred, warming the icy bedroom. Two nickel-plated photograph frames, empty of portraits, flanked a cut-glass decanter half filled with whisky. In an ashtray, filched from a local pub, two cigarette butts lay twisted. The quilt smelled musty and the sheets were yellow with much washing. On the room's only chair, a ragged wickerback, David had draped his suit and shirt. Holly's clothing lay in a heap upon the floor where he had tossed it piece by piece in the breathless act of revealing her body to his admiring gaze.

When he had touched her Holly's shame and fear had melted. Shivering, she had thrust herself against him, her mouth seeking his. His chest was sprinkled with brown hair, hard muscled, warm.

"You're so beautiful, Holly. I'm half afraid of you."

"David, I love . . . I've always loved you. I want you. Is that wrong of me?"

"No, no, my darling; that's how it should be."

"Do you want to . . . to look at . . . me?" she said. "Does it . . . is that what . . . ?"

"I thought you would be beautiful, but I didn't imagine how . . ."

"Will I go into bed?"

"Yes, darling. In bed."

Hugging the sheet to her chin, shivering now with the chill as well as the rush of sexual passion that had swept over her, Holly stared at the ceiling, at damp-patched plaster and chipped moulding. The stealthy sounds of David removing his trousers and undershorts seemed distant, unconnected with her.

The seediness of the room, the hour of the day, everything, in fact, was wrong. For all that, she had no feeling of martyrdom, of being wronged.

When he came to her and his skin touched hers, when his body lay against hers and the sheet and blanket were drawn up, they would be isolated, would be together in a binding moment of love, a fulfilment that not all the empty nickel picture frames or ticking tin clocks, not all the uncertainty and awkwardness could spoil. Later, when they were man and wife and the flat was filled with nice furniture and objets d'art, when they could be together every night in the privacy of this very room, then they would look back on the first time and laugh about it.

There was a split-second's dread for Holly, fear that she had made herself victim to a man she did not know. His persuasive gentleness had been replaced by need. Evidence of his passion frightened her. David was too experienced, however, to force her to yield to him at once. He touched her, caressed her, murmuring, kissing her hair, her mouth, ears and eyebrows. The response of her body seemed natural. She was no longer ashamed of its wild surprises. Kissing her breasts, stroking her thighs, he moved with patient thoroughness, reining in his passion, holding back his urgent desire. But it was not his considerate hesitations that brought Holly to surrender, rather the knowledge that he was denying himself for her, that she roused in him emotions so dominant and so powerful that they made him tremble and sweat.

Three or four times, he asked her, "Are you . . . are you ready, Holly?"

"Yes, darling. Dearest. Yes."

It did not occur to her that David had not planned it, that his preparations were incomplete or that he, like her, had cashed in on opportunity, seeking in their love-making a strength that he did not in fact possess. Sudden impulsive yielding made it all seem inevitable. It increased her response into heedless rapture as he entered her and brought her to fulfilment. Her unexpected torrent of need found release and, quickly, shook David from his pillar of gallantry. Experience and innocence merged, washed by surging waves of fevered blood. He bore down upon her. His ruthlessness and her passivity met and broke into crests of painful joy, receding only to mount again, and break, rise and roll and break, deep inside her loins. Then his muscles became taut. His weight crushed her. She heard him cry out, a long shuddering sound, and he lowered himself upon her, limp and spent. She held him with her arms, soothing him as gently as he had comforted her only minutes before.

"Did I . . . hurt you?" he asked.

"No."

"Are you all right?"

"Yes, darling."

He eased himself away from her. Reluctantly, she released him. She felt whole, complete. He sank back, head on the pillow, his eyes, strangely, swimming with tears.

Forgetful of herself, Holly turned on her elbow.

"David, what is it? What's wrong?"

He puffed out his cheeks, making his moustache flutter, and wiped his eyes with his forefinger.

"Are *you* all right?" Holly asked anxiously.

"Wonderful, my tiger. Wonderful."

"Why are you cryin'?"

"I don't know," he replied.

*   *   *

Christmas came and went. The year of 1919 ran out. Holly hardly noticed. For her, it was a period of trinkets and song, David, and more of David, of little gifts between them, secrets shared, of explorations and new fulfilments. They met in the morning in the flat in Wolfenden Street at nine o'clock and made love, leaving again not later than noon. There were no other rendezvous; no cocktails, no dinner engagements, no midnight suppers before slipping into bed. For all that, Holly was in a daze of delight. Within a week, she had begun to feather the drab nest with ornaments, cushions, kitchen goods and, of course, clean linen for the bed. It pleased her that she would not suffer sea-changes in Lambeth. She could take her own good time, build a home piece by piece free from her father's ill-tempered scorn, away from the taint of the man's house in Abraham's Box. Blinded by love, she did not discern the shadows or probe into David's night-time secrets, ask for an explanation of the curious deals that kept him from her. She trusted him, and stoutly commanded the sceptic in her to hold its tongue.

Convinced that what David was doing would be best for her too, she accepted the routines of the affair with gladness. She did not , therefore, allow herself to be stricken with misgivings when, for three days in a row, David did not show up in Wolfenden Street. Each day she waited until noon, then returned to the shop, disappointed but not dismayed. He was a busy chap, after all, occupied in making money so that they might buy the flat, or a grander house in Hampstead or Chelsea, perhaps. The lives of business men were not their own.

It was naive of Holly thus to anaesthetise her doubts, deaden her instincts and be quite so trusting.

Months later, when anger and shame had dwindled, she saw the process of disillusionment as a hard lesson, regarded the fleeting affair as an illustration of the uselessness of love and tried, as best she could, to learn from it. By will power and wits, she survived the two staggering blows that sent her reeling into the 1920s.

On January 2nd, 1920, David James Aspinall married Linsey Leigh-Jennings by special licence at a Croydon Registry Office.

On February 4th, Doctor Albert McCorkindale, a close friend of Emma Chubb, confirmed Holly's suspicion that she was six weeks pregnant.

PART THREE

1920

1

Postman's Knock

My dearest Holly,

How can words adequately convey the apology I must make and the forgiveness I must ask of you? As you will see I am in Dover, preparatory to leaving for a short sojourn in France. My wife is with me. I am married.

It was never my intention to deceive you just for what I could get. Everything I said was the absolute truth and came from my heart. I suspect it will be impossible for you to think fondly of me ever again and will be of little consolation to you to know that I will always cherish those few all-too-brief weeks we were together.

My wife is Linsey Leigh-Jennings – now Aspinall, of course. We were married at the Croydon Office of the Registrar yesterday afternoon. I am writing to tell my mother as she does not yet know of the event. A friend of mine and a friend of Linsey's acted as witnesses.

You will, I fear, condemn me as a cheat and a deceiver. I can hardly blame you. Once more may I stress that it was never my intention to seize advantage of your feelings towards me. Every promise I made was sincere at the time.

I cannot explain my reasons for marrying Linsey. It sounds silly to say she needs me more than you do – yet I can find no other motive for what I have done. From the bottom of my heart I can only repeat that I would not have hurt you for worlds, if there had been any way to avoid it.

Unless you feel impelled to make alternative arrangements, we will remain business partners. I promise I will not intervene in the running of the shop, will make no endeavour to see you, unless at your specific request. In view of the circumstances, I think that this is the best course for both of us. What passed between us will remain our secret, a few fleeting weeks of love that I will speak of to no one, not even Linsey.

The place in Wolfenden Street, our place, has the rent paid until July 1st, in advance. If you wish to make use of the flat in that period, do not fear that I will bother you there.

If you have urgent need to contact me, in a matter of business, say, Mr. Mumford will act as intermediary.

Although it is hardly an appropriate moment, my dearest, I cannot close this letter without telling you I will always regard you with great affection and respect. I pray that you will find a man more worthy of you, and will be happy with him.

Perhaps you have had a lucky escape.

David

January the first, 1920

My darling sweetheart, Ritchie,

I hope they will get this letter to you. It would be cruel if they did not let me tell you how I am feeling. They will read it before they give it to you I know but I do not care so long as they give it to you as it is. I do not care what any of them think about me. Mamma and Papa have been talking. They say you are wicked and you would have been better to have been in the army like a normal boy and to have fought for your country, died even, than bring such disgrace on your family. It was very difficult for me to keep hold on my tongue and not tell them about us. Your Grandpapa has managed to see me twice without them there. He told me you are well as can be expected in that place. I asked him if it was that I could visit you. He told me that it is one visit each month and I could not get away from here without we should tell all to Mamma and Papa. He said it would not be good to do that right now. I take his word for it. I ache for you, my love. I want to see you so much, so that I ache all over. I do not know what is happening, I want you so much. In school a girl called Amanda said she had been with her boy friend. She told me what she felt. That is how I feel though I have not been with you, as you know. For ever, I will wait to be with you until you are ready and I am not forced to stay here, if you understand what I mean, like we talked about so often. Only I know why you did what it was you did. It was for me. I know that and I love you more for it. I sit in my room and try to fall asleep to dream you are with me. I sometimes dream so hard I think you are there on the bed with me. I kiss you and hold you in my dream. Do you think of me often? I hope you do and you have time to think of me as I think of you – which is every day and every night. Though I do not believe in Him, I offer prayers for you, you will be not too fed up where you are. I cannot imagine what it is like in there. How is the grub? When you are free and we are together again I will make cherry strudel for you or lekach, like my mother has been teaching me to bake for New Year Festival. We will eat together every day when you are set free and we are together. I will be old enough and they will not stop me. It is an ache for me to write to you and to write down your name even. So I must sign off now and tell you that I love you, my dearest darling own sweetheart. I wait for you for ever, for nobody else ever fills my heart. Only my Ritchie – who is you, darling.

With all love,
Ruth

TO: –
Frederick Coe, Esquire,
Coe & Gifford Company, Ltd.,
14 Marigold Street,
Peckham,
London, S.E.   5th January, 1920

Dear Sir,
I am writing on behalf of Elkins & Beckman, Builders' Contractors, at the headed address, with respect of the advertisement for tenders pertaining to the completion of six private dwelling houses on the plot of land at South Moor Road and Bell Lane. We would esteem it a favour to be permitted to submit a quotation for completion work. Also we are prepared to give guarantees on completion dates, with financial adjustments in your favour should that date not be met.

A preliminary survey done by myself suggests that Messrs. Clark & Simmons have not only left the six houses incomplete at announcement of their bankruptcy, but they have not achieved safety standards required by recent act of parliament when it comes to laying of foundations. I appreciate that three of the dwellings are already erected and two others shelled. I would respectfully point out, however, that the Peckham New Town House Owners' and Tenants' Association are already making complaint about shoddy workmanship. Such a state of affairs cannot do anything but harm to your Company's reputation if and when the Association's complaints are made public.

Respectfully, may I suggest that our tenders include costing for necessary structural changes and strengthening to bring the dwellings into accord with regulations, therefore increasing their value.

As you will understand, no estimate can be given without detailed survey. If agreement in principle can be reached between us on the extent of requirements, we will arrange to send in a surveyor and estimator of our own within the week and will present precise elevations and costings shortly thereafter.

May I add, sir, that Elkins and Beckman would not be willing to make tender for the work if you conclude that structural repairs to the existing buildings are a needless expense. Quality is the keynote of our concern.

I hope to hear from you in the affirmative.

I am, sir, yours

Most Faithfully, A. MAURICE BECKMAN, Managing Partner.

Hotel Modesto,
Dover.
January 3rd, 1920

My dear Mother,

I have to tell you that I am now a married man. My fiancée, Linsey Leigh-Jennings, and I felt that we could wait no longer to tie the knot. This was duly done in the Croydon Registry Office yesterday, by special licence.

Now I realise you will be very disappointed not to have been present at the ceremony, that Andrea will be piqued and will try to make you angry with me too. This is a new century, however, and things are not done as they were in your day.

My wife and I will be on honeymoon in France for two weeks. When we return to London, I will bring Linsey to meet you. I am sure you and she will get along swimmingly. She is quite charming when you get to know her.

You may inform Andrea I have gone into business and I am doing very well at it. I will tell you all about it when I return to London. I am not sure yet where Linsey and I will be living – possibly Surrey, if we can find a suitable house. In case of emergency Mr. Mumford will be able to contact me.

I hope that you are in good health, Mother, and you will not hold the suddenness of our marriage against Linsey. It was one of those things that young people do on the spur of the moment. I am absolutely positive that Linsey will make me a good and loving wife. If she looks after me half as well as you looked after Daddy I will have no cause to repent at leisure. I am sure that she will.

Do take care of yourself and do not go out in this treacherous icy weather unaccompanied.

God Bless, David

P.S. I enjoyed our Christmas dinner. Next year you will have to set an extra place for your daughter-in-law and buy a larger turkey.   D.

TO: –
Albert R. Webster, Esquire,
19 New Road,
Peckham,
London, S.E.

Dear Mr. Webster,

I am writing to say thanks for telling me that the houses that Clark &
Simmons slung up are gerry-built. Paddy and I appreciate your tip
and, as you suggested, I have written to Fred Coe and told him he'd
better not settle for a plaster and paint job or you would have the
Peckham New Town Owners down on his neck like a shot. I agree
with you that Coe is a shifty individual but I think he will see sense in
having the job done properly now. I just hope that he does not take
the pip at Elkins & Beckman for pointing out the error of his
company's ways.

If opportunity arises and you can put in a good word for us without
seeming too obvious, I would appreciate it. We would not be selling
anybody a pup. I have the workers to be able to do a sound job on the
houses, quickly too, if we get any kind of a break with weather.

About your suggestion that Elkins & Beckman buy out the plot as it
stands and put the houses into shape on our own account, I doubt if
Coe would go for it. Besides, Paddy and I could not raise the asking
price. Our capital is completely tied up in the business. In a year or
two, we might consider that kind of thing, if there is any open land left
in Peckham by that time.

Once again, our thanks.

Yours faithfully,
MAURICE BECKMAN

12 Buck's Walk,
Lambeth,
London.
12/1/20

Dear Ritchie,

Your old man has told me they will not let you write more than one
letter each month and they censor everything. He told me you can get
in as many letters as you like, and I thought it might be nice for you to
hear from your old mate and know that he is thinking about you.

Jeff sends his regards as well. He is with me in the tannery as I am
writing this. We are just finished dinner. It is as cold as sin here. The
skins from the market were froze solid and we had to steam them.

The smell was terrible. Two of the batches got spoiled for anything. Corky was jumping mad. The man they have brought in your place is about thirty. He was with the Queen's Own in Flanders. His name is Inglis and he worked in Scotland at a tannery at a place called Barrhead before the war. Nobody here can make out what he is speaking about, he talks so queer. He talks not much really. He is not as good at getting things done right as you were.

It is very cold here. Can you read my writing? It is shaking, I know. Jeff wants to write to you but he said I do it better. I would send you something to eat but I do not know how do you do it. Jeff says that he will try to send a cake with a saw in it. Ha. Ha. Ha. Can we send you anything they will let you keep? You like nuts. I could buy you some if you can tell me how to get them inside to you.

Corky has just shouted. It is time to go.

Goodbye from Jeff and me. It will not be long, I hope.

Your friend, Stan.

P.S. *Everything is all right*.

Aspinall's Antiques,
Cardwell Place,
Pimlico,
London.
14th January, 1920

Dear Mr. King,

I am writing at Holly's behest to express her gratitude for your offer of four job lots of English china bric-à-brac. The price of eight pounds (£8.0.0.) has been pronounced very satisfactory and I will call at the Emporium to collect said lots on Wednesday morning, if that is convenient to you. A banker's cheque for the sum of eight pounds will be presented on receipt of the goods, that is, at time of collection.

Holly has asked me to convey her good wishes to you. Of late she has been rather under the weather; that is the reason she has not replied sooner to your communication and why I am acting as her temporary amanuensis. It is my belief that she has exerted herself too strenuously during the course of the past eighteen months and is in need of respite from the demands of business. She refuses to take a holiday but I have persuaded her to restrict her attendance here and her appearances at sales to a minimum until such times as she has recovered her strength.

May I say that I am personally appreciative of the kindness you have shown my granddaughter in matters of business. In this keenly competitive world of ours, such unselfishness is rare.

Yours sincerely, TAL KIRSANOFF

Mr. Leo Beckman,
Ambrahams Terace, Lambeth.
18th Janary, 1920 AD

My Belove Son,

I am sory I have not been up to Brickton to see you since yor unfortnate acident but I have been busy at the dock an in the house.

Maury will not come up neither. But he is difrent from what I am. *I have good reason an you know them???*

It was lonly without you Xmas. The bloks round Admarals Hat was askin how you was gettin on inside. They said it was a shame for you, inocent. I told them what had reely happened. They said it was them dirty dogs what didnt know right from wrong an should be locked up themselfs.

I have news for to tell you now.

Yor sister Holly Beckman has gorn off an left me in the lurch.

It is what you would ecspeck from that spoiled bratt. Yor granfather tells me there is no other man. He is a lyer.

Me an you know beter???

She is not loyle like you, my belove son. Tell them yor old Dad is alone in the world an see if they dont let you come home sooner. I hear they do that for some.

It has bin done???

You tell them dirty dogs it has bin done for them as what is no worse off than what I am.

Yor sister Holly Beckman. She has gorn to life with her nobs over Pimlicko.

You said it was onley a mater of time. I remember you said it. I listen to you, my belove son. It is onley you I got to listen to now.

She is not like you. She never had no respeck for me, not like what you done. *You know what I try to say???*

It is frezin cold out here. Mr. Blor says it would freze the noses of three brass monkeys. He did not sey that ecsackly but they would not let you reed what he reely seys. Coal can not be got anywhere. I got stiks from Millicans shop. He would onley give me three. She pays a room over there. *It will be ten shilings, at leest???* She give ten shilings to a stranger not her own father??? *Tell them dirty dogs that???*

I take a drink for you tonit in Admarals Hat. I think of you an wish you could be there to with me.

It is not like it was befor???

It was not you. I know that.

Maury has brot me a stickey stamp. I will sine of now, my belove son.

Yor Respeckfull Father,
Leo Beckman

Miss Andrea Aspinall,
24a Cardwell Place,
Pimlico,London.
January nineteenth

Dear David,

Mother was sensible enough to show me your letter. It is outrageous of you to suggest that I would attempt to poison her against you. However, your personal insults to my integrity are unimportant.

What is this nonsense abut your marriage to Leigh-Jennings? As you are lavish with details I am forced to the conclusion that you are legally bound to the woman and that nothing I can say or do will deter you.

I feel saddened by the fact that you did not see fit to consult with your sister and your mother before going into this venture. Is it possible that you were not in possession of your senses at the time. Perhaps intoxicated? I cannot believe that you were "swept off your feet" like some silly boy just out of school. You have "known" this woman too long for any "mystery" to have survived.

Really, I cannot comprehend it. Nor can I comprehend your secrecy in not informing us, your family, as to the nature of your business. Do you suppose that we, your family, have no interest in you or concern for your welfare? How you can shut us out of your life in this manner is more than I can grasp.

I would still like to know how much you received from the sale of your portion of the business. It appears that Beckman *retained* her quarter share. Do you realise the position this puts me in? I am living in a house on the sufferance of an owner that I do not even *know*.

If you were at all concerned for Mother's well-being you would be here with her now, attempting to discover who bought us out. Whoever it is, he has obviously not thought it worthwhile to purchase Beckman's share. Unless the girl is a better actress than I give her credit for, she too is in ignorance of the true facts. I questioned her closely last week but she was brazen and refused to tell me anything. To judge from her demeanour and her snappish manner with me she has reason to be very sure of herself, though she *professes* to know nothing.

It is imperative that we meet immediately upon your return to England, whenever that might be. It is ridiculous that I should have to forward letters to my brother through the offices of a solicitor. I don't know what Father would have to say to all this, if he was still alive. He was always far too indulgent with you, of course, which is, I imagine, what's wrong with you now.

Not a word about your discharge, except that embarrassing conversation during Christmas dinner. I have never been so humiliated as I was by your behaviour on that evening, your truculence to me, your lack of civility. Are you so ashamed of your so-called "profession" that you dare not even talk of it to your nearest?

In conclusion, let me warn you that Mother and I are not sufficiently well-off now to lend you money. I can be no plainer than that, can I, in stating that we are not in a position to advance you sums, no matter how small. I am tempted to say that you have made your bed and you may lie in it, but the phrase does not seem opportune in the light of recent events.

On your return, I would be obliged if you would notify me of your address so that we may arrange a meeting. Mother and I would prefer you *not* to come to the house with Leigh-Jennings as we have no particular desire to associate with her. A meeting between you and I is, however, *imperative and urgent*; we must somehow get to the bottom of this whole matter of the sale of the shop. The bewildering thing is the low rental set on the house and the beneficial lease. I am sure you know much more about it than you have so far admitted.

Knowing you, I suppose you will turn up in time to collect your share of the last half-year's profits. I am told that the sum is not large as Beckman saw fit to spend a great deal on stock, stock that has now been transferred to the new owner – at our expense, I might add.

I am not happy with this situation, and I am not at all satisfied with your casual attitude to a matter of such importance to your mother and to me.

There is nothing that I can say or do to hinder you going your own sweet way; your hasty marriage is only one example of your wilfulness. In the matter of business, however, I do have a say, and we must meet *as soon as possible*. I would, therefore, be obliged if you will notify me where you can be reached.

Your sister,
Andrea

Aspinall's Antiques,
Cardwell Place,
Pimlico,
London.
January 19th, 1920

Dear Christopher,
Herewith find enclosed ten volumes of works by Sir Walter Scott. I

think that some, if not all, are First Editions. I am no expert in books and I realise that bibliographers have a lot of difficulty in checking out points with Scott. I am sure that you will offer a fair price. The ten volumes came my way with a lot of furniture. I did not turn them down, as you can imagine.

I am sorry that I have not been round in person to have a look at your new premises. I hope that business is booming in Shepherd Market and that you are doing well. I am sure you deserve success.

If the Scott volumes are of use to you, please let me know your offer.

Yours sincerely,
Holly Beckman

22/1/20

Dear Stan, I can't tell if you'll get this letter. As you'll see from the paper it isn't anything that's going through the regular mail. I am having it smuggled out of this hole by a bloke who is leaving. He has promised me he will post it regular on the outside. It had to be folded small, so I hope you can read it. It is just to say thank you for your letter. It was nice to hear from the outside. It is bad in here, worse in some ways than you hear about. But not so bad in others. I have a cell with an old geezer who knew Shotten when he was young. He was a dipper, to hear him talk you would think he had dipped every pocket in England. He says he did the Prince of Wales once but only got a stickpin and a purse with ten bob in it. Can you believe it? I am going through this paper, so I must tell you what I want. What I want is for you to hold the money. It is no use even thinking of doing a bunk. Not that you would, would you? You know what I would do. Right? I don't need you to do anything else except hold the money till I get out of here, that will be September since I'm being a good boy and keeping my nose clean with the screws. Don't tell nobody about the money no matter who comes asking, even my old man or my Granpa. It is none of their business. Keep a weather eye for Jack Renzo or Chimp Seeman. I do *not* trust them though I kept my trap shut like I said I would – and they know it. But you are on the outside and they might take a fancy to see where the loot went. My advice is not to do nothing with nobody til I get out of here. I will see you right then, and that is a real promise. I am not finished. I am only just starting. Remember that. Keep your nose wiped and your fly buttoned. Your Good Friend, Ritchie.

Christopher Deems,
Bookseller,
4 Shepherd Market Lane,
London.
January 24th, 1920

Dear Victor,

The handbill for the Pilgrim Hall thing is hardly magnetic. Same old circus, it seems. I suppose Melanger will adopt his Albert Hall voice and deafen the flour-haired ladies in the front rows and that Estall will writhe through his Languid Nights in Ithaca yet again. It does not surprise me that Mad Jack could not steel himself to turn out for you. Graves, of course, is another matter. All is not well with him and, I suspect, departure is imminent. Who is this McIan fellow? I haven't heard of him. Your accompanying note was purposely vague; you will take the Inns of Court by storm with style of that order. But who is McIan? A khaki jackanapes mimicking the mighty? Will he speak with the voice of cannon in a Lothian brogue – or do you have a surprise for me? I am truly past surprises. Perhaps you are not, however, so here is a marvel for you to grunt at and shove around the Oxford wallow. Yes, I will condescend to appear. The guinea fee is the real attraction, you understand. However, I will not read new work. There is no new work, nothing new under the sun, only old songs and innocent expriences, the rusty ironies that they sheath. Slate me for fifteen minutes and I will stretch out my vowels like wet leather bootlaces and roll my consonants like gun-carriages and short change you if I can.

It is no more than you deserve for daubing in my name on your handbill after I had made it clear that I did not want to open my yawp in public ever again. Yes, I am aware that you are hell bent on restoring me, on drawing me from my shell like a hermit crab. I doubt if you understand the magnitude of the task that you have set yourself.

It is not a question of suffering or of despair; nor am I brooding like a mother hen, incubating in my nest of dung some fertile clutch of verses. All that is gone. Don't you believe me? God knows you examined me thoroughly enough during the vacation. I appreciated your help in the shop and your efforts to raise me up. But in the waiting, I am content. New rhymes and old flames are no answer to what ails me, Victor. I think you are right to be concerned. I am concerned myself – though that selfish indulgence too is a legacy of yesterday's morality. What is the life of one shy bookseller, after all?

If only there was something to leave behind, I would willingly set sail on an ebbing tide. From nothing into nothing, however, is too nebulous a track; even the wraithes would desert me on that downward path. Divine preservation; a purpose there? The godless man, too, may wait in hope of a sign that all was lost that once was.

Enough of this tick-tock-tick. I have work to do, honest labour with wrapping paper, string and sealing wax. Neat packages are some small comfort.

Fifteen minutes then between Estall and McIan on the fish-box in the Pilgrim Hall. Only for the sake of our friendship, though, which I trust you will not thus impose upon again.

Christopher

TO: –
Mr. Patrick Elkins.
Wednesday.

Dear Paddy,
Nora is quite right to keep you tucked up warm in bed. Better you act sensible now than hack for the rest of the winter and spread your mucky Irish germs round the lads. My sore throat is better, though I still cannot yell the odds very well. I am enclosing the letters relative to the Peckham contract. Bert Webster has been a good friend to us. As you will see from the attached he has put the fear into Coe and we have got an invite to make full survey and costing on the South Moor/Bell Lane scheme. We have to thank Webster for that, and Clark & Simmons for going bust when they did. Coe has agreed to let us re-lay the foundations but he will insist on best terms and a clause for delays in the contracts. While you are lying there in your scratcher, you might do some good by lighting candles for decent weather. If it snows for a long time in February or March we could follow Clark & Simmons down the drain.

But do not worry yourself, Paddy. I will make allowances for bad weather. Jim and Syd are good surveyors and know what is needed. They will do the best job for us. If we can pull this one off it will mean lots of money in the bank for us. It will give us a lot of influence too and that is also important.

Baxendale's shop is finished, you will be pleased to know.

I will come round to see you on Friday night, about supper time. Look after your health til you're better.

Yours,
Maurice

P.S.S. – Please Send Sausages???

Waldorf – Aldwych – Strand
29 Jan 20

My dear Holly,

We are back in London. It seems strange. We are staying here for a week or two until we find more suitable and permanent accommodation, perhaps in the country – but not too far out.

It's queer to be writing to you. I can't find the proper words. Really, I'm hoping that you will write, tell me all that's happening with the shop. The half yearly dividend will be distributed soon. I admit I could use it right now. Paris was very expensive, and not too pleasant. Too much "war" still in evidence. Not like dear old London.

I had hoped you might write to me care of Mr. Mumford, but I can't say that I blame you. It is asking a lot, I know. Will you write, even if it's just a short note telling me about the shop? Please, Holly, I would like to hear something from you. Please don't be afraid that I will try to see you. That would not be discreet. I realise the situation you are in and what you must think of me. But we are still partners, aren't we? I hope and pray that you might, in time, allow me to call myself your friend.

Are you using our place at all? I like to think of you there. Will you write? Please!

God Bless,
David

Aspinall's Antiques,
Cardwell Place,
Pimlico, London.
30th January, 1920

Dear David,

Messrs. Tolhurst & Burns, Ltd., Auditors and Accountants, of Alderman Road, Pimlico, have informed me that they will complete the auditing of the accounts of Aspinall's Antiques, for the period ending December 31st, 1919, not later than February 10th.

At my request Messrs. Tolhurst & Burns, Ltd., will present five sets of audited accounts, including balance sheets. Accounts will be presented in full to,

1)	David Aspinall	3)	Andrea Aspinall
2)	Thora Aspinall	4)	Holly Beckman

The fifth and final copy will be lodged with the bank. Also at my request, Messrs. Tolhurst & Burns, Ltd., will submit with the audited accounts a disbursement figure in four equal parts of the net profit for the half year, according to their final computation. As the employment of Messrs. Tolhurst & Burns, Ltd., was your suggestion, I assume that monies paid out on their calculation will be acceptable to you. I have, therefore, instructed the bank to send cheques for the relative sum to each of the four partners, as listed above. The cheque should reach you not later than the end of next month.

As you will see from the balance sheet, seven sums of money owing for the period to end December, 1919, have not yet been paid over and have been written down as carry-forward profits into the current year. As you are now three-part owner of Aspinall's Antiques, I have taken the liberty of dividing the total sum still owing by four and will instruct the bank to send a separate cheque to your mother and your sister for this quartered sum, thus clearing Aspinall's Antiques' debt to them. Your quarter share and my quarter share of the owed sum will be incorporated into the profit-and-loss account for the current year. I trust that this arrangement is satisfactory and meets with your approval.

In respect of the flat at 4b Wolfenden Street, of which you are nominally the tenant, I am grateful to you for offering it for my personal use. I have to inform you that I have taken up residence there and would consequently be grateful if you would arrange the transfer of the Rent Book into my name, as from February 1st, 1920. The arrangement can be done through my solicitor, Mr. Mumford. Though I appreciate your offer of rent-free accommodation at the above address for a further five months, under the circumstances I do not feel that it would be proper to accept. Mr. Mumford will negotiate with the landlord for a longer lease, in my name, as I intend to make my home there for some time to come. I would be obliged if all communication between us is conducted through Mr. Mumford's offices as I have no wish to have direct contact with you.

It only remains for me to congratulate you on your recent marriage and to wish you every happiness with your bride for the future.

Yours sincerely,
Miss Holly Beckman

Aspinall's Antiques
30/1/20

Dear Emma,

May I come and call on you tomorrow or the next day? I have a personal problem and would like your advice. I'm sorry to use you like this but there is no other woman to whom I can turn. I trust your discretion.

Yours,
Holly

2

Damaged Goods

PLUMP LITTLE ARMCHAIRS, love seats and pouffés upholstered in braided moquette, made Emma Chubb's parlour uncommonly crowded. Crown Derby vases and old Worcester ewers nudged shoulders with ebony photo frames on a three-shelved mantelpiece over a bow-fronted hearth. Within each frame sepia-tinted photographs were arranged with random indifference to period, a collage of Emma's happiest days from a slum childhood propped up by barrel-chested uncles in braces and big-bosomed aunts in canvas aprons through a host of holidays with Simon Black on seaside promenades, in punts and on plunging mountainsides. In all of the plates, Emma appeared to have been arrested in motion amid stolid surroundings. Even her companions of the moment had the posed immobility of landscape or furniture, but Emma, blurred, whirred among them like a buxom sprite.

The blazing coal fire was a welcome sight after the dead, cold street and the dead, cold waiting room of the doctor's residence, a dwarf mansion lost in tenements somewhere west of Whitechapel. Holly had returned in a state of numb shock, huddled in a corner of the taxicab while Emma hugged her and, for once, said nary a word.

Emma gave her a hot brandy and water and left her alone for a bit, seated, still in coat and hat, before the newly-lighted fire. Outside, the February afternoon closed iron talons on London. Sounds of the city became hoarse as if in anticipation of more fog and frost.

After ten minutes, Emma returned bearing a tray set with yellow buns and sardine sandwiches, two copper kettles and assorted tea things. She edged a drum-topped table from a corner. It squeaked like a pet on dolphin castors and clicked in a pleased way as she put the heavy tray upon it. Still without a word, Emma poured tea, put a sandwich and a bun on a plate and dumped the plate on Holly's lap.

"Eat," she said.

"I'm not hungry."

"Eat, it's the best thing."

"I'm keepin' you from your work, Emma."

"Stuff'n' nonsense," said Emma. "Get that lot down you. You'll feel more *compos mentis* then, and we can discuss what you're a-goin' to do about the comin' event."

"You won't tell anyone?"

"'Course I won't tell anyone. But it can't remain a secret for long, love. You'll be out like a balloon in three or four months. You're six weeks gone already, remember."

"I'm so ashamed."

"Why?"

"Because everybody'll think I'm . . . cheap."

"Everybody?"

"My grandfather, Maury my brother . . ."

"Snap to them," said Emma. "Anyhow, from what you've told me they'll stand by you come what may. What's really got you worried, Holly? Confide in Emma. She knows all about it."

"I won't be able t' manage the shop."

"What about your grandfather? Can't he cope for six months? Havin' a kid ain't the end of everythin'. It's not like you was a docker's missus an' could be sure you'd be saddled with one a year for the best part o' your life."

"You don't understand."

"Don't I?" said Emma. "Look, love, I understand more'n you think. I got myself in the family way – *twice*."

Holly looked up quickly. "But where are . . . ?"

"Had the first taken away – know what I mean – by the same doctor we visited today."

"Taken away?"

"He insisted on it."

"Who? The doctor?"

"No, the man, the daddy. He was married. Didn't want no more kids, 'specially one born out of the bed." Emma shrugged. "He arranged everythin' for me."

"What kind of man would do that?"

"He was a remittance man, lived on an income from his father. Had a nice house in Readin'. Fiddled about with antiques, paintin's mostly. Quite well off. I was his 'London companion' for nigh-on three years; younger than you even I was when it started. He treated me all right, really. Saw me through it. But he left me, after. When he knew I was all right, he posted me twenty pounds in an envelope with a letter of goodbye. Never saw him again. Missed him for a while."

"Taken away?" Holly repeated.

"Didn't hurt. It was done clean. Got me in the seventh week. Much later, an' it might've been dangerous."

"Emma, are you suggestin' I . . . ?"

"Drink your tea. There's real butter on that bun, plum jam, too."

"I won't do it, Emma," said Holly. "I won't have my baby taken away."

Emma Chubb nodded. She looked smooth and affable and, at that instant, sinister. "I'm not givin' advice, Holly. Just tellin' you what's what."

"*I won't do it.*"

"Second time was four years later. Little beggar almost took *me* off. Never told anybody this before – 'cept Simon."

"Was Mr. Black the father?"

"Simon? God, no!" Emma giggled, as if the idea of Simon Black being careless enough to spawn a bastard was ridiculous to the point of burlesque. "Happened before I met Simon. It was the man I worked for. In Chapman's. I was office skivvy, 'til he took up with me. He *owned* Chapman's. I wasn't the only girl he had out of there, neither. Couldn't even deceive myself he loved me. He also wanted me t'have the baby 'taken away'. Practically had a bill of account with a back-street midwife. But I'd heard rumours about 'er. Anyhow, just t'spite the old devil I ran off. Told myself I'd have the kid. Liked the idea of turnin' up in the office one fine day with a little kid the dead spit o' his Daddy in my arms. Didn't work out like I planned, though. I stayed with an aunt for my term. Fifth month, it happened. Bad. Lost the baby, near lost my life. Bled for nine days. Had to have bits o' me cut away."

"Emma, please, don't tell me any more."

"Can't have no more kids now. Best thing, really."

Pale as milk, Holly said, "Are you tellin' me I shouldn't *have* the baby."

"For your own good."

"What about the baby's good?"

"It ain't nothin' right now, not even as big as a skinned hare. No, Holly, the kid ain't got a claim on you just yet."

"I . . . I can sell my share of the shop. Would Mr. King . . . ?"

"Leave Kennedy out of it. That's my advice, Holly. Leave 'm out of it for now. Later, if you decide t' have the kid . . ." Emma Chubb frowned, considered, shook her head. "To be blunt, Kennedy won't want 'damaged goods'."

"But the shop, it's worth . . ."

"He never really wanted the shop, love. He only wanted you. But he's not a generous man, not that generous. He won't touch the kind of responsibility you'd be offerin'. Look, sell the shop back t' the Aspinalls. That's the ticket. Take the profit an' go off – maybe with your grandpa – 'till the baby's born. You'll have enough cash for that, if you live modest. I'd offer you space 'ere, but Simon wouldn't care for it."

"I have a place of my own; in Wolfenden Street."

"You want the baby, you want the shop, you want yer independence?" Emma pursed her lips and emitted a popping sound. "Want the lot, don't yer? Well, love, you can't have the lot – not now. You're goin' to have to make a choice. An' make it soon."

"I won't have an abortion, Emma."

Emma popped her lips again. "That's plain speakin'."

"It's what you meant, isn't it?"

"Yer." The woman settled her weight, putting aside the cup of luke-warm tea. "I gotta ask, Holly; who's the father?"

"I . . ."

"Won't tell a soul. Promise."

"He's married."

"I never took you for that kinda fool, love. Who is he, though?"

Calmly, Holly got to her feet. She laid plate and cup on the tray and brushed invisible crumbs from the skirts of her coat.

Placatingly, Emma held up her hands. "Don't go all huffy, Holly. I won't never ask again."

"Emma, what can I expect? I mean, what will the term be like? Will I be able to work for a while?"

"Depends. You look healthy enough t' me. You've been eatin' well, an' you're strong. You'll feel a bit 'off' some mornin's but that could be all."

"Will I be able to work?"

"No reason why not."

"Will Dr. McCorkindale look after me – not in that way; I mean, attend me?"

"That's his job, not t'other thing."

"He's not expensive, is he?"

"Not too expensive; not bleedin' Harley Street, like."

"I'm grateful t' you, Emma."

"But you won't confide in me?"

Holly wetted her lips. "Can I call on you again?"

"Any time; us women gotta stick together."

Holly said, "There are two things I won't do, not now an' not ever – I won't tell anybody the name of the father."

"That's your privilege, love. What's the other?"

"I won't give up my baby."

"Then you'll have t' sell the shop."

"Or find a husband," Holly said.

"Find a . . . What the 'ell do you mean, Holly?"

"What I say – find a husband, a father t' give my baby a name."

"In your condition? Gawd strewth, Holly! Men aren't that foolish! Damaged goods, love; you're damaged goods."

"I won't deceive anyone, Emma," Holly said.

"Then you'll never find a mug t'take you on."

"I might," Holly said.

She adjusted her hat. The paleness of her skin gave her eyes a lustre and sharpened the structure of her face. She looked ravishing, Emma thought. If the girl hadn't had one in the oven she could have had her pick of husbands.

"I'll sell my share of Aspinall's Antiques," Holly said.

"In the circumstances you won't get much."

"I'll get enough," said Holly. "Enough to buy a name for my baby."

Emma rose from the plump chair, fingers fluttering like a card dealer's, eyes round. "*Buy a name?*"

"Buy a husband," Holly said.

"But . . . but . . . who?"

"Anyone," Holly said. "I'm not fussy. Anyone who'll take me at a fair price."

"Gawd!" Emma gasped. "Gawd Almighty!"

"Did you mistake me for a loser, Emma?" Holly said. "Well, you're wrong. London's full of losers, but I was never earmarked t'be one of them. I'm not a little baa-lamb."

"A lamb?" Emma giggled nervously. "More like a tiger, I'd reckon."

"Don't say that," Holly snapped.

And then left Emma Chubb to return home to her spinster flat in Wolfenden Street.

●　●　●

Common sense dictated that she inform her allies of her predicament as soon as possible. Holly arranged supper for Tal and Maury with considerable care. She bought their favourite foods, two bottles of Chianti and a dozen bottles of ale. Grandfather Tal suspected that something was wrong, but not even he, shrewd though he was, guessed that Holly was carrying a child.

Tal had noted her absences from the shop and her preoccupied state when she returned from these morning jaunts. Though he did not question Holly, it occurred to him that she was meeting a man. Tal tried to imagine what kind of affair would be conducted before noon, for he had always considered mornings to be a most unromantic portion of the day. Perhaps, he conjectured, the man was married and was obliged to lead a double life. Holly's behaviour on the days following the doctor's confirmation of pregnancy threw Tal off the track; he observed that Holly had regained her appetite for work and assumed that the affair, if that's what it had been, had died a natural death. Holly was brisk, efficient and cheerful; herself again. Clearly, leaving Lambeth had been good for her after all.

David Aspinall's marriage to his mistress had been a shock to Holly and Tal supposed that she might have taken up with another man as a reaction to it. The Russian was secretly rather pleased that Aspinall had married; he was not the right sort of husband for Holly. She needed somebody stronger and more determined, with an intelligence to match her own.

Holly – though Tal was unaware of it – had to exercise every ounce of her intelligence to keep control of the situation in which she now found herself. Unmarried and pregnant though she was, she remained calm and not dismayed. Old wives' tales of "nature's retribution" did not trouble her in the least. She avoided slipping into the abyss of self-disgust. The doctor had informed her that she was in the best of health. She would carry the child and, when it was born, she would look after it *and* continue to run the shop – somehow. She did not need a protector, a breadwinner or a lover – only some man's name to link to her own and a marriage certificate to make her baby legitimate.

The Kirsanoff streak surfaced once more. In her way, Holly could be as ruthless as Ritchie or Maury. She liked to imagine that her mother, Huldah, would have approved.

Every word that Holly had said to Emma Chubb had been the truth as she saw it. She fully understood the magnitude of her self-appointed task but was steeled by the need to provide for the baby that was growing in her womb. She had become two people. She had no husband to share her love, so love folded inwards and wrapped itself snugly around the infant she cradled in her body. Everyting she did now would be shaped towards providing security for her son or daughter. It was almost as if she had conceived without intercourse, without David. Occasional waves of nausea, tiny lurchings in her belly she accepted gladly, signs that she would soon have a living being to love and care for and to be her companion.

All the diverse parts of Holly's life and character fitted into place around her unborn child.

She missed David. It would be crass not to admit it. But she did not pine for him as she might have done. She missed his cheerful company and his love-making but she did not feel that a prop had been struck from her existence. On the contrary, her real reason for wishing to find a husband to give her baby a name was intricately interwoven with a need to cut David Aspinall completely from her life.

There was no possibility of hiding her condition. Indeed, she did not wish to hide it. She would not burden her child with furtiveness and secrecy, would not make it unwanted. There had been no means of predicting the effect that motherhood would have on her.

Sharpened by deprivations in childhood and youth, Holly was acutely aware of the need to provide love and, out of love, security for herself and her infant. It was a challenge, a great, magnificent challenge. Holly rose to it gladly.

It was after ten o'clock before Tal and Maury declared themselves satisfied. There was hardly a crumb left on the plates on the table. Both wine bottles were empty. Maury moved from the table to the sofa that Holly had brought to the flat from the back store of the shop. The flat was clean now, cosy and bright, with new curtains, furniture hand-picked from salerooms, and a handful of pretty ornaments. She had cleaned the flat's two rooms herself, scrubbing floors, waxing linoleum, washing cornices and skirtings. In the spring, when her lease was secure, she would have it all nicely painted. She had had the original bed removed for scrap and had replaced it with a pinewood piece that fitted neatly into a corner.

It gave Holly a feeling of confidence to see her grandfather and her eldest brother taking their ease in *her* place.

Politely Tal burped into his fist as he settled himself in an armchair by the fire.

"I have not eaten so well in many years, Holly. I thank you."

"Me too," said Maury.

"Do you mind if I smoke my cigar?" asked Tal.

"Only if you accept one of these." Holly produced a small cedarwood box containing six pale brown Coronas. She passed it first to her grandfather, then to Maury. She lit the cigars for the men and stepped back, standing before them on the woollen-knit hearthrug as if it was a small stage.

"I didn't ask you here tonight just t' help me celebrate a house-warmin'," said Holly. "I want t' tell you both somethin' very important."

Grandpa Tal's eyes had become wary. He held the cigar in finger and thumb, oval tip resting against his bottom lip.

"I'm goin' to have a baby," Holly said.

Tal did not utter a word. He extended his left arm, palm spread, to hold Maury down in his seat.

Holly sucked in a deep breath. "The father is David Aspinall."

Maury shot to his feet. "I'll kill the bleedin' swine, the bastard. I'll. . ."

"No, Maury, no," Tal snapped.

"Good Christ! You're not goin' t' let 'im get away with it?" Maury stormed. "He's married, ain't he?"

"Yes," said Holly.

"Maury, sit down. The girl wants our help, do you not see."

"*Help? I'll smash his . . .*"

"Maury," Holly said, "stop makin' such a fuss. I wasn't a victim. He didn't seduce me. I slept with him because I wanted to."

"He only got married, what, three weeks ago," Maury shouted. "Did he know you was knocked up?"

"I'm not goin' to say another word 'til you sit down an' hold your hush," Holly told him.

Flushed, smouldering, Maury lowered himself on to the sofa. He remained taut and scowling, however.

"That's better," Holly said. "Now, I don't need anybody t' take vengeance on David Aspinall. What I do need is help, an' there's nobody else I can turn to right now except you two."

"If it's money," said Maury. "I got some."

"It isn't money," said Holly. "It's help of another kind."

"Tell us what you plan to do," said Tal.

"Promise you won't interrupt, Maury?" Holly asked.

"A'right, a'right."

"I've been to a reputable doctor. I *am* with child. Seven weeks gone. The baby'll be born in early September – possibly late August – seven months from now." Holly paused then declared. "I *will* have the baby. I will *not* have it 'removed'. I will *not* put it up for adoption."

"But you're . . . you're not bleedin' married," said Maury.

"I will be, long before the baby's due."

"But Aspinall's just got married, ain't he?"

"I'll marry somebody else."

"Who? Who?" Maury demanded.

"I don't know yet."

"What is this you are saying, Holly?"

"Don't be angry with me, Grandfather."

"I am not angry."

"My Gawd, Hol! You're takin' all this very cool." Maury shook his head in bewilderment.

"It's just as well I am," said Holly. "Oh, it was a shock, believe me, but it's not goin' to do me – or my baby – any good flyin' into a panic about it."

"You want to have the child?" said Tal, rhetorically.

"Yes, Grandpa, I want the child."

"No matter what it may cost you in happiness?"

"The mud-slingin', the gossip . . ." Maury muttered.

"Who'll gossip, Maury? Tell me, apart from the three of us in this room, who'll even care?"

"David Aspinall will care," said Tal.

"That's one reason I need to find somebody to marry me."

"Ah, I begin to see," said Tal. "David Aspinall will not know that it is his child?"

"I want nothin' from him; *nothing*."

"What about the shop? Don't Aspinall own it, near enough?" said Maury.

"He won't throw me out."

"He might buy you out," said Maury. "That sister of his, she's got her bleedin' knife in you already."

"Andrea has no say in shop business," said Holly.

"Even if he does not know that the child is his," said Tal, "young Aspinall may be ashamed enough of what he has done to stand up to his sister, to keep you on as manager and partner."

"He'd be even more liable, if you told him . . ." Maury began.

"He will *not* be told. He can think what he likes. *But he will never know for sure*. As far as I'm concerned, it'll be *my* baby."

"An' what about this husband you're goin' t' conjure up outta thin air?" said Maury. "He can count on 'is fingers; he'll know . . ."

"He'll know the truth when he marries me."

"But . . ."

Tal cut his grandson short. "What is it you propose, Holly?"

"To find somebody who'll marry me not for love, but for profit. I'll make it worth his while to stay with me until six months after the baby's born. After that, he may do as he wishes. He may sue me for divorce, anything. If I'm married, I can continue to work in Aspinall's for another five or six months, enough time to build up profit – my twenty-five percentage of the next half-year – and to stock the shop for the end of summer. I have a little money in the bank. I calculate I'll need two hundred pounds to see me through the time of the birth. If all goes well, I'll be able to return to work in a matter of a month. I can feed the baby and look after it just as well in the shop as anywhere."

"But you cannot attend sales," said Tal.

"Not 'til the baby's weaned," Holly agreed. "I *can* find somebody to bid, however, while I do markin' from catalogues."

"I can bid," said Tal. "There is no insurmountable problem on that score."

"Why d'you need t' marry at all?" asked Maury, with a trace of bitterness. "Seems you can handle everythin' on your own."

"I need a name for the baby. I need somebody with me durin' the last weeks of my pregnancy. We can live here."

"Before we discuss the man you intend to make your husband," said Tal, "let me ask you what will happen if David Aspinall refuses to keep you on?"

"He won't refuse."

"He may."

"If he does, I'll have money from the sale of my share of the shop to keep me goin'. I could live for a year on that."

"Why don't you hook yourself a millionaire?" said Maury. "Solve everythin'."

"It's no joke," said Holly.

"I'm not jokin'," said Maury. "You're sellin' yourself, love, that's what you're doin'."

"I've had a taste of the kind of life that a bit of money can bring," said Holly. "I never really asked t'be pushed up the ladder; that was Mr. Aspinall's doin'. But now I've seen what it's like, that's what I want. It's what I want for my baby, too. Think I intend t'let all this slip away from me, Maury? Think I want my child dragged up like we were?"

"Could've been worse," muttered Maury.

"Yes, but it could have been so much better," said Holly. "Don't you go all nostalgic on me, Maury Beckman. You're a fine one t'talk – workin' night an' day, buildin' up a business. What for?"

"It's what I like doin'."

"So what's the difference between us?"

"I'm not expectin'," Maury retorted.

Tal got to his feet. He placed the cigar in an ashtray on the mantelshelf then, with great deliberation, wiped his moustache with his forefinger. Taking Holly in his arms, he planted a kiss on each cheek. "Maury will help. I will help. You are right not to be ashamed, granddaughter. After what has gone on in this world the past eight years, what is there to fuss over? Let tongues wag. What do we care! Bring the child into the world. Do what you can for it from the beginning. At least it will have love."

Shaking his head in capitulation, Maury rose and kissed his sister too. "Sorry if I barked a bit, love. Your news caught me by surprise, that's all. If you're glad, then I'm glad for you. I just didn't think you was the . . . well, the type."

"Neither did I think I was the type," Holly admitted. "It . . . Oh, I dunno; it happened because I wanted it to. Queer thing about it, Maury, is that I don't regret it."

"I think I understand," said Maury.

Tal said, "Holly, how much money do you have?"

"Two hundred an' twenty pounds in the bank account," Holly answered. "I'll need every penny."

"An' more," said Maury. "Maybe I can extract a bit from the business."

Tal stroked his chin, removed the cigar from the ashtray, stuck it in his mouth and seated himself again. He crossed his legs, saying nothing. He was calculating what it would cost to bring his great-grandchild comfortably into the world and give the poor little beggar a name. If Holly was set on buying herself a husband, he would do what he could to see that she did not wind up with a fake.

"The prospective bridegroom, Holly?" Tal said at length. "Do you have anybody particular in view?"

"Yes," she said, without thinking. "Yes, I believe I do."

"May one ask the name of the lucky fellow?" said Tal.

"Not just yet," said Holly.

"Is he Jewish?"

"No, Grandfather."

Tal grunted in disappointment.

"Hoi," said Maury. "I've just 'ad a thought; who's goin' to'break the glad tidin's to Leo?"

"I will," said Holly. "But not until I've a husband along to protect me."

"He'll gloat, y'know," said Maury. "Pa'll gloat."

"Depends who my husband is," said Holly. "Everything seems to depend on that now."

After the hectic wave of selling that built up through November and had broken over Christmas, a natural seasonal recession followed. Dealers took stock. Catalogues were compiled. The expert and keenly competitive process of finding new specialised markets was attacked with vigour. During the remainder of the week, Holly's moods were erratic. One hour she would be brimful of exhilaration; the next, she would be in a trough of despair. Try as she would, she could not totally exclude David from her thoughts. A gesture of the will, not the heart, she forced herself to hate him – unsuccessfully.

At night when she lay alone in the pine bed in the flat in Wolfenden Street, she would relive the hours she had spent with him, closing her mind to the realisation that he lay now in another woman's arms.

The proud tradition of the Kirsanoffs was surfacing in Holly. She castigated herself for her weakness in yearning for a man who had shown himself to be so weak and selfish but, unwittingly, found herself measuring every possible husband against David.

London was full of men.

It would not be difficult to find one who would marry her, to "sell herself" as Maury, rather tactlessly, put it. Colonials were always in town in search of nice young girls to marry and carry off to the wilds of Australia or the backwood of Canada. Holly did not want to leave England, though she found one or two of the Colonial gentlemen attractive and charming.

On her night table was a single rose in a glass vase. It was all that remained of an extravagent bouquet given her by a Rhodesian farmer in appreciation of her help during an Eastern carpet sale. Jackie Walker, a bright, lean South African had treated her to dinner and had given clear indications that he was interested in Holly. Jackie Walker was still in London. He had given Holly the address of his sister's home in Earls Court in the hope that Holly would change her mind about seeing him again. Jackie Walker had made no bones about the fact that he was in England for six months to search for a young, good-looking, hard-working woman who would go back to South Africa as his bride.

But would Jackie Walker be willing to take on "damaged goods"? Holly doubted it very much and did not see the Rhodesian again.

If it came to it, Stan Nuttall would be only too glad to marry her, pregnant or not. She was sure that the Lambeth boy's compassion and devotion would withstand the shock of learning that she had got herself in trouble. But Stan was not for her, no matter how desperate she became. The eye-patch and the gloved hand she could surely learn to accept but she could not live with Stan knowing that he loved her and that she would never be able to return his love in any measure at all. Apart from that, she would never have the heart to walk out on him when the baby was born, and the thought of spending a lifetime with the unambitious Stan stuck, probably, in Lambeth filled her with horror. Marrying Stan would drag her back into Ritchie's influence and she emphatically wanted to shut Ritchie out.

Kennedy?

Kennedy King would not be likely to have her now. Besides, there had never been any mention of marriage in the hints that came from Kennedy and his ambassador. Holly wondered if Emma would report the latest turn-up to Kennedy immediately or if she would respect Holly's secret a while longer.

Marriage to Kennedy King would not be so bad. On the contrary, marriage to Kennedy would give her even closer contact with the trade. He had a certain charm, a kind of knowing innocence that Holly had come to find appealing. But Kennedy would never ever saddle himself with another man's child.

It would be wonderful to find somebody who had an affinity for antique dealing, somebody in the profession.

She could offer much; might even find herself coming to love the man.

Dreams again, silly impractical dreams.

Turning on her side Holly lifted a candlestick and brought from beneath it a handbill that had accompanied a business letter from Christopher Deems.

It had been Deems she'd had in mind when she told Grandpa Tal and Maury that there was a man she might marry. It was irrational to suppose that Deems had more than a passing interest in her.

A handbill for a poetry reading in the Pilgrim Hall had not been the only correspondence between them. In Deems' occasional letters, had she only imagined a quickening of interest? Was he merely being courteous in matters of business, or was there more? She had never felt inclined to find out. The strangeness, the massive sense of loneliness in the captain might, she thought hopefully, make him responsive to her plight.

The truth was – and she acknowledged it swiftly – that next to David, Christopher Deems was the only man she'd met who had stirred her emotionally. The faint sense of foreboding that she had ascribed to him, and his lingering effect upon her, she balanced against practical advantages. He was a poet. Poets, she believed, were used to eccentricity in their womenfolk. She convinced herself that beneath Deems' conservative manner there lurked a hunger for commitment and fresh adventure. Would he consider marriage to a pregnant Lambeth girl an adventure? Of all the men she knew, she could imagine only Deems responding intelligently and sympathetically to her proposition.

Apart from its oddness, however, what would be in it for him? What could she offer him?

As if in search of inspiration, she studied the handbill again.

VOICES OF WAR
Readings of Modern Poetry
by
Julian Melanger
John McIan
Frederick Estall
Christopher Deems

PILGRIM HALL

Wigmore Street, London, WC2
Doors Open – 7.30   February 10th, 1920

ADMISSION FREE

Across the bottom of the quarto yellow sheet was written: "Positively the last chance to hear the Bookseller pretend he's a Poet. If you care to attend, I'll reward you with supper afterwards." He had signed it, "Christopher".

Though the handbill had arrived folded into a letter about Scott first editions, on the day after she had learned of David's marriage, Holly had preserved it carefully. The gesture had been almost without purpose and certainly had no intent. It had occupied her mentally for no more than seconds. But she was glad of it now, could delude herself that she had intended all along to support the young poets, Deems in particular, during their recital in the Pilgrim Hall.

How, she wondered, had Christopher squared his conscience and what had persuaded him to appear in public when he had declared himself through with all poetry writing? Perhaps the scars of war were healing.

Holly sighed.

It was not Deems' adventure. It was Holly Beckman's. *She* needed *him* – not the other way about. She did not wish to make a fool of herself. But somehow she thought that Christopher Deems might listen without derision.

Sighing again, Holly slipped the handbill beneath her pillow. She switched out the lamp and turned on her back, settling down, hands folded gently on her tummy as if to assure the developing foetus that everything would be all right.

* * *

Paris had been a ghastly mistake, embodiment of many, many mistakes. France should have been avoided. Apart from the hideously uncomfortable rail journey and a bitter Channel crossing, the country was so badly scarred by war that David had been thrown into a mood of depression that not even Linsey at her most gay and provocative could lift.

It was much the same story in Dinant, where they retreated post haste when it became clear that Paris was more interested in the Council of the League of Nations than in providing for the comfort of a couple of honeymooners. At that season of the year Dinant was just as depressing as the capital, bleak, jaundiced, almost empty, in spite of the re-opening of a small casino at the rear of the Fontaine Hotel.

Shrouded in "the wrong aura" – Linsey's explanation – they had contrived to throw away three hundred pounds at the wheel before Linsey capitulated to David's suggestion that they pack up and return to London.

He could not even begin to explain to his wife that France was no longer a place of romance. The reality of limbless soldiers, blinded sailors and pilgrim bands of English widows visiting war graves compounded his sense of guilt and shame, weaving within him an intricate tapestry of self-disgust. The striding gun-metal waves of the Channel breaking on harbour walls and heavy debris of the defences boomed in his head. Cold salt winds scoured the corners of his mind. To all this Linsey was impervious. She was living an illusion. Her comparative sobriety revealed in full the incompatability of the union. Worse, it did not appear an illusion to her, neither the honeymoon nor the marriage itself, nor did she understand that he had gone through with the charade only out of pity and a profound fear that, without him, she would destroy herself.

More than once during the weeks in the Continent, it occurred to David that in many ways war had been preferable to peace. War had consolidated the fragmented nature of existence. Wasn't that just a high-falutin' way of saying he had been happier in the damned War Office than he had realised at the time? Pips, salutes, Brasso, leaky pens, blotting paper, filing cabinets, saucers browned by tea stains, floating with the butts of Gold Flake or Wild Woodbine; he missed the earthy humour of Sergeant Nairn and Corporal Rennie, the haw-haw-haw stupidity of his superior Major Hew Fulcher. He missed the brotherhood of mess, the freedom of barracks. Operating, as it were, on a divided front *had* been freedom of a very special sort.

God, he even missed his father.

Madcap capers had been innocent then; drinking, gambling, women, stamped with the War Office seal, *Approved Conduct for Subalterns*. He had been incorporated into the Big Show, the Grand

Adventure, in the company of men, without ever having to share their risks and sufferings. While Linsey slept under the French sampler that hung on the wall above the bed in the Fontaine Hotel, he had trudged alone around the Dinant headland, staring out across the scudding metallic sea. All alone.

The Aspinalls trailed back into London and headed for the Waldorf Hotel. It was plush enough to assuage David's doubts for a little while. It was London, after all, the upper tier. Rationing and shortages had eased a little; the food was excellent. He ate like an elephant, drank like a dromedary and, so Linsey said, made love like a bull. He *must* be happy. He had everything he'd always wanted.

In Christabel's they were made most welcome. The croupier asked them about Dinant. The Fish stood them "dinkies" to toast the marriage, his lipless mouth stretched in a cynical grin.

"Two sprigs of fern and a slice of lemon and you could sell that fellow by the pound," David said, later that morning when he and his wife were preparing for bed.

Linsey replied, "Poor old Fish. Please do not malign my second favourite man, darling."

"Which reminds me, dear," David said. "Did you ever think to inform your parents that you are a respectable married lady?"

Linsey squealed, tumbled into bed and pulled the satin sheets over her head, groaning. It was her only answer. The subject of her parents was not referred to again.

London was laden with tipsy Americans seeking to take on as much liquor as possible. Their nation had declared itself Dry only weeks before. Prohibition was being enforced with a bullying lack of justice that wrung the hearts of every English dipso and staggered those Yankee exiles who had supposed that President Wilson would come through with a last-minute reprieve.

Even although the Yankees refused to regard it as a gag any more, it was all fun. There was a rumour that Theo Willoughby had set sail for Chicago to put up for sale warehouse properties that one of his holding companies had thoughtfully acquired some years before. Another wild tale had him shipping Scotch across the Atlantic by tramp steamer from the Isle of Skye. But not much store was set by that one.

Linsey never mentioned Willoughby, never spoke of Mayfair. It was as if the flotsam of her past had been carried off on the river of time.

The Aspinalls spread their wings. They were to be seen in private gaming clubs and cellars like Brett's, rubbing shoulders with earls and dukes, international crooks and new millionaires, where money was scattered like confetti to blow along the cold pavements of the morning. Most of the smart set had fortunes begging to be squandered. Not so the Aspinalls. To pay the bills David took to gambling. He studied form, placed his bets by telephone and never saw a horse in the flesh. He lost just a little bit more than he ever won on the gee-gees but made up for it at cards, dice and roulette.

Linsey was much more at home with club and party gamblers, and her lucky streak did not desert her. David even began to be comfortable with their precarious way of life, to trust Linsey's uncanny instinct just as other men trusted the stable price of flax or coffee or a bull market in ferrous metals.

Only in the mornings, before Linsey had crawled out of bed, did the old David Aspinall walk with the new.

He suffered bad conscience about not visiting his mother and sister but consoled himself with the knowledge that it was his generosity that was supporting them. Besides, he could not bring himself to call at Cardwell Place in case he met Holly. It was Holly he wished to see – and Holly he must avoid.

Instead he went to an ex-officers' club in Venders Street and played billiards with other loose-enders who happened to be whiling away the drab morning hours, or picked up tips in the bar of the Bell where sporting gentlemen gathered for a pre-luncheon warmer.

It was in the latter stablishment that David encountered Lester Gosling. Lester had just taken purchase of a spanking Green Crouch motorcar and was very anxious to show it off to somebody. David volunteered. He spent the next hour holding on to his hat as the low-slung sports motorcar howled round Regent's Park circle, shot through St. John's Wood and up Primrose Hill.

Whipped raw by the cold wind, but incredibly toned up, the young men stopped off at the Two Barns and partook of sandwiches and toddy in the ingle-nook by the fire.

Lester was elfin, with feathery black hair, and eyebrows that looked as if they had been plucked and pencilled – though this was not the case. He had a very wide mouth and had once been described by a disapproving captain as looking "like a squirrel with its throat cut". Lester and David had always got on famously.

"Married the Lin gal, did you? Lucky pig! How was the dowry?" Lester asked in his shrill demanding voice.

"More than adequate," said David. "But do tell, old friend, how'd you acquire that dizzy machine? Grandma die?"

"Started with fifty quid," said Lester, smugly. "Hopped it up to a thousand. Splurged on the green-eyed beauty. Lost my heart, you might say."

"Some 'hoppin'," said David. "What were you hoppin' *on*, Lester?"

"Crown and Anchor."

"You scooped up a *thousand pounds* at the old C and A?"

"Walked straight out Monday and bought the green monster off the shelf."

"Where did you find a C and A game at those stakes?"

"Place in Newminster. Country house weekend. Hallet's the host's monniker. Jumped-up pig. Throws weekend parties just to drive his pig of a wife insane, you know. Great fun!" Lester said, "Why don't you come along on Saturday? Bring your wad, and your good lady wife. I'm sure Charlie wouldn't mind."

"Charlie Hallet," said David, "is an old acquaintance."

"There you are. Pick you up at nine, Saturday?"

"I used to have rather a flair for C and A."

"Try your luck. Can't do harm, can it?"

"No harm at all," said David. "Nine o'clock, then."

"Where?"

"Stayin' at the Waldorf."

"La-la-la," said Lester. "See you at the Waldorf. Wrap up well."

Gosling downed the last of his toddy. "Shall we toddle. Must be back by three. Mummy has the Polks comin' for tea. Tryin' to marry me off to Millicent-Ann. Might succeed, too."

"Drop me in Piccadilly," David said.

* * *

Holly's first tactical error was in arriving at the Pilgrim Hall in Wigmore Street dressed like a concert-goer. It was clear at once that Sunday-best respectability was not the style for an audience of poetry-lovers with an Oxford bias. A gulf divided the small crowd in the cold foyer. Holly had a foot in neither camp.

Short black marble columns topped by muscular Greeks and a floor of well-scrubbed marble provided an entranceway to three separate concert halls. "Voices of War" would be heard in the small room to the rear left but as that was the only event booked in for the evening, the audience gathered in the foyer looked very thin and overwhelmed. Two camps – elderly, powdered ladies, "spinsters to a man" as Victor Lawfeld called them, challenged casually dressed quasi-Bohemians. For leavening, there were six or seven officers in uniform, three or four young girls accompanied by aunts, and a "posse" – Lawfeld's word – of rusty academics intent on remaining modern at all costs.

As stated, admission was free. Programmes were offered at the price of sixpence. Holly purchased one at an unsteady card table that had been set up at the door of the hall. Inside she could make out rows of hard wooden benches, like church pews, a platform with a lectern and six chairs upon it, lit by two gigantic gas globes that hung like symbols of inspiration over the empty stage. The young man who sold her the programme wore a custard-coloured cardigan with a velvet port-wine cravat stuffed into the neck. He appeared to have no shirt on. He squinted at Holly through horn-rimmed spectacles as she dropped her sixpence into a tobacco tin by his elbow.

"Are you Caroline?"

"No, I'm not," said Holly.

"Are you not Melanger's sister?" It sounded like an accusation.

"No, I'm not."

"Will you sign the visitors' book – yonder."

The visitors' book lay open on another rickety card-table hard against the door of the hall. By it stood a young Jew, dressed in a tweed jacket, shirt and college tie.

Two ancient ladies bent over the visitors' book, an Oxford hard-back lecture pad.

"I don't have to put my age, do I, young man?"

"No, Miss Hatter, just your name and adddress, so that we may send you literature about poetry activities in London."

One elder gave away her signature with miserly distrust while the other, probably her sister, tapped her repeatedly on the shoulder, saying, "Write something nice. Write something nice for me."

When they had finished they doddered through the doorway into the hall.

The young man smiled at Holly and gave a little bow, without unfolding his arms. "Good evening. Is this your first attendance at an O.P.A. reading?"

"O.P.A.?" said Holly, pencil in hand.

"Oxford Poetry Association."

"Yes, it is."

"Do you mind signing the book?"

"Not at all."

He watched her, without appearing curious, and read her signature upside-down.

"Ah, *you're* Holly Beckman?"

"Yes."

"Christopher asked me to look out for you. He wasn't sure you would come. I'm Victor Lawfeld, by the way. For my sins, I helped arrange this feeble show."

He offered his hand. Holly shook it. The visitors' book was forgotten.

Lawfeld escorted her into the hall in person. "Christopher's sorry he couldn't meet you himself but he had to trot round to Carpenter's to rescue one of the readers."

"Which one – Melanger?"

"Fred Estall, in fact. Poor Fred is so fraught with insecurity – nerves – before readings that he hides out in public houses. He doesn't pickle himself or anything, that's more Melanger's trick, as you seem to know, but he *cowers*. Christopher can usually coax him out."

"Do you put on these . . . recitals often?"

"From time to time. Usually in Oxford. This is the first in Central London since the Armistice, in fact. I had hoped for a little more attention. Still, there's forty-one assorted inside – and that isn't *too* bad for a February night."

Lawfeld ushered Holly into an empty bench on the fifth row from the rear. "Do you want to sit closer to the front?"

"Will I be able to hear?"

"Yes, in fact. No whisperers tonight. Even Estall finds his lungs when he gets going. I'll join you shortly, if you don't mind," said Lawfeld. "Christopher asked me to keep an eye on you."

"Why?" asked Holly.

"I dunno. Because you're his only guest, I suppose. In fact, half of those here are friends and relatives of the poets, dunned into attending out of loyalty."

"What about the two old ladies?"

"Hatter and Hatter," said Lawfeld, smiling. "They attend *everything* poetical. Approve of nothing. I believe they are awaiting the reincarnation of Elizabeth Browning."

Holly laughed. She was sorry when Lawfeld excused himself to do duty as doorman. Holly took off her scarf and gloves, popped a peppermint into her mouth and settled to await the performance with a certain anticipation.

It was ten minutes to eight before the proceedings got under way. From behind a curtained door left of the platform five men, including Christopher, entered. Deems was dressed in a dark suit, the others in various loose "countrified" clothes. Melanger, a heavy-set man, older by ten years than the others, sported a bushy beard worn without a moustache. Fred Estall was visibly knotted by stage-fright. He sat close to Christopher who chatted to him lightly as the co-organiser of the reading, a waxy-skinned little man named Rothery, took his place at the lectern and riffled through reams of notes.

Clearing his throat, Rothery began his introduction. It was greeted in silence, apart from an occasional punctuation from one of the Hatter sisters, enquiring, "What does he say, Lettie? What does he say?" The volume of notes mercifully did not reflect itself in Rothery's remarks which were terse, almost diffident, as if he wished to be elsewhere.

To put him out of his misery, Fred Estall was invited to read first.

Estall began with a poem entitled "Street Finder". It concerned a soldier who imagines he has come home from the war to find his neighbourhood gone. It commenced simply enough, then became difficult, with clotted references to mythology stirred into the batter. Estall, however, was soon caught up in it. His rate of delivery increased, manuscript copy forgotten as he poured his creation at the audience in a loud, inflexionless voice. He seemed surprised to have reached the end and stepped back abruptly from the lectern, stunned by his own creativity.

There was a polite scattering of applause, though one of the officers was obviously so taken with the work that he boomed out appreciation from two big fists long after Estall had sneaked back to the lectern to continue his programme.

Estall's other poems were shorter. He read five in all. Apart from veiled hints, none of the others concerned war or warriors at all. Holly guessed that they had been written years ago before hostilities in Europe had flared up, perhaps while Estall, like the others present, had been an Oxford undergraduate.

After Estall, young John McIan's dry Scottish blurr defied the audience to interrupt while he chanted out eight tight little poems. Four were spoken in a dialect incomprehensible to the Lambeth girl. The others were odd, quirky, beautiful in their simplicity. For all his dryness, McIan was sufficiently intelligent to milk each subtle rhyme for all it was worth.

McIan's work was much appreciated by the girls and their aunts; McIan's London relatives as it happened. The uniforms in the audience sat in stony disapproval of the apparent slanders that McIan had inserted, besmirching the courage of men in the trenches. Later Holly discovered that only Deems and McIan had fought in Flanders.

It was a relief when Julian Melanger lumbered to the reading desk. He was a showman, flamboyant, expert, deliberately aggressive. A deep mellow voice enhanced his verse. He recited without reference to text, with, as Christopher put it "skin-deep passion". Holly, and most of the listeners, enjoyed it enormously. Sentiment dovetailed with sentimentality. His "literary" references were popular enough to be picked up by everyone present. There was a touch of French, a word of Latin, and a lot about Melanger's childhood spent among the "becks and hawk-billed rocks" of his native Yorkshire. References to war were historical, grand, triumphant. He received a rousing cheer from the voluble officer to swell the considerable applause.

It was at this point that Victor Lawfeld slid in beside Holly. The young woman was clapping her hands, like the rest.

Lawfeld smiled. "Did you enjoy it?"

"Yes."

"He's very practised," said Lawfeld. "Julian aims to be a major poet, in fact. He'll make it or go bust in the attempt. You watch, after the show he'll 'permit' himself to be taken over by the learned professors, lecturers and reviewers. Julian knows how to butter his bread."

"Don't you think he's a good poet, then?"

Lawfeld pursed his lips. "Good, yes. Very good, in fact. But not great."

"An' who would you say *is* a great poet?" asked Holly, feeling rather ashamed of her uninformed enthusiasm for Melanger.

"This one," said Lawfeld, pointing at the platform.

Christopher Deems had come to the lectern under cover of Melanger's acclaim.

He stood very straight, head lifted, eyes fixed on an invisible sphere fifteen feet above the heads. He waited two or three minutes until the audience settled. It might have been a trick, a ruse to gain attention. Holly doubted it.

"Voices of War," Deems said, half to himself. He gave a puffing sigh and, blinking, scanned the rows of faces with a faint smile. "I'm sorry that Wilfred Owen could not be with us tonight. I believe he is engaged elsewhere."

Gasps, murmurings, a seeping whisper of questions.

Audibly one Miss Hatter hopefully inquired of the other, "Is Wilfred Owen comin'? Did he say Wilfred Owen would be here?"

Deems glanced down at a tidy portfolio of notes.

He said, "The history of the poetical impulse is a tale of an individual's growing awareness of the world. Its meanings are equivocal, personal, relative to terms and times, weather and seasons, to tiny fragments of eternity embedded like glass in the innocent flesh of the soul. Emotions become cancerous in a slow erosion of reason.

In the end there is a clap . . ." Deems' cupped palms came together.
" . . . a clap that signifies the death of reason, host to the parasite that
we call the creative urge. Evocative images are reflections of the
growth of understanding in the individual. The responses they call
from other men and women are equations of the rate of growth in the
other men and women." He paused. "Tonight the Oxford Poetry
Association has invited me to have my say about war. Let me, if you
will, also have my say about peace in contrast. Before. And After.
Young Christopher Deems wrote thus."

Lawfeld sat forward, Holly forgotten. He rested his hands on the
back of the bench in front, chin on his knuckles, dark eyes fixed on
Deems.

""Mr. Proctor's Parlour"," Deems read from a page clipped from a
journal.

The poem was in perfectly rhymed verse, amusing and witty. He
read with a light touch, eight six-line verses, then skimmed the page
down and lifted another volume and began to read from it, raising his
voice over the applause.

""Lavender Castles"," Lawfeld muttered, frowning.

"Lavender Castles" was a clever romantic poem, a pastiche of
emotions too tender and too pronounced ever to have stirred in a
man's breast. Deems' tone was tender and sincere. Again he barely
hesitated between finishing the reading of one poem and commen-
cing the recitation of the next.

Voice ringing, rhythm accented, he began,

> "If I Had Rode with Hanson's Horse,
> Blown the Bugle, Drawn the Sword,"

Holly could see in her mind's eye the glorious vision that had
expanded in the young poet's brain. Brave banners and gallant
officers, prancing horses regimented into acts of vain courage. Colour
and glamour were stamped in every line, every syllable. As he read,
Christopher's features smoothed, his eyes shone, shoulders squared as
if he felt himself to be mounted on horseback. She was caught up in
the cadences, drawn on by them, like all the others in the Pilgrim Hall
– as Deems intended.

He was given a great show of appreciation, too loud to ignore. He
bowed and, without comment, exchanged one volume for another.
When the clapping diminished, he read then a poem that began,
"Young John Bull Strode Out One Noon."

The hair on the nape of Holly's neck rose involuntarily. She did not
understand the manner of the making of the piece but caught at once

the irony of contrast, the spurious heartiness that the stressing of the verse contained, down and down to the last two lines when, abrasively, the poet brought Death from the Front.

Melanger shook his head, pityingly, hinting at derision, as Deems concluded. John McIan had bridged his hand over his face, head lowered. One major flung himself from the bench and stalked indignantly from the hall, the doors slamming in his wake.

Deems lifted a third book, pages marked with tapers of torn newspaper and, more patiently, sinuously read in succession a series of three short poems, "Prime of Youth", "Cleaning Out" and "Small Justice Shown". Applause was sporadic, unsure, mitigated by restrained cries of "Shame on you, Captain," from the loud-mouthed major.

Glancing at Holly, Lawfeld said, "What now, I wonder."

Deems said, "I would like, in conclusion, to read three unpublished poems. They are not recent. They belong to another age. They were written by a man who is now departed but who exists, for me, as a troubled memory. There are, there will be, none to follow this."

Holly touched Lawfeld's shoulder. "Mr. Lawfeld, what does he. . ."

Gently Lawfeld touched a finger to his lips, then turned and leaned again.

The first of the series was entitled, "The Factory", soft as a pastel drawing, understated, shocking. Holly responded to the horror that had attended the poem's conception. A sudden wave of empathy for Deems, compassion that the words evoked, welled up in her. She felt her eyes swim, throat thicken, her nose grow stuffy.

But there were few in the Pilgrim Hall who felt that way. Even as Deems completed the fourth and final verse, two more officers marched up the aisle and left with noisy dignity. The ladies and little girls were bewildered. Only Deems' fellow poets, and three or four of the professorial gentlemen listened to the echo of the words, as if to distant music strange to their ears.

Like the first, the second piece in the sequence was typed on a foolscap sheet of yellow stock.

"The Magpies of Verdun".

It was clear and direct, a black statement on a white ground.

The audience responded in total silence.

No man left.

Deems licked his upper lip. He was sweating heavily. He wiped his fingertips on the lapels of his jacket. He lifted a third sheet of yellow paper. It was typed on both sides. His cheeks appeared caved, his eyes receded. Downcast shadows, suspended from the gas globes, lengthened on his flesh. He shifted his weight. He leaned for support on the lectern and gripped the foolscap in both hands. In that position, he read the poem.

"Wearing the Mask at Amiens".

It was long and complex, remote from anything in Holly's experience. She had read only inspirational verse and maudlin comedies printed in the popular press. Nothing had prepared her for the impact of Deems' intensely personal experience of a gas attack at Amiens, for the images that rang like fire bells as the poet expanded his fear of death in "the gagging rubber coffin of my mouth" to touch on moral cowardice cleansed by hatred of his fellow men. Like acrid smoke drifting across the verses, Holly remembered Maury's account of the blinded French boy. She saw not Deems, but Maury, and, for a single instant, was herself lost in the mud, in the mask, stumbling on in search of purpose.

Inured in suburban etiquette, old hands applauded. But the rapport had gone, wiped away by the stark visions that Deems had conjured up. To some, poetry itself had been sullied. They hurried off, muttering. To the remaining officers, nothing was quite clear. They departed wordlessly for the mess or nearby club to pick apart the poem and re-stitch it into a garment that suited their beliefs.

McIan was holding Deems by the shoulder, talking to him, the Scotsman's boyish features flushed. Melanger had walked away, steering Estall, to greet his university admirers at the steps. After a minute, Deems tactfully detached himself from McIan and vaulted down from the front of the stage. He walked quickly up the aisle and joined Lawfeld and Holly at the end of the row.

To Victor, he said, "Is that enough for you?"

"No, Chris," Lawfeld said. "It will never be enough."

"Get me out of here," Christopher said. "I can't breathe in this atmosphere."

Impulsively, Holly sought his arm and led him through the foyer into Wigmore Street.

* * *

"Come up, Holly," Christopher said.

They had walked from Wigmore Street across Oxford Street down North Audley Street past Grosvenor Square to Christopher's flat in Shepherd Market. Christopher had spoken hardly at all, except to say once, "Well, the weather's changed."

Sloughing off whatever suffering, or satisfaction, the performance in the Pilgrim Hall had engendered, he relaxed a little as the bustle of the city faded and they came to the insular streets of the Market. Holly respected his brooding silence. She had no illusions. If Christopher had not wanted her company he would have shaken her off as roughly as he had discarded his friends at the hall.

When they reached the doorway that led up to Christopher's flat, he invited her in. She baulked.

"It wouldn't be right, Christopher," Holly said.

"You've nothing to fear from me," he said. "I just don't want to be alone at present. Besides, I'll be surprised if Victor doesn't come down here after he has loosed himself from his duties."

"He seems like a nice man."

"He is – but he has a fixation about 'art'," said Deems. "He has very little creative talent; for that reason he puts poets on a pedestal."

"I think you're bein' unfair to him."

"Yes, I probably am. Will you come up for a while?"

"All right."

"Thank you."

The narrow stair smelled of cats and gas. The door to Deems' flat was painted bright green. Christopher unlocked it with a latchkey and ushered Holly ahead of him. He touched on the electric light from a panel of switches by the front door.

The house was exceptionally neat. There were many bookshelves and handsome old furnishings. Effortless taste, Holly thought. There was no specific design about the place. It had grown with the man.

"I'll make tea – or would you prefer a drink? I only have whisky, I'm afraid."

"Tea, please."

"Take off your coat. I shan't be long."

The kitchen was off to the rear, through three open doors. Holly could hear the sounds of kettle and gas stove, teacups. She removed her coat and draped it over a chair, seated herself by the coal fire, then got up and wandered round the room studying the bookshelves.

"Is this your own collection, or surplus stock?" she called out.

"Bit of both; mostly my own stuff," Christopher called back. It was the first time she had heard him raise his voice. It made him sound younger, more lively.

"You've always been a collector, then?"

He appeared in the doorway with two mugs of steaming tea and a tin of Claremount chocolate biscuits.

"Always," he said. "It's a nice vice, I suppose. Please don't ask me if I've read them all."

Holly smiled. "I wasn't goin' to."

"Thank God." Deems was making an effort at conversation, at conviviality. "Every gasman, every delivery boy who comes here trots out the same remark. But then you of all people must sympathise with the collector's urge – and its problems."

"I don't collect much personally," said Holly. "Trade books, that's about all. I can't afford it, really."

Christopher handed her the tea and pulled out a chair by the fire. He had banked the grate with fine dross and, mug in one hand, picked the poker from the companion and stirred up the fire. Flames fanned up at once. He put the poker back on its brass rack and offered Holly the Claremount tin. "Probably stale under the tinsel wrapping."

The girl took a triangular biscuit and unwrapped it. It was crisp and sweet. She ate it in two bites. "Is this the supper you promised me, Christopher?"

"Yes, I'm sorry. The reading took more out of me than I'd anticipated."

Holly grinned, forcing humour. "This ain't 'arf bad. Could choke dahn anuvver, though."

Christopher gave her the biscuit box. "Leave a couple for Victor."

"Are you sure he'll come?"

"Quite sure," said Christopher.

"Why – to talk over the readin'?"

Christopher said, "He's concerned about me. Thinks I shouldn't be left alone, too much or too long."

"He knows I'm with you, doesn't he?"

"That's another reason he'll abandon Fred and Julian and leave Rothery to count the take. He'll want to find out what you're like."

"Will he now? Why's that?"

"Because he's been the recipient of several years of legal training."

"Is *that* what he does?"

"And is consequently obsessed with the notion that everything can be reduced to a balance of cause and effect."

"I don't understand," Holly admitted, helping herself to a third chocolate biscuit.

"Victor is a bit of a nuisance," said Deems. "He mothers me dreadfully."

"*Mothers* you?"

"My real mother confines herself to looking after my bodily welfare. Collars and cuffs, ashtrays and crockery. She comes up from Oxford every couple of weeks and fusses about. Victor's mothering is *infinitely* more irritating. He is endeavouring to sweep away . . ."

Christopher hesitated, " . . . sweep away the cobwebs of war.",

"He admires you enormously."

"I know he admires me – for all the wrong reasons, really. But . . . Oh, I don't . . . Talk of something else, Holly."

"Lovely biscuits."

"Have another."

"I'll be sick if I do."

"In that case I'll remove temptation." He put the biscuit tin on the dresser, lit a cigarette and returned to the chair by the fire.

Conversation died completely in the lull.

Holly cleared her throat. "If Mr. Lawfeld annoys you so much, why did you agree t' do a readin' for him?"

Christopher's eyes closed, then opened again. For a moment, only a moment, Holly thought that he was going to snap at her and retreat into himself once more, perhaps even show her the door.

"Habit," Christopher finally answered.

"He's been a friend for a long time, hasn't he?"

"Yes, almost ten years."

"And it's as a friend that he worries about you."

"He had no right to force me to read for the O.P.A. He knew that I didn't want to, that I'd nothing to say."

"But you *did* say somethin'."

"Nobody heard."

"I heard."

Again that quick withdrawal, a stinging slight on the tip of his tongue, checked by an effort of will. "*Did* you understand?"

"No," said Holly. "But I think I understood enough t'know why your friend Victor's worried about you."

"He's worried in case I do not 'fulfil my promise'," said Christopher. "His concern is with poetry, as if poetry was some disembodied, ethereal creature that one kept in one's head like a dog in a kennel. He would sacrifice me for one more slim volume."

"And you don't believe in that kind of sacrifice?"

"Of course not. It's the epitome of the stupid Art-Conquers-All argument. I'm tired of Oxford polemics. Tired, tired."

"It strikes me," said Holly, "that you're doin' your best t'talk yourself out of your friendship with Mr. Lawfeld. Are you afraid?"

Christopher blinked, as he had done on the platform. He gave the young woman a sudden fierce concentration of interest. It was a glimpse of the Deems who had made his reputation in Oxford, of the Deems who had written wittily and wisely. Holly almost quailed before it. Until that instant they had been two people divided only by sex and personal circumstances. Now she saw how utterly removed from her world Deems really was. She felt a sorrowful sinking, a temporary loss of hope, and a welling of embarrassed inferiority. Lambeth, Leo, Ritchie, Brixton, bread an' drippin', Maury with his feet on the table; a world away from all that Christopher Deems had been shaped by.

"I . . . I have – nothing – to – fear." He made the statement in punctuated form, like a man in the dock insisting on his innocence.

"Don't you want t'write poetry any more?"

"Damnation, *no*! I don't *believe*. I don't *want* to do *anything*. I don't *need* anyone or anything."

Holly was not equipped to answer him. She had no knowledge of how the warped substances of memory oozed into the soul. Theology, psychology were high-falutin' subjects. She was just a working-class girl from the trackless wastes south of the Thames.

But she too was standing apart, severed from the person she had been.

"That's the difference," she said, "I do!"

The concentration levelled out; she had switched the emphasis away from him, pulled a curtain across the view of spiritual devastation that lay within him.

Rapping sounded from the front door, startling Christopher and Holly.

"Talk of the devil." Christopher got up to admit Lawfeld.

Holly was relieved.

Lawfeld threw his overcoat and scarf carelessly to the floor in a corner and advanced on the fire. "I had to walk. First had to reassure Freddie that he hadn't made a complete ass of himself, and that it would take years for him to acquire the panache of dear Julian. Slight case of hero-worship all round." He accepted the mug of tea that Deems brought him from the kitchen. "I'm afraid you've lost the most dogged disciple you ever had. I mean Estall, of course. Lost him totally."

Christopher shrugged.

"On the other hand, McIan is ready and willing to throw himself at your feet."

Christopher shrugged again.

In the gestures of indifference, however, Holly sensed an element of effort, of conscious pose.

She thought of the words of the poems – Verdun and Amiens – and their images of raging despair. Now that anger had cooled, what was left? Why did he refuse to try to restore the past? Was it too silly, too simple for him? Were the emotions that it held just crumbs and nibbled crusts after the great feast of self-searching that he had experienced in Flanders? From "Lavender Castles", to "The Factory" represented too sharp a drop for a man to make in so short a period of time. It was more than disillusionment that Christopher had endured. He had lost faith in everything. With puzzled shock Holly realised that he had told her as much.

"I assume," said Victor Lawfeld, "that having Young Lochinvar as a doormat is not to your liking?"

"I've nothing to offer McIan; neither advice, nor inspiration."

"Beyond technique lies personality, naked and unadorned," Victor quoted.

"If you keep citing those shop-soiled adages, Victor," said Christopher, "I'll be obliged to throw you bodily downstairs."

Lawfeld gulped tea and handed the mug over for a refill.

When Christopher had gone into the kitchen, Victor leaned over and in an anxious whisper asked Holly, "How is he?"

"He seems to be all right? Why?"

"Has he said much about tonight?"

"Not much."

"It may have been good for him," said Lawfeld. "I'm terribly glad you decided to come. I wish I could be sure reading in public is good for him."

"He doesn't want to do it."

"Oh, I know that; but I'm not going to let him surrender," said Lawfeld. "Sssssssshhhhh."

"Whispering?" said Christopher.

"I was making love to your young lady," Victor said.

"She isn't my . . ." Christopher checked himself.

"Took it very well." said Lawfeld. "Threatened to shoot me if I made so bold again. Declared herself madly in love with another."

Christopher had no patience with the game of flirtation; no more had Holly.

"Yes," Victor agreed with the unspoken criticism of his ruse. "Let's have none of that jolly nonsense. Fine at nineteen. Foolish at twenty-five." He angled himself towards Christopher. "You won't take me seriously, I realise, but may I say that I thought "Wearing the Mask" is the finest. . ."

Deems got to his feet, fists clenched.

Holly rose too. "Good. I'm glad you're up, Christopher. I'll have another biscuit after all."

* * *

It was a quarter to three in the morning before the couple left Shepherd Market. Holly was dizzy with the quality and quantity of conversations in which she had been involved. Christopher had been correct in his assessment of Victor's persistent curiosity. She had become the focus of it. He had questioned her closely about her family, her background, her ambitions. He had come very close indeed to being told off for impertinence; yet Holly could not bring herself to be offended by him. He made his interest in her so obvious, and somehow depersonalised. Perhaps, she thought, Victor is interrogating me on Christopher's behalf.

There was no talk of the reading, or of poetry, except in the most general terms. But Christopher in time relaxed sufficiently to take up the challenges that Victor threw down. He entered a prolonged and rambling argument about the impingement of the Bolshevist ideology upon the freedom of the individual, the damage that Lenin had done to the social advantages that the Mensheviki represented. Both men were careful to explain the terms of the debate to Holly and to listen to her views with interest. She learned during the course of the evening that Christopher held no degree from the University of Oxford. He had been reading History when war had broken out. He had volunteered for service as soon as he could. Victor had not been a fighting man. His brother Bram, a doctor, had volunteered for the RAMC. Bram had seen action in the Eastern zone and, later, in Flanders. Victor had been delegated to stay at home. He had been found a job that would ensure him of exemption from conscription; deputy plant manager in a small secret munitions factory not far from Birmingham. The reason for Bram Lawfeld's insistence that his younger brother remain in England was a gaggle of sisters – five in all – and a mother and father neither of whom kept good health. In fact, Lawfeld Pater had died in 1916 only a few months after Bram had been shipped overseas.

Christopher's case was different. There was only his mother, a woman, Lawfeld told Holly later, of innocent temperament. She did not understand war, nor the fact of Christopher's reputation as a poet, nor anything, really, about her son, except that he needed looking after. His father had died of a sudden stroke when Christopher was nine. There were no other children in the family. Money was not much in abundance. It had been a bit of a struggle for Christopher to attain an education. His mother had insisted upon it and had attenuated her own needs to meet the costs.

Not sleepy now, Victor and Holly loitered on the corner of Hyde Park. The air was clear. The wet winter earth of the park smelled fresh. A soft sifting frost, invisible to the eye, misted their clothing, and lamps and trees in the stand by Grosvenor Crescent. An indigenous matchseller, a woman as old as London, slept in a tent of greatcoats and ragged shawls hard by the arch, tray and stockbox propped up like a little barricade to keep wandering dogs at bay.

"You're a long way from home, Holly, are you not?" said Lawfeld. "I suppose the last bus has gone?"

"I'll walk a part of the way, then take a taxi."

"I'll walk with you, in fact – if you don't object."

"I'd welcome the company," said Holly. "I didn't realise that talkin' an' drinkin' tea could make you so intoxicated."

"I don't altogether relish the prospect of sharing a bed with Rothery in his uncle's house in Fulham. I suppose I can catch the milk train back to Oxford. Rothery will assume that I stayed over with Christopher or, being of that turn of mind, that I found a girl to occupy my attention."

"I suppose you have, in a way," said Holly.

"You're not being coquettish, are you?"

"Lord, no," said Holly, flushing. "I didn't mean that, at all."

"Have you been to Christopher's shop?" Tactfully Victor changed the subject.

"Not yet. What's it like?"

"Small, crowded. He does a fair bit of trade, though. The old ladies adore him. He finds them nice copies of novels by Miss Mitford and Mrs. Humphrey Ward, and remembers who likes what."

"The personal touch," said Holly. "He won't butter many buns with that kind of thing."

"In fact, the bulk of his stock is given over to historical works. If he sticks it, he'll probably specialise in history. It's what he knows best."

"If he sticks it? Do you think it's just a passin' fad?"

"I don't know what it is," said Lawfeld. "I don't even know why he's running a bookshop. He should be back at All Souls, like me, preparing for the Tripos. But . . ."

"But?" said Holly. "That's it, isn't it? It's the 'but' that bothers you?"

"Christopher is . . . In fact, I'm not sure *what* he is. Sick? Perhaps! I tried to persuade him to make an appointment with a colleague of my brother's, a chap who specialises in mental disorders. He's one of the enlightened school; none of your cold baths and regular exercise wallahs. But Christopher would have none of it."

"Is it shell-shock that's wrong with him?"

"Bram assures me that there are clear, discernible signs of shell-shock. Physically – regarding shell-shock as a disease of the nervous system – Christopher appears to be in good health. He was wounded in the thigh, but it was a simple enough thing and healed completely. No, in fact, I don't know *what's* really wrong with him."

"But something is?"

"Yes. Something."

"I didn't know him before," said Holly. "But there are times when he seems . . . not here. Was he always like that?"

"It's not vagueness. It's retreat," said Victor. "He isn't the Christopher I knew. The change is very marked, Holly – take my word for it. I'm frightened for him."

"Frightened?"

"Christopher no longer knows what he longs for in the depth of his soul."

"But the stress of the war . . . ?"

"According to Bram, relief from stress can result in emptiness. Ideals are the driving forces we need for survival. Christopher is simply 'holding on'. The bookshop is a charade, in fact, a mere occupation."

"In time, he may be all right."

"He needs new interests. His life is without meaning. He no longer gives anything in terms of creative activity. The poet's voice is still. I believe he feels that badly. It isn't just depression or a neurotic escape from responsibility. I think Christopher craves a responsibility large enough to revive his belief in the meaning and value and purpose of life. He won't discuss his war-time experiences. The only hint I've had of them came tonight, in "Magpies" and "Wearing the Mask". There's no published text of either poem, so that I can't begin to analyse them – I don't mean as poetry, I mean as peepholes into Christopher's sickness."

"But there are times when he seems . . . normal. Most times."

"Yes, but in those times he confronts his loss of volition, the meaninglessness of suffering itself. It's that confrontation that deepens his despair and sense of emptiness."

"Are there many ex-soldiers like Christopher?"

"According to my brother, more than you might suppose. Men who are living out their days in a vacuum."

"How horrible!" said Holly. "What can we do to help him?"

"Christopher seems attracted to you," Victor said. "I've no notion of what he seeks in a relationship. It may be that he covets your sense of purpose. I can't be at all sure."

"Do you want me to encourage him?"

"It's asking a lot."

"Less than you think, Victor."

He glanced at her. "Do you like him?"

"Yes."

"In spite of his strangeness?"

"Yes," said Holly. "But I'm not what I seem, Victor."

"Hm?"

It was in Holly's mind to blurt out the whole truth, but Victor Lawfeld was a stranger; Christopher's ally, not hers.

"It's complicated," said Holly.

"Because of your shop?"

"No, that's secondary."

"What then? Won't you tell me?"

"I wish I could," said Holly.

They had reached the vicinity of Victoria. Four cabs stood by an old iron horse-bus shelter. The drivers were gathered at the lighted front of a coffee stall. Urns gleamed under the paraffin lamps and the smell of frying bacon wafted out across the street. The street was not empty. Human jetsam had been washed here by the night's tide – runaways, cripples, vendors; a collection of queer birds, a negro waiter, three members of a third-rate dance band complete with instruments, four painted tarts, all drawn to the smell of stale smoke and hot coffee. A prankster in a wire-wheeled A.V. plywood monocar streaked down Victoria Street, parping impudently on the horn, startling the coven of tarts at the corner so that they screeched obscenities after the speed demon in his streamlined dart.

Holly said, "I'm tired, Victor. It's nearly four o'clock after all. I'm not used t' doin' without my sleep."

"Take a cab home from here. I'll pay."

"No need for that. I'm a business woman."

Victor touched her hand. "I'm glad we've had a chance to talk, Holly. You're a nice girl. Your friendship will be good for Christopher."

"I hope we meet again, Victor."

"I've the feeling that we will, in fact."

"Good night."

"Good night, Holly."

He opened a cab door for her and whistled through his fingers to attract the attention of the driver who came over from the stall, stuffing a bacon roll into his mouth. Victor leaned in the cab window. "Just remember Holly that Christopher is damaged. Be patient with him, please."

"I will," Holly said. "I promise."

3

Losers at Large

"WELL NOW, IF it ain't David an' his bran' new wife," said Charlie Hallet. "What a pleasure! Met my better 'arf, 'ave you?"

Mrs. Hallet was a great white pudding of a woman, neck and arms embedded with glittering gems as if she had been rolled in diamonds while still moist. She wore a long satin gown with a vee throat that showed off a mountainous bosom thrust up by an expensive corset. There seemed to be no place to look but into the puckered gulf of her cleavage. Her eyes were sad and hard. Her French maid had done a wonderful job with puffs, sponges and brushes; even so Winifred Hallet's face had no character, only a seedy vulgarity that might once have been pretty.

"Came with my pal Lester? Glad to see you. Ain't yer glad t'see them, ol' Dutch, wot?" Charlie gushed, laying on the common accent thickly.

"Charmed, I'm sure."

A peculiar and – initially – inexplicable flush of anger stole over David. It was Hallet, Hallet and Linsey – a thing of minute gestures, attitudes; if the cold breathtakingly fast drive up from London hadn't sobered and sharpened his wits he might never have noticed it at all. Hallet smirked knowingly.

Linsey did not meet the man's eye. After a pause, she was condescendingly effusive with the great white pudding, complimenting her on the decor of the house, her dress. Hostess and lady guest walked a little way into the morning room to the left of the hall. Here a portable bar had been wheeled into a central position and, against a backdrop of French windows and a terrace flanked by potted plants, snug for the winter in canvas sacks that made them resemble limbless dwarves, the new arrivals were reviving themselves with rainbow-coloured drinks.

Lester Gosling had one nerve in his body, and that was in his bladder. The hair-raising ride in the Crouch had tweaked it into protest. On arrival he had headed straight for the ground-floor cloakroom to see a man about a dog.

Charlie took David on a short tour of the hall.

Hired flunkies in Regency costume, including one black boy and a mandatory Chinese, sloped about with silver trays of canapes and, as Charlie put it, "chopped omelette", sweatmeats and fluted glasses of champagne. The butler in charge was resident manager of Hallet's country seat. He lorded it over everyone, including guests, and ruled the house in Charlie's absence with a rod of iron, keeping Winnie in a state of awed obedience.

"Nice little wifie, you got yourself," Charlie said.

"Thank you," David replied.

"Keep you on your toes."

"I'm sure she will."

"Not egzactly a homemaker, though."

"Suits my style."

"Yer," said Charlie. "Upstairs you'll find the sports."

"Sports?"

"Your sort, David; big spendin' boys. I reckon Lester told yer about the activity 'ere. That's the real fun, ain't it? Leave the girlies for another time."

"What's the game?" David asked.

"Uh? Oh, yer, the game! Cards, Newmarket, Nap, Chase the Lady."

"Old Maid and Snap?"

"Bit tame for you, David? Is that what you're sayin'? Crown an' Anchor more t'yer taste? The stakes get 'eavy, I warn yer."

"I like it heavy."

"Developed into quite a fast chap, ain't yer? Nothin' like the hin'fluhence of a filly ter make the stallion sit up, right?"

"Don't push it, Charlie."

"Ain't me that's pushin' it. I 'pushed' it already, all I want."

David glanced at him, anger charging his system.

Hallet jerked his thumb. "Drinks an' grub in there. Dancin' in the drawin' room."

On cue a negro jazz band broke into "Alligator Rag."

Charlie grinned. "See. Only the very best.

"Why do you do it, Charlie?" David asked.

"Do it? Throw an occasional party? Keeps the Missus 'appy." Charlie looked beyond David to the door. One of the flunkies was admitting a Midlands cotton baron, a giggling flapper dangling on each arm. "Brought 'is own entertainment, I see. Fussy dog, ol' Smedley. Yer, keeps the Missus amused. An' attracts old friends – know what I mean? Old friends."

Hallet patted him on the shoulder and slid past him, calling, "Winnie, the door," to attract his wife to her duties.

David loitered at the foot of the stairs.

Peach garland carpet covered the treads between white-painted banisters. White-painted? Beneath the white paint was an example of fine Jacobean carving. Holly would have been furious at such barbaric maltreatment of ancient craftsmanship.

Holly. He shook his head.

Linsey – his wife – was his true concern.

Sprawling on the staircase was a young man. His face seemed faintly familiar. Full length, belly down, he propped elbows on the edge of the landing, as if to pay obeisance to a bust of Cleo on a mock-Greek pedestal that ornamented the corner. Four cocktail glasses were arranged before him. Curious, David leaned on the newel-post. The young lounger paid him not the slightest attention. He was counting money. Scowling with concentration, he arranged fivers into piles, one before each conical glass. Above him was a girl. She stood straight as a larch, arms by her sides, legs beautifully shaped by silk stockings, line of thighs, stomach and breasts tantalisingly draped in fine chiffon. She was dark-haired, young, innocent, sullen.

"Eyes front," commanded Lester Gosling who had stolen up on David. "She is not for mere mortals like thee or me."

"Who is she?"

"That is Lisbeth, she of the fabled hymen. Dear sweet virginal Lisbeth. Not quite right in the head, old son."

Immediately David identified the money-counter: Edward Quillam. No anaemic earl, Quillam had won the Victoria Cross in gallant action at Aubers Ridge, in exchange for most of his intestines and one kidney. He subsisted now on a diet of steamed turbot and milk sops. He was his sister's guardian, her champion and, it was said, slept with her whenever propriety allowed. Who else but a fey sister could warm the bed of a man who did not want to be a hero but a boy again?

The strains of "Alligator Rag" grew louder.

"Going up?" said Lester.

"Think I'll have a drink first."

"Sound idea," said Lester. "Where's Linsey?"

"Probably at the bar."

"Told you it was quite a dolly place."

"Yes, Hallet does things well."

"What'll you have?"

"Whisky-soda."

David separated himself from Lester, leaving the young man to wend his way into the morning room. He had spotted Linsey on the edge of the dance floor, her body moving in tempo to the music. Somebody would pick her up soon, whirl her into the dancers. How many people were here all told? Thirty or thirty-five couples in the huge room, a dozen more by the bar. How many upstairs? By midnight the house would be full of people; the London set safe here from the untimely intervention of police.

Stepping into the drawing room, David took his wife by the arm and drew her into an alcove by the long, white-painted seventeenth-century dresser whose shelves were crammed with the bric-à-brac that Winifred Hallet had acquired and would not part with or even decently hide. Two greenhouse rubber plants did their best to veil the tasteless collection with their fleshy fronds.

"I want you with me upstairs," David said.

"Is there a bed?" said Linsey.

"You know perfectly well what I mean. We didn't come here for fun."

"Speak for yourself, darling."

"I want you at the table, where I can see you?"

"Don't you trust me."

"I don't trust Hallet."

"You've no need to fret about Charlie. He's not interested in me any more."

"I think he is."

"The green-eyed monster, David?"

"And don't drink too much."

"Don't you tell me what to do."

"Let's go upstairs. That's where the money is."

"Later, David. I'm not in the mood."

"Well damned-well *get* in the mood."

"Charlie isn't interested in me, not any more," Linsey repeated.

"He . . . Never mind. I don't like the fellow. In fact, I detest him. Let's do what we came for, and clear out."

"What will your old chum Lester have to say? It's his vehicle, in case you'd forgotten," Linsey said.

"I don't mean leave now. There's activity upstairs, apparently."

"Activity downstairs, too."

"Linsey, you're not. . .you can't be. . ."

"Tiddles? How could I? In ten minutes?"

"You look it."

She crossed her eyes, screwed up her nose and tugged her mouth with her fingertips. She stuck out her tongue and waggled it at him. It was obscene, not comical.

He gripped her hand firmly. "Let's try our luck at the Crown and Anchor."

"You go."

"Both of us. You're my lucky mascot."

Sulkily, the woman agreed to accompany him.

Without waiting for Lester to return with his drink, David led his wife upstairs.

Quillam and his sister had left the staircase.

Gambling was taking place in two of the smaller rooms on the west wing of the mansion. Squared by four corridors the upper storey of the house had master and guest bedrooms to the east and north and, occupying the whole of the southern aspect, Charlie Hallet's 'office', a sanctuary for which not even Iron-rod, the butler, possessed a key.

Two rooms were quite sufficient for the fifteen or twenty people addicted to the fall of cards or dice. In the first room were three card parties. As Hallet had catalogued them, the games being played were pure lotteries, requiring little skill: Newmarket, Nap, Find the Lady. There was much noise in this apartment, whooping laughter, shouting of bets. Males and females were mixed in the ratio of half and half. When David put his head around the door, somebody – an acquaintance from the club – called out, "Come an' join us, old fruit." David smiled, shook his head and, taking Linsey's hand, walked along the corridor to seek out Crown and Anchor.

It was quieter next door. In one corner three stuffy gentlemen and an elderly woman were playing bridge. Principal activity, however, was focused on a rectangular table quilted with green baize and boxed around with strips of teak. Hanging shades, lowered on chains, spread light evenly over the table. Nine people were seated round the table. David had no trouble in finding a chair. He drew Linsey to his side, seated himself and brought out one of the packets of pound notes that he had made up before leaving the Waldorf. He lit a cigarette and watched the cast of the dice for a while, discreetly studying the faces of his fellow bettors.

Quillam was there, his sister seated beside him. Her eyes followed every movement of the silver dice, though she did not seem to be otherwise involved in her brother's changing fortunes.

The table was de luxe stuff, probably specially commissioned; a far cry from the scruffy little boards that he had seen in use in back offices and dormitories through the war years. No doubt Quillam had crouched in sandbagged caverns under pounding guns and wagered on boards even more creased and stained.

It was an exceedingly easy game to understand, requiring only three dice and a 'layout'. The layout was of card or cotton fabric marked off with six squares. In each square was printed a symbol matched by an identical set of symbols on the facets of the dice – Heart, Diamond, Spade, Club, Crown, Anchor. Bets were laid on combinations of symbols made against the "House" or "Banker", the person who held the dice cup at the time.

Without looking up, Quillam said, "No limit, old chap."

The Banker began with a stake as large or as small as he or she wished it to be and held the cup as long as that stake lasted, or until the end of a round of the table. The cup was passed on to the Banker's left, and could be refused. Though wagers were made between the Banker and each member of the school individually there were many cross-bets, side-bets and 'covers', private arrangements between participating players. On exceptionally high Banks, the House might lay off "against all odds" to cover against absolute ruin. Among experts the game progressed at great speed, requiring a maximum of concentration. Unlike roulette, Crown and Anchor boasted few formalities, few "breathing spaces" for the gamblers. In a prolonged session, the drain on nervous energy was considerable.

Linsey nudged David's arm. "Go on. What are you waiting for, darling? Spring?"

David said, "Pass."

Betting opportunity shifted to the man on his left.

The Banker was a beefy matron with a ruby pin on the bodice of her velvet gown, another clipped to an aigrette of white ostrich feathers that nodded from her tinted blue hair. Inviting the man on David's left to wager with her she rattled the dice cup. He was a rumpled scholar with pince-nez and a bald spot, not old though.

In single notes he laid down ten pounds on a complicated bet. "Let her go."

Dice struck the raised lip of the table. Almost without thought, the pince-nez took in fourteen pounds.

In David's ear, Linsey whispered, "What did he do?"

"Sssssh," said David, gently.

"Bit o' skill there, Doctor." The matron had a coarse accent. She did not attempt to disguise it. It transpired that she was the wife of one of the bridge players.

The kitty, the Banker's stake, still stood large. Betting went around the lower arc of the table, nothing grand. The matron passed on the cup to Quillam, stating, as she tucked the notes into her purse, "Well, that'll keep the cats in cream, won't it?"

"Not 'arf, Dora," said Quillam, in friendly fashion.

He fanned fivers in neat array upon the kitty box.

"How much?" asked David.

"Two hundred," said Quillam.

"Oh, dear me!" said the pince-nez. "It's going awfully high, awfully early."

"Don't worry, you'll still be here at breakfast, Claude," said Quillam. "You always are."

"Two hundred won't bust anyone," said a youngish fellow with tight sandy curls and a pitted complexion. "I was led to believe I'd see some real sport here."

"Oh, you will, you will," Quillam promised. "The bet is with you, I believe."

"Two hundred."

"Whole Bank," said Quillam. "Heart, Diamond, Club – even pay."

Quillam handed the dice-cup to his sister. She gave him a loving smile, tossed her pretty head, enclosed the silver cup in her hands and shook it like a cocktail mixer.

"Do put a jig in it," said the youngish fellow. "I rather want the House."

"Manners," said Quillam, sternly.

Dice pattered – Spade, Spade, Anchor.

"Thank you kindly," Quillam shifted the youngish fellow's notes into the kitty box. "Four hundred the whole bank."

When David's turn came, he laid fifty on Anchor.

The dice showed Club, Anchor, Anchor.

"Two to one," said Quillam.

David plucked one hundred pounds from the kitty box, saying, "Winner's choice, Quillam?"

"If you wish?"

"My fifty on a heart."

Quillam's sister mixed the dice and spinkled them upon the table. Linsey muttered, "You should have stayed on Anchor."

"Club, Club, *Heart*, indeed," Quillam read.

David removed fifty from the kitty box and his own fifty from the board. "Enough – for the moment."

"Warming up," said pince-nez. He arranged another complicated wager that netted him another four pounds.

Betting shifted to two young women, playing separately. They were "lookers", and knew it. Neither spoke to the other, though occasionally their hands would touch. Clinging dresses showed off their breasts. They lost a tenner each.

Randolph Galt and his fiancée agreed on a mutual flutter on Crown and Anchor and kissed goodbye, mutually, to Randolph's daddy's money. The fiancée consoled Randolph with a sip of champagne.

At the end of his round Quillam relinquished the cup, and took away over four hundred pounds, one way and another. He gave Lisbeth the profit to salt in her long silvery purse.

The evening wore on.

Lester Gosling found his way to the table.

David had a poor round as House.

Linsey chivvied him with knee and elbow, complaining at his "niggardly" betting.

The youngish fellow, by showing off, broke himself before midnight and wafted off into oblivion, six hundred quid lighter. Claude's luck held. He did not push it, took his tiny profits with regularity and rode out Quillam's jibes with good humour. Dora, the matron, enjoyed herself enormously.

At one o'clock a flunkey brought in a tray of coffee and canapés and there was a slight pause in play and a lot of remarks about wishing to purchase a canine pet and visiting relatives in Persia. Quillam's sister was despatched to find a glass of milk, then Quillam thought better of it and chased after her to bring her back upstairs. Linsey complained that this was the dullest party she'd ever been to. Enclosed in a world of their own the two young "lookers" fed each other canapés and licked each other's fingertips while Randolph Galt, to his fiancée's chagrin, could not take his eyes off them.

Some time after one, Charlie Hallet joined the school. He bet in quirky bursts of rashness and caution, and David thought that he was the worse for drink. Charlie stood two Banks of one hundred pounds each, and lost both before the rounds were through. He did not seem to mind. At two o'clock, Charlie excused himself, and the table thinned to eight players. Tightly cocooned now, intent upon winning, they were oblivious to the jumping rhythm of the dancers that pulsed up from below and the shouts of laughter from the corridor outside.

David had the Bank when Linsey left him.

*   *   *

David did not clearly know how long his wife had been gone from his side. Later he surmised that it had been, at most, an hour. Absorbed in the game, he hardly gave her a passing thought, vaguely assuring himself that she would be dancing or drinking, downstairs, that she would return when the fancy took her.

If he had been losing, it might have been a different story. But he had hold of a winning thread and little packages of five pound notes dispersed in various pockets were building up. Like Quillam, he kept a check on his winnings by this means. Like Quillam, he found his concentration growing as night progressed into the wee small hours and the rhythm of the game seeped into his brain. He did not drink alcohol but stimulated himself with liberal helpings from a silver tassie of coffee that bubbled on a hot plate on a corner table. He smoked constantly, though tobacco was beginning to make his eyes water and his throat raw. Physical discomforts were part of the job.

Lester Gosling said, "Lend me a couple of hundred, old son, will you? I'll give you a marker, if that's agreeable."

David said, "I don't believe in lendin' money to losers, Lester."

"Come on, old son; I'm your chauffeur, remember?"

"How do I know you're good for two hundred?"

"Really! The motor is worth much more than that."

David gave Lester four little packages and received in exchange a leaf torn from Lester's notebook: "I. O. David Aspinall the Sum of Two Hundred Pounds – £200/0/0 – Feb. 18th, 1920." It was signed with the Gosling scribble.

Two hundred went quickly as Lester, like a fool, tried to recoup his losses by heavy betting against the odds. Chaps like Lester were easy meat for Quillam. Even hearty old Dora could suck the Goslings of this world dry without much effort.

"Another hundred, David, please."

"This is the last, Lester. I'm not encouragin' your craziness after that."

"Sure, yes, that's perfectly all right. Do I get the hundred?"

"Your marker, please."

If it came to it, he could put the markers into the kitty box against Quillam. Quillam would accept them.

It probably wouldn't reach that stage. He was over five hundred up on the night's play and had adopted a more conservative style of play, lowering his wagers and choosing short odds. He could not be sure how much Quillam was out, but had the feeling that the war hero had dipped a couple of hundred. Claude too had lost impetus, had been unable to resist the temptation to increase stakes, though he should have known better.

Three Crowns on eighteen faces. Quillam's sister had the cup. Her young breasts shook under the chiffon. A single Crown would pay out six to one. David placed fifty against the House on a Crown, with no covering bet. He lost to two Spades and an Anchor. Quillam had a good round all told, dipping sixty pounds to Dora, taking from all the others. He elected to hold the cup.

Once more David bet fifty on a single Crown. He won. He claimed the privilege of holding the bet.

Quillam nodded; that's what he would have done too.

"Same Crown?" he asked.

"Yes. Fifty at six to one. You'll take it?" said David.

After checking his stake, Quillam said, "I've three hundred and twenty there. Do you want to clean me out?"

"Not particularly. Fifty will do."

"Stir the pot, Lisbeth," Quillam told his sister. He drank milk from a glass. It left a pale crescent on his upper lip that he dabbed at with a handkerchief as dice scattered and clicked across the board.

"Diamond, Spade. . ."

"Crown," said David.

"You've the luck of the Devil," said Claude.

David removed his winnings from the kitty box, leaving two fivers and ten sad singles there.

Quillam looked up. He was facing the door. It was not a casual intruder, not some drunk in search of the boys' room, or a pair of new lovers seeking the solitude of a bedroom.

David glanced over his shoulder.

Winifred Hallet was framed in the doorway. Behind her the light in the corridor seemed brilliant, making geometric shafts through the smokey haze, like sunlight through mist. Her arms were crossed over her huge bosom. For once, her dull features had taken on character.

"Mr. Aspinall, will you come?"

"What?" said David, stupidly. "What's wrong?

"Your wife."

"What?"

Quillam said, "Has there been an accident?"

Winifred Hallet said, "Come with me, Mr. Aspinall."

Leaving his money on the table, David rose and, in a kind of waking dream, followed the woman along the corridor and across the breadth of the mansion into the east wing. Corridor lights here were less garish. A staircase plunged away on the left, dropping into dimness; to the kitchens, perhaps. He was alone with her, shut off. Like a drum heard from distant clearings, the din of a party throbbed below. She led him round a corner. Two hothouse plants, in brass tubs, masked a window. By the window was a door, at the end of a cul-de-sac. Winifred Hallet stopped before the door and, staring at it, murmured, "Your wife is in there."

"What's wrong with her?"

"She's with my 'usband."

"Are you sure?"

"Yer."

"Mrs. Hallet, perhaps . . . "

"Open it."

"Mrs. Hallet . . . "

"*Open it*. Are *you* such a bleedin' *coward*"

Reluctantly David put his hand upon the door knob. He turned it stealthily. The woman pushed him from behind. He was projected forward through the opening door into the bedroom.

The bed was low and ultra modern, an oval with an oval headboard of quilted silk that matched the pattern of the silken counterpane, a weird tomato red, like a gigantic bloodstain. Two shaded lamps poured light down upon the bed. The scene was repeated again and again in amber-tinted mirrors that panelled the walls of the alcove.

Two people lay on the counterpane: Hallet and Linsey – neither undressed – Hallet's trousers lowered, dress shirt's skirts white against hairy thighs; Linsey's dress and unbuttoned camiknickers rolled tightly across her belly, breasts spilling from the unstrapped yoke, thighs naked above her stocking-tops – Hallet and Linsey.

It was no drunken rape. She kneeled on him. He lay with hands behind his head on the blood-red bolster. His cheeks were flushed, lips open, showing tongue. Linsey's arms braced, hips moving in wild surges. Tossing her head, hair ragged, mascara slimy with perspiration, the young woman was too far gone to notice the intruders.

And Charlie Hallet did not care.

It was, David thought, as if Hallet had planned this corrupt farce to rub his wife's nose in infidelity, in depravity. Hallet's yellow eyes swivelled towards the door. Though he saw them, recognised them, he did not attempt to rise. He gave no sign of contrition or alarm. Indeed, he grinned wolfishly as the young woman bucked and squirmed upon him, and, with a sudden, brief groan, reached climax.

"Gawd! Gawd! Charlie not *this*, not *this* far," Winifred gasped and turned her face away.

Hallet pushed the young woman from him. The dismissive gesture snapped David's horrified immobility. He stepped forward, caught Linsey by the waist, lifted her away, dropped her on to the floor, then reached for Hallet. Hallet drove himself up on his elbows, cheeks as scarlet as the counterpane. Lowering his head he rammed his brow into David's face. Blinded by pain, David flinched.

Hallet rolled out of the bed. One hand hauled up his trousers as he danced out of range, shouting, "*Are you' appy now, you cow. Is this what yer wanted t'see? Yer old man on the bloody job?*" Winifred stumbled, supporting her weight against the wall, face averted as he hopped to her like a hobgoblin, yelling. '*Now you've seen, now will yer leave me be. I can still do it, you bitch.*"

Sobbing Linsey sprawled on the floor by the foot of the bed, face buried on the crook of her elbow. In partial nakedness she looked defenceless. Blood smeared David's mouth and nose. He shook his head and wiped his nose on his cuff. He left Hallet to scream hatred at his wife. He stooped and lifted Linsey, smoothing down her dress as best he could. She flopped against him. Her fevered eyes were large, lips slack. The perfume of her body mingled with sour sweat.

"I'm sorry, sorry, Dav . . . sorry sorry sorry sorry sorry."

"Get up. Can you?"

Then Hallet was on him. "*She done it willin'. She came t'me. I 'ad 'er before. I pay for the bleedin' privilege.*"

Blood flowed thickly over David's moustache. He could taste salt. He licked his lip, wiped his face once more with his cuff.

"*Touch me,*" Hallet told him, "*an' I'll ruin yer.*"

"What did you give her?"

"*What she wanted.*"

"Cocaine?"

"*She came t'me. She wanted it.*"

Winifred Hallet slid down the wall into a fat crumpled heap, racked by sobs.

"You're an animal, Hallet."

"Maybe so, maybe so, but you *need* me. Yer little wifie *needed* me. Think on that, sonnie. *I can give 'er what you can't.*"

David lifted Linsey. He smoothed the dress again and slid the straps of the bodice over her shoulders. She was slack, silent, leaning on him. He helped her out of the bedroom into the corridor and along it to the top of the kitchen staircase. He thanked God that the ugly scene had attracted no attention. He could not have held his rage in check against the gibbering apes of Hallet's set. He would have thrashed one or more, or all, if they had appeared to goggle at the "diversion". He lead Linsey down the staircase into a small oak-panelled hallway. Another flight down would be the kitchen.

In the hallway, a young man pressed an older woman into the darkest corner, his hands groping over her body. She roared softly in response to his attack, her own needs not yet fulfilled.

"Find your own spot," the young man growled as David guided Linsey past them to the narrow outside door.

Cold night air enveloped them. David put Linsey in front of him and slammed the door. Off to the right he could make out the brilliant windows of morning room and dining room. Streaming light seemed to shiver with strident sound as the party sprawled from the dance hall. In a motorcar with the top propped up, hard by the ivy-covered gable, a couple were making love. David could see nothing except one long silk-clad leg cocked over the window ledge, silver slipper dangling by a fragile strap. The motorcar rocked on its springs, groaning as if it, too, had been cajoled into entering the act.

Still mute, Linsey leaned on him.

Disentangling her arm from his shoulder, he released her.

"Wait here."

" . . . sor . . . sor . . . sor . . . sor . . . "

"Linsey, do you understand? Wait for me here."

He pushed her down. She sat on the step, shoulders and head against the stone balluster, profile defined by black-shadowed ivy.

David went into the house again. He climbed the main staircase. He pushed his way into the gaming room.

Lester got to his feet. "Dear God, old son! What the Deuce?"

David removed Gosling's two markers and tossed them on the board.

"Those in exchange for the use of your motorcar."

"But . . . "

"I need it, Lester. I've got to get Linsey out of here and back to London."

"Gosling, don't argue, old man," said Quillam, briskly, "Give him the ignition key. I'll see you safe back to Piccadilly."

"Well, it ain't worth it. Three hund . . . "

"Now, Lester."

Lester Gosling had been taught how to obey. He handed David the wire from which the spindle key hung. "Want a hand to start her up?"

"I'll manage."

As David turned to hurry from the room, Quillam called, "Aspinall, wait." He came from the table and stuffed David's winnings into the pocket of his dinner jacket, saying, "Is your wife all right?"

"Yes."

"Can I help?"

"No, Quillam. Thanks."

David hurried downstairs by the back way.

The lovers in the hallway had been replaced by a quartet who waltzed round and round on the parquet, heads on each others shoulders, like some fantastical beast with eight limbs. Roughly, David pushed past them.

Linsey was where he had left her.

She giggled when he touched her. "Thought you'd gone, darling."

Shock was wearing off, leaving the cocaine's effortless poison to numb her system. David envied her guiltless state. Bodily he lifted her into his arms and carried her along the gravel path towards the ranks of parked cars below the terrace wall. Several were occupied. Squeals. Laughter. Profanities. Linsey snuggled against him, secure in his arms.

"Hm, Daddy! My Daddy," she crooned, smiling.

He kicked open the passenger door of the Green Crouch and put her in as best he could. He had no anger to spare for her. Desolation froze his soul like icy vapour. He fiddled with the key until the engine fired than he switched on the big bullfrog lamps, cleaving the light out across the lawn. Behind him Hallet's mansion palpitated. Doors flung open, revellers tumbled down stairs, holding above them a negro saxophone player, his golden instrument glinting like a gigantic hook.

Squirting gravel, tyres bit and flung the Crouch away from the house.

Linsey was shaken in her moonbeam sleep by scythings of cold air. The motorcar hurtled down the driveway between trees and out of the gates into the Newminster lane.

David riveted his fingers to the big leather steering wheel.

Darkness split into etched visions of withered weeds and stark hedgerows, barred gates and gnarled tree trunks. He had no clear idea where this road would lead him, only the notion that it headed south, back to London, back to Pimlico.

Linsey whimpered. "Cold. Cold."

"Blanket." He drew a travelling rug from the dickey seat and dropped it on her. She hugged it, turned and slept.

Powering the low-slung car, David drove on and on and on, into the bitter winter night.

●　　　●　　　●

The mileometer told David that they were not too far from London. The sports car had devoured the miles of country road hungrily. Headlamps slashed through darkness, picking out rabbits or startled hares, a cock pheasant once. Horses shied away from the roadside like ghosts. Villages and little towns fled past. He followed signs – *London. London. London* – in a state of numbness, suspended in the car, attached to reality by naked, frozen fingers wrapped around the wheel. He hardly noticed the intense cold that ate into the nerves of his bruised face. His eyes had stopped watering. Besides him was no wife, only a bundle wrapped in a travelling rug. He could see nothing except knees and one foot, shoe fallen into the well of the passenger compartment. Eyes fastened on the road ahead, feet worked the pedals, knees in that awkward hunched position that was a feature of Lester's speedster. He did not notice that Linsey had wakened.

Hauling herself up she clutched his arm.

The Crouch slithered and weaved across the road.

Stripped elms, an alderbrake, a five-barred gate jumped out at David — Norman church with pretty spire visible against a frosty haze – a fleeting glint of light on a frozen pond – two large cottages sleeping close by the road, snug behind privets.

He shook her off.

She gripped his shoulder, struggling in the seat.

Once more he shook her off.

"Oh . . . *God!*" She groaned, then loudly repeated, "*Oh, God!*"

She was shuddering with cold, dress puffed out by streams of wind whipped back from the bonnet, funnelling around the windshield. Tense now, David drew himself closer to the wheel, tightening his hold. Below, his feet stabbed accelerator, clutch, brake – clutch, brake, accelerator. As if it had a will of its own and was reluctant to be checked in its wild dash for the city the Crouch responded skittishly. *London:* signpost quaint, tilted. Behind it, a lane. A mile on, a bone-white post, an inn-board hanging from wrought-iron escutcheon varnished by frost.

"*David! Oh, God! I'm dying!*"

"We'll be home soon," he shouted.

Floods of air made his teeth ache. He hurt. She had drawn him into hurting. Wrenching the gear stick he tramped on the accelerator.

"*I'm sick. I'm sick. I'm sick.*"

He fought her off. Her arm snaked around his throat, body rubbed against his chest. He thrust her off, roughly, holding her away.

"*Sick. I'm sick.*"

Banks of withered grass; a thorn hedge rimed with frost.

Frost thickening the air, palpable and clinging.

Railway bridge; the thrum of the Crouch's engine ripped out behind, an echo, lost. Road twisted, straightened, curved. Rose, beech tree, willow; a pond again, reeds like knives.

"*Sick! Sick! David! Christ have Mercy! David!*"

He glanced down. She was huddled in the foot-well, a white envelope in her hand, tearing at it, stuffing torn paper into her mouth.

Reaching, he caught a fistful of her hair and pulled her head back. A tiny puff of moonbeam, like a whiff of cartridge smoke, blew from the corner of the shredded envelope.

"No more, Linsey. No more dope."

The wheel leapt and shuddered. He stamped on the brake pedal, almost driving it through the floor.

She was on him like a predator, a jaguar or leopard, sleek, lithe, all claws, tearing, gouging at his face, screaming in rage at the loss of the few pale grains of dust. Nails dug into his eyes. Punching her breasts, he fought to control the wheel. But the Crouch was gone, tyres spinning on the frosty road. Great naked trees with womanly boles stooped over the verge. He fought his wife, fury unleashed in a moment of sheer savagery as the motor spun, slewed, slithered, and covered a hundred yards broadside, not slowing at all. Out of one eye, David watched it. He was caught in an eddy of disbelief, a sluggish whorl of time, an infinite allowance in which to calculate that all was for the best.

The Crouch curved up the banking. Flighted in a low spiral, it almost cleared the thorn hedge.

Speared on the wing, it was brought down by trailing oak branches. The bonnet cracked into them. The spiral was reversed, the free-flying bulk of Lester Gosling's sportster twisted round an opposite axis. The massive torque began to break up the frame even before it struck the oak tree. Sounds were sharp as pistol fire. David felt a wash of pain – then release as he was snatched from the unhinged door and shaken on to hard winter stubble.

The oak tree seemed a long way off.

One lamp, unrooted, burned still, bathing the corn stalks with mild light. David smelled the sweet reek of petroleum fumes.

Rising, he staggered across rutted ground.

Linsey was draped over the passenger door, head hanging, arms trailing. He lifted her, tugging. Could not free her. He kicked at the buckled door until it sprang loose. He tried to draw her out. Metal wreckage pinned her hips. Fumes made him giddy. Breathing through bloody lips he clambered over her, slid his arms beneath her flanks, and manoeuvered her free. Greasy with blood, skirts and stockings ripped. The Crouch, or what was left of it, sank under his weight as he hoisted his wife over the debris and pitched full length upon the ground. Panting he lay on top of her. Her eyes were closed. Blood seeped from a jagged wound across her brow. It had flensed away a furrow of hair. There was blood on her lips too.

Behind him the Crouch burst softly into flame.

Dragging the woman, David crawled away.

Heat and light from the burning wreckage was pleasantly sensual, almost heady. The car did not explode. David propped Linsey on a quilt of grasses by the base of the hedge. The ground was cold, not moist. He put his head down. He noticed how heat melted the frost fur on the leaves of grass. He was bleeding from the chest and side. There was very little pain. He felt weak but serene. Apart from the seeping wound on her forehead, Linsey was undamaged – above the waist. Below, was a bloody mess. He did not look down there.

Crouching over her, he said, "Come on, darling. Come on. Give me a smile."

Linsey did not answer him – ever again.

Twenty minutes later a commercial traveller heading north in a bouncy little Trojan spotted smoke, stopped and found the couple in distress hard against the hedgerow.

At twenty-five minutes past five o'clock on Sunday morning, David and Linsey Aspinall were carried into the tiled receiving room of Howewood Cottage Hospital where two local doctors and a nursing staff of three did all that they could to pull the young couple back from the brink of the grave.

* * *

News of David's accident brought Thora Aspinall to the point of collapse. On Sunday morning, when the police arrived at the house in Cardwell Place, Thora was alone. When Andrea returned from church – fortunately with Miles in tow – it was to find Thora locked in her bedroom. It was inconsiderate of the local constable to leave the woman alone at such a time, though she had given every appearance of accepting the grim news stoically.

"Mother, what is it? What's wrong?" Andrea called through the door. "Are you ill?"

"Mother, will you open this door?"

"Listen," Miles touched his fiancée's arm. "She's saying something."

"David . . . "

"What about David, mother?"

"Accident."

"Oh, dear God! Please, mother, open the door."

"She . . . she . . . brought it on him."

"What's she saying?" asked Andrea.

"I think she means Linsey, blames Linsey."

"Miles, break the lock."

"Of course."

Three hours later, in a hired motorcar, Thora, Andrea and Miles reached the quaint edifice of Howewood Cottage Hospital. On explaining who they were, they were admitted at once to a private ward in the convalescents' wing.

There was frost upon the windows, for the room faced north and received no sun during the short winter day. The vista of leafless larches, infertile flowerbeds and dun-coloured lawns was depressing. Icy daylight was reflected in glassware on the stand by David's bed and seemed to seep into the sheets and pillow-slips, into the young man's flesh.

Thora kissed her son on the brow.

To Andrea's surprise her brother opened his eyes. He pushed himself up, quite brightly. "Mother. It's good to see you. Sorry for all this fuss. Miles, Andrea, how are you?"

"David, David," Thora sobbed.

"Now, now, Mother. None of that. I'm not so bad, really."

Seated on a wooden chair, close to the bed, Thora held her son's hand and wept soundlessly while David conversed in a remarkably animated manner with Andrea and Miles.

In answer to their enquiries, he told them, "Ice on the road. The motor just took off. Couple of cracked ribs. Lost some blood. I'll be right as rain in a day or two, so they tell me. I say, Miles, you wouldn't have a gasper on you, by any chance?"

Miles gave him a cigarette.

"What about . . . her?" said Andrea.

David blew out smoke. He picked a shred of tobacco from the tip of his tongue and patted his mother's hand absently.

"Your wife *was* with you, wasn't she?" Andrea said.

"The motor's a write-off," said David. "Expect I'll have a visit from Lester Gosling's insurance agent. Pray God Lester's insured against third-party risk."

"David – your wife," Miles reminded him.

"I know it's a dreadful chore, Howewood being so far out of the city," said David, "but I'd be grateful if somebody would fetch down a dressin'-gown and socks, shirt, trousers, that sort of thing. I'll be up and about tomorrow, I expect."

"I'll bring what you need, son," Thora promised.

"Thank you, mother." He took in a lungful of smoke, coughed, winced and slumped back on the pillow, head against the iron bedstead. He turned his face to the window. Staring out across the lawn to the larches, his eyes filled with tears. "She'll. . .she'll probably die."

"Oh, I say, David!" Miles exclaimed. "Are you sure?"

"The doctor spoke to me this morning. Gives me little hope for

Lin's life. She's still unconscious. Her legs – smashed. Her head, her brain – injured." David looked down at his mother's round hat. "You never met her, mother, did you?"

"I'll meet her when she's better."

Andrea had sense enough to hold her tongue, this was neither the time nor the place for recriminations.

"Has surgery been performed?"

"Two emergency operations."

"Can she be moved?" Miles said.

"To London, you mean?"

"Guy's or the Royal. If it's a question of money. . ."

"Money!" said David. "God, no! It's not a question of money. If she . . . if she survives tonight . . . then . . . I . . . I really don't know what will happen."

"Try to look on the bright side, dear,"

Leaving Andrea and Thora, Miles went off in search of a doctor. Instead, he found Matron, a pleasant dumpling of a woman bursting with optimism.

"Mrs. Aspinall? Well, no, can't let you see her, sir. You're not her brother, are you?"

"No, no relation," said Miles. "How bad is her condition?"

"She's comfortable, comfortable."

"Can she be moved, to a London hospital, say?"

"Certainly not. The lady's in no fit condition to travel. I'm sure Doctor Mayes would forbid it. Didn't her husband tell you how badly injured she is?"

"I was hoping for more positive information."

"She's comatose. She might remain so for several days." said the matron. "Once she's conscious, then a programme of rebuilding her broken bones will be undertaken – by any surgeon you see fit to engage."

"Her legs – are they badly damaged?"

"To be perfectly honest with you, sir, I have my doubts if the lady will ever walk again."

•   •   •

The first intimation Holly received that fate had dealt another queer card came at eight-thirty the following morning. Even before Mrs. Hodge had time to pant down the iron staircase bearing the dreadful news, Holly was confronted by an ambulance as she rounded the corner into Cardwell Place. The vehicle was drawn up outside the shop. She ran towards it. Stretcher-bearers emerged from the entrance and slid their burden into the back of the ambulance. Holding a leather bag in her hands, Andrea followed them. She waited until the stretcher was safely aboard then held out the bag to one of the men. "You may need this. It's my mother's handbag. All the particulars that will be required are inside."

The man looked surprised. "Ain't you comin' with 'er?"

"Not immediately. I assume that I cannot contribute to the care and attention that my mother will receive?"

"Well, missus, I wouldn't know nothin' about that."

"I'll be along presently."

The man shrugged. Carrying the handbag he went round to the driving compartment and climbed in.

As the ambulance took off, Holly stepped between Andrea and the doorway. Not bothering to hide her contempt, Holly said, "How can you let her go alone?"

"I've a number of things to do here," said Andrea.

"What can be more important than your mother's health?"

"There isn't much wrong with her," said Andrea. "Oh, I don't mean she's shamming. It's just the strain that's been too much for her. It's simple emotional exhaustion."

"Who says so?"

"The doctor."

"Have you notified David?"

Malevolence lit Andrea's eyes. She glanced up and down Cardwell Place. Freezing traces of fog shut off both ends of the road. Out of it came the growl of Monday morning traffic. Two or three curious neighbours loitered at doorways. One of the shopkeepers, a vinter, had come out on the step to see what the fuss was about.

"I'm not discussing my business in public." Andrea said. "Open the shop."

Holly did so, laying the gate to one side.

Once within the darkness of the shop, Andrea wasted no time, and no tact, in giving Holly the details of David's accident.

"Is he goin' to recover?" Holly asked.

"Of course he's going to recover. Oh, yes, my dear brother will recover to rue the day he married that . . . that . . . "

"How can you say such a thing?" Holly demanded. "She may be dyin' right now. May be dead for all you know."

"I doubt it. Her kind don't die. She'll be back in the swim, dragging my brother down, before long."

"Why do you hate her so much?" Holly interrupted.

"It's no concern of yours, Beckman. I hope this fearful fright will have brought our David to his senses. If he's any brains left he'll divorce her, pull himself together and start building a worthwhile life!"

Andrea's face was harder than Holly ever remembered it. In spite of the hour, she was dressed in modern fashion. After telephoning the doctor, she must have left her mother and taken time to tog herself up. Deep-crowned hat, short skirt and straight lines of the mode gave her an angularity at odds with her ripeness.

"I will see to it," said Andrea," that David does not shame us again. It's this place, this shop. We don't need it. I'll strenuously advise him to move, with mother and I, to Brighton. Perhaps to Bath."

"What will your Mr. Walshott have to say to that? I thought you were gettin' married soon."

"That's no concern of yours, either, Beckman. I'll never understand how you persuaded David to buy the business. Oh, yes, that also came out in the wash. Thought he'd pamper and protect you, did you? Well, precious little protection you can expect from him now!"

"Andrea," said Holly, "you're a cow."

The eyes did not lose their glitter, the lips their smile. It had taken the destruction of her brother's marriage and the eroding of her mother's health to bring Andrea into a position of dominance in the family circle. Her whole demeanour said it was worth it.

"I guarantee we'll be shut of this place within six months," said Andrea. "And you with it, Beckman."

"It'll be your loss," said Holly.

"And if *she* dies . . . well, so much the better, perhaps."

"Do you mean your mother?"

"My . . . *How dare you?* I mean that gold-digging little minx who vampired my brother into her bed. Do you suppose there was anything else in it except crude physical attraction?"

"Get out, Andrea."

"I beg you pardon."

"I don't have to listen to this. Get out of my shop at once."

"I'm going. I have," Andrea was armoured by triumph, "better things to do."

Behind her, Holly closed and locked the shop door.

When Wilf arrived, three or four minutes later, he got no answer to his knocking. Holly was in the back store, weeping, not for herself, however, but for David who, it seemed, had lost everything – including his unborn child.

* * *

Little news of David and his wife filtered down to Holly during the beginning of March. Dog days of winter in the city were never much fun but this year especially a pall of gloom hung over Cardwell Place. Though Holly saw little of Mrs. Hodge and nothing at all of Andrea she was conscious of the empty apartments upstairs.

Cold grey weather continued, spiced with one or two watery glints of sunshine to remind Londoners that spring in its own sweet time would bloom in the parks again. As was her habit, Holly threw herself into work. She was surprisingly energetic, though the baby within her body was making itself felt. When she stood before the mirror in her bedroom, she remarked the thickening about her waist and the portly protrusion at her midriff. She could no longer risk wearing tight skirts and planed blouses. With each passing day she become more conscious of the pressure of time upon her. Still she vacillated, pretending that she would make good her boast to Emma Chubb, would search out a husband, once the next sale had been and gone, the goods purchased, washed, priced – and sold. The latest Aspinall catalogue was well forward. She was selling regularly from the client-book, stirring the profit, as Tal put it, back into the shop like a big pot of *borsch*.

But it was David who filled her thoughts. From Mrs Hodge – who had wheedled it out of Andrea – Holly learned that Linsey Aspinall had been transferred from the Howewood to St. Agnes Hospital in Marylebone, were two famous surgeons had operated upon her. The prognosis was not encouraging. It was unlikely that she would regain the use of her legs. As if that wasn't bad enough, Mrs. Hodge had got the impression that there was "something wrong wiff the pore girl's 'ead." It seemed that David's wife would not only be a bed-ridden cripple for the rest of her life but would always be mentally handicapped. It would have been better, Mrs. Hodge hinted, for her to have died. She would be no better than a cabbage, until the day she passed on. If Holly had encountered Andrea she would have asked her point blank for information. But the woman was seldom in Cardwell Place these days.

News concerning Thora was more encouraging. She was in a nursing home near Brighton, suffering from nervous debility. The "change of air", however, had been beneficial and she seemed to be recovering quite nicely. David's "secret" ownership of the shop had, of course, been revealed.

One diversion – though that was hardly an appropriate word – came in the unexpected form of Christopher Deems. He indicated his willingness to establish and maintain some sort of relationship with Holly. They lunched together three or four times. He listened with interest to her conversations about the antique trade, and the importance of the latest catalogue.

"Why is this one so important?" he asked.

"It just is."

"Are you planning an expansion?"

Holly smiled at the irony. She shook her head. "I want to take some time off in the autumn. I'd like to have the shop well stocked an' the annual turnover bumped up before I do."

"Going on holiday?" asked Deems.

"Yes."

"Abroad?"

"I'm not sure, yet."

"Are you going alone?"

"You're very inquisitive, Christopher," said Holly. "When I ask things about you, you hedge."

"Do I? I'm not the only one; you're hedging now."

"I've been workin' too hard. I'm takin' myself out of London for a month."

"In the autumn?"

"Before the summer's out."

"The season will still be in full swing."

"My grandfather will look after things in Cardwell Place."

"He seems a very competent fellow," said Deems.

"He'd be flattered to hear you say so, Christopher. He admires your poetry greatly."

Deems' eyes become veiled.

Holly said, "You don't have to listen to me for the next minute or two, because I'm going t' talk to you about your writings."

"Please don't."

"Why are you so shy about them?"

"The poems are no longer a part of me."

"I think they are."

"What do you know about such things. You're . . . "

"I'm what? A common shop girl?"

"I didn't mean that. If it's any consolation, I find all talk of literature, my own writings in particular, extremely boring."

"Why?"

"Please, Holly, change the subject."

She had depressed him. He stopped eating and angled his chair away from her to look out over the half screen at the street, studying buses, motorcars and horse carts, as if to record them indelibly in his memory.

"I'll change the subject in a minute, Christopher."

"God, you're stubborn."

"Victor sent me your books, your poems."

"Oh, he would!"

"I agree with him."

"On what particular topic?"

"You are a fine poet."

"How many poets have you read?"

"Not many, that's true."

"In that case, you have no standard of comparison, Tell me more about your catalogue."

"Did you always write about war?"

"I . . . " Deems clenched his fists.

"In your very first book, through that poem, "Beowulf's Last Speech," I could see right into you, Christopher. Is that not good poetry?"

"It depends what you find in there. In my case – nothing. Just silly lies, Holly. Illusions."

"What's wrong with illusions?"

"Illusions are for innocent children, not grown men."

"I have illusions, Christopher."

"Yes, I know."

"Do you think I'm a child?"

"I can't . . . I won't talk about it, Holly."

"Another poem – "The Stars Throw Down Their Spears" – how old were you when you wrote that?"

"Twenty-one or two. It's also a child's poem."

"It doesn't read like it."

"I must get back to the shop. I'm not like you, I have to close up when I take French leave. Business is lost."

"I would have been proud to have written that poem."

"I was proud once. But I deceived myself, fostering an illusion that now seems quite hideous."

"About the glory of war?"

"Glory. War isn't . . . mankind isn't . . . " He got to this feet, dropping his table napkin and spoon and, in agitation, spilling coffee from the cups. "I must go back."

"Wait, Christopher," said Holly. "Please, sit down an' finish your lunch. I'll pour you more coffee."

His distress was not feigned. She had touched him, had gained reaction. The fact that he seated himself again and allowed her to replenish his cup was a small victory for her.

"Why do you come round to the shop, Christopher? Is it because you think I'm too stupid to talk about poetry or to ask you about the war?"

"Holly, I'm *trying,* trying so hard to like you."

"Why?"

"You and Victor are the only real friends I have."

"Did Victor suggest you see me, meet me?"

"I wanted to see you again."

"Christopher, what is it about me that makes you afraid?"

"I'm not afraid, not of you. I am of myself. Me."

"Isn't that selfish?"

"I've learned to be selfish."

"I don't think you're selfish."

"Christopher Deems – bachelor. Christopher Deems – bookseller. That's the whole story."

"Holly Beckman – business woman. Holly Beckman – antique dealer. Holly Beckman – unmarried girl. *Not* the whole story. I wish to God it was."

"You have your grandfather, your brothers."

"You have your mother," said Holly, "an' Victor – an' me.".

"There are others, Holly, others you know nothing about."

"Friends."

"Companions." Christopher glanced at his wristwatch. "Now, this time, really! I must get back to the shop. The ladies drop in on their way to tea. I like to be there. It wouldn't do to show them a closed door."

"Right," said Holly.

They stood on the pavement outside Miss Sinclair's. An abrasive wind hurtled up from the river.

"Will you walk back?" Holly asked.

"It only takes a quarter of an hour. My allocation of fresh air."

"Don't catch a chill."

"Unfortunately I never catch anything."

"May I call round at the shop some afternoon?"

"Please do," said Christopher.

"Are you bein' polite or do you mean it?"

"I mean it, Holly. Come any afternoon, or evening. I'm usually there."

"Thank you for lunch, Christopher."

"Thank you for putting up with my tantrums."

"Christopher?"

"Yes."

"I won't ask you about poetry again."

A brewer's cart lurched noisily past, trailed by three impatient motorists, all pumping their horns. Christopher's overcoat collar was turned up. The wind made his eyes water a little.

Raising his voice above the hubbub of traffic, he told her, "There's nothing behind the mask, Holly. You must understand that. Nothing behind the mask."

She was startled by his assumption that she needed a warning, that their relationship had advanced that far. He touched his hat courteously, as if he had just bid her an amicable goodbye.

"We'll see, Christopher," Holly said as, with a wave, he walked off towards Victoria. "There may be more than you think."

* * *

Howard Leigh-Jennings had a large equine face ravaged by inner tensions. He was tall and had acquired a dowager's hump that thrust his face forward in a challenging manner. From the very moment that they met, David was afraid of him. He regretted the impulse that had driven him to seek an interview with his father-in-law in the office in a granite block off Regent Terrace.

Leigh-Jennings wore a dark blue suit over a striped flannel shirt, coarse enough to have fitted a convict. In contrast to the shirt his collar was a narrow white band, the tie a black shoelace with a knot no larger than a peanut. The backs of Leigh-Jennings' hands were downed with hair and, though it was morning, dark shadow had already begun to creep across his jowls.

A pert little secretary with frizzy hair showed David through two anterooms packed with mahogany filing cases into Mr. Leigh-Jennings' sanctum. David had no notion of the nature of Leigh-Jennings' business, except that it concerned shipping. The office gave nothing away, being neither pompous nor comfortable, only a place where work was done. On a heavy Victorian desk wire trays and spring-clip folders were strewn. There was much evidence of rollers and stamps, tobacco jars bristling with pens and pencils. Light from tall windows overlooking the Terrace fell obliquely on the desk, embellished by four pools of yellow from commercial lamps propped among the paper.

Leigh-Jennings did not rise to greet his son-in-law. He sat dourly in his leather chair, lifted a briar pipe from an ashtray, struck a match and lit the plug of tobacco. With a sudden, habitual motion he knocked his spectacles from his nose and let them hang from his neck on a brown cord.

Nervously David seated himself on the room's one vacant chair, directly before the desk. He was looking into the light, could see the shape of the man but no detail.

"What do you want?" Leigh-Jennings rumbled.

"I . . . I'm Linsey's husband."

"I know who you are."

"Ah!"

"What do you want?" Leigh-Jennings repeated.

"I . . . I . . . have some very distressing news, sir."

"Is she dead?"

"What? No, no, Lin's not dead."

"Well – what?"

"She's in a private ward in Saint . . . "

"I know where she is."

"I take it then that you are aware of her serious condition, sir?"

"Yes."

David paused, awaiting expressions of sympathy or regret, a gesture of concern. Puffs of acrid smoke curled from the pipe bowl as Leigh-Jennings got it going and, settling in his chair, appeared to have nothing much on his mind except the flavour of his tobacco. David licked his dry lips. "I assume your source of information is accurate?"

"Yes."

"In that case you'll know all about the accident."

"I'm not interested in your sordid story."

"Ah!"

"You came for a reason, young man, what is it?"

"Your daughter – Linsey – she may be permanently crippled."

"Cerebral concussion, damage to the anterior lobe of the brain, is usually inoperable," said Leigh-Jennings.

"And her poor legs, too."

"Left knee-cap and right femur."

"If you don't mind my saying so, sir, you don't seem much upset."

"Why should I be upset?"

"She's your daughter."

"She *was* my daughter," said Leigh-Jennings.

"Do you mean you can actually . . . actually cut her right out of your thoughts, sever all feeling for your own flesh and blood?"

"I have done so."

"Then there's no point in my staying."

The man removed the pipe stem from his mouth. "Did you expect me to say 'I forgive her for all the hurt she's caused me'? Is that what you'd hoped? For myself, young man, I might be inclined to generosity. But I've seen how hurtful Linsey's behaviour has been to her mother. I'm afraid I cannot regard what's happened as any more than a reaping."

"She's young, she . . . "

"You seem to love her?"

"I do," David lied.

"Then look after her, what's left of her."

"I intend to."

"But you'll get no help from me, young man. Not one penny."

"Do you suppose that's why I came here today?"

"What other reason?"

David got to his feet. "Out of decency. Out of respect."

"Respect! Pshaw! What does that word mean these days?" Leigh-Jennings put the pipe in an ashtray and leaned his arms on the desk, staring up at his son-in-law. "She's your wife. You are her mate. You're two of a kind. If she requires expensive medical attention, constant nursing – and I have it on good authority that she will – then it's up to *you* to provide it."

"What if I abandon her?"

"There are public wards."

"*Public wards!*" David was horrified. "No wife of mine will be condemned to a public ward."

"See to it then that you don't fail her as she failed me," Leigh-Jennings said. "In my opinion it'll make no difference to Linsey where she is. She'll hardly be aware of her surroundings. However, if the idea of confining your wife in anything less than elegant surroundings fills you with dismay, young man, you have my permission to cosset her for the rest of her life."

"I have your permission, but not your help. Oh, that is kind of you, sir! Most generous and kind! Most bloody fatherly!"

"I will not pick up the pieces, Aspinall, not for your benefit. My . . . Linsey is beyond any aid I can give."

"I can see why she hates you."

Leigh-Jennings looked down at his hands. "She doesn't hate me – not now. She has no feelings now – not for me, not for you. She is safe from both of us."

"Won't you even visit her?"

"No."

"How . . . how . . . ?"

"Don't you see? Don't you see at all?"

"No, sir. I do not."

"Then we have no more to say to each other."

"So it would seem. Good day, sir."

"Goodbye, Mr. Aspinall."

David clattered angrily out of the granite block and into the Terrace, his mind racing desperately, his strapped ribs aching. He felt weak with temper at the man's unnatural behaviour, weaker still at the thought that he was saddled with the massive responsibility of maintaining Linsey for five years or ten, or twenty. She would require doctors, nurses, a place in a comfortable and well-equipped nursing home, all of which would cost money; not just a few hundred down, but week-after-week, month-after-month, for ever. And he would never be free of her. She had chained him to her, shackled him with pounds and shillings. As he hurried up the Terrace towards Holborn, David's eyes swam with tears of self-pity.

In the Victorian office, at the great littered desk, Howard Leigh Jennings wept too, for the daughter he had lost so many years ago.

*   *   *

"One thing's clear," said Andrea. "You can't stay here."

"Nothing wrong with the Waldorf," David replied.

"Better come home."

"Better?"

"It'll cost you virtually nothing to live at home; besides mother needs you."

"Mother's perfectly all right where she is."

"But it is costing a small fortune to keep her there."

"Don't I know it!"

"I haven't got it," said Andrea. "At least not enough of it."

"Marry Walshott then."

"Are you suggesting that I marry just to obtain . . . favours?"

"I've enough to do finding cash to cover Lin's medical expenses. Add a monthly fee for mother, and I'll be broke in three months," said David.

"In that case you must find a remunerative job."

"Really? Must I?"

"What will it take to teach you your lesson? Do you intend, still, to throw away good money in gambling?"

"Andrea, I didn't invite you to tea just to listen to a rant against my way of life. Believe it or not, I agree with you. I'm not saying I intend to do what you suggest – about finding a job, I mean – but I must cut down on expenses."

"*Are* you coming home, David?"

"There are certain problems."

"What problems? The accommodation is quite large enough for the three of us. Miles suggests, in fact, that we try to find a place in the country – a cottage or such like – for mother. He feels that she would be happier there, away from all the memories Pimlico holds. She's always liked the country."

"Get rid of her, Andrea; isn't that what you mean?"

"Talking to you, David, is like addressing a brick wall."

"Frankly, mother is the least of my concerns. It's true that she needs rest and a clean break from that dismal house.

"You *do* agree with me?"

"Finding money for a country cottage is beyond me at the moment."

"Sell the shop."

"Oh, God, not that again!"

"What alternative have we?"

"One moment you're suggesting I come home to live, next it's "Sell the shop" – that means the house, too, Andrea." David drank from the cup on the tray on the low table. He lit his third cigarette since Andrea had arrived in the Waldorf's tea lounge. "When, tell me, do you plan to marry Miles?"

"Soon."

"This year?"

"We haven't finally decided."

"If you wait until his old aunt pops off you could be fifty or sixty yourself."

"I am not marrying Miles simply to take on the burden of his mad auntie," said Andrea. "Don't side-step the issue, David. You're awfully good at it. But not this afternoon, please."

"The doctors inform me that in three weeks Linsey will be as recovered, shall we say, as she's ever liable to be. Once I've found a suitable, and not *too* expensive, nursing home for her, then I'll pack up and come home. Is that what you want to hear?"

"And *do* what?"

"Perhaps I'll go into the trade."

"Trade; what trade?"

"Antiques."

"You know precious little about them."

"Holly does. I can keep the books – and learn."

"Holly?" Andrea's eyes clouded. "Work with Holly Beckman?"

"Listen, Andrea, I have money. No assets to speak of except the shop and the house. But I do have money. The cost of keeping Linsey in a nursing home will be a considerable drain on my resources, but I can meet it, I'm sure, provided I live modestly – and if I start out with enough capital to establish myself properly."

"Mumbo-jumbo, mumbo-jumbo," said Andrea. "I've heard it all before."

"This time I mean it. There are things you don't know about."

"Debts?"

"Yes, debts."

"How much?"

"Not financial debts. Obligations; difficulties."

"Why don't you confide in Miles?"

"I'm quite capable of handling my own affairs."

"See what happens when you do?"

"What the deuce d'you mean, Andrea?"

"Poor Linsey – reduced to a cabbage."

"Surely you don't blame me for that?"

"You were driving the car, weren't you?"

"*You do blame me.*" David's hands began to tremble.

"If you hadn't been at that . . . that place – drinking, I suppose – and if you hadn't driven that sportscar . . . "

She was . . . Lin was . . . "

"Pull yourself together, David. It's time somebody made you face the truth. *It was your fault.* You must shoulder the blame like a man."

"Christ!"

"People are staring at us."

"All right, all right, all right! While we're in the business of dishing out home truths, let me put one to you – why haven't you married Walshott? Are you afraid he'll damage your delicate sensibilities? Yes, flush, look injured. I don't care. If you marry Miles – which is patently what he wants – then *I'll* look after mother, *and* Linsey, *and* the shop."

"So I'm the fly in the ointment, am I? I'm to be made the scapegoat for your foolishness, your *depravities.* We're not all *obsessed* with . . . with . . . with sex. Miles and I have the kind of relationship that a . . . a . . . a . . . *creature* like you cannot understand."

"I'll take care of my responsibilities – my poor wife, my mother, my father's business. But I will *not* take care of you, Andrea. I want no part of you, to be saddled with your nagging, petty ways for ever. I owe *you* nothing. Not one single solitary damned thing."

"It . . . it doesn't *suit* me to marry."

"Miles' old aunt is just an excuse."

"Don't start that again. I won't sit here and listen to you besmirch my love for Miles – and his love for me – with obscene remarks. I will *not* be your excuse."

"I don't need an excuse," David said. "I've a perfectly valid excuse lying in a bed in St. Agnes's Hospital."

"Is that all she is to you now – just another excuse?"

"At least I loved her. *Loved.* Had pleasure. I have that to remember. What, Andrea, do you have?"

"You'll find another woman, won't you?"

"Yes," David said. "Yes, yes. Is that what you want to hear?"

"Is sex that important to you?"

"No," David answered. "Love is."

* * *

"Well, I'm sorry, old sport, but you know how it is?" Lester Gosling said. "At a time like this I wouldn't for worlds bother you with such a trivial thing if I wasn't a tiny bit desparate. Easy come, easy go is all very well in theory but, boiled down, a thousand pounds – call it seven hundred – ain't somethin' one lets slide. It's the insurance company, you see. Kicking up stink about the Crouch, old son. Written off, 'fraid. Hardly worth towing in. Oh, yes, my markers cover a bit of it. But remember you traded me two back for the use of the machine. Everybody will vouch for that. And the rest don't cover the value of the Crouch – so the insurance company says. It wasn't a simple sort of loan, but you *are* responsible for the car. Quillam, I'm sure, would be prepared to swear to it in court. Not that it'll come to court. Let's call it six hundred, shall we? I think that's fair, don't you? At a time like this, it's boorish to prat on about chink. But you know how it is? If it's inconvenient, I'll take it in instalments. Prefer the lot, actually, being a bit short right now. Shall we say your cheque for five hundred and call it quits?"

* * *

The wheel glittered as it spun. David placed plaques neatly before him. He took out his cigarette case, extracted a tube and lit it. He watched the wheel turn, the ball drop, the rake jab out.

"'Ow is Madam?" Daniel asked.

"As well as can be expected, thanks."

"*Rien n'va plus.*"

David put one hundred pounds on number eleven.

The ball bedded in number nineteen.

David put one hundred pounds on number eleven.

The ball bedded in number four.

David put fifty pounds on red.

Black showed.

He was aware of a presence at his left elbow. He glanced up with intense flooding optimism. The woman was beautiful, lithe – not Linsey.

"*Monsieur Aspinall?*"

"Yes, Daniel. Red, if you please."

Black showed.

David took a second envelope, containing two hundred and fifty pounds, from his pocket. He thought of going back to the desk to change it into plaques and chips, but he was indifferent to formalities, plain lazy.

"Cash bet?" he asked

"*Oui, monsieur.* If you wish," the croupier said.

David put fifty pounds on number eleven.

He did not even have to look at the wheel to know that the ball would bed elsewhere.

* * *

A cap of white plaster covered her hair. She looked like a nun. Her eyes were open, pupils blue and innocent. A thoughtful nurse had used pencil on her brows, put a touch of lipstick on her mouth. The cage that kept the weight of the blankets from her legs was removed during visiting periods. She lay flat on her back with the blanket drawn up to her breasts, white sheets folded in perfect symmetry. Her arms were by her side on top of the scarlet blanket. Her nails had been clipped but not polished. All the functions of her body continued. Hair grew, nails grew, saliva flushed her mouth, digestive juices coped with a light diet and, weirdly, cells poisoned by alcohol and cocaine had revived from exhaustion and brought a bloom to her skin. Motionless, emotionless, Linsey had never looked more beautiful or more desirable.

Outside mad winds bowed the saplings and whirled the wraithes of last autumn's leaves over the high brick wall of the Mackenzie Nursing Home.

The curtains were of white net. A grid of chicken wire was fixed to the outside of the window, in case of accidents. The private room was furnished with blonde-wood furniture, like a nursery. It even had a big coloured picture of woodland creatures on the wall opposite the bed. There was a coal fire in the white fireplace, though the afternoon

was not cold and snowdrops and crocuses along the country road that
lead out from Leatherhead had popped up at last.

As David stood by the window, looking out, it occurred to him that
there was no healing value in the country setting. Fresh air would not
cure his wife. Natural beauty would not give her balm, bring her
more tranquillity than crushed brain tissue had done already. It
would have been more convenient to dump – to put – her into one of
the grim London establishments.

She had been here now for eight days.

He caught a train down from Waterloo every other afternoon.

He glanced at his watch.

There were fifty minutes left of the two-hour visiting period.

At least when he had called on his mother near Brighton, she had
been able to talk to him, to shed a few tears, squeeze out a few wan
smiles, touch his hand, kiss his cheek, pour him tea in the faintly
musty, chintz-draped lounge that overlooked the Downs and a band
of the sea.

He listened to his watch ticking.

He would come only once in the week, as from next Saturday.

Later, he might come only once a month.

There was no point in visiting.

If he had been lying there, how often would Linsey have visited
him? Once the drama was out of it, the novelty, she would have tired
quickly of loyalty. He tried not to be mean. There was nothing to be
gained by such speculation. No more was there anything to be gained
by standing here at this window, or sitting in that wooden chair, by
the side of a . . . a . . . She did not recognise him. She had no memory.
The pathways from her senses dribbled out in a cascade of bruised
and wasted tissue.

In time. In time. In time.

Hearty doctors repeated the phrase to keep him optimistic, to keep
him coming down. The sheer futility of it increased his boredom, and
boredom made him angry.

"Hasn't she been a good girl today, Mr. Aspinall. Ate all her nice
oxtail soup like a big girl. Ate her potatoes too. And didn't she enjoy
her semolina? Didn't she now? I'll just tuck her in, shall I? You know, I
think it does her good to have you here. They sense it, you know.
Would you like to wait and see how she eats her tea?"

"The trains – I'm afraid I can't."

"Sure, and we understand," the nurse would say to the thing in the
bed. "Don't we understand? Hubby's got lots of things to do up in
town. We understand."

He hated the nurse.

Hated her schoolgirl phrases and her constant cheerfulness.

He listened to his watch ticking.

Once a month would be enough.

Once a year.

"We understand. We understand. We understand."

Jerking round from the window, he glanced nervously at the closed door, then stepped to the bed. He leaned on it, his face above Linscy's, scowling down at her. He could see reflections of the square panes of the window on her eyes, the indistinct warped shadow that was himself.

"Linsey? Linsey?"

How sweet am I, head in the sky.

"It's David. David. Don't you know me? Your husband?"

Head in the sky, how sweet am I.

He touched her shoulders, ran his fingers down her arms, took her hands in his. It was like holding a pair of empty kidskin gloves. Warm. Slack.

"I've moved out of the Waldorf. If you want me, I'm staying in a small place in the Gloucester Road. Cumbria House. Welsh couple run it. It isn't too bad, really. Quite cheap, too. My room is clean, quiet. The breakfast's ample. I eat out. Linsey?"

How sweet.

"I went to Christabel's last night. The croupier asked after you. Didn't do so well. Dropped six hundred. Have to put a stop to that. Can you do anything for me, do you think? A piece of magic for me, tiger?"

Am I, head.

"Linsey, do you hear me?"

In the sky.

"Andrea wants me to go home. Mother's all right. She'll be back from Brighton in a fortnight. Back to Cardwell Place. She just needed a change of scene, to get away from London, from the shop. From bloody Andrea, I suppose. From me. From you. From all of us. Andrea wants me to go home. I might. What do you say? What do you say, Linsey?"

Head.

"Please. Tell me what I should do, Linsey, please? Squeeze my hand. Here. See. Squeeze. Like that. Squeeze it. Please?"

In the sky.

How sweet.

"Do you know, have you any idea, what it's costing to keep you here? Do you think, Andrea does, that I'm made of money? The gambling-thing, oh, that's hopeless, it's useless, always was. Fun, though, while it lasted. You were right to take what you could get. Why did you do it with Charlie Hallet, why did you, was it just for the damned moonbeam? If you hadn't . . . Linsey? Please? Linsey? Tell me."

Am I.

He ran out of words, There was no response at all. Not even a faint flick, a moistness of the eyes, a tremor of the tongue or a spasm of the fingers, however involuntary, gave him a lever for imagination.

Leaning, he kissed her on the brow, then, roughly, on the lips. He held the kiss, pressing hard, then more gently until he tenderly withdrew. Head cocked he stared quizically into her vacant eyes.

The princess still slept.

When the nurse bustled in half an hour later, Mrs. Aspinall was alone.

Hubby had gone back to town by an early train.

* * *

It was coincidence that Holly was immersed in Christopher Deems' first poetical collection when rapping sounded on the door of the flat in Wolfenden Street. Catalogues and dozens of books on antiques abounded in the flat now. She had picked up a couple of cheap bookcases to keep the hoard in order. It was to Christopher's poems that she turned, however, when the hour was late and she sat by the fire in her woolly dressing-gown. She had acquired works by other poets too, coaxed into a study of Deems' contemporaries. She kept this new interest to herself, storing away the little magazines that she purchased from the Poetry Bookshop just in case Grandpa Tal or Maury happened to drop by and see them – or worse, in case Christopher ever called unexpectedly.

Though other poems moved her, none had the effect of Christopher's compositions. She had almost memorised "San Souci" and "Young John Bull," so often had she mulled over their subtle rhythms. But that evening it was the simpler romantic cadences of the early love poem, "Lavender Castles," that filled her mind.

The pounding on the door frightened her.

She dropped the book to the table and got to her feet, drawing the dressing-gown tightly around her, one arm low across her stomach as if to protect the baby snuggled within her.

Perhaps she should pretend to be out. But the caller would surely have seen the light in the transom above the door. It flickered into her thoughts that it might be one of Ritchie's hoodlum cronies, might be Ritchie, escaped from Brixton, on the run, armed with a gun. She hugged herself tighter as the pounding continued.

She padded into the short corridor that served as a hall.

"Who is it?"

"Holly, Holly. It's me. It's David."

Nausea caught her, a response to shock.

"Please Holly, let me in for a moment."

"I'm . . . I've . . . got . . . I can't."

"Please. Only for a moment."

"Go away, David." She found Courage. "*Go away.*"

Fists beat upon the door, shaking the panels, making lock and chain rattle.

"*I must see you.*"

Sickness increased. She gagged, then it waned, leaving shiveriness in its wake.

"*I must talk to you, Holly.*"

"I'm not dressed."

"Put something on, then. Don't turn me away."

The pleading in his voice distressed her. She wrestled with commonsense and, losing the contest, opened the door of the flat.

For no good reason she had expected to be confronted by a dishevelled wreck. Not so. David was dressed in an expensive dinner suit and immaculately groomed.

"I had to talk to you, Holly. Had to talk to somebody."

"How are you?"

"What?"

"I heard you'd been hurt."

"Hurt? What, yes. I'm all right. My ribs are mending." He glanced round the living room. "I can hardly believe it's the same place. What a difference you've made to it. The woman's touch, hm?"

"Your wife, how is she?"

"Not so good, alas."

David stared at her. She pulled the collar of the gown across her breasts, self-consciously aware of her thickening waist. She did not even consider the fact that he had caught her without make-up, with her hair uncombed.

"May I sit down for a bit?" he asked.

There was no mark of suffering on him. It was as if the supplicant at the closed door and the man she'd admitted were two different people. He appeared to be as suave and self-possessed as ever, perhaps even more so. She responded with a nod at one of the chairs by the hearth. She did not seat herself. She was suddenly conscious of the poetry book bridged on the arm of the chair. It had a mauve cover and a paper title label. *Poems by Christopher Deems*. She was inclined to remove it, but hesitated, not wishing to draw David's attention to it. He paid it no heed, however, watching her almost furtively as she moved away from the hearth, saying, "Would you like tea? Coffee, perhaps?"

"Nothing, Holly. Just your company for half an hour."

"It's late, David. I don't want you to stay."

"Stay? Oh, no. No." He said it as if the thought hadn't entered his mind. "That's not why I came, tiger."

"Why did you come, David? There's nothing between us. There can never be anything between us, ever again."

"Because of my wife, do you mean?"

"Because you cheated me," said Holly, coldly.

"Can we not still be friends?"

"Don't be so stupid," Holly snapped. "You've only been married three months. Your wife – I'm sorry about what happened to her, but she's still your wife. Always will be, I suppose, unless you plan to abandon her the way you abandoned me."

"Come on, old tiger! It wasn't that serious."

"Not to you, perhaps. But to me . . . " Holly cut off her angry tirade. "No, David, you're right. It wasn't *that* serious. I should thank you."

"Thank me?"

"For givin' me confidence."

"Confidence?"

"Never mind. Tell me how is Mrs. Aspinall, your mother?"

"Mother's well enough. She'll be home in a week or so," he said, adding, "but Linsey will never be well again."

"I'm sorry to hear it."

"I can't believe you mean it."

Holly shrugged. "I wouldn't wish harm on anyone."

"Not even me?"

"David, why did you come here?"

"To see you again."

"I told you – there's nothin' between us."

"The shop . . . ?"

"The shop," said Holly, "is bein' well taken care of. You get your share of the profit. Are you satisfied?"

"I'm considerin' taking a more active part in running the business."

"Is that your sister's idea?"

"Andrea still wants me to sell. She has very positive plans for my future but they don't include keepin' shop."

"Sell if you wish."

Her reply startled him. "I thought Aspinall's was the most important thing in your life, Holly?"

"A shop's a shop. I've other things to think about."

"How would you live, if I sold? King – you'd go to Kennedy King, wouldn't you? I suppose he's made you an offer."

"I've a more important thing to occupy me than antiques." Holly sensed that she had fallen into vindictiveness. Under the circumstances nobody would deny her right to take revenge upon him. "But, since you're the owner, let me make it clear that the business is on a solid footing. My grandfather will be able to keep it tickin' over during August an' September. After that, I'll be back in charge."

"What . . . what the hell . . . ?"

"I'm taking a couple of months off – to have a baby."

David reared back as if she had struck him. Drained of blood, his face, turned the colour of whey. His lips gaped in disbelief. "Your baby?"

"Half of August an'all of September," said Holly. "The stock's well up. We've a new catalogue in the pipeline, so . . . "

Reaching for her, he rose. She did not flinch away but held him back with both hands. The dressing-gown swayed open. He blinked, gaze drawn to the plump swelling curve of her body.

"*Why didn't you tell me*'" he cried

"Why should I? It's none of your business."

"My child – none of my . . . ?"

"It isn't your child."

"You *bitch!* You're *lying*."

"You're not the father."

"I was the first man you ever had."

"Yes, David, but not the last."

"*You sly bitch*," he cried. "It *is* my child."

"What did you expect me to do? Lock myself up, just because you threw me over? You were kind enough to give me this flat. I was glad of it, believe me,"

"Who is he? Who the devil *is* he?"

"No one you know," said Holly.

"Why hasn't he married you? Is he married already?"

"No," said Holly. "Perhaps we will marry. Perhaps we won't."

"But you're expecting a child?"

"You, of all people, shouldn't be shocked. I don't really see what difference it makes to anythin' – especially to you. If you don't think I'm fit to look after the shop then you're at liberty . . . "

"Damn the shop. Who is the man?" David shouted.

"I met him before you . . . before we. At a sale. I met him at a sale. He was a friend when I needed a friend. It seemed natural we should. . ."

"It's that swine King, isn't it? Isn't is Kennedy King. *You sold yourself to King.*"

"Is that all you think of me?"

"You gave yourself to *me* without much hesitation."

"You shouldn't have said that."

"Andrea was right – you're a trollop, a cheap, dirty little trollop. God, why did I ever think we might . . . "

"I loved you, David."

"You didn't. Don't lie. You let me have you just for what you could get out of me. If you'd loved me you wouldn't have thrown yourself under this other fellow."

"He's been a friend for a long time. He's a friend now. He won't let me down, whatever happens. He won't cheat me, David."

"I should have listened to Andrea. She was right all along." He paused, scowling. "You're fibbing, Holly. It *is* my baby."

"No, David."

"Then tell me the father's name."

"No."

He grabbed her, crushing her against him, all his despair, his hopeless confusion exploding. He caught fistfuls of her hair, dragging her head back. "*Who is he? Who is he? You're mine, Holly. You've always been mine. You always will be. I've nobody else now. Nobody. I thought you loved me. You told me you loved me. I was counting on you.*"

Holly did not fight him. She let him cling to her, abuse her, shake her like a rag doll as all the pent-up guilt and the frustrations of loss ripped through him.

"*I would have come back to you, don't you know that? Linsey was nothing to me. And now she's as good as dead; in a year, in just a year, I would have. Why didn't you wait? Why did you have to? I don't believe you, you bitch. I don't believe there's anyone but me.*"

"You're wrong, David."

Holding her, brow against her hair, he moaned, "Nothing, nothing left."

"You'd better go."

"Where? Go where?"

"I don't know," Holly said. "One of your hotels. Home to Cardwell Place. I don't care. But get out of here, will you? I can't give you what you're lookin' for."

"Holly, I don't care about the child. I mean it. Let me, let's begin again. Forget this man."

"*Get out. Get out.*"

She pushed him violently from her. He stumbled on the small table, sending a cocoa mug and a pile of poetry books to the rug. Braced on his elbows, lolling half on the chair, he said, "My God, there *is* another man, and you *do* love him'"

"Yes," said Holly. "Yes. Now, please, get out."

The door slammed behind him. The *Poems of Christopher Deems* slipped slowly from the chair and fell into the soggy cocoa stain on the rug. Quickly Holly plucked up the book, dabbing the pages against her dressing-gown to absorb the milky brown moisture. She held the book against her breast, weeping at the lies that David had forced her into, at the loss of her last illusions.

"Lavender Castles" toppled soundlessly in the brisk spring night. They would never be built again upon the same foundation.

Tomorrow she would call on Christopher.

He was her last hope.

4

The Bargain

THE BOOKSHOP IN Shepherd Market was a suitable setting for the proposal. It was Christopher's retreat. If he was comfortable anywhere, it was in the tiny back room of his shop. Holly was surprised at how small the establishment was. No soaring walls of calf-bound volumes here: one could reach top shelves by standing on tiptoe. Library ladders were merely to assist elderly and undersized customers and to provide impromptu seating for browsers. A table set with wrapping paper, string in a painted tin, scissors and an invoice tablet, was tucked into a corner. From behind this table Christopher sold his wares.

But it was the books, not the customers, that gave the shop its character. Fat books, thin books, books in cloth, books in buckram, some in leather, were built into every nook and cranny, spines all neatly outward. Card labels printed bold-faced in Indian ink gave rapid references – Biography: History, Elizabethan: History, Victorian: French: Sporting: Classics: Travel, by country: Art, by subject. There were rows of novels to entertain the ladies of Mayfair and Park Lane, housekeepers, aged aunts, grandmothers to the flimsy generation, spinsters living in the lovely past.

Close by the door a penny stall promised bargains. The shoebox window was draped with brown baize and housed a handsome set of Ouida's works bound in half blue morocco, Surtees in scarlet, Charles Lever in turf green, two picture books of London tabbed open to the best plates, three volumes on old theatre and a tiger-striped monster of a book on hunting in India. A tall display held random titles designed to appeal to passers-by. Already, Holly felt, the shop had a settled air, a slow-breathing quality, sleepy but mannerly, like a butler in late evening. From such a place a man of modest habits might skim off a modest living with a modest outlay of energy.

Christopher was in the back room. Here was a wicker chair, much battered, a kneehole desk, filing boxes, and umpteen columns of books waiting to be priced and allocated, more bundles marked with labels ready for invoicing, wrapping and dispatch. Christopher wore a chunky cardigan with suede patches on the elbows, and a pair of grey trousers. He was printing labels with a fountain pen, checking off letters of order and postcards of requests that small advertisements had brought his way. He seemed pleased to see Holly. He wiped the pen-nib, capped it and stuck the pen in his cardigan pocket.

Outside in the shop were two browsers, both women.

"What do you think of it, Holly?" Christopher asked. There was little or no eagerness in his tone, no pride.

"Smaller than I imagined. What's your store space like?"

"What you see here."

"Is that enough?"

"It's enough for me. I don't intend to expand."

"What was the shop before?"

"Would you believe that it belonged to a man who made high-button boots."

"A shoemaker'" said Holly. "What happened to him?"

"Oh, he was very old and childless; he died just before the war. The shop's lain empty ever since. I have it on a year-by-year lease."

"In case you want to give up?"

Christopher did not answer the question. He offered her tea. She said that she did not want tea.

It was four o'clock exactly. The light in the street was grey with the threat of rain but strong with the imminent onset of spring. One of the ladies in the shop cleared her throat to attract Christopher's attention. He went out through the doorless opening to serve her. Holly waited, watching him, her nervousness mounting.

So far she had no foundation for her assumption that Christopher would not laugh her to scorn or fly into a temper at the sheer outrageousness of her proposal. It was – now she thought of it – hardly a proposal at all. It was not even a fair exchange. What had she to offer in return for marriage? Why should he be interested in her? The uniqueness of the situation, however, could not be totalled in ordinary emotional coinage. Victor Lawfeld's warnings, and his obvious matchmaking intentions, kept hope alive in her – the threat as much as the promise. There was the spice of danger in what she was about to do, more danger than in her brief love affair with David.

Holly watched Christopher bow to the old lady and open the shop door for her. She went out carrying a wrapped volume. Christopher returned. He removed a deep drawer from the desk and dropped a florin into a wooden bowl hidden beneath the drawer. All in all, Holly noticed there could not have been more than a pound in silver in the bowl.

"You won't get rich from passin' trade, Christopher."

"I don't want to get rich, Holly."

"I see. It's a labour of love?"

"A gesture of survival," he said, lightly. "What about you – do you want to get rich?"

"I did."

"You no longer have that ambition?"

"I certainly don't want to be poor again."

"I wonder if James Aspinall did you a service, or if he would have been wiser to have left well alone."

"I'd have been workin' in a factory by this time."

"Not you, Holly. You have too much sense of where you're going."

"Where am I going?"

"Bond Street." Christopher made it clear that he was teasing.

"That's only a label for other things," Holly said.

"Security, is that what you're after?"

"Probably."

"Security's a luxury," Christopher said. "Purpose is all."

She blinked, then fixed her gaze on the fountain pen clipped in the breast pocket of his heavy cableknit cardigan. The garment made Christopher appear less like a wraithe. It gave him a dependable ordinariness that Holly, at that instant, feared.

"My purpose, Christopher, is to find a father for the baby I'm carryin'." Cheeks pink, Holly did not dare glance up.

Christopher's silence was not one of horror, not even of shock. He was smiling. His eyes had taken on a light of enthusiasm that she had detected there only once or twice before.

"Does Victor Lawfeld know of this?" Christopher asked.

"No, of course he doesn't." Holly was startled. "Why should he know? I haven't gone about tellin' everybody."

"When's the baby due."

"In August, late August."

Deems nodded, smiling. It was as if he had found a new irony, a pleasantly sardonic revelation, in Holly's declaration.

"I'm glad you find it funny," she snapped, totally put out by his reaction and his question about Lawfeld.

Did he think that Victor Lawfeld and she had had an affair? No, that was obviously nonsense. Why did he bring up Lawfeld's name? Why, too, was he smiling? In challenging him, she veiled her own motives still more.

Christopher stuck his fists into the pockets of the cardigan. The smile still flickered. He seemed – he *was* – glad for her.

"Pregnant!" he said. "Pregnant!"

Holly curbed another outburst.

Christopher asked, "Almost, what, four months?"

"Yes."

"Five to carry. It's not long, Holly, not long at all. How do you feel?"

"As right as rain."

"That's good." He laughed, rubbing his forefinger across his nose. "You, of all people."

"I need somebody to marry me," Holly said. "I'm not interested in the baby's father. I don't particularly want to talk about him, unless you really want to know. But I'm determined, really determined that this little mite isn't goin' to be deprived of anythin' just because it's mother happened to be a fool."

Christopher said, "A name – is that all you require?"

"I can look after the bread and butter."

Christopher was caught up in her now. "Of course. You'll organise the shop so that you can take a couple of months off – who'll look after things? Your grandfather? Then you'll be back in harness.

There are worse places than antiques shops to bring up an infant."

"The baby won't suffer," said Holly.

"Of course it won't – on the contrary," said Christopher.

"Now do you see?"

"It's not a mate you require, Holly, only a husband?"

"I'd keep my side of the bargain."

"Bargain?"

"I'd be a wife to the man in every respect."

"Are we talking personally?"

"Do you think I'm calculatin'?"

"I do."

"Cold-blooded?"

"No, not cold-blooded, Holly; not that."

"If I asked *you*, say, would *you* think it was a bargain?"

"I'm not the same as other men," said Christopher. "In my case, yes, it would be a bargain, a very great bargain. But I would be getting the best of it."

"Why?"

"Is it *my* name you want, Holly? Is that it?" Christopher asked. "Would you accept me?"

"I would."

"I'm flattered."

"Flattered?" said Holly. "Christopher, I'm carryin' another man's baby. I'm no catch at all. Even without that, I wouldn't be much to write home about."

"I don't care who fathered the child," Christopher said. "But don't sell yourself short, Holly Beckman. You have one great prize, a dowry gift, if you like – you still believe life has meaning. There's no emptiness in you, in head or heart."

"Christopher, would you do it? Marry me? If it didn't suit, then you could go off, separate, divorce me. I'd never try to hold you against your will."

"I wish you *could* hold me, Holly," Christopher said. "I must tell you this, make it clear to you. I don't think even you can hold me. I want you to remember that. Now do you still want the use of my name?"

"Yes," Holly said.

Christopher took his hands from his pockets and turned them palms uppermost and looked down at them, fingers spread.

They were trembling.

At long last. Human essences flowed sluggishly in him again. He felt stirrings of will, the strength that she, without knowledge, had imparted. When the will grew vigorous and strength increased, he would complete the journey that he had interrupted in the salient north of Bullecourt.

Holly Beckman would give him something to leave behind.

One man's marker on the road to the redoubt.

"Christopher, do you mean it? Will you really marry me?"

"Yes," the captain said. "But we'd better make it soon."

* * *

Leo Beckman was tugged reluctantly from the company of his bosom pals and led off by the old Russian to seek a modicum of peace and quiet in the snug of the Admiral's Hat. The fact that Tal Kirsanoff was not only friendly in his attitude but offered to buy a pint worried Leo. He could smell bad news a mile off and his father-in-law's unusual behaviour reeked of it.

The snug was fairly private. Ethel Sykes was there with old Ma Jem, warming up cold gossip over port and lemon; and Jock Caldwell, who, being a Scot, thought himself a cut above the Lambeth scruff. Jock was knocking back Old Mull in a favourite corner by the fire.

Daylight had faded but there was enough of a moon to bathe the street and backlight the ornate stained glass of the snug window so that faint rainbow patches lay like puddles on the marble table.

Tal settled into the corner with a sigh. He had not yet shed his moulding sheepskin coat and he looked huge, stuffed into the padded bench. He offered Leo a cheroot which Leo refused, preferring instead a Woodbine from his own crumpled five-packet. Tal struck a match and held the flame out for his son-in-law. He was too bleedin' smug, the old Jew. Beer backed up in Leo's throat. He belched rudely, catching the wilting fag between his teeth. Tal puffed out cheroot smoke. It was an expensive roll, glossy leaf, must have cost all of a shilling. Next time he had the chance, Leo promised himself, he would have a prowl round the old geezer's room, see if he could half-inch one or two of the smokes to save for Ritchie's return and the whopping big booze-up he would throw that night. He pined for Ritchie. He ascribed to his missing son all sorts of filial virtues that memory should have watered down. Maury? Hardly ever saw him these days. When they did happen to run into each other in the house, Maury only grunted in response to Leo's attempts at conversation.

"How yer doin' then, son?"

Grunt.

"Makin' yer pile, are yer, son?"

Grunt.

"Gotta coupler bob for yer old ..."

Grunt, grunt.

Wherever Maurice's big body was, his mind was elsewhere. Even Leo sensed the impenetrability of his eldest's thoughts which, he reckoned, lay behind brick walls and shop frontages or buried in pyramids of sand and plaster.

Now and again, when loneliness gnawed at laziness, Leo would pen a letter to Brixton Jail and bare his soul to Ritchie.

Ritchie seldom bothered to reply, and then only on a prison postcard in chopped sentiments in which even Leo recognised a tinge of sarcasm: "Dear Father, I am well and I am eating well and changing my socks regular. Have a pint for me at the Hat. Hope this finds you as it leaves me, Ritchie." The very colour of the postcard was the colour of confinement, a grainy grey-brown. Leo left visiting to Tal. The trail to Brixton was not for him.

And there was her, Holly. She had never once come home to see him. Not one bleedin' time, not even at Xmas, like you'd expect. Her name never crossed his lips. He did not enquire after her from Kirsanoff, or ask about the shop. In fact, he had put Holly far out of his thoughts, there being nothing to be gained in that connection.

"Raise your glass, Leo," Kirsanoff commanded. "Join me in a happy toast."

"What's this then; what's all this?"

"To your daughter, my granddaughter."

"What's the 'ell's she been ..."

"Wedding bells."

Beer backed up again on Leo. He belched and swallowed but, this time, the acid sensation did not ease but wriggled down his gullet into the pit of his stomach. He betrayed no surprise at Kirsanoff's news, though he *was* surprised. A faint selfish sense of loss, an unexpected emotion, plagued him.

"Knocked up, is she?"

"I thought you might want to gift her something."

"Eh?"

"A wedding gift. Fathers usually give their daughters wedding gifts," Kirsanoff said.

"Ain't got no money for that sorta bilge."

"At least drink to her health and happiness, Leo. That won't cost you anything."

Leo dipped his face to his glass and supped without lifting.

"I knew you would be pleased for her," said Kirsanoff.

"He a nob?"

"Beg pardon?"

"The bloke; well-orf?"

"Very well-off," Kirsanoff said. "Shall I tell you about him?"

"Don't care, one way or t'other."

"I'll tell you, anyhow. You don't have to listen, of course. But I'll tell you," said Kirsanoff. "His name is Christopher Deems. He owns a shop."

"Might've bleedin' known!"

"He was a captain in the war. Fought very bravely."

"Yer, millions did."

"He's an Oxford man."

"Londoner's not good enough for 'er."

"And he's a famous poet."

"Gawd!"

"The wedding will be in two weeks time; a quiet affair."

"Cheap," said Leo. "Them rich geezers is allers cheap."

"Close friends only. Holly asked me to ask you to come."

"Where?"

"The Hildebrand Hotel, in Galt Street, off the Strand."

"Hilabran' Hotel? Gawd!"

"Holly would like you to be there, Leo."

Curiosity nagged him, mingled with shame and an overwhelming dread that he would look like what he was in posh company. Confused, his stomach paining him, he gulped down beer and pushed the mug at the old man. "I'll 'ave another."

Kirsanoff signalled to the barmaid who was keeping an eye on the Snug. She brought a fresh-pulled pint for Leo. He did not say any more until Leo had scooped up half the liquid in the glass.

Leo was fighting a war with himself. If he went to the wedding he'd need to get togged up. He hated getting togged up. Free feed, free booze, though. Would have to buy her a present. Only right. Bride's father. Gawd strewth, make a speech! Meet the 'groom, though. New son-in-law might be generous, good for a backhander now and again.

No. It wouldn't change anything. The bridegroom was posh, and posh meant thrifty. How the 'ell had she managed it? He glanced furtively at Kirsanoff who was watching him with a mild expression that Leo misinterpreted as patronising.

"What day?" he growled.

"It will be Wednesday, afternoon."

"Tell 'er I won't be there. Can't take the time orf. Nobody pays me when I'm orf."

"Your daughter's wedding, Leo?"

"Yer. Well, she went 'er own way. Couldn't even come see me, like. Couldn't come tell me 'erself." He swallowed the rest of the pint and pushed himself to his feet. "She can get spliced without my 'elp."

"That is what I told her," Kirsanoff said. "But she insisted that you be asked."

"Ain't goin' t'be there." Leo belched once more. "An' that's flat."

"Very well," Kirsanoff said. "I'll inform Holly that you feel you would rather not come but that you send her your very best wishes."

Leo did not answer. He pushed his way from the snug and returned to his cronies at the public bar. Within minutes, however, he was bending their ears with the news that his daughter – you remember our Hol – was engaged to a war hero who ran a chain of stores all across Oxfordshire.

"Allers 'ad it in 'er," Leo bragged. "Well, I wish 'er luck."

"Be all dickied up for the weddin', Leo."

With rueful forbearance, Leo grinned. "Never got asked. Don't mind. Not my place t' spoil 'er life. No matter what she done ter me, I wish 'er all the luck in the world."

"Yer too good by 'alf, Leo."

"Yer," Leo said, accepting the free pint that was passed his way. "It's me forgivin' nature, that's what it is."

*   *   *

At first sight the Crabtree Club did not strike Holly as a place in which Christopher would choose to celebrate. Reached by a narrow back staircase in an old building in Greek Street, Soho, it offered open house to anyone interested in the arts. The steering committee was so wary of the charge of being upper-class, however, that any patron who put in an appearance wearing evening dress was fined the sum of one shilling. Holly's fears that the evening would be stuffy vanished as soon as she entered the brightly-lit room and saw couples dancing the fox-trot to the music of a small but enthusiastic band.

"It's a fairly unique establishment," Christopher explained as they threaded their way to a table.

"I recognise so many famous faces."

Christopher held out a chair for her. "That's Compton Mackenzie, the writer. Over there – Randall Cecil, son of Lord Willum. Do you know the lady he's dancing with?"

"It's Evelyn Laye. I've seen her picture in magazines. Oh, my goodness!"

"In the corner; rather shy?"

"Leslie Howard," said Holly.

"Those who wish to dance are perfectly at liberty to do so, provided they behave themselves. But its conversation that draws most of the artists and writers. They meet, quite informally, at those two large tables in the back alcove. When I was . . . before the war, I used to love visiting the Crabtree when I was in town. The continuity of history, and all that. Swinburne sat there. Browning was a member. Oscar Wilde, before the pack caught up with him. Tennyson." He looked up at the doorway. "And talking of famous men – here's Victor."

Lawfeld wore a yellow silk cravat printed with red kidney beans as a concession to Bohemianism. He did not appear at home here, though, as he came to Christopher's table, he exchanged greetings with several of the habitués and even paused for a word with an elderly and very distinguished-looking gentleman who, Christopher explained, was the current literary editor of *The Times*. Lawfeld greeted Christopher warmly, and, after asking permission, kissed Holly on the cheek.

"Supper – what would you like?" Christopher asked.

"Something light. An omelette."

While the snack was being prepared, Christopher chatted with Victor about Oxford, gently putting down Victor's attempts to be effusive about the unexpected engagement and the coming marriage.

It was Holly who sided with Victor, ganged up, as it were, on Christopher and brought the subject into the open.

"You will be my best man, Victor, won't you?" Christopher asked. "After all, you are in part way responsible."

"I'd be delighted," Victor said.

Holly said, "I wish I'd a friend like you, Victor. As it is I'll have to make do with an acquaintance."

"The best maid?" Victor said.

"Yes. Emma Chubb."

Christopher glanced quickly at Holly. "In that case, my Uncle Kennedy had better receive an invitation."

"You don't mind, do you?" said Holly.

"It'll keep mother happy. She's always been quite fond of the old charlatan."

"Why do you call him that?" asked Victor.

"He's a self-centred rogue," said Christopher. "I never did trust him."

"He enjoys life," said Holly.

"Do you like him?" asked Christopher.

Holly did not know how to answer. "He's been kind to me, Christopher."

"I suspect he wanted you," said Christopher.

"Wanted . . .?"

"To be his mistress."

Victor cleared his throat. "Don't much care for the turn of phrase, old chap."

"Christopher's right," said Holly. "Not that Mr. King ever behaved badly, but it was, well, 'suggested' that I might do myself a good turn by . . . ."

"You, ah, didn't . . . I mean, ah, weren't inclined . . ." said Victor.

"No." Holly did not resent the question. It was difficult to be offended by Victor's interest in her. He was, she felt, now protecting not only his friend Christopher but had assumed, already, some measure of responsibility for her, as Christopher's bride-to-be. Even so she was astonished when, without preliminary, Christopher suddenly announced, "Holly's expecting a child, Victor. Hence the reason for our abrupt decision to marry."

Lawfeld flushed. "But . . . but I didn't realise . . . you'd known each other so . . . so well."

Holly kept still, saying nothing. Totally unprepared, she was uncertain as to whether Christopher wished to absolve himself from the stigma of having seduced her, or to claim intimacy far beyond his right. Why did he drag the secret into the open – to damn her, or to damn himself?

"My child, of course," said Christopher.

Still at a loss, Lawfeld stammered, "Con . . . congratulations".

"You see, Victor, you don't have to fret about my mental health. I've found my own salvation."

"Well, all sorts of felicitations are in order," said Victor. There was a tinge of sorrow in his tone; perhaps he had become adjusted to thinking of himself as guardian over the wounded poet and could not rapidly divorce the power of that role from thankfulness that Christopher was capable of ruling his own destiny.

"I . . . I'd no notion of what was in the wind. Still it's marvellous. How do you feel, Holly?"

"It's kind of everybody to be so fussed about my health," said Holly. "I'm fine. I'm not made of glass, you know."

"At least Christopher's still enough of a gentleman to do the right thing," said Victor. "By God if he hadn't I'd have horsewhipped him myself."

"It was me who wouldn't agree to settin' a weddin' date," said Holly. "Funny, it took pregnancy to bring me to my senses."

Victor did not quite swallow the lie. The tone of the supper party remained brittle and uncertain.

It was not until many months later that Holly saw the evening in its true perspective and realised how deftly Christopher had charged Victor with her safe keeping.

* * *

On the first day of April, Holly and Christopher Deems were married in the Marylebone Registry Office. Grandpa Tal, Christopher's mother, Maury, Lawfeld and Emma Chubb attended the civil ceremony and – as odd an assortment as you could shake together, according to Christopher – crammed into a hired motorcar for the short drive to the Hildebrand Hotel where a private luncheon had been arranged. Kennedy King and Simon Black were waiting there. Leo did not turn up. To her surprise, Holly regretted his absence.

Mrs. Deems was a plump, fussy, vague lady who obviously adored Christopher. Holly feared that the woman would be possessive and bitter, but this proved not to be the case. Oozing avuncular bonhomie, King presented the couple with a pair of silver castors that had once been used by George the First – an authentic history in a brown envelope confirmed the claim. Tal and Maury had clubbed together to meet the cost of the luncheon. "Only right an' proper, ain't it, Holly?" In addition Maury gave his sister and her husband a "Letter of Services" in which he promised to decorate the apartment in Shepherd Market where the couple planned to make their home. Grandpa Tal parted with the tiny gold coach, fitted neatly into a minute velvet box made by Mendel Erbach. Holly was touched, more so as the old Russian made it clear that he was "passing it on" to his great-grandchild, that she and her husband were only temporary keepers. From Emma Chubb and Simon Black came a Canton vase of exquisite finish. Victor Lawfeld's present to the happy couple was a cradle of carved, painted pine, delivered from an import house in Portsmouth on the day before the wedding. There was no doubt that Victor had gone to endless pains to acquire the nursery furniture which, he said, was the work of a Bavarian woodcarver now in exile in France. Naturally this fine gift was not put on show with the others on a side table in the Hildebrand, though everybody there, including Mrs. Deems, was told of it by Christopher.

No secret was made of the bride's condition. The guests were trusted friends, open-minded, and affectionate.

Only Emma was so overwhelmed by curiosity that she tried to wheedle precise details of the liason from Holly. Holly told outright lies convincingly, keeping her part of the bargain with Christopher.

"No, Emma, I didn't have to buy a husband after all."

"It's him, then, if you know what I mean?"

"Yes."

"But you told me he was already married."

"I told you a lie. I didn't want to marry him just then."

"What changed your mind?"

"Christopher changed it for me."

"He's very forceful, under that quiet manner. What a sly puss you've been, Holly Beckman. What are your plans, if you don't mind my askin'?"

"Christopher will continue with the bookshop. I'll run Aspinall's, as long as I can. Grandfather will keep the shop open while I'm havin' the baby."

"Got it all nicely worked out, I see."

"What's wrong with that?"

"Not a thing, not a thing."

Holly was not as settled as she should have been, nor as full of joy. A sense of loss hung over the events of that strange day. In the presence of the Registrar she had been aware of it. Not even Christopher's graciousness could quite shield her from it.

A large bare room, high windows, polished wood floor, it was an institution, like marriage itself. Necessary certificates. Names of the witnesses – all too much like the sealing and signing of a contract. That's what it was, of course, a bond of marriage. Holly was too conscious of the situation, the oddness of its origins to be comfortable. The mood did not lift in the Hildebrand. She had made a contract for her child, offered herself up to a man she hardly knew. What puzzled her most of all, now that the event was over, was why he had taken her on such ridiculous terms. What did he want from her? Security, a home, sex? Or in the depths of him was there something more, some other purpose.

At half-past three the newly-weds left the Hildebrand by taxicab for Euston Station. There they caught the evening train to Edinburgh to spend a four-day honeymoon.

* * *

My Dearest Darling,

I see how your sister got married. I wish it was you and me. Mamma says she had to get married and it will square her and serve her right. I think it is wonderful!! It is one thing Mamma could not stop, if it was to happen to us. It is a nice thought.

Now I am counting the days until your are free to be with me. We will not waste no more time. I will be eighteen. They can't stop us.

Do you still want me as much as I want you?

Papa has won the argument. Mamma still wants me to go off to a school in Yorkshire to finish my education, really to get me out of London. Mamma shouted and bullied him but he did not give in, as usual. I will not leave London. She wants me under her thumb, like Papa is. But I will go to college in London, not far away, and come home every night just like I do right now. I am to learn to be a secretary. Papa says it is a fine thing for a girl to have something on her fingertips, like to work a typewriter and shorthand and bookkeeping. I have done some at school. It is not hard just boring. Papa says a girl like me will always find a good job with the right class of firm, if I can do these things. Two years to get the certificate, it will take. Two years, five days a week. Like school again. I have been to see it and to book a place for the autumn term. Believe me it is like another prison, my darling. It is Scott's Commercial College in the Millbank.

Your sister has got married to a man who was a hero in the war so Papa told me. Is it all true? I do not care about how a hero is. It is you I want and will always want – my dearest – my darling.

I kiss you a thousand times. I count the days until your are with me. We will not wait then. I love you.   Your Own, Ruth

* * *

Ritchie looked pale and haggard. He brushed aside Tal's anxious enquiries about his health, assuring his grandfather that it was only prison pallor and the after effects of a quinsy throat. He sounded husky still, and his quickness had deserted him, the glitter gone from his eyes. He seemed disinterested in the outside world, even in hearing what the old man had to tell him about Ruth. It was an effort to sustain the half hour's conversation. For the first time, Tal felt a welling of sympathy for the young man.

He had told him about Holly's marriage; not, however, about her pregnancy. Ritchie was too close to Leo. Besides, Ritchie betrayed little interest in his sister's affairs.

Tal said, "Never mind, lad, it will soon be time for your release. You will be eating French's saveloys again before you know it."

"All bleedin' summer yet," said Ritchie. "Gawd! I ain't but half through."

"They will give you time off for good behaviour, will they not?"

"I've kept my nose clean."

"You see. It will not be long. Five months."

"All bleedin' summer," Ritchie repeated.

"I have never seen you so down."

The young man hesitated. His fingers plucked at the stiff and slightly frayed collar of the prison suit. He glanced along the row of tables at the warder who stood by the door then slid his gaze to the uniform who sat on a chair under the huge barred window. He leaned a little closer to his grandfather.

"Got nightmares. Me! Think the bad throat had somethin' to do with it. Maybe the rat poison they gave me for medicine. Nightmares! Gawd, I'm scared to go to sleep."

"Would it help to talk of them."

"I see her dead. I see her lyin' there on a carpet, dead."

"Who?"

"Ruth."

"Ah!"

"Oh, Christ! I'm scared t' sleep."

"You have been quite sick, Ritchie. That is the reason. In a day or two it will pass."

"You don't understand."

"Would it help if I . . . if I somehow managed to bring her here for a visit?"

"*No.*" Ritchie shouted.

The warder stood on tiptoe and craned his neck to see what the source of the disturbance might be. Ritchie and Tal remained silent, staring back at the warder. His eye remained upon them.

In a low voice, Ritchie said, "No, I don't want her here. She mustn't see me like this, mustn't see me 'til I'm right again."

"What do you plan to do when you are released."

"Stay free."

"No more 'business', Ritchie?"

A scornful little smile twisted Ritchie's mouth. "I ain't never comin' back inside, Grandpa."

"And Ruth, what in God's name will you do about Ruth?"

"I got plans."

"Tilly will . . ."

"Eff Tilly."

"You will have to find a job. I suspect that it will be difficult. I am not sure, but perhaps Maury might be persuaded . . ."

"Work for Maury? You're kiddin' me, old man: what'm I gonna do, heft a bloody spade for three nicker a week an' say thanks Maury, you're a proper toff?"

"You'll have to find work – if you want to keep Ruth well."

"I got money."

"It will not last long, lad. Prices today . . ."

"Yer, yer. But I got money, an' money makes money."

Tal said, "Just how much did you manage to put away?"

Slyly, Ritchie said, "Enough."

"The proceeds?"

"Yer, the proceeds."

"Is it safe?"

"As 'ouses." Ritchie appeared more cheerful all of a sudden. "What's bleedin' more, I know where I can mill out a fortune. *That's* what's on, old man."

"But you said . . ."

"Then it's me an' Ruth for the off."

Fear came into Tal Kirsanoff's heart. He alone knew how many jobs his grandson had pulled, details of dates and times. How many of those jobs were still listed in police records? He was aware of the enormous power he had over the young man, a weapon that Ritchie did not know existed. What increased his fear was the sheer naked hatred in Ritchie's voice. Tal backed down before it.

"I know who got me in 'ere," Ritchie said. "They didn't exactly shop me, but they're bloody lemon-squeezers. They got, an' they keep."

"God in Heaven, Ritchie!" Tal said. "What is it you . . . ?"

A round metal bell on the brickwork clanged deafeningly, obliterating Tal's protests. He stared at his grandson in perplexity. Warders and guards were clumping among the tables now, tapping shoulders, shouting, "Time's up, move along. Now then, move along. Prisoners to cells. Move along."

The young man stood. The crushing weight of defeat seemed to have lifted from his shoulders. He swaggered a little, grinning the old cockey grin. "Thanks for comin'. You cheered me up no end, grand-dad."

"Ritchie . . . !"

"No more nightmares now. Not for me." He began to move off, while Tal Kirsanoff, as instructed, waited at the table, watching his grandson edge into the shuffling line of prisoners.

"Nightmares," Ritchie called, with a parting wink, "for somebody else."

•   •   •

They did not sleep together. Holly understood Christopher's reluctance to take her as a husband would. Undressed, her condition was obvious. He must feel that she was already more of a mother than a wife. Restraint did not impair their relationship. On the contrary it seemed to deepen it, drawing them into a bond of companionship where tenderness was more important than sexual release.

During their brief honeymoon, Mr. and Mrs. Deems wandered the streets of Edinburgh and explored the many antique shops and book stores to be found in the Scottish capital. They made the long train journey back to London on Sunday and were established in their new home in Shepherd Market in time for a late dinner.

Holly's skills as a cook had not had much opportunity to develop in Lambeth but Christopher declared himself to be perfectly happy to dine on plain fare.

Two single divans had been set up in the bedroom. Holly was in bed when Christopher came to her and, stooping, kissed her on the mouth. She misinterpreted the touch of his hands, the lingering warmth of his lips.

"I'll make it up to you Christopher," she murmured.

"Oh, that!" he said. "You've nothing *to* make up. Besides, it's a privilege to watch the process of motherhood."

"Even though it's not your child?

"Possession," Deems said, "is nine points of the law."

He kissed her again, shed his dressing-gown and climbed into the adjacent bed. "I fought for things less worthy; to make a mark on a sectional map, to stick a pin in a board. Senseless ownership of a strip of mud or a burned out trench. No meaning. No meaning at all. Love of country was a lie, hatred of Jerry an excuse. When you suffered enough, the cause of your suffering became yours. You owned it, possessed it. You would not give up the ownership to some fat Whitehall toad – not to your Colonel, or your General, or your King." Hands folded behind his head, he stared at the ceiling. "I couldn't envisage anything beyond the falling of the dusk each night. My friends were the dead. You loved them because you had been ready to die for and with them. But when it didn't happen, there was loss, Holly, loss so fierce, so intense, so enduring . . . Oh, I don't know."

"Has it passed now, Christopher, that feeling?"

"No."

Holly could see the sorrow in his eyes. How many nights had he lain in his greatcoat on a dirty cot under a roof of mud and rotting sandbags listening to sounds of destruction, yearning for the only identity that had any validity in those hellish fields. Christopher was not at all like Maury. Her brother had sought sanctuary in hate,

Christopher in love – the love of a few acres of earth where his companions lay, their wasted spirits beckoning him.

"I'm glad you're here, Holly." He glanced across at her. She stretched out her hand, seeking his touch. He gripped her fingers in his fist. "Patterns, habits were not enough. I thought that nothing would be enough. No purpose. Cheated and deceived by materialistic men in power. Robbed of any kind of future. I carried eternity around on my back along with the memories of all the men that had died for a future they did not believe in. Oh, that's despair! But you can't be expected to understand."

"I don't pretend to, Christopher."

"What is the worst thing that could happen to you?"

"Losin' my baby."

"What if I'd asked you that question six months ago?"

"My answer would have been different."

"Reasons for living are relative," Christopher sighed. "What would your answer have been?"

Holly hesitated, then replied, "Losin' my shop."

"And now, that's no longer important."

"No longer so important."

"You do like your trinkets, your antiques?"

"Yes, I do."

"Frail, fragile things. They need taking care of too, I suppose."

"And books?"

"Hardly," Christopher said. "They aren't things in themselves. They represent worlds of ideas, fading, changing, constantly renovating themselves. Shelves of them, thousands, hundreds of thousands – like the regiments of all the wars there ever were."

"Collecting antiques," said Holly, "can be a reason for living. I know men and women who think of very little but chasin' some beautiful object that they desire."

"It's as good a thing as any," Christopher said.

"Christopher, can I give you what you want?"

"I believe you can."

"What is it?"

"You can protect me from failure."

"Failure?"

"You'll never fail, Holly. You're too full of purpose to let despair catch you out."

"Failure? Is that what you hold against yourself?"

"Yes, failure to live up to my dreams."

"Your dreams were false, you say so yourself."

"But they were *mine*. Fragile as one of your porcelain vases or fluted drinking glasses. I saw them smashed, Holly, and I did nothing to prevent it."

"What more could you have done, Christopher?"

"I could have died."

"Don't say that! *Don't ever say that!*"

"Why – because you love me?"

"Because there's *something*, Christopher. Between us, there's something. I want it to grow, change, get better."

"And you do *not* encompass failure," said Deems. "So, I'd better toe the line, hadn't I?"

The bantering tone told Holly that they had touched enough for one night, that the sharing of secrets between them would be a prolonged process. She squeezed his hand.

"Yes, you'd jolly well better," she told him.

The following morning they breakfasted early and went their separate ways to work.

*   *   *

Aspinall's summer catalogue was a monument of good taste and astute pricing. Industry had brought the articles into the shop. The young woman's growing experience had enabled her to seek out only the finest examples to offer to her clients.

Kennedy King was most impressed. He even went so far as to invite Holly and Christopher to dinner just to laud praises on the pair and to study the phenomenon of their marriage with a certain degree of envy. He could not fathom what had enabled his dour nephew to acquire such a piece as Holly Beckman. King had to admit, however, that the couple seemed to have sufficient confidence to make the marriage stick. Later, after he had returned to his bachelor apartments in Chelsea and had settled before the fire in the library, he studied the thick and undeniably handsome catalogue with great care, as if he might extract from it the secret of the young woman's Midas touch. King had no doubt at all that, in a year or two, he would be sharing the Bond Street market with Mrs. Deems. It would be only a matter of time until she roped Christopher into helping her and bred, almost incidentally, a whole gaggle of little Deems children to establish a dynasty of up-market dealers.

If he had been younger, and a shade less fussy, he might have captured Holly for himself. King consoled himself with the thought that the woman's energy, and talent, might have proved too disruptive an influence on a man of his age. Besides, he had status and wealth already. With the catalogue open on his knee, he imagined Emma and Simon and the machinery of that relationship. So different, so brittle. Yet both Holly and Emma were typical of post-war women; he did not quite comprehend them. Twenty years back he would have been able to purchase either one of them. Plump Edwardian Emma, garrulous and eager, quiet and assured Holly: how both might have added the missing element into his life, helped alleviate the tedium of always having his own way. But Simon had one, Christopher the other, and poor old King had to be content with his fine Chelsea house and his bank accounts.

Once more he studied the catalogue on his knee – a fine collection, all of a piece. He appreciated wholeness, completeness, and the patient attention to detail that had gone into its compilation. He poured himself another brandy and, with his fat gold-nibbed fountain pen, began to mark off items that he wanted for himself, destroying the collection even as it had been built to be destroyed.

Nine weeks later, in the midst of a July heatwave, Kennedy King took purchase of three-quarters of Aspinalls and bought himself into the family.

* * *

News of Holly's marriage halted David's descent into ruin. He was gambling with determined abandon, dropping more than he could afford. He had promised himself that when a certain level – never quite defined – was reached he would quit his current life style and return, still in control, to Cardwell Place. There, out of sheer necessity, he would knit the loose ends of his past into a modest garment for the future. In the meantime he continued to stay in Cumbria House in Gloucester Place and spent his days much as he had done before the accident. Looming over him, however, was the shadow of his crippled wife. Though Linsey could not utter an intelligible word of reproach, she seemed able to reach her thoughts across the ether, to torment him with her vicious laughter, disturb his sleep with taunts and his waking hours with threats. He could hear her voice distinctly in his head, a clear high-pitched fully verbalised sound amid the hive-like hum of confusion. Holly might have saved him, provided the strength he needed in that terrible time. But Holly had stunned him with her rejection. In some ways he blamed poor Linsey for the fate that had befallen her, absolving himself from guilt. But he could hardly discredit Holly in that manner. In a sense, with Linsey, he was paying off old debts; with Holly he would be opening a new account.

Money was immaterial. He spent it in exactly the same manner as he had acquired it, with careful arithmetic, always aware of just how much had gone sloshing down the drain and how much was left to meet Lin's hospital bills, his mother's nursing-home demands and to keep a roof over his head. He did not take the shop profits into account, of course. They would remain intact, his backfall, emergency rations. They would start him off anew – when the day arrived.

Holly's marriage washed away the sandcastles he had built, and left him utterly lost.

Acting against his first panic-stricken impulse to shout and rage against his sister – who had thoughtfully telephoned him the news – David immediately retreated to his narrow hotel room and extracted a box-file from the foot of the wardrobe. The file contained reams of financial data, all of which, really, could have been condensed and put down on a couple of ledger sheets. In calculations and projections, however, David found comfort. He spread the papers on the bed, taking some up onto the square table and, with coloured pencils, worked and reworked the bookkeeping. When sums could no longer keep anger at bay, he bathed and dressed himself in nattiest style and went out to the club to eat a late supper and play a few frames of billiards with the lizards.

Dignity, that's the ticket.

I'm a gentleman. I must accept inevitable reversals.

He soaked his positive thoughts in best Scotch whisky and fell asleep on the billiard-room sofa where the night porter, a kindly devil, left him at peace until the soft light of early morning wakened him.

David drifted out into the quiet pastel streets. He walked by a roundabout route, heading vaguely for his hotel in Gloucester Place. But Pimlico drew him. He slunk past the shuttered shop and peeped up at the blinds of the upstairs apartments where his sister and mother slept. Fifteen minutes later, in a kind of trance, he found himself on a bench in Hyde Park with his head in his hands and his cheeks dew-wet with tears. Early dog-walkers ignored him. White tie and tails made him a familiar anachronism, a sight more sad than picturesque there in warming sunshine against glistening grasses and leaf-bud, the Serpentine still as a mirror behind him.

It was over. He had lost his retreat position. With a shuddering sigh, he wiped his eyes and fumbled for his cigarettes. He lit one. He got to his feet. His head ached. Brightening sunlight made his eyes water again. He began to drag himself towards the gate, anxious now to be out of the daylight, shaded, alone. It was a moment of revelation, of decision. For all his sickness and self-disgust, David was aware of the nature of choice. All it would take to keep him free was money. He must pay for Linsey, pay for his mother, pay, pay, pay. With money. But neither wife nor mother had a chain on him now. He could do as he wished. He had a grand set of excuses for going to the dogs. He might become a drunkard. He might sleep with all the Bohemian women that had ever briefly caught his fancy. He might scrounge free dinners, become a weekend guest on the Home Counties circuit, provided he minded his manners and did not whine. He might even find himself an amiable job through one or other of his acquaintances. Charlie Hallet would fix him up – he could extract a tithe from Hallet, if he wanted to. Hallet owned more than Hallet could ever pay. But none of it appealed. Indeed, the very thought of that kind of life disgusted him. It was Linsey's pattern. Not Holly's. He had lost them both and missed both more than he had imagined possible. By marrying her lover, Holly had denied him an opportunity to redress the wrongs that he had done her, done to himself. She was another man's wife. All he was to her now was the owner of her place of business. How much did the shop still matter?

There were no pieces left worth picking up.

It was over, all over.

He must buy himself a new beginning.

David reached Cumbria House. He let himself in with his latchkey, making no noise. But Mr. Evans was up already and, peering out of the kitchen, recognised his resident guest and, being a believer in flaming youth, took mercy on him.

"Had a rough night, Mr. Aspinall?"

"Very rough, Mr. Evans."

"Going for a lie down?"

"Yes."

"Come an' have a bite of breakfast first, there's a suggestion."

So David ate kippers and toast, drank coffee and chatted to Mr. Evans for a while, then went upstairs to his room just as the other guests were rising to prepare for the day's work ahead.

He no longer felt sick, or even sleepy.

He undressed, put on his bathrobe and seated himself at the bedtable. He opened a new pad of stationery, uncapped his fountain pen and, after a few false starts, began to write off his losses.

* * *

David did not let the grass grow under his feet. Within a week he had squared his debts with the remainder of his savings and had spoken with Mr. Mumford about selling out the shop and domestic premises. Mumford had condemned David's haste, had pointed out that Miss Beckman – Pardon, Mrs. Deems – should in fairness be given first refusal. Grudgingly, David agreed to Mumford notifying Holly of the intended sale. In due course Mumford reported back. It seemed that Mrs. Deems did not care unduly. Ownership and possession were less important to her now. Here Mumford was not quite as sure of his judgment as he led David to believe. Holly's love of Aspinall's had not diminished. It was true that she had other things in her life – not least the baby and Christopher – but buying and selling antiques allowed her to exercise judgment and flair in an area that was almost exclusively the province of men. She was beginning to build a reputation. Her appearances at sales, even before her pregnancy became obvious, earned her glances from vendors and dealers. She was in no way put out to overhear disgruntled West End purchasers complain, "Damn it to hell, that Beckman gal seems to be everywhere." Bidding and competition had come to mean something in themselves. She was conscious of the stir she caused with her bow-fronted dress and waddling gait. She enjoyed attention, was proud of it. Within the enclaves of London dealers she had friends – Emma and Kennedy King, lesser mortals like Mr. Draper and Mr. Spence. Pregnancy and marriage only served to increase her mystique within the club of the London antique trade. She was reputed to be able to spot bargains by sniffing the pages of a catalogue, to have stolen the hearts of the flintiest auctioneers. More importantly, she was constantly enlarging her client-list, and had been given first refusals on several private collections of porcelain and chinaware. She was known to be honest, and to produce some of the handsomest trade catalogues in town.

But it was her nose for a bargain that was her most enviable asset. Evidence of this was provided when she attended a sale in one of the large houses in the Green Park area. Excitement that the sale initially engendered lessened when it was seen that the majority of the lots were very ordinary indeed. "Crafty old devil, that Lord Merriman; got rid of the quality stuff years ago." The opinion was shared by all the dealers present. Faithful to her credo that it was provident to cater to the lower end of the trade as well as the high, Holly had marked off umpteen lots that she considered worth purchasing, plus a couple of portraits in fine Dutch frames, half a dozen pieces of silver plate and a Queen Anne fire-basket of unusual design. In a bucket of odds she had also spotted a little Chinese vase. Almost circular in shape it was weakly enamelled in shades of yellow, blue and gold. Though the colours were not classic *famille verte*, Holly studied the vase covertly and at length. The gold was tinged with traces of a brick-red substance. She longed to take out her glass and give the vase extra close scrutiny, but she dared not. The corridors of the Merriman mansion were thronged with eagle-eyed dealers. If she paid undue attention to the vase it would attract notice. Dismissively, she put it back into the basket, and, puffing, got up from her knees. She had been careful to show no excitement at her discovery.

It was not until after 1720 that the rose tint had been added to the enamels that had become famous as *famille rose*. The Chinese vase, however, clearly pre-dated that period. Holly suspected that it was one of the early experiments in the fashioning of the style. If so, the unprepóssessing piece could be worth quite a deal of money. She prayed that nobody else had detected the item or realised its significance. It was a great relief when Holly heard the *chack* of the auctioneer's gavel and his declaration, "Sold to Aspinall's for seven pounds, four shillings."

The following morning she traced references, quoted them in full in a letter to a Mr. Mitchell of Deal and offered him the vase at sixty pounds. Mr. Mitchell accepted by return. More profits seeped into Aspinall's.

Christopher was amazed at his wife's industry, but a little concerned that she would overstrain herself. His anxiety in this respect increased as spring moved into summer and Holly's tummy burgeoned like the park trees, becoming heavier with each passing day. Though the heat distressed her she did not complain and went about her various duties, as wife as well as business woman, with no sign of flagging. At Christopher's insistence, however, she did not work late, and was forbidden to go within a mile of Cardwell Place on Sundays. To ensure that his wife rested, Christopher took her up to Oxfordshire to visit his mother.

Mrs. Louisa Deems lived in a terraced house in the small town of Maldenhill, in a fold of the Chilterns. It was an odd locale, rustic yet suburban, with fashionable conversions beyond the river bridge and on the upper side of the High Street. Regular train services to London had opened the countryside. Several politicians had homes in the district. They rode up to the House on Mondays and returned to their Westminster widows on Fridays. The Deems family had been the first owners of the large terrace house. Christopher's ancestors had been a sub-branch of the famous Squires of Little Lee Grange. A plantation of cousins and distant kin still farmed the Lee Grange policies.

Mrs. Deems lived in a world of her own. Her only interests outwith the little town where she had been born and raised came through Christopher. But she did not really understand her son, though she attended on him with adoring servility, and obviously embarrassed him by her attention. Holly was incorporated into Mrs. Deems' environment not as an intruder or usurper but as a simple appendage to Christopher's antipodean existence. Holly had the peculiar feeling that Christopher did not exist for Mrs. Deems except when he visited the house in Maldenhall. Even Uncle Kennedy was imprisoned in "My mother's own Never-Never Land", as Christopher, sardonically, termed it. It occurred to Holly on the occasion of their second visit that Christopher might find his mother's nostalgia consoling – but he did not. Oxford had been the first great rent in the fabric of his life, the War the second. Nothing his mother could say or do could restore the pleasant, drifting, idle state of boyhood in the country township. Her garrulous reveries, her feyness, chimed ironic counterpoints to Christopher's experiences of the world.

The contrast between Christopher's upbringing and Holly's own was never more obvious than during those Sunday visits to Maldenhall. Holly would be settled in the secluded garden, Mrs. Deems would serve her hand and foot, with tea, home-made lemonade, with more tea, with a cold luncheon, trotting in and out of the house's back door with a restless rhythm that Holly soon found wearing. Noting this, Christopher curtailed the visits.

Contact with Holly's family was confined to Maury and Tal. Christopher did not press his wife to take him to meet Leo. Perhaps Maury's scathing sarcasm about his father put Christopher off. More likely, he sensed Holly's antipathy to Lambeth and the embodiment of its worse aspects in Leo Beckman. Little was said about Ritchie. Holly knew that her grandfather still visited her brother from time to time, but she did not enquire after him. She wished to exclude these reminders of her past from her present contentment. Besides, she still felt threatened – by Ritchie in particular. Tal's silence seemed to confirm her belief that her brother had not repented or turned from his criminal intent.

During the months of April, May and June, Holly heard little of David. Occasionally Mrs. Hodge disgorged a casual item of gossip, but David's influence on Holly waned with each passing week. She no longer thought of him with bitterness. Christopher and the baby claimed most of her attention. There were occasions when she quite forgot that Christopher was not the father of the infant snuggled in her womb.

The flat in Shepherd Market had become her home. She had given up her own place in Wolfenden Street without regret. Maury had done out Christopher's gloomy rooms, had even rearranged the bookshelving, clearing one of the bedrooms to serve as a nursery "when the time came for the little beggar to show his nose". Like Tal and Christopher, Maury invariably referred to the baby as a male. Holly was not so sure. Dr. McCorkindale would make no prediction, though he declared that it would be a large and healthy specimen, if the evidence of its Mamma was anything to go by.

Towards the end of the hot month of June, however, when Holly felt that she was sailing serenely towards the day at the end of August when her happiness would become complete, David Aspinall once more entered her life.

* * *

"It's perfectly simple, Andrea," David said. "I've done exactly as you wished. I've put both the shop and house up for sale."

"Why?" his sister snapped.

It was a still, stifling evening in Cardwell Place. The odour of the Thames, lentic and baking at low tide, penetrated all quarters of the city. For days now there had been no breath of wind in London's streets. The trees in the parks hung motionless and exhausted. Summer visitors to the metropolis sought refuge in cafes and dark picture palaces and came out, like moths, only when evening cooled the fierce stone heat. Brewers and ice-cream manufacturers were making a fortune. Vendors of paper parasols, lemonade fizz and sunshade hats lined every main thoroughfare.

The legions of unemployed were less evident in the heart of London than elsewhere in Britain. Middle-class adherents like Andrea remained oblivious to the larger issues of the day. As always Andrea's focus was narrowly set on maintaining stability and in widening her "circle" to include as many members of the wealthy upper crust as Miles could introduce. She had got over her libidinous phase, no longer felt or acted flirtatious, and generally behaved to Miles Walshott as she would have done to a husband with whom she had grown slightly bored.

David answered her question. "Because I need the capital."

"Would you throw mother out?"

"I've found a cottage for mother, in Hampshire."

"What about me?"

"It's not a large cottage, Andrea, but it'll do for both of you," David said. "It *was* your idea in the first place."

"Not Hampshire?"

"Village called Dreyborough, not far from Winchester. Pretty place. The cottage has two bedrooms and all mod. cons."

"What would I do in Hampshire?"

"Look after Mother."

Thora said, "It would be nice, Andrea, 'specially in this warm weather."

Son and daughter glanced at the woman in her chair by the fireplace, then ignored her.

Thora did not speak again.

The prospect of living in a cottage pleased Thora. She had enjoyed herself in the nursing home near Brighton and had not missed London or her children at all. The break with Cardwell Place had brought home to her how dependent she had been on James to create a centre for her life. The shop without him was much like a mausoleum. She had no friends in the city, and preferred the blue skies and fresh breezes of the country. She had struck up friendships with several of the ladies and gentlemen at the nursing home, and had resented being brought back to the city. During her holiday, it had became clear that Andrea and David did not need her. She could make no contribution to their welfare. She felt sad for poor David and his wife. But in the changes that had taken place in England too much had been lost, and that loss seemed to be reflected in her own losses. She was not really old. Once she had been set free from Cardwell Place she would soon settle again. A cottage in Hampshire sounded ideal. She nodded to herself, following the rest of the conversation only in a general way.

In the dark drawing room, David's voice was like that of a stranger, harsh and forceful; Andrea's replies peevish. "I will not be packed off to the cabbage patch just to suit your latest whim, David."

"Then make alternative arrangements," said David.

"Why don't you sell the shop, and let us keep the house?"

"You might find yourself living above a whole clan of Beckman's relatives, you know."

"That isn't funny!"

"I can't afford to keep you any longer. You're an able-bodied woman, Andrea. It's time to fend for yourself."

"What will Beckman have to say about it? Has she been told yet?"

"Mrs. Deems, as I believe she now is, will be offered the option to take purchase of the entire property, including the portion of the business that I now own. If she is unwillin' or unable to buy, then she must agree to accept her quarter share of the business, and cannot impede the sale."

"Do you think she will buy?"

"I doubt it very much, Andrea."

"How much will the whole lot fetch?"

"I've no idea; several thousand pounds."

"The house, I suppose, is worth more than the business."

"The lease is not paid up, not near it," said David. "That apart, I should make a decent thing on it, as well as on the business as a going concern."

"I see that you have frittered away . . . ."

"I've no intention of bickering with you, Andrea. It's time to be rid of this place. Mother will enjoy the country; you said so yourself.

"That just leaves the problem of what's to become of me."

"Do stop carping. Walshott will look after you. Perhaps you can persuade him to put you up in a little flat."

"That is a nasty suggestion, David."

"Marry him, then."

Andrea bit her lip. She was closer to tears than she had been in years. David's sudden, if not entirely unexpected announcement had highlighted her vulnerability. Throughout her youth and young womanhood she has been kept. She had considered it her right to be preserved from the vicissitudes of earning a living. She had been reared as a lady. Her ornamental function had remained largely unchallenged. It was her role, her purpose. She could visualise no other. But Hampshire? There she would be exposed, would quickly deteriorate into a spinster. Her mother would become dependent upon her. The whole thing would rapidly harden. Yes, in Hampshire that's what she would become – a fossil.

"How much will I make from the sale?" she asked.

David's brows rose. "You? Nothing. You've had your share. In fact, you've been living on my charity, more or less, for the last half year. I bought you out, paid you a generous sum for your quarter share. Besides, I'm hoping to purchase mother's cottage outright, to make sure that she never has to be without a home."

"What will she live on?"

"I'll make her a small allowance. Miles will help out."

"Miles is not a charitable instit . . ."

"Not what I meant," David interrupted. "Miles will arrange to put some of my money in a fund for mother. She has a little income as it is. She'll have quite sufficient for her needs."

"Why are you doing this?"

"I'll tell you," said David. "I'm doing it because I don't trust myself."

"Now that *is* sensible."

"All I have left is this house and the shop. If the money from the sale . . . well, if I get my hands on it . . . Look, Andrea, I've *got* to clear out. Don't you see. Linsey doesn't need me and . . ."

"How can you say that?"

"Because it's true. She may live for a year – for ten. But she doesn't know me, doesn't recognise me. She must stay where she is, nursed constantly. My sole duty to Linsey is to see that the remainder of her days are passed just where she is. Eventually there may be some sort of progress, but I doubt it. I have a wife, but I have no wife."

"I suppose you'll take a mistress."

"No, Andrea. I will not take a mistress. Apart from anything else, I couldn't afford to keep one."

"That didn't stop you in the past."

"For twenty years, Andrea, I've been listening to you complaining. I'm tired of it. Yes, I've made a fearful mess of things. I admit it. But just take a close look at your own situation. How much better is it?"

"Miles . . ."

"Go to Miles, then. God help him, he's all you've got."

"David! Oh, David! I'm afraid."

"Please don't blubber. I'm not impressed by your crocodile tears, Andrea. You've certain responsibilities too. It's up to you to see mother settled in Hampshire. I assume you're not so thoughtless as just to dump her there."

"But this, this is my *home*."

"This was the home of a boy called David and a girl called Andrea. They're part of history now."

"How soon will . . . ?"

"As soon as Mr. Mumford finds a buyer willing to pay my price."

* * *

Holly handed the letter to Christopher.

She had hurried round to the bookshop, leaving Tal in charge at Cardwell Place. It had not occurred to her to telephone Christopher. She was perspiring, her cheeks beetroot red. Christopher escorted her into the back shop where it was cool and made her a cup of sweet tea, reading the letter as he did so.

"Calm down, Holly," Christopher said. "You must take more care in this weather not to become so excited."

"I can't help it. Mr. Mumford's letter . . ."

"Yes, I see it."

Christopher put the teapot by the side of the gas ring and went over and kneeled in front of his wife. He patted her stomach. "Aspinall's doesn't matter to the person in there, does it? What does matter is your racing pulse and raised temperature."

Holly nodded. She breathed deeply, deliberately relaxing as she had been taught to do by a manual that Doctor McCorkindale had recommended. Christopher held her hands. She could feel the strength flowing from him, and assurance that she was not obliged to face such problems all by herself.

Eventually, without speaking, he got up and poured tea and gave it to her. He seated himself on the edge of the work table, the letter in his hand.

"It's obvious that David Aspinall doesn't intend that you should buy the business. If he wanted you to have it then surely he would have separated the domestic lease from the shop property. He assumes that we won't be able to raise the cash."

"He's right, Christopher."

"The point is, do you want to? Do you want to own Aspinall's?"

"I don't know how to answer."

"Why are you so upset, Holly?"

"It came as a shock, that's all."

"You do want it, don't you?"

"I never thought of myself workin' anywhere else."

"Holly, when the child comes . . ."

"I know, I know."

". . . you won't have the same . . ."

"Yes, Christopher, I know all that."

"You *do* want Aspinall's."

"It's the first thing in my life I ever owned, that was really and truly mine. Mr. A. entrusted it to me. He was the first person ever to have faith in me. I don't think he ever envisaged the shop bein' sold."

"But it's Mr. A.'s son that's doing the selling."

"Oh, it's silly anyway," said Holly. "David will sell out. At least I'll have my share of the business end. Perhaps I could take it in stock, start up on my own, lease a little property near here."

"But that isn't what you want, is it?" Christopher insisted.

"No."

"Leave it to me."

"Christopher?"

"We can't afford Aspinall's price – but Uncle Kennedy can."

"Your uncle? He won't want it now."

"I'm sure he can be persuaded," said Christopher.

"I'm not sure I'd want to be Kennedy King's employee."

"I won't be asking for you," said Christopher. "I'll be asking for me."

"What?"

"Pimlico isn't such a bad place to bring up a child."

"You mean *all* of it? The house too?"

"Why not?" said Christopher. "A family business. There would be enough in it for all of us, wouldn't there?"

"But, the bookshop?"

Christopher smiled. "I'll raise about three hundred on sale of my stock. It'll help us furnish Cardwell Place."

"And you would work with me?"

"Much more convenient," said Christopher.

"Oh, Christopher, do you mean you intend to stay with me – after?"

"After?"

"After my baby's born?"

"Of course," said Deems.

"I thought . . . I thought you'd leave me."

The man was silent, drawn into himself again for an instant. In the bookshop somebody accidentally dropped a volume. The sound was intrusive, the small faint bump on the uncarpeted floor and the creak of library steps as the browser guiltily replaced the volume was audible too.

"Yes, Holly," Christopher said. "I did intend to leave you."

"Victor warned me."

"Victor is too shrewd sometimes," said Christopher. "I'd have been gone by now, Holly, if you hadn't come to my rescue. You see, it meant nothing to me to give your child a name, my name. It rather pleased me, in fact, to leave that much behind."

"What are you sayin'?"

"A wife and child! You'd have been secure enough."

"I don't want you to go, Christopher. I don't care where we live, what we do, you and I, but I don't want you to leave me. Not now, not ever," Holly cried. "I'm fallin' in love with you, whether you like it or not."

"That," said Christopher, "was not part of the bargain."

"What do I care about the bargain?" said Holly. "I was afraid of bein' hurt. Instead, I'm in love with you. What a ridiculous thing to happen, isn't it?"

"Ridiculous!" Christopher Deems agreed.

* * *

"As it happens," said Kennedy King, "Mumford, the lawyer, has already been in touch with me regarding the purchase of Aspinall's."

"And what reply did you give him?" Christopher enquired.

"I asked for a fortnight to consider it."

"I rather got the impression that you were keen to establish a branch in Pimlico?"

Uncle Kennedy squinted doubtfully at his nephew. How much had the Beckman girl told her husband of his one-time intentions?

King said, "Keen is perhaps too strong a word, Christopher. Couple of years ago I had a fancy . . . I was *inclined* to support Holly Beckman. I'd no idea that the girl would become your wife."

"How does that alter things?"

"Um, well, as a wife and mother she may have too many distractions to manage one of my shops properly."

"Come now, Uncle, you know Holly better than that. She's dedicated. Besides, it's the day-to-day running of the shop that takes up time, not so much buying and pricing. Am I right?"

"Holly isn't the only trained dealer in London."

"But she is one of the best?"

"Potentially, potentially."

"You don't really approve of women in business, do you?"

"Unfair," King protested. "Many a small shop in England today is supported by the wife or daughter of the owner. No, I see no reason why Holly should not succeed in building a business."

"Will you help her; help *us* is what I really mean?"

"You've changed, Christopher, do you know that?"

"I've marriage to thank for that."

"Ambition's infectious," said King. "Very well, tell me what you'd expect from me?"

"Negotiate with David Aspinall for the business, including the large flat above the shop. Holly and I will pool our financial resources and will lease the flat from you at a suitable rental."

"Suitable to whom?"

"An estate agent will give us current value."

"Um! Very well! Go on."

"You will hold the lease on the property. Stock and general shop furnishing will be valued separately. Holly will take a twenty-five per cent share."

"Transfer her present quarter holding?"

"Exactly," said Christopher.

"You might starve."

"Do you really think so?"

Uncle Kennedy allowed himself a smile. "No, I don't think so.

Holly will draw a managerial salary, in addition to her percentage of profits, but do *you* propose to live a life of luxury, Christopher, penning a few poems for *Punch* or the *Lady* to keep yourself in tobacco?"

"The latest catalogue, the Aspinall summer catalogue. . ."

"I take your point. You wish to indicate that Aspinall's can support Holly *and* you quite comfortably."

"And old man Kirsanoff."

"A staff of four? It's rather tall for such a small establishment."

"Volume of trade . . ."

King waved his plump hand. "You're beginning to sound just like that young wife of yours. God, what drive that child has. First she snares James Aspinall; now she snares you."

"I object to the word 'snare'."

"Don't fly off the handle, Christopher. I know almost as much about Holly Beckman as you do."

"If any snaring was done, uncle, it was me that laid the trap. I was no bargain."

"No argument."

"How much *do* you know about Holly, uncle?"

"I know that she has a brother presently serving a jail sentence for robbery."

"Holly has no contact with him."

"Blood, Christopher, is thicker than water."

"What do you know of blood, uncle? I think we may take it that Ritchie Beckman will not be admitted to Holly's life, or mine."

"Nevertheless . . ."

"Uncle Kennedy, are you scraping for an excuse to turn down the offer? If so, have no hesitation, not on our account."

"What *would* you do if Aspinall's was sold to a stranger?"

"Invest Holly's quarter share of the profits in buying a business of our own."

"Antiques or books?"

"I haven't discussed it with Holly. Probably books for a year or so, then, perhaps, a gradual shift into antique dealing."

"Unless your wife is burdened with another small child by that time?"

"I see I've misjudged you, uncle," said Christopher. "I had hoped that you might help us – and do yourself some good in the process. It's patently obvious you don't think Holly and I are a good bet."

"On the contrary," said Kennedy King, smugly. "I think the pair of you together – now that you've wakened up, shall we say – are an excellent bet. I warn you, uncle or not, I'll extract my pound of flesh from both of you."

"Do we have an agreement?" asked Christopher.

"We do," said Kennedy King.

* * *

Wilf was pegging the leg of a small eighteenth-century Dutch commode that Holly strongly suspected of being a fake and had consequently given over to her assistant to practise his skills as a repairer. Wilf was delighted to splash about the glue pot and manipulate some old tools that Mendel Erbach had given him. But pegging was a noisy business and Holly had formed the opinion that hammering and banging were really the sources of Wilf's pleasure, not the satisfaction of doing a solid job on the pretty piece of furniture. She was, she had to admit, a little irritable that day. The suffocating heat was getting her down. With only four weeks of her pregnancy to run, she was enormously heavy. In fact she felt as if her body had been possessed by a lively young bullock whose sharp hoofs jabbed into her every time she moved. She could not find a comfortable position in which to sleep, even to rest. Concentrating on business matters was exceedingly difficult. Christopher was highly sympathetic but, now that he had shaken off the iron chains of defeatism and snapped the manacles of indifference, he had become a dynamo of energy, unexpectedly altered from the brooding, introspective ex-captain that Holly had married. Even Victor was flabbergasted at the changes in his friend. He congratulated Holly, as if it was somehow all her doing, a piece of female magic wrought by wand and incantation, and egged her on, in Christopher's absence, to "get the lad back to writing poetry". This undertaking was more than Holly felt capable of giving. She informed Victor that she had married a man, not a poet.

"Perhaps when we're settled in Cardwell Place he'll take up writing again," she said, since Victor looked so disappointed.

"And when will that be?"

"In six months, or a year."

"Well, I suppose it's better than nothing."

"Really, Victor, what right have you t' regard Christopher as nothing but a source of literature. Isn't he entitled to do as he wishes? 'Strewth, only six months ago you were afraid he'd . . ."

"You're right, of course," Victor agreed. "It's such a relief just to see him happy, and busy. Even at Oxford, before the damned war got him, he wasn't like this. Love of a good woman is a great restorer it seems."

"You should try it, Victor."

"Try what?"

"The love of a good woman. No sayin' how you'd turn out."

"For the moment," Victor said, "the Law must be my bride."

"How dull!"

"Agreed. But it won't be long now. Soon I'll be able to join the row of hopeful young acolytes at the back of the Old Bailey, and – perhaps – take a little time off to search the waving meadows for a Muse."

"A nice Jewish Muse?"

"I'm not fussy," said Lawfeld, "so long as she can cook."

"I don't feel much like a Muse right now," said Holly.

"Must say, you're a bit more Earth Motherish than Ethereal."

"You're a great comfort, Victor."

"What are you going to call the little chap?"

"Christopher suggests Belshazzer."

"Hm, yes, I like it," Victor Lawfeld said, and Holly threw a wicker letter rack at him.

But Victor's visits to London were limited by his studies and the vicissitudes of his private life, about which he seldom spoke. Holly missed his company. She had grown fond of Lawfeld. Now, with August come and deliverance not far off, she was relieved that Victor was not in London. She had no patience with anyone, and was not at all sure that Victor would be tolerant of her moods. She had even bitten Grandpa Tal's nose off for nothing at all. But Tal Kirsanoff was experienced in matters relating to women and did not take offence. Instead he would go quietly off and make her an orange juice or pour her a glass of buttermilk. Holly, then, would feel fearfully contrite, would shed a few tears against the old man's chest while he patted her and assured her that all pregnancies he had ever witnessed were wearisome but would be considered worth the discomfort when the little mite arrived.

"Then you will have your hands full, Holly."

"Oh, grandfather, I hope I can cope."

"Christopher and I will help."

"I know, I know, but . . ."

"Remember how young you are still."

"I don't think of myself as young."

"Nonetheless, you are. It is as well, my child, that you have all that energy to spare."

"But there's so much to do."

"Would you prefer to be a lady like Andrea Aspinall," said Tal Kirsanoff, "with nothing to do all day long but think of means to fill in the hours? Is that what you would have?"

"No."

"To be back in Lambeth, living in the Box, working in the medicine factory; would you have that?"

"I wouldn't change a thing," said Holly, "except the weather. Why couldn't I have carried during the winter?"

"It is nature that chooses," said Tal.

"A shop to run, stock to buy, orders to see to, and now a new house – I don't think I can cope unless I get some sleep, and I'm not sleepin' at all."

"Shop and house," said Tal, "will be taken care of, Holly, without much intervention on your part. The baby is your business now."

"That's it," said Holly, with a sniffle. "I'm not even sure I want the baby any more."

Tal understood that heresy too. He patted his granddaughter again, let her weep for a minute or two, then, innocently, asked her advice about a matter of bookkeeping and gradually wooed her from her depression.

It was Holly's last tantrum.

At three o'clock next morning, the heatwave broke in a violent thunderstorm. Lightning shredded the cloud that had built up over Southern England and folded over London in massive creases. The rolling thunder cracks wakened Holly from a light doze. Sticky with perspiration, her back aching, she propped herself on the pillows, knees drawn up. The bedroom was illuminated by a brilliant flash and Holly saw Christopher crouched on the rug, arms wrapped over his head.

He wore only pyjama trousers. The muscles of his back and shoulders were rigid with terror. When thunder boomed over the rooftops once more, he pressed his face into his thighs, his naked spine curved like a bow. Holly's fear of the elements was minimal, a slight apprehension lessened still more by the sound of cooling rain tapping on the windowpanes.

Holly hoisted herself from the bed and got down on all fours by her husband's side. Sweat varnished his pale flesh. Cotton pyjamas clung to him. Holly was not distressed by her husband's terror. She saw it in true relation to his war experiences. Three years – as Maury kept reminding her – was not long when it came to the healing of mental wounds. In Christopher's response to the storm, Holly recognised catharsis at work. Hauling a lightweight blanket from her bed she pulled it over Christopher, over herself. Within the tent, his abject fear was contained and shared. Holly put her arms about her husband, pressing herself against him, the blanket taut and encompassing.

Thunder pealed overhead. Three, four, five jagged zippers of lightning spilled white light under the hem of the blanket. Three, four, five times thunder built to a deafening crest of sound, broke and swallowed its own echoes. Whipping across the roofs like great strings of beads, driving against the panes like fusillades of glass cartridges, rain beat down upon the dusty city. Holly rocked her husband in her arms. She did not flinch now, did not resist sharing his experiences. She had never felt closer to the shy, damaged being that hid in Christopher's body. Soldier, captain, failed leader, the voice struck dumb. This was the man who had chosen her, accepted her.

As the storm slackened and trudged south, out of earshot, Holly's sense of wholeness increased. Inside his shell of terror, Christopher was touched by a similar emotion. Part of him had yielded to irrational fear and he could no longer mask his shame, from Holly. He had no need. She felt him slacken, rock-hard muscles quiver, head loll against her cheek, wetting her with his sweat. In the darkness of the tent she could not see his face. Only his posture told her that the terror had gone out of him and that, in its wake, was a degree of peace that he had not known in a long time.

Outside, rain veiled the dawn. Its cleansing brought an immediate coolness, almost a chill, to the atmosphere.

Christopher got to his knees. He leaned weakly against the side of the bed. Holly went to the bureau and brought from it a whisky flask and a glass that were kept there. She poured neat spirits into the glass and gave it to her husband.

"Drinking," he said, hoarsely, "at four o'clock in the morning. How depraved!"

"I'll make some tea."

"Yes, darling."

When Holly returned to the bedroom with the tea, Christopher had lit the bed lamp and was seated in the chair by the wardrobe, the blanket over his shoulders. The empty glass was on the table and he had a cigarette in his fingers.

"I'm sorry."

"Don't be," said Holly. "Has it happened before?"

"Not like that," he answered. "I'm sorry if it frightened you."

"I'm not afraid, Christopher."

"I knew it was thunder, only thunder, but . . ."

"It reminded you of the guns."

He took the mug of hot sweet tea in both hands and leaned forward. His features were drawn but composed. Parched by his ordeal, he gulped the tea.

"Yes, the guns," he said. "I lost control, Holly."

"I'm glad I was here, Christopher." Holly seated herself on the bed. Rain slashed fiercely against the windows. A strong buffeting wind backed it, enlivening the enervating air of the city. Holly found a comfortable position, a pillow against her side. She leaned close to her husband. "I'm glad you didn't have to be alone."

"It's degrading, though."

"Much less degradin' than the things that started it."

"A motion of clouds?"

"You know perfectly well what I mean."

"War," said Christopher. "Yes."

Holly did not try to draw him. In time he would confide in her, talk out the horror.

Christopher lit another cigarette. He put down the mug and lay back in the chair, legs stretched.

"I honestly thought I was going insane," he said. "I was a walking dead man, a marionette jerking myself through a daily performance, trying to salvage my capacity for a belief in instinct, in creativeness, in purpose for existence. Everything I had seen, Holly, everything I had been forced to do – and had forced myself to do – was a negation of my true feelings. I had repudiated my inner being – or so the doctors would say, if I dared consult doctors. I knew they couldn't help me. How could they understand that it wasn't what I had brought *back* from Verdun, Amiens and the ridge at Bullecourt that was poisoning me but what I had *left* there – scraps and flakes, like skin flayed away inch by inch over the course of forty-one eternal months."

"Maury told me some of it, Christopher."

"Oh, war-time experiences are all much the same." Christopher studied the tip of his cigarette. "Much the same, much the same whoever you talk to. It was the kind of man you were to begin with, before you put on the King's uniform and shouldered your rifle, that made the difference. Your brother Maury was no less sensitive than I was – and no more so. But he clutched the wild, sick romanticism of combat, he welcomed blood, earth, killing. The miracle is that when the war ended he was able to shake it off, to integrate himself so quickly and thoroughly into civilian life and become a purposeful member of society again."

"He did it by hard work," said Holly. "Even that didn't save him from the dark, I don't think."

"Ah, but Maury was more clever than I," said Christopher. "He didn't drown his contempt for human kind in a larger contempt for himself."

"Is that how you survived?" asked Holly. "Is that what you meant when you said that you were a failure?"

"I adjusted well to war. I was an excellent officer. Gallant. Brave. Never showed my other self, my true self. I lived by the reality of that infernal zone. It didn't occur to me, Holly, that I would be one of the survivors, that a bullet or a shell or a bottomless pit of mud would not end it for me. I didn't realise that I would be called upon to adjust again, to change again, to become what I had been before. I'd dealt successfully with the world as it was in Flanders. How could I deal with the fantasy that was England, Oxford, the Strand? Bank Holidays and Christmas? Poetry readings in the Pilgrim Hall? I couldn't grow *back* into the young man I'd been before – and yet that was what was expected, demanded of me." Christopher paused. "I'd have shouldered any kind of suffering, Holly, if I could have found meaning in it. But there was meaning in the sufferings of war only in the context of war. Do you see? I intellectualise, I rationalise; that's all I'm capable of doing."

"Even now, Christopher?"

His eyes narrowed. His cheekbones caught the light of the lamp and the stark reflection of the cold, dim light of the window, one warm, the other icy.

"No, you're right; not now," Christopher said. "A year ago I wouldn't have let my fear of thunder show. I would still have been *Captain* Deems; in control, waving the flag, wearing the mask. I would have been the empty shell of the leader of warriors."

"But the shell wasn't empty, was it?" said Holly.

"It was, it was, almost to the moment when . . . when I asked you to marry me," Christopher said.

"Because – or in spite of – the fact that I was carryin' another man's child?"

Christopher smiled. "We are all other men's children, Holly, all strangers in spirit to ourselves. There's no rational process by which I can grasp the meaning of what you brought me, or why I need you and your child. It's transcendant, beyond my comprehension. And yet, perhaps, I've found what I longed to find in the very act of commitment. I think that's what came out of it, what you brought me, something accessible only to a dormant emotional core in me that I'd forgotten existed."

"Is it enough?"

"Yes, it's enough, Holly."

"Is it love? Is that what you found?"

"Perhaps. But not, Holly, as a means to an end. At best it was a desperate gesture, that's all."

"What if it hadn't worked?"

"I would have killed myself."

"A last grand gesture?"

"Yes."

"Didn't it occur to you that I'd be hurt?"

"Yes."

"But you risked it."

"Yes."

"Is that the truth?"

"That's the truth, Holly. Do you despise me for it?"

"How can I despise you? It was a mutual bargain, Christopher. In any case, I had – I dunno – an intuition, a feeling that we might not be long with each other."

"I won't leave you, Holly. I love you too much to hurt you now."

"Will you love the baby too? It'll be a person soon, not just a concept. It'll be a livin' *being*, Christopher. But it won't be your flesh and blood. Can you be certain you haven't misjudged your reaction?"

"There was no deception on your part, Holly. Deception would have been dangerous, I admit. But you didn't endeavour to cheat me. Really, I'm the deceiver. If I'd failed to find in you what . . ."

"Please, darling, don't say it," Holly broke in.

"I could never have found for myself what you've given me, Holly. The baby's part of that, an inseparable part. It'll be my child as much as yours. I'll be its father and will love it the way a father should. What does blood matter? Blood's only a thin substance that fills the veins. I've seen too much of it to hold it in awe." He leaned towards her, taking her hand in his. "You're cold, darling. Into bed with you."

"God, it's wonderful to feel cool," said Holly, as she slipped between the sheets.

Christopher put the blanket over her, then stretched himself out on it, face on the pillow close to his wife's. Gently he placed his palm against her stomach. "It's stopped kicking. Is that as it should be?"

"Hm," said Holly. "It's quite usual at this stage. Gatherin' its strength to be born. What do you hope it'll be, Christopher? A girl?"

"I hope it's a boy, of course. Every man, even a poet, wants a son to call his own."

* * *

Christopher Deems had his wish. On August 29th, in a ward in the Queen Victoria Maternity Hospital, Holly was delivered of a male child after a labour lasting some seven hours. The baby was sound and healthy and weighed eight pounds and three ounces at birth.

In the course of the next week, Holly and the baby were visited by friends and relatives all bringing small tokens of congratulation. Emma Chubb came up with a hand-crocheted jacket, Kennedy King with two twenty-two carat gold sovereigns in a velvet case, Tal with an engraved silver spoon and Maury with an engraved silver dish. Victor, who was angling to be godfather, brought a magnificent silver carriage clock, with the date and time of young Master Deems' birth etched on the base.

Leo Beckman betrayed no apparent interest in his grandson's arrival, or his daughter's welfare. Apart from that, however, everything seemed to augur well for the baby's future, and the happiness of his parents, Holly and Christopher Deems. But, on September 21st, Ritchie Beckman was released from Brixton Prison and returned, unannounced, to Lambeth.

5

Lavender Castles

FOR ANDREA ASPINALL there were fleeting moments of regret as the men from Pickfords man-handled furniture down the staircase and into the pantechnicon that would transport the smaller items to Hampshire and drop off the larger pieces at Miles' house in Hampstead where they would be stored in the large dry attic –

assuming that Miles could find a means of getting them up there. Thora Aspinall, of course, shed tears by the bucketful during the course of the morning. David was too occupied in supervising Andrea who was supervising the removal team to spare much time for his mother. Besides, there was little he could do, except mutter words of comfort. He was not immune to sentiment but the deed had been forced upon him, so he told himself. The transaction had been accomplished much more swiftly than anyone had a right to expect. Once it was done, it could not be undone. Besides, nobody wanted it undone. Mother's tears and Andrea's occasional contrivance at a sniffle were minor. All of them, really, wanted shot of the place.

David was relieved that Holly was not present. He had no wish to meet her again, to have to enquire about her baby – a boy at that – and make polite noises like a mere acquaintance. He did not know whether he was furious with Holly or jealous of the happiness she appeared to have found with the Deems fellow.

Via the redoubtable Mr. Mumford, David had been informed that Holly would remain as manager at Cardwell Place and would also lease the domestic apartments. David had suspected that some such move might be in the wind. When it came about, however, he could not help nursing a sense of grievance, as if the young woman had bested him. As usual, Andrea was much less rational about it, and less reticent. Abruptly she switched her viewpoint. Neglecting to take into account the fact that she had been the instigator of the removal, she acted as if Holly had robbed the Aspinalls of their birthright. David was in no mood to defend Holly or her husband. Apart from pointing out that Kennedy King was now Beckman's uncle-by-marriage, he did not make a case for the new tenants.

To transport his mother and sister to Hampshire, David had rented a small upright Morris motorcar. A bit of a banger, it had just sufficient stamina to tootle the three of them, plus a quantity of personal luggage, to Dreyborough. They had lunch at a local tavern and refreshed themselves by splitting a bottle of wine. The final leg of the journey was accomplished in bright sunshine. Thora was as excited as a child on a trip to the seaside, and delighted to reach her cottage a mile or so out of the village.

It stood in a half acre of brambley garden, quaint and a good deal more accommodating than it looked. David helped his mother and sister settle in, then loitered by the gate until the Pickfords' van arrived. It was after five o'clock before everything was in place. The Aspinalls had tea together, with groceries that David had thoughtfully purchased at the village shop. For the first time since James had died, almost three years ago, Thora was genuinely happy. Even Andrea had not the heart to complain too volubly in her mother's presence.

She escorted her brother to the motorcar in the lane by the gate. "How long do you expect me to stay here?"

It was a beautiful tranquil evening, breathlessly still, the sky liquid with colour, shadows of trees and shrubs large and dense upon the watered surface of the road. Moths drifted soundlessly in the fragrant air.

"That's rather up to you, Andrea."

"Up to me?"

"I ask only that you stay with mother until she makes a few friends. Shouldn't be long, by the look of it. She has neighbours only a hundred yards round the corner, a pleasant couple. Quarter of mile in the other direction, there's a farm. I'll arrange to have a telephone installed so that she won't be cut off. Grocer, baker and butcher all deliver. Local bus passes the end of the lane twice a day."

"You haven't answered my question."

"The final deed is being drawn up. I'll post mother the original. Mumford will hold the other copies. The cottage is in mother's name. Money . . ."

"David, how long will I be here?"

"I repeat, Andrea, that's wholly up to you."

"You're *forcing* me to marry Miles."

"I'm not forcing you to do anything."

"Did Miles put you up to it?"

"Good God, no."

"What's *that* supposed to mean?"

"You may have to do a little ladylike shadow-boxing now, Andrea," said David. "I have the feeling even the loyal Miles may slip through your fingers if you're not careful."

"Miles and I . . ."

"Oh, I don't give a damn about your pet neuroses," David interrupted. "If you won't marry, and don't like it here, find yourself a job in town and rent a little flat."

"A job?"

"On the other hand, if you want to turn your hand to gardening and become a leading light in the life of Dreyborough, I think there's enough interest due on the investments to keep both Mother and you fairly comfortable."

"Don't be smug, David."

"Andrea, I'm not smug. Just weary."

"I suppose you're hurrying off to some night club now," the woman said. "You won't be weary there, will you?"

"As a matter of fact I'm going straight home to my room in the Cumbria – to sleep." David opened the door of the Morris and slid in behind the wheel. Through the window he waved to his mother who was leaning through the open window of the living room. She looked cheerful and already very much at home. Birds warbled, and in the distance a pheasant *chuck-chuck-churred*. "Goodbye, Andrea."

"When will you come again?"

"Sunday – probably."

He started the engine, eased the clutch and coaxed the motorcar forward on to the crown of the lane. He tooted the horn twice and waved again.

In the mirror, he could see his sister, tall, elegant and entirely out of place in the setting of a pastoral evening.

He didn't care.

In three or four months, he would be rid of them all.

The following morning, he dropped the keys for the doors of Cardwell Place into Mr. Mumford's office and, with apparent indifference, left the rest of the transaction to the lawyer.

* * *

The taxicab drew up in Cardwell Place. Christopher Deems was first out. He opened the passenger door and, with great solicitude, helped his wife alight. She had not yet recovered her strength and an autumnal breeze that bowled up from Hyde Park and cut into a wedge on the corner of the British Linen Bank made her sway a little. The first crisp leaves, like cornflakes from a new packet, tumbled along the pavement. Holly turned her back to the wind. Shoulders hunched, she protected the shawl-clad bundle in her arms. Gloved hand and broad lapel kept the draught from her son's sleeping face. Under a dainty bonnet, amid fine angora woollen and lace-edged swaddling, there was precious little to see of young Master Deems. A bright pink nose was incorporated into a frown of such concentration that, according to Christopher, "the chap must already be composing a Byronic epic in preparation for the day when somebody teaches him to write". As Holly stepped gingerly across the pavement towards the open door of the shop, Master Deems gave a wistful sigh – he had been fed in the comfort of the Queen Victoria at one o'clock and it was now only a quarter to two – and snuggled deeper into the wrappings, to withdraw, with dour mischievousness, from his great-grandfather's looming features.

The old man peeped over the edge of Holly's lapel. "Fast asleep," said Tal Kirsanoff. "I've yet to see him awake."

"Hardly ever awake," said Christopher. "Except in the wee small hours of the morning. Saves all his strength to swell the dawn chorus."

"So would you if you were hungry," said Holly.

Tal closed the shop door. The ringing of the bell seemed to impinge upon the infant's consciousness. His eyelids flickered, his lips parted. He gave a faint whimper of displeasure, then fell asleep once more.

"We'll call him Towzer, I think," said Christopher, "after Pavlov's favourite dog."

"We'll call him Christopher – after his father," said Holly. Decisiveness had been evident in her manner since the birth. "No Russian dogs – and no peculiar poets."

"Yes, dear." Christopher winked at Tal who was hovering by his granddaughter in a state of quiet enchantment with the new arrival. "Whatever you say."

"Come out of there, Wilf." Holly had spotted the lad peering from behind the packing bench in the recesses of the back store. "Don't be shy. Come an'meet Christopher."

Wilf approached as if Holly held a bomb not a baby in the shawl, and, from a safe distance, standing on tiptoe, inspected the bonnet.

"This is Wilf," said Holly to her son. "When you're older, he'll read you the Comic Cuts. Won't you, Wilf?"

"Yus, mizz."

Holly headed towards the iron staircase. "Has Mr. Kirsanoff been keepin' you busy while I've been gone, Wilf?"

"Yusss."

"Well, that's good," said Holly. "Now, no more hammerin' and bangin', Wilf, not while baby's upstairs. Don't make any more noise down here than you can help."

"Noah, mizz." To show that he had received the message and understood it, Wilf stole back to the packing bench on the points of his boots.

Holly had hardly spared a glance for the shop. Tal was not disappointed in her lack of interest. After all she had only been absent for nine days and very little had changed in that short time. Besides, she would be more concerned with inspecting the arrangements that had been made for the baby's comfort in the apartments upstairs. It also occurred to the old man that Holly might find it very strange, and perhaps a bit disconcerting, to climb the iron staircase as mistress of the house, not as an unwelcome shop servant. It would take the young woman some weeks to adjust. In the interim he would see to it that the shop was kept spick and span, the books up-to-date and that Wilf did not kick up a racket. In the whirl of arrangements, Christopher had so far spent little time on the shop floor, though he and Tal had got along well.

Cautiously, Holly cradled the baby in the crook of her left arm and steadied herself with her right hand on the iron railing.

"I see you sold the Sutherland table," she said.

"Mr. Riceman bought it," Tal told her.

"Who bought the Lowestoft circular bowl?"

"A man off the street," Tal answered. "He paid the fifty pounds in cash from a great horse wad. I think he was a dealer, though he did not ask for discount."

"He got no bargain there." Holly progressed up four steps, before resting her hip against the rail again. "I'll look over all the sales slips tomorrow or the next day," she said, and with an effort, got herself up the remaining steps to the landing and, with Christopher's aid, through the door into the apartment.

In the limited time at his disposal, Christopher had performed wonders with the decoration and furnishing of the main rooms. Maury had found him four reliable men who, for a bob or two, were willing to turn their hands to almost any job. With the assistance of the out-of-work tradesmen, Christopher had cleaned the apartments from top to bottom. He had concentrated his efforts on the large bedroom and kitchen, wisely reckoning that Holly would want to have a say in choosing the decor for the public rooms. The floor of the long broken corridor had been waxed and polished and laid with a new runner carpet of sober Turkey on a No Creep Felt Underbase. Corridor walls had been washed; the original paper had come up an attractive pattern and would do until the spring. The kitchen had been scoured and scrubbed, new linoleum laid, new curtains hung and a thick rug placed in front of the range. Through the good offices of Tal a table, four dining chairs and two comfortable armchairs had been bought secondhand. There was a special low, armless chair, one of a pair, from which Holly could feed, change and bath the baby. In the meantime, the master bedroom would also serve as young Christopher's nursery. It had been thoroughly done over. Old paper had been stripped from the walls; the woodwork had been repainted in Devon Cream, a tint that went perfectly with the inexpensive wallpaper that Christopher had chosen and that the four odd-jobbers had hung so neatly.

"Fish?" Holly sniffed.

"It's the paste," said Christopher. "It'll take a day or two to dry out. Do you like it, on the whole?"

He switched on the electric light.

The roof no longer seemed oppressive. Bright paper and new curtains had lifted it. Bow-fronted chest-of-drawers, convex mirror, shieldback chairs and the heavy double bed with its needlework panel headboard had all gone. Holly hesitated, waiting for ghosts of the past to drift out at her. The ghosts remained immured behind the new wallpaper, however. All memory of Mr. A. had been removed with the antique bed. It was not a room of which Holly could disapprove. Cream-coloured rugs were scattered on the pea-green carpet, and the painted cradle, quilted and padded, stood ready to receive its tiny tenant.

The large double bed was brand new, Christopher's one extravagance.

"I thought," Christopher said, following the direction of his wife's gaze, "that we would be more comfortable together."

"Yes," said Holly. "Provided you don't mind bein' disturbed when I get up to feed the baby."

"Oh, in six months or so the chap'll have a nursery of his own," said Christopher lightly. "The room next door will do very well."

"You've made a good job of things, Christopher."

"Everything's at sixes and sevens, really," Christopher said. "I think, however, that I've sold the bookshop as a going concern. I advertised it in the newspapers and had several genuine replies. On the strength of that, the bank advanced me enough money to buy furniture. The rest we can acquire over the course of the winter. There's still my flat, of course. I've hopes that it may go, as it stands, with the bookshop. The prospective purchaser is from Glastonbury. He'll be looking for a place in London."

"I'm happy t'leave it all to you," said Holly. "Now, if you don't mind, darling, I'll put this little puddin' into his new crib and have a bit of a lie down myself for half an hour."

When young Master Deems was snug in the painted cradle, Holly took off her dress and shoes and lay under the coverlet of the new bed. Christopher went off to make tea and prepare the evening meal, in spite of his wife's protests that she was the woman of the house.

Holly was glad of the time alone. Lying there in the strange room in the Aspinalls' apartments, she had an opportunity to come to terms with the perspectives of her life. Turning her head on the pillow, she looked down at the Bavarian crib by her side. She listened hard for the sound of Christopher's breathing then, knowing how silly she was, lifted herself on her elbow so that she could see the baby's face. Sound asleep, and snoring faintly. Relieved, she laid her head on her arm. Her breasts were tender and heavy with milk; otherwise she felt fine. Around her she could hear the sounds of the menfolk and, listening hard, the distant *tang* of the shop door bell below.

It was peculiar, really, Holly thought drowsily, how no lingering traces of the Aspinalls remained here. It was as if Andrea, Thora and James had blown away like clouds.

And David?

She opened her eyes and frowned slightly at her son, at David's son.

Only with an effort of the intellect could she convince herself that the baby had been fathered by David Aspinall. In her heart, she thought of the infant as Christopher's natural heir.

At that moment, Holly Deems was happy. She had everything in life she wanted, much more than she deserved. Sighing, she drifted off to sleep. Christopher did not waken her to drink the tea he'd made.

* * *

The woodland path was dry and well-defined, otherwise Andrea would not have followed it. Miles had suggested that they stroll down to the village but Andrea had developed a pathological hatred of Dreyborough and made no bones about the fact that she despised the natives.

"On Thursday," she told her fiancé, "I went into the butcher's shop to order steak and kidney – Mother seems obsessed with baking these days and wanted to make a pie – and you should have *seen* the way they looked at me. Those lumpy farmers' wives in their dirty skirts and boots, they looked at me as if I'd come from Africa or from the moon. They turned up their noses at me. *They. At me.* I ask you, Miles! Even the butcher was barely civil. If there was any option at all I'd take our trade elsewhere. The trouble is that there's no competition. And he knows it, that butcher. Shop's quite filthy too. Flies everywhere. Two dirty cats *inside* the window. In London . . ."

"Yes," said Miles, wearily. "But this is the country. Things are done a little differently here. Besides, you're not giving it much of a chance, Andrea. You've only been here a week or so."

"It seems like an eternity."

"Your mother..."

"Oh, yes, mother loves it. I cannot understand why. Truly, Miles, I cannot fathom what she finds so attractive about all this, this *countryside*."

"It is peaceful, you must admit, and very beautiful."

Miles waved his hand at the vista of a vast patch of corn rippling in the evening breeze. The low contours of hills in the distance were blue beneath the westering sun. Ring doves called in the deep green depths of the oakwood and flowering weeds and wild flowers scattered colour along both sides of the winding pathway.

"There's just nothing *here*, Miles. Can't imagine what you see in it. Would *you* like to live here, in that pokey little cottage?"

Miles had the temerity to consider his reply. "Well," he answered, with a cautious attempt at wit, "it *is* rather far from the Connaught, I confess."

"The Connaught. Oh, the Connaught!" said Andrea, as if he had mentioned Eden to Eve Cast Out. "Lord, what I wouldn't give to be able to pop into the Connaught for tea."

"You're not in exile, Andrea. I mean, they won't arrest you if you come up to London. Next week, why don't you? Take a couple of days. *Stay* at the Connaught."

"Money," said Andrea, "is no longer available. My brother has seen to that. David's got rid of me – and a very thorough job he's made of it, by the looks of it."

They had reached a fork in the woodland track marked by the bole of a huge grey elm whose leaf-laden boughs were slung across the clearing. Doves and wood-pigeons broke suddenly from cover in the tree, whirring and coo-rooring in all directions.

"Damn these creatures," Andrea said, startled.

"They're only birds, dear," said Miles. "I was always partial to pigeon-pie myself. However – money. David hasn't left you *too* badly off, considering. The investments are very *secure*."

"Secure! Is that all you can say?"

Miles plucked a grass stem, breaking it neatly from the clump with his thumbnail. He put the stem in his mouth. "Shall we take this path, or that one?"

"I don't care."

"Which one goes to the top of the hill, I wonder?"

"What's so attractive about the top of a hill?"

"The view might be rather nice," said Miles. "What do you say, dear? This one?"

"If you wish."

"Money. Yes. If it'll help, you could be my guest at the Connaught."

"That wouldn't be very seemly."

"Oh, I dunno. These days I doubt if anyone would be morally outraged. After all it's not as if I'd be there, not overnight, at any rate."

To Miles Walshott's astonishment, Andrea reached for his hand. She drew it to her side, bringing him close to her. Her tone was syrupy. Good God, she actually batted her eyelashes. The sun of the past week had lightly tanned her arms. She wore a silk blouse with a powderblue jumper draped across her shoulders. In coming close, the jumper slipped. She caught it and held it in her left hand. The neck of the blouse was fashionably deep and exposed an unfashionable amount of cleavage.

"I wouldn't object, darling," Andrea was saying, while Miles tried to fall into some kind of step with her along the path that led away behind the elm.

"Hm? What?"

"If you did stay overnight with me."

"Bit inconsistent, Andrea! What?" he muttered.

"In for a penny, in for a pound."

"Could be misconstrued."

"Lord, Miles, we've been engaged for years."

"I don't understand you, my dear. There are times when you leave me at a loss for words."

"You have that effect on me too," Andrea simpered. "It *is* a lovely evening, now that you mention it."

"There. You've done it again."

"A woman is entitled to her moods, Miles."

"I've never seen you in this sort of mood before."

"Touch me, Miles."

"What?"

"Touch me."

"Andrea, for God's sake! What's got into you?"

"There's nobody about."

"It's a public footpath, you know."

"Behind the tree, among the twigs."

"Andrea!"

"Don't you love me, Miles?"

"That isn't the point."

"Don't tell me you respect me. I want more than that."

"Andrea, please!"

"Here. The leaves will hide us. Not a soul for miles and miles around. Touch me. Nobody will see."

"Touch you *where?*" said Miles, in confusion.

With a clawing motion Andrea wrenched at the throat of her

blouse. Tiny pearl buttons popped. Two, three of them fell into the grass at the base of the tree. She pulled Miles with her as she sank back into the branches and rested her shoulders against the huge smooth trunk.

"Here, Miles. Now, Miles. Feel me. See, I'm a woman."

"Good God!"

"Look, look."

"Andrea, don't! *Oh, hell!*"

His hands closed over her breasts. He thrust himself against her, as much to shock her into behaving sensibly as out of desire. Her breasts seemed to pulse against his palms. He had a totally uncharacteristic urge to inflict pain on her, to crush the womanly flesh until she begged for mercy – or kicked him in the shins and ran shrieking back to her blasted mother in her blasted rustic retreat and refused, ever, to see him again. But he was surprised on two counts that had little or nothing to do with his first primitive instinct. Andrea did not fly into a rage of revulsion at his violent caress. On the contrary, her head tipped back and she gave a long, loud groan while he, staring in disbelief, watched his hands begin to shape and stroke her white flesh, rubbing the dark nipples to make them stand erect. Andrea groaned again, very loudly, and, clasping his head in her hands, hauled his mouth to hers.

Miles did not allow himself to be encumbered by ghastly recollections of his mother drowning his father, his Aunt Cordelia's lewd disparagements or any of the arid female relatives who had dried out his male responses like leather bootlaces. His nervous system temporarily ruled his intelligence. Revolution had taken place within his tidy brain. The secluded green fecundity of the Hampshire woodland – Miles later explained by way of apology – had brought out the beast in him.

He groped his right hand over Andrea's stomach, insinuated it under her skirt, slithered it up the length of her thigh. Andrea was both soft and hard. Firm fleshed. Warm, damp, demanding. Demented by greed, she closed her knees on his expeditionary fingers, trapping them at source. For her it may have begun as a cunning exercise in enticement but now that she had lost control, she was as selfish as ever.

Miles took her maidenhead without much awkwardness, far too carried away on tides of need to pay any attention to objective reality, the comical sight they must have presented, Andrea with skirts rolled around her waist, he with braces dangling and a great deal of very white flesh visible. So much noise did Andrea make that the doves and wood-pigeons stayed well clear, and even furry little squirrels stole off to nibble in other trees. Down among the elm's gnarled roots, cushioned on velvet grass, vetches and melancholy thistles, Andrea made sure of her man.

The couple did not forget themselves again. There were no more sessions of passionate love-making. A month later, Andrea had the audacity to marry in maidenly white, a bit of hypocrisy that did not cause the roof of St. Luke's, Hampstead, to fall on bride, groom and assembled guests, and that everybody present took for granted.

By mid-October Mr. and Mrs. Walshott were in residence in the Walshott house in Hampstead, sharing with a cook, a maid, Mrs. Owens and mad old Aunt Cordelia all the pleasures of domestic bliss, while down in Dreyborough Thora Aspinall, relieved, got on with the business of making up to the butcher.

* * *

As autumn stole into Cardwell Place the Deems family got on with the daily round. To Holly's surprise - but to nobody else's - she was more occupied with the baby than with shop matters. Anticipating this turn of events, Christopher had hastened the sale of his bookshop and the flat in Shepherd Market and threw himself wholeheartedly into learning the antique trade from scratch. He did not have to be taught how to run a shop. He was his wife's equal in keeping necessary accounts, in correct invoicing and prompt payment of bills. He also had an easy manner that made him popular with customers, the more so as he did not pretend to be an expert and deferred all difficult decisions to his wife.

Christopher was not entirely a novice, however. He brought a considerable knowledge of militaria with him from his young manhood and, by dint of a few experimental purchases, proved capable of developing this line on his own. Mainly, though, he was dependent on Holly's directions. He took no liberties with the prices that she marked in sale catalogues, and studied her detailed notes with great attention before bidding. Christopher learned how to consult reference sources to solve problems of identification and valuation. The field was so vast, however, that he soon understood why James Aspinall had rated Holly so highly. The young woman had an almost encyclopaedic knowledge of certain specialised subjects and broad background in most others. Whatever she read, saw or heard relating to the history, construction and worth of any antique object seemed to slot itself into her memory to be called forth when required. It was a knack that Christopher could never hope to emulate, though he applied himself diligently to the task.

Tal was general overseer of the shop. Wilf Akers did the heavy work. Instead of dropping during the transitional period, monthly turnover increased. Kennedy King called frequently. He would do a little tour of the shop and lug off three or four pieces in exchange for a slip – pretentiously termed an Interbranch Exchange Note – for the cost price value. Uncle Kennedy was much more interested in Christopher than in Holly's stock. He would make the shop inspections rapidly and hurry upstairs to take tea with Holly and dangle ribbons or strings of bells over his totally disinterested nephew.

If any lingering sexual attraction towards Holly remained in Kennedy, he gave no sign of it. On the contrary, he appeared to be relieved to be offered the role of uncle and to have an excuse for lowering his guard with Holly and the infant.

Christopher explained. "I do believe my dear uncle prefers being a family friend to being a roué. Perhaps this will persuade him to find himself a wife and have a family of his own."

To a stranger Mrs. and Mr. Christopher Deems appeared to live a rather dull life, to be almost too compatible. In their leisure time, however, they visited the Lyceum cinema and laughed at Keaton and Harold Lloyd or suffered with Mary Pickford. On occasion Christopher would purchase tickets for a West End theatre and they would make an evening of it. Only in the privacy of their bedroom was the marriage less than satisfactory, but even there the couple had reached a point of understanding that would lead in time to a merging of passion with tenderness.

Holly had to admit, however, that she felt just a little tied. Christopher suggested employing a housemaid, but Holly was reluctant to commit them to any further expense until the returns for the Christmas period had been audited. She managed well enough, though lunch was always rough and ready and dinner not always punctual. Christopher's army training stood him in good stead and he was more than willing to pitch in with tasks that many a man would have considered beneath his dignity.

"Perhaps we should advertise for a shop assistant and keep you as the maid, Christopher," Holly said, and got her nose tickled with a feather duster for the very suggestion.

Master Deems grew and became more active.

Emma Chubb declared that the child was obviously destined to be a coal-heaver or perhaps a furniture remover.

Victor Lawfeld had him marked down to play blocker for Oxford on the rugby football field.

Uncle Maury saw him as a potential hod-carrier, and Grandpa Tal recalled that his own father had been a giant of a man and as strong as a bear.

Uncle Ritchie had no opinion. He had never clapped eyes on his new nephew, and had no wish to do so.

Since his release from Brixton Ritchie had remained incarcerated in Abraham's Box and, so far as anyone knew, had never so much as crossed the threshold to join his bewildered Pa for a pint in the Admiral's Hat.

* * *

"How long you gonna keep this up?" Leo asked, apologetically. "I mean, ain't none o' my business, really, right, but what's got you too scared t'even step outside?"

"I told you, Pa. I don't want nobody t'know I'm out."

"I never told nobody."

"Be bleedin' sure you don't, or I'll cut . . . Never mind. Just be bleedin' sure you don't."

"Sure, Ritchie."

"You give Stan Nuttall my message?"

"Last Tuesday, like I told you."

"He's takin' his sweet time."

"Stan ain't at your beck an' call now, son. He's got hisself a girl."

"Yer, I thought that might be it. Who?"

"Some bint from down the Borough Road."

"With a wooden leg an' a wig, I suppose," said Ritchie.

"She's a widder, so I 'eard."

"She can't be fussy, takin' on the Baron."

"Got kids'n'all."

"Is Stan livin' with 'er?"

"On'n'orf, so I 'eard."

"Well, the Borough Road ain't the bleedin' end o' the world," said Ritchie. "Bastard better show up 'ere by Sat'day."

"What's so special 'bout Sat'day?"

"I give 'im ten days, an' ten days is up Sat'day."

Ritchie's tone silenced his father, bringing the conversation over the breakfast table to an abrupt termination.

Ritchie buried himself again in the *News* and Leo, disconcerted by his son's truculent behaviour, eventually went off to work.

* * *

Lugging a battered suitcase in one hand, with a pair of working boots slung round his neck by the laces and his army kitbag, stuffed full, hefted over his shoulder, Maury bumped down the narrow staircase. It was approximately a quarter to two on Saturday afternoon. He had entered the house only fifteen minutes before. Going directly to his room he had paid no attention to his brother who, with a copy of *The Human Bat* folded over his face, was lying full-length on the living-room couch in a state of suspended animation. Maury had intended to be gone before his Pa got in from the early shift, but he had been delayed at a job in New Cross and was running an hour late in his plans for the day.

Even when Maury came clumping downstairs, Ritchie did not lift a corner of the lurid comic paper. The sounds, though unusual, were not those he was waiting to hear and, like a cat, he completely ignored every intrusion on his senses that did not relate directly to him.

As Maury reached the hall, however, the outside door opened and Leo, in overalls, jacket and cap, entered. Father and son had no alternative but to confront each other. There was no space in the tiny hall for sidestepping.

"What the bleedin' 'ell . . .?" Leo began.

"I'm leavin'."

"When you be back?"

"I won't be back."

"Eh?"

"You 'eard, Pa. I'm leavin' for good," said Maury.

"Gawd strewth!"

"On the run, Maury?" Ritchie had glided unseen to the door of the living room and leaned there, smirking.

"Room's clean. Month's 'ouse-keepin's on the dresser under the bowl," said Maury.

"But . . . but where . . .?" Leo blustered.

"Gotta place of my own in Peckham," said Maury. "Put down a deposit, an' raised a mortgage through the firm."

"But...but Maury, son, don't yer like it 'ere?" said Leo.

Ritchie sniggered. His easy charm had gone, chafed off by his months in prison. He said, "Can't bring 'is tarts 'ere, Pa. Needs a cosy nook t' take 'is fancy women to."

"Fancy women?" said Leo. "You gotta fancy woman, Maury?"

"Nope," said Maury. "But I gotta nice little villa in my name, an' that's where I'm stayin' from now on."

"Cost a bleedin' fortune," said Leo. "What about me?"

"This place ain't big enough for you, him an'me," said Maury.

"*It's yer bleedin' 'ome,*" Leo shouted.

"If y' need me for anythin' urgent, leave word at the yard. Paddy Elkins 'as my new address." Pushing the suitcase ahead of him, Maury nudged his father aside and unlatched the front door.

"When'll I see yer?" Leo asked.

"I'll be around."

"Peckham? What yer want t'buy an 'ouse in Peckham for?" Leo trailed Maury on to the pavement. "I mean ter say, what's so bloody marvellous about bloody Peckham? The bloody, bleedin' sticks, it is. Peckham! Maury?"

Maury was already striding down the street, stepping over children who, in spite of the cold, were sprawled on the pavement like casualties or squatted like pygmies at the base of the lampstandards. Maury carried his burdens as if they were weightless, moving fast away from the irate figure by the open door of No. 5.

Women, leaning from groundfloor windows, said, "Nice day, Maury." Maury answered them – "Nice day" – without breaking stride, while the women's heads turned left and looked on down at old man Beckman doin' his conker.

"Maury! Maury! You 'ear me, Maury?"

Maury went around the corner by the Hat.

Leo threw his greasy haversack to the pavement and kicked it violently against the wall; then, sheepish at his public outburst of temper, stooped, picked it up and dived indoors, slamming the door behind him.

Ritchie was seated on the stairs. He wore a collarless shirt, baggy trousers and black canvas plimsolls without laces. He hadn't shaved in a week, though his hair was still short. Leo stared at his only remaining child, seeing him with great clarity for a split-second, a lean, mean, heartless little rat-bag, grinning like a split seam. Leo closed his eyes quickly. When he opened them again Ritchie had moved back into the living room.

"First 'er, now 'im," said Leo. "It'll be you next, suppose?"

"Right, right you are," said Ritchie from the kitchen.

Leo rubbed his face with his hand and braced his elbow on the unsteady post at the foot of the stairs. He glanced upstairs. Maury's room door was wide open. Light from the window, the colour of lye soap, flooded down. The room looked hideously empty.

"Wouldn't 'ave been this if his mother'd been alive."

The sizzle of meat in a frying pan and the sudden strong odour of cooking drew Leo into the living room.

There were little holes in the fabric of the home-place. Things were missing – a photograph of Holly, brass letter-rack, tin cigarette box and a matchbox holder with a picture of Lords Cricket Ground on it. With a sense of shock, Leo realised that these objects had belonged to Maury. They had accumulated so gradually in the house that he had thought of them as his. But they'd been Maury's all along, the boy's private property. He looked around; no socks over the fireguard rail, no big brown handkerchiefs drying on the string by the window, no boots, stuffed with newspaper, down by the side of the hearth.

Maury *had* gone.

Ritchie came through the curtain with a plate in his hand. He also carried a knife and fork and a bottle of pickled cabbage. He put them on the newspaper that served as a table cover.

A faint blue haze emanated from the scullery, savoury and pungent enough to stir Leo's appetite. He tugged off his cap and jacket, tossed them on to the couch.

"That for me, son? That my dinner, then?"

Ritchie laughed, pulled out a chair and slid on to it.

"Don't be bloody stupid!" he said, and, while Leo watched, quickly demolished two pork chops smothered in pickled red cabbage. He mopped up gravy with a slice of bread.

Sitting back, Ritchie lit a Woodbine. He blew smoke in his father's direction.

At a loss, Leo had seated himself on the edge of the armchair by the empty grate.

"Listen," Ritchie told him, fumbling in his pocket as he spoke. "Here's half a dollar. When Stan Nuttall turns up, you buzz off. Right?"

"But I ain't 'ad me dinner yet."

"Buzz off, Pa."

"Sure, son," said Leo. "Whatever you say."

He had lost one son and daughter already, through no fault of his own. He must do his level best to see that Ritchie did not leave him too, though in his bones he knew that Ritchie would be long gone by Christmas and he would be alone – apart from Kirsanoff, who didn't count.

"You want me t' buzz off now?"

"Yer, why don't you," Ritchie said.

* * *

Stan Nuttall held out his hand without removing the grey suede glove that covered it. "Ritchie, it's good t' see yer."

"Took your time spreadin' the welcome mat, though."

Ritchie did not shake hands. Turning from the door he led his former accomplice into the living room. It was after six and darkness was down over Lambeth. Curtains were drawn, dirty dishes cleared from the table. Ritchie had even tidied up the room a little, not because of Stan's impending visit but simply out of boredom.

"I was just obeyin' your instructions, Ritchie," said Stan. "I mean, I was led t' believe you didn't want me rushin' at things an' runnin' round 'ere right off. That's what yer old man told me, anyhow."

"Yer, yer," said Ritchie. "You're 'ere now, so I don't suppose it matters. I just didn't want nobody knowin' I was back on the streets, like."

"I ain't 'eard a whisper, Ritchie."

"Well, you wouldn't, Stan," said Ritchie. "Shotten's boys don't hang out down the Borough Road, do they?"

"Right you are."

Stan wore a long ex-army trenchcoat with a broad belt and a profusion of flaps. His shoes were new, brown brogues with welted tongues. He put his hand into the inside pocket of the coat and extracted a package wrapped in crisp mauve paper, sealed with four rubber bands. "I brought the money, like you asked."

Ritchie took the package, seated himself at the table and undid the bands. "Spent your share already, have yer?"

"Some," said Stan.

"Need more, now you got a bedmate t' support?"

"Listen," said Stan. "Ritchie, listen. I'm glad yer out the nick, but future plans . . . well, I . . ."

"Gone respectable?"

Glumly Stan nodded.

He had expected to discover changes in his friend but not to such an alarming degree. Ritchie was like a section of naked wire through which an electric current might crackle at any moment.

Behind the eyepatch, Stan's scarred lid itched.

"It's okay," Ritchie said. "I mean it, mate. No strings. You done what I asked, an' you're in the clear. I ain't goin' t' twist yer arm."

"It's all there, Ritchie. Every penny."

Ritchie stripped away the mauve tissue and looked down at the banknotes. "Renzo or Seaman ever come sniffin' round?"

"Not near me," said Stan.

"They're too bleedin' passive," said Ritchie. "I don't like it."

"I don't see what Shotten's got against yer, Ritch. I mean, you done the work, took the tumble an' kept a stitched mouth. He can't 'ave nothin' against yer."

"Not yet, maybe," said Ritchie.

He ran his pinkie up the side of the wad of notes, not counting, merely caressing them. He knew to the penny how much was there and was sure of Stan's loyalty. The money excited him, though he did not show it. Possession of the money brought his plan into perspective, gave it substance. It was only a matter of patience now, of not allowing his desire to be with Ruth to spoil everything. He had learned a lot in Brixton, about crime, about Vince Shotten, about himself; most of all about patience.

"Didn't tell Jeff I was out, did yer?"

"Nope," said Stan. "Didn't even tell Marigold."

"Marigold?"

"From the Borough Road," said Stan.

Ritchie glanced round. "Weddin' bells?"

"Some time," said Stan. "She's shy. Besides she collects a widder's pension. Ain't much, but it's always money."

"Pa said there was kids?"

"Two girls."

"A whole family ready an' waitin'," said Ritchie. "Still slavin' away in the tannery, are yer?"

"Stuck there, looks like."

"No more blags, no more easy money?" It was framed as a question. Stan took it seriously.

"Can't risk it, Ritchie. I got too much t' lose now. I don't even drink no more."

"Marigold must be a corker."

"She don't mind about the eye, or the 'and. Even the kids don't mind; they're only young, 'course. I, well, I can't let them down."

"Heard about our Holly?"

"Married, with a kid."

"Yer," said Ritchie, diffidently. "Got knocked up by some toff. Leaseways he married 'er. She was never one t' get caught out. Cumin' cow."

"Don't you go gettin' caught out, Ritchie."

"I won't." Ritchie got to his feet, leaving the banknotes on the table. He had a five-pound note in his fingers and extended it towards Stan. "Take it, mate. It's for Marigold. Buy her a bottle of scent an' a buncha flowers. Somethin' for the kids an' all."

Stan hesitated then took the note and transferred it to his pocket. "Thanks, Ritchie. I will get them somethin'."

"Just don't say it came from me."

"Ritchie, what's up?"

"Up?"

"Why're you hidin' out?"

"I got somethin' t' do," Ritchie said. "I don't want Shotten's boys gettin' windy."

"Somethin' violent, Ritchie?"

"After – I'll be on me merry way, Stan. I'd tell you, but it's best you know nothin'. If Shotten sends his chimps round, you tell 'em you ain't seen me since I come out. Tell 'em you didn't even know I *was* out. Do it right. Convince them."

"It's Shotten you're scared of?"

"Not scared of," said Ritchie.

"Gawd! It's Shotten you're after."

"Best get outa 'ere, Stan."

"Ritchie. Take care."

"An' you, Stan."

*   *   *

It was late on Saturday night before Tal Kirsanoff returned from Pimlico. He felt rather pleased with himself. He had been in sole charge of his great-grandson for all of three hours. Though the little fellow hadn't raised a whimper in all of that time, Tal prided himself that he had done his job very well indeed. It was good for Holly to get out of the house. She had taken some persuading but he and Christopher had worked on her. broken down her maternal concern until finally she had acknowledged that popping round to the new French restaurant in Anson Street, only twenty minutes' walk from Cardwell Place, could not be construed as deserting her child. It was the first evening out that Christopher and Holly had had since the baby's birth. Both of them enjoyed it hugely, though Holly had come upstairs again in a state of anxiety, convinced that young Christopher must have smothered in her absence. Calmly Tal had assured Holly that the infant was sleeping soundly and had been no trouble at all, neglecting to mention, of course, that he had stolen through to the bedroom every five minutes stung by the same silly fear.

Christopher had brought the old man back a bowl filled with *Supreme de Volaille Alexandra* – chicken breasts in Mornay sauce – and a half bottle of wine as payment for his services. The young couple and the old man had sat around the kitchen stove chatting for over an hour while Tal shifted the delicious supper dish and Holly fed the baby. It was after midnight before he left to catch the last bus across the river to the Lambeth depot, and returned home to the Box.

Ritchie was waiting up for him.

"Knew about Maury, didn't yer? Knew he was leavin'?"

"Yes."

"Didn't say nothin', did yer?"

"It was not my place."

Ritchie shrugged. "Goin' up the ladder, is our Maury."

"He works very hard."

"Like our Holly."

"She also works hard."

"Implyin' I don't."

"I have not seen any sign of industry on your part, Ritchie."

"I suppose you're entitled t' wig me off. You done all right by me, Gran'pa. I got no complaints."

"Where is your father?"

"Upstairs in 'is bed. Drunk as a bleedin' lord."

"What do you want from me, Ritchie?"

"Suspicious old cove ain't you?"

"You haven't exchanged two civil words with me since you were released from Brixton. I cannot believe that you waited up for me out of kindness."

"Want t' thank you."

"Thank me?" Tal was astonished.

"Yer, you're the only one o' the lot o' them that done anythin' for me. You could've shopped me. I know that. You could've given the coppers enough information t' send me up for five years."

"You are my grandson, Ritchie."

"Don't seem like it. Don't feel like it, know what I mean?"

Tal nodded. "I'm afraid I do. Now, out with it; what favour do you require of me? Has it to do with Ruth Erbach?"

"You know I've been lyin' very low," said Ritchie.

"Yes."

"I've been waitin' on money comin'."

"From Stan Nuttall? He was your holder, was he not?"

"No flies on you, right enough. Yer, Stan come through tonight."

"Are you planning another job?"

"Now, now! Shouldn't ask that, Gran'pa. Matter of fact, I'm plannin' a little holiday. I'm leavin' first thing in the mornin'. Be gone about a week."

"Alone?"

"I ain't takin' Ruth with me – not this time. So you won't be confronted with Tilly ready t' claw yer eyes out for aidin' and abettin'."

"Not this time?"

"Tell Leo I'll be back. Tell Leo t' keep 'is trap shut."

"Why did you not tell him yourself?"

"He ain't too bright, case you hadn't noticed," Ritchie said "Now, I know what's on yer mind, Gran'pa. Think I'm goin' out on a tickle, don't yer? Well, I'm not. I'm plannin' on leavin' the country, discreet, like."

"But you have a prison record, Ritchie. How will you obtain an exit visa?"

"Got friends, up in Scotland. I can buy the papers I need."

"Are you going alone – not now, when you emigrate?"

Ritchie smiled. "What d' you think?"

"You pulled a lot of jobs, Ritchie," said Tal. "Do not think that I do not know how many. I kept a record."

"Thought you 'ad."

"I don't know why. Perhaps I intended to use it someday to wring money from you."

"You ain't cut out t'be a blackmailer."

"It is not necessary. If it had been necessary, perhaps I would have used it."

"Necessary?"

"To obtain finance from you for your sister, or for Maury."

"*Them!*"

"I have done no less for you, Ritchie, if you recall."

"Yer, that's true."

"It is your plan to elope with Ruth Erbach, to go to a foreign country with her and to start a new life together?"

"Somethin' like that."

"When?"

"Soon as I can arrange it."

"Do you want me to break the news to Tilly and Mendel."

"Gawd, no! I wouldn't put *that* on to anybody. Nope, I'll leave word, tell them m'self."

"Tilly will bring the law down upon you."

"We'll be gone by that time, Ruth'n'me."

"Tilly is very determined."

"Tilly's also stupid," said Ritchie. "She can't see what she done t' Ruth."

"Tilly is possessive, I do admit."

"Driven Ruth to me. Think I'd 'ave got much in that direction if Ruth 'ad 'ad choice?"

"How can one answer that question?"

"How, indeed, can one answer that question," said Ritchie, imitating the Russian's formal manner of speech. "Don't matter."

"What do you want from me? You haven't told me yet."

"There might be another kinda stir when I go."

"Stir? How do you mean?"

"People come lookin' for me; not the law."

"Criminals?"

"Maybe – maybe not. Tell them I gone t' France. That's all you know, Gran'pa. Gone t' France. They won't lean too 'eavy on yer if you give 'em somethin'."

Tal said nothing.

He felt cold suddenly, though the fire had warmed the living room and he had not yet taken off his overcoat. The chill came from within, sudden dread of involvement with Ritchie's dark affairs. Deceiving Tilly and Mendel was bad enough. However, he had a certain sympathy for the girl, for Ruth. He could pretend that he was little more than an innocent go-between. After all, Ritchie's ardour was equally matched by Ruth's.

It was a strange passion that had grown up between them, but he, being Russian, understood it. Denial had strengthened their love for each other until it had become all-consuming. In Ritchie now there was no room for compromise, no room even for cockiness, the brashness, the arrogance of youth. He had waited almost as long as he could bear. The girl was of an age. There was something strangely honest in the love between his grandson and Tilly Erbach's daughter. He regretted that Tilly and Mendel would be hurt, grievously at that, but as Ritchie had been quick to point out, the Erbachs had brought it on themselves. Only an elopement would suffice. There could be no amicable solution. Condoning Ritchie's affair with Ruth was one thing, however, becoming involved with men like Vincent Shotten was another. Fear stayed with him. He was not reassured by Ritchie's indication that Shotten would probably not bother the family.

"Tell 'em I've gone t' France,,' Ritchie repeated. "Tell 'em I was careless, left a fake passport lyin' about. Tickets. Get 'em off yer back any way you can, Gran'pa."

"Is that the favour?"

"Last thing I'll ever ask yer t'do for me."

"Have I a choice?"

"Nope." Ritchie reached up to the shelf over the fireplace and took down the cigar box in which Tal kept his smokes. He flipped up the lid of the box and held it out to the old man. "A present, Gran'pa, from me t' you."

There were banknotes in the box, many of them.

Tal's features hardened. He snatched the box from his grandson's grasp and upturned it, spilling banknotes and cigar stumps on to the dirty carpet. He dropped the box after them and got to his feet. "Is *this* what you think of me? Am I only to be *bought*? How *dare* you? I would have done as you asked of me because I am your *grandfather*, not because you give me presents. I do not *need* your dirty money, Ritchie. I do not *want* it."

The young man's cheeks flushed. For once he was ashamed of himself, and his misjudgment. But he had forgotten how to apologise. "Sod you, then, old man."

"Tonight, you thanked me. That I accept. I am glad to accept. But payment – no, *never*. Ah, it makes me *sick* that you would think of me so."

"Listen, Gran'pa . . ."

"I have no more time for you, Ritchie. Good night."

"Wait, look, I . . ."

Tal turned and stalked out of the living room. Ritchie heard him clumping up the narrow stairs, the creak of his weight upon the ceiling, then the attic door slamming.

He looked down at the scattered banknotes on the carpet and, shrugging, stooped to pick them up. As he did so he was struck by a sudden vivid recollection of the Jewish fence lying bleeding on the floor of the stinking house in Shadwell. He had not thought of Steiner in months, not since he'd been sick with 'flu in Brixton and the dreams had tormented him. But he had a quick flickering vision of the Jew now, and the eye of God on the lintel. He even glanced up at the door of the living room.

Shaddai.

He wondered if the old Russian was overhead, giving him a forked sign with his fingers and muttering potent Yiddish curses.

Superstitious guff!

He did not believe a word of it. Anyhow, Kirsanoff was blood kin, too steeped in religious manure to risk calling on God and Abraham, Moses and Isaac and all the rest of that Old Testament gang to avenge a hurt to his pride. Even so – Ritchie's eyes travelled over the piebald ceiling with its layer of fine grime and fuzzy strings of spiders' webs adhering to greasy stains – he could no longer hear the old man moving.

Oh, Gawd! Suppose he had died, the way Fielding had died? Oh, Gawd! Oh, Gawd, not him! Not Gran'pa!

Being cooped up had done it. Hunger for Ruth. He was going

coconuts. Shut up, first in Brixton, now here in Abraham's bloody Box, he was sailing round the loop. He held himself still, listening, straining. The silence from up above was complete. He could not even hear his father's spluttering snores.

Suppose? Like Fielding?

He rushed out of the living room and took the stairs two at a time. Even as he ran he knew how lunatic it was, how totally crazy. He did not knock but threw open the attic door.

The lamp was lit. The old man had tossed the sheepskin overcoat on to a chair. He was seated on the side of the bed with a book in his hands. He glanced up, startled, at Ritchie's intrusion. Ritchie did not enter the room.

"What is it now?" Tal Kirsanoff asked.

"Are . . . are you all right?"

In the book were photographs, some of them faded to pale sepia phantoms, hardly distinguishable. On the bed by the old man's side were other portraits – his wife, maybe, and Holly.

"I . . . You didn't make no noise," said Ritchie, accusingly.

"Am I usually noisy?"

"No, but I . . ."

"I understand," Tal Kirsanoff said. "Good night again, grandson."

"Goodnight," said Ritchie. "Take it easy. Right?"

"Right," said Gran'pa Tal, and smiled.

* * *

The golden leaves of late October filled the swales of St. James's Park, oldest of London's pleasure grounds. Once wildfowl and pretty ducks had shaken feathers on the red shale pathways and a sheet of ornamental water had provided a mirror for the trees. During the War the lake had been drained and covered with the temporary buildings of government departments so that even now the view from the suspension bridge was a reminder of sacrifice and ugliness. Above the trees, however, the Palace caught the rays of the afternoon sun and the wood-paved Mall was carpeted with the broad leaves of the plane trees as if guardsmen out of St. James's courts had scattered unmilitary tokens of the season in great armfuls. Autumn, not spring, seemed to suit this part of Royal London best, Holly thought. She wondered when the authorities would demolish the temporary sheds and once more give the ducks a home. Christopher would enjoy coming down to feed the quackers before going on to see if the King was at home in Buckingham Palace. She could imagine her son in warm red woollen coat and pantaloons, a big white knitted "tammy" on his head, gloves tied by a tape to his collar. She would make a point of being free every weekday afternoon – at least until he went to school.

The baby-carriage was a high-wheeled Swann. It rode easily and was not too awkward on kerbs. Though Holly had full possession of the wooden handle, Emma Chubb shared command, one gloved hand on the curved iron. If not the captain of the expedition Emma considered herself its navigator and helmsman. Out of kindess Holly would let Emma "have a shot" of the baby-carriage on their second turn of the path by Birdcage Walk. Head high, Emma would fairly race along, secretly hoping that passers-by would think the baby belonged to her and that Holly was just a nursemaid.

Though his eyes were open, Christopher betrayed no interest in the passing scene. Emma and Holly, however, pretended that certain developmental movements of the baby's eyes represented awareness, even amusement. There was no doubt that the afternoon walk kept the infant contented for, awake or asleep, there was never a sound of complaint while the Swann was in motion.

They were heading up the centre of the park towards Buckingham Palace, into slanting sunlight, when David caught up with them.

He wore a broadcloth thigh-length topcoat and tweed trousers, new but not expensive. He had had to step it out, it seemed, to catch the baby-walkers and was breathless as he came abreast of the women. Stooping slightly, cocking his head, he looked into their faces. Coincidence was possible but not probable; Holly suspected that David had contrived the meeting. Perhaps he had even followed them from Cardwell Place.

"Holly?" David raised his hat politely. "I thought I recognised you. Couldn't let you pass without saying hello."

"Do you know Miss Chubb?"

"Miss Chubb." David raised his hat again, not even glancing at Holly's companion. His attention was drawn magnetically to the baby. Manifest in excessive courtesy and a stilted manner, his composure was not sufficient to mask his curiosity.

"Is this your son?" he asked.

"Master Christopher Deems," said Emma, since Holly did not answer immediately.

"May I?" said David.

"Yes," said Holly.

David took off his hat and leaned against the side of the carriage, staring down at the baby. Holly straightened the little angora bonnet, squaring it across the infant's brow. Young Christopher scowled, wrinkled his nose and gave a discontented bleat.

"He likes us to keep movin', Mr. Aspinall," said Emma.

"Oh, I see," said David, still staring. "Well, if I may, I'll walk with you as far as the gate."

"If you an' Holly want to have a a chat," said Emma, "I'll take the little chap once around the lake."

"No, Emma," Holly said. "It's time we were headin' home. But, please, David, do walk to the gate with us, if you wish."

"You look well, Holly."

"Motherhood agrees with her," said Emma. "Don't it?"

Reluctantly Holly yielded the handle to Emma. She could think of no other means of preventing the woman dominating the conversation. Instinctively she realised that David had contrived the meeting. He wanted to see the child; she could not find it in her heart to deny him. Confused, she released the handle, a gesture that seemed to weaken her defence against David's influence. She did not love him now. But no more did she hate him.

Boldly pushing the baby-carriage, Emma led off.

David and Holly followed a few steps behind Emma's dash for the gate, falling in with her striding pace.

"Haven't seen you since you became owner of the shop," said David. "Is business booming?"

"Kennedy King's the owner," said Holly. "I'm just the manager."

"But you live above the shop?"

"Yes. It's very comfortable."

"We always found it so."

"An' convenient, under the circumstances."

"Do you know, I've never had the pleasure of meeting your husband."

"Haven't you?" said Holly.

"Is the baby like him? It's hard to tell at that age."

"Opinions differ," said Holly. "How are your mother an' sister?"

"Andrea's married; did you know that?"

"I'd heard."

"Not before time, I say," David added. "Mother – she's never been better. I saw her on Sunday."

"She likes country life, then?"

"Adores it."

"An' your wife – is there any improvement?"

"None."

Obvious questions had been asked and answered. Emma was

clucking and chucking at Christopher, patently not listening to the couple behind her. The gate seemed very close. David had given no reason for prolonging their meeting. He would have to leave them, or make his intentions too obvious.

Without warning, he gripped Holly's arm and halted her. Startled, Holly glimpsed Emma and the pram going on, then she was looking up into David's eyes.

"Yes, I followed you," David said.

"David, please, it's . . ."

"I wanted to see you just once more."

"David, it's all over; everythin's changed."

"I sail for Hong Kong next Wednesday."

"Hong Kong? But David what about your wife?"

"It won't matter to Linsey whether I'm in Hong Kong or Hampshire. I've taken on commitments, Holly, and the best-paying job I could find is in Hong Kong. Miles Walshott recommended me. It's with a large firm of shipping agents. I'm to be assistant cashier; *the* assistant cashier. Promotional opportunities are excellent. Apparently, my superior is due to retire in three years. If I prove myself reliable, I should find myself in charge."

Emma had stopped just inside the gate.

Holly could hear Christopher's war cries of annoyance at the cessation of the soothing rocking of the carriage. She was torn between that cry and David. His news seemed so final, so ambitious. But Emma's croonings did not appear to pacify the infant. The crying became loud and sore.

"I'm glad, David," Holly touched his arm.

"I couldn't stay in London," said David. "Not after all that's happened. Over there, at least I'll be my own man."

"David, I must go."

"Of course," said David. "May I . . . may I write to you now and then?"

"No, David. Please don't."

"I understand."

He lifted his hat once more, and took her hand. He did not shake it, but squeezed it as if to reassure her that he would not interrupt the flow of her life again.

"Look after Aspinall's," David said. "Dad always wanted you to have it."

"Goodbye, David."

"Goodbye."

She left him.

She took the handle of the baby-carriage and steered out of the park gates on to the pavement. Christopher stopped wailing at once. Holly did not turn round.

"Well, that was a surprise, you meetin' him like that," said Emma, probingly.

"Oh, I think he wanted to meet me," said Holly.

"Really?"

"We were friends once – but never close. He's leavin' for a new job in Hong Kong next week," said Holly.

"Best place for him," Emma declared.

"Yes, Emma," Holly said. "I think you may be right."

* * *

Once, and only once, did Andrea Aspinall rebel against the outrages that dear old eccentric Aunt Cordelia perpetrated upon her. Miles had made it plain that she, Andrea, had taken the marriage vow in full cognizance of the facts of his domestic situation and that, while he would certainly welcome a complete redoing of the Hampstead house, he would brook no suggestion that Cordelia be brushed into an asylum.

"She *is* my last surviving relative, dearest. I will not discard her," he explained. "Not even for you."

During the first month of connubial bliss Andrea was preoccupied with supervision of interior decorators and the arrival of vanloads of new furnishings from posh West End stores. It excited her almost as much to buy suites and tables and odd bits of things for the house as it did to buy hats and gowns. Miles was generous in his allowances. When he returned from the office each evening they would dine together in the dining room. And Andrea would flirt with him, if she was in the mood. And Miles would suggest that they go to bed quite early, since there didn't seem to be much else to do.

But Aunt Cordelia could not be ignored. Not only did the old woman have the run of the first floor, she also had an innate sense of timing. Just as Andrea had wooed Miles into an interested frame of mind and was slithering out of her Parisian nightdress, the wicked old woman would take it into her head to sing herself to sleep. Aunt Cordelia had a voice like a sergeant-major and could carry a tune no further than the first bar. In compensation, however, she had a head full of obscene lyrics that she'd picked up from her first nurse. Nurse Runcorn and Aunt Cordelia had spent many a happy afternoon blending their voices in ballads so blue that they would have made an

Irish navvy blush. The servants had finally ganged up on Nurse Runcorn and, in spite of Cordelia's vehement protests and sulks, Miles had been forced to dismiss her. Nurse Runcorn's legacy had remained. Quite frequently Cordelia would throw herself into performances of ditties both nautical and naughty, particularly when she wanted to annoy her nephew or, as now, her nephew's wife.

Andrea realised that she was an ideal victim. She could not pretend to be amused, could not indulgently humour the old woman. She reacted with anger and indignation – which, of course, was precisely what gave the old woman pleasure.

Miles was not an ardent lover. He had to be coaxed. Magical spells were completely broken whenever Auntie twanged her vocal cords.

There was no simple solution. Andrea spoke of doing out the cellars for the aged but that idea was not ever on, really. No other area of the house was sufficiently remote to baffle the bellowing solos that recounted in graphic detail the adventures of "Peg-leg Dan", the "Wallasy Maid" and the crew of the "Good Ship Venus". Though Mrs. Owens was not shocked by Anglo-Saxon rhymes, she was rendered near speechless at the quality of Cordelia's voice. Being Welsh, she found the lack of pitch and timbre an offence against decency.

Threats and punishments, the withdrawal of alcoholic beverages, sweet reasonings and towering rages, by Miles and Mrs. Owens in turn, hadn't the slightest effect on Cordelia. By hook or by crook, in any manner possible, the old woman was determined to drive her nephew's stiff-necked cow of a wife insane.

Confrontation was inevitable. Andrea could not live under the shadow of Aunt Cordelia for long. She *would* be mistress of all she surveyed. Miles must choose. Miles must be rid of Cordelia, or find himself without a wife. Andrea repeated the sentiment to herself, quietly, twice a day. She practised adamant poses before her cheval glass. She wanted the mansion – and Miles. She had never learned to compromise. Even in the matter of the shop she had, by devious roundabout way, got what she wanted in the end.

In spite of her determination, Andrea prevaricated. Each passing day, let alone week, strained her temper. Each passing hour, let alone day, played on her nerves. She was all ears, all eyes for Cordelia or, worse, one of Cordelia's practical jokes which were so varied and imaginative that they never failed to make Andrea shriek – a clockwork mouse under the lid of the cheeseboard, a salt cube in the sugar basin, a rubber frog floating in the downstairs you-know-what, an exploding cigarette in the silver box in the drawing room – Miles got the worst of that one – and all kinds of other proprietary horrors.

Where Cordelia laid hands on such infuriating toys nobody could discover. She never went out and received no mail. The servants swore on their knees before Andrea that they did not smuggle in the goods. The whole thing remained a mystery. But the havoc played on Andrea's nerves was obvious. Sniffing, touching, tasting, peering, probing and prying into every item of food, every drink, every article of clothing and piece of furniture became normal behaviour for Walshott's wife, *chez* Walshott. She would flinch at every noise, quiver before opening cupboards and enter the you-know-what with the deliberation of a sapper crossing a minefield. It all got a bit much, really. Once, during a Savoy lunch in company with her husband and an aristocratic client, Andrea felt compelled to have her orange sorbet cut into pieces by the waiter at a separate table and then spent three or four seconds sniffing each part like a basset hound before cautiously spooning it into her mouth.

That particular night Miles had yet another serious word with his aunt in the privacy of her room. He told Andrea that he had threatened her with expulsion if she did not immediately mend her ways and cease her attacks.

For six days and nights peace reigned in the Walshott household. Andrea's confidence began to seep back. She even began to impress her will upon the sluts and slovens of her domestic staff. She still suspected that one or two of them were in cahoots with Cordelia, acting as supply agents for the squalid joke objects and the bottles of gin that the old lady had secreted about the house.

For six evenings, however, Miles and Andrea dined quietly and without interruption. Andrea informed Miles that if Aunt Cordelia continued to behave herself for another two months perhaps they might risk entertaining. There were *so* many people to whom they owed dinner, said Andrea. After all they had a beautiful home. Could he blame her for wanting to show it off? No dearest, said Miles, privately thinking that two months was an eternity in context and that it was always most calm just before the storm. Besides Miles had recognised the source of the practical jokes. They came from an extra large De-Luxe Boy's Box of Tricks that Cordelia had given him as a Christmas present many years ago and that he, being bashful, had never dared use. Where his aunt had hidden the thing, though, he could not wring from her, nor could he quite remember, alas, what other parlour terrors had been tucked away in the gaudy compendium.

In a peculiar way Miles did not wholly disapprove of his aunt's badgering of Andrea. He would never have been courageous enough to undertake the role of Petruccio off his own bat, but that did not hinder him appreciating some of the changes that were taking place in his bride. Andrea's spitfire tempers had been diminished and, if not tamed, at least she had been somewhat gentled by her inability to contrive a suitable method of counterattack. She was even beginning to treat Miles like a refuge and not a lackey. He rather liked that, to be truthful. Beneath her aggressive, self-assertive carapace Andrea was rather vulnerable and the gradual appearance of that vulnerable streak made Miles feel more manly. The six-day lull in Cordelia's war against his wife had not been the result of a dire threat by Miles. Aunt Cordelia might be mad as a hatter but she wasn't stupid. She cackled away to herself in the privacy of her suite at the thought of the masterstroke she had planned and the item from the extra large De-Luxe Boy's Box of Tricks that she had saved until last.

November closed in. To Andrea, the day of her wedding to Miles seemed far off. David called upon them that evening. Though he would not wait for dinner, over drinks in the library he had informed them of his imminent departure for Hong Kong. The very thought of Hong Kong made Andrea shudder. Miles had been instrumental in finding her brother the job. She believed Miles when he told her that it entailed hard work and a strict code of behaviour; the English community in the Far East would ensure that David behaved himself.

In spite of her callousness Andrea could not help but think of Linsey Leigh-Jennings – an Aspinall now – in a sterile room in a nursing home. She had always been a little jealous of Linsey. The punishment for naughtiness was exceedingly excessive, in Andrea's opinion. Even so, she had bidden her brother farewell without regret. David and she had never been temperamentally in tune. Now that mother was settled, there was nothing David could do for her that Miles could not do much more efficiently.

Her brother's departure, however, had a retroactive effect. Seated by candlelight at the long dining table in the company of her husband, Andrea was suddenly seized by a feeling of panic at the thought that she was Miles's prisoner and would remain in this house through middle-age, into senility. By rapid turns, she felt abandoned and cared-for, imprisoned and free. To steady her mood and regain her sense of purpose, she encouraged Miles to drink deep of the table wine and to ply himself – and her – with Napoleon brandy.

By half-past eleven, with furry fog rubbing itself on the windows and infiltrating into the corners of the hall, Andrea had relaxed into a state of amorousness. She needed to be needed by her husband, assured that she was attractive and retained a unique power over him, the same kind of fundamental power that the Leigh-Jennings girl had exercised on David to make him her slave.

She joined Miles on the leather sofa before the fire and leaned her large body against him. Miles had unbuttoned his waistcoat and loosened his collar stud. He was smoking a large cigar but politely held it away from his wife and angled his head from her every time he took a puff.

"Where's your aunt?" Andrea asked, in a low voice.

"Tucked up safe and sound, I expect," said Miles.

"The servants?"

"Dismissed to their various corners."

"Miles, let's go to bed."

"Hm! Are you sleepy, dear?"

"No."

"Don't you feel like a hand at cribbage?"

"No, darling, I do not feel like a hand at cribbage."

"Another drink?"

"Miles, I want to go to bed."

Lazily Miles got to his feet. He went through the nightly ritual of checking ashtrays and banking down fires, putting up guards, locking the outside doors. Andrea waited for him at the foot of the stairs and, hugging his arm, accompanied him through the corridor to the ground-floor bedroom at the rear of the house.

The bathroom was en suite and while Miles went through a second ritual of brushing his teeth and putting on his pyjamas and robe, Andrea quickly changed into a sheer silk nightgown, dabbed her bosom with exotic perfume, tidied her hair and got between the sheets. She put out all lights except the one by the bed so that its radiance was cast upon her, making her appear sensual and romantic. Napoleon brandy still coursed through her system. She felt almost as passionate as she had done that summer afternoon in the wilds of Hampshire.

Miles appeared from the bathroom, closed the door, stepped to the bed and took off his robe. He contemplated his wife for a moment, then walked around the bottom of the bed and slid in beside her. She sank against the pillows.

"Put the light off, Andrea."

"Let's be daring, dearest; leave it on."

"Hm!"

"Touch me, Miles. Kiss me."

Miles was not reluctant. He met her halfway, slipping his arms about her and drawing her to him. She fumbled to free the buttons of his pyjama jacket, to nuzzle her breasts against his chest. She was unpardonably stimulated.

"Now, darling. Now."

She lay back while Miles, humped beneath the bedclothes, prepared himself and put himself in position. Andrea's head tilted backwards against the headboard and, even as Miles joined with her, she found herself staring at the legs of a gigantic hairy creature perched above her on the rail of the four-poster, its body crouched under the curtain.

She opened her lips. No sound came.

Her eyes widened in horror.

Miles lurched against her and the violent motion wakened the creature. With a limber jerk it shot from its hiding place and swooped down on Andrea, monstrous swollen limbs dangling, hairy body curved. It brushed her once then swung on, jigged round Miles's ears and returned to stuff its tail into Andrea's face.

"Dear God!" Miles ejaculated, and, waving his arms, tumbled from elbows and knees and rolled on to his side. "Dear God, what . . . what . . . what the devil!"

Andrea was transfixed.

The obscene creature danced and bobbed above her. A hybrid, a cross between a monkey and a spider, it was suspended on a long black rubber band fastened to the upper bedpost, lips peeled back in a hideous red leer, evil green eyes glowing in the half-dark. Worst of all, strung between its paws was a banner of white paper on which was printed in jet black ink, "Do be Quick. I'm Dying for It."

It was Christmas dinner all over again, only worse, much worse. No exploding pudding could have had the effect of that monster on unsuspecting Andrea. She might have shrieked herself into a swoon if it hadn't been for Miles. Her dear husband was curled into a foetal ball, knuckles shoved between his teeth, face scarlet. He uttered odd little uck-uck-uck-uck noises. Clearly he was in the throes of a heart seizure.

Andrea bounced up.

"Miles, Miles, Miles: are you dying? The doctor, oh God, the doctor. Don't die, Miles. Please don't die!"

The stockbroker could hold his breath no longer. He unfurled suddenly and flopped on his back, head on his wife's lap, face directly beneath her breasts. He tried to restrain himself, but the effort was too great. Even as Andrea stretched out her hand to touch him, he let out a violent bray of laughter. It was succeeded by snorts and wheezes, hoots and howls, so explosive and painful that he was thrown off the bed on to the carpet by them.

"Your . . . your . . . your . . . face.   Your . . . face,   d . . . d . . . . . . dearest. God, your face, Andrea. I . . . n . . . n . . . never saw . . . saw anything l . . . like it. Ha-ha-ha-ha-ha-ha-noooooo, ho-ho-ho. No. N . . . n . . . never did. Oh, oooooooooh, ooooooh, ha-ha-ha-ha. Oh, Andrea, did you . . . *Ah-ha-ha-oooh*."

"Miles, you're laughing?"

"Yes, yes, yesssssss. I'm s . . . s . . . sorry. Can't h . . . help . . . *canthelpit*."

"Miles, you are laughing at me?"

"AH-AH-AH-AH, HAAAAAAAAAAA. OH. OH. OH. HEEEE-EEEEE."

She beat her fists upon his arms, then, wriggling and stretching, battered the top of his head. None of it seemed to have any effect, except to make the furry creature entangle itself in Andrea's hair again. She tore at it, dismembered it, and hurled the limbs and tail at Miles who had tipped over backwards and was prone upon the carpet, racked by mirth. She flung herself from the bed, stood on him.

"Oh.Oh.Oh.Oh.Andrea! Oh.Oh.Oh.Oh!"

Miles hadn't the strength to twist out of her way. But Andrea was no longer intent upon choking him. She made a bee-line for the little dressing room and hauled out her clothes, talking at him as she whipped off her nightdress and jumped into anything she could find to cover her nakedness. She did not shout nor shrill. She spoke in a whispered staccato that her poor prostrated husband could barely hear let alone decode.

As she dumped clothing into an alligator suitcase, Andrea said, "You knew all along it was her, your aunt, I think you even bought the bloody stuff for her, I know you buy her the bloody booze, you bastard. Good God, what do you take me for, do you think, the pair of you, I'm going to live in this lunatic asylum and be your victim, is that you still laughing, you bastard? YOU BASTARD. Do you hear me, Miles? I hope you do because it's the last you'll hear of me, you or your precious *bloody*, BLOODY, aunt, I think the whole family's insane, INSANE, do you hear me? Goodbye, Miles, don't bother to see me out, I'll find my own way out, thank you, then you can have a drink with that old bitch, OLD BITCH, upstairs and tell her how funny it was."

The speech carried Andrea out of the bedroom and along the corridor. She lugged the alligator suitcase and trailed a fur stole that was all she could find in the darkness of the dressing room. She was vaguely aware that Mrs. Owens and a maid were peering down at her from between the rails of the banister and thought that she could discern Cordelia's manic laughter echoing along the first floor.

As she crossed the hall to the front door she remembered that Miles had locked it and had hung the key on the hook in the kitchen. She did not hesitate. She veered to her right, bashed open the library door with the case and marched across the room to the window bay. Sweeping back the velvet curtain, she groped for the patented burglar-proof bolt, twisted and released it, yanked up the long window, flung the case out and, with the stole bundled in her arms, stepped over the sill into the garden. She found the case, hoisted it up and strode off between the evergreens towards the gate.

Behind her, Miles lowered the window and secured the bolt. He was still in pyjamas and had not even paused to put on his robe. He stood in the bay for a moment watching his wife wrestle with the latch of the big front gate then, as she vanished into the street, he let the curtain fall.

Going back into the library, he poked up the fire, found his brandy glass and poured himself a snort. With a final exhausted giggle, he settled down on the leather sofa to await Andrea's inevitable return.

It took Andrea an hour to realise that she had nowhere to go. Hampshire and Mother? Even if she could have got there at that hour of the night, Andrea had no wish to lose face to that degree, particularly with Thora. Hotel? She had not thought to bring money with her. Besides she looked so dishevelled and disreputable that she would not be likely to obtain a room in any decent hotel without creating a scene. She was in no state to create a scene. The suitcase became heavier with every passing minute. She was cold. The stole did not protect her legs and feet from the November chill. David? She did not even know where her brother stayed.

Lost, humiliated and utterly alone, Andrea trudged round the streets of Hampstead until she found herself once more back in Laurel Row. She rested, sitting on the wall, screened from the house by the dense mass of the hedges, hoping, rather forlornly, that Miles would be scouting the neighbourhood in search of her.

At length she rose, let herself through the front gate and walked disconsolately to the door. She rang the bell. No lights showed in the hall. She rang the bell again. The house remained silent.

"Miles," she hissed. "Miles, it's me. I've come back."

Once more, she tugged on the bell-pull, heard the jangle of the Victorian brass clapper in the depths of the kitchen.

How could he fail to hear it?

Perhaps everybody had been dispatched to search for her.

Surely not Aunt Cordelia; or Mrs. Owens.

"It's me – Mrs. Walshott. Let me in this instant."

She stepped back out of the portico and surveyed the facade above her. Not a light showed, not even in the servants' attic.

"Andrea, I say, Andrea."

Her heart leapt. She ran around the side of the house to the library and there found light, a long slat of it projecting across the lawn.

"Miles? Miles, is it you? Do let me in."

He had closed the window again, though she could see him standing close to the glass on the inside, the cheerful blaze of the fire behind him darting points of light upon the panes.

"I've . . . I've . . . Let me in, Miles. Open the door."

Miles shook his head.

"Miles, for God's sake!"

She could just make out his words. "Why – have – you – come – back?"

"Miles, don't be silly. This is my home."

"Why – did – you – leave – it?"

"Miles, what are you doing? Let me in this instant."

"I'll – consider – it."

"Miles Walshott, you listen to me. . ."

He lifted the window six inches and, stooping, said, "I'm sick and tired of listening to you, Andrea. Why should I let you in? You packed up and walked out. Left me, your husband."

"But your aunt, that . . . incident . . ."

"Annoying, I agree," said Miles.

"Let me in."

"Hm?"

She broke, begged, half-kneeling against the sill. "Please, Miles, please, please, let me in."

"Why, Andrea, did you come back?"

"I had nowhere else to go."

"So, this house is only a refuge? I'm only a refuge?"

"No, dearest, no, of course not."

"You married me because you had nowhere slse to go? Am I correct, Andrea?"

"Miles, I love you."

"I can't hear you."

"I love you, Miles."

He pushed up the window, took her hands and assisted her into the house, saying, "I won't stand for it again, Andrea. Even if you do say you love me."

"It was that . . . that thing. I lost my head completely."

He closed the window, slipped the stole from her shoulders and, with his arm about her, took her close to the fire.

"Andrea, I am your husband. I deserve respect."

"I . . . all I ask is a little peace. I'm not like you; I can't laugh at things."

Miles drew her on to the couch and put his arms about her.

"You mean you can't stand to be made to look a fool, Andrea."

"Is that so wrong of me?"

"Of course not. But you make a fool of me."

"Never, Miles. Never."

"You see; you're not even aware of it."

"Miles, I'd never do that."

"We're two of a kind, I fear," said Miles. "For all that, I've been made a fool of too often, Andrea. I'm not a joke. I can see the funny side of things, but I am not a joke."

"Miles." She wept.

Her husband comforted her. "I realise that Aunt Cordelia – much as I like the old goose – cannot remain here. I'll arrange for her to be put into a home."

"Must it be a home?"

"I suppose she might be all right in a place of her own."

"With Mrs. Owens."

"If I can persuade Mrs. Owens to stay. However, I'll arrange something, Andrea."

"You won't . . . won't put me out?"

"Not," said Miles, touching her nose, "if you behave yourself."

"Thank you, dearest. Thank you."

"Now, shall we go upstairs to bed?"

"Is that . . . thing gone?" asked Andrea.

"All gone," said Miles and, quite firmly, escorted his wife from the library.

* * *

"What is wrong with you, Mendel Erbach?" Tilly demanded. "How can you sit there, so calm, when your little girl might be lost?"

"She is not lost, Tilly. She is most like enjoyin' herself."

"Six o'clock on a winter Saturday night; she is three and one half hours late, up in the city, an' you say not to worry my head? Is that a responsible father talkin', I ask?"

"She 'll have gone to see the shops, Tilly."

"Ruth never does that."

"Ruth is a grown woman now. Maybe she meets friends."

"Friends? What friends?"

"From the typewritin' school. She must have friends, Tilly. It's right for a girl her age to have friends."

"*Boy* friends?" said Tilly. "*Boy friends,* you mean?"

"Boy, girl – just friends."

"Have I not been a good mother to her, she should want to chase after boys?"

"You, me – we have nothin' to do with it. It's nature, Tilly. She's close to nineteen years old."

"A child."

"Ruth is no child now, Mother. Only in your eyes, is she still a child."

"So I'm the one to blame for what has happened to her?"

"Nothin' has happened to her. She will be home soon."

"I should never have listened to you, Mendel Erbach. She should not have gone to that typewritin' school. It is full of boys."

"You don't want ever to be a grandma, Tilly?"

"Sure, I want to be a grandma – but not tonight."

"We *buy* Ruth a baby, from Silverdale and Baur's? If she wants to find a husband, first she gotta meet boys."

"I'm glad her upbringing was not left to you, Mendel."

"Tilly, that is enough."

"Six o'clock, Saturday! Where *is* she? She never done this before."

"Maybe she go to a picture house."

"Picture house? You know what goes on in picture houses?"

"Alas, I only hear," said Mendel. "Look, what d'you want me to do, Tilly?"

"Go tell the police."

"Tell them what?"

"Our girl is missin', you ask what you gotta tell the police? Maybe she's been *taken*. Maybe she's in a box on a ship headin' for . . . how would I know . . . for Damascus, someplace."

"Tilly, Tilly! What a condition you got yourself into. Sit down. Drink tea, eat fish. Ruth'll come home soon."

"You won't go to the police for me?"

"Look, I tell you, nine o'clock, I go to the police."

"Three *hours,* Mendel! What could happen, think, to a young girl in three hours?"

"She could enjoy herself," said Mendel Erbach. "I go to the police at nine o'clock, not one minute before."

"Eh-eh-eyyyya," said Tilly, wringing her hands.

"Ruth is fine," said Mendel. "Take my word for it, mother; your little girl is just fine."

• • •

Fortress-like, the Staffa Hotel in Hare Street, Soho, protected its inhabitants' anonymity. Thick walls and dusty plush muffled private communication between the temporary occupants of its rooms. There was no meal service to speak of and the day porter was a wizened little budgerigar of a man who had been at the job so long that nothing surprised him. Even so he let his rheumy eyes trail over the young Jewess as he handed a room key to her companion and took a ten shilling note in exchange.

"Got 'till seven," the porter said. "After's extra."

Ritchie scribbled the name "Carter" in the dog-eared notebook that passed for a register, and led Ruth upstairs. No daylight penetrated the claustrophobic corridors and the rooms were sealed against the intrusions of the afternoon by ancient crushed-velvet curtains.

The short evening dwindled into darkness.

Neither the man nor the young woman locked together on the bed noticed the passage of time.

Eventually the budgerigar banged his fist on the door and shouted, "Ten minutes, you in there. Ten minutes an' it's extra."

Sated with his loved one's body, Ritchie was lying languidly against her touching her eyebrows with his fingertips.

Hoarsely he answered. "Yer, we hear yer."

Ruth stirred. "Have we got to leave, Ritchie? Can't we stay here, just stay here for ever?"

"We'll be together soon, darlin'," Ritchie told her.

He got up and began to dress.

"I never thought it would be so marvellous," Ruth said.

"It was, wasn't it? Marvellous," said Ritchie.

"Can't we go off – t'night, Ritchie? I can't wait any longer t' be with you. I want you all the time."

"This time next week, we'll be together," Ritchie leaned on the rumpled bed to kiss her brow. "After next Saturday, we'll never be separated again. It'll be you'n'me every night, every day."

"I worry, my darlin'," the girl said. "I worry somethin' 'll happen; it won't go right."

"It'll go right," said Ritchie. "You know what you've gotta do?"

"How can I not see you for a whole week?"

"We've waited two years," said Ritchie. "A week's all it'll take. We don't want t' have t' meet in dumps like this again. After next Saturday, sweetheart, it'll all be different. I promise."

"I believe you."

"Put your clothes on," said Ritchie. "You don't want to make your Ma too mad."

"She'll be mad already," said Ruth, rolling out of the bed and beginning, unselfconsciously, to dress in front of her lover. "She'll be bleedin' furious. I don't care."

"Tell me again," said Ritchie. "Last time, darlin'; tell me what you've gotta do?"

"Nine o'clock next Saturday. . ."

"No earlier," said Ritchie. "Not a minute earlier."

"Nine o'clock, I put on my warmest coat an' pack a case with my best clothes an' I slip out the house without them knowin' it."

"Can you manage that?"

"Yer, I'll manage. Don't fret, love," said Ruth. "I take a taxi from the stance at Eadie's to Euston railway station. I meet you in front of the bookin' offices."

"The train for Glasgow leaves, ten o'clock," said Ritchie. "You gotta whole hour t' get there. I'll be waitin' with the tickets. We get on the ten o'clock train t' Glasgow, arrive there early Sunday. I got rooms booked for Sunday. Monday we find ourselves a proper place for three or four weeks 'til the papers come through, then we sail for Canada."

"The ring, tell me about the ring, Ritchie."

"I gotta ring for you. We'll be married, only nobody else'll know about it. Just you'n'me. The Scotch geezer, brother of a bloke I met in prison, don't even know my proper name. But he'll see us right about the papers we need to leave the country."

"Mamma'll search."

"Your Ma won't find us," said Ritchie. "Nobody'll find us."

"I don't like leavin' a note."

"Ruth, you must do what I tell yer. Leave a note. Tell them you run off with Tal Kirsanoff's grandson, an' you've gone t' France on the boat with him. My grandpa'll collect what comes from yer Ma."

Ruth chuckled. "I wouldn't be in his shoes, not for anythin'."

Ritchie took the girl in his arms.

The budgerigar rapped again on the door. "Five minutes, sonny."

She kissed him again and again, until, with an effort of will, Ritchie pushed her away.

"Is everythin' clear, Ruth?"

"I won't let you down, my love," she said.

"Got your story made up?"

"She won't believe me."

"Don't matter now," said Ritchie.

They left the Staffa Hotel together and walked through Soho to Oxford Street where Ritchie saw her safely on to an omnibus that would take her home.

Ruth leaned from the top deck and blew him wild kisses, not caring who saw or what anyone thought.

"Next Saturday, my darlin'," she called out, as the bus gathered speed.

"Next Saturday," said Ritchie and waved until she was out of sight.

* * *

"Out. She says she's been out. You hear, father? We worry ourselves sick today an' answers, 'I been out. *Where?*"

Ruth said, "I went shoppin', Mamma."

"Shoppin'! You hear, Mendel? All right, what did you buy, uh? Where is the parcels?"

"Window shoppin', Mamma, with two friends from school."

"Boys?"

"Girls, Mamma."

"Their names?"

Mendel said, "Let her eat supper, Mamma."

"Their names?"

"May Wattis and Ruth Wiseman; I met them. . ."

"Three girls on the loose up town . . ." said Tilly.

". . . at the typewritin' school. We walked around, ate tea in Lyons . . ."

"Is that what girls do now?" Tilly cried. "Why d'you do this to me. What's wrong with you, Ruth? You used to be a good girl. Now you go paradin' round the streets, into tearooms, like a tart."

"Tilly. . ." Mendel tried vainly to restrain his wife.

"Like a tart. There *was* a boy, uh? Wasn't there a boy, maybe more than one boy – *Goyim?* They give you money?"

"*Don't talk to me like that,*" Ruth shouted.

"You shout at *me*, your Mamma? You hear, Mendel!"

"All you think about is money, money, money," Ruth said. "You never think about me. I got to do somethin' on my own. Look, Mamma . . ."

But she had raised her voice, exerted her personality, demonstrated that she had grown up. The day had come, the day Tilly had dreaded, when her baby, her doll-child, would come to life in front of her eyes and would walk away from her.

Tilly swung her arm. It was a well-muscled arm attached to a hard fist, the palm calloused. It struck Ruth flat on the left cheek and snapped the girl's head away, pulling again as Tilly, with no apparent sign of temper, only cruel calculation, brought round her right and jerked the girl's head back with a second blow. Finger marks glowed instantly upon the girl's pale flesh.

Mendel was on his feet at once. He caught his wife by the shoulder and drew her down into the kitchen chair. "No, Tilly. No, that's enough. She does not deserve such punishment."

"I spoiled her," said Tilly, nodding. "Ay-ey, I spoiled her. Now I'm to reap the reward."

To Ruth, Mendel said, "Your Mamma 's upset. She thought somethin' bad had happened to you because you were late. Do not blame her."

Tilly said, "Blame me? What's that you say, Mendel Erbach? Blame me? Was it me who was out street walkin' all day an' half the night, uh?"

"Ruth, go up to your room," said Mendel. "Soon I bring you a nice supper."

"Let her find her own suppers from now on," Tilly said.

"Go, Ruth."

Face inflamed and head still ringing, Ruth moved silently out of the kitchen and made her way up the narrow stairs to her bedroom, her sanctuary. She hurt. But she did not cry. She did not have to fight tears. She felt quite dry inside. She threw herself on the bed, hands beneath her, pressing on the place where Ritchie had been, feeling the soft, gelatinous heat there again. She groaned. The ache of fulfilment cancelled out the pain in her head, the rage at her mother, and her father's weakness. Papa should have protected her. He should not have stood for it.

On her back now, Ruth smiled to herself, looking up at the darkness in the corners of the room. She felt triumphant.

It was not what Mamma had imagined.

It was worse, much worse.

And come Saturday, the pair of them would really have something to wail about.

After Saturday, she would never see either of them again.

* * *

Prison – or love-making – had left its mark on Ritchie. It took him twice as long as he had anticipated to enter the big Victorian house in the Swanpond Road in the wee small hours of Sunday. It was a former brewer's mansion, close enough to the Southwark-Peckham Brewery to contain the sour yeasty odour of fermenting hops in corridors, lounges, nursery and even the bedrooms. It was the bedrooms that gave Ritchie most problems. The owner and his wife were in residence. He was obliged to do his work while they slept. But Ritchie took nothing away. He did not steal so much as a cigarette or a walnut. He left no record at all of his visit. He was after information.

He was inside the mansion for almost two hours and did not get home to the Box until five a.m. He set the alarm clock on his dresser, rolled into bed and slept until half-past eleven, when he rose, he washed, shaved and dressed himself in the new hopsack suit that he had bought during his visit to Glasgow. He took time and trouble with grooming. Studying himself in the mirror in Holly's room, he had to admit that he looked real smart. His skin was pasty and there were puffy ash-grey smudges under his eyes but quality tailoring suited him.

One o'clock on the nose Ritchie reached Polmar's English Chop House in a narrow throughway called Turpentine Lane, not far from the Elephant. Polmar's was an establishment of many rooms, decorated with gilt-framed prints of thoroughbreds, pugilists, whippets and wrestlers. There was a lot of brasswork, brown leather and old red tile, and, it being November, a fire in every room.

Ritchie was met by Mannie Polmar, the elder, and given a warm welcome considering he was a stranger. He was shown into the snug, while Mannie Polmar went off to see if Jack Renzo was taking dinner with his brother in the back parlour.

There was no doubt in Ritchie's mind that the Renzos would be taking dinner; it had been a fraternal habit for years and hardly a Sunday passed without the meet being kept. Mannie came back with Jack Renzo and, the snug being quiet, Ritchie bought drinks, apologised for taking Jack from his dinner and said he wouldn't keep him long.

They sat in a corner, protected by the curved leather wings of a bench and the bottle-glass of the street window.

"I didn't even know you was out, Ritchie."

"No reason t' tell anyone, Jack."

"If you're lookin' for business . . ."

Ritchie spread his hands, indicating the hopsack suit. "Does it look like I'm broke?"

"Seems Brixton never done you any harm. What's the shout?"

"I gotta load for you, Jack."

"What sort of gear?"

"Only the best. You got my word on it. Only the very, very best."

"Where's it stashed?"

Ritchie smiled. "West o' here, Jack."

"Right-o. We'll fix delivery."

"Hold it," said Ritchie. "One thing I never learned in Brixton was blind trust. I call the tune, Jack. Believe me, you won't regret it." He took a folded sheet of paper from his inside pocket and read from it, in a low voice. "Three furs, one mink-skin. Two half fur jackets. Diamond ear-rings, three pairs. Set matching dress necklace, gold an' diamonds, ring an' bracelet. Pendant ear-rings – this big."

"Get off!"

"Pigeons' eggs, I'm tellin' you," said Ritchie. He continued to read from the inventory. "Gold cig case, four gold watches, solid twenty-two gold signet ring, pearl stick-pin."

"What the hell've you done – Clarence House?"

"Interested?"

"Naturally."

"Lots more." Ritchie read again from the itemised list of the objects in the house in Swanpond Road.

"Where's it from?" Renzo asked.

"Various places," said Ritchie. "If y' want t' know, Jack, I made a purchase. I used my savin's on it."

"You've *got* all this gear?"

"Sure."

Renzo had to work had to hide his eagerness. "Well, I reckon we'd be interested. Need to value it first."

"I'm sellin' it in two lots." Ritchie put away the paper. "It's take it or leave it. No room for negotiation. You don't want the stuff, plenty folk across the river'll jump at it."

"Vince don't like being' told what t' do."

"Don't tell Vince, then."

"What?"

"I bought this haul for an old song," said Ritchie. "Never mind how; that's water under the bridge. Terms are these – I bring you one batch next Saturday evenin'. You get to examine it on the spot. Bring anybody you like t' help. But I want one thousand pounds for it. No more; no less. No barter; no argument. One thousand quid, Jack, is the price o' the first delivery. Cash on the barrel."

"A thousand quid! God, Ritchie, that's a mountain of money!"

"Stuff's worth it, three times over. Don't take my word for it, Jack. You'll get t' see it all, by electric light – but nobody leaves the premises, an' none of the gear goes out neither. Those are my terms."

"Ritchie, you wouldn't be tryin' to pull a fob job on me?"

"I done a stretch; I don't want no more," said Ritchie. "Besides, take as long as you want t' hive off the first lot – then give me the word an' I'll deliver the second."

"Same terms?"

"Same terms."

"Supposin' I don't make my profit on . . ."

"I told yer, Jack. It's no quibble. You'll make yer profit three times over, that's guaranteed."

"Vince'll want details before he parts with ten buckets."

"Takin' it through Vince, are yer?" Ritchie raised his eyebrows.

"How else?"

"Well, I thought yer might buy first." Ritchie shrugged.

"Buy personally?"

"I ain't goin' t'tell Vince – not if you don't want me to."

"Buy first, then resell to Vince," Renzo mused.

"You've done it before."

"What if I come unstuck?"

"Won't come unstuck with me, Jack. I don't want flayed."

Jack Renzo made his decision. "I'll take it, Ritchie."

"Upstairs room, the Baronspark Hotel, River Street."

"What's wrong with the Shears?"

"Nothin' – but Vince has got ears everywhere," said Ritchie. "Make it the Shears if y' like."

"Make it the Baronspark," said Renzo. "But no funny business, Ritchie. I'll have Aleric with me an' he's still got a score to settle with you."

"Bring who yer like," said Ritchie. "Just be there at seven-thirty sharp – with the thousand quid."

"What night, again?"

"Saturday," said Ritchie.

* * *

After the baby's midday feed, Christopher carried the painted cradle downstairs into the shop and there Holly put the baby down. Young Master Deems was not much of a one for a siesta and would sleep for no more than a couple of hours. Even so, he was prone to nap during the afternoon walk and, the weather being cold and none too bright,

Holly would not keep him out for long. Once the baby was tucked up snug in the niche by the high desk, Holly settled to her day's tasks. She did not concern herself with the steady stream of customers. Christopher and Tal were quite capable of handling routine sales. She paused once or twice to have a friendly word with dealers who had come in, to show them the baby with as much pride as she might have allowed them a peep at a priceless objet d'art. Christopher did not steal Holly's thunder, though he sauntered close at hand to pick up stray compliments.

"Bonnie wee laddie," declared Mr. McClure.

"'An'some little beggar," declared Mr. Marlowe.

"Sterlin' quality there, Holly, my dear," declared Mr. Levin.

And each of them, being old school, slipped a silver florin under the end of the shawl, discreetly and without fuss.

Christopher Deems the Second took the birth gifts as his due and did not cease his gentle snoring.

At two-thirty, Christopher Deems the First left to catch the three o'clock auction sale at Scott's, in Dartington Street. Holly had dropped in yesterday, on her way back from the park, and had spotted a nice eighteenth century mirror, framed in gilt gesso, that she thought might do for upstairs if the price was right. She had priced fifteen other items, including a Charles II tankard with authentic Ram's Head marks that she could re-sell through King's to an old established client. Scott's was not on Kennedy King's beat, and Emma and Simon Black had gone up to York for a house sale. With the price-list in his pocket, Christopher went off, leaving Tal to hold the fort for the later part of the afternoon.

Shortly after Christopher's departure, the shop being temporarily deserted, Tal came up to the desk where Holly was writing letters of quotation.

"Holly," said the old man. "I told you that your brother, Ritchie, is out of prison?"

"What of it?"

"I believe he is going to leave London."

"Thank God," said Holly.

"Why do you say that?"

"I dunno, Grandpa. I just feel safer when Ritchie's not hangin' around. Ever since he tried to palm off those ear-rings on me, I've been suspicious. It wouldn't stop him, knowin' I could get into serious bother for re-sellin'. If he did manage to sell me somethin' an' it was discovered, we'd be hard put to it to convince the police I'd bought in innocence."

"He has been very quiet since his return," said Tal. "I believe Brixton frightened him."

"Our Ritchie – frightened? I doubt it."

"He has not said so directly, but it is my opinion he will be leaving London, perhaps England, in the near future."

"He can't go far enough to suit me."

"There may be . . ."

Holly glanced up from her letter. "What's up?"

It had been in Tal's mind to tell Holly about the plans Ritchie had made concerning Ruth Erbach but the old man checked himself. He still had faint hopes that he might dissuade Ritchie from going through with it – though he could see no manner in which he could bring pressure to bear on his grandson. Tilly and Mendel would blame the Beckmans, and Holly would lose two good friends in the trade. Still, skilled though the Erbachs were, they were not the only restorers in London, and they had never been particularly cheap.

"Nothing, Holly," Tal answered.

"Ritchie bothers you too, doesn't he?"

"It is true. I have been closer to him than any of you, but I still do not know him. He is unpredictable, Holly."

"If you ask me he's just plain wicked. Maury wouldn't take him on, would he?"

"Perhaps – if Ritchie had wished it."

"Just what *is* Ritchie goin' to do?"

"I think he intends to take his money. . . ."

"His money?"

"The money he made from theft," said Tal. "Stan Nuttall kept it safe while Ritchie was in prison."

"I didn't know about that."

"You had no reason to know," said Tal. "Besides, you were occupied with your own concerns, Holly. I thought it best not to involve you in your brother's affairs."

"Oh, I don't care about him," said Holly, waving the pen and making a blot on the letter below the letterhead. She dabbed at it angrily with a blotting pad then, after inspecting it, crumpled up the letter and dropped it into the wastepaper basket beneath the desk. "I don't even want to talk about him."

"Are you happy, Holly?"

The question surprised her. It was one of Tal's favourites, but it was many, many months since he had put it to her. In addition, there was a seriousness in his tone that prevented a casual answer. She bit the end of the pen-holder and looked down at the baby in its cradle. "I'm so happy, I'm almost afraid."

"You too?"

"What d'you mean, Grandpa?"

"I am anxious, Holly – without reason."

"About me?"

"No. I can't put my finger upon it."

The old Russian and the young woman stared at each other and their apprehension was, for an instant, palpable. Then the shop bell rang and a couple of well-dressed ladies came in obviously expecting immediate service and the moment was lost.

For all that, Holly felt suddenly oppressed by the shop and, in a strange mood, transferred her sleeping son to his perambulator, put on her overcoat, gloves and hat and, with a curt goodbye to Tal, left Cardwell Place quickly for the fresh air of St. James's Park.

* * *

The trunks had been packed with the new tropical clothes that he had been advised to buy in London and ship over with him. He had also bought eight hefty volumes on various aspects of accounting and on shipping matters and intended to spend the voyage in study and comparative seclusion. The company were paying his passage. They had not stinted in that department, reserving a first-class cabin on a second-class passenger liner that, from what he could gather, was carrying a load of middle-class sun-worshippers on a world cruise. No doubt there would be much drinking, dancing and gambling. David felt uneasy at the very thought. He would read his textbooks and diligently avoid social entanglements. With luck, he thought dolefully, I might even be seasick. I'm a young man on the threshhold of a new career. I won't allow myself to wreck things before I even have a chance to get there.

Bearing his weaknesses in mind, David had arranged for his savings to be transferred directly to the Bank of Hong Kong. He took with him only sufficient for his needs – and that did not include high-stake bridge, backgammon or – God forbid – roulette. Once he got to Hong Kong, was drawn into the job, he would be all right, but the voyage, the luxury, the idleness, would surely strain his resistance. By Wednesday afternoon, David was praying for gales in the Atlantic, hurricanes round the Cape of Good Hope and at least a couple of typhoons to whip up the Indian Ocean.

As he travelled down to Leatherhead, however, England seemed as placid as a piece of faded tapestry. In his mind's eye he imagined the deck of the Cunarder washed by nothing more distracting than tropical moonlight. He felt like a man on the eve of a battle, nervous and very anxious to be getting on with it.

He had almost forgotten Linsey these past few hectic weeks. He had visited her only twice.

Guilt touched him not at all.

It made not the slightest difference to Linsey whether anybody visited her or not. Why the Devil should he feel ashamed because a gang of paid nurses disapproved of his so-called "neglect"? Really, there was nothing *to* neglect. It was like visiting a grave.

He had informed the matron of his intention to work abroad. She had sniffed and said, "It's up to you, I suppose, Mr. Aspinall. It's up to you." And he had answered, brusquely, "It is, indeed, up to me."

If it hadn't been for Linsey, he would not be leaving England at all.

Calling on Lin was the very last thing he had to do. He would travel directly on to Southampton by train and 'bus and would spend the night on board the ship. He could not believe that he would not see Piccadilly or the Strand, Pimlico or Hampstead, Mayfair or St. James's for at least three years. The fact that he carried no luggage with him – it had gone off in advance by rail – increased the dream-like unreality.

"You're early, Mr. Aspinall."

"I can't stay very long. I'm catching a boat tonight."

"Oh, a boat is it. Yes, of course. Tonight."

They let him into the private room.

Nothing had changed, except the view from the window. Winter's early frosts had peeled the landscape to tendon and bone. It was flat, dull, lifeless.

Linsey was propped up in bed. Big hard bolsters jammed under her shoulders made her arms jut out, her head lag to one side. The nurses no longer bothered to paint her face or fingernails and, weirdly, she did not look young now. Though there was no precise evidence of physical change in her appearance, something had gone, something that had fluttered for the past months like a small invisible flame, warming the empty corners of her being.

Logically, David told himself that the doctors had been trying out some new treatment on her and that what he saw was the result of their experiments. Negative, of course. Just as he'd entered the room, however, he had been gripped by panic; she was going to be sitting up, smiling; she would extend her arms to him and give him one of her lascivious winks. He did not want a miracle. The very thought of it filled him with dread. If Linsey was better, if any degree of progress had been wrung from her dumb body and numb brain, how could he abandon her? He would have to be cruel, as cruel as Linsey would have been. And if . . . and if . . . if she *was* sitting up, smiling, it would be all over; Hong Kong, the job, the new beginning.

So relieved was he to find her still shackled in her deep disordered dungeon of silence that he was almost gay in her presence; so gay that he felt heartless and, after prattling on to her for ten minutes, could take no more of the nine-tailed lash with which he scourged himself in this white room, and, without ceremony, kissed her cool brow and left.

The following morning, the liner nosed out with the tide from the bustling pier and David, who had hardly slept a wink, stood at the rail and watched the well-wishers slide away from him.

Miles and Andrea had talked of coming down to see him off, but he had dissuaded them.

Even now, after all that had happened, David Aspinall wanted only one person to shed a tear for him, and that person was presently in Pimlico taking breakfast with her husband.

Some day. Some year. In a decade or two, when the world had stood itself on its head again, he might come back and she might come to love him once more.

The horn barked and bellowed deafeningly. The tugs responded. Involuntarily David put his hands to his ears, pushed himself from the rail and went below.

* * *

"What's this?" Leo enquired.

"Fifty quid," Ritchie answered.

"Wha' for?"

"Beer money."

"Fifty quidsworth?"

"I'm goin' away."

"How long you be this time?"

"Dunno."

"Where?" Leo asked in sepulchral tones.

"France."

"Strewth! Bit late for the fightin', ain't yer, son?"

"Ha-ha," said Ritchie. "Goin' down South where it's warm. Look for work there; hotel, maybe, where they speakee de An-glash."

"Nothin' for you down there," said Leo, without an ounce of

conviction. He knew there was no point in trying to put the boy off. He'd been expecting it. This wasn't like it'd been with Maury. He could always go round and see Maury if things got desperate. But Ritchie was off like a whippet from a trap and he understood only too well that he might not see his beloved son for years. "Nothin' worth stealin' in France."

"In that case, I'll shove on some place else."

"Give you yer money back if you'll stay."

Ritchie laughed and buffed his father lightly on the chest. "Yer a stupid old begger, Pa, know that?"

"I know, I know, but . . ."

"Grandpa's still 'ere. He'll tuck you in when yer sloshed an' see you don't starve t' death. He's all right, y'know."

"Kirsanoff ain't my flesh'n'blood, like you, son."

"Holly an' Maury . . ."

"Stuck up, the both o' them," Leo sulked.

"Yer, but they done all right, didn't they?"

"For themselfs, just for themselfs."

"Give's yer 'and, Pa," said Ritchie in his broadest South London accent, sticking out his right fist with gruff manliness.

"'Ere, yer don't mean t' say yer leavin' right now, on a Sat'day afternoon?"

"Right now."

"Where's yer bags."

"I'm goin' as I stand," said Ritchie. "Give's yer bleedin' paw."

Leo shook his son's hand then, in a sudden and surprising welter of sentiment, clasped the skinny young man to his chest and hugged him furiously.

It lasted three or four seconds and made both father and son decidedly embarrassed.

Without another word Ritchie left No. 5 Ambraham's Terrace and set off for the Baronspark Hotel in River Street to prepare himself for the biggest night of his life.

• • •

To Ritchie's disappointment the man of the house was not at home that late Saturday evening. The long brick garage had one empty slot. The brand new, just-out-of-the-factory forty horse-power Lanchester tourer that had been the talk of The Shears and Mallet was missing, though the little side-valve Singer Ten was still there, personal transport now for the lady. The absence of the man of the house added an unknown factor into Ritchie's plans. He could not be sure when the man would return and, in a strategy as finely worked out as his, an extra ten or fifteen minutes advantage might make all the difference. But it was too late to pull out. Besides, nothing was ever gained without a bit of risk.

Ritchie carried the huge soft leather suitcase round to the back entrance via a trellissed walk that ran between the side wall of the garage and a strip of flower garden under the street wall. An electric bulb in a frosted globe shed light over the flagged yard. Washing hung neatly on a length of line strung between a hook and a pole. Two five-quart milk churns and a row of mops and brooms stood by the door of the laundry house. Within, through squared windows, Ritchie glimpsed the activity of the kitchen. He could smell the aroma of roasting beef, overlaying the yeasty atmosphere of the brewery a quarter mile away. Ritchie rapped on the door with the butt of the military Colt revolver he had removed from the pocket of his pilot's jacket.

When a maid, in white apron and geranium cap, opened the door, Ritchie thrust the barrel of the revolver into her face and pushed her back into the kitchen. He had not been down here during his nocturnal reconnaissance, but he had detailed in his mind the several things that he must look for immediately. They were not difficult to find.

The cook was caught between a chopping block and the stove. She had a huge brown bowl in her hands, filled with crushed herbs and onion rings. Like all the servants, high and low, the cook was too hard-bitten to seek refuge in hysterics.

Cook, maid and – by sheer good luck – the butler were all in the kitchen when Ritchie entered. He kept the revolver six inches from the maid's head, set down the suitcase and came out to one side of the girl to give himself a clear line of fire on the butler and the cook.

"Put the bowl down," he said.

The cook put the bowl on the nearest table and raised her hands to shoulder level. The butler had been decanting spirits from three big bottles into crystal containers in a silverware rack. He was small, squat, balding, and livid at the outrageous intrusion into his domain.

Ritchie pointed. "You. Not one bleedin' word. Not one foot wrong, or yer all dead."

"You must be off yer bleedin' 'ead," the cook said.

She reminded Ritchie of the prison visitor who came with the chaplain and handed out evangelical tracts, not in the least soft or saintly but a tartar with hawk-eyes and a mouth like a razor slash not properly stitched.

"You should know whose 'ouse this is." The butler managed to choke back his spleen and sound calm.

"I know whose 'ouse it is," said Ritchie. "How many more servants upstairs? You." He brushed the maid's waxy nose with the tip of the revolver. "You tell me."

"Only one," she answered at once. "Maggie's got 'er day off, every fifth Sat'day, like."

"The other one, man'r woman?"

"It's a boy, a kid," said the cook.

"Where is 'e right now?"

"Puttin' on a fire in the dinin' room," said the cook.

The butler had not yet raised his hands. He kept them low. In dark striped wastcoat and white shirt with arm-bands, he looked like a bartender in a Saturday matinee cowboy picture.

Ritchie said, "You. Where's the missus an' 'er kids?"

"Upstairs," the butler replied.

"Where?"

"First floor, 'er bedroom."

"Doin' what?"

"I dunno."

"Ain't there a nanny?" asked Ritchie.

"No," said the butler.

"Yer," said the maid.

"Which is it?" said Ritchie.

"Nanny's lyin' down," said the cook. "Gotta touch o' 'flu, like. Been lyin' down all arternoon."

"Where's 'er room?"

"Second floor," said the maid.

Ritchie did not engage in idle conversation. He had marked the kitchen's two entrances and the door to the cellar. He had also noticed the key-board on the wall close to the short, broad stairs that led up, he assumed, to the house proper. He said to the maid, "Go over there. Get me the cellar key. Quick."

The girl did exactly as he'd asked, returning with a long oiled key attached to a wooden slat on which was painted the word "Stillroom."

"I said the cellar."

"T'is the bloody cellar, y' ignorant tyke," said the cook.

"Where decent folks keep the wine cool," said the maid.

At that moment, the sound of boots thumping on the stairs accompanied the clang of a shovel in a bucket. Almost at once the boy, not more than fifteen and small for his age, came rattling down the stairs straight into the kitchen. His hands were black, his sleeves rolled up and he had soot smudges on both cheeks.

"Time that chimbley wuz swept," he said, then stopped in his tracks.

"Right, son, not a word," Ritchie told him.

He had them more or less where he wanted them now. The butler was still looking for his chance, but that chance would not come. They were all veterans of hard times, even the boy. They knew what was going on, sensed that Ritchie was fully aware of what he was doing and that he would not hesitate to fire the revolver, to wound or to kill.

"Is there an electrical light in the cel . . . the stillroom?" he asked, addressing the maid.

"Yer, two."

"All of yer, round the back o' the table and int' the stillroom. Put the lights on."

Ritchie kept the servants' dinner table, in the centre of the room, between him and the domestics. They did as he'd commanded without protest, the boy still carrying the bucket and shovel. The butler went in last. Ritchie followed him, stepping quickly. Before the butler could react, Ritchie brought the butt of the Colt down hard upon his head.

The butler groaned and pitched forward into the cook who shouted, "Y' rotten liddle bast'ad. He wasn't goin' t' cause no trouble."

"Makes sure, don't it?" said Ritchie.

He stepped over the butler's unconscious body and surveyed the stillroom. It was a tee-shaped cellar, with two doors in the deep wall which, when opened, revealed a coal hole and a log cupboard. Wine was racked along the short gable, and a couple of big kegs of beer stood upright. There were other bits and pieces of stuff, including three straw-stuffed boxes of spirits. But there was no window, not even a decent vent, and no fireplace that might have given the boy an escape route.

Ritchie broke both light bulbs one after the other and went out into the kitchen again, locking the stillroom door behind him. He dropped the key into the heart of the fire in the cooking stove, shifted off the pots so that nothing would burn and the smell attract attention, then he lifted the suitcase and took the keys, all ten of them, from the board and put them into his pocket. He paused. From inside the stillroom he could hear the sounds of the boy wailing and the cook's deep voice trying to comfort him, assuring him, probably, that he was no longer in danger.

The broad stairs led to a small landing. Narrow wooden stairs went left, almost certainly a back route to the servants' quarters on the second floor. To the right was a carpeted flight leading into a lighted hall, the main hall. Ritchie hesitated, then, very quietly, taking his time, he negotiated the suitcase up the wooden staircase, past a heavy door – first floor – to another heavy unpainted door through which he eased himself.

The corridor was gloomy, lit by two gas mantles and no other lighting. The flames were turned down low. The corridor was not wide. Surprisingly, it was carpeted with a cheap runner. There were five doors. He cursed his stupidity. He should have asked the girl which one was the nanny's room.

Hardly breathing, he stole along the corridor, paused outside each door, listened, heard nothing. He left the suitcase against the wall at the top of the main stairs, returned along the corridor, and listened again. A slight sound. Stooping, Ritchie peered through the keyhole. There was a key in the lock on the inside; maybe nannies had that privilege. He shifted the Colt to his left hand and tapped lightly with his knuckles on the door. The sounds became louder. Glass tinkling. Footsteps. Shuffling movements.

"Gawd! Did the nanny have a fancy-man in there?

"Who is it?"

Ritchie put his face into the sleeve of his pilot's coat and said, "Cook."

"Cookie, is that you?"

"Hmmmph."

The nanny was a woman in her thirties, dark-haired, handsome and full breasted. She had pulled a woollen robe over her nightgown and had socks and slippers on her feet. Her hair was down, and she smelled strongly of gin and Friar's Balsam. Ritchie shot out his right hand and closed his fingers across her mouth. He rammed the heel of his hand hard against her teeth, making her gag too much to bite him. He threw himself in on her, waltzing her round so that he could put his left arm around her throat and let her see the revolver. She was sweating in great heavy droplets, her skin greasy. A stuffed nose made breathing difficult and she choked as Ritchie doubled her up and ran her across the room – which was surprisingly large – and into the wall beside a huge Victorian wardrobe.

One wardrobe door was a dress mirror, the other showed the beautiful burled grain of the wood. There was an ornate brass lock with a key in it. Ritchie pinned the nanny against the wall and groped for the key. He turned it and let the door swing open. Dresses, a uniform, two overcoats hung inside. It was commodious enough, however, for the woman to fit in without having to curl up. Still holding her mouth, he hauled her away from the wall and thrust her into the wardrobe and, just as she let out her first strangulated, wheezing shriek, boomed the door shut and locked it. He put the key in his pocket, switched off the gas fire and the two gaslight mantles, making sure they were sealed, then hurried out into the corridor, picked up the case and padded down to the first floor.

Having heard some unusual noise, the lady of the house had obligingly opened the door of the master bedroom, but, finding nothing to draw her further, she had returned to the game she was playing with her children. Clothing from her cupboards was strewn on the bed, including the two fur coats that Ritchie had spotted. It was a dressing up parade that mother had devised to keep her offspring entertained, though, by the laughter, it seemed that mother was enjoying it too.

The woman was not at all what Ritchie expected. She was young – hardly older than he was – and slender, with fine ash-blonde hair and a heart-shaped face. She looked posh. One of the children, the nine-year-old boy, resembled his mother. The girl had her father's colouring, being dark-haired and sallow. She was not more than six years of age, too young to be afraid of a man with a gun.

The woman was seated on the bed, sorting out a wispy chiffon dress, measuring it against herself. The boy was on the bed too, with a full-length coat of Canadian red fox fur cowled over his head. Beneath it, he made growling noises. Cross-legged on the floor, the little girl was primping up a posy of velvet flowers and trying to fix them to the band of a huge summer-yellow hat.

Ritchie said, "Don't make no noise, please."

The woman put her hand to her mouth. For a split second, she seemed to be about to scream her head off, then thought better of it. She was even cooler than the maid servant had been. Perhaps she sensed that Ritchie would do them no physical harm – provided they co-operated. Clearly, the trappings of wealth meant little to her in real terms, otherwise she would not have made playthings of such expensive garments.

The muffled voice of the boy came from beneath the fur. "What is it, Mummy? Is it Daddy?"

"No, dear. It's . . . a gentleman has come to take away some things."

The boy's head popped out. He stared at Ritchie. "What things?"

The woman put her hand on the boy's head, holding him still. She extended the other hand, saying quietly to the girl, "Teresa, come here, please. Come, sit with Mummy."

The little girl looked up at Ritchie, smiling. "Paul has a gun just like that," she said.

"Tessie, don't talk to him," said the boy, Paul. He was still within the folds of the coat. Maybe, Ritchie thought, it makes him feel protected.

"Do you know," said the woman, as the girl rose and toddled to the side of the bed, "to whom this house belongs?"

"That's why I'm here," said Ritchie.

"My daddy will . . ." said the boy.

Ritchie said, "Never mind about that, kid." He opened the suitcase, kneeling on the floor. "you, lady, you know what I want."

"My jewellery, I suppose?"

"All the small stuff," said Ritchie. "An' I mean all of it."

"There isn't much. My husband keeps it in the ba . . ."

"*Gerroff!*" said Ritchie. "Lady, I been 'ere. I know what's what. Right, up you get. Pull the drawers out, all o' them. Put the jewellery in the suitcase. Don't burke me, neither. I ain't scrupulous about who I shoot."

"Does your gun have bullets in it?" asked the boy.

Ritchie ignored him. He had no intention of conversing with kids. He didn't much like kids. He would shoot the boy, if he had to. He would shoot the boy before he would shoot the woman. She could be of use.

He remained on the floor, supported on one knee, and gestured with the Colt, indicating that the woman should do as he had asked. She hesitated, stooped and lifted the girl up on to the bed. She drew the Canadian red fox fur from around the boy's body. The boy flattened himself on the silk counterpane. The woman touched both children. "Now, Paul – you too Teresa – I want you to be very well behaved, to sit on the bed and not to move until Mummy has finished what she has to do. Paul?"

"Is he *robbing* us?" said Paul.

"Just do as Mummy says. Please."

"Yes, Mummy." Paul twisted into a sitting position, legs straight out before him, and took his sister's hand. "Sit still, Tessie, or the man will shoot you."

Tessie began to cry. Paul hugged her awkwardly.

The woman did not attempt to comfort them. She looked ugly for a moment, until Ritchie said, "Careful. Be careful," and then she got control again.

She crossed the room to the dressing-table with its shell-shaped mirror and many drawers. She picked stuff from the drawers quickly and brought it to Ritchie who had her put it straight into the suitcase.

"Nanny will . . ." the boy said.

"Nanny's busy," said Ritchie. "Don't talk, kid."

The woman did not try to deceive him. She was more thorough than Ritchie would have believed possible, even lifting out the false bottoms of shallow drawers to expose fine jewels that he had failed to discover during his stealthy reconnaissance. He was almost moved to thank her, then to jeer at her; but he did neither thing, merely nodding as she lowered long pendants and heavy necklaces into the case.

It was a treasure trove, all right. Madness to keep such stuff unguarded in a private house in the heart of South London, a kind of conceit. The pick of the best of the crop, creamed off and held as an investment. Nobody would ever know. No doubt, there were faked receipts to authenticate ownership and placate imprudent policemen.

As the large suitcase began to fill up, Ritchie could not help grinning. It contained a mass of gold and silver, tangled with diamonds, sapphires, and rubies, gleaming with pearls.

Stupid. Plain bloody stupid.

On an open market he could have got four times a thousand quid for the haul even as it was. But a thousand was what he'd asked for, and a thousand would do. He would keep back six or eight of the really prime pieces, give them to Ruth to pass off as her own when they shipped out for Canada. That slender drop-stone pendant would look beautiful around his Ruth's throat.

Ritchie shook himself out of his daydream.

The woman – unbidden – had gone to the tall chest of drawers and was unloading her husband's jewellery from the third drawer down, items that Ritchie had marked – cufflinks, watches, stickpin, signet rings.

Quite suddenly it was over.

The woman returned to stand by the side of the bed. Stroking her daughter's dark hair, she told Ritchie, "That's all, all you can carry off in a suitcase, at any rate."

"Wish I'd time to do a full job, lady," said Ritchie. "I'd like to relieve you o' the silverware downstairs, but I ain't a glutton. I'll 'ave the furs, though."

"Mummy. He's stealing all your belongings," the boy complained.

Ritchie suppressed a sudden urge to slap the kid's kisser.

He was a whiner; whining about his rights, his entitlements. Inbred greed was all it was. If he'd been nineteen, not nine, he would have been riled enough to try something on, gun or not – then Ritchie would have had an excuse to shoot him.

The woman got the furs as commanded. She folded them and stuffed them into the big canvas kitbag that Ritchie had brought along inside the suitcase.

Ritchie locked the suitcase and strapped it, roped up the throat of the kitbag. He told the woman to take the children and go into the fitted wardrobe that covered the whole of the bedroom's inner wall. The girl wept loudly and the woman lifted her into her arms, pushing the angry little boy before her.

"*I won't. I won't. I won't,*" the boy raged.

"You'd bloody better," said Ritchie.

Wisely the woman thrust the boy out of sight into the depths of the wardrobe. Ritchie could hear him shouting, more in fear than in temper now, "I hate you. I hate you."

The woman stepped inside and turned to look out at Ritchie.

Ritchie grinned again, winked, pulled the door and locked it.

Carrying suitcase and kitbag, the revolver tucked in the pocket of the pilot's coat, he hurried back down the servants' stairs and out of the house by the kitchen entrance. In the stillroom, the butler, recovered, was bellowing for help.

Ritchie hesitated at the door of the garage.

He half-expected to see the Lanchester tourer prowling in through the gates. But his luck held good. He was clear of the vicinity of the house in seconds and on his way, not to the Baronspark Hotel, but to the smaller, seedier Atlanta, a mere half block down River Street from the place of his meet with Renzo.

There he emptied the suitcase, sorted out all the items that bore a tell-tale monogram and stuffed them under the mattress, writing them off. He took out two pendants and a diamond cluster, two rings and a solid gold cigarette case, wrapped them in a handkerchief and tucked them into the front band of his underpants. Next, he shaved himself and changed into a new dark suit and matching overcoat. He hung the furs in the upright wardrobe and put the case in the foot of the wardrobe, went out and locked the door, leaving the overhead electric light burning.

Empty-handed, he walked the couple of hundred yards from the Atlanta to the Baronspark. River Street was not busy, not down this end; there were few public houses and the commercial hotels did not serve particularly good dinners. It was easy to spot Seaman and another chimpanzee lurking by the pillars of an office block. Ritchie tightened his fingers on the butt of the Colt in his overcoat pocket. He did not feel afraid. He was completely calm.

It was twenty minutes past seven o'clock.

He went into the foyer of the Baronspark, crossed to the desk and asked the clerk for his room key. The clerk did not meet his eye as he gave him the key.

"Anybody call?" Ritchie asked.

"No, Mr. Brown."

He wondered what technique Renzo had used on the clerk. Bribery, threat – or a little bit of both?

Didn't matter.

Ritchie went up to his room.

Renzo and two other men were there. Ritchie's travelling case had been taken from under the bed and opened, the contents examined. The room had also been done over, though there were precious few hiding places in it.

Renzo was seated on the room's only chair.

Ritchie said, "Find anythin' interestin', Jack?"

"Not a bloody thing, Ritchie."

Ritchie kept his hand in his pocket. "Won't do no good t' rough me up, Jack. Besides, it'd be cuttin' your own throat. Only got half the gear on offer. Next month I'll 'ave a little army of my own t' see that everythin's done nice an' proper."

"Where's the gear?"

"Show me the money."

"Addie, show him the cash," said Renzo.

Addie was a small, middle-aged prune of a man. Ritchie had seen him around the Shears. An embezzler, he had served time many years ago and was employed now by Shotten as a toter and calculator. The other man might have been Addie's twin, only his hair was pure white and he had an even beakier nose. He would be the valuator.

Addie took out a wallet of brown buckram, flipped it open and held it out to Ritchie who saw a sheaf of banknotes, thick and colourful.

"Count them out on to the bed, Addie," Ritchie said.

Renzo nodded.

Addie counted out one thousand pounds, laying the notes in rows across the cheap cotton counterpane.

Ritchie said, "Right. I'll take you t' the gear now."

They went downstairs and across the foyer. Ritchie did not turn in his room key and the clerk did not have the gall to ask for it.

As they walked up the pavement to the Atlanta, Ritchie and Jack

Renzo behind Addie and his colleague, Ritchie said, "I know where Seaman is, Jack. You wouldn't intend anythin' nasty, like?"

"Just protection," said Renzo. "Carryin' a thousand needs a bodyguard."

"Sure," said Ritchie.

In the room in the Atlanta, the valuator went to work. He had all the tools of his trade in his pockets, the glass, the gramme-scales, and a couple of little dishes of chemical paste. Ritchie did not understand the method, and he did not care. His only concern was in case Renzo, or the valuator, recognised any of the articles. The transaction, however, was carried out smoothly and amicably.

"What about it?" Jack Renzo asked, when the man had laid the last jewelled item back into the suitcase and was tucking away his tools.

Nobody had even bothered to examine the furs.

"Pay 'im the thousand, Jack," the valuator said.

Renzo did not question the man's judgment.

"Pay him, Addie."

Addie handed Ritchie the wallet containing one thousand pounds in banknotes.

"Thanks, Jack," said Ritchie.

"My pleasure," Jack Renzo said.

Fifteen minutes after the men had left with the suitcase and the kitbag, Ritchie Beckman laid a pound note across the palm of the Atlanta's porter and was shown out through the hotel's back kitchens into an alley that led him, unseen, into adjacent Batsford Road, and clean away.

* * *

Habit took Tilly to Ruth's bedroom around ten o'clock. Corrupted by seventeen years of motherly love, Ruth had come to regard Mamma's good night kiss as a cover for spying, an intervention into her privacy as dictatorial as any that Ritchie might have known in Brixton prison. Ten o'clock – seven minutes after, to be exact – was too late an hour for Tilly to do anything practical to prevent her daughter plunging into a folly that, in Tilly's view, amounted to outrageous defiance.

Though the letter told Mamma and Papa all they needed to know, Tilly was so incredulous that she had Mendel in the street and whistling for a taxicab before he even had time to change out of his house slippers or wash the glue from his hands. On the dining-room table, together with the plate that contained Ruth's supper, a shell-framed mirror remained in a state of half repair, while the Erbachs shot over to Ambraham's Terrace to take revenge on the Beckmans.

Leo, in fact, knew the Erbachs hardly at all. Besides, he would have been hard put to it to recognise even familiar faces so much beer had he poured across his throat in the Admiral's Hat that evening.

Beer did not help him drown the sorrow that wriggled about in him, like a spider in a wash-pipe. His bravura performance in front of his mates was not particularly convincing. The drunker he got the more outrageous his lies, until his contradictions far outstripped his imagination and he became, even to his cronies, boring. There was no Ritchie to see him down the street, and Leo was obliged to fend for himself, with only the walls of the houses for support. He groped his way from the public house and reached the door of Number 5 just as Mendel and Tilly Erbach got out of the taxicab.

"That's 'im," Tilly cried. "That's the father."

Inside, in the living room, Tal Kirsanoff had been pottering about, putting coals on the fire, warming baked beans in a pot and making toast on the grate, all, more or less, at the same time. He heard Tilly's voice clearly even at the back of the house. The woman was trumpeting like an elephant, making incoherent sounds of fury and recrimination as she whacked the soggy Leo about the head with her handbag and urged Mendel to kick the truth out of the man.

Mendel was too gentle, and at this point too bewildered, to obey his wife's injunctions. All he wanted was to find out what the Beckman boy intended to do with his Ruth, if there was any honour at all in the chap's intentions. It had already occurred to Mendel – as it had not occurred to Tilly – that Ruth had left the nest of her own volition. The letter had been unequivocal. She had gone off with Ritchie Beckman of her own free will. She had even written his name with beligerent pride, underlining it four times. Without being capable of a full analysis, Mendel caught enough of the drift of the message to realise that it took two to make an affair and the same number to contrive an elopement. During the taxicab ride, while Tilly boiled like a lidless kettle, Mendel was sunk in his own thoughts. He found that he could grasp his daughter's motives for this sudden turning against her home and parents, and was more puzzled by the fact that she had ever got to meet the young man long enough for an attraction to flower than by the flowering itself.

Mendel did not know Ritchie well.

In spite of the bare bones of Ritchie's biography – his criminal record – Mendel was willing to make the one last gesture of love that an indulgent father can make to a spoiled daughter: to let her marry the man she fancied. But not Tilly. Never Tilly. In jumping out of the back window and sneaking off with her boy friend, Ruth had cheated Tilly out of years of enjoyable suffering, out of plot and counter-plot, out of the star performance for which all the rest had been but rehearsal – the Mother of the Bride. It was a role that Tilly would never have a chance to play now.

Mendel's only real regret was that he would not have an opportunity to wish his daughter well, and press a few quid into her hand.

With Ruth gone, especially under such circumstances, he stood alone against Tilly, a prospect that pleased the generous restorer less than greatly.

When Tal Kirsanoff opened the door to see what all the racket was about, Leo toppled against him. He was not really hurt, but the catch of Tilly's handbag had torn his earlobe and blood was running dramatically down his neck. Leo was making odd gobbling noises. He rolled past Tal, fell and crawled up the hall, on to the stairs, seeking the refuge of an upstairs room.

Tal put out both hands, gripped the doorposts and barred Tilly's pursuit of Leo with his big ursine body. She hit him on the chest with the handbag; flapping blows, made weak by her earlier explosions of rage.

Leaning out of range of the swinging bag, Mendel said, "It is our Ruth. She has left home."

"*With your grandson, may he rot,*" Tilly shouted.

"Is it true, Tal?" asked Mendel, apologetically.

"*It is true. Our Ruth would not write lies.*"

"Come in off the street," said Tal.

He caught Tilly, imprisoned her flailing fists, and drew the woman into the hallway. Mendel followed, closing the door behind him.

Leo had reached the landing. On all fours he rested, peering back under his armpit at the wild Jewish woman below. He wanted none of this. He was a poor old man, who'd done nobody wrong. Why should he suffer? He began to blub, and went on blubbing, ignored by the trio in the hall below. Restraining Tilly from making further assaults, Tal took her into the living room.

Darting her head about, Tilly shouted. "*Where are they?*"

"Not here, Tilly," Tal answered.

"It's true, Tal, is it not?" said Mendel. "They've gone."

"*You are hidin' them.*"

"No, Tilly; my grandson has gone from this house. He told us that he was leaving for France, to look for work there."

"*France? Oi-oi-oi! She will die in France, so far from her Mamma.*"

"Is it true?" Mendel repeated. "Have they run off?"

"Yes, my friend," said Tal.

"*You knew?*"

"I did not know that they intended to run off together."

"*You knew?*"

Tilly struggled. Tal did not release her. Mendel too had come forward and put his arm about her. She kicked like a pony, and her husband spread his legs. He was afraid now, afraid that she would do herself harm. Her sallow skin had darkened to the colour of a victoria plum, her eyes popping like pickled eggs. Her throat worked, her mouth champed and yet no words came. She had become speechless with rage at Tal's duplicity; more, she had accepted the blunt fact that her Ruth had left her to go off, unwed, with a man.

Leo's wailing from the landing had become insistent. A neighbour through the wall was rapping with a broom handle on the ceiling. Tal ignored both interruptions. He too was concerned with Tilly.

"Take her, Mendel."

Tilly's outburst of tears was not unexpected. It came as a relief to her husband and to Tal Kirsanoff. The old Russian found the remains of a bottle of whisky in a cupboard and dispensed a glass for the woman, then he went into the kitchen and made tea, judiciously leaving Mendel to calm and comfort his wife. But when Tilly had pulled herself together there was a return to temper, more calculating now and evidently directed at Tal.

As best he could, without actually lying, Tal told the couple that he had been aware that Ritchie and Ruth were acquainted. He denied that he had been a party to the elopement and said nothing about his function as go-between.

It was a jagged conversation. Though saddened by the turn of events, Mendel did not hold Tal to blame. Tilly, on the other hand, was obsessed with the need to find someone upon whom to lay her guilt. Tal was as good as any. Later, Mendel sensed, she would turn on him. Leo had given up his piteous cry for attention, had taken himself into Maury's room and had fallen asleep on the bed there, covered by an army greatcoat.

It was after midnight when Mendel suggested to Tilly that they had best be going home.

"There is work to do tomorrow."

"Work; why do we work now, husband? Uh? Who do we work for? I ask, where has honest labour got us? She's gone away. Nothing, we bought nothing with our work."

Tal said, "You have a good business. Perhaps Ruth will come back."

"Come back." Tilly was on her feet now. "You think I take her back, after what she does to us. Believe me, Kirsanoff, I tell her what she can do. Anyhow, you think this . . . this thief you call a grandson, you think we hand him over our business? He's not even a decent Jew."

"Tilly, we must go."

"I go when I have said what I have to say. You hear me, Kirsanoff?"

"I hear, Tilly."

"I'd burn down our workshop before I'd let it fall to your precious grandson. Not for the likes of him did my husband an' me work our fingers t' the knuckle, scratch an' save our money. Not for some *mensch* t' come along, take it for his own, an' call himself our son."

"Tal, we thank you for. . ." Mendel began.

"We thank him for nothin'," Tilly rasped.

"Tilly, if it had not been Tal's boy, it would have been another – maybe somebody worse."

"Who else would have taken our Ruth away like the thief he is? No," said Tilly. "No, she will not love him for long. An' when she comes crawlin' back t' me, I tell her then. Eeh-yeh, I tell her, believe me!"

Tal did not answer. He was too appalled at the depth of her hatred. He did not doubt her word. It was no casual threat, made in the heat of the moment. Tilly Erbach meant what she said. She would carry the threat for ever, uphold her promise. If Ruth ever should return, with or without Ritchie, Tal had no doubt that the girl would find the house door firmly shut in her face. He could not understand such mentality – but then he had never carried the burden that Tilly now bore. Not with his father, or his mother, his brothers, wife, daughter or grandchildren. Even with Ritchie he had somehow always known where he stood and what he could and could not do to steer the boy. Tilly Erbach's bitterness would not diminish. As weeks gave to months and months to years it would turn more sour, until it burned in her heart and made all hope of happiness impossible. It was not Tilly that Kirsanoff pitied, but poor Mendel. If he felt any guilt over his sly part in the affair it was for what it would do to Mendel.

Tal saw them to the door. He accepted Tilly's parting curses and Mendel's murmured apologies in silence. He watched them walk off down the Terrace, the woman gripping her husband's arm with a vice-like fist, then he went indoors.

Tea consoled him. He sat up very late by the fire in the living room, drinking cup after cup, smoking all the stumps of cheroots in the box, brooding. He heard clocks strike and the Terrace and the back lane quieten, night-sounds become faint, trains and trams travelling their iron rails, distant as memories. He had taken his part in the trivial history of his family. It had wearied him more than all the travails of his youth and young manhood, but try as he would he could not square the Erbach's present misery or make it add up to more than a fraction of all the suffering that had swirled around him during his seventy-four years on earth.

The boy, Ritchie, was wicked but – it must be said – he loved the girl. Ruth was no more selfish than her mother had taught her to be.

As the night deepened, Tal thought soothingly of his grand-daughter, and his place in her life, of the comfortable shop in Pimlico, across the river. Holly had given him more than he had ever given her, he supposed. For all her drive and purpose, she had not cast him aside when her need of him was through.

Smiling to himself, the old man dozed in the chair by the embers, untroubled by Ritchie, the Erbachs and Leo Beckman, safe with Holly and his great-grandson, in the haven that her industry had made.

*   *   *

It was Sunday afternoon before Jack Renzo surfaced. He had spent Saturday night with his brother, Sydney, the bookmaker. They had kicked over the traces with a couple of stunners picked up in a Leicester Square sporting club. Sydney had put up half the money for Beckman's goods, including running expenses, which meant hire fees for Addie, the valuator and the heavy brigade. All in all it had set the Renzo brothers back a mighty six hundred and fifty pounds each. But it was worth it, well worth it, they both agreed.

Jack had dismissed his squad soon after leaving the Baronspark Hotel. He had no intention of trying to diddle Ritchie Beckman. The kid had always been hot. Renzo respected his excessive caution. He accepted that Beckman had divided the hoard into two lots. Beckman was obviously hooked into a strong line in quality goods. There was no reason, as far as Jack Renzo could see, why he should not act as middle-man and slice a profit from both ends of the transaction.

As the brothers gloated over the goods in the bookmaker's bachelor apartment off the Waterloo Road, Jack explained how he intended to offer the gear piecemeal to Vince over the next three or four months, claiming that he'd got it from different thieves. He could sell it to Vince at under market price, and still cream off a high return.

Jack left Sydney with the girls, and walked to Polmar's English Chop House to take a quick bite of lunch before he toddled down to the Shears to set up a meet with Vince. Though it was his general policy not to carry stolen goods on his person, he felt cocky enough to disobey his rule that Sunday afternoon. He had brought along seven of the best items of jewellery to show to Vince.

It was a clear bright November day, with a nip in the air. The exercises of the night had not tired Renzo. On the contrary he felt spruce and bushy-tailed. He took off his hat and overcoat and wished old Ma Polmar the best of the day. Jack Renzo was too full of his own cleverness to notice that the Chop House was quieter than usual. Mannie seemed liverish but did his host act well enough. He ushered Jack into the smallest of the dining rooms. There was beef on the carver, chicken and goose on salvers on the dresser, and a huge cooked ham, dressed with paper frills and garnished with green stuff. A fire cast reflections on brasswork and picture glasses.

At a table by the fire Vince Shotten sat alone.

That fact, of itself, did not immediately alert Jack Renzo. It was not unknown for Vince to slip down to the Chop House for lunch; occasionally he even brought his wife.

"Vince," said Renzo heartily. "Just the man I want to see."

"Sit down, Jack."

The old leather chair creaked as Renzo seated himself across the oak table from his boss. Behind him, Mannie Polmar quietly closed the connecting door.

Shotten was very still. Coal-black eyes were sleepy. His full underlip was pressed tight against his teeth. There was a tiny fleck of blood on the cleft of his chin where his razor had nicked. His hands rested on the tablecloth, thick smooth fingers curled.

Instinctively Jack Renzo realised that he had been found out. As he had made no pitch, however, and named no price, he was still in the clear. He had conducted on-the-spot deals before. It was the manner of the job, his style. He thanked God, though, that he hadn't breezed in with his brother in tow, crowing. After all, he had already hinted that he had something for Shotten. All he had to do now was lay off the whole collection at the price he'd paid Beckman, take his usual percentage, and write it off to experience. Vince would not hold it against him. Vince had no reason to be displeased with him.

"I hear you did a deal last night, Jack."

"Yer – a good one."

"Got the stuff?"

"There's a ton of it, Vince."

"Where is it?"

"At my brother's place."

"How much did you pay out?"

"Thousand."

"It's a lotta money," said Shotten.

"It's a whale of a lot of gear, believe me, Vince."

"Furs?"

"Yer."

"Rings?"

"Some, yer."

"Pendants, necklaces, watches, links?"

"Who told you, Vince?"

"Who'd you buy from?"

"Did Aleric tell you?"

"I prefer to hear it from you, Jack."

"I bought from Beckman. Ritchie Beckman."

"I thought he was inside."

"He got out."

"You never told me, Jack."

"Didn't know, did I? What's . . . what's up?"

"Do you think I'm gonna pay a thousand for this lot?"

"Well, it's a bargain, Vince."

"Show me your samples."

Nervously Jack Renzo dipped into his side pocket and fished out a diamond clip. He held it in the flat of his palm. "I had the stuff checked. It's all genuine."

"Sure, it's genuine." Shotten glanced at the clip almost disinterestedly. "Think I'd pay cash for anythin' that wasn't genuine?"

Shotten's hand closed on the dinner fork. Before Renzo could move, he had been caught by the necktie and hauled across the table, spilling the cruet and tipping over wine glasses. The tines of the fork were an inch from his eyes.

"*My bloody house he robbed,*" Shotten snarled. "*My stuff he stole. My wife he terrified half to death.*" He flung Renzo back so forcefully that the chair tipped and the stunned man skidded to the wooden floor. He had no opportunity to recover. Shotten stood over him, a foot planted on his chest. "*Beckman done over my house. And you, you stupid bastard, bought the damned stuff from him.*"

"I didn't know, Vince. I swear to God, I didn't know."

"Get up, Renzo. I wanna talk to you."

Renzo struggled to his feet. The fork was still in Shotten's hand.

"I'll . . . I'll . . . I'll find him, Vince. Honest to God. I'll find the little swine."

Shotten shook his head. "Anybody smart enough to do what he did ain't gonna be easy to find. Oh, yes, Jack; you're gonna look. You're gonna search 'til you're blue in the face. But I doubt if you'll track him down. One thousand quid, he's got. He can run a long, long way on that."

"The . . . the thousand. . ."

"It ain't my thousand," said Shotten.

"But. . ."

"I never traded with Ritchie Beckman," said Shotten.

"But Vince, it's . . ."

"I want all my possessions returned, Jack. All in good order, every last piece. Got it?"

"Yes, yes, Vince. Sure. Yes."

"Then you take Aleric and you ferret around, and see if Beckman left any clues."

"What if . . . what if . . ."

"What if he has got clean away?"

"Yes, Vince."

"Then leave a message," Vince Shotten said.

"I know what you mean," said Renzo.

* * *

They took Leo in the street outside the Hat. Renzo personally thumped him, while all Leo's mates looked on. Kids stood around, fingers in their mouths, noses running. Women leaned out of the ground floor windows, tutting.

"I dunno. I dunno," Leo yelled.

Seaman caught the little docker, shook him until his teeth rattled then flung him again into the wall.

Renzo got down on one knee. "Where's your boy?

"Went off with a girl," said Leo, covering his head with his arms, talking to the pavement. "Went off yest'day afternoon. Said he was goin' t' France."

"France?" Renzo frowned.

Seaman kicked Leo's back. Leo howled.

"France?" Renzo repeated.

"*France*." Leo shouted. "*With a girl*."

"What girl?"

"Name's Erbach. A cow. A cow, I tell yer. Ruth Erbach. Gotter cow for a mother, too. Erbach. That's who yer want. Tilly Erbach."

"Where's she live?" asked Seaman.

Unhesitatingly Leo told him.

* * *

"Hands off my Mendel," Tilly Erbach said.

"Then talk."

"You want Beckman? I want Beckman."

"Help us find 'im then."

"Stole my daughter. Stole my Ruth."

"Sure. Right," said Aleric Seaman.

"Take your paws off," said Tilly. "I got nothin' I hide from you. You find him, you bring him back 'ere. I give him worse than you. You bring my girl back 'ere, I got money for you."

"Where did they go?" Renzo asked.

"France."

"How d'you know."

"She said so in a letter. Made no secret. Crowed about it," said Tilly.

Mendel said, "My daughter, she left a letter for us. They have gone to France. To the South, I expect, where it is warm. The young man appears to have money."

"He's got money all right," said Renzo.

"You had trouble from him, too?" said Tilly. "I tell you who knows everything. I tell you who put him up to it, in cahoots with him all the time. No joke. I tell you."

"No, Tilly. No."

"Tal Kirsanoff," said Tilly Erbach.

"It is not true," said Mendel.

"Tal Kirsanoff knows everythin'," said Tilly.

"Ritchie's grandad," said Seaman.

"Where's he at?" asked Renzo.

"With the sister, in Cardwell Place," said Tilly. "Pimlico, it is."

"Tilly, what have you done," Mendel groaned.

"Done us a favour, guv'nor," said Seaman.

"The shop," said Renzo. "We can leave our message at the antique shop."

* * *

Though busy putting the finishing touches to his villa in Peckham Maury had marked out Sunday to call on his sister in Pimlico. He took along his tool bag and, as if he could not let a day go past without keeping his hand in, went through the shop and house doing the odd jobs that Christopher, being "all thumbs", tended to put off – fitting shelves, shaving drawers, changing tap washers, inserting plugs, hooks and picture fitments. There was more to it, of course, than a handyman's visit. Maury had caught wind of his brother's latest escapade, at least the part of it involving Ruth Erbach.

Leo had screwed up his nerve to use the telephone in the public call box in the yard of the Hat and had given Maury a garbled tale about Ritchie having run off with the girl, and what was Maury going to do about it. Maury wasn't going to do anything about it. Leo bored Maury. Boredom was the only word for it. His father was a self-pitying semi-drunkard whom Maury had written off. But Maury was cautious about writing off Ritchie. He wished to learn the truth. He knew that Grandpa Tal would be at the antique shop on Sunday afternoon; that was the main attraction.

Number 5 Ambraham's Terrace had become even more dismal since Holly and Maury had departed. Tal spent very little time there now. It had been the old man's habit to call in at Cardwell Place on Sunday and do the sort of things that might be expected of a venerable relative, even if he did also happen to be an employee. He could hardly wait for young Christopher to grow up. In a year or so, what fun they would have! As it was, Tal Kirsanoff enjoyed just being near the little chap, quite happy to sit by the cradle singing, in a low growling voice, ancient Russian sleep-songs that he had not had occasion to remember since Holly was an infant.

In preparation for the Sunday visit Holly made a huge pot of curried veal and a cold chocolate souffle. The family ate lunch in style in the apartment's dining room. Later, around nine o'clock, Christopher and Holly would walk round to Mario's or Irwin's for a bite of supper while Tal, in his element, regaled his granddaughter's son with stirring tales of Cossack horsemen, a rehearsal for the age of comprehension. But that Sunday, lunch was prolonged, the shop's paperwork neglected.

Tal Kirsanoff kept nothing back from Holly and Maury. He told them all he knew of Ritchie's passion for the Erbach girl and how he had acted as a go-between, once he was certain that Ruth Erbach was a willing partner in the affair. He told them everything, up to and including the events of the previous night, when Tilly Erbach had descended on Ambraham's Terrace and had taken revenge on the innocent Leo.

Only Maury found the story funny.

Holly was concerned and Christopher, who had listened without saying a word, sympathised with his wife's feelings.

"But where did Ritchie get the money?" asked Holly.

"From theft," said Maury. "I expect one of his mates kept it for 'im while he was doin' his bird."

"Stan Nuttall, I believe," said Tal.

"What will happen now?" asked Holly.

Tal shrugged. "It is possible we will hear no more of Ritchie and his lady."

"No such luck," said Maury.

"From what you've said Tal," put in Christopher, "it seems to me that Ritchie might go abroad."

"How can he?" said Maury. "Him an' his prison record."

"There are ways," said Christopher. "Forged documents can be purchased for a price."

"How do you know?" Holly asked.

"Everybody knows that," said Christopher. "Money, these days, is the only key. It can open all doors."

"Right," said Maury.

"Grandfather, you don't suppose Ritchie's still in London?" Holly asked.

"I think he has gone," said Tal. "He talked of the South of France, but it is my opinion that he intends to make his way to another country; America perhaps."

"A land of opportunity," said Christopher.

"An' what about the girl?" said Maury. "Will he do the right thing by 'er, or will he shed 'er once he's had what he wants?"

"Strange as it may seem, I believe our Ritchie loves her," Tal answered.

"Didn't even know he 'ad an 'eart," said Maury.

Christopher said, "I assume we'll have to find another restorer to do our shop work, Holly."

"No two ways about that," said Holly. "Tilly Erbach'll never forgive us for what Ritchie did."

"You are right," said Tal. "I am sorry to lose such old friends."

"That bleedin' selfish brother o' mine's to blame," said Maury.

"His money won't last for ever," said Holly. "He'll go somewhere warm an' dry, for his asthma, an' have a long honeymoon, never thinkin' about tomorrow."

"I don't agree. Our Ritchie's a planner," said Maury. "He'll be on the scout for opportunities. He'll 'ave somethin' in mind, some grand scheme – dishonest, most like."

"Is that what you predict for him?" said Holly. "Prison in another country?"

Maury shrugged. "Don't much care, Hol. I suppose I'm as selfish as he is, in my own way. I got a good business, fairly solidly established, an' a nice house o' my own in a nice town. In three, four years Paddy Elkins'll sell out his share an' go off t'Ireland t' see out his days on his son's farm. An' I'll 'ave the lot. It'll all be mine. What Ritchie does won't 'ardly affect me."

"I wish I could be sure, Maury," said Holly.

"You worried about Ritch?" said Maury.

"No, I . . . I dunno."

"Shall I make coffee now?" asked Christopher.

"Yes, please, love," Holly answered.

Throughout the rest of the afternoon, the Beckmans did what the Beckmans did best – they worked. It did not seem like work, exactly, more like the employment of time in industrious ways.

While Holly took the baby for an afternoon walk, Tal and Christopher went down into the back store and emptied four large cartons of assorted porcelain and china that Holly had bought from a private house in Islington. She had paid a generous sum to the woman, a war widow, who knew nothing whatsoever about the value of her late husband's collection. The husband had been a master printer with his own small business in Fleet Street, and collecting had been his hobby. From the straw and stripped paper packing, Christopher and Tal carefully removed the objects. Holly had been thinking of compiling a collection of English porcelains for a special catalogue. It was clear that her main field of interest lay in pottery, porcelain and china. The Islington purchase included Bow, Chelsea and Derby figures.

Christopher carried them to the deep tub, lined with two old blankets, where they would be carefully washed; an exercise that his wife would probably supervise.

He held up a yellow bunting. "This is Bow, isn't it, Tal?"

Tal peered at it. "I do believe it is."

"This," said Christopher, holding two redbreasts, "is Chelsea?"

"With the raised anchor mark?"

"Indeed, it has."

"We are learning, you see," said Tal.

"I can understand the attraction," said Christopher. "I'm beginning to find antique dealing rather exciting."

"Holly's enthusiasm is infectious."

"My uncle made a very shrewd move, I think."

"Not only your uncle, surely?" said Tal.

"I did, too," said Christopher.

He laid the fragile little birds side by side on a strip of grey felt and returned to the packing bench. He put his hand on the old man's shoulder.

"Do you know what Holly means to me?" he said.

"Yes."

"Truly, Tal; do you?"

"I know that you love her very much."

"Very much," said Christopher. "It isn't the done thing for a husband to prattle about love. It would make me a laughing-stock in the officers' club. But I don't care about the damned officers' club."

"What of your poetry?"

"Oh, that?" said Christopher. "You know, I'd almost forgotten that I was once considered a fair poet."

"Is it good to neglect such a talent?"

"There are too many other things in life." Christopher was not being defensive now. "In time, perhaps it will come back to me. It belongs to a period in my life that almost sucked me under, Tal, years, like quicksand, in which I almost suffocated. I feel solid ground beneath me now. You can't imagine how odd that feeling is."

Tal was silent for a moment, then, dusting straw from a small jug, held it on the palm of his hand for Christopher's inspection. "What do you make of this?"

"Not as pretty as some," said Christopher, inspecting it.

"Perhaps not," said Tal. "But, in my opinion, it is worth more than the rest put together. I have the feeling that it is quite rare, and consequently valuable."

"What makes you say that?"

"Unless I am mistaken, it is a 'goat-and-bee' jug. See how fine the creamy white paste is. And this triangle mark?"

"Can you identify it, Tal?"

"Not I – but I suspect that Holly can."

Christopher took the jug from the old Russian's hand and carried it to the sink. He paused to examine the little object, to marvel at its cunning perfection. It was like a poem – not elaborate, yet subtle and enduring and, to the understanding eye, beautiful.

Standing by the sink, under a tin-shaded bulb, Christopher Deems felt the first quickening of a line of poetry. It was patently inspired by the 'goat-and-bee' jug, in juxtaposition to the harsh realities that had made up the lunch-table talk. Greedy passions and the fine white jug twined in helical patterns in his mind. Christopher recoiled, dropping the creative process down into his subconscious, while the surface of his thinking busied itself, not with nebulous images, but with wondering when his wife and son would return from the park. But as he put down the jug and returned to the bench to see what Tal had unearthed, he was silent, the inner voice speaking once again, vocalising feelings that he had considered not dormant but dead.

He did not flinch from it, however. In his heart, he was glad. In a week, or a month or a year even, the words would emerge and he would put them down on paper – a scrap of realised thought, an evocation of experience. Even if the poem came to nothing, it was a sign that he, Christopher Deems, had come fully to life again.

Later that night, without stating his reason, he took Holly and her brother to supper at Mario's, not knowing that chance had finally found him out and had, at last, devised the only threnody which would lure the captain away.

*   *   *

Mario's was in Queen Charlotte Road, not far off. Tal contended that he would be satisfied with another helping of the curried veal and the remains of the chocolate souffle later in the evening. Soon after the others left, he gently carried the baby's cradle into the big kitchen at the rear of the house and settled comfortably in an armchair with his feet propped on the brass rail of the hob. Maury had brought him a dozen cigars and he smoked one slowly, relaxing. Bathed and fed, young Christopher slept soundly, the painted cradle placed in a corner away from draughts.

It was some time after ten o'clock when Tal, who was beginning to think about supper, was disturbed by an unfamiliar noise. There was a bit of wind to the front of the house. Curling up from Chelsea and the Grosvenor Canal, it brought the sound of trains and other faint breaths of city traffic through the clear winter-Sunday air. Pulling his cardigan about him, Tal checked his great-grandson, dropped the lid on the opening of the grate, then wandered out into the corridor that crossed the apartment to doors above stairs, one flight leading steeply down to the street, the other to the shop.

Imagination played strange tricks on Tal. He could have sworn he heard someone calling his name – not Holly, Maury, Christopher, though, not friends. Strangers, with coaxing, cajoling voices.

"Kirsanoff. Kirsanoff."

The old man rubbed his brow with his thumb. He had had nothing at all to drink, except a glass of white wine at lunch. He could feel his joints stiffening with tension, and his heart fluttered and became loud in his chest.

"Kir . . . san . . . noff."

The voice was close at hand.

"Tal Kirsanoff."

He crept along the corridor.

The voice was sibilent, and quite insistent – yet spectral, not real. For all his pragmatism, Tal was afraid. Ancient superstitions had been rubbed into his soul early in life and they showed their vivid hues again now.

Was this, he wondered, how death came for old men?

Overlaid by the little shouts and sighings of the night wind, the voice spoke in English, however, with a South London accent at that.

"Tal Kirsanoff."

From behind the door to the shop, it came.

Tal turned the key and pulled the door inwards.

The man had been waiting for him. He was standing down one step from the iron landing, a large hulking fellow in a cut-away coat of heavy green tweed. The shop was in darkness, save for stray shafts of light from the street lamps.

Involuntarily Tal began to close the door. The intruder was too fast for him, too strong. Even in the prime of his youth, Tal doubted if he could have matched the power of the man. He glimpsed a fair, ham-like face, with a Teutonic squareness to it, as the head thrust up and broad shoulders followed arms between door and post.

The struggle lasted only a couple of seconds, Tal pushing against the stranger's weight, then yielding. Fists closed on the lapels of his cardigan. He was dragged forward, arms stuck out, and slammed into the high black iron railing that overlooked the shop. All the air was knocked from his lungs. He felt pain in his ribs. Even so, he swung round and jabbed. He was too slow, far too cumbersome. The stranger chuckled, ducked and caught his hand, pulling him away from the rail and pitching him down the spiral staircase.

"Got 'im, Jack," the man called out in a gutteral whisper.

"Are you sure it's Kirsanoff?"

"Can't be two geezers this old on the premises."

"Bring him down."

"What about the others?"

Braced against the iron bannister, reined back by the man's bundled grip on his cardigan, Tal was suspended.

He shouted, "There are no others. I am alone."

He was thinking dazedly of the baby. In the moments after the initial shock he could think of nothing but the baby. He genuinely believed that these men had come to harm his great-grandson.

"Better not be lyin', granddad," the stranger said.

"No one. No one."

"Come on, Aleric. Bring him down here so's I can talk to him," Jack Renzo ordered.

Aleric Seaman was enjoying himself. He prodded the old man with his knee and drove him on down the twisting staircase, flinging him out at the bottom into a Louis XV marquetry table that the Erbachs had restored only last month. The table cracked as Tal sprawled on to it and the top tilted sliding him to the floor amid a collection of goblets and wine glasses. He rolled over. His left hand was cut and his cheek was grazed. He heard the table crack again under his knees and he strove to get to his feet, to fight back.

Seaman gave him no opportunity to gather his wits. Though Tal was no lightweight, Seaman wadded the cardigan into his fists and hauled the old Russian to a standing position.

"Not so loud, Aleric. Take him in the back."

Tal was thrust forward once more. His hip caught the edge of a mahogany three-tier stand and tipped it over. A Bristol glass finger-bowl and a Cranberry water jug shattered as they struck the floor. The clatter of pewter and old Sheffield plate an instant later told him that his captor had completed the destruction with senseless clumsiness.

"Hold it down, Aleric, for God's sake."

Then Tal was round the corner of the back store, where it was pitch dark. He could smell resins, soaps and spirits very distinctly, as if fear had sharpened his senses. He could see virtually nothing, though, except the hulking shape of the man directly behind him. He swung at that shape, and made contact.

"Bleedin' 'ell."

"What's up?"

"The old beggar's still got lead in 'is pencil. He 'it me."

"Wait, I've found the light."

The dim bulb in its tin shade over the sink went on.

Without releasing his hold on Tal, Seaman dabbed at his nose with his sleeve. "Bleedin' 'ell. He got me." He glared at Tal. "You'll pay twice over for that, you old beggar."

Renzo came over. Tal was backed into the corner. Overhead were shelves with bric-à-brac on them. To his left, a rack for drying china and porcelain, and empty boxes. The packing bench was behind the strangers. He blinked. His eyes were watering. He blinked again.

"You should never 'ave got smart with Mr. Shotten," Jack Renzo said. "It don't pay to get smart with men like him."

"I . . . I do not . . . not know what you are talking about."

"Hark at 'im," said Seaman, and punched Tal's ribs.

The old man winced, but did not buckle. He was trying to clear his head, to put his thoughts together, find out what the assault meant and what purpose the men had in coming here. Vaguely, he connected them with Ritchie. Shotten: Ritchie. What had Ritchie done now?

Seaman punched him a second time.

Jack Renzo drew Seaman back. "That's enough for now, Aleric. He's gonna talk to us, ain't he? He'll tell us what we need to know."

"Wha . . . what?" Tal's body hurt. He felt nauseous. His head was swimming.

"We know you helped Ritchie. We got reliable information, you helped that thievin' little swine set it up."

"Ritchie? No, I . . . I do not know what . . . Ritchie is gone."

"We know that much. Where's he gone?"

"I cannot . . ."

Renzo was very close to him, pinning him in the corner. He prayed to God that Christopher would not cry now. If they brought Christopher down, he would tell them. But tell them *what?* All loyalty to Ritchie vanished.

"He has gone to France, to the South of France," Tal said, head lowered. "He has taken a girl with him. I knew of his romance . . ."

"Ain't that sweet?" said Seaman.

"Shut it, Aleric."

". . . his . . . of this girl. But I did not know that he intended to run off with her."

"He's lyin'," said Seaman. "It's a carve-up. Beckman ain't no more in France than I am."

"He told me," Tal said, "Told me little, very little."

"You were in it with him," said Renzo. "Admit it."

"Come on, old man," said Seaman. "Can't y' see, we aim t' find yer precious boy."

"He's gone," said Tal. "Ritchie has gone. You must believe me."

"Where?"

"He told me . . . the . . . to France. What has he done?"

"Don't play the bleedin' innocent," said Seaman.

"Aleric, just hold it down," said Renzo. "Is that right, Kirsanoff? Is what you say right? You didn't know what he was up to, what he planned to do before he skipped?"

"No. I swear to you. . ."

"I'll get it outta him," said Seaman.

Renzo took a pace back, pushing Seaman away. "Listen, that's what Vince said – said Beckman'd he clean away, out the country. This old bloke knows nothing, Aleric. We're not going to find Ritchie."

"Then we'll do the other."

Renzo nodded. "Leave a message."

"Here?"

"Right here."

"What with?"

"Use your loaf," said Renzo. "See what's back there? Varnish, wax, coal-oil – like a tinder box, it is."

Seaman dabbed his nose again, and grinned. "Right you are, Jack."

Tal raised his hands and gripped the edge of the shelves. He pushed up then flung his weight forward, bringing the shelves away from the angle-irons, projecting them, and their contents, forward onto the head and shoulders of the man called Jack. Bottles, vases, jugs, dented pewter pots and wooden quaichs, a Victorian metronome in a heavy case, the brass horn of a broken polyphone, a Regency box and Georgian cheese coaster, brass letter scales and copper inkwells, candlesticks and picture frames, kettles, unwashed beakers and three big chamber pots all rained down on Renzo who staggered beneath the onslaught, reeled back and fell to his knees.

Tal hunched his shoulders to protect his head. He swung and locked his arms around the post of the drying rack and hauled at it, bringing it away from the wooden pins that held it to the brick. There were only a few small objects on its quilted slats but the rack itself was the weapon he sought and he lumbered forward with it and swung again and hurled it at the men.

The one called Aleric was too quick. He side-stepped and, as Tal swayed and stumbled in the wake of the massive exertion, brought his bunched fists scything down on the old man's neck, just above the ear. Tal fought against darkness for a moment, arms thrashing sluggishly, pawing the air, then Seaman struck him again, and he fell to the stone floor, insensible.

* * *

Seaman pulled Renzo to his feet. His boss was bleeding from a contused wound on his jaw and his cheekbone was split where the edge of the rack had caught him. He doubled over with pain, then straightened. When Seaman read the expression on his face he knew that they were going to leave a proper message, a message that Ritchie would hear even if he had gone to the bleedin' moon.

"Burn it," Renzo hissed. "Burn it."

Seaman swung round. First he reached for a large red tin that bore a new paper label: "Real Turpentine". He shook it and heard the viscous gurgle that told him the can was almost full. He opened it and sloshed it round the packing bench and the cartons, the broken rack, not caring that it dribbled over the old man. He put the tin down, still with some of the liquid in it. He searched the shelf, found a dark bottle, uncorked it, sniffed, recoiled and then poured the contents – white spirit – into the chests of straw and paper strips that stood by the bench.

In pain, Renzo had gone out into the shop. "Here, out here. Make a bloody good job of it," he called. "I'll teach Beckman and his damned family not to cross me again."

Seaman took more tins and bottles from the shelf. Napthalene, Scotch Glue, Linseed Oil, Etherol Cleaner and a small bottle of surgical spirit with which he would shortly soak a swansdown cloth to make a fuse. He took the turpentine can too and used it liberally, jerking the tin in all directions.

"Where's the old man?" Renzo asked.

"In the back. Want 'im out?"

"No. Leave him," Renzo said.

It did not take long for Seaman to do his work. He tossed away the last bottle, smashing the leaded glass front of a cabinet with it, then stopped. He glanced behind him. Jack Renzo had opened the front door on its broken lock. The gate was still in place but it would only take them a second to scale it. Renzo was peering out into the street.

"Right?" said Seaman. "All clear?"

"Yes."

When Seaman struck the first match, Jack Renzo climbed the gate.

Flame bloomed. Cupping the match in his palm until it was well lit, Seaman did not hurry. He dropped it on to the cloth impregnated with spirit. It wafted into a pale blue flame, then gave a soft rasping sound and burst fully alight. Seaman tossed it into the storeroom where it spread its flames with no impediment. He struck another half dozen matches and laid them here and there about the shop, watching each to ensure that it had caught.

The fires grew quite bright, bathing his face. He could feel the exciting warmth on his skin.

"Come on. Come on."

Renzo jigged on the pavement outside the shop.

Seaman came out of his trance. He scattered the contents of the matchbox in all directions then turned and ran through the door, swarmed over the gate, and, without waiting for Renzo, headed towards the corner. He paused there, skipping, until Renzo caught up with him.

Behind the men, already, the glow of the fire was apparent through the windows of Aspinall's Antique Shop, and draughts of thin grey smoke puffed from the door.

"'Ere," said Seaman. "Don't suppose there *was* anybody upstairs?"

"Couldn't have been," Jack Renzo said.

"Well, if there is," said Seaman, going round the corner, "I wouldn't give tuppence for their bleedin' chances now."

*   *   *

The commotion in Cardwell Place attracted neighbours from supper and lured small boys from their beds. A horse-cart blocked the westward entrance. Its owner, a greengrocer plodding home from Kent with a load of potatoes, had abandoned his vehicle to goggle at the spectacle of some poor blighter's shop going up in smoke. Shopkeepers who lived adjacent to Aspinall's Antiques were howling for the fire-brigade and running agitatedly up and down the pavements in search of buckets of water to damp down their frontages. Within minutes of Seaman's match being struck, seconds after the arsonists had vanished round the corner, Cardwell Place had been transformed from a quiet backwater into a bustling thoroughfare with the immediate vicinity of the antique shop its only unoccupied area.

Nobody ventured close to the building, though there were shouts of, "Where's the owner? Somebody fetch the owner. Ain't nobody seen the woman or her old man?" And, as the glow within the cavern of the shop became brighter, cries of, "Evacuate the houses. Get everybody out. Is there anybody inside? Maybe they've all been smovvered."

Small boys, who had escaped their bedrooms by devious means, nudged each other in delight. The ragamuffin chorus in nightshirts and jackets, boots unlaced, exchanged information on combustion.

"It'll blow up, like. You'll see. Any minute."

"Noah, they'll come an' put it out."

"Gotta motor engine now, wiff a pump that don't need no men."

"Listen, you'll 'ear the bell."

"Be too late. Be all gorn by then."

"Maybe somebody's in there – roastin' alive."

"Cor blimey! Think o' that!"

Several events occurred in rapid succession, a series of happenings so dramatic that the public hardly had had time to take in the sequence, let alone savour it. First a policeman arrived – a patrolling constable who had smelled smoke and followed the tide of sightseers.

"Keep back there. Make way for the law. Did anybody send for the brigade? Did anybody?" he shouted, standing with arms akimbo not ten yards from the frontage.

In fact, at that period the fire was still contained within the shop, and had not spread up into the apartment. But the glow was considerable, already hot enough to outline, black on dusky red, the shapes of furniture within the shop and the aperture, like a proscenium arch, that led into the back store. Observers remarked to each other that, by the look of it, the fire had started back there and had really got a grip on the bricklined interior.

The second incident was startling and rather horrifying. Nobody expected it. Even the constable, who was just beginning to recall his drills and consider a heroic gesture or two, did not seriously imagine that anyone was inside the place. Then out of the fiery grotto stumbled a figure. Clothing smoked like grey fur. The ursine silhouette resembled a stuffed bear stepped down from its pedestal. Swaying, pawing the air, shambling, a dumb brute blinded by smoke and fear and pain, it thrust through the clumps of living flame that bloomed in the body of the shop until it crashed against the outer gate at the doorway. It hung there, then, with a pathetic heave of the shoulders and a raising of the arms, tilted back its head and roared, "HELP ME."

"Gawd save us! It's Mr. Kirsanoff."

Aid was instantly forthcoming. A dozen men ran forward, braving radiant waves of heat. Three sprightly youngsters vaulted over the barrier to give the old man a shove so muscular that it lifted him clear up and down into the waiting arms of the rescuers. A blanket appeared out of the crowd. It was wrapped round him to extinguish his smouldering garments. His hair was frizzed, his flesh blackened. His eyes stared wildly out of the sooty mask. His mouth looked wet and red, like a wound.

He yammered, "The boy, the baby, upstairs, the baby."

No doubt the constable would have lead a volunteer force into the house by the street stair but the third and fourth events happened before the old man's appalling news had time to sink in.

Two men and a woman, running hard, came up Cardwell Place, pushed through the ring of spectators into the clearing in front of the shop.

"That's 'er, that's the owner!"

"Don't she look dreadful!"

"Who's the other geezer!"

"'Usband."

"An' the big feller?"

"Dunno!"

At that same moment the motorised fire-brigade, followed by a horse-drawn salvage van, hurtled round the corner from Pimlico Road Station and, skidding, ran smack into the greengrocer's cart, tipping it over and sending a rubble of potatoes across the cobbles. The terrified horse, strangled by its halter, reared and twisted, dragging the drop-side of the cart and one wheel into and partly under the steaming bonnet of the fire-engine where, crushed by half a ton of brasswork and water tanks, it jammed. The horse screamed hideously, endeavoured to bolt and, with a sudden slide, broke its back and fell, dying, across the width of the road.

Fire chief and salvage master were on the spot at once. Cursing, shouting commands, they urged their crews to manhandle the damned hulking carcass to one side, to get under the motor and clear the wreckage, to make room, let the brigade through.

Most of the crowd, while noting the accident and the delay it caused, were engrossed in another happening right there in front of their eyes.

Somebody was going in.

Somebody was really going into the blazing building.

"Who? Who is it?"

"Her 'usband."

*   *   *

From the moment they turned the corner, caught sight of the crowd and the canopy of smoke, Christopher knew that Aspinall's was ablaze. Holly sensed it too, even before intelligence, confirmed by locational signs, told her that it was her shop that was burning. Holding her overcoat skirts up she was the first to run, Maury and Christopher following. Quickly overtaking her, they sprinted ahead to clear a path through the throng.

Tal had just been helped over the gate. Muffled in a blanket, he was laid out on the pavement fifteen or twenty yards to the right of the glowing shop front.

Holly headed straight for her grandfather, yelling, "Where's the baby? Where's Christopher?"

The constable and a rough couple of lads tried to hold her back. There were shouts of protest. "It's Miss Beckman. It's the owner. Let'r through."

Leaning from the waist, Holly gaped at the old man. "Grandfather? Please God! Oh, please, God, please!" She searched the faces around her for answers.

The constable announced. "Doctor wanted. Doctor wanted. Is there a doctor 'ere."

There was no response.

Maury was in front of the shop, dangerously close. He had stripped off his jacket and wrapped it around his arm. Hopping about, shielding his face, he tried to see into the shop.

The interior was almost incandescent. Flames had flooded up from the centre of the shop. The panes of the apartment contained a dull oven-like redness, threatening an imminent spread of the fire. The shop's contents were already destroyed. Sensibly, Maury retreated from the immediate vicinity. A split-second later the windows shattered as if a shell had struck them.

The crowd ooooooooooooow-ed and tripped back over itself as slivers of broken glass hurled outwards and a series of small dense explosions shook the street.

"Gas! Strewth, it's gas!"

"Got the gas main!'

"Gawd save us!"

"Gas mains gone! Run for yer lives!"

A few cowardly souls fled, then, rather ashamed of themselves, returned a minute or two later when it became clear that, so far, the gas main remained intact. Besides, was it likely that the constable would let them all hang around if there was any serious danger of a whopping big blow-out?

All of this hubbub crystalised in Christopher's consciousness. He saw every detail with staggering clarity while he stood by Holly's side staring up at the apartment windows. Already he had noticed the dark funnel of the street stairs. He glanced down. His wife had fallen to her knees beside the old man and had lifted his head in her hands. Tal's lips moved.

Holly shrieked, flung herself up and back.

Christopher cried, "Maury. Stop her."

Maury was picking himself up. His flight had ended in a spill and he had sprawled headlong on the cobbles, breaking his fall on his arms. He had no alternative but to tackle Holly.

He caught his sister around the waist.

She slapped and clawed at him, crying, "*Baby. My baby's up-stairs.*"

Maury held on grimly.

Christopher snared Holly's arm. He whipped her round and slapped her stingingly across her face.

"Did Tal tell you exactly where the baby is?" he demanded. "Holly, for God's sake, listen. Where is the baby? What room?"

"MY BABY. MY BABY. MY LITTLE BOY'S IN THERE!"

Christopher caught the back of her neck, held her thrashing head still and slapped her once more.

"*Holly. Think. Talk. Tell me.*"

"The kitchen, he's in the kitchen, dearest, please get my baby out, my baby I want him I want. Christopher?"

Softly, Christopher said, "Yes, darling. I'll fetch him out."

To two women in the crowd, wives of neighbouring shopkeepers, Christopher said, "Take care of her. Don't let her come after me, whatever you do."

"Right you are, Mr. Deems."

He pushed Holly away. The women caught her, each taking an arm, restraining the young woman as she lunged to free herself and run into the blazing building.

Christopher tried to ignore his wife's desperate cries.

Taking off his jacket he cowled it over his head.

"Maury," he said. "I'm going up the street stairs. Will you back me up?"

"But what about the firemen; they're trained for . . ."

"My son's in there," Christopher said.

"Gawd, yer! What am I thinkin' about?"

Christopher turned. He looked directly at Holly. She had given up the struggle. She sagged against the women, neck elongated, hair tousled, coat flapping wide about her legs.

"Christopher! Christopher!"

"I love you," he said.

He pivoted and drove forward under the flames that snaked from the shop's front window. Fanned by a breeze and the intense combusion of the fire in the store, black smoke had squeezed into the stairwell. The heat was almost unbearable. The light below was sickly, like the sweat of a French town, wounded by shellfire, bleeding up on to leaden cloud.

"Watch the door, how y' open it." Maury was directly behind him, crouched, jacket over his head.

They had made the stairs three at a time, cleaving through the smoke. The taste of it, acrid rasp on the back of the throat, smarting eyes – both men had lived with such discomforts for months on end. It meant little. Christopher could feel the sergeant hard against his haunches, keeping contact, as he would have done if this had been a night patrol between the lines. The growl of the fire grew louder, fluctuated, dwindled, swelled up again, rapidly advancing.

Head down under the shelter of his arm, Christopher fitted the key into the lock, turned it and eased the door open. He expected a vivid streak of flame to meet his eyes but, with relief, saw nothing but a potted plant on an ugly wooden column that had been left behind by the Aspinalls and that he had not had the heart to toss out.

"It's all right, Maury."

"Go in slow."

The men slipped through the door and closed it behind them to seal the corridor.

Smoke clotted the corridor's end. A great pulsing fire blister had formed on the door above the shop. Even as Christopher ran forward the blister burst, spattering gouts of flame into the house.

Apparently the fire had hauled itself up the interior wall, using the trunk of the chimney as access. Beams and joists were charred by the heat. The deadly gaseous hiss of sparkled varnish and greasy paint indicated that the domestic apartments were in a volatile state and might explode into a raging inferno at any moment. The smoke was less severe than the men had anticipated, however. It had not yet massed into the choking cloud that would poison their lungs and starve them of oxygen. Even so, they proceeded cautiously towards the kitchen.

In the centre of his mind Christopher formed an image of the shop over which they walked. He knew that only a thin crust kept them above that hell. He had walked over thinner crusts in his time, brazenly and optimistically. But then there had been no child, return had not been required. Now there was his son, Holly's son. He could not fail to do what was demanded of him. Unlike the obedience he had shown to the programmers of the war, his doggedness now was powered by desperation, not hopelessness. He had a duty to Holly, to the child, even to Maury. The sum of his responsibilities weighed on him and made him, in those moments, cautious of his own safety. To fail gloriously would not be good enough. Living was important. The design now was small and fine enough to encompass him; he could identify his part in it only too well.

Maury punched him on the shoulder. He glanced round. Out of the bedroom, a long tongue of amber flame had emerged into the corridor. Where the door to the spiral staircase had been was a forest of flames, standing upright, heavy and massy, alive with sound.

"Stay here, Maury." The captain gestured; dumb-show commands.

Maury nodded.

In the half minute since they had entered the apartments fire had swarmed up around them. Beneath their feet the blackened carpet smoked. The floorboards shifted like a ship's deck.

"It'll go any second," Maury shouted.

"Wait here."

Crouched low, Christopher ran towards the flames, and ducked around the kitchen door.

The large room was burning. All burning. Beneath the quarter ton of iron cooking range, the beams had sagged. Horns of flame spiked hearth and mantel. Fed by melting gas pipes they grew longer and more flexible even as he watched. The whole inner wall was disintegrating before Christopher's eyes.

In the painted cradle, out of the draught, the baby howled. Christopher could see little fists raised, protesting at the world's neglect.

Curtains across the window billowed inwards suddenly. A storm of broken glass blasted across the room. The captain was puzzled by its direction, until he realised that fire had swept from the shop below via the intricate branches of the gas supply pipe. He stepped across the floor. It felt like brash ice under his feet. The heat was so intense that he feared he might swoon with it. Fierce spots of pain on his flesh were caused by spores of burning paint and jetting sparks. He was not even aware of them, any more than he had been aware of the Maxim's bullets ripping through the ground mist that morning at Bullecourt. Only this time he had to come through, had to return, not to the comradely arms of the dead, but to a street in Pimlico, to the young woman who waited there for him.

> *If I had rode with Hanson's Horse,*
> *Blown the Bugle, Drawn the Sword.*

Like the short cape of a Royal Hussar the tweed jacket swung about his shoulders. He lifted the baby. Enclosing its tiny fists, he peered down, smiling, into its face. Fear, innate even in an infant, had contorted his features. But there was no evidence of injury, or of suffocation.

Christopher – the young 'un – wailed.

The captain put him into the folds of the jacket and lightly turned the lapels over his face. The baby howled even louder. Stooped, the captain headed for the kitchen door.

> *Lancer, Lancer charging down*
> *The lithe, flamboyant pennants of the dawn.*

He stepped into the corridor.

Beneath his heels the floor collapsed, ripping away ahead of him. The fissure was brick-red and straw-yellow, the heat searing. Involuntarily Christopher stepped back on to the heavy wooden spar on which the kitchen door was propped, protecting the baby with his body.

There was nothing but colour now. Colour and hellish heat. Heat more intense than anything he had ever imagined. It was like being thrust into the heart of a furnace. His flesh felt stretched by it, hair scorched, eyes and mouth, even lungs, dried out. He kept his arms around the baby, and sucked in the heat, sucked in the little oxygen it contained.

His trousers were burning.

He blanked out pain. He did not yield to it. No more did he yield to his desire for ease, for peace, to be at one again with all the lost batallions of the boys he had known, victims of the deceiver. He would not permit himself to be deceived.

He poked his head from the shelter of the doorway.

Maury was a brown silhouette, away beyond the gaping hole in the floor, through which, like sea-spray, sparks shot up. He could see past the broken ends of the beams, down into the depths of the shop, to phantom shapes of chairs and sofas, tables and cabinets, grey, red, brown and molten yellow in the hollow place beneath.

He knew that he had very little time.

There was no hope of exit across the kitchen. No retreat.

He did not quibble with his fear or argue with his experience.

Cloth had adhered to the flesh of his legs. He could not feel his feet or ankles. He refused to identify with his agony. Refused. Inturned his thinking. The poet's trick come back at last.

Down close to his belly, he snuggled the child.

Moving, he stepped out into the corridor, braced one sticky forearm against the decaying wall. Maury had not deserted him.

Easy, easy now, sir. I'll have you off of there in a jiffy.

Crawling, jacket wrapped round his head like a veil, Maury had advanced as far as he dared. He was on the edge, the fire spitting up at him, roasting him. He could not hold consciousness for more than two or three seconds. The big main beam would go soon. Even before it gave, Maury would have to retreat. He was beckoning, arms pulling, drawing Christopher to him, begging the captain to do the impossible.

Christopher closed his fist on his breast, the baby pinned possessively against his chest.

I've lost a glove. Suspended on the wire.

Smaller and smaller, the tiny black dot of the glove on the wire in the mist.

"Give him to me. Christ, give him to me."

Through the uproar of the fire, the sergeant's voice was barely audible.

Christopher spread his legs over the gulf, jerked three strides, cocking his knees, bridging the width from wall to wall. Flames consumed him. The pain was great, too great to ignore; a stern and commanding reality compared to the mind's faint torments and the petty anguish of survival.

He slipped.

He extended his right arm.

The jacket, the bundle, the baby – poised. Maury stretched out. Christopher felt the weight lift, the burden being taken from him. He slipped again, smearing down the inner wall, not even seeking purchase, a hold. His dying brain, dying heart welled with delight at raw red glory. He saw Maury vanish down the stairwell, the baby tucked close to his chest.

Sailing past Freddie.

Sailing past George.

Christopher fell. The weight of the burning wall toppled on to him and carried him down to the space below.

The Shoemaker sat up.

"Captain Deems?" he said, in his flat Fenland voice. "Captain Deems, sir, is that you?"

1921 – A Postscript

By APRIL THE business was settled and the dreary days of Afterwards had closed round Holly just as they had enveloped the warriors, widows and orphans of the larger conflict. She had to learn to live without him – and in the learning came to love him more and more.

By returning to stay with her father in Ambraham's Terrace, Holly had hoped to shake off the poignant memories of her brief marriage to Christopher Deems. But after a time she came to cherish the memories and to realise that they had become part of her. She shed few tears for her captain and the lost promise of the days that never came. She had his courage as an example and her mourning for Christopher was clear and soft, balm for its own wound. In Lambeth the loss of Grandfather Tal made itself more obviously felt and it was for the company of the old Russian that Holly most often longed.

Investigations into the cause of fire and an official enquiry into the deaths reported no positive conclusions. Mr. Kirsanoff had succumbed to a heart seizure only minutes before the ambulance had arrived in Cardwell Place. Mr. Deems had perished within the burning shell of the shop. There was nothing much left to salvage from the blaze, apart from a few oddments that miraculously survived and that King's insurance company sold off to defray a little of their heavy financial loss on the policy claim.

What had started the fire?

Expert opinion suggested that a volatile fluid in the store had been ignited, perhaps by a careless cigar stub or match. It was duly noted in relevant documents that Mr. Kirsanoff had been well on in years and not quite as mentally alert as he might have been. Mercifully the Pimlico Fire Service had managed to contain the flames and only superficial damage had been done to adjacent premises. The fire master declared that it could have been much worse. None of the public enquiries reached deep enough into circumstances to unearth Seaman, Renzo or Vince Shotten.

Holly and Maury did not accept the public findings at face value.

Not for a moment did Holly believe that Grandfather Tal had been carelessly responsible for the fire and she held no resentment against him. On the contrary, it was the thought of the courage that the two men had displayed that helped her, in due course, to pull herself out of depression and begin to shape her life to new patterns. That's what Tal and Christopher would have expected her to do; she would not disappoint them.

To Maury Beckman the whole thing was too much of a coincidence. Somehow, Maury reckoned, Ritchie had a part in it, Ritchie and his criminal acquaintances. Maury had sufficient experience to recognise vengeance when he saw it. Given opportunity, he might have made discreet enquiries of his own, probing into Jack Renzo's and Vince Shotten's participation in the events of that night. Jack Renzo, however, did not go scot-free. Whatever web of circumstances bound them together soon strangled Renzo. In March Maury heard that Renzo and his side-kick Aleric Seaman had gone missing. In early May, Seaman's swollen corpse was washed up on the spars of the naval pier near Greenwich, his throat cut from ear to ear. The murder remained unsolved.

Jack Renzo's body was never found, though word was out that the fence was dead. Even his bookmaker brother stopped making a noise about it. Vincent Shotten and Ritchie Beckman escaped obvious punishment. But Maury was convinced that their time, too, would come; somewhere, somehow, the debts would be paid and justice done.

Four years were to pass before anything was heard of Ritchie and Ruth. Late in 1924 Mendel Erbach received a letter from his daughter. Postmarked Toronto, it was casual and uninformative, obviously intended to establish contact and no more. In it Ruth said that she was married, and very happy, and had seen a lot of the world. Though she sent her love, she did not say that she missed them and Mendel, after much soul-searching, did not show the letter to Tillie or even tell her of it.

In that same year a letter also found its way to Maury, via Elkins' old yard. It gave the address of a hotel in Vancouver. The quality of the headed notepaper suggested that Ritchie was far above the breadline and doing well for himself. Ritchie's letter was even less informative than Ruth's. In it Ritchie asked for news, not of his father and sister, but of Vincent Shotten's criminal empire. By 1924 the events of that November night back in 1920 seemed, to Maury at least, like history; Holly had settled, might even be said to be thriving, and Maury kept the letter to himself. He did not, of course, bother to reply.

Though young Christopher had emerged virtually unscathed, Maury had been rather severely burned in the Cardwell Place tragedy. It had been a full year before he regained full use of his hands and the period of enforced idleness – no hammers, chisels or shovels – resulted in a change of direction. He was forced to concentrate his considerable energies on supervising an expanding building business. In fact, by the time his hands had healed, he was too much the gentleman to soil his cuffs with manual labour.

Though Leo gladly accepted his daughter's return and quickly grew fond of his grandson, he knew that Holly's sojourn in Lambeth would not last long. Naturally, Maury offered to take Holly over to his place in Peckham; the bungalow was quite large enough for three, particularly as he had no immediate plans to look for a wife. For reasons too subtle to explain, Holly would not go. Lambeth seemed to offer her the maximum degree of comfort that it was possible to find in the twelve months following her husband's death. Eventually Maury gave up trying to persuade her. He settled instead for acting on her behalf in all matters pertaining to the will and the division of the monies paid out to Kennedy King by the insurance company.

Kennedy was a good friend to Holly. Chaperoned by Emma, he often visited Holly in Lambeth. He offered her a holding in his company instead of her twenty-five per cent share of the insurance. He made the offer too soon, however, and Holly listlessly refused. Next, Kennedy tempted her with the managership of a branch he planned to open in Sedbar Street; Holly expressed no interest. Eventually Kennedy broke down and, to everybody's astonishment, tried to persuade the young widow to come and live with him – on a platonic basis – in his museum-piece house in Chelsea. It was no secret that Kennedy loved Holly almost as much as he adored his nephew's child. Never had Kennedy's life seemed so empty. He made the offer several times. Each time Holly gently refused.

Only Emma's shrewd prediction that Holly would "come out of it" in her own good time, and that Kennedy should exercise patience, cooled the dealer's embarrassing ardour and persuaded him to play a waiting game. The lure of the trade would prove too strong for Holly in time and he, Emma said, might have what he wanted then.

Tal had been buried in the Jewish cemetery at Comstock Road in South Lambeth. There was a little headstone commemorating his date and place of birth, and that of his death. Sometimes, on her walks, Holly would push the baby carriage down that far, would stand in the deserted place for a while and talk to the stone. Fortunately that phase did not last and, before April, she had begun to converse with baby Christopher instead.

It was Christopher who became the centre of Holly's life. It was Christopher who brought her from lonely seclusion in Lambeth and back, out of necessity, into the antique trade. She was determined, grimly and passionately determined, that her child would have the best life had to offer. He would have opportunity, every possible opportunity, and the cosy wrap of wealth. It was not, perhaps, what her husband would have wanted for the boy, but it was the best she could provide in lieu of a proper father. It was the pattern she designed for herself in the quiet solemn months of 1921. By the end of the year, Holly was ready to begin again.

Captain Deem's body had been taken in a sealed coffin to rest close to his father in the Maldenhall churchyard. It was his mother's wish that this be done and Holly, at that low period, had no will to resist the older woman's request. Later, she regretted her capitulation. Maldenhall seemed such a long way off. Besides, Mrs. Deems had become openly hostile to Holly, as if she somehow blamed her for her son's death. After Mr. Mumford had settled the legalities, there was no further communication between the women.

It was three years after old Mrs. Deems passed on, in 1931, that Holly made her very first visit to her husband's grave. It being high summer, she stayed awhile and left a bunch of hand-picked wild flowers on the lush grass there. By that time, she had grown strong again, and her fine handsome harum-scarum son had grown into boyhood. Young Christopher had turned out well, secure in his mother's love and protective of her. He had not been spoiled by the privileges he enjoyed, and was not at all dismissive of his father's reputation which Kennedy King kept alive for him in tales and stories and readings from the more stirring poems.

Nobody told young Chris of the bargain, however.

The bargain remained Holly Beckman Deems' secret, shared only with Maury – and with David, ten thousand miles away on the other side of the world.

PART FOUR

1921